Praise for Robin Hobb's Liveship Traders Trilogy

Ship of Magic

Mad Ship

Ship of Destiny

"In today's crowded fantasy market, Robin Hobb's books are diamonds in a sea of zircons."
—George R. R. Martin

"A truly extraordinary saga...the characterizations are consistently superb, and [Hobb] animates everything with the love for and knowledge of the sea. If Patrick O'Brian were to turn to writing high fantasy, he might produce something like this. Kudos to the author, and encore!" —*Booklist*

"Hobb gives us her usual marvelously coherent setting and intriguing, multidimensional characters who refuse to be pigeonholed.... A new series sure to please fantasy fans." —*Publishers Weekly*

"Rich, complex... [Hobb's] plotting is complex but tightly controlled, and her descriptive powers match her excellent visual imagination. But her chief virtue is that she delineates character extremely well." —*Interzone*

BOOKS BY ROBIN HOBB

*Fool's Quest
*Fool's Assassin

THE FARSEER TRILOGY
* Assassin's Apprentice
* Royal Assassin
* Assassin's Quest

THE LIVESHIP TRADERS TRILOGY
* Ship of Magic
* Mad Ship
* Ship of Destiny

THE TAWNY MAN TRILOGY
* Fool's Errand
* Golden Fool
* Fool's Fate

THE SOLDIER SON TRILOGY
Shaman's Crossing
Forest Mage
Renegade's Magic

THE RAIN WILDS CHRONICLE
Dragon Keeper
Dragon Haven
City of Dragons
Blood of Dragons

*AVAILABLE FROM RANDOM HOUSE

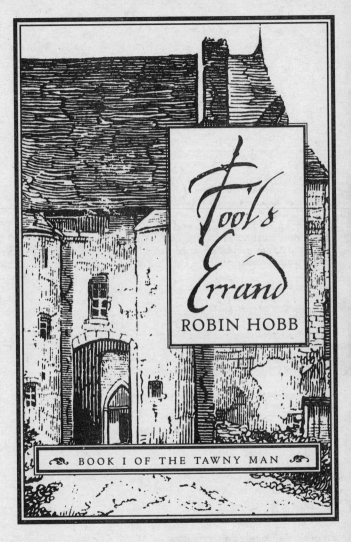

Fool's Errand

ROBIN HOBB

BOOK I OF THE TAWNY MAN

DEL REY • NEW YORK

2015 Del Rey Mass Market Edition

Copyright © 2002 by Robin Hobb

All rights reserved.

Published in the United States by Del Rey, an imprint of Random House, a division of Penguin Random House Company LLC, New York.

DEL REY and the HOUSE colophon are registered trademarks of Penguin Random House LLC.

Originally published in hardcover in the United States by Bantam Spectra, an imprint of Random House, a division of Penguin Random House LLC, in 2002.

ISBN 978-0-553-58244-4
eBook ISBN 978-0-553-89704-3

Cover art by Alejandro Colucci

Printed in the United States of America

www.delreybooks.com

21 20 19 18 17 16 15 14 13

for

RUTH AND

HER LOYAL STRIPERS,

ALEXANDER AND

CRUSADES

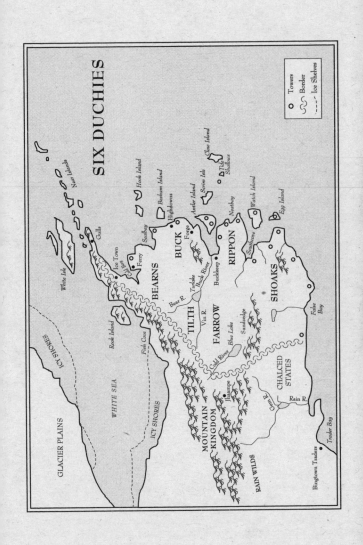

chapter I

CHADE FALLSTAR

Is time the wheel that turns, or the track it leaves behind?
                                   ❧ KELSTAR'S RIDDLE

He came one late, wet spring, and brought the wide world back to my doorstep. I was thirty-five that year. When I was twenty, I would have considered a man of my current age to be teetering on the verge of dotage. These days, it seemed neither young nor old to me, but a suspension between the two. I no longer had the excuse of callow youth, and I could not yet claim the eccentricities of age. In many ways, I was no longer sure what I thought of myself. Sometimes it seemed that my life was slowly disappearing behind me, fading like footprints in the rain, until perhaps I had always been the quiet man living an unremarkable life in a cottage between the forest and the sea.

I lay abed that morning, listening to the small sounds that sometimes brought me peace. The wolf breathed steadily before the softly crackling hearth fire. I quested toward him with our shared Wit magic, and gently brushed his sleeping thoughts. He dreamed of running over snow-smooth rolling hills with a pack. For Nighteyes, it was a dream of silence, cold, and swiftness. Softly I withdrew my touch and left him to his private peace.

Outside my small window, the returning birds sang their challenges to one another. There was a light wind, and whenever it stirred the trees, they released a fresh shower of last night's rain to patter on the wet sward. The trees were silver birches, four of them. They had been little more than sticks when I had planted them. Now their airy foliage cast a pleasant light shade outside my bedroom window. I closed my eyes and could almost feel the flicker of the light on my eyelids. I would not get up, not just yet.

I had had a bad evening the night before, and had had to face it alone. My boy, Hap, had gone off gallivanting with Starling almost three weeks ago, and still had not returned. I could not blame him. My quiet reclusive life was beginning to chafe his young shoulders. Starling's stories of life at Buckkeep, painted with all the skill of her minstrel ways, created pictures too vivid for him to ignore. So I had reluctantly let her take him to Buckkeep for a holiday, that he might see for himself a Springfest there, eat a carris-seed-topped cake, watch a puppet show, mayhap kiss a girl. Hap had grown past the point where regular meals and a warm bed were enough to content him. I had told myself it was time I thought of letting him go, of finding him an apprenticeship with a good carpenter or joiner. He showed a knack for such things, and the sooner a lad took to a trade, the better he learned it. But I was not ready to let him go just yet. For now I would enjoy a month of peace and solitude, and recall how to do things for myself. Nighteyes and I had each other for company. What more could we need?

Yet no sooner were they gone than the little house seemed too quiet. The boy's excitement at leaving had been too reminiscent of how I myself had once felt about Springfests and the like. Puppet shows and carris-seed cakes and girls to kiss all brought back vivid memories I thought I had long ago drowned. Perhaps it was those memories that birthed dreams too vivid to ignore. Twice I had awakened sweating and shaking with my muscles clenched. I had enjoyed years of respite from such unquiet, but in the past four years, my old fixation had returned. Of late, it came and went, with no pattern I could discern. It was almost as if the old Skill magic had suddenly recalled me and was reaching to drag me out of my peace and solitude. Days that had been as smooth and alike as beads on a string were now disrupted by its call. Sometimes the Skill-hunger ate at me as a canker eats sound flesh. Other times, it was no more than a few nights of yearning, vivid dreams. If the boy had been home, I probably could have shaken off the Skill's persistent plucking at me. But he was gone, and so yesterday evening I had given in to the unvanquished addiction such dreams stirred. I had walked down to the sea cliffs, sat on the bench my boy had made for me, and stretched out my magic over the waves. The wolf had sat beside me for a time, his look one of ancient rebuke. I tried to ignore him. "No worse than your penchant for bothering porcupines," I pointed out to him.

Save that their quills can be pulled out. What stabs you only goes deeper and festers. His deep eyes glanced past mine as he shared his pointed thoughts.

Why don't you go hunt a rabbit?

You've sent the boy and his bow away.

"You could run it down yourself, you know. Time was when you did that."

Time was when you went with me to hunt. Why don't we go and do that, instead of this fruitless seeking? When will you accept that there is no one out there who can hear you?

I just have to . . . try.

Why? Is my companionship not enough for you?

It is enough for me. You are always enough for me. I opened myself wider to the Wit-bond we shared and tried to let him feel how the Skill tugged at me. *It is the magic that wants this, not me.*

Take it away. I do not want to see that. And when I had closed that part of myself to him, he asked piteously, *Will it never leave us alone?*

I had no answer to that. After a time, the wolf lay down, put his great head on his paws, and closed his eyes. I knew he would stay by me because he feared for me. Twice the winter before last, I had overindulged in Skilling, burning physical energy in that mental reaching until I had been unable even to totter back to the house on my own. Nighteyes had had to fetch Hap both times. This time we were alone.

I knew it was foolish and useless. I also knew I could not stop myself. Like a starving man who eats grass to appease the terrible emptiness in his belly, so I reached out with the Skill, touching the lives that passed within my reach. I could brush their thoughts and temporarily appease the great craving that filled me with emptiness. I could know a little of the family out for a windy day's fishing. I could know the worries of a captain whose cargo was just a bit heavier than his ship would carry well. The mate on the same ship was worried about the man her daughter wished to marry; he was a lazy fellow for all of his pretty ways. The ship's boy was cursing his luck; they'd get to Buckkeep Town too late for Springfest. There'd be nothing left but withered garlands browning in the gutters by the time he got there. It was always his luck.

There was a certain sparse distraction to these knowings. It restored to me the sense that the world was larger than the four walls of my house, larger even than the confines of my own garden. But it was not the same as true Skilling. It could not compare to that moment of completion when minds joined and one sensed the wholeness of the world as a great entity in which one's own body was no more than a mote of dust.

The wolf's firm teeth on my wrist had stirred me from my reaching. *Come on. That's enough. If you collapse down here, you'll spend a cold wet night. I am not the boy, to drag you to your feet. Come on, now.*

I had risen, seeing blackness at the edges of my vision when I first stood. It had passed, but not the blackness of spirit that came in its wake. I had followed the wolf back through the gathering dark beneath the dripping trees, back to where my fire had burned low in the hearth and the candles guttered on the table. I made myself elfbark tea, black and bitter, knowing it would only make my spirit more desolate, but knowing also that it would appease my aching head. I had burned away the nervous energy of the elfbark by working on a scroll describing the stone game and how it was played. I had tried several times before to complete such a treatise and each time given it up as hopeless. One could only learn to play it by playing it, I told myself. This time I was adding to the text a set of illustrations, to show how a typical game might progress. When I set it aside just before dawn was breaking, it seemed only the stupidest of my latest attempts. I went to bed more early than late.

I awoke to half the morning gone. In the far corner of the yard, the chickens were scratching and gossiping among themselves. The rooster crowed once. I groaned. I should get up. I should check for eggs and scatter a handful of grain to keep the poultry tamed. The garden was just sprouting. It needed weeding already, and I should reseed the row of fesk that the slugs had eaten. I needed to gather some more of the purple flag while it was still in bloom; my last attempt at an ink from it had gone awry, but I wanted to try again. There was wood to split and stack. Porridge to cook, a hearth to sweep. And I should climb the ash tree over the chicken house and cut off that one cracked limb before a storm brought it down on the chicken house itself.

And we should go down to the river and see if the early fish runs have begun yet. Fresh fish would be good. Nighteyes added his own concerns to my mental list.

Last year you nearly died from eating rotten fish.

All the more reason to go now, while they are fresh and jumping. You could use the boy's spear.

And get soaked and chilled.

Better soaked and chilled than hungry.

I rolled over and went back to sleep. So I'd be lazy one morning. Who'd know or care? The chickens? It seemed but moments later that his thoughts nudged me.

My brother, awake. A strange horse comes.

I was instantly alert. The slant of light in my window

told me that hours had passed. I rose, dragged a robe over my head, belted it, and thrust my feet into my summer shoes. They were little more than leather soles with a few straps to keep them on my feet. I pushed my hair back from my face. I rubbed my sandy eyes. "Go see who it is," I bade Nighteyes.

See for yourself. He's nearly to the door.

I was expecting no one. Starling came thrice or four times a year, to visit for a few days and bring me gossip and fine paper and good wine, but she and Hap would not be returning so soon. Other visitors to my door were rare. There was Baylor who had his cot and hogs in the next vale, but he did not own a horse. A tinker came by twice a year. He had found me first by accident in a thunderstorm when his horse had gone lame and my light through the trees had drawn him from the road. Since his visit, I'd had other visits from similar travelers. The tinker had carved a curled cat, the sign of a hospitable house, on a tree beside the trail that led to my cabin. I had found it, but left it intact, to beckon an occasional visitor to my door.

So this caller was probably a lost traveler, or a road-weary trader. I told myself a guest might be a pleasant distraction, but the thought was less than convincing.

I heard the horse halt outside and the small sounds of a man dismounting.

The Gray One, the wolf growled low.

My heart near stopped in my chest. I opened the door slowly as the old man was reaching to knock at it. He peered at me, and then his smile broke forth. "Fitz, my boy. Ah, Fitz!"

He reached to embrace me. For an instant, I stood frozen, unable to move. I did not know what I felt. That my old mentor had tracked me down after all these years was frightening. There would be a reason, something more than simply seeing me again. But I also felt that leap of kinship, that sudden stirring of interest that Chade had always roused in me. When I had been a boy at Buckkeep, his secret summons would come at night, bidding me climb the concealed stair to his lair in the tower above my room. There he mixed his poisons and taught me the assassin's trade and made me irrevocably his. Always my heart had beaten faster at the opening of that secret door. Despite all the years and the pain, he still affected me that way. Secrets and the promise of adventure clung to him.

So I found myself reaching out to grasp his stooping shoulders and pull him to me in a hug. Skinny, the old man was getting skinny again, as bony as he had been when I first met him. But now I was the recluse in the worn robe of gray wool. He was dressed in royal blue leggings and a doublet of the same with slashed insets of green that sparked off his eyes. His riding boots were black leather, as were the soft gloves he wore. His cloak of green matched the insets in his doublet and was lined with fur. White lace spilled from his collar and sleeves. The scattered scars that had once shamed him into hiding had faded to a pale speckling on his weathered face. His white hair hung loose to his shoulders and was curled above his brow. There were emeralds in his earrings, and another one set squarely in the center of the gold band at his throat.

The old assassin smiled mockingly as he saw me take in his splendor. "Ah, but a queen's councillor must look the part, if he is to get the respect both he and she deserve in his dealings."

"I see," I said faintly, and then, finding my tongue, "Come in, do come in. I fear you will find my home a bit ruder than what you have obviously become accustomed to, but you are welcome all the same."

"I did not come to quibble about your house, boy. I came to see you."

"Boy?" I asked him quietly as I smiled and showed him in.

"Ah, well. To me, always, perhaps. It is one of the advantages of age, I can call anyone almost anything I please, and no one dares challenge me. Ah, you have the wolf still,

I see. Nighteyes, was it? Up in years a bit now; I don't recall that white on your muzzle. Come here now, there's a good fellow. Fitz, would you mind seeing to my horse? I've been all morning in the saddle, and spent last night at a perfectly wretched inn. I'm a bit stiff, you know. And just bring in my saddlebags, would you? There's a good lad."

He stooped to scratch the wolf's ears, his back to me, confident I would obey him. And I grinned and did. The black mare he'd ridden was a fine animal, amiable and willing. There is always a pleasure to caring for a creature of that quality. I watered her well, gave her some of the chickens' grain, and turned her into the pony's empty paddock. The saddlebags that I carried back to the house were heavy and one sloshed promisingly.

I entered to find Chade in my study, sitting at my writing desk, poring over my papers as if they were his own. "Ah, there you are. Thank you, Fitz. This, now, this is the stone game, isn't it? The one Kettle taught you, to help you focus your mind away from the Skill-road? Fascinating. I'd like to have this one when you are finished with it."

"If you wish," I said quietly. I knew a moment's unease. He tossed out words and names I had buried and left undisturbed. Kettle. The Skill-road. I pushed them back into the past. "It's not Fitz anymore," I said pleasantly. "It's Tom Badgerlock."

"Oh?"

I touched the streak of white in my hair from my scar. "For this. People remember the name. I tell them I was born with the white streak, and so my parents named me."

"I see," he said noncommittally. "Well, it makes sense, and it's sensible." He leaned back in my wooden chair. It creaked. "There's brandy in those bags, if you've cups for us. And some of old Sara's ginger cakes . . . I doubt you'd expect me to remember how fond you were of those. Probably a bit squashed, but it's the taste that matters with those." The wolf had already sat up. He came to place his nose on the edge of the table. It pointed directly at the bags.

"So. Sara is still cook at Buckkeep?" I asked as I looked for two presentable cups. Chipped crockery didn't bother me, but I was suddenly reluctant to set it out for Chade.

Chade left the study and came to my kitchen table. "Oh, not really. Her old feet bother her if she stands too long. She has a big cushioned chair, set up on a platform in the corner of the kitchen. She supervises from there. She cooks the things she enjoys cooking, the fancy pastries, the spiced cakes, and the sweets. There's a young man named Duff does most of the daily cooking now." He was unpacking the saddlebags as he spoke. He set out two bottles marked as Sandsedge brandy. I could not remember the last time I'd tasted that. The ginger cakes, a bit squashed as foretold, emerged, spilling crumbs from the linen he'd wrapped them in. The wolf sniffed deeply, then began salivating. "His favorites too, I see," Chade observed dryly, and tossed him one. The wolf caught it neatly and carried it off to devour on the hearthrug.

The saddlebags gave up their other treasures quickly. A sheaf of fine paper, pots of blue, red, and green inks. A fat ginger root, just starting to sprout, ready to be potted for the summer. Some packets of spices. A rare luxury for me, a round ripe cheese. And in a little wooden chest, other items, hauntingly strange in their familiarity. Small things I had thought long lost to me. A ring that had belonged to Prince Rurisk of the Mountain Kingdom. The arrowhead that had pierced the Prince's chest and nearly been the death of him. A small carved box, made by my hands years ago, to contain my poisons. I opened it. It was empty. I put the lid back on the box and set it down on the table. I looked at him. He was not just one old man come to visit me. He brought all of my past trailing along behind him as an embroidered train follows a woman into a hall. When I let him into my door, I had let in my old world with him.

"Why?" I asked quietly. "Why, after all these years, have you sought me out?"

"Oh, well." Chade drew a chair up to the table and sat

down with a sigh. He unstoppered the brandy and poured for both of us. "A dozen reasons. I saw your boy with Starling. And I knew at once who he was. Not that he looks like you, any more than Nettle looks like Burrich. But he has your mannerisms, your way of holding back and looking at a thing, with his head cocked just so before he decides whether he'll be drawn in. He put me so much in mind of you at that age that—"

"You've seen Nettle," I cut in quietly. It was not a question.

"Of course," he replied as quietly. "Would you like to know about her?"

I did not trust my tongue to answer. All my old cautions warned me against evincing too great an interest in her. Yet I felt a prickle of foreknowledge that Nettle, my daughter whom I had never seen except in visions, was the reason Chade had come here. I looked at my cup and weighed the merits of brandy for breakfast. Then I thought again of Nettle, the bastard I had unwillingly abandoned before her birth. I drank. I had forgotten how smooth Sandsedge brandy was. Its warmth spread through me as rapidly as youthful lust.

Chade was merciful, in that he did not force me to voice my interest. "She looks much like you, in a skinny, female way," he said, then smiled to see me bristle. "But, strange to tell, she resembles Burrich even more. She has more of his mannerisms and habits of speech than any of his five sons."

"Five!" I exclaimed in astonishment.

Chade grinned. "Five boys, and all as respectful and deferential to their father as any man could wish. Not at all like Nettle. She has mastered that black look of Burrich's and gives it right back to him when he scowls at her. Which is seldom. I won't say she's his favorite, but I think she wins more of his favor by standing up to him than all the boys do with their earnest respect. She has Burrich's impatience, and his keen sense of right and wrong. And all your stubbornness, but perhaps she learned that from Burrich as well."

"You saw Burrich then?" He had raised me, and now he raised my daughter as his own. He'd taken to wife the woman I'd seemingly abandoned. They both thought me dead. Their lives had gone on without me. To hear of them mingled pain with fondness. I chased the taste of it away with Sandsedge brandy.

"It would have been impossible to see Nettle, save that I saw Burrich also. He watches over her like, well, like her father. He's well. His limp has not improved with the years. But he is seldom afoot, so it seems to bother him little. It is horses with him, always horses, as it always was." He cleared his throat. "You do know that the Queen and I saw to it that both Ruddy's and Sooty's colts were given over to him? Well, he's founded his livelihood on those two stud horses. The mare you unsaddled, Ember, I got her from him. He trains as well as breeds horses now. He will never be a wealthy man, for the moment he has a coin to spare, it goes for another horse or to buy more pasturage. But when I asked him how he did, he told me, 'Well enough.'"

"And what did Burrich say of your visit?" I asked. I was proud I could speak with an unchoked voice.

Chade grinned again, but there was a rueful edge to it. "After he got over the shock of seeing me, he was most courteous and welcoming. And as he walked me out to my horse the next morning, which one of the twins, Nim I think, had saddled for me, he quietly promised that he'd kill me before he'd brook any interference with Nettle. He spoke the words regretfully, but with great sincerity. I didn't doubt them from him, so I don't need them repeated from you."

"Does she know Burrich is not her father? Does she know anything of me?" Question after question sprang to my mind. I thrust them away. I hated the avidity with which I had asked those two, but I could not resist. It was like the Skill addiction, this hunger to know, finally *know* these things after all the years.

Chade looked aside from me and sipped his brandy. "I don't know. She calls him Papa. She loves him fiercely, with absolutely no reservations. Oh, she disagrees with him, but it is about things rather than about Burrich himself. I'm afraid that with her mother, things are stormier. Nettle has no interest in bees or candles, but Molly would like to see her daughter follow her in her trade. As stubborn as Nettle is, I think Molly will have to be content with a son or two instead." He glanced out the window. He added quietly, "We did not speak your name when Nettle was present."

I turned my cup in my hands. "What things do interest her?"

"Horses. Hawks. Swords. At fifteen, I expected at least some talk of young men from her, but she seems to have no use for them. Perhaps the woman in her hasn't wakened yet, or perhaps she has too many brothers to have any romantic illusions about boys. She would like to run away to Buckkeep and join one of the guard companies. She knows Burrich was Stablemaster there once. One of the reasons I went to see him was to make Kettricken's offer of that position again. Burrich refused it. Nettle cannot understand why."

"I do."

"As do I. But when I visited, I told him that I could make a place for Nettle there, even if he chose not to go. She could page for me, if nothing else, though I am sure Queen Kettricken would love to have her. Let her see the way of a keep and a city, let her have a taste of life at Court, I told him. Burrich turned it down instantly, and seemed almost offended that I'd offered it."

Without intending, I breathed out softly in relief. Chade took another sip of his brandy and sat regarding me. Waiting. He knew my next question as well as I did. Why? Why did he seek out Burrich, why did he offer to take Nettle to Buckkeep? I took more of my own brandy and considered the old man. Old. Yes, but not as some men get old. His hair had gone completely white, but the green of his eyes seemed to burn all the fiercer beneath those snowy locks. I wondered how hard he fought his body to keep the stoop in his shoulders from becoming a curl, what drugs he took to prolong his vigor and what those drugs cost him in other ways. He was older than King Shrewd, and Shrewd was all these many years dead. Bastard royalty of the same lineage as myself, he seemed to thrive on intrigue and strife as I had not. I had fled the court and all it contained. Chade had chosen to stay, and make himself indispensable to yet another generation of Farseers.

"So. And how is Patience these days?" I chose my question with care. News of my father's wife was well wide of what I wished to know, but I could use his answer to venture closer.

"Lady Patience? Ah, well, it has been some months since I have seen her. Over a year, now that I think of it. She resides at Tradeford, you know. She rules there, and quite well. Odd, when you think of it. When she was indeed queen and wed to your father, she never asserted herself. Widowed, she was well content to be eccentric Lady Patience. But when all others fled, she became queen in fact if not by title at Buckkeep. Queen Kettricken was wise to give her a domain of her own, for she never again could have abided at Buckkeep as less than queen."

"And Prince Dutiful?"

"As like his father as he can be," Chade observed, shaking his head. I watched him closely, wondering how the old man intended the remark. How much did he know? He frowned as he continued. "The Queen needs to let him out a bit. The folk speak of Dutiful as they did of your father, Chivalry. 'Correct to a fault,' they say and almost have the truth of it, I fear."

There had been a very slight change in his voice. "Almost?" I asked quietly.

Chade gave me a smile that was almost apologetic. "Of late the boy has not been himself. He has always been a solitary lad—but that goes with being the sole prince. He has always had to keep his position in mind, always had to take care that he was not seen to favor one companion over another. It has made him introspective. But recently he has shifted to a darker temperament. He is distracted and moody, so caught up in his inner thoughts that he seems completely unaware of what is going on in the lives of those around him. He is not discourteous or uncaring; at least, not deliberately. But . . ."

"He's what, fourteen?" I asked. "He does not sound so different from Hap, of late. I've been thinking much the same things about him; that I need to let him out a bit. It's time he got out and learned something new, from someone other than myself."

Chade nodded. "I think you are absolutely correct. Queen Kettricken and I have reached the same decision about Prince Dutiful."

His tone made me suspect I had just run my head into the snare. "Oh?" I said carefully.

"Oh?" Chade mimicked me, and then leaned forward to tip more brandy into his glass. He grinned, letting me know the game was at an end. "Oh, yes. You've no doubt guessed it. We would like to have you come back to Buckkeep and instruct the Prince in the Skill. And Nettle too, if Burrich can be persuaded to let her go and if she has any aptitude for it."

"No." I said the word quickly before I could be seduced. I am not sure how definitive my answer sounded. No sooner had Chade broached the idea than desire for it surged in me. It was the answer, the so-simple answer after all these years. Train up a new coterie of Skill-users. I knew Chade had the scrolls and tablets relating to the Skill magic. Galen the Skillmaster and then Prince Regal had wrongfully withheld them from us, so many years ago. But now I could study them, I could learn more and I could train up others, not as Galen had done, but correctly. Prince Dutiful would have a Skilled coterie to aid and protect him, and I would have an end to my loneliness. There would be someone to reach back when I reached out.

And both my children would know me, as a person if not as their father.

Chade was as sly as ever. He must have sensed my ambivalence. He left my denial hanging alone in the air between us. He held his cup in both hands. He glanced down at it briefly, putting me sharply in mind of Verity. Then he looked up again, his green eyes meeting mine without hesitation. He asked no questions, he made no demands. All he had to do was wait.

Knowing his tactic did not shield me against it. "You know I cannot. You know all the reasons I should not."

He shook his head slightly. "Not really. Why should Prince Dutiful be denied his birthright as a Farseer?" More softly he added, "Or Nettle?"

"Birthright?" I tried for a bitter laugh. "It's more like a family disease, Chade. It's a hunger, and when you are taught how to satisfy it, it becomes an addiction. An addiction that can become strong enough eventually to set your feet on the paths that lead past the Mountain Kingdom. You saw what became of Verity. The Skill devoured him. He turned it to his own ends; he made his dragon and poured himself into it. He saved the Six Duchies. But even if there had been no Red Ships to battle, Verity would eventually have gone to the Mountains. That place called him. It is the ordained end for any Skilled one."

"I understand your fears," he confessed quietly. "But I think you are wrong. I believe Galen deliberately instilled that fear in you. He limited what you learned, and he battered fear into you. But I've read the Skill-scrolls. I haven't deciphered all that they tell, but I know it is so much more than simply being able to communicate across a distance. With the Skill, a man can prolong his own life and health. It can enhance a speaker's powers of persuasion. Your training . . . I don't know how far it went, but I'll wager Galen taught you as little as he could." I could hear the excitement building in the old man's voice, as if he spoke of a hidden treasure. "There is so much to the Skill, so much. Some scrolls imply that the Skill can be used as a healing tool, not only to find out exactly what is wrong with an injured warrior, but actually to encourage the healing of those hurts. A strong Skilled one can see through another's eyes, hear what that other hears and feels. And—"

"Chade." The softness of my voice cut him off. I had known a moment of outrage when he admitted he'd read the scrolls. He'd had no right, I'd thought, and then known that if his Queen gave them to him to read, he had as much right as anyone. Who else should read them? There was no Skillmaster anymore. That line of ability had died out. No. I had killed it. Killed off, one by one, the last trained Skillusers, the last coterie ever created at Buckkeep. They had been faithless to their King, so I had destroyed them and the magic with them. The part of me that was rational knew that it was magic better left dead. "I am no Skillmaster, Chade. It's not only that my knowledge of the Skill is incomplete, but that my talent was erratic. If you've read the scrolls, then I'm sure you've discovered for yourself, or heard from Kettricken, that using elfbark is the worst thing a Skilled one can do. It suppresses or kills the talent. I've tried to stay away from it; I don't like what it does to me. But even the bleakness it brings on is better than the Skillhunger. Sometimes I've used elfbark steadily for days at a time, when the craving was bad." I looked away from the concern on his face. "Whatever talent I ever had is probably stunted beyond recall now."

His voice was soft as he observed, "It seems to me that your continued craving would indicate the opposite, Fitz. I'm sorry to hear you've been suffering; we truly had no idea. I had assumed the Skill-hunger would be like a man's craving for drink or smoke, and that after a period of enforced abstinence, the longing would grow less."

"No. It does not. Sometimes it lies dormant. Months

pass, even years. Then, for no reason I can tell, it stirs to life again." I squeezed my eyes shut for an instant. Talking about it, thinking about it was like prodding at a boil. "Chade. I know that this is why you came all this way to find me. And you've heard me say no. Now can we speak of other things? This conversation . . . pains me."

For a time he was silent. There was a false heartiness in his voice when he abruptly said, "Of course we can. I told Kettricken that I doubted you'd fall in with our plan." He gave a brief sigh. "I'll simply have to do the best I can with what I've gleaned from the scrolls. Now. I've had my say. What would you like to hear about?"

"You can't mean that you'll try to teach Dutiful the Skill from what you've read in some old scrolls?" I was suddenly on the edge of anger.

"You leave me no choice," he pointed out pleasantly.

"Do you grasp the danger you'd be exposing him to? The Skill draws a man, Chade. It pulls at the mind and heart like a lodestone. He will want to be one with it. If the Prince yields to that attraction for even an instant while he's learning, he'll be gone. And there will be no Skilled one to go after him, to put him back together and drag him from the current."

I could tell from the expression on Chade's face that he had no understanding of what I was telling him. He only replied stubbornly, "What I read in the scrolls is that there is danger to leaving one with a strong Skill-talent completely untrained. In some cases, such youngsters have begun to Skill almost instinctively, but with no concept of the danger or how to control it. I should think that even a little knowledge might be better than to leave the young Prince in total ignorance."

I opened my mouth to speak, then shut it again. I drew a deep breath and let it out slowly. "I won't be drawn into it, Chade. I refuse. Years ago I promised myself. I sat by Will and watched him die. I didn't kill him. Because I'd promised myself I was no longer an assassin, and no longer a tool.

I won't be manipulated and I won't be used. I've made enough sacrifices. I think I've earned this retirement. And if you and Kettricken disagree with that and no longer wish to provide me with coin, well, I can cope with that as well."

As well to have that out in the open. The first time I'd found a bag of coins by my bed after Starling had visited, I was insulted. I'd hoarded the affront for months until she visited me again. She'd only laughed at me, and told me they weren't largesse from her for my services, if that's what I'd thought, but a pension from the Six Duchies. That was when I'd forced myself to admit that whatever Starling knew of me, Chade knew as well. He was also the source of the fine paper and good inks she sometimes brought. She probably reported to him each time she returned to Buckkeep. I'd told myself it didn't bother me. But now I wondered if all those years of keeping track of me had been Chade waiting for me to be useful again. I think he read my face.

"Fitz, Fitz, calm down." The old man reached across the table to pat my hand reassuringly. "There's been no talk of anything like that. We are both well aware of not only what we owe you, but also what the whole Six Duchies owes you. As long as you live, the Six Duchies will provide for you. As for Prince Dutiful's training, put it out of your head. It's not truly your concern at all."

Once again, I wondered uneasily how much he knew. Then I steeled myself. "As you say, it's not truly my concern. All I can do is warn you to be cautious."

"Ah, Fitz, have you ever known me to be otherwise?" His eyes smiled at me over the rim of his cup.

I set it aside, but forbidding myself the idea was like tearing a tree up by the roots. Part of it was my fear that Chade's inexperienced tutelage of the young Prince would lead him into danger. But by far the biggest part of my desire to teach a new coterie was simply so that I could furnish myself with a way to satisfy my own craving. Having recognized that, there was no way I could in good conscience inflict this addiction on another generation.

Chade was as good as his word. He spoke no more about Skilling. Instead, we talked for hours of all the folk I had once known at Buckkeep and what had become of them. Blade was a grandfather, and Lacey was plagued with aching joints that had finally forced her to set her endless tatting aside. Hands was the Stablemaster at Buckkeep now. He had married an inland woman with fiery red hair and a temper to match. All of their children had red hair. She kept Hands on a short leash, and according to Chade, he seemed only happier for it. Of late, she was nagging him to return to Farrow, her homeland, and he seemed prone to indulge her; thus Chade's trip to see Burrich and offer him his old position again. So on and on, he peeled callus away from my memories and brought all the old faces fresh to my mind again. It made me ache for Buckkeep and I could not forbear to ask my questions. When we ran out of folk to gossip about, I walked him about my place as if we were two old aunties visiting one another. I showed him my chickens and my birch trees, my garden and my walks. I showed him my work shed, where I made the dyes and colored inks that Hap took to market for me. Those, at least, surprised him. "I brought you inks from Buckkeep, but now I wonder if your own are not the better." He patted my shoulder, just as he once had when I mixed a poison correctly, and the old wash of pleasure at his pride in me rushed through me.

I showed him probably far more than I intended. When he looked at my herb beds, he no doubt marked the preponderance of sedatives and painkillers among my drug plants. When I showed him my bench on the cliffs overlooking the sea, he even said quietly, "Yes, Verity would have liked this." But despite what he saw and guessed, he spoke no more of the Skill.

We stayed up late that night, and I taught him the basics of Kettle's stone game. Nighteyes grew bored with our long talk and went hunting. I sensed a bit of jealousy from the wolf, but resolved to settle it with him later. When we set our game aside, I turned our talk to Chade himself and how he fared. He smilingly conceded that he enjoyed his return to court and society. He spoke to me, as he seldom had before, of his youth. He'd led a gay life before his mishandling of a potion had scarred him and made him so ashamed of his appearance that he had retreated into a secretive shadow life as a king's assassin. In these late years, he seemed to have resumed the life of that young man who had so enjoyed dancing and private dinners with witty ladies. I was glad for him, and spoke mostly in jest when I asked, "But how then do you fit in your quiet work for the crown, with all these other assignations and entertainments?"

His reply was frank. "I manage. And my current apprentice is proving both quick and adept. The time will not be long before I can set those old tasks completely into younger hands."

I knew an unsettling moment of jealousy that he had taken another in my place. An instant later, I recognized how foolish that was. The Farseers would ever have need of a man capable of quietly dispensing the King's Justice. I had declared I would no longer be a royal assassin; that did not mean the need for one had disappeared. I tried to recover my aplomb. "Then the old experiments and lessons still continue in the tower."

He nodded once, gravely. "They do. As a matter of fact . . ." He rose suddenly from his seat by the fire. Out of long habit reawakened, we had resumed our old postures, him sitting in a chair before the fire and me on the hearth by his feet. Only at that moment did I realize how odd that was, and wonder at how natural it had seemed. I shook my head at myself as Chade rummaged through the saddlebags on the table. He came out with a stained flask of hard leather. "I brought this to show to you, and then in all our talk, I nearly forgot it. You recall my fascination with unnatural fires and smokes and the like?"

I rolled my eyes. His "fascination" had scorched us both more than once. I refused the memory of the last time I had witnessed his fire magic: he had made the torches of Buckkeep burn blue and sputter on the night Prince Regal falsely declared himself the immediate heir to the Farseer crown. That night had also seen the murder of King Shrewd and my subsequent arrest for it.

If Chade made that connection, he gave no sign of it. He returned eagerly to the fireside with his flask. "Have you a twist of paper? I didn't bring any."

I found him some, and watched dubiously as he took a long strip of my paper, folded it lengthwise, and then judiciously tapped a measure of powder down the groove of the fold. Carefully he folded the paper over it, folded it again, and then secured it with a spiraling twist. "Now watch this!" he invited me eagerly.

I watched with trepidation as he set the paper into the fire on the hearth. But whatever it was supposed to do, flash or sparkle or make a smoke, it didn't. The paper turned brown, caught fire, and burned. There was a slight stink of sulfur. That was all. I raised an eyebrow at Chade.

"That's not right!" he protested, flustered. Working swiftly, he prepared another twist of paper, but this time he was more generous with the powder from the small flask. He set the paper in the hottest part of the fire. I leaned back from the hearth, braced for the effect, but again we were disappointed. I rubbed my mouth to cover a grin at the chagrin on his face.

"You'll think I've lost my touch!" he declared.

"Oh, never that," I responded, but it was hard to keep the mirth from my voice. This time the paper he prepared was more like a fat tube, and powder leaked from it as he twisted it closed. I stood up and retreated from the fireplace as he set it onto the flames. But as before, it only burned.

He gave a great snort of disgust. He peered down the dark neck of the small flask, then shook it. With an exclamation of disgust, he stoppered it. "Damp got into it somehow. Well. That's spoiled my show." He tossed the flask into the fire, a mark of high dudgeon for Chade.

As I sat back down by the hearth, I sensed the keenness

of his disappointment and felt a touch of pity for the old man. I tried to take the sting from it. "It reminds me of the time I confused the smoke powder with the powdered lancet root. Do you remember that? My eyes watered for hours."

He gave a short laugh. "I do." He was silent for a time, smiling to himself. I knew his mind wandered back to our old days together. Then he leaned forward to set his hand to my shoulder. "Fitz," he demanded earnestly, his eyes locking with mine. "I never deceived you, did I? I was fair. I told you what I was teaching you, from the very beginning."

I saw then the lump of the scar between us. I put my hand up to cover his. His knuckles were bony, his skin gone papery thin. I looked back into the flames as I spoke to him. "You were always honest with me, Chade. If anyone deceived me, it was myself. We each served our King, and did what we must in that cause. I won't come back to Buckkeep. But it's not because of anything you did, but only because of who I've become. I bear you no ill will, for anything."

I turned to look up at him. His face was very grave, and I saw in his eyes what he had not said to me. He missed me. His asking me to return to Buckkeep was as much for himself as for any other reason. I discovered then a small share of healing and peace. I was still loved, by Chade at least. It moved me and I felt my throat tighten with it. I tried to find lighter words. "You never claimed that being your apprentice would give me a calm, safe life."

As if to confirm those words, a sudden flash erupted from my fire. If my face had not been turned toward Chade, I suppose I might have been blinded. As it was, a blast like lightning and thunder together deafened me. Flying coals and sparks stung me, and the fire roared suddenly like an angry beast. We both sprang to our feet and scrambled back from the fireplace. An instant later, a fall of soot from my neglected chimney put out most of the hearth fire. Chade and I scurried about the room, stamping out the glowing sparks and kicking pieces of burning flask back onto the hearth before the floor could take fire. The door burst open under Nighteyes' assault on it. He flew into the room, claws scrabbling for purchase as he slid to a halt.

"I'm fine, I'm fine," I assured him, and then realized I was yelling past the ringing in my ears. Nighteyes gave a disgusted snort at the smell in the room. Without even sharing a thought with me, he stalked back into the night.

Chade suddenly slapped me several times on the shoulder. "Putting out a coal," he assured me loudly. It took us some time to restore order and renew the fire in its rightful place. Even so, he pulled his chair back from it, and I did not sit down on the hearth. "Was that what the powder was supposed to do?" I asked belatedly when we were resettled with more Sandsedge brandy.

"No! El's balls, boy, do you think I'd deliberately do that in your hearth? What I'd been producing before was a sudden flash of white light, almost blinding. The powder shouldn't have done that. Still. I wonder why it did. What was different? Damn. I wish I could remember what I last stored in that flask . . ." He knit his brows and stared fiercely into the flames, and I knew his new apprentice would be put to puzzling out just what had caused that blast. I did not envy him the series of experiments that would undoubtedly follow.

He spent the night at my cottage, taking my bed while I made do with Hap's. But when we arose the next morning, we both knew the visit was at an end. There suddenly seemed to be nothing else to discuss, and little point to talking about anything. A sort of bleakness rose in me. Why should I ask after folk I'd never see again; why should he tell me of the current crop of political intrigues when they had no touch on my life at all? For one long afternoon and evening, our lives had meshed again, but now as the gray day dawned, he watched me go about my homely tasks; drawing water and throwing feed to my poultry, cooking breakfast for us and washing up the crockery. We seemed to grow more distant with every awkward silence. Almost I began to wish he had not come.

After breakfast, he said he must be on his way and I did not try to dissuade him. I promised him he should have the game scroll when it was finished. I gave him several vellums I had written on dosages for sedative teas, and some roots for starts of the few herbs in my garden that he did not already know. I gave him several vials of different-colored ink. The closest he came to trying to change my mind was when he observed that there was a better market for such things in Buckkeep. I only nodded, and said I might send Hap there sometimes. Then I saddled and bridled the fine mare and brought her around for him. He hugged me goodbye, mounted, and left. I watched as he rode down the path. Beside me, Nighteyes slipped his head under my hand.

You regret this?

I regret many things. But I know that if I went with him and did as he wishes, I would eventually regret that much more. Yet I could not move from where I stood, staring after him. It wasn't too late, I tempted myself. One shout, and he'd turn about and come back. I clenched my jaws.

Nighteyes flipped my hand with his nose. *Come on. Let's go hunting. No boy, no bows. Just you and I.*

"Sounds good," I heard myself say. And we did, and we even caught a fine spring rabbit. It felt good to stretch my muscles and prove that I could still do it. I decided I was not an old man, not yet, and that I, as much as Hap, needed to get out and do some new things. Learn something new. That had always been Patience's cure for boredom. That evening as I looked about my cottage, it seemed suffocating rather than snug. What had been familiar and cozy a few nights ago now seemed threadbare and dull. I knew it was just the contrast between Chade's stories of Buckkeep and my own staid life. But restlessness, once awakened, is a powerful thing.

I tried to think when I had last slept anywhere other than my own bed. Mine was a settled life. At harvesttime each year, I took to the road for a month, hiring out to work the hayfields or the grain harvest or as an apple picker. The extra coins were welcome. I had used to go into Howsbay twice a year, to trade my inks and dyes for fabric for clothing and pots and things of that ilk. The last two years, I had sent the boy on his fat old pony. My life had settled into routine so deeply that I had not even noticed it.

So. What do you want to do? Nighteyes stretched and then yawned in resignation.

I don't know, I admitted to the old wolf. *Something different. How would you feel about wandering the world for a bit?*

For a time, he retreated into that part of his mind that was his alone. Then he asked, somewhat testily, *Would we both be afoot, or do you expect me to keep pace with a horse all day?*

That's a fair question. If we both went afoot?

If you must, he conceded grudgingly. *You're thinking about that place, back in the Mountains, aren't you?*

The ancient city? Yes.

He did not oppose me. *Will we be taking the boy?*

I think we'll leave Hap here to do for himself for a bit. It might be good for him. And someone has to look after the chickens.

So I suppose we won't be leaving until the boy comes back?

I nodded to that. I wondered if I had taken complete leave of my senses.

I wondered if we would ever come back at all.

chapter II

STARLING

*Starling Birdsong, minstrel to Queen Kettricken, has inspired
as many songs as she has written. Legendary as Queen
Kettricken's companion on her quest for Elderling aid during the
Red Ship War, she extended her service to the Farseer throne
for decades during the rebuilding of the Six Duchies. Gifted
with the knack of being at home in any company, she was
indispensable to the Queen in the unsettled years that followed
the Cleansing of Buck. The minstrel was trusted not only with
treaties and settlements between nobles, but with offers of
amnesty to robber bands and smuggler families. She herself
made songs of many of these missions, but one can be sure that
she had other endeavors, carried out in secret for the Farseer
reign, and far too sensitive to ever become the subject of verse.*

Starling kept Hap with her for a full two months. My
amusement at his extended absence changed first to irritation and then annoyance. The annoyance was mostly with
myself. I had not realized how much I had come to depend
on the boy's strong back until I had to bend mine to the
tasks I'd delegated to him. But it was not just the boy's ordinary chores that I undertook during that extra month of his
absence. Chade's visit had awakened something in me. I
had no name for it, but it seemed a demon that gnawed at
me, showing me every shabby aspect of my small holding.
The peace of my isolated home now seemed idle complacency. Had it truly been a year since I had shoved a rock under the sagging porch step and promised myself I'd fix it
later? No, it had been closer to a year and a half.

I put the porch to rights, and then not only shoveled out the chicken house but washed it down with lye-water before gathering fresh reeds to floor it. I fixed the leaking roof on my work shed, and finally cut the hole and put in the greased skin window I'd been promising myself for two years. I gave the cottage a more thorough spring-cleaning than it had had in years. I cut down the cracked ash limb, dropping it neatly through the roof of the freshly cleaned chicken house. I reroofed the chicken house. I was just finishing that task when Nighteyes told me he heard horses. I clambered down, picked up my shirt, and walked around to the front of the cottage to greet Starling and Hap as they came up the trail.

I do not know if it was our time apart, or my newly seeded restlessness, but I suddenly saw Hap and Starling as if they were strangers. It was not just the new garb Hap wore, although that accentuated his long legs and broadening shoulders. He looked comical atop the fat old pony, a fact I am sure he appreciated. The pony was as ill-suited to the growing youth as the child's bed in my cottage and my sedate lifestyle. I suddenly perceived that I could not rightfully ask him to stay home and watch the chickens while I went adventuring. In fact, if I did not soon send him out to seek his own fortune, the mild discontent I saw in his mismatched eyes at his homecoming would soon become bitter disappointment in his life. Hap had been a good companion for me; the foundling I had taken in had, perhaps, rescued me as much as I had rescued him. It would be far better for me to send this young man out into the world while we both still liked one another rather than wait until I was a burdensome duty to his young shoulders.

Not just Hap had changed in my eyes. Starling was vibrant as ever, grinning as she flung a leg over her horse and slid down from him. Yet as she came toward me with her arms flung wide to hug me, I realized how little I knew of her present life. I looked down into her merry dark eyes and noted for the first time the crow's-feet beginning at the corners. Her garb had become richer over the years, the quality of her mounts better, and her jewelry more costly. Today her thick dark hair was secured with a clasp of heavy silver. Clearly, she prospered. Three or four times a year, she would descend on me, to stay a few days and overturn my calm life with her stories and songs. For the days she was there, she would insist on spicing the food to her taste, she would scatter an overlay of her possessions upon my table and desk and floor, and my bed would no longer be a place to seek when I was exhausted. The days that immediately followed her departure would remind me of a country road with dust hanging heavy in the air in the wake of a puppeteer's caravan. I would have the same sense of choked breath and hazed vision until I once more settled into my humdrum routine.

I hugged her back, hard, smelling both dust and perfume in her hair. She stepped away from me, looked up into my face, and immediately demanded, "What's wrong? Something's different."

I smiled ruefully. "I'll tell you later," I promised, and we both knew that it would be one of our late-night conversations.

"Go wash," she agreed. "You smell like my horse." She gave me a slight push, and I stepped clear of her to greet Hap.

"So, lad, how was it? Did a Buckkeep Springfest live up to Starling's tales?"

"It was good," he said neutrally. He gave me one full look, and his mismatched eyes, one brown, one blue, were full of torment.

"Hap?" I began concernedly, but he shrugged away from me before I could touch his shoulder.

He walked away from me, but perhaps he regretted his surly greeting, for a moment later he croaked, "I'm going to the stream to wash. I'm covered in road dust."

Go with him. I'm not sure what's wrong, but he needs a friend.

Preferably one that can't ask questions, Nighteyes agreed.

Head low, tail straight out, he followed the boy. In his own way, he was as fond of Hap as I was, and had had as much to do with his raising.

When they were out of eyeshot, I turned back to Starling. "Do you know what that was about?"

She shrugged, a twisted smile on her lips. "He's fifteen. Does a sullen mood have to be about anything at that age? Don't bother yourself over it. It could be anything: a girl at Springfest who didn't kiss him, or one who did. Leaving Buckkeep or coming home. A bad sausage for breakfast. Leave him alone. He'll be fine."

I looked after him as he and the wolf vanished into the trees. "Perhaps I remember being fifteen a bit differently from you," I commented.

I saw to her horse and Clover the pony while Starling went into the cottage, reflecting as I did so that no matter what my mood, Burrich would have ordered me to see to my horse before I wandered off. Well, I was not Burrich, I thought to myself. I wondered if he held the same line of discipline with Nettle and Chivalry and Nim as he had with me, and then wished I had asked Chade the rest of his children's names. By the time the horses were comfortable, I was wishing that Chade had not come. His visit had stirred too many old memories to the surface. Resolutely, I pushed them away. Bones fifteen years old, the wolf would have told me. I touched minds with him briefly. Hap had splashed some water on his face, and strode off into the woods, muttering and walking so carelessly that there was no chance they'd see any game. I sighed for them both, and went into the cottage.

Inside, Starling had dumped the contents of her saddlebags on the table. Her discarded boots were lying across the doorsill; her cloak festooned a chair. The kettle was just starting to boil. She stood on a stool before my cupboard. As I came in, she held out a small brown crock to me. "Is this tea any good still? It smells odd."

"It's excellent, when I'm in enough pain to choke it

down. Come down from there." I set my hands to her waist and lifted her easily, though the old scar on my back gave a twinge as I set her on the floor. "Sit. I'll make the tea. Tell me about Springfest."

So she did, while I clattered out my few cups, cut slices from my last loaf, and put the rabbit stew to warm. Her tales of Buckkeep were the kind I had become accustomed to hearing from her: she spoke of minstrels who had performed well or badly, gossiped of lords and ladies I had never known, and condemned or praised food from various nobles' tables where she had guested. She told each tale wittily, making me laugh or shake my head as it called for, with nary a pang of the pain that Chade had wakened in me. I supposed it was because he had spoken of the folk we had both known and loved, and told his stories from that intimate perspective. It was not Buckkeep itself or city life that I pined for, but my childhood days and the friends I had known. In that I was safe; it was impossible to return to that time. Only a few of those folk even knew that I still lived, and that was as I wished it to be. I said as much to Starling: "Sometimes your tales tug at my heart and make me wish I could return to Buckkeep. But that is a world closed to me now."

She frowned at me. "I don't see why."

I laughed aloud. "You don't think anyone would be surprised to see me alive?"

She cocked her head and stared at me frankly. "I think there would be few, even of your old friends, who would recognize you. Most recall you as an unscarred youth. The broken nose, the slash down your face, even the white in your hair might alone be disguise enough. Then, you dressed as a prince's son; now you wear the garb of a peasant. Then, you moved with a warrior's grace. Now, well, in the mornings or on a cold day, you move with an old man's caution." She shook her head with regret as she added, "You have taken no care for your appearance, nor have the years been kind to you. You could add five or even ten years to your age, and no one would question it."

This blunt appraisal from my lover stung. "Well, that's good to know," I replied wryly. I took the kettle from the fire, not wanting to meet her eyes just then.

She mistook my words and tone. "Yes. And when you add in that people see what they expect to see, and they do not expect to see you alive . . . I think you could venture it. Are you considering a return to Buckkeep, then?"

"No." I heard the shortness of the word, but could think of nothing to add to it. It did not seem to bother her.

"A pity. You miss so much, living alone like this." She launched immediately into an account of the Springfest dancing. Despite my soured mood, I had to smile at her account of Chade beseeched to dance by a young admirer of sixteen summers. She was right. I would have loved to have been there.

As I prepared food for all of us, I found my mind straying to the old torment of "what if." What if I had been able to return to Buckkeep with my Queen and Starling? What if I had come home to Molly and our child? And always, no matter how I twisted the pretense, it ended in disaster. If I had returned to Buckkeep, alive when all believed me executed for practicing the Wit, I would have brought only division at a time when Kettricken was trying to reunify the land. There would have been a faction who would have favored me over her, for bastard though I was, I was a Farseer by blood while she reigned only by virtue of marriage. A stronger faction would have been in favor of executing me again, and more thoroughly.

And if I had gone back to Molly and the child, returned to carry her off to be mine? I suppose I could have, if I had no care for anyone but myself. She and Burrich had both given me up for dead. The woman who had been my wife in all but name, and the man who had raised me and been my friend had turned to one another. He had kept a roof over Molly's head, and seen that she was fed and warm while my child grew within her. With his own hands, he had delivered my bastard. Together they had kept Nettle from Regal's men. Burrich had claimed both woman and child as his own, not only to protect them, but to love them. I could have gone back to them, to make them both faithless in their own eyes. I could have made their bond a shameful thing. Burrich would have left Molly and Nettle to me. His harsh sense of honor would not have allowed him to do otherwise. And ever after, I could have wondered if she compared me to him, if the love they had shared was stronger and more honest than . . .

"You're burning the stew," Starling pointed out in annoyance.

I was. I served us from the top of the pot, and joined her at the table. I pushed all pasts, both real and imagined, aside. I did not need to think of them. I had Starling to busy my mind. As was customary, I was the listener and she was the teller of tales. She began a long account of some upstart minstrel at Springfest who had not only dared to sing one of her songs, with only a verse or two changed, but then had claimed ownership of it. She gestured with her bread as she spoke, and almost managed to catch me up in the story. But my own memories of other Springfests kept intruding. Had I lost all content in the simple life I had created for myself? The boy and the wolf had been enough for me for many years. What ailed me now?

I went from that to yet another discordant thought. Where was Hap? I had brewed tea for the three of us, and portioned out food for three as well. Hap was always ravenous after any sort of a task or journey. It was distracting that he could not get past his bad mood to come and join us. As Starling spoke on, I found my eyes straying repeatedly to his untouched bowl of stew. She caught me at it.

"Don't fret about him," she told me almost testily. "He's a boy, with a boy's sulky ways. When he's hungry enough, he'll come in."

Or he'll ruin perfectly good fish by burning it over a fire. The wolf's thought came in response to my Wit questing toward him. They were down by the creek. Hap had made a temporary spear out of a stick, and the wolf had simply plunged into the water to hunt along the undercut banks. When the fish ran thick, it was not difficult for him to corner one there, to plunge his head under the water and seize it in his jaws. The cold water made his joints ache, but the boy's fire would soon warm him. They were fine. *Don't worry.*

Useless advice, but I pretended to take it. We finished eating, and I cleared the dishes away. While I tidied, Starling sat on the hearth by the evening fire, picking at her harp until the random notes turned into the old song about the miller's daughter. When everything was put to rights, I joined her there with a cup of Sandsedge brandy for each of us. I sat in a chair, but she sat near the fire on the floor. She leaned back against my legs as she played. I watched her hands on the strings, marking the crookedness where once her fingers had been broken, as a warning to me. At the end of her song, I leaned down and kissed her. She kissed me back, setting the harp aside and making a more thorough job of it.

She stood then and took my hands to pull me to my feet. As I followed her into my bedroom, she observed, "You're pensive tonight."

I made some small sound of agreement. Sharing that she had bruised my feelings earlier would have seemed sniveling and childish. Did I want her to lie to me, to tell me that I was still young and comely when obviously I was not? Time had had its way with me. That was all, and to be expected. Even so, Starling kept coming back to me. Through all the years, she'd kept returning to me and to my bed. That had to count for something.

"You were going to tell me about something?" she prompted.

"Later," I told her. The past clutched at me, but I put its greedy fingers aside, determined to immerse myself in the present. This life was not so bad. It was simple and uncluttered, without conflict. Wasn't this the life I had always dreamed of? A life where I made my decisions for myself?

And I was not alone, really. I had Nighteyes and Hap, and Starling, when she came to me. I opened her vest and then her blouse to bare her breasts while she unbuttoned my shirt. She embraced me, rubbing against me with the unabashed pleasure of a purring cat. I clasped her to me and lowered my face to kiss the top of her head. This too was simple and all the sweeter for it. My freshly stuffed mattress was deep and fragrant as the meadow grass and herbs that filled it. We tumbled into it. For a time, I stopped thinking at all, as I tried to persuade both of us that despite appearances, I was a young man still.

A while later, I lingered in the hinterlands of sleep. Sometimes I think there is more rest in that place between wakefulness and sleep than there is in true sleep. The mind walks in the twilight of both states, and finds the truths that are hidden alike by daylight and dreams. Things we are not ready to know abide in that place, awaiting that unguarded frame of mind.

I came awake. My eyes were open, studying the details of my darkened room before I realized that sleep had fled. Starling's wide-flung arm was across my chest. In her sleep, she had kicked the blanket away from both of us. Night hid her careless nakedness, cloaking her in shadows. I lay still, hearing her breathe and smelling her sweat mixed with her perfume, and wondered what had wakened me. I could not put my finger on it, yet neither could I close my eyes again. I slid out from under her arm and stood up beside my bed. In the darkness I groped for my discarded shirt and leggings.

The coals of the hearth fire gave hesitant light to the main room, but I did not linger there. I opened the door and stepped barefoot into the mild spring night. I stood still a moment, letting my eyes adjust, and then made my way away from the cottage and garden and down to the stream bank. The path was cool hard mud underfoot, well packed by my daily trips to fetch water. The trees met overhead, and there was no moon, but my feet and my nose knew the way as well as my eyes did. All I had to do was follow my

Wit to my wolf. Soon I picked out the orange glow of Hap's dwindled fire, and the lingering scent of cooked fish.

They slept by the fire, the wolf curled nose to tail and Hap wrapped around him, his arm around Nighteyes' neck. Nighteyes opened his eyes as I approached, but did not stir. *I told you not to worry.*

I'm not worried. I'm just here. Hap had left some sticks of wood near the fire. I added them to the coals. I sat and watched the fire lick along them. Light came up with the warmth. I knew the boy was awake. One can't be raised with a wolf without picking up some of his wariness. I waited for him.

"It's not you. Not just you, anyway."

I didn't look at Hap, even when he spoke. Some things are better said to the dark. I waited. Silence can ask all the questions, where the tongue is prone to ask only the wrong one.

"I have to know," he burst out suddenly. My heart seized up at the question to come. In some corner of my soul, I had always dreaded him asking it. I should not have let him go to Springfest, I thought wildly. If I had kept him here, my secret would never have been threatened.

But that was not the question he asked.

"Did you know that Starling is married?"

I looked at him then, and my face must have answered for me. He closed his eyes in sympathy. "I'm sorry," he said quietly. "I should have known you didn't. I should have found a better way to tell you."

And the simple comfort of a woman who came to my arms when she would, because she desired to be with me, and the sweet evenings of tales and music by the fire, and her dark merry eyes looking up into mine were suddenly guilty and deceptive and furtive. I was as foolish as I had ever been, no, even stupider, for the gullibility of a boy is fatuousness in a man. Married. Starling married. She had thought no one would ever want to marry her, for she was barren. She had told me that she had to make her own way with her songs, for there would never be a man to care for her, nor children to provide for her old age. Probably, when she had told me those things, she had believed they were true. My folly had been in thinking that truth would never change.

Nighteyes had risen and stretched stiffly. Now he came to lie down beside me. He set his head on my knee. *I don't understand. You are ill?*

No. Just stupid.

Ah. Nothing new there. Well, you haven't died from that so far.

But sometimes it has been a near thing. I took a breath. "Tell me about it." I didn't want to hear it, but I knew he had to tell it. Better to get it over with.

Hap came with a sigh, to sit on the other side of Nighteyes. He picked up a twig from the ground beside him and teased the fire with it. "I don't think she meant for me to find out. Her husband doesn't live at Buckkeep. He traveled in to surprise her, to spend Springfest with her." As he spoke, the twig caught fire. He tossed it in. His fingers wandered to idly groom Nighteyes.

I pictured some honest old farmer, wed to a minstrel in the quiet years of his life, perhaps with grown children from an earlier marriage. He loved her, then, to make a trip to Buckkeep to surprise her. Springfest was traditionally for lovers, old and new.

"His name is Dewin," Hap went on. "And he's some sort of kin to Prince Dutiful. A distant cousin or something. He's a tall man, always dressed very grand. He wore a cloak, twice as big around as it need be, collared with fur. And he wears silver on both wrists. He's strong, too. At the Springfest dancing, he lifted Starling right up and swung her around, and all the folk stood back to watch them." Hap was watching my face as he spoke. I think he found my obvious dismay comforting. "I should have known you didn't know. You wouldn't cuckold a grand man like that."

"I wouldn't cuckold any man," I managed to say. "Not knowingly."

He sighed as if relieved. "So you've taught me." Boyishly, his mind instantly reverted to how it had affected him. "I was upset when I saw them kiss. I'd never seen anyone except you and Starling kiss like that. I thought she was betraying you, and then when I heard him introduced as her husband . . ." He cocked his head at me. "It really hurt my feelings. I thought then that you knew and didn't care. I thought that perhaps all these years you had taught me one thing, and done another. I wondered if you thought me so dull I'd never discover it, if you and Starling laughed about it as if it were a joke for me to be so stupid. It built up in my mind until I began to question everything you'd ever taught me about anything." He looked back at the fire. "It felt horrible, to be so betrayed."

I was glad to hear him sort it out this way. Better far that he consider only what it meant to him, rather than how it could cut me. Let him follow his own thoughts where they would lead. My own mind was moving in another direction, creaking like an old cart dragged out of a shed and newly greased for spring. I resisted the turning of the wheels that led me to an inevitable conclusion. Starling was married. Why not? She'd had nothing to lose and all to gain. A comfortable home with her grand lord, some minor title no doubt, wealth and security for her old age, and for him, a lovely and charming wife, a celebrated minstrel, and he could bask in her reflected glory and enjoy the envy of other men.

And when she wearied of him, she could take to the road as minstrels always did, and have a fling with me, and neither man ever the wiser. Neither? Could I assume there were only two of us?

"Did you think you were the only one she bedded?"

A direct-spoken lad, Hap. I wondered what questions he had asked Starling on the ride home.

"I suppose I didn't think about it at all," I admitted. So many things were easier to live with if you didn't give them much thought. I suppose I had known that Starling shared herself with other men. She was a minstrel; they did such things. So I had excused my bedding her to myself, and indirectly to Hap. She never spoke of it, I never asked, and her other lovers were hypothetical beings, faceless, and bodiless. They were certainly not husbands, however. She was vowed to him, and him to her. That made all the difference to me.

"What will you do now?"

An excellent question. One I had been carefully not considering. "I'm not sure," I lied.

"Starling said that it was none of my business; that it hurt no one. She said that if I told you, I'd be the cruel one, hurting you, not her. She said that she'd always been careful not to hurt you, that you'd had enough pain in your life. When I said that you had a right to know, she said you had a greater right not to know."

Starling's clever tongue. She'd left him no way to feel right about himself. Hap looked at me now, his mismatched eyes loyal as a hound's, and waited for me to pass judgment on him. I told him the truth. "I'd rather know the truth from you than have you watch me be deceived."

"Have I hurt you, then?"

I shook my head slowly. "I've hurt myself, boy." And I had. I'd never been a minstrel; I had no right to a minstrel's ways. Those who make a living with their fingers and tongues have flintier hearts than the rest of us, I suppose. "Sooner a kindly wolverine than a faithful minstrel," so the saying goes. I wondered if Starling's husband paid heed to it.

"I thought you would be angry. She warned me that you might get angry enough to hurt her."

"Did you believe that?" That stung as sharply as the revelation.

He took a quick breath, hesitated again, then said quickly, "You've a temper. And I've never had to tell you something that might hurt you. Something that might make you feel stupid."

Perceptive lad. More so than I had thought. "I am angry, Hap. I'm angry at myself."

He looked at the fire. "I feel selfish, because I feel better now."

"I'm glad you feel better. I'm glad things are easy between us again. Now. Set all that aside and tell me about the rest of Springfest. What did you think of Buckkeep Town?"

So he talked and I listened. He'd seen Buckkeep and Springfest with a boy's eyes, and as he spoke I realized how greatly both castle and town had changed since my days there. From his descriptions, I knew the city had managed to grow, clawing out building space from the harsh cliffs above it, and expanding out onto pilings. He described floating taverns and mercantiles. He talked too of traders from Bingtown and the islands beyond it, as well as those from the Out Islands. Buckkeep Town had increased its stature as a trade port. When he spoke of the Great Hall of Buckkeep and the room where he had stayed as Starling's guest, I recognized that a great deal had changed up at the keep as well. He spoke of carpets and fountains, rich hangings on every wall, and cushioned chairs and glittering chandeliers. His descriptions put me more in mind of Regal's fine manor at Tradeford than the stark fortress I had once called home. I suspected Chade's influence there as much as Kettricken's. The old assassin had always been fond of fine things, not to mention comfort. I had already resolved never to return to Buckkeep. Why should it be so daunting to learn that the place I recalled, that stark fortress of black stone, did not really even exist anymore?

Hap had other tales, too, of the towns they had passed through on their way to Buckkeep and back again. One he told me put a cold chill in my belly. "I got scared near to death one morning at Hardin's Spit," he began, and I did not recognize the name of the village. I had known, dimly, that many folk who had fled the coast during the Red Ship years had returned to found new towns, not always on the ashes of the old. I nodded as if I knew of the place. Probably the last time I had been through it, it had been no more than a wide place in the road. Hap's eyes were wide as he spoke, and I knew he had, for the moment, forgotten all about Starling's deception.

"It was on our way to Springfest. We had spent the night at the inn there, Starling singing for our supper and a room, and they were all so kind and well spoken to us there that I thought Hardin's Spit a very fine place. In the common room, when Starling was not singing, I heard angry talk about a Witted one who had been taken for magicking cows so they would not yield, but I paid little attention to it. It just seemed men talking too loud after too much beer. The inn gave us an upstairs room. I woke up early, much too early for Starling, but I could not sleep anymore. So I sat by the window and watched the folk come and go in the streets below. Outside, in the square, folk began to gather. I thought it might be a market or a spring fair. But then they dragged a woman out there, all bruised and bloody. They tied her to a whipping post, and I thought they would flog her. Then I noticed that some of those gathered had brought full baskets of stones. I woke Starling and asked her what it was all about, but she bade me be quiet, there was nothing either of us could do about it. She told me to come away from the window, but I did not. I could not. I could not believe it could happen; I kept thinking someone would come and make them all stop. Tom, she was tied there, helpless. Some man came up and read from a scroll. Then he stood back, and they stoned her."

He stopped speaking. He knew that in the villages there were harsh punishments for horse thieves and murderers. He'd heard of floggings and hangings. But he'd never had to watch one. He swallowed in the silence between us. Cold crept through me. Nighteyes whined, and I set a hand to him.

It could just as well be you.

I know.

Hap took a deep breath. "I thought I should go down there, that someone should do something, but I was too scared. I was shamed to be so scared, but I couldn't make myself move. I just stood there and watched, and the stones hit her. And she kept trying to hide her head in her arms. I felt sick. Then I heard a sound such as I had never heard before, as if a river rushed through the air. The morning sky dimmed, as if storm clouds were blowing in, but there was no wind. It was crows, Tom, a flood of black birds. I'd never seen so many, cawing and screeching, just as they do when they find an eagle or a hawk and set out to roust it. Only they weren't after an eagle. They rose out of the hills behind the town and filled the sky, like a black blanket flapping on a clothesline. Then they suddenly fell on the crowd, diving and cawing. I saw one land in a woman's hair and strike at her eyes with his beak. People were running in every direction, screaming and slapping at the birds. They spooked a team and the horses went crazy, dragging their wagon right through the crowd. Everyone was screaming. Even Starling got up to come to the window. Soon the streets were empty of everything save the birds. They perched everywhere, on roofs and window ledges, and they filled the trees so that the branches drooped with their weight. The woman who had been tied, the Witted one, she was gone. Just the bloody ropes were left there, tied to the post. Then all at once, all the birds just lifted and took flight. And then they were gone." His voice dropped to a hush. "Later that morning, the innkeeper said that he deemed she had just turned into a bird and flown off with the others."

Later, I told myself. Later I would tell him that wasn't true, that she might have called the birds down to help her escape but that not even Witted ones could change their shapes like that. Later I would tell him he was not a coward for not going down there, that they would only have stoned him alongside her. Later. This story he was telling now was like poison running from a wound. Best to let it drain unhindered.

I picked up the trail of his words again. ". . . And they call themselves Old Blood. The innkeeper said they've begun to have high ideas of themselves. They'd like to come to power, he says, like they did in the days when the Piebald Prince ruled. But if they do, they'll take vengeance on us all. Those that don't have the Wit magic will be their slaves. And if any try to defy them, they'll be thrown to the Witted ones' beasts." His voice died away to a whisper. He cleared his throat. "Starling told me that that was stupid, that Witted folk aren't like that. She said that mostly they just want to be left alone to live quietly."

I cleared my throat. I was surprised at the rush of gratitude I felt toward Starling. "Well. She's a minstrel. They know many kinds of folk, and have many odd corners of knowledge. So you can believe what she told you."

He had given me far too much to think about. I could scarcely keep my mind on the rest of his tales. He was intrigued by some wild story that Bingtown was hatching dragons and that soon towns could buy a Bingtown dragon for a watch beast. I assured him that I had seen real dragons, and that such tales were not to be believed. More realistic were the rumors that Bingtown's war with Chalced might spread to the Six Duchies. "Would a war come here?" he wanted to know. Young as he was, he had only vague but frightening memories of our war with the Red Ships. Still, he was a boy, and a war seemed as interesting an event as Springfest.

"'Sooner or later, there is always war with Chalced,'" I quoted the old proverb to him. "Even when we are not at war with Chalced, there are always border skirmishes and a certain amount of piracy and raiding. Don't let it worry you. Shoaks and Rippon duchies always take the brunt of it, with relish. Shoaks Duchy would like nothing better than to carve themselves another chunk out of the Duke of Chalced's lands."

So the conversation moved to safer and more prosaic news of his Springfest. He told of jugglers who hurled flaming clubs and bare blades hand to hand, recounted the best jests from a bawdy puppet show he'd seen, and told me of a pretty hedge-witch named Jinna who had sold him a charm against pickpockets and promised someday to visit us here. I laughed aloud when he told me that within the hour, the charm had been plucked from him by a sneak thief. He'd eaten pickled fish and liked it very much until he had too much wine one evening and vomited them together. He swore he'd never be able to eat it again. I let him talk on, glad he was finally taking pleasure in sharing his Buckkeep adventures with me. Yet, every story he told me showed me more plainly that my simple life was no longer suitable for Hap. It was time I found him an apprenticeship and let him strike out on his own.

For an instant, it was like standing on the lip of an abyss. I must turn Hap over to a master who could teach him a true trade, and I must set Starling out of my life, as well. I knew that if I turned her out of my bed, she would not humble herself to come back to me as a friend. All the simple comfort of our companionship of the last few years would vanish. Hap's voice pattered on, his words falling around me like a soft rain. I would miss the boy.

I felt the warm weight of the wolf's head as he set it on my knee. He stared steadily into the fire. *Once you dreamed of a time when it would be only you and me.*

A Wit-bond leaves very little room for polite deception. *I never expected to hunger so for the company of my own kind,* I admitted.

A brief lambent glance from his deep eyes. *Only we are our own kind. That has always been the problem with the links we sought to forge with others. They were wolves or they were human. But they were never our own kind. Not even those who call themselves Old Blood are as deeply twined as we.*

I knew he spoke true. I set my hand to his broad skull and silked his ear through my fingers. I did not think at all.

He could not let it be. *Change comes upon us again, Changer. I can feel it at the edge of the horizon, almost smell it. It is like a bigger predator come into our hunting territory. Do not you feel it?*

I feel nothing.

But he heard the lie. He sighed out a heavy breath.

chapter III

PARTINGS

The Wit is a dirty magic, most often afflicting the children of an unclean household. Although it is often blamed on having congress with beasts, there are other sources for this low magic. A wise parent will not allow his child to play with puppies or kittens that are still at suckle, nor permit his offspring to sleep where an animal sleeps. A child's sleeping mind is most vulnerable to invasion by the dreams of a beast, and hence to taking the tongue of an animal as the language of his heart. Often this foul magic will afflict generations of a household due to their filthy habits, but it is not unknown for a Wit child to suddenly appear in the midst of families of the best blood. When this happens, the parents must harden their hearts and do what must be done, for the sake of all the family's children. They should look too amongst their servants to see whose malice or carelessness is the source of this contagion, and the offender should be dealt with accordingly.

    SARCOGIN'S "DISEASES AND AFFLICTIONS"

Shortly before the first dawn birds began to call, Hap drowsed off again. I sat for a brief time by his fire, watching him. The anxiety was smoothed from his face. Hap was a calm and simple boy who had never enjoyed conflict. He was not a boy for secrets. I was glad that his telling me about Starling had put him at peace with himself. My own route to peace would be a rockier path.

I left him sleeping in the early sunlight by the dying fire. "Keep watch over him," I told Nighteyes. I could feel the aching in the wolf's hips, echoing the gnawing pain in my scarred back. Nights in the open were not gentle to either of us anymore. Yet, I would have gladly lain down on the cold damp earth rather than go back to my cottage and confront Starling. Sooner is usually better than later when it comes to facing unpleasantness, I told myself. Walking like a very old man, I returned to the cottage.

I stopped at the henhouse for eggs. My flock was already up and scratching. The rooster flew to the top of the mended roof, flapped his wings twice, and crowed lustily. Morning. Yes. One I dreaded.

Inside the cottage, I poked up the fire and put the eggs to boil. I took out my last loaf of bread, the cheese that Chade had brought, and tea herbs. Starling was never an early riser. I had plenty of time to think of what I would say, and what I would not say. As I put the room to rights, mostly picking up her scattered belongings, my mind wandered back over the years we had shared. Over a decade it had been, of knowing one another. Of *thinking* I knew her, I corrected myself. Then I damned myself for a liar. I did know her. I picked her discarded cloak from the chair. Her scent was trapped in its good wool. A very fine quality, I told myself. Her husband provided her with the best. The worst part of this was that what Starling had done did not surprise me. I was ashamed only of myself, that I had not foreseen it.

For six years after the Cleansing of Buck, I had moved alone through the world. I made no contact with anyone who had known me at Buckkeep. My life as a Farseer, as Prince Chivalry's bastard, as Chade's apprentice assassin, was dead to me. I became Tom Badgerlock, and entered wholeheartedly into that new life. As I had long dreamed, I traveled, and my decisions were shared only with my wolf. I found a sort of peace within myself. This is not to say that I didn't miss those I had loved at Buckkeep. I did, sometimes savagely. But in missing them, I also discovered my freedom from my past. A hungry man can long for hot meat and gravy without disdaining the simple pleasures of bread and cheese. I put together a life for myself, and if it lacked much of what had been sweet in my old life, it also provided simple pleasures the old life had long denied me. I had been content.

Then, one foggy morning about a year after I had settled into the cottage near the ruins of Forge, the wolf and I returned from a hunt to find change waiting in ambush for us. A yearling deer was heavy on my shoulders, making my old arrow scar ache and twinge. I was trying to decide if the comfort of a long soak in hot water was worth the pain of hauling the buckets and the wait for the water to heat when I heard the unmistakable sound of a shod hoof against stone. I eased our kill to the ground, and then Nighteyes and I ghosted a wide circle around the hut. There was nothing to see but a horse, still saddled, tied to a tree near my door. The rider was likely within our home. The horse flicked her ears as we sidled closer, aware of me, but not yet certain of alarm.

Hang back, my brother. If the horse scents wolf, she will neigh. If I go very softly, I might get close enough to see inside before she gives any warning.

Silent as the fog that cloaked us both, Nighteyes withdrew into a swirl of gray. I circled to the back of our cottage and then glided down to stand close to one wall. I could hear the intruder inside. A thief? I heard the clack of crockery, and the sound of water being poured. A thump was someone tossing a log on my fire. I knit my brows in puzzlement. Whoever it was, he seemed to be making himself at home. An instant later, I heard a voice lift in the refrain of an old song, and my heart turned over in me. Despite the years that had passed, I recognized Starling's voice.

The howling bitch, Nighteyes confirmed for me. He'd caught her scent. As always, I winced wryly at how the wolf thought of the minstrel.

Let me go first. Despite knowing who it was, I was still wary as I approached my own door. This was no accident. She'd tracked me down. Why? What did she want of me?

"Starling," I said as I opened the door. She spun to confront me, teapot in hand. Her eyes traveled me swiftly, then met my eyes and, "Fitz!" she exclaimed happily, and lunged at me. She embraced me, and after a moment, I put my arms around her as well. She hugged me hard. Like most Buck women, she was small and dark, but I felt her wiry strength in her embrace.

"Hello," I said uncertainly, looking down at the top of her head.

She tilted her face up at me. "Hello?" she said incredulously. She laughed aloud at my expression. "Hello?" She leaned away from me to set the teapot on the table. Then she reached up, seized my face between her hands, and pulled me down to be kissed. I had just come in from the damp and the cold. The contrast between that and her warm mouth on mine was astonishing, as amazing as having a woman in my arms. She held me close and it was as if life itself embraced me again. Her scent intoxicated me. Heat rushed through me and my heart raced. I took my mouth from hers. "Starling," I began.

"No," she said firmly. She glanced over my shoulder, then took both my hands and tugged me toward the sleeping alcove off the main room. I lurched after her, drunken with surprise. She halted by my bed and unbuttoned her shirt. When I just stared at her dumbly, she laughed and reached up to untie the laces of mine. "Don't talk yet," she warned me. And she lifted my chilled hand and set it on one of her bared breasts.

At that moment, Nighteyes shouldered the door open and came into the cabin. Cold billowed into the warm room as fog. For an instant, he just looked at us. Then he shook the moisture from his coat. It was Starling's turn to freeze. "The wolf. I'd almost forgotten . . . you still have him?"

"We are still together. Of course." I started to lift my hand from her breast, but she caught my hand and held it there.

"I don't mind. I suppose." She looked uncomfortable. "But does he have to . . . be here?"

Nighteyes gave another shake. He looked at Starling and away. The chill in the room was not just from the door standing open. *The meat will be cold and stiff if I wait for you.*

Then don't wait, I suggested, stung.

He drifted back outside into the fog. I sensed him closing his mind to us. Jealousy, or courtesy, I wondered. I crossed the room and shut the door. I stood by it, troubled by Nighteyes' reaction. Starling's arms came around me from behind and when I turned to her embrace, she was naked and waiting. I made no decision. That joining had happened between us in much the same way as night falls upon the land.

Thinking back on it, I wondered if she had planned it that way. Probably not. Starling had taken that part of my life with no more thought than she would give to picking a berry by the roadside. It was there, it was sweet, why not have it? We had become lovers with no declaration of love, as if our bedding were inevitable. Did I love her, even now, after all the years of her coming and going from my life?

Thinking such thoughts was as eerie as handling the artifacts Chade had brought from my old life. Once, such thoughts had seemed so important to me. Questions of love and honor and duty . . . I loved Molly, did Molly love me? Did I love her more than I loved my King, was she more important to me than my duty? As a youth, I had agonized over those questions, but with Starling, I had never even asked them until now.

Yet as ever, the answers were elusive. I loved her, not as a person carefully chosen to share my life, but as a familiar part of my existence. To lose her would be like losing the hearth from the room. I had come to rely on her intermittent warmth. I knew that I had to tell her that I could not continue as before. The dread I felt reminded me of how time had dragged and how I had clenched my soul against the healer digging the arrowhead from my back. I felt the same stiff apprehension of great pain to come.

I heard the rustling of my bedding as she awoke. Her footfall was light on the floor behind me. I did not turn to her as I poured the water over the tea. I suddenly could not look at her. Yet she did not come to me or touch me. After a pause, she spoke.

"So. Hap told you."

"Yes," I replied evenly.

"And you're determined to let it ruin everything between us."

There seemed no answer to that.

Anger surged into her voice. "You've changed your name, but after all these years, you've not changed your ways. Tom Badgerlock is just as straitlaced a prude as FitzChivalry Farseer was."

"Don't," I warned her, not of her tone but of that name. We had always taken great pains that Hap knew me only as Tom. I knew it was no accident that she spoke that name aloud now, but a reminder that she held my secrets.

"I won't," she assured me, but it was a knife sheathed. "I but remind you that you lead two lives, and you lead them very well. Why begrudge that to me?"

"I don't think of it that way. This is the only life I have now. And I but try to do by your husband as I would wish another man to do by me. Or will you tell me that he knows of me, and does not care?"

"Exactly the opposite. He does not know, and therefore does not care. And if you look at it carefully, you will see it comes out to exactly the same thing."

"Not for me."

"Well, for a time it was the same for you. Until Hap saw fit to ruin it. You've inflicted your stiff standards on yet another young man. I hope you take great pride in knowing you've raised another moralistic, judgmental prig like yourself." Her words slapped me as she began to slam about the room, throwing her things together. I finally turned to look at her. Her color was very high, her hair tousled from sleep. She wore only my shirt. The hem of it grazed her thighs. She halted when I turned to look at her and stared back at me. She drew herself up, as if to be sure I must see all I was refusing. "What does it hurt?" she demanded.

"Your husband, if he ever gets word of it," I said quietly. "Hap gave me to understand he's a noble of some kind. Gossip can do more damage to that kind of man than a knife. Consider his dignity, the dignity of his house. Don't make him some old fool taken with a lively younger woman . . ."

"Old fool?" She looked perplexed. "I don't . . . Hap told you he was old?"

I felt off balance. "He said he was a grand man . . ."

"Grand, yes, but scarcely old. Quite the opposite." She smiled oddly, caught between pride and embarrassment. "He's twenty-four, Fitz. A fine dancer and strong as a young bull. What did you think, that I'd pastured myself out to warm some elderly lord's bed?"

I had. "I thought—"

She was suddenly almost defiant, as if I had belittled her. "He's handsome and he's charming, and he could have had his pick of any number of women. He chose me. And in my own way, I do, truly, love him. He makes me feel young and desirable and capable of real passion."

"What did I make you feel?" I asked unwillingly, my voice low. I knew I was inviting more pain but I couldn't stop myself.

That puzzled her for a moment. "Comfortable," she said at last, with no thought for my feelings. "Accepted and valued." She smiled suddenly, and her expression cut me. "Generous, giving you what no one else would. And more. Worldly and adventurous. Like a bright songbird come to visit a wren."

"You were that," I conceded. I looked away from her, toward the window. "But no more, Starling. Never again. Perhaps you think my life a poor thing, but it is mine. I won't steal the crumbs from another man's table. I have that much pride."

"You can't afford that kind of pride," she said bluntly. She pushed her hair back from her face. "Look around you, Fitz. A dozen years on your own, and what do you have? A cottage in the forest, and a handful of chickens. What do you have for brightness or warmth or sweetness? Only me. Perhaps it's only a day or two of my life, here and there, but I'm the only real person in your life." Her voice grew harder. "Crumbs from another man's table are better than starving. You need me."

"Hap. Nighteyes," I pointed out coldly.

She dismissed them. "An orphan boy I brought you and a decrepit wolf."

That she should disparage them so not only affronted me, it forced me to face how differently we perceived things. I suppose that if we had lived together, day in and day out, such disagreements would have manifested themselves long ago. But the interludes we had shared had not been ones of philosophical discussions, or even practical considerations. We had come together at her convenience, to share my bed and my table. She had slept and eaten and sung and watched me at my tasks in a life she didn't share. The minor disagreements we had were forgotten between one visit and the next. She had brought me Hap as if he were a stray kitten, and given no thought since then as to what we might have become to one another. This quarrel was not only ending what we had shared, but exposing that we had truly shared very little at all. I felt twice devastated by it. Bitter words from a past life came back to me. The Fool had warned me: "She has no true affection for Fitz, you know, only for being able to say she knew FitzChivalry." Perhaps, despite all the years we'd shared, that was still true.

I held my tongue for fear of all I might say; I think she mistook my silence for a wavering in my resolve. She suddenly took a deep breath. She smiled at me wearily. "Oh, Fitz. We need one another in ways neither of us likes to admit." She gave a small sigh. "Make breakfast. I'm going to get dressed. Things always seem worst in the morning on an empty stomach." She left the room.

A fatalistic patience came over me. I set out the breakfast things as she dressed. I knew I had reached my decision. It was as if Hap's words last night had extinguished a candle inside me. My feelings for Starling had changed that completely. We sat at table together, and she tried to make all seem as it had before, but I kept thinking, This is probably the last time I'll watch how she swirls her tea to cool it, or how she waves her bread about as she talks. I let her talk, and she kept her words to inconsequential things, trying to fix my interest on where she planned to go next, and what Lady Amity had worn to some occasion. The more she talked, the farther away she seemed from me. As I watched her, I had the strangest sense of something forgotten, something missed. She took another piece of cheese, alternating bites of it and the bread.

A sudden realization trickled through me like a drop of cold water down the spine. I interrupted her.

"You knew Chade was coming to see me."

A fraction of a second too late, she lifted her brows in surprise. "Chade? Here?"

These were habits of mind I thought I had discarded. Ways of thinking, taught to me painstakingly by a skilled mentor in the hours between dusk and dawn during the years of my youth. It was a way of sifting facts and assembling them, a training that let the mind make swift leaps to conclusions that were not conjectures. Begin with a simple observation. Starling had not commented on the cheese. Any cheese was a luxury for the boy and me, let alone a fine ripe cheese like this one. She should have been surprised to see it on my table, but she was not. She had said nothing of the Sandsedge brandy last night. Because neither had surprised her. I was both astonished and pleased, in a horrified way, at how swiftly my mind leapt from point to point, until I suddenly looked down on the inevitable landscape the facts formed. "You've never offered to take Hap anywhere before this. You took the boy off to Buckkeep so that Chade could see me alone." One possible conclusion from that chilled me. "In case he had to kill me. There would be no witnesses."

"Fitz!" she rebuked me, both angry and shocked.

I almost didn't hear her. Once the pebbles of thought had started bouncing, the avalanche of conclusions was bound to follow. "All these years. All your visits. You've been his eyes on me, haven't you? Tell me. Do you check on Burrich and Nettle several times a year as well?"

She looked at me coldly, denying nothing. "I had to seek them out. To give Burrich the horses. You wanted me to do that."

Yes. My mind raced on. The horses would have served as a perfect introduction. Any other gift, Burrich would have refused. But Ruddy was rightfully his, a gift from Verity. All those years ago, Starling had told him that the Queen had sent Sooty's colt as well, in token of services done for the Farseers. I looked at her, waiting for the rest. She was a minstrel. She loved to talk. All I nèed do was provide the silence.

She set her bread down. "When I am in that area, I visit them, yes. And when I return to Buckkeep, if Chade knows I have been there, he asks after them. Just as he asks after you."

"And the Fool? Do you know his whereabouts as well?"

"No." The answer was succinct, and I believed it true. But she was a minstrel, and for her the power of a secret was always in the telling of it. She had to add, "But I think that Burrich does. Once or twice, when I have visited there, there have been toys about, far finer than anything Burrich could afford for Nettle. One was a doll that put me very much in mind of the Fool's puppets. Another time, there was a string of wooden beads, each carved like a little face."

That was interesting, but I did not let it show in my eyes. I asked her directly the question that was foremost on my mind. "Why would Chade consider me a threat to the Farseers? It is the only reason I know that might make him think he must kill me."

Something akin to pity came into her face. "You truly believe that, don't you? That Chade could kill you. That I would help by luring the boy away."

"I know Chade."

"And he knows you." The words were almost an accusation. "He once told me that you were incapable of completely trusting anyone. That wanting to trust, and fearing to, would always divide your soul. No. I think the old man simply wanted to see you alone so he could speak freely to you. To have you to himself, and to see for himself how you were doing, after all your years of silence."

She had a minstrel's way with words and tone. She made it seem as if my avoiding Buckkeep had been both rude and cruel to my friends. The truth was that it had been a matter of survival.

"What did Chade talk about with you?" she asked, too casually.

I met her gaze steadily. "I think you know," I replied, wondering if she did.

Her expression changed and I could see her mind working. So. Chade hadn't entrusted the truth of his mission to her. However, she was bright and quick and had many of the pieces. I waited for her to put it together.

"Old Blood," she said quietly. "The Piebald threats."

There have been many times in my life when I have been shocked and have had to conceal it. That time, I think, was most difficult for me. She watched my face carefully as she spoke. "It is a trouble that has been brewing for a time, and looks to be coming to a boil now. At Springfest, on the Night of the Minstrels, where all vie to perform for their monarch, one minstrel sang the old song about the Piebald Prince. You recall it?"

I did. It told of a princess carried off by a Witted one in the form of a piebald stallion. Once they were alone, he took his man's shape and seduced her. She gave birth to a bastard son, mottled dark and light just as his sire had been. By treachery and spite, her bastard came to the throne, to rule cruelly with the aid of his Witted cohorts. The entire kingdom had suffered, until, so the song said, his cousin, of pure Farseer blood, had rallied six nobles' sons to his cause. At the summer solstice, when the sun stood at noon and the Piebald Prince's powers were weakest, they fell upon him and slew him. They hanged him, then chopped his body to pieces, and then burned the pieces over water, to wash his spirit far away lest it find a home in some beast's body. The song's method of dealing with the Piebald Prince had become the traditional way to be surely rid of Witted ones. Regal had been very disappointed that he had not been able to serve me so.

"Not my favorite song," I said quietly.

"Understandably. However, Slek sang it well, to much applause, more than his voice truly merits. He has that quaver at the end of his notes that some find endearing, but in truth is the sign of a voice with poor control . . ." She suddenly realized she was wandering from her topic. "Feelings run high against the Witted these days. The Witted ones have been restless of late, and one hears wild tales. I have heard that in one village where a Witted man was hanged and burned, all the sheep died four days later. Just dropped in the fields. Folk said it was his family's revenge. But when they went for vengeance against his kin, they found them long gone. There was a scroll left tacked to the door of their house. All it said was, 'You deserved it.' There have been other incidents as well."

I met her eyes. "So Hap told me," I admitted.

She nodded curtly. She rose from the table and stepped clear of it. A minstrel to the bone, she had a story to tell, and demanded a stage for it. "Well. After Slek sang 'The Piebald Prince,' another minstrel came forward. He was very young, and perhaps that was why he was so foolish. He doffed his cap to Queen Kettricken, and then said he would

follow 'The Piebald Prince' with another song, of more recent vintage. When he said he had heard it first in a hamlet
of Witted folk, muttering ran through the crowd. All have
heard rumors of such places, but never have I heard someone claim to have been to one. When the mutter died, he
launched into a song I had never heard before. The tune
was derivative, but the words were new to me, as raw as his
voice." She cocked her head at me and regarded me speculatively. "This song was of Chivalry's Bastard. It touched on
all he had done before his Witted taint was revealed. He
even stole a phrase or two from my song 'Antler Island
Tower,' if you can believe the gall of that! Then, this song
went on that this 'Farseer's son with Old Blood blessed, of
royal blood and wild, the best' had not died in the Pretender's dungeon. According to this song, the Bastard had
lived, and been true to his father's family. The minstrel sang
that when King Verity went off to seek the Elderlings, the
Bastard rose from his grave to rally to his rightful King's aid.
The minstrel sang a stirring scene of how the Bastard called
Verity back through the gates of death, to show him a garden of stone dragons that could be wakened to the Six
Duchies' cause. That, at least, had the ring of truth to it. It
made me sit up and wonder, even if his voice was growing
hoarse by then." She paused, waiting for me to speak, but I
had no words. She shrugged, then observed caustically, "If
you wanted a song made of those days, you might have
thought of me first. I was there, you know. In fact, it was
why I was there. And I am a far better minstrel than that
boy was." There was a quiver of jealous outrage in her voice.

"I had nothing to do with that song, as I'm sure you
must realize. I wish no one had ever heard it."

"Well, you've little enough to worry about there." She
said the words with deep satisfaction. "I'd never heard it before that day, nor since. It was not well made, the tune did
not fit the theme, the words were ragged, the—"

"Starling."

"Oh, very well. He gave the song the traditional heroic

ending. That if ever the Farseer crown demanded it, the
true-hearted Witted Bastard would return to aid the kingdom. At the end of the song, some of the Springfest crowd
yelled insults at him and someone said he was likely Witted
himself and fit for burning. Queen Kettricken commanded
them to silence, but at the end of the evening, she gave him
no purse as she did the other minstrels."

I kept silent, passing no judgment on that. When I did
not rise to her bait, Starling added, "Because he had vanished
when it came time for her to reward those who had pleased
her. She called his name first, but no one knew where he had
gone. His name was unfamiliar to me. Tagsson."

Son of Tag, grandson of Reaver, I could have told her.
And both Reaver and Tag had been very able members of
Verity's Buckkeep guard. My mind reached back through
the years to find Tag's face as he knelt before Verity in the
Stone Garden before the gates of death. Yes, so I supposed
it had looked to him, Verity stepping out from the stark
black Skill-pillar and into the uncertain circle of the firelight. Tag had recognized his King, despite all hardship had
done to Verity. He had proclaimed his loyalty to him, and
Verity had sent him on his way, bidding him return to
Buckkeep and tell all there that the rightful King would return. In thinking back on it, I was almost certain that
Verity had arrived at Buckkeep before the soldier did. Dragons a-wing are a deal faster than a man on foot.

I had not known Tag had recognized me as well. Who
could ever have foreseen he would pass on that tale, let
alone that he would have a minstrel for a son?

"I see that you know him," Starling said quietly.

I glanced at her to find her eyes reading my face greedily. I sighed. "I know no Tagsson. I'm afraid my mind wandered back to something you said earlier. The Witted have
grown restless. Why?"

She lifted an eyebrow at me. "I thought you would better know than I."

"I lead a solitary life, Starling, as well you know. I'm in

a poor position to hear tidings of any kind, save what you bring me." It was my turn to study her. "And this was information you never shared with me."

She looked away from me and I wondered: had she decided to keep it from me? Had Chade bade her not speak of it to me? Or had it been crowded from her mind by her stories of nobles she had played for, and acclaim she had received? "It isn't a pretty tale. I suppose it began a year and a half ago . . . perhaps two. It seemed to me then that I began to hear more often of Witted ones being found out and punished. Or killed. You know how people are, Fitz. For a time after the Red Ship War, I am sure they had their glut of killing and blood. But when the enemy is finally driven far from your shore, and your houses are restored and your fields begin to yield and your flocks to increase, why, then it becomes time to find fault with your neighbors again. I think Regal wakened a lust for blood sport in the Six Duchies, with his King's Circle and justice by combat. I wonder if we shall ever be truly free of that legacy."

She had touched an old nightmare. The King's Circle at Tradeford, the caged beasts and the smell of Old Blood, trial by battle . . . the memory washed through me, leaving sickness in its wake.

"Two years ago . . . yes," Starling continued. She moved restlessly about the room as she considered it. "That was when the old hatred of Witted folk flared up again. The Queen spoke out against it, for your sake I imagine. She is a beloved queen, and she has wrought many changes during her rule, but in this, tradition runs too deep. The folk in the village think, Well, what can she know of our ways, Mountain-bred as she is? So although Queen Kettricken did not countenance it, the hounding of the Witted went on as it always has. Then, in Trenury in Farrow, about a year and a half ago, there was a horrifying incident. As the story came to Buckkeep, a Witted girl had a fox as her beast, and she cared not where it hunted so long as the blood ran every night."

I interrupted her. "A pet fox?"

"Not exactly common. It was even more suspect that the girl who had this fox was neither of noble blood nor wealthy. What business had a farmer's child with such a beast? The rumors spread. The poultry flocks of the village folk near Trenury suffered the most, but the final blow was when something got into Lord Doplin's aviary and made dinner of his songbirds and imported Rain Wilds fowl. He sent his huntsmen after the girl and fox said to be at the root of it, and they were run down, not gently, and brought before Lord Doplin. She swore it was none of her fox's doing, she swore she was not Witted, but when the hot irons were put to the fox, it is said that she screamed as loudly as the beast did. Then, to close the circle of his proof, Doplin had the nails drawn from the girl's fingers and toes, and the fox likewise shrieked with her."

"A moment." Her words dizzied me. I could imagine it too well.

"I shall finish it swiftly. They died, slowly. But the next night, more of Doplin's songbirds were slain, and an old huntsman said it was a weasel, not a fox, for a weasel but drinks the blood whereas a fox would have taken the birds to pieces. I think it was the injustice of her death as much as the cruelty of it that roused the Witted against him. The next day, Doplin's own dog snapped at him. Doplin had both his dog and his dogboy put down. He claimed that when he walked through his stables, every one of his horses went wild-eyed at his passage, laying back ears and kicking their stall walls. He had two stableboys hanged over water and burned. He claimed flies began to flock to his kitchen so that he found them dead daily in his food, and that . . ."

I shook my head at her. "That is the wildness of a man's uneasy conscience, not the work of any Witted ones I have ever known."

She shrugged. "In any case, the folk cried out to the Queen for justice when over a dozen of his lesser servants had been tortured or killed. And she sent Chade."

I leaned back in my chair and crossed my arms on my chest. So. The old assassin was still the bearer of the Farseer justice. I wondered who had accompanied him to do the quiet work. "What happened?" I asked, as if I did not know.

"Chade made a simple solution to it all. By the Queen's order, he forbade Doplin to keep horse, hawk, or hound, or beast or bird of any kind in his manor. He cannot ride, hawk, or hunt in any form. Chade even forbade him and all who live in his keep the eating of any flesh or fish for a year."

"That will make for a dreary holding."

"It is said among the minstrels that no one guests with Doplin anymore unless they must, that his servants are few and surly, and that he has lost his stature with the other nobles since his hospitality has become such a threadbare welcome. And Chade forced him to pay blood-gold, not only to the families of the slain servants, but to the family of the fox-girl."

"Did they take it?"

"The servants' families did. It was only fair. The fox-girl's family was gone, dead or fled, no one could or would say. Chade demanded that the blood money for her be given to the Queen's counting-man, to be held for the family." She shrugged. "That should have settled it. But from that time to now, the incidents have multiplied. Not just the scourings for Witted ones, but the revenge the Witted wreak in turn on their tormentors."

I frowned. "I don't see why any of that would provoke further uprisings among the Witted. It seems to me Doplin was justly punished."

"And some say more severely than he deserved, but Chade was unrelenting. Nor did he stop with that. Shortly after that, all six Dukes received scrolls from Queen Kettricken, saying that to be Witted was no crime, save that a Witted one used it for evil ends. She told the Dukes they must forbid their nobles and lords to execute Witted ones, save that their crimes had been proven against them as surely as any ordinary man's crimes. The edict did not sit well, as you can imagine. Where it is not ignored, proof of a man's guilt is always ample after his death. Instead of calming feelings, the Queen's declaration seemed to wake all the old feelings against the Witted ones.

"But among the Witted, it has seemed to rally them to defiance. They do not suffer their blood to be executed without a fight. Sometimes they are content merely to free their own before they can be killed, but often enough they strike back in vengeance. Almost any time there is an execution of a Witted one, some evil swiftly befalls those responsible. Their cattle die or diseased rats bite their children. Always it has to do with animals. In one village, the river fish they depended on simply did not migrate that year. Their nets hung empty and the folk went hungry."

"Ridiculous. Folk claim happenstance is malice. The Witted do not have the kind of powers you are ascribing to them." I spoke with great surety.

She gave me a disdainful look. "Then why do the Piebalds claim credit for such acts, if the work is not theirs?"

"The Piebalds? Who are the Piebalds?"

She lifted one shoulder in a shrug. "No one knows. They do not announce themselves. They leave messages pegged to inn doors or trees, and send missives to the nobles. They always sing the same tune with different words: 'Such a one was killed unjustly, for no crime but merely for possessing Old Blood magic. Now our wrath falls on you. When the Piebald Prince returns, he will have no mercy on you.' And it is signed with no name, but only an image of a piebald stallion. It makes folk furious.

"The Queen has refused to send out her guard to hunt them down. So now the gossip among some of the nobility is that Queen Kettricken herself is at fault for the increased executions of Witted ones, for her punishing of Lord Doplin has made them think they have the right to their perverted magic." At my scowl, she reminded me, "A minstrel but repeats what she has heard. I do not create the rumors, nor put words in people's mouths." She came closer to me and, from behind me, set her hands on my shoulders. She bent down, her cheek by mine. Gently, she added, "After all the years we have been together, surely you know by now that I do not consider you tainted." She kissed my cheek.

Our current conversation had almost driven my resolve from my mind. Nearly, I took her in my arms. Instead, I stood, awkwardly, for she was right behind my chair. When she tried to embrace me, I chilled my heart. I set her at arm's length from me. "You are not mine," I told her quietly.

"Nor am I *his*!" she blazed at me suddenly. Her dark eyes shone with her anger. "I belong to myself, and I shall decide who shares my body. It hurts nothing for me to be with both of you. I will not get pregnant by either of you. If any man could get me with child, it would have happened long ago. So what does it matter whose bed I share?"

She was quick-witted and words served her tongue far better than mine. I had no clever reply. So I echoed her own words. "I too belong to myself, and I decide who will share my body. And I will not share it with another man's wife."

I think then that she finally believed it. I had set her belongings in a neat pile beside the hearth. She flung herself to her knees beside it. Snatching up her saddle pack, she began to stuff it furiously. "I don't know why I ever bothered with you," she muttered.

Mishap, true to his name, chose that moment to enter the cabin. The wolf was at his heels. At the sight of Starling's angry face, Hap turned to me. "Should I leave?" he asked baldly.

"No!" Starling spat the word. "You get to stay. I'm the one he's throwing out. Thanks to you. You might ponder a moment or two, Hap, on what would have become of you if I had left you digging in that village garbage heap. I deserved gratitude from you, not this betrayal!"

The boy's eyes went wide. Nothing she had ever done, not even how she had deceived me, angered me as much as witnessing her hurt him. He gave me a stricken look, as if he expected I too would turn on him. Then he bolted out of the door. Nighteyes gave me a baleful look, then spun to follow him.

I'll come soon. Let me finish this first.

Better you had never started it.

I let his rebuke hang unanswered, for there was no good reply to it. Starling glared up at me, and as I glowered back, I saw something almost like fear pass over her face. I crossed my arms on my chest. "Best you were gone," I said tightly. The wary look in her eye was as great an insult to me as the abuse she had flung at Hap. I left the cabin and went to fetch her horse. A fine horse and a fine saddle, doubtless both gifts from a fine young man. The animal sensed my agitation and pranced restlessly as I saddled her. I took a breath, gathered control over myself, and set my hand to the horse. I sent calmness to her. In doing so, I calmed myself. I stroked her sleek neck. She turned to whuffle her nose against my shirt. I sighed. "Take care of her, would you? For she takes no care with herself."

I had no bond with the creature, and my words were only reassuring sounds to her. I sensed in return her acceptance of my mastery. I led her to the front of the cottage and stood outside, holding her reins. In a moment, Starling appeared on the porch. "Can't wait for me to leave, can you?" she observed bitterly. She threw her pack across the saddle, unsettling the horse once more.

"That's not true and you know it," I replied. I tried to keep my voice level and calm. The pain I had been denying broke through my humiliation at how gullible I had been, and my anger that she had used me so. Our bond had not been a tender, heartfelt love; rather it had been a companionship that had included the sharing of our bodies and the trust of sleeping in one another's arms. The betrayal of a friend differs from the treachery of a lover only in the degree of pain, not the kind. I suddenly knew I had just lied to her; I desperately wanted her to leave. Her presence was like an arrow standing in a wound; it could not be healed until she was gone.

Nevertheless, I tried to think of some significant words, something that would salvage the good part of what we had shared. But nothing came to me, and in the end I stood dumbly by as she snatched the reins from my hand and mounted. She looked down on me from the animal's back. I am sure she felt some pain, but her face showed only her anger that I had thwarted her will. She shook her head at me.

"You could have been someone. Regardless of how you were born, they gave you every chance of making something of yourself. You could have mattered. But this is what you chose. Remember that. You chose this."

She tugged the horse's head around, not so badly as to injure her mouth, but rougher than she needed to be. Then she kicked the horse to a trot and rode away from me. I watched her go. She did not look back. Despite my pain, I felt, not the regret of an ending, but the foreboding of a beginning. A shiver ran over me, as if the Fool himself stood at my elbow and whispered words at my ear. "Do not you sense it? A crossroads, a vertex, a vortex. All paths change from here."

I turned, but there was no one there. I glanced at the sky. Dark clouds were hastening from the south; already the tips of the trees were stirring with the oncoming squall. Starling would begin her journey with a drenching. I told myself I took no satisfaction in that, and went looking for Hap.

chapter IV

THE HEDGE-WITCH

There was a hedge-witch in those parts, Silva Copperleaf by name, whose charms were of such a strength that their potency lasted not just from year to year, but continued to protect the folk who possessed them for generations. It is said that she made for Baldric Farseer a marvelous sieve such that it purified all waters that passed through it. This was a great boon for a king so often threatened by poisoners.

Above the gate of the walled town of Eklse, she hung a charm against pestilence, and for many years the grain bins were free of rats and the stables clean of fleas and other vermin. The town prospered under this protection, until the town elders foolishly built a second gate in their walls, to admit more trade. This opened a way for pestilence to enter the town, and all there perished from the second wave of the Blood Plague.

    SELKIN'S "TRAVELS IN THE SIX DUCHIES"

High summer found Hap and me just as it had found us for the last seven years. There was a garden to tend, poultry to mind, and fish to salt and smoke against winter's need. Day followed day in its round of chores and meals, sleeping and waking. Starling's departure, I told myself, had effectively quenched the restlessness that Chade's visit had sparked. I had spoken to Hap, in a desultory way, of putting him out to an apprenticeship. With an enthusiasm that surprised me, he told me of a cabinetmaker in Buckkeep whose work he had greatly admired. I balked at that, having no desire to visit Buckkeep Town, but I think he suspected I could not pay such a high prentice fee as a fine workman like Gindast could demand. In that, he was likely correct. When I asked him of any other woodworkers he had noticed, he stoutly replied that there was a boatbuilder in Hammerby Cove whose work was often praised. Perhaps we might try there. This was a far humbler master than the cabinetmaker in Buckkeep. I uneasily wondered if the boy was not tailoring his dreams to the depths of my pockets. His apprenticeship would determine the course of his life's work. I didn't want my lack of coin to condemn him to a trade he found merely tolerable.

Yet despite the boy's interest, the apprenticeship remained a topic for late-night talks by the hearth and little more. Oh, I set aside the small store of coins that remained to me against a prentice fee. I even told the boy that we would make do with fewer eggs for meals if he wished to let the hens set some. There was always a market for chickens, and whatever he got for them he could save toward his fee. Even then, I wondered if it would be enough to buy him a good place. Willing hands and a strong back could buy a lad an apprenticeship, it was true, but the better artisans and craftsmen usually demanded a fee before they would take a likely boy into their shops. It was the way of Buck. The secrets of a man's trade and the good livelihood he made at it were not to be carelessly given to strangers. If parents loved their children, they either raised them in their own trades, or paid well to see them apprenticed to those who had mastered other arts. Despite the humbleness of our fortunes, I was determined to see Hap well placed. That, I told myself, was why I delayed, to muster more coin. It was not that I dreaded parting with the boy. Only that I wished to do well by him.

The wolf did not ask me about the journey I had earlier proposed. I think that, in his heart, he was relieved to see it postponed. There were days when I felt that Starling's words had made an old man of me. Years had done that in truth to the wolf. I suspected he was very old for his kind, though I had no idea how long a wild wolf usually lived. I wondered, sometimes, if our bond did not lend him an unnatural vitality. Once it even crossed my mind that perhaps he used up my years to lengthen his own. Yet that thought came not with any resentment that he might borrow my days but with hope that we might still have a good long span together. For once the boy was apprenticed out, whom else did I have in the world besides Nighteyes?

For a time, I wondered if Chade might come to call again, now that he knew the way, but the long days of summer simmered away and the trail to our cabin remained empty. I went to market with the boy twice, taking fledged chickens and my inks and dyes and such roots and herbs as I thought might be unusual there. Nighteyes was as pleased to remain at home, for he disliked not only the long walk to the trade crossroads but the dust and noise and confusion of the crowded market. I felt much the same about it but forced myself to go anyway. We did not do as well as I had hoped, for folk at the small market we frequented were more accustomed to trade in goods than to buy with coin. Still, I was pleasantly surprised at how many folk recalled Tom Badgerlock, and commented that it was good to see me come to market again.

It was the second time we went to market that we chanced to meet Hap's hedge-witch from Buckkeep. We had set our wares out on the tail of our pony cart in the market. Midway through the morning, she found us there, exclaiming with pleasure at seeing Hap again. I stood quietly to one side, watching them talk. He had told me Jinna was pretty, and so she was, but I confess I was startled to find her closer to my age than his. I had supposed her a girl who had turned his head when they met in Buckkeep. Instead she was a woman nearing her middle years, with hazel eyes, a scattering of freckles, and curly hair that shaded from auburn to brown. She had the round and pleasant figure of a mature woman. When he told her that her charm against pickpockets had been stolen from him before the day was out, she laughed aloud, an open hearty laugh. Then she calmly replied to him that that was exactly how the charm was intended to work. His purse had been protected when the thief took the charm instead of it.

When Hap glanced about to include me in the conversation, her eyes had already found me. She was regarding me with that expression parents usually reserve for possibly dangerous strangers. When I smiled and nodded to Hap's introduction and offered her good day, she visibly relaxed and her smile expanded to include me. She stepped closer as she did so, peering up at my face, and I realized her eyesight was not keen.

She had brought her wares to market, and spread her mat in the shadow of our cart. Hap helped her arrange her charms and potents, and the two of them made a merry day of our marketing after that, exchanging news since Springfest. I listened in as Hap told her of his apprenticeship plans. When he spoke to Jinna, it became very clear to me just how much he had wished for the cabinetmaker in Buckkeep rather than the boatbuilder in Hammerby Cove. I found myself pondering if there was yet some way it might be arranged, not only the higher fee but for someone other than myself to negotiate the apprenticeship on his behalf. Could Chade be persuaded to help me in such an endeavor? From there my mind wandered to what the old man might ask of me in return. I was deep in such thoughts when Hap's elbow in my ribs jolted me from my wandering.

"Tom!" he protested, and I instantly perceived that in some way I had embarrassed him. Jinna was looking at both of us expectantly.

"Yes?"

"See, I told you it would be fine with him," Hap crowed.

"Well, I do thank you, as long as you are sure it would be no trouble," Jinna replied. "It's a long road, with inns both far spaced and expensive to one such as myself."

I nodded my agreement to the statement, and in the next few minutes of conversation, I realized that Hap had extended the hospitality of our cottage to her the next time she happened to pass our way. I privately sighed. Hap loved the novelty of our occasional guests, but I still regarded any new stranger as a potential risk. I wondered how long I would have to live before my secrets were so old that they no longer mattered.

I smiled and nodded as they conversed, but added little. Instead, I found myself studying her as Chade had taught me but I found nothing to suggest she was anything other than the hedge-witch she claimed to be.

Which is to say that I knew very little of her at all. Hedge-witches and -wizards are fairly common at any market, fair, or festival. Unlike the Skill, common folk attach no awe to hedge-magic. Unlike the Wit, it does not mark the practitioner for execution. Most folk seem to regard it with both tolerance and skepticism. Some of those who claim the magic are complete and unapologetic charlatans. These are the ones who pull eggs from the ears of the gullible, tell fortunes of vast riches and lofty marriages for milkmaids, sell love potions that are mostly lavender and chamomile, and peddle luck charms made from dismembered rabbits. They are harmless enough, I suppose.

Jinna was not, however, one of those. She had no friendly patter of talk to attract the passing folk, nor was she dressed in the gaudy veils and jewelry that such frauds usually affected. She was clad as simply as a forester, her tunic shades of green over buckskin-brown trousers and soft shoes. The charms she had set out for sale were concealed within the traditional bags of colored fabric: pink for love charms, red to rouse lagging passions, green for good crops, and other colors whose significance I did not know. She offered packets of dried herbs as well. Most were ones I knew and they were correctly labeled as to their virtues: slippery-elm bark for sore throats, raspberry leaves for morning sickness and the like. Mixed amongst the herbs were fine crystals of something which Jinna claimed increased their potency. I suspected salt or sugar. Several pottery dishes on her mat held polished disks of jade or jasper or ivory, inscribed with runes for luck or fertility or peace of mind. These were less expensive than the constructed charms, for they were merely general good wishes, though for an extra copper or two Jinna would "hone" the pocket stone to the individual customer's desire.

She did a fairly lively trade as the long morning ventured toward afternoon. Several times customers inquired about the covered charms, and at least three made purchases with good silver. If there was a magic to the gadgets she sold them, it was one that neither my Wit nor my Skill could detect. I caught a glimpse of one of the charms; it was an intricate assembly of glittering beads and small rods of wood and, I thought, a tuft of feathers. She sold it to a man wishing to attract good fortune to himself and his home as he sought a wife. He was a broad man, muscled as a plowman and homely as a sod roof. He looked about my age, and I silently wished him well in his quest.

The market was well into its day when Baylor arrived. He came with his cart and ox, and six trussed piglets to sell. I did not know the man well, despite the fact that he was as close to a neighbor as Hap and I had. He lived in the next vale and ran his hogs there. I seldom saw him. In the fall, we sometimes made a trade, a slaughter-pig in exchange for chickens or labor or smoked fish. Baylor was a little man, skinny but strong, and ever suspicious. He gave us a glare for a greeting. Then, despite the close quarters, he forced his cart into place alongside ours. I did not welcome his company. The Wit gives one an empathy for other living creatures. I had learned to shield myself from it, but could not close it off completely. I knew that his ox was rubbed raw by the badly fitting harness, and felt the terror and discomfort of the immobilized and sun-scorched piglets in the cart.

So it was as much self-defense as neighborliness for me

to greet him with, "Good to see you again, Baylor. Fine litter of piglets. Best get some water into them to make them lively, and they should fetch a good price."

He gave them a careless glance. "No sense stirring them up, or taking the chance they'll get loose. Like as not they'll be meat before the day is out anyway."

I took a breath, and with an effort kept from speaking. The Wit is more curse than gift, I sometimes think. Perhaps the hardest part of possessing it is witnessing so completely the casual cruelty of humans. Some speak of the savagery of beasts. I will ever prefer that to the thoughtless contempt some men have toward animals.

I was willing to let our conversation end, but he came to inspect our trade goods. He made a small disparaging noise, as if surprised we had bothered to come to market at all. Then, catching my eye, he observed heavily, "These are good piglets, but there were three more in the litter. One was bigger than these."

Then he paused, waiting. His eyes never left my face. Uncertain of what he expected, I replied, "Sounds like a nice, big litter."

"Aye. It was. Until the three disappeared."

"A shame," I rejoined. When he kept his stare on me, I added, "Lost while ranging with the sow, were they?"

He nodded. "One day there were ten. The next day, seven."

I shook my head. "A shame."

He took a step closer to me. "You and the boy. You wouldn't have happened to see them? I know sometimes my sow ranges almost to your stream."

"I haven't." I turned to Hap. The boy had an apprehensive look on his face. I noticed that Jinna and her customer had fallen silent, their interest caught by Baylor's intent tone. I hated to be the center of such attention. I felt the blood begin to rise in me, but I pleasantly asked my boy, "Hap, have you seen any sign of three of Baylor's piglets?"

"Not so much as a track or a pile of dung," he replied

gravely. He held himself very still when he spoke, as if a sudden movement could precipitate danger.

I turned back to Baylor. "Sorry," I said.

"Well." He observed heavily, "That's strange, isn't it? I know you and your boy and that dog of yours range all about those hills. I would have thought you'd have seen something." His remark was oddly pointed. "And if you saw them, you'd know them for mine. You'd know they weren't strays, free for the taking." His eyes had never left my face.

I shrugged, trying to keep my calm. But now other folk were pausing in their business, watching and listening. Baylor's eyes suddenly ranged round the audience, and then came back to me.

"So you're sure you haven't seen my pigs? Not found one stuck or hurt somewhere? Not found it dead and used it for dog meat?"

It was my turn to glance about. Hap's face had gone red. Jinna looked distinctly uncomfortable. My anger surged that this man would dare to accuse me of theft, no matter how indirect his words were. I took a breath and managed to hold my temper. In a low, gratingly civil voice, I replied, "I haven't seen your pigs, Baylor."

"You're sure?" He took a step closer to me, mistaking my courtesy for passivity. "Because it strikes me odd, three disappearing all at once. A wolf might take one, or one the sow might misplace, but not three. You haven't seen them?"

I had been leaning on the tail of the cart. I stood up straight, to my full height, my feet set solidly wide. Despite my effort at control, I could feel my chest and neck growing tight with anger.

Once, long ago, I had been beaten badly, to the point of death. Men seem to react to that experience in one of two ways. Some become cowed by it, never to offer physical resistance again. For a time, I had known that abject fear. Life had forced me to recover from it: I had learned a new reaction. The man who becomes most efficiently vicious first is most likely to be the man left standing. I had learned to be that man. "I'm getting tired of that question," I warned him in a low growl.

In the busy market, a quiet circle surrounded us. Not only Jinna and her customer were silent, but across the way the cheese merchant stared at us, and a baker's boy with a tray full of fresh wares stood silent and gawking. Hap was still, eyes wide, face gone to white and red. But most revealing was the change in Baylor's face. If a snarling bear had suddenly towered over him, he could not have looked more cowed. He fell back a step, and looked aside at the dust. "Well. Of course, if you haven't seen them, well, then—"

"I haven't seen them." I spoke forcefully, cutting him off. The sounds of the market had retreated into a distant hum. I saw only Baylor. I stalked a step closer.

"Well." He backed another pace, and dodged around his ox so the beast was between us. "I didn't think you had, of course. You'd have chased them back my way, for certain. But I wanted to let you know about it. Odd, isn't it, for three to go missing at once? Thought I'd let you know, in case you'd had chickens disappearing." From conciliating his voice went suddenly to conspiring. "Like as not we've had Witted ones about in our hills, thieving my beasts as only they can. They wouldn't have to chase them down, just spell the sow and the piglets and walk right off with them. Everyone knows they can do that. Like as not—"

My temper flared. I managed to divert it into words. I spoke quietly, biting off each word. "Like as not the piglets fell down a creek bank and were swept away, or got separated from the sow. There's fox and cats and wolverine in those hills. If you want to be sure of your stock, keep a better watch on them."

"I had a calf go missing this spring," the cheese merchant suddenly said. "Cow strayed off pregnant, and came home two days later, empty as a barrel." He shook his head. "Never found a trace of that calf. But I did find a burnt-out firepit."

"Witted ones," the baker's boy chimed in sagely. "They caught one over to Hardin's Spit the other day, but she got away. No telling where she is now. Or where she was!" His eyes gleamed with the joy of his suspicions.

"Well, that explains it, then," Baylor exclaimed. He shot a triumphant look my way, then hastily looked aside from my expression. "That's the way of it, then, Tom Badgerlock. And I only wanted to warn you, as neighbors do for one another. You keep good watch on those chickens of yours." He nodded judiciously, and across the way, the cheese merchant nodded as well.

"My cousin was there, at Hardin's Spit. He saw that Wit whore just sprout feathers and fly. The ropes fell away from her and off she went."

I didn't even turn my head to see who spoke. The normal movement and noise of the market had resumed around us, but now the gossip hummed with jolly hatred of the Witted. I stood isolated, the warm summer sun beating down on my head just as it did the hapless piglets in Baylor's cart. The surging of my heart was like a shaking inside me. The moment in which I might have killed him had passed like a fever breaking. I saw Hap wipe sweat from his brow. Jinna put a hand on his shoulder and said something quietly to him. He shook his head, his lips white. Then he looked at me and gave me a shaky smile. It was over.

But the gossip in the market went on. All around me, the market chuckled along, healed by the prospect of a common enemy. It made me queasy, and I felt small and shamed that I did not shout out at the injustice of it all. Instead, I took up Clover's lead. "Mind our trade, Hap. I'm going to water the pony."

Hap, still silent and grave, nodded to me. I felt his eyes on me as I led Clover away. I took my time at the task, and when I came back, Baylor made a point of smiling and greeting me. All I could manage was a nod. It was a relief when a butcher bought all Baylor's piglets on condition that he deliver them to the man's shop. As the sore ox and the miserable piglets left, I let out a sigh. My back ached with the tension I'd been holding.

"Pleasant fellow," Jinna observed quietly. Hap laughed aloud, and even I broke a sour smile. Later we shared our hard-boiled eggs, bread, and salt fish with her. She had a pouch of dried apples and a smoked sausage. We made a picnic of it, and when I laughed at some jest of Hap's, she made me blush by saying, "You look a vicious man when you scowl, Tom Badgerlock. And when you knot your fists, I'd not want to know you. Yet when you smile or laugh aloud, your eyes put the lie to that look."

Hap snickered to see me flush, and the rest of the day passed in good companionship and friendly barter. As the market day wound to a close, Jinna had done well for herself. Her supply of charms had dwindled measurably. "Soon it will be time to go back to Buckkeep Town, and turn my hand to making more. It suits me better than the selling, though I do like traveling about and meeting new folk," she observed as she packed up what was left of her wares.

Hap and I had exchanged most of our goods for things we could use at home, but had gained little in actual coin for his apprenticeship fee. He tried to keep the disappointment from his face but I saw the shadow of his worry in his eyes. What if our coins were not sufficient even for the boatbuilder? What then of his apprenticeship? The question haunted me as well.

Yet neither of us voiced it. We slept in our cart to save the cost of an inn and left the next morning for home. Jinna came by to bid us farewell and Hap reminded her of his offer of hospitality. She assured him she would remember, but her eyes caught at mine as she did so, as if uncertain of how truly welcome she would be. Perforce I must nod and smile and add my hope that we would see her soon.

We had a fine day for the journey home. There were high clouds and a light wind to keep the summer day from being oppressive. We nibbled at the honeycomb that Hap had received for one of his chickens. We talked of nothing: that the market was much larger than the first time I had been there, that the town had grown, that the road was more traveled than it had been last year. Neither of us spoke of Baylor. We passed the fork in the road that once would have taken us to Forge. Grass grew on that trail. Hap asked if I thought folk would ever settle there again. I said I hoped not, but that sooner or later, the iron ore would bring someone with a short memory there. From there, we progressed to tales of what had happened at Forge and the hardships of the Red Ship War. I told them all as tales I had heard from another, not because I enjoyed the telling of them, but because it was history the boy should know. It was something everyone in the Six Duchies should always recall, and again I resolved to make an attempt at a history of that time. I thought of my many brave beginnings, of the stacked scrolls that rolled about on the shelves above my desk, and wondered if I would ever complete any of them.

An abrupt question from Hap broke me rudely from my musing.

"Was I a Red Ship bastard, Tom?"

My mouth hung ajar. All my old pain at that word shone fresh in Hap's mismatched eyes. Mishap, his mother had named him. Starling had found him, a scavenging orphan that no one in his village would claim. That was as much as I knew of him. I forced honesty. "I don't know, Hap. You could have been Raider-born." I used the kinder term.

He stared straight ahead now, walking steadily as he spoke. "Starling said I was. I'm an age to be one, and it might be why no one save you would take me in. I'd like to know. I'd like to know who I am."

"Oh," I finally said into the dangling silence.

He nodded hard, twice. His voice was tight when he added, "When I said I'd have to tell you about her, Starling said I had the same Forged heart as my raping father."

I suddenly wished he were smaller, so I could catch him up mid-stride and hug him. Instead, I put my arm around his shoulders and forced him to a halt. The pony ambled along without us. I didn't make him meet my eyes nor did I let my voice become too grave. "I'm going to give you a gift, son. This is knowledge it took me twenty years to gain, so appreciate that I'm giving it to you while you're young." I took a breath. "It doesn't matter who a man's father is. Your parents made a child, but it's up to you to make the man you'll be." I held his gaze for a moment. Then, "Come on. Let's go home."

We walked on, my arm across his shoulders for a time, until he reached up to clap me on the shoulder. I let him go then, to walk on his own and silently finish his thinking. It was the best I could do for him. My thoughts of Starling were not charitable.

Night caught us before we reached the cottage, but there was a moon and both of us knew the road. The old pony meandered along placidly and the clopping of her hooves and the creaking of the two-wheeled cart made an odd sort of music. A summer rain began to fall, damping the dust and cooling the night. Not far from home, Nighteyes came nonchalantly to meet us, as if mere chance had brought him out upon the road. We journeyed companionably together, the boy in silence, the wolf and I in the effortless communion of the Wit. We absorbed the other's experiences of the day like an indrawn breath. He could not grasp my worry for the boy's future.

He can hunt and he can fish. What more does he need to know? Why send one of our own off to another pack, to learn their ways? We are diminished by the loss of his strength. We grow no younger, you and I.

My brother, that is perhaps the strongest reason why he should go. He must begin to make his own way in the world, so that when the time comes for him to take a mate, he can provide well for her and their children.

What of you and me? We will not help him in that providing? We will not watch the cubs while he hunts, or bring back our kill to share? Are we not pack with him?

Among human packs, this is the way of it. It was an answer I had given him many times in our years together. I knew how he interpreted it. It was a human custom that made no sense, and he need not waste time trying to understand it.

What of us, then, when he is gone?

I've told you. Perhaps we shall travel again.

Ah, yes. Leave a cozy den and a predictable food supply. That makes as much sense as sending the boy away.

I let his thought hang unanswered, for he was right. Perhaps the restlessness Chade had stirred in me had been the last gasp of my youth. Perhaps I should have bought that wife-finding charm from Jinna. From time to time I had considered the idea of looking for a wife, but it seemed too perfunctory a way to take a mate. Some did so, I knew, merely seeking out a woman or man who had similar goals and no excessively irritating habits. Such partnerships often grew into loving relationships. But having once experienced a relationship not only founded on years of knowing one another but blessed with the heady intoxication of genuine love, I did not think I could ever settle for anything else. It would not be fair to ask another woman to live in Molly's shadow. In all the years that Starling had intermittently shared herself with me, I had never thought to ask her to marry me. That thought gave me pause for a moment: had Starling ever hoped that I would? Then the moment of wondering passed and I smiled grimly to myself. No. Starling would have found such an offer baffling, if not laughable.

The last part of our journey was darker, for the track to our cottage was narrow and overshadowed on both sides by trees. Rain dripped from the leaves. The cart jounced along. "Should have brought a lantern," Hap observed, and I grunted agreement. Our cottage was a darker hummock in the shadowed hollow we called home.

I went inside and kindled a fire and put our traded goods away. Hap took a light and settled the pony. Nighteyes

immediately sighed down onto the hearth, as close to the
fire as he could get without singeing his coat. I put on the
kettle and added the few coins we had gained to Hap's small
hoard. It wasn't going to be enough, I grudgingly admitted.
Even if Hap and I hired ourselves out the rest of the summer
to bring in hay and other crops, it still wouldn't be enough.
Nor could we both work that way, unless we were resigned
to our own chickens and garden perishing from neglect. Yet
if only one of us hired out, it might be another year, perhaps
longer, before we had saved enough.

"I should have started saving for this years ago," I observed sourly as Hap came in from outside. He set the
lantern on its shelf before dropping into the other chair. I
nodded at the pot on the table and he poured himself a cup
of tea. The stacked coins on the table were a pitiful wall between us.

"Too late to think that way," he observed as he took up
his cup. "We have to start from where we are."

"Exactly. Do you think you and Nighteyes could manage here for the rest of the summer while I hired out?"

He met my gaze levelly. "Why should you be the one to
hire out? The money would go for *my* apprenticeship."

I experienced an odd little shift in perception. Because
I was "bigger and stronger and could earn more" was no
longer true. His shoulders were as wide as mine, and in any
test of endurance, his young back would probably hold out
better. He grinned sympathetically as he saw me grasp what
he already knew. "Perhaps because it is something that I'd
like to give you," I said quietly, and he nodded, understanding what those words really meant.

"You've already given me more than I could ever pay
back. Including the ability to go after this for myself."

Those were the words we went to bed on, and I was
smiling as I closed my eyes. There is monstrous vanity in
the pride we take in our children, I told myself. I had bum-
bled along with Hap, never really giving much thought to
what I was or was not teaching him about being a man.

Then one evening, a young man meets my eyes and tells me that he can fend for himself if he needs to, and I feel the warm flush of success. The boy had raised himself, I told myself, but I still smiled as I fell asleep.

Perhaps my expansive mood left me more open than usual, for I Skill-dreamed that night. Such dreams occasionally came to me, more taunting my addiction than assuaging it, for they were uncontrollable things that offered brief glimpses with none of the satisfaction of full contact. Yet this dream was tantalizing with possibility, for I felt that I rode with an individual mind rather than sampling the stray thoughts of a crowd.

It seemed as much memory as vision. In the dream, I ghosted through the Great Hall at Buckkeep. Scores of elegant folk decked out in their finest clothes filled the hall. Music wafted through the air and I glimpsed dancers, but I moved slowly through standing folk conversing with one another. Some turned to greet me as I passed, and I murmured my responses, but my eyes never lingered on their faces. I did not wish to be here; I could not have been more uninterested. For a moment, my eye was caught by a fall of gleaming bronze hair. The girl's back was to me. Several rings rode on the slender hand that lifted to nervously tug her collar straight. As if she felt my gaze, she turned. She had caught my eyes on her, and she blushed pink as she curtseyed deeply to me. I bowed to her, proffered some greeting, and moved on through the crowd. I could feel her looking after me; it annoyed me.

Even more annoying was to see Chade, so tall and elegant as he stood on the dais beside and slightly behind the Queen's chair. He too had been watching me. He bent now to whisper something in her ear, and her eyes came unerringly to me. A small gesture of her hand beckoned me to join them there. My heart sank. Would I never have time that was my own, to do as I pleased? Bleakly and slowly, I moved to obey her.

Then the dream changed, as dreams will. I sprawled on

a blanket before a hearth. I was bored. It was so unfair. Below, they danced, they ate, and here I was ... A ripple in the dream. No. Not bored, simply not engaged with anything. Idly I unsheathed my claws and inspected them. A bit of bird down was caught under one of them. I freed it, then cleaned my whole paw thoroughly before dozing off before the fire again.

What was that? Amusement tinged the sleepy thought from Nighteyes, but to reply to him would have required more effort than I was willing to make. I grumbled at him, rolled over, and burrowed back into sleep.

In the morning I wondered at my dream but briefly, dismissing it as a mixture of errant Skill and my own boyhood memories of Buckkeep mingling with my ambitions for Hap. As I did the morning chores, the dwindling firewood stack caught my attention. It needed replenishing, not only for the sake of summer's cooking and night comfort, but to begin a hoard against winter's deep cold. I went in to breakfast, thinking I would attend to it that day.

Hap's neatly packed carry-sack leaned beside the door. The lad himself had a freshly washed and brushed air to him. He grinned at me, suppressed excitement in his smile as he dolloped porridge into our bowls. I sat down at my place at the table and he took his place opposite me. "Today?" I asked him, trying to keep reluctance from my voice.

"I can't start sooner," he pointed out pleasantly. "At market, I heard the hay was standing ready at Cormen. That's only two days from here."

I nodded slowly, at a loss for words. He was right. More than right, he was eager. Let him go, I counseled myself, and bit back my objections. "I suppose there's no sense in delaying it," I managed to say. He took this as both encouragement and an endorsement. As we ate, he speculated that he could work the hay at Cormen, and then perhaps go on to Divden and see if there was more work to be had there.

"Divden?"

"Three days past Cormen. Jinna told us about it, re-member? She said their barley fields looked like an ocean when the wind stirred the growing grain. So I thought I might try there."

"Sounds promising," I agreed. "And then you'd come home?"

He nodded slowly. "Unless I heard of more work."

"Of course. Unless you heard of more work."

In a few short hours, Hap was gone. I'd made him pack extra food, and take some of the coins with him in case of extreme need. He'd been impatient with my caution. He'd sleep by the roadside, he told me, not in inns. He told me that Queen Kettricken's patrols kept the highwaymen down, and that robbers would not bother with poor prey like himself. He assured me that he would be fine. At Nighteyes' insistence, I asked him if he wouldn't take the wolf with him. He smiled indulgently at this, and paused at the door to scratch Nighteyes' ears. "It might be a bit much for the old fellow," he suggested gently. "Best he stays here where you two can look after one another until I get back."

As we stood together and watched our boy walk down the lane to the main road, I wondered if I had ever been so insufferably young and sure of myself, but the ache in my heart had the pleasant afterglow of pride.

The rest of the day was oddly difficult to fill. There was work to be done, but I could not settle into it. Several times, I came back to myself, realizing I was simply staring off into the distance. I walked to the cliffs twice, for no more reason than to look out over the sea, and once to the end of our lane to look up and down the road in both directions. There was not even dust hanging in the air. All was still and silent as far as I could see. The wolf trailed me disconsolately. I be-gan a half-dozen tasks and left them all half-done. I found myself listening, and waiting, without knowing for what. In the midst of splitting and stacking firewood, I halted. Care-fully not thinking, I raised my axe and drove it into the chopping block. I picked up my shirt, slung it over my sweaty shoulder, and headed toward the cliffs.

Nighteyes was suddenly in front of me. *What are you doing?*

Taking a short rest.

No you're not. You're going down to the cliffs, to Skill.

I rubbed the palms of my hands down the sides of my trousers. My thoughts were formless. "I was just going there for the breeze."

Once you're there, you'll try to Skill. You know you will. I can feel your hunger as plainly as you do. My brother, please. Please don't.

His thought rode on a keening whine. Never had I seen him so desperate to dissuade me. It puzzled me. "Then I won't, if it worries you so."

I wrenched my axe out of the chopping block and went back to work. After a time, I became aware I was attacking the wood with ferocity far beyond the task's need. I finished splitting the tumble of logs and began the tedious chore of stacking it so it would dry and yet shed rain. When that was done, I picked up my shirt. Without thinking, I turned toward the sea cliffs. Instantly the wolf was blocking my path.

Don't do this, brother.

I already told you I wouldn't. I turned aside from him, denying the frustration I felt. I weeded the garden. I hauled water from the stream to replenish the kitchen barrel. I dug a new pit, moved the privy, and filled the old pit with clean earth. In short, I burned through work as a lightning fire burns through a summer meadow. My back and arms ached, not just with weariness but with the complaints of old injuries, and still I dared not be still. The Skill-hunger tugged at me, refusing to be ignored.

As evening came, the wolf and I went fishing for our supper. Cooking for one person seemed foolish, yet I forced myself to set out a decent meal and to eat it. I tidied up and then sat down. The long hours of the evening stretched before me. I set out vellum and inks, but could not settle to the task of writing anything. My thoughts would not order themselves. I finally dragged out the mending and began to doggedly patch, sew, or darn every garment that needed it.

Finally, when my work began to blear before my eyes, I went to bed. I lay on my back, my arm flung over my face, and tried to ignore the fishhooks that were set and dragging at my soul. Nighteyes dropped beside the bed with a sigh. I trailed my other arm over the side of the bed, resting my hand on his head. I wondered when we had crossed the line from solitude to loneliness.

It's not loneliness that eats at you like this.

There seemed nothing to say to that. I passed a difficult night. I forced myself out of bed shortly after dawn. For the next few days, I spent the mornings cutting alder for the smokehouse, and the afternoons catching fish to smoke. The wolf gorged himself on entrails, but still watched greedily as I salted the slabs of red fish and hung them on hooks over the slow fire. I put more green alder on to thicken the smoke and shut the door tightly. Late one afternoon, I was at the rain barrel, washing slime, scales, and salt from my hands when Nighteyes suddenly turned his head toward the lane.

Someone comes.

Hap? Hope surged in me.

No.

I was surprised at the strength of my disappointment. I felt an echo of the same from the wolf. We were both staring down the shaded lane when Jinna came in sight. She paused a moment, unnerved perhaps by the intensity of our gazes, then lifted a hand in greeting. "Hello, Tom Badgerlock! Here I am, to take up your offer of hospitality."

A friend of Hap's, I explained to Nighteyes. He still hung back and regarded her warily as I went to meet her.

"Welcome. I didn't expect to see you so soon," I said, and then heard the awkwardness of my words. "An unexpected pleasure is always the most welcome," I added to mend the moment, and then realized that such gallantry was just as inappropriate. Had I completely forgotten how to deal with people?

But Jinna's smile put me at ease. "Seldom do I hear such honesty harnessed with such fair words, Tom Badgerlock. Is that water cool?"

Without waiting for an answer, she strode up to the rain barrel, unknotting the kerchief at her throat as she did so. She walked like a woman used to the road, weary at the end of the day, but not overly taxed by her journey. The bulging pack high on her back was a natural part of her. She damped her kerchief and wiped the dust from her face and hands. Moistening it more generously, she wiped the back of her neck and her throat. "Oh, that's better," she sighed gratefully. She turned to me with a smile that crinkled the corners of her eyes. "At the end of a long day's walk, I envy folk like you with a settled life and a place to call your own."

"I assure you, folk like me just as often wonder if life would not be sweeter as travelers. Won't you come in and be comfortable? I was just about to start the evening meal."

"Many thanks." As she followed me to the door of the cabin, Nighteyes shadowed us at a discreet distance. Without turning to look at him directly, she observed, "A bit unusual, a wolf as a watchdog."

I often lied to people, insisting that Nighteyes was merely a dog that looked like a wolf. Something told me this would be an insult to Jinna. I gave her the truth. "I adopted him as a cub. He's been a good companion to me."

"So Hap told me. And that he does not like to be stared at by strangers, but will come to me when he's made up his mind about me. And as usual, I'm telling a tale by starting in the middle. I passed Hap upon the road a few days ago. He was in high spirits, with every confidence that he will find work and do well. I do believe he will; the boy has such a friendly, engaging manner that I cannot imagine anyone not welcoming him. He assured me again of a warm welcome here, and of course he spoke true."

She followed me into my cabin. She slung her pack to

the floor and leaned it up against the wall, then straightened and stretched her back with a relieved groan. "Well. What are we cooking? You may as well let me help, for I'm never content to sit still in a kitchen. Fish? Oh, I've a wonderful herb for fish. Have you a heavy pot with a tight-fitting lid?"

With the ease of the naturally gregarious, she took over half the dinner chores. I had not shared kitchen tasks with a woman since my year among the Witted folk, and even then, Holly had been a near-silent companion at such times. Jinna talked on, clattering pots and pans and filling my small home with her bustle and friendly gossip. She had the rare knack of coming into my territory and handling my possessions without me feeling displaced or uneasy. My feelings bled over to Nighteyes. He soon ventured into the cabin, and assumed his customary attentive post by the table. She was unruffled by his intent stare, and accepted his adeptness at catching the fish trimmings she tossed his way. The fish was soon simmering in a pot with her herbs. I raided my garden for young carrots and fresh greens while she fried thick slabs of bread in lard.

It seemed that dinner appeared on the table with no real effort from anyone. Nor had she neglected to prepare bread for the wolf as well, though I think Nighteyes ate it more out of sociability than hunger. The poached fish was moist and savory, spiced as much with her conversation as the herbs. She did not chatter endlessly, but her stories encouraged responses, and she listened with as much appreciation as she gave to the food. The dishes were cleared from the table with as little effort. When I brought out the Sandsedge brandy, she exclaimed delightedly, "Now, this is the perfect end to a good meal."

She took her brandy to the hearth. Our cooking fire had burned low. She added another piece of wood, more for light than warmth, and settled herself on the floor beside the wolf. Nighteyes didn't even twitch an ear. She sipped her brandy, gave an appreciative sigh, then gestured with her cup. My scroll-cluttered desk was just visible through the open door of my study. "I knew you made inks and dyes, but from what I see, you employ them as well. Are you a scribe of some kind?"

I gave a desultory shrug. "Of sorts," I admitted. "I do not attempt the fancy work, though I do simple illustration. My lettering is no better than passable. For me, there is a satisfaction in taking knowledge and committing it to paper, where it is accessible to all."

"To any who can read," Jinna amended my words.

"That is true," I conceded.

She cocked her head at me and smiled. "I don't think I approve."

I was startled, not just that she disagreed with such a thing, but that she could do it so pleasantly. "Why not?"

"Perhaps knowledge should not be available to all. Perhaps it should be earned, parceled out from master to worthy student only, rather than committed to paper where anyone who chances upon it may claim it for himself."

"I confess to some of the same doubts myself," I replied, thinking of the Skill-scrolls that Chade now studied. "And yet I have known of cases in which a master died an untimely death, and all she knew went with her, before it could be passed on to her chosen pupil. Generations of knowledge were lost in one death."

She was silent for a time. "Tragic," she admitted at last. "For though masters of a skill may share a great deal of knowledge, each has his own secrets, destined only for his own apprentices."

"Consider someone such as yourself," I went on, pushing my advantage in the discussion. "You practice a trade that is as much an art, woven of secrets and skills shared only by those others who practice hedge-magic. You have no apprentice at all that I have seen. Yet I would wager there are aspects of your magic that are yours alone, ones that would die with you if you perished tonight."

She looked at me for a still moment, then took another

sip of her brandy. "There's a chill thought to dream on," she replied wryly. "Yet there is this also, Tom. I have no letters. I could not put my knowledge in such a form, unless someone such as yourself aided me. And then I would not be certain if you had truly put down what I know, or what you thought I had told you. That is half of teaching an apprentice: making sure the youngster learns what you said, not what she thinks you said."

"Very true," I had to agree. How often had I thought I understood Chade's directions, only to come to disaster when I tried to mix the concoction on my own? Another little ripple of uneasiness went through me, as I thought of Chade trying to teach Prince Dutiful from the scrolls. Would he teach what some forgotten Skillmaster had committed to paper, or only his understanding of it? I pulled my thoughts back from the unsettling notion. I had no duty there. I had warned him; that was as much as I could do.

Conversation lagged after that, and Jinna soon sought rest in Hap's bed. Nighteyes and I went out to shut up the chicken house for the night and make our evening round of our smallholding. All was well and calm in the peaceful summer night. I cast one longing look toward the cliffs. The waves would be lace-edged silver tonight. I forbade it to myself and felt Nighteyes' relief at my decision. We added more green alder branches to the slow fire in the smokehouse. "Bedtime," I decided.

On nights such as this, we used to hunt together.

That we did. It would be a good night for hunting. The moon will make the game restless and easy to see.

Nevertheless, he followed me as I turned back toward the hut. Regardless of how well we both recalled it, neither of us were the young wolves we once had been. Our bellies were full, the hearth was warm, and rest might ease the dull ache in Nighteyes' haunches. Dreams of hunting would have to suffice tonight.

I awoke to the morning sounds of Jinna ladling water into a kettle. When I came out into the kitchen, she had already set the kettle to boil over the stirred fire. She looked over her shoulder as she was slicing bread. "I hope you don't feel that I've made myself too much at home," she offered.

"Not at all," I replied, but it did feel a bit odd. By the time I had seen to my animals and returned with the day's eggs, hot food was steaming on the table. When we had eaten, she helped with the tidying up.

She offered me thanks for the hospitality, and added, "Before I go, perhaps we might do a bit of trading. Would you consider a charm or two from my stock in exchange for some of your yellow and blue inks?"

I found that I was glad to delay her leaving, not only because her company was pleasant, but because I had always been intrigued by hedge-magic. Here was an opportunity, perhaps, for a closer look at the tools of her trade. We went first to my workbench in the shed, where I packaged up pots of yellow, blue, and a small quantity of red ink for her. As I sealed the pots with wooden stoppers and wax, she explained that using colors on some of her charms seemed to increase their efficacy, but that this was an area in which she was still making discoveries. I nodded to her words, but much as I longed to, I refrained from asking more details. It did not seem polite.

When we returned to the house, she set the pots of dye on the table, and opened her own pack. She spread a number of her bagged charms on the table. "What will you choose, Tom Badgerlock?" she asked with a smile. "I have charms for verdant gardens, for hunter's luck, for healthy babes—that's small use to you, let me put that one back. Ah. Here's one you might find useful."

She whisked the cover off a charm. As she did so, Nighteyes let out a low growl. His hackles stood as he stalked to the door and nosed it open. I found myself backing away from the object she revealed. Short rods of wood marked with shrieking black symbols were fastened to each other at chaotic angles. Ominous beads were dangerously interspersed with them. A few tortured tufts of fur, twisted and fixed with pitch, clung to it. The object both offended and distressed me. I would have fled if I had dared take my eyes off it. I abruptly felt the wall of the cabin against my back. I pressed against it, knowing that there was a better path to escape, but unable to think what it was.

"I beg your pardon." Jinna's gentle words came from a vast distance. I blinked, and the object was gone, mantled in cloth and hidden from my sight. Outside the door, Nighteyes' low growl rose to a whistling whine and ceased. I felt as if I had surfaced from deep waters. "It had not occurred to me," Jinna apologized as she thrust the charm deep into her pack. "It's intended to keep predators away from chicken houses and sheep pens," she explained.

I got my breath back. Her gaze did not meet mine. Apprehension hung like a miasma between us. I was Witted, and now she knew it. How would she employ that knowledge? Would she merely be disgusted? Frightened? Scared enough to bring destruction down on me? I imagined Hap returning to a burned-out cabin.

Jinna suddenly looked up and met my eyes as if she had overheard my thoughts. "A man is as he is made. A man can't help how he's made."

"That's so," I muttered in response, shamed at how relieved I felt. I managed to step away from the wall and toward the table. She didn't look at me. She rooted through her pack as if the incident had never occurred.

"So, then, let's just find you something a bit more appropriate." She sorted through her bagged charms, stopping sometimes to pinch at the contents to freshen her memory of what was inside. She chose one in a green pouch and placed it on the table. "Will you take one to hang near your garden, to encourage your green things to prosper?"

I nodded mutely, still recovering from my fear. Moments ago, I would have doubted the power of her charms. Now I almost feared their potency. I clenched my teeth as she unveiled the garden charm, but as I stared at it, I felt nothing. When I met her eyes, I found sympathy there. Her gentle smile was reassuring.

"You'll have to give me your hand so I can tune it to you. Then we'll take it outside and adjust it for your garden. Half this charm is for the garden, and half for the gardener. It's that which is between the gardener and his bit of soil that makes a garden. Give me your hands."

She seated herself at my table and held her own hands out to me, palms up. I took the chair opposite hers and, after an awkward hesitation, placed my palms atop hers.

"Not that way. A man's life and ways are told in the palms of his hands, not the backs."

Obediently, I turned my hands over. In my apprentice days, Chade had taught me to read hands, not to tell fortunes, but to tell a man's past. The calluses of a sword differed from those of a scribe's pen or a farmer's hoe. She bent close over my hands, staring at them intently. As she scanned my palms, I wondered if her eyes would discover the axe I had once borne, or the oar I had wielded. Instead, she studied my right hand intently, frowned, then transferred her gaze to my left. When she looked up at me, her face was a picture. The smile that twisted her face was a rueful one.

"You're an odd one, Tom, and no mistake! Were they not both at the ends of your arms, I'd say these were the hands of two different men. It's said that your left hand tells what you were born with, and your right hand what you have made of yourself, but even so, such differences in a man's two hands I've seldom seen! Look what I see in this hand. A tender-hearted boy. A sensitive young man. And then . . . Your lifeline stops short on your left hand." As she spoke, she let go of my right hand. She set her forefinger to my left palm, and her nail traced a tickling line to where my life ended. "Were you Hap's age, I'd be fearing I was looking at a young man soon to die. But as you're sitting there across from me, and your right hand bears a nice long lifeline, we'll go by it, shall we?" She released my left hand, and took my right in both of hers.

"I suppose so," I conceded uncomfortably. It was not only her words that made me ill at ease. The simple warm pressure of her hands gripping mine had made me suddenly aware of Jinna as a woman. I was experiencing a very adolescent response to it. I shifted in my chair. The knowing smile that flickered over her face discomfited me even more.

"So. An avid gardener, I see, one devoted to the knowing of many herbs and their uses."

I made a neutral noise. She had seen my garden, and could be speculating based on what grew there. She studied my right hand a bit more, sweeping her thumb across it to smooth the lesser lines away, and then cupping my fingers in her own and encouraging my hand to close slightly to deepen the folds. "Left or right, it's not an easy hand to read, Tom." She frowned to herself, and compared the two again. "By your left hand, I'd say you'd had a sweet and true love in your short life. A love that ended only in your death. Yet here in your right hand, I see a love that wends its way in and out of all your many years. That faithful heart has been absent for a time, but is soon to return to you again." She lifted her clear hazel eyes to mine to see if she had scored true. I shrugged one shoulder. Had Hap been telling her tales of Starling? Scarcely what I would call a faithful heart. When I said nothing, she returned her attention to my hands, her gaze going from one to the other. She frowned slightly, raising a furrow between her brows. "Look here. See this? Anger and fear, shackled together in a dark chain . . . it follows your lifeline, a black shadow over it."

I pushed aside the uneasiness her words roused in me. I leaned forward to look into my own hand. "It's probably just dirt," I offered.

She gave a small snort of amusement and shook her head again. But she did not return to her ominous peering. Instead she covered my hand with her own and met my eyes. "Never have I seen two palms so unlike on the same man. I suspect that sometimes you wonder if you even know who you are yourself."

"I'm sure every man wonders that from time to time." It was oddly difficult to meet her nearsighted gaze.

"Hm. But you, perhaps, have more honest reason to wonder it than others. Well," she sighed. "Let me see what I can do."

She released my hands, and I drew them back. I rubbed them together under the table as if to erase the tickling of her touch. She took up her charm, turned it several times, and then unfastened a string. She changed the order of the beads on the string, and added an extra brown bead from her pack. She retied the string, and then took out the pot of yellow ink I had traded her. Dipping a fine brush in it, she outlined several black runes on one of the dowels, bending close over it to peer at her work. She spoke as she worked. "When next I come to visit, I expect you to tell me this has been your best year ever for plants that bear their fruits aboveground where the sun ripens them." She blew on the charm to dry the ink, then put away both pot and brush. "Come, now, we have to adjust this to the garden."

Outside, she sent me to find and cut a forked branch at least as tall as myself. When I returned with it, I found she had dug a hole at the southeast corner of my garden plot. I set the pole in it as she directed, and filled in the hole. She hung the charm from the right fork of the branch. When the wind stirred it, the beads rattled gently and a small bell chimed. She tapped the bell with a fingertip. "It discourages some birds."

"Thank you."

"You're welcome. This is a good spot for one of my charms. It pleases me to leave it here. And when next I come, I shall be interested to see how well it has worked for you."

It was the second time she had mentioned visiting again. The ghost of my court manners nudged me. "And when next you come, you shall find yourself as welcome as you were this time. I shall look forward to your visit."

The smile she gave me dimpled her cheeks more deeply. "Thank you, Tom. I shall certainly stop here again." She cocked her head at me and spoke with sudden frankness. "I know you are a lonely man, Tom. That won't always be so. I could tell that, at first, you doubted the power of my charms. You still doubt the truth of what I can see in the palm of a man's hand. I don't. Your one true love is stitched in and out and through your life. Love will return to you. Don't doubt that."

Her hazel eyes met mine so earnestly that I could neither laugh nor frown at her. So I nodded mutely. As she shouldered her pack and strode off down the lane, I watched her go. Her words tugged at me, and hopes long denied struggled to grow. I thrust them away from me. Molly and Burrich belonged to one another now. There was no place for me in their lives.

I squared my shoulders. I had chores to do, wood to stack, fish to put by, and a roof to mend. It was another fine summer day. Best use it while I had it, for while summer smiles, winter is never far away.

chapter V

THE TAWNY MAN

There is some indication, in the earliest accounts of the territories that eventually became the Six Duchies, that the Wit was not always a despised magic. These accounts are fragmentary, and the translations of these old scrolls are often disputed, but most of the master scribes will agree that at one time there were settlements where the preponderance of folk were born with the Wit and actively practiced its magic. Some of these scrolls would indicate that these folk were the original inhabitants of the lands. This may be the source of the name that the Witted people apply to themselves: Old Blood.

In those times, the lands were not so settled. Folk relied more on hunting and collecting of wild bounty than on harvesting what they had themselves planted. Perhaps in those days a bond between a man and a beast did not seem so uncanny, for folk provided for themselves much as the wild creatures did.

Even in more recent histories, accounts of Witted folk being slain for their magic are rare. Indeed, that these executions are recorded at all would seem to indicate that they were unusual, and hence noteworthy. It is not until after the brief reign of King Charger, the so-called Piebald Prince, that we find the Wit referred to with loathing and an assumption that its practice merits death. Following his reign, there are accounts of widespread slaughter of Witted folk. In some cases, entire villages were put to death. After that time of carnage, either those of Old Blood were rare, or too wary to admit that they carried the Wit magic.

Beautiful summer days followed, one after another, like blue and green beads on a string. There was nothing wrong with my life. I worked in my garden, I finished the repairs to my long-neglected cottage, and in the early mornings and the summer twilight, I hunted with the wolf. I filled my days with good and simple things. The weather held fine. I had the warmth of the sun on my shoulders as I labored, the swiftness of wind against my cheeks when I walked the sea cliffs in the evening, and the richness of the loamy earth in my garden. Peace but waited for me to give myself up to it. The fault was in me that I held back from it.

Some days, I was almost content. The garden grew well, the pea pods swelling fat, the beans racing up their trellis. There was meat to eat as well as some to set by, and daily the cottage became more snug and tidy. I took pride in what I accomplished. Yet sometimes I would find myself standing by Jinna's charm in the garden, idly spinning the beads on it as I gazed toward the lane. Waiting. It was not so bad to wait for Hap to return when I was not so aware of waiting. But waiting for the boy's return became an allegory for my whole life. When he did come back, what then? It was a question I had to ask myself. If he had succeeded, he would return only to leave again. It was what I should hope for. If he had not succeeded in earning his prentice fee, then I would have to rack my wits for another way to gain the money. And all the while, I would be waiting still. Waiting for Hap to return would transform itself into waiting for Hap to leave. Then what? Then . . . something more, my heart suggested, then it would be time for something more, but I could not put my finger on what stirred this restlessness in my soul. At the moments when I became conscious of that suspension, all of life chafed against me. Then the wolf would heave himself to his feet with a sigh and come to lean against me. A thrust of his muzzle would put his broad-skulled head under my hand.

Stop longing. You poison today's ease, reaching always for tomorrow. The boy will come back when he comes back. What is there to grieve over in that? There is nothing wrong with either of us. Tomorrow will come soon enough, one way or another.

I knew he was right, and I would, usually, shake it off and go back to my chores. Once, I admit, I walked down to my bench overlooking the sea. But all I did was sit down on it and stare out across the water. I did not attempt to Skill. Perhaps, after all the years, I was finally learning that there was no comfort for loneliness in such reaching.

The weather continued fine, each morning a cool, fresh gift. Evenings, I reflected as I took slabs of fish from their hooks inside the smoker, were more precious than gifts. They were rest earned and tasks completed. They were satisfaction, when I let them be. The fish were done to my liking, a hard shiny red on the outside, but enough moisture left trapped within to keep a good flavor. I dropped the last slab into a net bag. There were already four such bags hanging from the rafters in the cottage. This would finish what I knew we needed for the winter. The wolf followed me inside and watched me climb up on the table to hang the fish. I spoke over my shoulder to him. "Shall we get up early tomorrow and go looking for a wild pig?"

I didn't lose any wild pigs. Did you?

I looked down at him in surprise. It was a refusal, couched as humor, but a refusal all the same. I had expected wild enthusiasm. In truth, I myself had little appetite for such a strenuous hunt as a pig would demand. I had offered it to the wolf in the hope of pleasing him. I had sensed a certain listlessness in him of late, and suspected that he mourned Hap's absence. The boy had been a lively hunting companion for him. I feared that in comparison, I was rather dull. I know he felt my query as I gazed at him, but he had retreated into his own mind, leaving only a distracted haze of thoughts.

"Are you well?" I asked him anxiously.

He turned his head sharply toward the door. *Someone comes.*

"Hap?" I jumped down to the floor.

A *horse*.

I had left the door ajar. He went to it and peered out, ears pricked. I joined him. A moment passed, and then I heard the steady thudding of hoofbeats. *Starling?*

Not the howling bitch. He did not disguise his relief that it was not the minstrel. That stung a bit. Only recently had I fully realized how much he had disliked her. I said nothing aloud, nor did I form the thought toward him, but he knew. He cast me an apologetic glance, then ghosted out of the house.

I stepped out onto the porch and waited, listening. A good horse. Even at this time of day, there was life in its step. As horse and rider came into view, I took a breath at the sight of the animal. The quality of her breeding shouted from her every line. She was white. Her snowy mane and tail flowed as if she had been groomed but moments before. Silky black tassels bound in her mane complemented the black and silver of her harness. She was not a large mare, but there was fire in the way she turned a knowing eye and a wary ear toward the invisible wolf that flanked her through the wood. She was alert without being afraid. She began to lift her hooves a bit higher, as if to assure Nighteyes that she had plenty of energy to either fight or flee.

The rider was fully worthy of the horse. He sat her well, and I sensed a man in harmony with his mount. His garments were black, trimmed in silver, as were his boots. It sounds a somber combination, did not the silver run riot as embroidery around his summer cloak, and silver edge the white lace at his cuffs and throat. Silver bound his fair hair back from his high brow. Fine black gloves coated his hands like a second skin. He was a slender youth, but just as the lightness of his horse prompted one to think of swiftness, so did his slimness call to mind agility rather than fragility. His skin was a sun-kissed gold, as was his hair, and his features were fine. The tawny man approached silently save for the rhythmic striking of his horse's hooves. When he drew near, he reined in his beast with a touch, and sat looking down on me with amber eyes. He smiled.

Something turned over in my heart.

I moistened my lips, but could find no words, nor breath to utter them if I had. My heart told me one thing, my eyes another. Slowly the smile faded from his face and his eyes. A still mask replaced it. When he spoke, his voice was low, his words emotionless. "Have you no greeting for me, Fitz?"

I opened my mouth, then helplessly spread wide my arms. At the gesture that said all I had no words for, an answering look lit his face. He glowed as if a light had been kindled in him. He did not dismount but flung himself from his horse toward me, a launch aided by Nighteyes' sudden charge from the wood toward him. The horse snorted in alarm and crow-hopped. The Fool came free of his saddle with rather more energy than he had intended, but, agile as ever, he landed on the balls of his feet. The horse shied away, but none of us paid her any attention. In one step, I caught him up. I enfolded him in my arms as the wolf gamboled about us like a puppy.

"Oh, Fool," I choked. "It cannot be you, yet it is. And I do not care how."

He flung his arms around my neck. He hugged me fiercely, Burrich's earring pressing cold against my neck. For a long instant, he clung to me like a woman, until the wolf insistently thrust himself between us. Then the Fool went down on one knee in the dust, careless of his fine clothes as he clasped the wolf about his neck. "Nighteyes!" he whispered in savage satisfaction. "I had not thought to see you again. Well met, old friend." He buried his face in the wolf's ruff, wiping away tears. I did not think less of him for them. My own ran unchecked down my face.

He flowed to his feet, every nuance of his grace as familiar to me as the drawing of breath. He cupped the back of my head and, in his old way, pressed his brow to mine. His breath smelled of honey and apricot brandy. Had he fortified himself against this meeting? After a moment he drew back from me but kept a grip on my shoulders. He stared at me, his eyes touching the white streak in my hair and running familiarly over the scars on my face. I stared just as avidly, not just at how he had changed, his coloring gone from white to tawny, but at how he had not changed. He looked as callow a youth as when I had last seen him near fifteen years ago. No lines marred his face.

He cleared his throat. "Well. Will you ask me in?" he demanded.

"Of course. As soon as we've seen to your horse," I replied huskily.

The wide grin that lit his face erased all years and distance between us. "You've not changed a bit, Fitz. Horses first, as it ever was with you."

"Not changed?" I shook my head at him. "You are the one who looks not a day older. But all else . . ." I shook my head helplessly as I sidled toward his horse. She high-stepped away, maintaining the distance. "You've gone gold, Fool. And you dress as richly as Regal once did. When first I saw you, I did not know you."

He gave a sigh of relief that was half a laugh. "Then it was not as I feared, that you were wary of welcoming me?"

Such a question did not even deserve an answer. I ignored it, advancing again on the horse. She turned her head, putting the reins just out of my reach. She kept the wolf in view. I could feel the Fool watching us with amusement. "Nighteyes, you are not helping and you know it!" I exclaimed in annoyance. The wolf dropped his head and gave me a knowing glance, but he stopped his stalking.

I could put her in the barn myself if you but gave me the chance.

The Fool cocked his head slightly, regarding us both quizzically. I felt something from him: the thinnest knife-edge of shared awareness. I almost forgot the horse. Without volition, I touched the mark he had left upon me so long ago; the silver fingerprints on my wrist, long faded to a pale gray. He smiled again, and lifted one gloved hand, the finger extended toward me, as if he would renew that touch. "All down the years," he said, his voice going golden as his skin. "You have been with me, as close as the tips of my fingers, even when we were years and seas apart. Your being was like the hum of a plucked string at the edge of my hearing, or a scent carried on a breeze. Did not you feel it so?"

I took a breath, fearing my words would hurt him. "No," I said quietly. "I wish it had been so. Too often I felt myself completely alone save for Nighteyes. Too often I've sat at the cliff's edge, reaching out to touch anyone, anywhere, yet never sensing that anyone reached back to me."

He shook his head at that. "Had I possessed the Skill in truth, you would have known I was there. At your very fingertips, but mute."

I felt an odd easing in my heart at his words, for no reason I could name. Then he made an odd sound, between a cluck and a chirrup, and the horse immediately came to him to nuzzle his outstretched hand. He passed her reins to me, knowing I was itching to handle her. "Take her. Ride her to the end of your lane and back. I'll wager you've never ridden her like in your life."

The moment her reins were in my hands, the mare came to me. She put her nose against my chest, and took my scent in and out of her flaring nostrils. Then she lifted her muzzle to my jaw and gave me a slight push, as if urging me to give in to the Fool's temptation. "Do you know how long it has been since I was astride any kind of a horse?" I asked them both.

"Too long. Take her," he urged me. It was a boy's thing to do, this immediate offering to share a prized possession, and my heart answered it, knowing that no matter how long or how far apart we had been, nothing important had changed between us.

I did not wait to be invited again. I set my foot to the stirrup and mounted her, and despite all the years, I could feel every difference there was between this mare and my old horse, Sooty. She was smaller, finer-boned, and narrower between my thighs. I felt clumsy and heavy-handed as I urged her forward, then spun her about with a touch of the rein. I shifted my weight and took in the rein and she backed without hesitation. A foolish grin came over my face. "She could equal Buckkeep's best when Burrich had the stables prime," I admitted to him. I set my hand to her withers, and felt the dancing flame of her eager little mind. There was no apprehension in her, only curiosity. The wolf sat on the porch watching me gravely.

"Take her down the lane," the Fool urged me, his grin mirroring mine. "And give her a free head. Let her show you what she can do."

"What's her name?"

"Malta. I named her myself. I bought her in Shoaks, on my way here."

I nodded to myself. In Shoaks, they bred their horses small and light for traveling their broad and windswept plains. She'd be an easy keeper, requiring little feed to keep her moving day after day. I leaned forward slightly. "Malta," I said, and she heard permission in her name. She sprang forward and we were off.

If her day's journey to reach my cabin had wearied her, she did not show it. Rather it was as if she had grown restive with her steady pace and now relished the chance to stretch her muscles. We flowed beneath the overarching trees, and her hooves making music on the hard-packed earth woke a like song in my heart.

Where my lane met the road, I pulled her in. She was not even blowing; instead she arched her neck and gave the tiniest tug at her bit to let me know she would be glad to continue. I held her still, and looked both up and down the road. Odd, how that small change in perspective altered my whole sense of the world around me. Astride this fine animal, the road was like a ribbon unfurled before me. The day was fading, but even so I blinked in the gentling light, seeing possibilities in the blueing hills and the mountains edging into the evening horizon. The horse between my thighs brought the whole world closer to my door. I sat her quietly, and let my eyes travel a road that could eventually take me back to Buckkeep, or indeed to anywhere in the entire world. My quiet life in the cabin with Hap seemed as tight and confining as an outworn skin. I longed to writhe like a snake and cast it off, to emerge gleaming and new into a wider world.

Malta shook her head, mane and tassels flying, awakening me to how long I had sat and stared. The sun was kissing the horizon. The horse ventured a step or two against my firm rein. She had a will of her own, and was as willing to gallop down the road as to walk sedately back to my cabin. So we compromised; I turned her back up my lane, but let her set her own pace. This proved to be a rhythmic canter. When I pulled her in before my cabin, the Fool peeked out the door at me. "I've put the kettle on," he called. "Bring in my saddle pack, would you? There's Bingtown coffee in it."

I stabled Malta beside the pony and gave her fresh water and such hay as I had. It was not much; the pony was an adept forager, and did not mind the scrubby pasturage on the hillside behind the cabin. The Fool's sumptuous tack gleamed oddly against the rough walls. I slung his saddle pack over my shoulder. The summer dusk was thickening as I made my way back to my cabin. There were lights in the windows and the pleasant clatter of cooking pots. As I entered to set the pack on my table, the wolf was sprawled before the fire drying his damp fur and the Fool was stepping around him to set a kettle on the hook. I blinked my eyes, and for an instant I was back in the Fool's hut in the Mountains, healing from my old injury while he stood between the world and me that I might rest. Then as now he created reality around himself, bringing order and peace to a small island of warm firelight and the simple smell of hearth bread cooking.

He swung his pale eyes to meet mine, the gold of them mirroring the firelight. Light ran up his cheekbones and dwindled as it merged with his hair. I gave my head a small shake. "In the space of a sundown, you show me the wide world from a horse's back, and the soul of the world within my own walls."

"Oh, my friend," he said quietly. No more than that needed to be said.

We are whole.

The Fool cocked his head to that thought. He looked like a man trying to recall something important. I shared a glance with the wolf. He was right. Like sundered pieces of crockery that snick back together so precisely that the crack becomes invisible, the Fool joined us and completed us. Whereas Chade's visit had filled me with questions and needs, the Fool's presence was in itself an answer and a satisfaction.

He had made free with my garden and my pantry. There were new potatoes and carrots and little purple and white turnips simmering in one pot. Fresh fish layered with basil steamed and rattled a tight-fitting lid. When I raised my brows to that, the Fool merely observed, "The wolf seems to recall my fondness for fresh fish." Nighteyes set his ears back and lolled his tongue out at me. Hearth cakes and blackberry preserves rounded out our simple meal. He had ferreted out my Sandsedge brandy. It waited on the table.

He dug through his pack and produced a cloth bag of dark beans shining with oil. "Smell this," he demanded, and then put me to crushing the beans while he filled my last available pot with water and set it to boil. There was little conversation. He hummed to himself and the fire crackled while pot lids tapped and occasional escaping drips steamed away on the fire. The pestle against the mortar made a homey sound as I ground the aromatic beans. We moved for a space in wolf time, in the contentment of the present, not worrying about what had passed or what was to come. That evening remains for me always a moment to cherish, as golden and fragrant as brandy in crystal glasses.

With a knack I've never attained, the Fool made all the food ready at once, so that the deep brown coffee steamed alongside the fish and the vegetables, while a stack of hearth cakes held their warmth under a clean cloth. We sat down to the table together, and the Fool set out a slab of the tender fish for the wolf, who dutifully ate it though he would have preferred it raw and cold. The cabin door stood open on a starry night; the fellowship of shared food on a pleasantly mild evening filled the house and overflowed.

We heaped the dirty dishes aside to deal with later, and took more coffee out onto the porch. It was my first experience of the foreign stuff. The hot brown liquid smelled better than it tasted, but sharpened the mind pleasantly. Somehow we ended up walking down to the stream together, our cups warm in our hands. The wolf drank long there of the cool water, and then we strolled back, to pause by the garden. The Fool spun the beads on Jinna's charm as I told him the tale of it. He flicked the bell with a long fingertip, and a single silver chime spun spreading into the night. We visited his horse, and I shut the door on the chicken house to keep the poultry safe for the night. We wandered back to the cabin and I sat down on the edge of the porch. Without a word, the Fool took my empty cup back into the house.

When he returned, Sandsedge brandy brimmed the cup. He sat down beside me on one side; the wolf claimed a place on the other side, and set his head on my knee. I took a sip of the brandy, silked the wolf's ears through my fingers, and waited. The Fool gave a small sigh. "I stayed away from you as long as I could." He offered the words like an apology.

I lifted an eyebrow to that. "Any time that you returned to visit me would not have been too soon. I often wondered what had become of you."

He nodded gravely. "I stayed away, hoping that you would finally find a measure of peace and contentment."

"I did," I assured him. "I have."

"And now I have returned to take it away from you." He did not look at me as he said those words. He stared off into the night, at the darkness beneath the crowding trees. He swung his legs like a child, and then took a sip of his brandy.

My heart gave a little lurch. I had thought he had come to see me for my own sake. Carefully I asked, "Chade sent you, then? To ask me to come back to Buckkeep? I gave him my answer."

"Did you? Ah." He paused a moment, swirling the brandy in his cup as he pondered. "I should have known that he would have been here already. No, my friend, I have not seen Chade in all these years. But that he has sought you out but proves what I dreaded. A time is upon us when the White Prophet must once more employ his Catalyst. Believe me, if there were any other way, if I could leave you in peace, I would. Truly I would."

"What do you need of me?" I asked him in a low voice. But he was no better at giving me a straight answer now than when he had been King Shrewd's Fool and I was the King's bastard grandson.

"I need what I have always needed from you, ever since I discovered that you existed. If I am to change time in its course, if I am to set the world on a truer path than it has ever followed before, then I must have you. Your life is the wedge I use to make the future jump from its rut."

He looked at my disgruntled face and laughed aloud at me. "I try, Fitz, indeed I do. I speak as plainly as I can, but your ears will not believe what they hear. I first came to the Six Duchies, and to Shrewd's court all those years ago, to seek a way to fend off a disaster. I came not knowing how I would do it, only that I must. And what did I discover? You. A bastard, but nonetheless an heir to the Farseer line. In no future that I had glimpsed had I seen you, yet when I recalled all I knew of the prophecies of my kind, I discovered you, again and again. In sideways mentions and sly hints, there you were. And so I did all that I could to keep you alive, which mostly was bestirring you to keep yourself alive. I groped through the mists with no more than a snail's glinting trail of prescience to guide me. I acted based on what I knew I must prevent, rather than what I must cause. We cheated all those other futures. I urged you into danger and I dragged you back from death, heedless of what it cost you in pain and scars and dreams denied. Yet you survived, and when all the cataclysms of the Cleansing of Buck were done, there was a trueborn heir to the Farseer line. Because of you. And suddenly it was as if I were lifted onto a peak above a valley brimmed with fog. I do not say that my eyes can pierce the fog; only that I stand above it and see, in the vast distance, the peaks of a new and possible future. A future founded on you."

He looked at me with golden eyes that seemed almost luminous in the dim light from the open door. He just looked at me, and I suddenly felt old and the arrow scar by my spine gave me a twist of pain that made me catch my breath for an instant. A throb like a dull red foreboding followed it. I told myself I had sat too long in one position; that was all.

"Well?" he prompted me. His eyes moved over my face almost hungrily.

"I think I need more brandy," I confessed, for somehow my cup had become empty.

He drained his own cup and took mine. When he rose, the wolf and I did also. We followed him into the cabin. He rucked about in his pack and took out a bottle. It was about a quarter empty. I tucked the observation away in my mind; so he had fortified himself against this meeting. I wondered what part of it he had dreaded. He uncorked the bottle and refilled both our cups. My chair and Hap's stool were by the hearth, but we ended up sitting on the hearthstones by the dying fire. With a heavy sigh the wolf stretched out between us, his head in my lap. I rubbed his head, and caught a sudden twinge of pain from him. I moved my hand down him to his hip joints and massaged them gently. Nighteyes gave a low groan as the touch eased him.

How bad is it?

Mind your own business.

You are my business.

Sharing pain doesn't lessen it.

I'm not sure about that.

"He's getting old." The Fool interrupted our chained thoughts.

"So am I," I pointed out. "You, however, look as young as ever."

"Yet I'm substantially older than both of you put together. And tonight I feel every one of my years." As if to give the lie to his own words, he lithely drew his knees up tight to his chest and rested his chin atop them as he hugged his own legs.

If you drank some willow-bark tea, it might ease you.

Spare me your swill and keep rubbing.

A small smile bowed the Fool's mouth. "I can almost hear you two. It's like a gnat humming near my ear, or the itch of something forgotten. Or trying to recall the sweet taste of something from a passing whiff of its fragrance." His golden eyes suddenly met mine squarely. "It makes me feel lonely."

"I'm sorry," I said, not knowing what else I could say. That Nighteyes and I spoke as we did was not an effort to exclude him from our circle. It was that our circle made us one in a fundamental way we could not share.

Yet once we did, Nighteyes reminded me. *Once we did, and it was good.*

I do not think that I glanced at the Fool's gloved hand. Perhaps he was closer to us than he realized, for he lifted his hand and tugged the finely woven glove from it. His long-fingered, elegant hand emerged. Once, a chance touch of his had brushed his fingers against Verity's Skill-impregnated hands. That touch had silvered his fingers, and given him a tactile Skill that let him know the history of things simply by touching them. I turned my own wrist to look down at it. Dusky gray fingerprints still marked the inside of my wrist where he had touched me. For a time, our minds had been joined, almost as if he and Nighteyes and I were a true Skill coterie. But the silver on his fingers had faded, as had the fingerprints on my wrist and the link that had bonded us.

He lifted one slender finger as if in a warning. Then he turned his hand and extended it to me as if he proffered an invisible gift on those outstretched fingertips. I closed my eyes to steady myself against the temptation. I shook my head slowly. "It would not be wise," I said thickly.

"And a Fool is supposed to be wise?"

"You have always been the wisest creature I've known." I opened my eyes to his earnest gaze. "I want it as I want breath itself, Fool. Take it away, please."

"If you're sure . . . no, that was a cruel question. Look, it is gone." He gloved the hand, held it up to show me, and then clasped it with his naked one.

"Thank you." I took a long sip of my brandy, and tasted a summer orchard and bees bumbling in the hot sunshine among the ripe and fallen fruit. Honey and apricots danced along the edges of my tongue. It was decadently good. "I've never tasted anything like this," I observed, glad to change the subject.

"Ah, yes. I'm afraid I've spoiled myself, now that I can afford the best. There's a good stock of it in Bingtown, awaiting a message from me to tell them where to ship it."

I cocked my head at him, trying to find the jest in his words. Slowly it sank in that he was speaking the plain truth. The fine clothes, the blooded horse, exotic Bingtown coffee, and now this . . . "You're rich?" I hazarded sagely.

"The word doesn't touch the reality." Pink suffused his amber cheeks. He looked almost chagrined to admit it.

"Tell!" I demanded, grinning at his good fortune.

He shook his head. "Far too long a tale. Let me condense it for you. Friends insisted on sharing with me a windfall of wealth. I doubt that even they knew the full value of all they pressed upon me. I've a friend in a trading town, far to the south, and as she sells it off for the best prices such rare goods can command, she sends me letters of credit to Bingtown." He shook his head ruefully, appalled at his good fortune. "No matter how well I spend it, there always seems to be more."

"I am glad for you," I said with heartfelt sincerity.

He smiled. "I knew you would be. Yet, the strangest part perhaps is that it changes nothing. Whether I sleep on spun gold or straw, my destiny remains the same. As does yours."

So we were back to that again. I summoned all my strength and resolve. "No, Fool," I said firmly. "I won't be pulled back into Buckkeep politics. I have a life of my own now, and it is here."

He cocked his head at me, and a shadow of his old jester's smile widened his lips. "Ah, Fitz, you've always had a life of your own. That is, precisely, your problem. You've always had a destiny. As for it being here . . ." He shied a look around the room. "*Here* is no more than where you happen to be standing at the moment. Or sitting." He took a long breath. "I haven't come to drag you back into anything, Fitz. Time has brought me here. It's carried you here as well. Just as it brought Chade, and other twists to your fortunes of late. Am I wrong?"

He was not. The entire summer had been one large kink in my smoothly coiling life. I didn't reply but I didn't need to. He already knew the answer. He leaned back, stretching his long legs out before him. He nibbled at his ungloved thumb thoughtfully, then leaned his head back against the chair and closed his eyes.

"I dreamed of you once," I said suddenly. I had not been planning to say the words.

He opened one cat-yellow eye. "I think we had this conversation before. A long time ago."

"No. This is different. I didn't know it was you until just now. Or maybe I did." It had been a restless night, years ago, and when I awakened the dream had clung to my mind like pitch on my hands. I had known it was significant, and yet the snatch of what I had seen had made so little sense, I could not grasp its significance. "I didn't know you had gone golden, you see. But now, when you leaned back with your eyes closed . . . You—or someone—were lying on a rough wooden floor. Your eyes were closed; you were sick or injured. A man leaned over you. I felt he wanted to hurt you. So I . . ."

I had repelled at him, using the Wit in a way I had not for years. A rough thrust of animal presence to shove him away, to express dominance of him in a way he could not understand, yet hated. The hatred was proportionate to his fear. The Fool was silent, waiting for me.

"I pushed him away from you. He was angry, hating you, wanting to hurt you. But I pressed on his mind that he had to go and fetch help for you. He had to tell someone that you needed help. He resented what I did to him, but he had to obey me."

"Because you Skill-burned it into him," the Fool said quietly.

"Perhaps," I admitted unwillingly. Certainly the next day had been one long torment of headache and Skill-hunger. The thought made me uneasy. I had been telling myself that I could not Skill that way. Certain other dreams stirred uneasily in my memory. I pushed them down again. No, I promised myself. They were not the same.

"It was the deck of a ship," he said quietly. "And it's quite likely you saved my life." He took a breath. "I thought something like that might have happened. It never made sense to me that he didn't get rid of me when he could have. Sometimes, when I was most alone, I mocked myself that I could cling to such a hope. That I could believe I was so important to anyone that he would travel in his dreams to protect me."

"You should have known better than that," I said quietly.

"Should I?" The question was almost a challenge. He gave me the most direct look I had ever received from him. I did not understand the hurt I saw in his eyes, nor the hope. He needed something from me, but I wasn't sure what it was. I tried to find something to say, but before I could, the moment seemed to pass. He looked away from me, releasing me from his plea. When his eyes came back to mine, he changed both his expression and the subject.

"So. What happened to you after I flew away?"

The question took me aback. "I thought . . . but you said you had not seen Chade for years. How did you know how to find me, then?"

By way of answer, he closed his eyes, and then brought his left and right forefingers together to meet before him. He opened his eyes and smiled at me. I knew it was as much answer as I would get.

"I scarcely know where to begin."

"I do. With more brandy."

He flowed effortlessly to his feet. I let him take my empty cup. I set a hand on Nighteyes' head and felt him hovering between sleep and wakefulness. If his hips still troubled him, he was concealing it well. He was getting better and better at holding himself apart from me. I wondered why he concealed his pain.

Do you wish to share your aching back with me? Leave me alone and stop borrowing trouble. Not every problem in the world belongs to you. He lifted his head from my knee and with a deep sigh stretched out more fully before the hearth. Like a curtain falling between us, he masked himself once more.

I rose slowly, one hand pressed against my back to still my own ache. The wolf was right. Sometimes there was little point to sharing pain. The Fool refilled both our cups with his apricot brandy. I sat down at the table and he set mine before me. His own he kept in his hand as he wandered about the room. He paused before Verity's unfinished map of the Six Duchies on my wall, glanced into the nook that was Hap's sleeping alcove, and then leaned in the door of my bedchamber. When Hap had come to live with me, I had added an additional chamber that I referred to as my study. It had its own small hearth, as well as my desk and a scroll rack. The Fool paused at the door to it, then stepped boldly inside. I watched him. It was like watching a cat explore a strange house. He touched nothing, yet appeared to see everything. "A lot of scrolls," he observed from the other room.

I raised my voice to reach him. "I've been trying to write a history of the Six Duchies. It was something that Patience and Fedwren proposed years ago, back when I was a boy. It helps to occupy my time of an evening."

"I see. May I?"

I nodded. He seated himself at my desk, and unrolled the scroll on the stone game. "Ah, yes, I remember this."

"Chade wants it when I am finished with it. I've sent him things, from time to time, via Starling. But up until a month or so ago, I hadn't seen him since we parted in the Mountains."

"Ah. But you had seen Starling." His back was to me. I wondered what expression he wore. The Fool and the minstrel had never gotten along well together. For a time, they had made an uneasy truce, but I had always been a bone of contention between them. The Fool had never approved of my friendship with Starling, had never believed she had my best interests at heart. That didn't make it any easier to let him know he had always been right.

"For a time, I saw Starling. On and off for, what, seven or eight years. She was the one who brought Hap to me about seven years ago. He's just turned fifteen. He's not home right now; he's hired out in the hopes of gaining more coin for an apprenticeship fee. He wants to be a cabinet-maker. He does good work, for a lad; both the desk and the scroll rack are his work. Yet I don't know if he has the patience for detail that a good joiner must have. Still, it's what his heart is set on, and he wants to apprentice to a cabinetmaker in Buckkeep Town. Gindast is the joiner's name, and he's a master. Even I have heard of him. If I had realized Hap would set his heart so high, I'd have saved more over the years. But—"

"Starling?" His query reined me back from my musings on the boy.

It was hard to admit it. "She's married now. I don't know how long. The boy found it out when he went to Springfest at Buckkeep with her. He came home and told me." I shrugged one shoulder. "I had to end it between us. She knew I would when I found out. It still made her angry. She couldn't understand why it couldn't continue, as long as her husband never found out."

"That's Starling." His voice was oddly nonjudgmental, as if he commiserated with me over a garden blight. He turned in the chair to look at me over his shoulder. "And you're all right?"

I cleared my throat. "I've kept busy. And not thought about it much."

"Because she felt no shame at all, you think it must all belong to you. People like her are so adept at passing on blame. This is a lovely red ink on this. Where did you get it?"

"I made it."

"Did you?" Curious as a child, he unstopped one of the ink bottles on my desk and stuck in his little finger. It came out tipped in scarlet. He regarded it for a moment. "I kept Burrich's earring," he suddenly admitted. "I never took it to Molly."

"I see that. I'm just as glad you didn't. It's better that neither of them know I survived."

"Ah. Another question answered." He drew a snowy kerchief from inside his pocket and ruined it by wiping the red ink from his finger. "So. Are you going to tell me all the events in order, or must I pry bits out of you one at a time?"

I sighed. I dreaded recalling those times. Chade had been willing to accept an account of the events that related to the Farseer reign. The Fool would want more than that. Even as I cringed from it, I could not evade the notion that somehow I owed him that telling. "I'll try. But I'm tired, and we've had too much brandy, and it's far too much to tell in one evening."

He tipped back in my chair. "Were you expecting me to leave tomorrow?"

"I thought you might." I watched his face as I added, "I didn't hope it."

He accepted me at my word. "That's good, then, for you would have hoped in vain. To bed with you, Fitz. I'll take the boy's cot. Tomorrow is soon enough to begin to fill in nearly fifteen years of absence."

The Fool's apricot brandy was more potent than the Sandsedge, or perhaps I was simply wearier than usual. I staggered to my room, dragged off my shirt, and dropped into my bed. I lay there, the room rocking gently around me, and listened to his light footfalls as he moved about in the main room, extinguishing candles and pulling in the latchstring. Perhaps only I could have seen the slight unsteadiness in his movements. Then he sat down in my chair and stretched his legs toward the fire. At his feet, the wolf groaned and shifted in his sleep. I touched minds gently with Nighteyes; he was deeply asleep and welling contentment.

I closed my eyes, but the room spun sickeningly. I opened them a crack and stared at the Fool. He sat very still as he stared into the fire, but the dancing light of the flames lent their motion to his features. The angles of his face were hidden and then revealed as the shadows shifted. The gold of his skin and eyes seemed a trick of the firelight, but I knew they were not.

It was hard to realize he was no longer the impish jester who had both served and protected King Shrewd for all those years. His body had not changed, save in coloring. His graceful, long-fingered hands dangled off the arms of the chair. His hair, once as pale and airy as dandelion fluff, was now bound back from his face and confined to a golden queue. He closed his eyes and leaned his head back against the chair. Firelight bronzed his aristocratic profile. His present grand clothes might recall his old winter motley of black and white, but I wagered he would never again wear bells and ribbons and carry a rat-headed scepter. His lively wit and sharp tongue no longer influenced the course of political events. His life was his own now. I tried to imagine him as a wealthy man, able to travel and live as he pleased. A sudden thought jolted me from my complacency.

"Fool?" I called aloud in the darkened room.

"What?" He did not open his eyes but his ready reply showed he had not yet slipped toward sleep.

"You are not the Fool anymore. What do they call you these days?"

A slow smile curved his lips in profile. "What does who call me when?"

He spoke in the baiting tone of the jester he had been. If I tried to sort out that question, he would tumble me in verbal acrobatics until I gave up hoping for an answer. I refused to be drawn into his game. I rephrased my question. "I should not call you Fool anymore. What do you want me to call you?"

"Ah, what do I want *you* to call me now? I see. An entirely different question." Mockery made music in his voice.

I drew a breath and made my question as plain as possible. "What is your name, your real name?"

"Ah." His manner was suddenly grave. He took a slow breath. "My name. As in what my mother called me at my birth?"

"Yes." And then I held my breath. He spoke seldom of his childhood. I suddenly realized the immensity of what I had asked him. It was the old naming magic: if I know how you are truly named, I have power over you. If I tell you my name, I grant you that power. Like all direct questions I had ever asked the Fool, I both dreaded and longed for the answer.

"And if I tell you, you would call me by that name?" His inflection told me to weigh my answer.

That gave me pause. His name was his, and not for me to bandy about. But, "In private, only. And only if you wished me to," I offered solemnly. I considered the words as binding as a vow.

"Ah." He turned to face me. His face lit with delight. "Oh, but I would," he assured me.

"Then?" I asked again. I was suddenly uneasy, certain that somehow he had bested me yet again.

"The name my mother gave me, I give now to you, to call me by in private." He took a breath and turned back to the fire. He closed his eyes again but his grin grew even wider. "Beloved. She called me only 'Beloved.'"

"Fool!" I protested.

He laughed, a deep rich chuckle of pure enjoyment, completely pleased with himself. "She did," he insisted.

"Fool, I'm serious." The room had begun to revolve slowly around me. If I did not go to sleep soon, I would be sick.

"And you think I am not?" He gave a theatrical sigh. "Well, if you cannot call me 'Beloved,' then I suppose you should continue to call me 'Fool.' For I am ever the Fool to your Fitz."

"Tom Badgerlock."

"What?"

"I am Tom Badgerlock now. It is how I am known."

He was silent for a time. Then, "Not by me," he replied decisively. "If you insist we must both take different names now, then I shall call you 'Beloved.' And whenever I call you that, you may call me 'Fool.'" He opened his eyes and rolled his head to look at me. He simpered a lovesick smile, then heaved an exaggerated sigh. "Good night, Beloved. We have been apart far too long."

I capitulated. Conversation was hopeless when he got into these moods. "Good night, Fool." I rolled over in my bed and closed my eyes. If he made any response, I was asleep before he uttered it.

chapter VI

THE QUIET YEARS

I was born a bastard. The first six years of my life, I spent in the Mountain Kingdom with my mother. I have no clear recollections of that time. At six, my grandfather took me to the fort at Moonseye, and there turned me over to my paternal uncle, Verity Farseer. The revelation of my existence was the personal and political failure that led my father to renounce his claim to the Farseer throne and retire completely from court life. My care was initially given over to Burrich, the Stablemaster at Buckkeep. Later, King Shrewd saw fit to claim my loyalty, and apprentice me to his court assassin. With the death of Shrewd, by the treachery of his youngest son, Regal, my loyalty passed to King Verity. Him I followed and served until the time I witnessed him pour his life and essence into a dragon of carved stone. Thus was Verity as Dragon animated, and thus were the Six Duchies saved from the depredations of the Red Ship Raiders of the Out Islands, for Verity as Dragon led the ancient Elderling dragons as they cleansed the Six Duchies of the invaders. Following that service to my King, injured in both body and spirit, I withdrew from court and society for fifteen years. I believed I would never return.

In those years, I attempted to write a history of the Six Duchies, and an accounting of my own life. In that time, I also obtained and studied various scrolls and writings on a wide variety of topics. The disparity of these pursuits was actually a concerted effort on my part to track down the truth. I strove to find and examine the pieces and forces that had determined why my life had gone as it had. Yet the more I studied and the more I entrusted my thoughts to paper, the more truth eluded me. What life showed me, in my years apart from the world, was that no man ever gets to know the whole of a truth. All I had once believed of all my experiences and myself, time alone illuminated anew. What had seemed clearly lit plunged into shadow, and details I had considered trivial leapt into prominence.

Burrich the Stablemaster, the man who raised me, once warned me, "When you cut pieces from the truth to avoid sounding like a fool, you end up sounding like a moron instead." I have discovered that to be true, from firsthand experience. Yet even without deliberately attempting to cut and discard pieces of a story, years after giving a full and just accounting of an event, a man may discover himself a liar. Such lies happen not by intent, but purely by virtue of the facts he was not privy to at the time he wrote, or by being ignorant of the significance of trivial events. No one is pleased to discover himself in such a strait, but any man who claims never to have experienced it is but stacking one lie on top of another.

My efforts at writing a history of the Six Duchies were based on oral accounts and the old scrolls that I had had access to. Even as I set pen to paper, I knew I might be perpetuating another man's error. I had not realized that my efforts to recount my own life might be subject to the same flaw. The truth, I discovered, is a tree that grows as a man gains access to experience. A child sees the acorn of his daily life, but a man looks back on the oak.

No man can return to being a boy. But there are interludes in a man's life when, for a time, he can recapture the feeling that the world is a forgiving place and that he is immortal. I have always believed that was the essence of boyhood: believing that mistakes could not be fatal. The Fool brought that old optimism out in me again, and even the wolf seemed puppyish and fey for the days he was with us.

The Fool did not intrude into our lives. I made no

adaptations or adjustments. He simply joined us, setting his schedule to ours and making my work his own. He was invariably stirring before I was. I would awake to find the door of my study and my bedroom door open, and like as not the outside door open as well. From my bed, I would see him sitting cross-legged like a tailor on my chair before my desk. He was always washed and dressed to face the day. His elegant clothes disappeared after that first day, replaced with simple jerkins and trousers, or the evening comfort of a robe. The moment I was awake, he was aware of my presence, and would lift his eyes to mine before I spoke. He was always reading, either the scrolls or documents that I had painstakingly acquired, or those composed by me. Some of those scrolls were my failed attempts at a history of the Six Duchies. Others were my disjointed efforts to make sense of my own life by setting it onto paper. He would lift an eyebrow to my wakefulness, and then carefully restore the scroll to precisely where it had been. Had he chosen to do so, he could have left me ignorant of his perusal of my journals. Instead, he showed his respect by never questioning me about what he had read. The private thoughts that I had committed to paper remained private, my secrets sealed behind the Fool's lips.

He dropped effortlessly into my life, filling a place that I had not perceived was vacant. While he stayed with me, I almost forgot to miss Hap, save that I hungered so to show the boy off to him. I know I spoke often of him. Sometimes the Fool worked alongside me in the garden or as I repaired the stone and log paddock. When it was a task for one man, such as digging the new postholes, he perched nearby and watched. Our talk at such times was simple, relating to the task at hand, or the easy banter of men who have shared a boyhood. If ever I tried to turn our talk to serious matters, he deflected my questions with his drollery. We took turns on Malta, for the Fool bragged she could jump anything, and a series of makeshift barriers across my lane soon proved this was so. The spirited little horse seemed to enjoy it as much as we did.

After our evening meal, we sometimes walked the cliffs, or clambered down to stroll the beaches as the tide retreated. In the changing of the light, we hunted rabbits with the wolf, and came home to set a hearth fire more for cheer than warmth. The Fool had brought more than one bottle of the apricot brandy, and his voice was as fine as ever. Evenings were his turn to sing, and talk, and tell stories, both amazing and amusing. Some seemed to be drawn from his own adventures; others were obviously folklore acquired along the way. His graceful hands were more articulate than the puppets he once had fashioned, and his mobile face could portray every character in the tales he told.

It was only in the late evening hours, when the fire had burned to coals and his face was more shadow than shape, that he led my talk where he would go. That first evening, in a quiet voice mellowed by brandy, he observed, "Have you any idea how hard it was for me to let Girl-on-a-Dragon carry me off and leave you behind? I had to believe that the wheels were in motion, and you would live. It taxed my faith in myself to the utmost to fly off and leave you there."

"Your faith in yourself?" I demanded, feigning insult. "Had you no faith in me?" The Fool had spread Hap's bedding on the floor before the hearth, and we had abandoned our chairs to sprawl in the dubious comfort there. The wolf, his nose on his paws, dozed on my left side while on my right, the Fool leaned on his elbows, chin propped in his hands. He gazed into the fire, his lifted feet waving vaguely.

The last flames of the fire danced merrily in his eyes. "In you? Well. I shall say only that I took great comfort in the wolf at your side."

In that, his confidence was not misplaced, the wolf observed wryly.

I thought you were asleep.

I'm trying to be.

The Fool's voice was almost dreamy as he went on, "You had survived every cataclysmic event that I had ever glimpsed for you. So I left you, forcing myself to believe that there was a period of quiet in store for you. Perhaps, even, a time of peace."

"There was. After a fashion." I took a breath. I nearly told him of my death watch by Will. Almost, I told him of how I had reached through Will with the Skill magic, finally to seize control of Regal's mind and work my will on him. I let the breath out. He didn't need to hear that; I didn't need to relive it. "I found peace. A bit at a time. In pieces." I grinned foolishly to myself. Odd, the small things that are amusing when one has had enough to drink.

I found myself speaking of my year in the Mountains. I told him how we had returned to the valley where the hot springs flowed, and of the simple hut I had built against the coming of winter. The seasons turn more quickly in the high country. One morning the leaves of birch trees are veined in yellow, and the alder has gone red in the night. A few more nights, and they are bare-fingered branches reaching toward a cold blue sky. The evergreens hunch themselves against the oncoming winter. Then the snow comes, to cloak the world in forgiving white.

I told him of hunting the days away with Nighteyes as my sole companion. Healing and peace were the most elusive of the prey I stalked. We lived simply, as predators with no loyalties save to one another. That absolute solitude was the best balm for the wounds I had taken to both my body and my soul. Such injuries do not truly heal but I learned to live with my scars, much as Burrich once learned to tolerate his game leg. We hunted deer and rabbit. I came to accept that I had died, that I had lost my life in every way that mattered. Winter winds blew around our small shelter, and I understood that Molly was no longer mine. Brief things were those winter days, pauses of sunlight on glittering white snow before the long, blue-fingered dusks returned to draw the deep nights close to us. I learned to cushion my loss with the knowledge that my little daughter would grow up in the shelter of Burrich's good right arm, much as I myself had.

I had tried to rid myself of my memories of Molly. The stabbing pain of recalling her abused trust of me was the brightest gem in a glittering necklace of painful memories. As much as I had always longed to be freed of my duties and obligations, being released from such bonds was as much a severing as an emancipation. As the brief days of winter alternated with the long, cold nights, I numbered to myself those I had lost. Those who still knew I lived did not even take up the fingers of one hand. The Fool, Queen Kettricken, the minstrel Starling, and through those three, Chade: those were the four who knew of my existence. A few others had seen me alive, amongst them Hands the Stablemaster and one Tag Reaverson, a guardsman, but the circumstances of those brief meetings were such that any tales of my survival were unlikely to be believed.

All others who had known me, including those who had loved me best, believed me dead. Nor could I return to prove them wrong. I had been executed once for practicing Wit magic. I would not chance a more thorough death. Yet even if that taint could be lifted from my name, I could not return to Burrich and Molly. To do so would destroy all of us. Even if Molly had been able to tolerate my Beast Magic and my many deceptions of her, how could any of us untangle her subsequent marriage to Burrich? To confront Burrich with his usurpation of my wife and my child would destroy him. Could I found future happiness on that? Could Molly?

"I tried to comfort myself with the thought that they were safe and happy."

"Could not you reach out with the Skill, to assure yourself of that?"

The shadows of the room had deepened and the Fool's

eyes were fixed on the fire. It was as if I recounted my history to myself.

"I could claim I learned the discipline to leave them to their privacy. In truth, I think I feared it would drive me mad, to witness love shared between them."

I watched the fire as I spoke of those days, yet I felt the Fool's eyes turn to me. I did not turn toward him. I did not want to see pity there. I had grown past the need for anyone's pity.

"I found peace," I told him. "A bit at a time, but it came to me. There was a morning when Nighteyes and I were returning from a dawn hunt. We'd had a good hunt, and taken a mountain goat that the heavy snows of winter had pushed down from the heights. The hill was steep as we worked our way down, the gutted carcass was heavy, and the skin of my face was stiff as a mask from the cold burning down from the clear blue sky. I could see a thin tendril of smoke rising from my chimney, and just beyond my hut, the foggy steam rose off the nearby hot springs. At the top of the last hill, I paused to catch my breath and stretch my back."

It all came back so clearly to me. Nighteyes had halted beside me, panting clouds. I'd swathed my lower face in the edge of my cloak; now it was half-frozen to my beard. I looked down, and knew that we had meat for days, our small cabin was tight against winter's cold clench, and we were nearly home. Cold and weary as I was, satisfaction was still uppermost in my mind. I hefted my kill to my shoulders. *Almost home,* I told Nighteyes.

Almost home, he had echoed. And in the sharing of that thought, I sensed a meaning that no man's voice could have put into it. Home. A finality. A place to belong. The humble cottage was home now, a comforting destination where I expected to find all I needed. As I stood staring down at it, I felt a twinge of conscience as for some forgotten obligation. It took me a moment to grasp what was missing. The whole of a night had passed and I had not once thought of Molly. Where had my yearning and sense of loss gone? What sort of shallow fellow was I, to let go of that mourning and think only of the dawn's hunting? Deliberately I turned my thoughts to the place and the people who were once encompassed in the word HOME.

When I wallow in something dead to reawaken the savor of it, you rebuke me.

I turned to look at Nighteyes but he refused the eye contact. He sat in the snow, ears pricked forward toward our hut. The unpleasant little winter wind stirred his thick ruff, but could not penetrate to his skin.

Meaning? I pressed him, though his meaning was perfectly clear.

You should leave off sniffing the carcass of your old life, my brother. You may enjoy unending pain. I do not. There is no shame in walking away from bones, Changer. He finally swiveled his head to stare at me from his deep-set eyes. *Nor is there any special wisdom in injuring oneself over and over. What is your loyalty to that pain? To abandon it will not lessen you.*

Then he had stood, shaken his coat free of snow, and trotted resolutely down the snowy hillside. I had followed him more slowly.

I finally glanced over at the Fool. He looked at me but his eyes were unreadable in the darkness. "I think that was the first bit of peace I found. Not that I take any credit for discovering it. Nighteyes had to point it out to me. Perhaps to another man it would have been obvious. Leave old pains alone. When they cease coming to call, do not invite them back."

His voice was very soft in the dim room. "There is nothing dishonorable about abandoning pain. Sometimes peace is most quickly found when a man simply stops avoiding it." He shifted slightly in the dark. "And you never again lay awake all night, staring at darkness and thinking of them."

I snorted softly. "I wish. But the most I can say is that I

stopped deliberately provoking that melancholy. When summer finally came and we moved on, it was like leaving a cast-off skin." I let a silence follow my words.

"So you left the Mountains and came back to Buck."

He knew I had not; it was just his little prod to get me talking again.

"Not right away. Nighteyes didn't approve, but I felt I could not leave the Mountains until I had retraced some of our journey there. I went back to the quarry, back to where Verity had carved his dragon. I stood on the spot. It was just a flat, bare place hemmed in by the towering quarry walls under a slate-gray sky. There was no sign of all that had happened there, just the piles of chips and a few worn tools. I walked through our campsite. I knew the flattened tents and the possessions scattered about had once been ours, but most of them had lost their significance. They were graying rags, sodden and slumped. I found a few things I took with me . . . the pieces for Kettle's stone game, I took those." I took a breath. "And I walked down to where Carrod had died. His body was as we had left it, gone to bones and bits of moldering cloth. No animals had disturbed it. They don't like the Skill-road, you know."

"I know," he admitted quietly. I felt he had walked with me through that abandoned quarry.

"I stood a long time looking at those bones. I tried to remember Carrod as he had been when I first met him, but I couldn't. But looking at his bones was like a confirmation. It all had truly happened, and it all was truly finished. The events and the place, I could walk away from. I could leave it behind now and it could not get up and follow me."

Nighteyes groaned in his sleep. I set a hand on his side, glad to feel him so near in both touch and mind. He had not approved of me visiting the quarry. He had disliked journeying along the Skill-road, even though my ability to retain my sense of self against its siren call had increased. He was even more disgruntled when I insisted I must return to the Stone Garden, as well.

There was a small sound, the chink of the bottle against the cup's lip as the Fool replenished our brandy. His silence was an invitation for me to speak on.

"The dragons had gone back to where we first found them. I visited them there. The forest was gradually taking them back again, grass sprouting tall around them and vines creeping over them. They were just as beautiful and just as haunting as when we first discovered them there. And just as still."

They had broken holes in the forest canopy when they had left their slumbers and arisen to fight for Buck. Their return had been no gentler, and thus sunlight fell in shafts, penetrating the lush growth to gild each gleaming dragon. I walked amongst them, and as before, I felt the ghostly stir of Wit-life within the deeply slumbering statues. I found King Wisdom's antlered dragon; I dared to set my bare hand to his shoulder. I felt only the finely carved scales, cold and hard as the stone they had been fashioned from. They were all there: the boar dragon, the winged cat, all the widely divergent forms carved by both Elderlings and Skill coteries.

"I saw Girl-on-a-Dragon there." I smiled at the flames. "She sleeps well. The human figure is sprawled forward now, her arms twined lovingly around the neck of the dragon she bestrides still." Her I had feared to touch; I recalled too clearly her hunger for memories, and how I had fed her with mine. Perhaps I feared as much to regain what I once had willingly given her. I slipped past her silently, but Nighteyes stalked past her, hackles abristle, showing every white tooth he possessed in a snarl. The wolf had known what I truly sought.

"Verity," the Fool said softly, as if confirming my unspoken thought.

"Verity," I agreed. "My King." I sighed and took up my tale.

I had found him there. When I saw Verity's turquoise hide gleaming in the dappling summer shade, Nighteyes sat down and curled his tail tidily around his forefeet. He would come no closer. I felt the silence of his thoughts as he carefully granted me the privacy of my mind. I approached Verity-as-dragon slowly, my heart thundering in my throat. There, in a body carved of Skill and stone, slept the man who had been my King. For his sake, I had taken hurts so grievous that both my mind and my body would bear the scars until the day I died. Yet as I drew near to the still form, I felt tears prick my eyes, and knew only longing for his familiar voice.

"Verity?" I asked hoarsely. My soul strained toward him, word, Wit, and Skill seeking for my King. I did not find him. I set my hands flat to his cold shoulder, pressed my brow against that hard form, and reached again, recklessly. I sensed him then, but it was a far and thin glimpse of what he had been. As well to say one touches the sun when one cups a dapple of forest light in the palm of a hand. "Verity, please," I begged him, and reached yet again with every drop of the Skill that was in me.

When I came to myself, I was crumpled beside his dragon. Nighteyes had not moved from where he kept his vigil. "He's gone," I told him, uselessly, needlessly. "Verity's gone."

I bowed my head to my knees and I wept then, mourning my King as I never had the day his human body had vanished into his dragon form.

I paused in my telling to clear my throat. I drank a bit of the Fool's brandy. I set down my cup and found the Fool looking at me. He had moved closer to hear my hoarse words, and the firelight gilded his skin, but could not reveal what was behind his eyes.

"I think that was when I fully acknowledged that my old life was completely reduced to ashes. If Verity had remained in some form I could reach, if he had still existed to partner me in the Skill, then I think some part of me would have wanted to remain FitzChivalry Farseer. But he did not. The end of my King was also the end of me. When I rose and walked away from the Stone Garden, I knew I truly had what I had longed for all those years: the chance to determine for myself who I was, and a time in which to live my own life as I chose. From now on, I alone would make my decisions."

Almost, the wolf derided me. I ignored him to speak to the Fool. "I stopped at one more place before we left the Mountains. I think you will recall it. The pillar where I saw you change."

He nodded silently and I spoke on.

When we came to the place where a tall Skill-stone stood at a crossroads, I halted, beset by temptation. Memories washed over me. The first time I had come here, it had been with Starling and Kettle, with the Fool and Queen Kettricken, searching for King Verity. Here we had paused, and in a flash of waking-dream, I had seen the verdant forest replaced with a teeming marketplace. Where the Fool had perched atop a stone pillar, a woman stood, like him in white skin and near-colorless eyes. In that other place and time, she had been crowned with a wooden circlet carved with rooster heads and decorated with tail feathers. Like the Fool, her antics had held the crowd's attention. All that I had glimpsed in a moment, like a brief glance through some otherworldly window. Then, in the blinking of an eye, it had all changed back, and I had seen the stunned Fool topple from his precarious perch. Yet he seemed to have shared that brief vision of another time and folk.

The mystery of that moment was what drew me back to the place. The black monolith that presided over that circle of stones stood impervious to moss or lichen, the glyphs carved in its faces beckoning me to destinations unknown. I knew it now for what it was, as I had not when I had first encountered one of the Skill-gates. I circled it slowly. I recognized the symbol that would take me back to the stone quarry. Another, I was almost sure, would bear me back to the deserted Elderling city. Without thinking, I lifted a finger to trace the rune.

Despite his size, Nighteyes can move swiftly and near silently. He seized my wrist in his jaws as he sprang between me and the obelisk. I fell with him to keep his teeth from tearing my flesh. We finished with me on my back on the ground. He stood beside but not quite over me, still gripping my wrist in his jaws. *You will not do that.*

"I didn't intend to use the stone. Only to touch it."

It is not a thing to trust. I have been inside the blackness within the stone. If I must follow you there again, for the sake of your life, then you know I would. But do not ask me to follow you there for puppy curiosity.

Would you mind if I went to the city for a short time, alone?

Alone? You know there is no true "alone" for either of us anymore.

I let you go alone to try a time with the wolf pack.

It is not at all the same, and you know it.

I did. He released my wrist and I stood and brushed myself off. We spoke no more about it. That is one of the best things about the Wit. There is absolutely no need for long and painfully detailed discussions to be sure of understanding one another. Once, years ago, he had left me to run with his own kind. When he had returned, it was his unspoken assertion that he belonged more with me than he did with them. In the years since, we had grown ever closer. As he had once pointed out to me, I was no longer completely a man, nor was he a wolf. Nor were we truly separate entities. This was not a case of him overriding my decision. It was more like debating with myself as to the wisdom of an action. Yet in that brief confrontation, we both faced what we had avoided considering. "Our bond was becoming deeper and more complicated. Neither of us was certain of how to deal with it."

The wolf lifted his head. His deep eyes stared into mine. We shared the misgiving, but he left the decision to me.

Should I tell the Fool where we had gone next and all we had learned? Was my experience among the Old Blood folk completely mine to share? The secrets I held protected many lives. For myself, I was willing to put my entire existence trustingly in the Fool's hands. But did I have the right to share secrets that were not exclusively mine?

I don't know how the Fool interpreted my hesitation. I suspect he took it for something other than my own uncertainty.

"You are right," he declared abruptly. He lifted his cup and drained off the last of his brandy. He set the cup firmly on the floor, then rotated one graceful hand, to halt it with one slender forefinger held aloft in a gesture long familiar to me. *Wait*, it bade me.

As if drawn by a puppeteer's strings, he flowed fluidly to his feet. The room was in darkness, yet he crossed it unerringly to his pack. I heard him rustling through it. A short time later, he returned to the fireside with a canvas sack. He sat down close beside me, as if he were about to reveal secrets too intimate even for darkness to share. The sack in his lap was worn and stained. He tugged open the drawstringed mouth of it, and pulled out something wrapped in beautiful cloth. I gasped as he undid the folds of it. Never had I seen so liquid a fabric, nor so intricate a design worked in such brilliant colors. Even in the muted light of the dying fire, the reds blazed and the yellows shimmered. With that length of textile, he could have purchased the favor of any lord.

Yet this wondrous cloth was not what he wished to show me. He unwound it from what it protected, heedless of how the glorious stuff pooled to the rough floor beside him. I leaned closer, holding my breath, to see what greater wonder it might reveal. The last supple length of it slithered away. I leaned closer, puzzled, to be sure of what I was seeing.

"I thought I had dreamed that," I said at last.

"You did. We did."

The wooden crown in his hands showed the wear of years. Gone were the bright feathers and paint that had once lent it color. It was a simple thing of carved wood, skillfully wrought, but austere in its beauty.

"You had it made?" I guessed.

"I found it," he returned. He took a breath, then said shakily, "Or perhaps it found me."

I waited for him to say more but he did not. I put out a hand to touch it, and he made a tiny motion as if to keep it to himself. An instant later, he relented. He held it out to me. As I took it into my hands, I realized that in sharing this he offered me far more of himself, even more than the sharing of his horse. I turned the ancient thing in my hands, discovering traces of bright paint still trapped in the graven lines of the rooster heads. Two of the heads still possessed winking gem eyes. Holes in the brim of the crown showed where each tail feather would have been set. I did not know the wood it was carved from. Light but strong, it seemed to whisper against my fingers, hissing secrets in a tongue I did not know.

I proffered it back to him. "Put it on," I said quietly.

He took the crown. I saw him swallow. "Are you sure?" he asked me quietly. "I have tried it upon my head, I will admit. Nothing happened. But with us both here, the White Prophet and his Catalyst . . . Fitz, it may be that we tempt a magic neither one of us understands. Time and again, I have searched my memory, but in no prophecy I was ever taught did I find mention of this crown. I have no idea what it signifies, or if it signifies anything at all. You recall your vision of me; I have only the haziest of memories of it, like a butterfly of a dream, too fragile to recapture yet wondrous in its flight."

I said nothing. His hands, as golden as they had once been white, held the crown before him. In silence, we dared ourselves, curiosity warring with caution. In the end, given who we were, there could only be one outcome. A slow, reckless grin spread over his face. Thus, I recalled, had he smiled the night he set his Skilled fingers to the carven flesh of Girl-on-a-dragon. Recalling the agony we had inadvertently caused, I knew a sudden moment of apprehension. But before I could speak, he lifted the crown aloft and set it upon his head. I caught my breath.

Nothing happened.

I stared at him, torn between relief and disappointment. For an instant, silence held between us. Then he began to snicker. In an instant, laughter burst from both of us. The tension broken, we both laughed until the tears streamed down our cheeks. When our mirth subsided, I looked at the Fool, still crowned with wood, still my friend as he had always been. He wiped tears from his eyes.

"You know, last month my rooster lost most of his tail to a scuffle with a weasel. Hap picked up the feathers. Shall we try them in the crown?"

He lifted it from his head and regarded it with mock regret. "Tomorrow, perhaps. And perhaps I shall steal some of your inks as well, and redo the colors. Do you recall them at all?"

I shrugged. "I'd trust your own eye for that, Fool. You always had a gift for such things."

He bowed his head with grave exaggeration to my compliment. He twitched the fabric from the floor and began to rewrap the crown. The fire was little more than embers now, casting a ruddy glow over both of us. I looked at him for a long moment. In this light, I could pretend his coloring had not changed, that he was the white-skinned jester of my boyhood, and hence, that I was still as young as he was. He glanced over at me, caught my eyes on him, and stared back at me, a strange avidity in his face. His look was so intense I glanced aside from it. A moment later, he spoke.

"So. After the Mountains, you went . . . ?"

I picked up my brandy cup. It was empty. I wondered

how much I had drunk, and suddenly knew it was more than enough for one evening. "Tomorrow, Fool. Tomorrow. Give me a night to sleep on it, and ponder how best to tell it."

One long-fingered hand closed suddenly about my wrist. As always, his flesh was cool against mine. "Ponder, Fitz. But as you do so, do not forget . . ." Words seemed suddenly to fail him. His eyes gazed once more into mine. His tone changed to a quiet plea. "Tell me all you can, in good conscience. For I never know what it is I need to hear until I have heard it."

Again, the fervor of his stare unnerved me. "Riddles," I scoffed, trying to speak lightly. Instead, the word seemed to come out as a confirmation of his own.

"Riddles," he agreed. "Riddles to which we are the answers, if only we can discover the questions." He looked down at his grip on my wrist, and released me. He rose suddenly, graceful as a cat. He stretched, a sinuous writhing that looked as if he unfastened his bones from his joints and then put himself together again. He looked down on me fondly. "Go to bed, Fitz," he told me as if I were a child. "Rest while you can. I need to stay up a bit longer and think. If I can. The brandy has quite gone to my head."

"Mine as well," I agreed. He offered a hand and I took it. He drew me easily to my feet, his strength, as always, surprising in one so slightly built. I staggered a step sideways and he moved with me, then caught my elbow, righting me. "Care to dance?" I jested feebly as he steadied me.

"We already do," he responded, almost seriously. As if he bade farewell to a dance partner, he pantomimed a courtly bow over my hand as I drew my fingers from his grip. "Dream of me," he added melodramatically.

"Good night," I replied, stoically refusing to be baited. As I headed toward my bed, the wolf rose with a groan and followed me. He seldom slept more than an arm's reach from my side. In my room, I let my clothes drop where they would before pulling on a nightshirt and falling into bed. The wolf had already found his place on the cool floor beside it. I closed my eyes and let my arm fall so that my fingers just brushed his ruff.

"Sleep well, Fitz," the Fool offered. I opened my eyes a crack. He had resumed his chair before the dying fire and smiled at me through the open door of my room. "I'll keep watch," he offered dramatically. I shook my head at his nonsense and flapped a hand in his direction. Sleep swallowed me.

chapter VII

HEART OF A WOLF

One of the most basic misunderstandings of the Wit is that it is a power given to a human that can be imposed on a beast. In almost all the cautionary tales one hears about the Wit, the story involves an evil person who uses his power over animals or birds to harm his human neighbors. In many of these stories, the just fate of the evil magicker is that his beast servants rise up against him to bring him down to their level, thus revealing him to those he has maligned.

The reality is that Wit magic is as much a province of animals as of humans. Not all humans evince the ability to form the special bond with an animal that is at the heart of the Wit. Nor does every animal have the full capacity for that bond. Of those creatures that possess the capacity, an even smaller number desire such a bond with a human. For the bond to form, it must be mutual and equal between the partners. Amongst Witted families, when the youngster comes of age, he is sent forth on a sort of quest to seek an animal companion. He does not go out, select a capable beast, and then bend it to his will. Rather the hope is that the human will encounter a like-minded creature, either wild or domestic, that is interested in establishing a Wit-bond. Simply put, for a Wit-bond to be established, the animal must be as gifted as the human. Although a Witted human can achieve some level of communication with almost any animal, no bond will be formed unless the animal shares a like talent and inclination.

Yet in any relationship there is always the capacity for abuse. Just as a husband may beat his wife, or a wife pare her husband's soul with belittlement, so may a human dominate his Wit partner. Perhaps the most common form *of this is when a Witted human selects a beast partner when the creature is far too young to realize the magnitude of that life decision. Rarer are the cases in which animals debase or dictate to their bond-partner, but they are not unknown. Among the Old Blood, the common ballad of Roving Grayson is said to be derived from a tale of a man so foolish as to bond with a wild gander, and ever after spent his life in following the seasons as his bird did.*

🐾 BADGERLOCK'S "OLD BLOOD TALES"

Morning came, too bright and too early, on the third day of the Fool's visit. He was awake before me, and if the brandy or the late night held any consequences for him, he did not betray them. The day already promised to be hot, so he had kept the cook fire small, just enough to boil a kettle for porridge. Outside, I turned the chickens out for the day, and took the pony and the Fool's horse out to an open hillside facing the sea. I turned the pony loose but picketed Malta. She gave me a reproachful look at that, but went to grazing as if the tufty grass were exactly what she desired. I stood for a time, overlooking the calm sea. Under the bright morning sun, it looked like hammered blue metal. A very light breeze came off it and stirred my hair. I felt as if someone had spoken words aloud to me and I echoed them. "Time for a change."

A *changing time*, the wolf echoed me in return. And yet that was not quite what I had said, but it felt truer. I stretched, rolling my shoulders, and letting the little wind blow away my headache. I looked at my hands held out before me, and then stared at them. They were a farmer's hands, tough and callused, stained dark with earth and weather. I scratched at my bristly face; I had not taken the care to shave in days. My clothes were clean and serviceable, yet like my hands they were stained with the marks of my daily work, and patched besides. All that had seemed comfortable and set a moment before suddenly seemed a disguise, a costume donned to protect me through my quiet years of rest. I suddenly longed to break out of my life and become, not Fitz as I had been, but Fitz as he might have been, had I not died to the world. A strange shiver ran over me. I was reminded, suddenly, of a summer morning in my childhood when I had watched a butterfly twitch and tear its way out of its chrysalis. Had it felt so, as if the stillness and translucency that had wrapped and protected it had abruptly become too confining to bear?

I took a deep breath and held it, then sighed it out. I expected my sudden discontent to disperse with it, and most of it did. But not all. A changing time, the wolf had said. "So. What are we changing into, then?"

You? I don't know. I know only that you change, and sometimes it frightens me. As for me, the change is simpler. I grow old.

I glanced over at the wolf. "So do I," I pointed out.

No. You do not. You are aging, but you are not getting old as I am getting old. This is true and we both know it.

There seemed little point in denying it. "So?" I challenged him, bravado masking my sudden uneasiness.

So we approach a time of decision. And it should be something we decide, not something that we let happen to us. I think you should tell the Fool about our time among the Old Blood. Not because he will or can decide for us, but because we both think better when we share thoughts with him.

This was a carefully structured thought from the wolf, an almost too-human reasoning from the part of me that ran on four legs. I went down on one knee suddenly beside him and flung my arms around his neck. Frightened for no reason I dared name, I hugged him tight, as if I could pull him inside my chest and hold him there forever. He tolerated it for a moment, then flung his head down and bucked clear of me. He leapt away from me, then stopped. He shook himself all over to settle his rumpled coat, then stared out over the sea as if surveying new hunting terrain. I drew a breath and spoke. "I'll tell him. Tonight."

He gave me a glance over his shoulder, nose held low and ears forward. His eyes were alight. A flash of his old mischief danced there. *I know you will, little brother. Don't fear.*

Then, in a leap of grace that belied his dog's years, he whipped away from me and became a gray streak that vanished suddenly amongst the scrubby brush and tussocky grasses of the gentle hillside. My eyes could not find him, so clever was he, but my heart went with him as it always did. My heart, I told myself, would always be able to find him, would always find a place where we still touched and merged. I sent the thought after him, but he made no reply to it.

I returned to the cottage. I gathered the day's eggs from the chicken house and took them in. The Fool coddled eggs in the coals on the hearth while I brewed tea. We carried our food outside into the blue morning, and the Fool and I broke our fasts sitting on the porch. The wind off the water didn't reach my little vale. The leaves of the trees hung motionless. Only the chickens clucked and scratched in the dusty yard. I had not realized how prolonged my silence had been until the Fool broke it. "It's pleasant here," he observed, waving his spoon at the surrounding trees. "The stream, the forest, the beach cliffs nearby. I can see why you prefer it to Buckkeep."

He had always possessed a knack for turning my thoughts upside down. "I'm not sure that I prefer it," I replied slowly. "I never thought of comparing the two and then choosing where I would live. The first time I spent a winter here, it was because a bad storm caught us, and in seeking shelter under the trees, we found an old cart track. It led us to an abandoned cottage—this one—and we came inside." I shrugged a shoulder. "We've been here ever since."

He cocked his head at me. "So, with all the wide world to choose from, you didn't choose at all. You simply stopped wandering one day."

"I suppose so." I nearly halted the next words that came to my lips, for they seemed to have no bearing on the topic. "Forge is just down the road from here."

"And it drew you here?"

"I don't think so. I did go back to it, to look at the ruins and recall it. No one lives there now. Usually, a place like that, folk would have scavenged the ruins. Not Forge."

"Too many evil memories associated with that place," the Fool confirmed. "Forge was just the beginning, but folk remember it the best, and gave its name to the scourge that followed. I wonder how many folk were Forged, all told?"

I shifted uneasily, then rose to take the Fool's empty dish. Even now, I did not like to recall those days. The Red Ships had raided our shores for years, stealing our wealth. It was only when they began to steal the humanity of our people that we had risen in full wrath against them. They had begun that evil at Forge, kidnapping village folk and returning them to their kin as soulless monsters. Once, it had been my task to track down and kill Forged ones; one of many quiet, nasty tasks for the King's assassin. But that was years ago, I told myself. That Fitz no longer existed. "It was a long time ago," I reminded the Fool. "It's over and done with now."

"So some say. Others disagree. Some still cling to their hatred of the Outislanders and say that even the dragons we sent them were too merciful. Others, of course, say we should put that war behind us, as Six Duchies and Outislanders have always moved from war to trade. On my way here, there was tavern talk that Queen Kettricken seeks to buy both peace and a trade alliance with the Outislanders. I've heard it said she will marry Prince Dutiful off to an Out Islands narcheska, to cement the treaty bond she has proposed."

"Narcheska?"

He lifted his eyebrows. "A sort of princess, I assume. At the very least, a daughter of some powerful noble."

"Well. So." I tried not to show how this news unsettled me. "It will not be the first time that diplomacy was secured in such a way. Consider how Kettricken came to be Verity's wife. To confirm our alliance with the Mountain Kingdom was the intent of that marriage. Yet it worked out to be far more than that."

"It did, indeed," the Fool replied agreeably, but his neutral words left me pondering.

I took our bowls inside and washed them out. I wondered how Dutiful felt about being used as barter to secure a treaty, then pushed the thought from my mind. Kettricken would have raised him in the Mountain way, to believe that the ruler was always the servant of the people. Dutiful would be, well, dutiful, I told myself. No doubt he would accept it without question, just as Kettricken had accepted her arranged marriage to Verity. I noted that the water barrel was nearly empty already. The Fool had always been ardent in his washing and scrubbing, using three times as much water as any other man I knew. I picked up the buckets and went back outside. "I'm going to fetch more water."

He hopped nimbly to his feet. "I'll come along."

So he followed me down the dapple-shaded path to the stream, and to the place I had dug out and lined with stone so that I could fill my buckets more easily. He took the opportunity to splash his hands clean, and to drink deeply of the cold, sweet water. When he straightened up, he looked around suddenly. "Where is Nighteyes?"

I stood up with the buckets, their weight balancing one another. "Oh, he likes to go off on his own sometimes. He—"

Then pain lanced through me. I dropped my brimming buckets, and clutched at my throat for an instant before I realized the discomfort was not my own. The Fool's gaze met mine, his golden skin gone sallow. I think he felt a shadow of my fear. I reached for Nighteyes, found him, and set off at a run.

I followed no path through the forest, and the underbrush caught at me, seeking to bar my headlong flight. I crashed through it, heedless of my clothes and skin. The wolf could not breathe; his tortured gasping taunted my body's frantic gulping of air. I struggled to keep his panic from becoming my own. I drew my knife as I ran, ready for whatever enemy had attacked him. But when I burst from the trees into the clearing near the beaver pond, I saw him writhing alone by the shore. With one paw, he was clawing at his mouth; his jaws were stretched wide. Half of a large fish lay on the pebbled shore beside him. He backed jerkily in circles, shaking his head from side to side, trying to dislodge what choked him.

I threw myself to my knees beside him. "Don't fight me!" I begged him, but I do not think he could heed me. Red panic drenched his thoughts. I tried to put an arm around him to steady him, but he flung himself clear of me. He shook his head wildly, but could not clear his throat. I launched myself at him, throwing him to the ground. I landed on his ribs, and inadvertently saved his life. The press of my body on his chest pushed the fish clogging his throat up into his mouth. Heedless of his teeth, I reached into his mouth and clawed it free. I flung it from us. I felt him gasp in a breath. I lifted my body off his. He staggered to his feet. I felt I did not have the strength to stand.

"Choking on fish!" I exclaimed shakily. "I might have known! Teach you to be so greedy in your gulping."

I took a deep breath of my own, relieved beyond words. However, my relief was short-lived. The wolf stood, took two staggering steps, then collapsed brokenly to the ground. He was no longer choking, but pain blossomed heavily inside him.

"What is it? What's wrong with him?" the Fool demanded behind me. I had not even been aware that he had followed me. I had no time for him now. I scrabbled over to my companion. Fearfully I set a hand to him, and felt that touch amplify our bond. Pain squeezed him, deep in his chest. It hurt so that he could scarcely breathe. His heart thundered unevenly in his ears. His parted eyelids revealed only the roll of his eyes. His tongue sprawled limply from his mouth.

"Nighteyes! My brother!" I shouted the words, but I knew he scarcely heard them. I reached after him, willing my strength to him, and felt an unbelievable thing. He evaded me. He drew back from my reaching, refusing, as much as his weakness allowed him, that link we had shared so long. As he concealed his thoughts, I felt him slipping away from me into a grayness I could not penetrate.

It was intolerable.

"No!" I howled, and flung my awareness after his. When I could not make that gray barrier yield to my Wit, I Skilled into it, heedlessly and instinctively using every magic I possessed to reach him. And reach the wolf I did. I was suddenly with him, my consciousness meshed with his in a way I had never known before. His body was my own.

Long years ago, when Regal had killed me, I had fled the battered husk of my own flesh and taken shelter within Nighteyes. I shared residence with the wolf in his body, perceiving his thoughts, seeing the world through his eyes. I had ridden with him, a passenger in his life. Eventually, Burrich and Chade had called us both back to my graveside, and restored me to my own cold flesh.

This was not that. No. Now I had made his body my own, my human awareness overpowering his wolfness. I settled into him and forced calm upon his frenzied struggling. I ignored his distaste for what I did; it was necessary, I told him. If I did not do this, he would die. He stopped resisting me, but it was not concession. Instead, it was as if he disdainfully abandoned what I had taken from him. I would worry about it later. Offending him was the least of my concerns. It was strange to be in his body that way, rather like donning another man's clothing. I was aware of every piece of him, nails to tail-tip. Air poured strangely over my tongue, and even in my distress, the scents of the day spoke sharply to me. I could smell the sweat of my Fitz self nearby, and I was dimly aware of the Fool crouching over that body, shaking it. I had no time for that now. I had discovered the source of this body's pain. It centered in my shuddering heart. My forcing calm on the wolf had already aided him somewhat, but the limping, uneven beat of his blood spoke ominously of something gone savagely wrong.

Peering down into a cellar is very different from climbing down inside it and looking around. It is a poor explanation, but the best I can offer. From feeling the wolf's heart, I suddenly *became* the wolf's heart. I did not know how I did it; it was as if I leaned desperately against a locked door, knowing my salvation was on the other side, and that door suddenly gave way. I became his heart and knew my function in his body, and knew, also, that my function was impeded. Muscle had grown thin with age, and weary. As heart, I steadied myself and sought feebly for a more even beat. When I achieved that, the press of pain eased, and I went to work.

Nighteyes had retreated to some far corner of our awareness. I let him sulk there, focusing only on what I must do. To what can I compare what I did? Weaving? Building a brick wall? Perhaps it was more like darning the worn heel of a sock. I sensed that I constructed, or rather reconstructed that which had become weakened. I also knew that it was not I, Fitz, who did this, but rather that as part of a wolf's body, I guided that body through a familiar dance. With my focus, it did its task more swiftly. That was all, I told myself uneasily, yet I sensed that somewhere, someone must pay for this hastening of the body's work.

When I felt the work was complete, I stepped back. I was "heart" no longer, but felt with pride its new strength and steadiness. Yet, with that awareness came a sudden jolt of fear. I was not in my own body; I had no idea what had been happening to my own body all the while I had been within Nighteyes. I had no concept of how much time had passed. In perplexity, I reached for Nighteyes, but he held himself aloof from me.

I only did this to help you, I protested.

He kept his silence. I could not tell his thoughts clearly, but his emotions were plain. He was as insulted and affronted as I had ever felt him.

Fine, then, I told him icily. *Have it your way.* Angrily I withdrew.

At least, I attempted to withdraw. Suddenly everything was very confusing. I knew I had to go somewhere, but "somewhere" and "go" were not concepts that seemed to apply. It recalled me somewhat to the sensation of being caught unprepared in the full flood of Skill. That river of magic could tatter an inexperienced user's self to threads, could unfurl a man across the waters of consciousness until he had no self-awareness left. This was different, in that I did not feel spread out and tattering, but trapped in a tangle of myself, bobbing in the current with nowhere to anchor myself save in Nighteyes' body. I could hear the Fool calling my name, but that did me no good, for I heard his voice with Nighteyes' ears.

You see, the wolf observed woefully. *See what you have done to us? I tried to warn you, I tried to keep you out.*

I can correct it, I asserted wildly. We both knew that I did not lie so much as frantically strive that my thought be true.

I divorced myself from his body. I gave up his senses, refused touch and sight and hearing, denied the dust on my tongue and the scent of my nearby body. I pulled my awareness free of his, but then hung there, suspended. I did not know how to get back into my own body.

Then I felt something, a tiny twitch, smaller than if someone had plucked a thread from my shirt. It reached for me, crawling out to me from my true body. To clutch at it was like snatching after a sunbeam. I struggled wildly to grasp it, then subsided back into my formless self, feeling that my snatching at it had only dispersed that faint sending. I held my awareness still and small, waiting as a cat lurks beside a mousehole. The twitching came again, faint as moonlight through leaves. I forced myself to keep still, forced calmness on myself as I allowed it to find me. Like fine gold thread, it touched me at last. It probed me, and when it was sure of me, it picked at me, pulling me unevenly toward itself. The tug was insistent, yet it had no more strength than a hair. I could do nothing to aid it without destroying it. Instead, I must hang suspended, fearing that the touch would break, as it drew me uncertainly away from the wolf and toward myself. Faster it drew me, and then suddenly I could flow of my own volition.

I abruptly knew the cramped form of my own body. I poured into myself, horrified at how cold and stiff the physical confines of my soul had become. My eyes were sticky and dry from being open and unblinking. At first, I could see nothing. Nor could I speak, for my mouth and throat were likewise dried to leather. I tried to roll over, but my muscles were cramped and unyielding. I could do no more than writhe feebly. Yet even my pain was a blessing, for it was my own, the sensation of my own flesh connecting to my own mind. I gave a hoarse croak of relief.

The Fool's cupped hands trickled water over my lips and eventually down my throat. Sight came back to me, blurry at first, but enough to reveal that the sun was far past the noon. I had been out of my body for hours. After a time, I could sit up. I reached immediately for Nighteyes. He sprawled beside me still. He did not sleep. His state of unconsciousness was deeper than that. By touching him, I could sense him as a tiny mote of awareness, buried deep. I felt the steady throb of his pulse and knew immense satisfaction. I nudged at his awareness.

Go away! He was still angry with me. I could not care. His lungs worked, his heart beat steadily now. Exhausted as he was, disoriented as I was, still it was all worth it if his life had been saved.

A time later, I located the Fool. He knelt beside me, his arm around my shoulders. I had not been aware of him steadying me. I wobbled my head to look at him. His face sagged with weariness and his brow was creased with pain, but he managed a lopsided smile. "I did not know if I could do it. But it was the only thing I could think of to try."

After a few moments, his words made sense to me. I looked down at my wrist. His fingerprints were renewed there; not silver as they were the first time he Skill-touched me, but a darker shade of gray than they had been for some time. The thread of awareness that linked us had become one strand stronger. I was appalled at what he had done.

"Thank you. I suppose." I offered the words ungraciously. I felt invaded. I resented that he had touched me in such a way, without my consent. It was childish, but I had not the strength to reach past it just then.

He laughed aloud at me, but I could hear the edge of hysteria in it. "I did not think you would like it. Yet, my friend, I could not help myself. I had to do it." He drew a ragged breath. His voice was softer as he added, "And so it begins again, already. Scarcely two days am I at your side, and fate reaches for you. Will this always be the cost for us? Must I always dangle you over death's jaws in an effort to lure this world into a better course?" His grip on my shoulders tightened. "Ah, Fitz. How can you continually forgive what I do to you?"

I could not forgive it. I did not say so. I looked away from him. "I need a moment to myself. Please."

A bubble of silence met my words. Then, "Of course." He let his arm fall away from my shoulders and abruptly stood clear of me. It was a relief. His touch on me had been heightening the Skill-bond between us. It made me feel vulnerable. He did not know how to reach across it and plunder my mind, but that did not lessen my fear. A knife to my throat was a threat, even if the hand that held it had only the best of intentions.

I tried to ignore the other side of that coin. The Fool

had no concept of how open he was to me just then. The sense of it taunted me, tempting me to attempt a fuller joining. All I would have to do was bid him lay his fingers once more on my wrist. I knew what I could have done with that touch. I could have swept across and into him, known all his secrets, taken all his strength. I could have made his body an extension of my own, used his life and his days for my own purpose.

It was a shameful hunger to feel. I had seen what became of those who yielded to it. How could I forgive him for making me feel it?

My skull throbbed with the familiar pain of a Skill-headache, while my body ached as if I had fought a battle. I felt raw to the world, and even his friend's touch chafed me. I lurched to my feet and staggered toward the water. I tried to kneel by the stream's edge, but it was easier to lie on my belly and suck water up into my parched mouth. Once my thirst was assuaged, I splashed my face. I rubbed the water over my face and hair, and then knuckled my eyes until tears ran. The moisture felt good and my vision cleared.

I looked at the slack body of my wolf, and then glanced at the Fool. He stood small, his shoulders rounded, his mouth pinched tight. I had hurt him. I felt regret at that. He had intended only good, yet a stubborn part of me still resented what he had done. I sought for some justification to cling to that stupidity. There was none. Nevertheless, sometimes knowing one has no right to be angry does not disperse all the anger. "That's better," I said, and shook the water from my hair, as if I could convince us both that only my thirst had troubled me. The Fool made no reply.

I took a double handful of water to the wolf, and sat by him, to let it trickle over his still-lolling tongue. After a bit, he stirred feebly, enough to pull his tongue back into his mouth.

I made another effort for the Fool. "I know that you did what you did to save my life. Thank you."

He saved both our lives. He spared us continuing in a way that would have destroyed us both. The wolf did not open his eyes, but his thought was strong with passion.

However, what he did—

Was it worse than what you did to me?

I had no answer for that. I could not be sorry that I had kept him alive. Yet—

It was easier to speak to the Fool than follow that thought. "You saved both our lives. I had gone . . . somehow, I had gone inside Nighteyes. With the Skill, I think." A flash of insight broke my words. Was this what Chade had spoken of to me, that the Skill could be used to heal? I shuddered. I had imagined it as a sharing of strength, but what I had done—I pushed the knowledge away. "I had to try and save him. And . . . I did help him. But then I could not find my way out of him. If you hadn't drawn me back . . ." I let the words trail off. There was no quick way to explain what he had rescued us from. I knew now, with certainty, that I would tell him the tale of our year among the Old Blood. "Let's go back to the cabin. There is elfbark there, for tea. And I need rest as much as Nighteyes does."

"And I, also," the Fool acceded faintly.

I glanced over him, noting the gray pallor of fatigue that drooped his face and the deep lines clenched in his brow. Guilt washed through me. Untrained and unaided, he had used the Skill to pull me back into my own body. The magic was not in his blood as it was in mine; he had no hereditary predilection for it. All he had possessed was the ancient Skill marks on his fingers, the memento of his accidental brush against Verity's Skill-encrusted hands. That and the feeble bond we had once shared through that touch were his only tools as he had risked himself to draw me back. Neither fear nor ignorance had stopped him. He had not known the full danger of what he did. I could not decide if that made his act less brave or more so. And all I had done was rebuke him for it.

I recalled the first time that Verity had used my strength to further his own Skill. I had collapsed from the drain of it. Yet the Fool still stood, swaying slightly, but he stood. And he made no complaint of the pain that must be playing hammer and tongs on his brain. Not for the first time, I marveled at the toughness that resided in his slender body. He must have sensed my eyes on him, for he turned his gaze to mine. I attempted a smile. He answered it with a wry grimace.

Nighteyes rolled onto his belly, then lurched to his feet. Wobbly as a new foal, he tottered to the water and drank. Satisfying his thirst made both of us feel better, yet my legs still trembled with weariness.

"It's going to be a long walk back to the cabin," I observed.

The Fool's voice was neutral, yet almost normal as he asked, "Can you make it?"

"With some help." I held my hand up to him and he came to take it and draw me to my feet. He held my arm and walked beside me, but I think he leaned on me more than I did on him. The wolf trod slowly after us. I set my teeth and my resolve, and did not reach out to him through that Skill-link that hung between us like a silver chain. I could resist that temptation, I told myself. Verity had. So could I.

The Fool broke the sun-dappled silence of the forest. "I thought you were having a seizure at first, as used to fell you. But then you lay so still . . . I feared you were dying. Your eyes were open and staring. I could not find your pulse. But every now and then, your body would twitch and gasp in some air." He paused. "I could get no response from you. It was the only thing I could think of to do, to plunge in after you."

His words horrified me. I was not sure that I wanted to know what my body did when I was out of it. "It was probably the only way to save my life."

"And mine," he said quietly. "For despite what it costs

either of us, I must keep you alive. You are the wedge I must use, Fitz. And for that, I am sorrier than I can ever say."

He turned his head as he spoke to me. The openness of that golden gaze combined with the bond between us, gold and silver twining. I recognized and rejected a truth I did not want to know.

Behind us, the wolf paced slowly, his head hanging.

chapter VIII

OLD BLOOD

". . . And I trust the hounds will reach you in good health along with this missive. If it be otherwise, please have a bird sent me with such tidings, that I may advise you as to their care. In closing, I ask that you please pass on my regards to Lord Chivalry Farseer. Inform him, with my greetings, that the colt he entrusted to my care still suffers from too abrupt a weaning from his dam. In nature, he is skittish and suspicious, but we shall hope that gentle treatment and patience coupled with a firm hand will cure him of this. He has also a stubborn streak, most vexatious to his trainer, but this, I believe, we may attribute to his sharing his sire's temperament. Discipline may supplant it with strength of spirit. I remain, as always, his most humble servant.

My best wishes also to your mistress and children, Tallman, and I look forward, when next you come to Buckkeep, to settling our wager regarding my Vixen's tenacity on a scent as opposed to your Stubtail."

BURRICH, STABLEMASTER, BUCKKEEP
FROM A MISSIVE SENT TO TALLMAN,
STABLEMASTER, WITHYWOODS

By the time we reached the cabin, darkness threatened the edges of my vision. I gripped the Fool's slender shoulder and steered him toward the door. He stumbled up the steps. The wolf followed us. I pushed the Fool toward a chair and he dropped into it. Nighteyes went straight to my bedchamber and clambered up onto my bed. He made a brief show of rucking up the blankets, then settled into it and dropped into a limp sleep. I quested toward him with the Wit, but found him closed to me. I had to be content with watching the rhythmic rise and fall of his ribs as I built up the fire and put a kettle on to boil. Each step of the simple tasks required all my concentration. The thundering of pain in my head demanded I simply drop in my tracks, yet I could not allow myself to do that.

At the table, the Fool had pillowed his head on his arms, the picture of misery. As I took down my supply of elfbark, he rolled his head to watch me. The Fool made a face at his bitter memory of the dark, dried bark. "So you keep a supply at hand, do you?" His question came out as a croak.

"I do," I conceded, measuring out the bark. I began to grind it with a mortar and pestle. As soon as some was powdered, I dipped my finger into it and touched it to the side of my tongue. I felt a brief easing of the pain.

"And you use it often?"

"Only when I must."

He took a deep breath and let it out. Then he stood reluctantly, and found mugs for both of us. When the water boiled, I prepared a strong pot of elfbark tea. The drug would ease the headache of Skilling, but leave behind both a jittery restlessness and a morose spirit. I had heard tales that the slave owners of Chalced gave it to their slaves, to increase their stamina at the same time that it drained their will to escape. Using elfbark is said to become a habit, but I have never found it so. Perhaps regular forced use of it could create a craving, but my own use of it has always been as a remedy. It is also said to extinguish the ability to Skill in the young, and to cripple its growth for older Skill users. That I might have considered a blessing, but my experience has been that elfbark can deaden the ability to Skill without easing the craving to do so.

I poured two mugs of it after the bark had steeped, and sweetened both with honey. I thought of going to the garden for mint. It seemed much too far away. I set a mug before the Fool and took a seat across from him.

He lifted his mug in a mocking toast. "To us: the White Prophet and his Catalyst."

I lifted mine. "The Fool and the Fitz," I amended his words, and touched my mug to his.

I took a sip. The elfbark spread bitterness all through my mouth. As I swallowed it, I felt my throat tighten in its wake. The Fool watched me drink, then took a mouthful of his own. He grimaced at it, but almost immediately, the lines in his brow relaxed somewhat. He frowned at his mug. "Is there no other way to get the benefit of this?"

I grinned sourly. "I was desperate enough, once, to simply chew the bark. It cut the insides of my cheeks to ribbons and left my mouth so puckered with bitterness I could scarcely drink water to get rid of the taste."

"Ah." He added another liberal dollop of honey to his, drank from the mug, and scowled.

A little silence fell. The edge of uneasiness hovered between us still. No apology would clear it, but perhaps an explanation would. I glanced over at the wolf sleeping on my bed. I cleared my throat. "Well. After we left the Mountain Kingdom, we journeyed back to the borders of Buck."

The Fool lifted his eyes to mine. He propped his chin on one hand and looked at me, giving me his absolute and silent attention. He waited as I found my words. They did not come easily. Slowly I strung together for him the tale of those days.

Nighteyes and I had not hurried our journey. It took us the better part of a year of wandering by a very roundabout path through the Mountains and across the wide plains of Farrow before we returned to the vicinity of Crowsneck in Buck. Autumn had just begun, her warnings when we reached the low-roofed log and stone cabin built into the rise of the forested hill. The great evergreens stood impervious to autumn's threats, but frost had just touched the leaves of the small bushes and plants that grew on the mossy roof, outlining some in yellow and blushing others to red. The wide door stood open to the cool afternoon, and a ripple of near-invisible smoke rose from the squat chimney. There was no need to knock or call. The Old Blood folk within knew we were there, as surely as I could sense that both Rolf and Holly were within. Unsurprised, Black Rolf came to the threshold. He stood in the cavernous dark of his cabin and frowned out at us.

"So, you've finally realized you need to learn what I can teach you," he greeted us. The stink of bear hung about the place, making both Nighteyes and me uneasy. Yet I still had nodded.

He laughed aloud, and his welcoming grin divided the forest of his black beard. I had forgotten the size of the hulking man. He lumbered out and engulfed me in a friendly hug that near cracked my ribs. Almost, I felt the thought he sent to Hilda, the bear that was his bond-animal.

"Old Blood welcomes Old Blood." Holly emerged to greet us gravely. Rolf's wife was as slender and quiet as I recalled her. Her Wit-beast, Sleet, rode on her wrist. Her hawk fixed me with one bright eye, then took flight as she drew closer to us. She smiled and shook her head to watch him go. Her greeting was more restrained than Rolf's, yet somehow warmer. "Well met and welcome," she offered us. She turned her head slightly and sent us a sideways glance from her dark eyes. A quick smile lit her face even as she ducked her head to conceal it. She stood beside Rolf, as slight as he was broad. She preened her short, sleek hair back from her face. "Come within and share food," she invited.

"And then we shall take a walk, find a good place for your den, and start building it," Rolf offered, blunt and direct as always. He glanced up through the forest roof at the overcast sky. "Winter draws nigh. You were foolish to delay so long."

And as simply as that, we became part of the Witted folk who lived in the area outlying Crowsneck. They were forest-dwellers, going into the town only for those things they could not make for themselves. They kept their magic concealed from the town-dwellers, for to be Witted was to invite the rope and the blade to your door. Not that Rolf and Holly or any of the others referred to themselves as Witted. That was the epithet flung by those who both hated and feared Beast Magic; it was a taunt to be hung by. Amongst themselves, they spoke of their kind as Old Blood, and pitied any children born to them who could not bond with an animal, mind and spirit, as ordinary folk might pity a child born blind or deaf.

There were not many of the Old Blood; no more than five families, spread far and wide in the forests about Crowsneck. Persecution had taught them not to dwell too closely together. They recognized one another, and that was enough community for them. Old Blood families generally practiced the solitary trades that permitted them to live apart from ordinary folk and yet close enough to barter and enjoy the benefits of a town. They were woodcutters and fur trappers, and the like. One family lived with their otters near a clay bank, and made exquisitely graceful pottery. One old man, bonded with a boar, lived amply on the coin the richer folk of the town paid him for the truffles he foraged. By and large, they were a peaceful folk, a people who accepted their roles as members of the natural world without disdain. It could not be said that they felt the same about humanity in general. From them, I heard and sensed much disapproval for folk who lived cheek by jowl in the towns and thought of animals as mere servants or pets, "dumb" beasts. They disparaged too those of Old Blood who lived amongst ordinary folk and denied their magic to do so. Often it was assumed I came of such a family, and it was difficult to dispel such ideas without revealing too much of the truth about myself.

"And did you succeed in that?" the Fool asked quietly.

I had the uneasy feeling he was asking the question because he knew I had not. I sighed. "In fact, that was the most difficult line I walked. In the months that passed, I wondered if I had not made a great error in coming back amongst them. Years before, when I had first met them, Rolf and Holly had known that my name was Fitz. They had known, too, of my hatred for Regal. From that knowledge to identifying me as Fitz the Wit Bastard was a tiny step. I knew that Rolf took it, for he attempted to talk of it with me one day. I told him flatly that he was mistaken, that it was a great and unfortunate coincidence both of name and bond-beast that had caused me a great deal of trouble in my lifetime. I was so adamant on the point that even that blunt soul soon realized he would never badger me into admitting otherwise. I lied, and he knew I lied, but I made it clear that it must be taken as truth between us, and so we left it. Holly, I am certain, knew as much but never spoke of it. I did not think the others in the community made the connection. I introduced myself as Tom, and so they all called me, even Holly and Rolf. Fitz, I prayed, would stay dead and buried."

"So they knew." The Fool confirmed his suspicion. "That group, at least, knew that Fitz, Chivalry's bastard, did not die."

I shrugged a shoulder. It surprised me that the old epithet still stung as it did, even from his lips. Surely I had grown past that. Once, I had thought of myself only as "the bastard." But I had long ago got past that and realized that a man was what he made of himself, not what he was born. I suddenly recalled how the hedge-witch had puzzled over my disparate palms. I resisted the impulse to look at my own hands and instead poured us both more of the elfbark brew. Then I rose to rummage through my larder to see what I could find to drive the bitter taste from my mouth. I picked up the Sandsedge brandy, then determinedly set it back again. Instead, I found the last of the cheese, a bit hard but still flavorful, and half a loaf of bread. We had not eaten since breaking our fast that morning. Now that my headache was quieting, I found myself ravenously hungry. The Fool shared my appetite, for as I whittled hunks off the cheese, he sliced thick slabs off the bread.

My story hung unfinished in the air between us.

I sighed. "There was little I could do about what they knew or didn't know, save deny it. Nighteyes and I needed what they knew. They alone could teach us what we had to learn."

He nodded, and stacked cheese atop bread before biting into it. He waited for me to continue.

The words came to me slowly. I did not like to recall that year. Nonetheless, I learned much, not just from Rolf's deliberate teaching, but by simple exposure to the Old Blood community. "Rolf was not the best of teachers. He was short-tempered and impatient, especially around mealtimes, much inclined to cuff and growl, and sometimes roar his frustration at a slow student. He simply could not grasp how completely ignorant I was of Old Blood ways and customs. I suppose by his lights I was as ill-mannered as a deliberately rude child. My 'loud' Wit-conversations with Nighteyes spoiled hunting for other bonded predators. I had never known that we must announce our presence through the Wit if we shifted territory. In my days at Buckkeep, I had never even known that community existed among the Witted ones, let alone that they had customs of their own."

"Wait," the Fool interrupted me. "Then you are saying that Witted ones can share thoughts with each other, just as thoughts can be exchanged through the Skill." He seemed very excited at the idea.

"No." I shook my head. "It's not like that. I can sense if another Witted one is speaking with his bond-beast . . . if they are careless and free in their conversing, as Nighteyes and I used to be. Then I will be aware of the Wit being used, even though I am not privy to the thoughts they share. It's like the humming of a harp string." I smiled ruefully. "That was how Burrich kept guard on me, to be sure I was not indulging in the Wit, once he was aware I had it. He kept his own walls firm against it. He did not use it, and he tried to screen himself from the beasts that reached toward him with it. For a long time, that kept him ignorant of my use of it. He had set Wit-walls, similar to the Skill-walls that Verity taught me to set. But once he realized I was Witted, I think he lowered them, to oversee me." I paused at the Fool's puzzled gaze. "Do you understand?"

"Not completely. But enough to take your meaning. But . . . can you overhear another Witted one's beast speaking to that Witted one, then?"

I shook my head again, then nearly laughed at his baffled look. "It seems so natural to me, it is difficult to put it into words." I pondered a bit. "Imagine that you and I shared a personal language, one that only we two could interpret."

"Perhaps we do," he offered with a smile.

I continued doggedly. "The thoughts that Nighteyes and I share are our thoughts, and largely incomprehensible to anyone who overhears us using the Wit. That language has always been our own, but Rolf taught us to direct our thoughts specifically to one another, rather than flinging our Wit wide to the world. Another Witted one might be aware of us if he were specifically listening for us, but generally, our communication now blends with all the Wit-whispering of the rest of the world."

The Fool's brow was furrowed. "So only Nighteyes can speak to you?"

"Nighteyes speaks most clearly to me. Sometimes, another creature, not bonded to me, will share thoughts with me, but the meaning is usually hard to follow; rather like trying to communicate with someone who speaks a foreign but similar language. There can be much hand waving and raised voices repeating words and gesturing. One catches the gist of the meaning with none of the niceties." I paused and pondered. "I think it is easier if the animal is bonded to another Witted one. Rolf's bear spoke to me once. And a ferret. And between Nighteyes and Burrich . . . it must have been oddly humiliating to Burrich, but he let Nighteyes speak to him when I was in Regal's dungeons.

The understanding was imperfect, but it was good enough that Burrich and he could plot together to save me."

I wandered for a time in that memory, then pulled myself back to my tale. "Rolf taught me the basic courtesy of the Old Blood folk but he did not teach us gently; he was as prone to chastise before we were aware of our errors as afterward. Nighteyes was more tolerant of him than I was, perhaps because he was more amenable to a pack hierarchy. I think it was more difficult for me to learn from him, for I had grown accustomed to a certain amount of adult dignity. Had I come to him younger, I might have accepted more blindly the roughness of his teaching. My experiences of the preceding years had left me violent toward any person who showed aggression toward me. I think the first time I snarled back at him after he shouted at me for some error, it shocked him. He was cold and distant with me for the remainder of the day, and I perceived I must bow my head to his rough ways if I were to learn from him. And so I did, but it was like learning to control my temper all over again. As it was, I was often hard-pressed to quell my anger toward him. His impatience with my slowness frustrated me as much as my 'human thinking' baffled him. On his worst days, he reminded me of the Skillmaster Galen, and he seemed as narrow-minded and cruel as he spoke spitefully of how badly educated I had been amongst the un-Blooded. I resented that he should speak so of folk that I regarded as my own. I knew too that he thought me a suspicious and distrustful man who never completely lowered all my barriers to him. I held back much from him, that is true. He demanded to know of my upbringing, of what I could recall of my parents, of when I had first felt my Old Blood stir in me. None of the sparse answers I gave him pleased him, and yet I could not go into detail without betraying too much of whom and what I had been. The little I did tell him provoked him so much that I am sure a fuller tale would have disgusted him. He approved that Burrich had prevented me from bonding young, and yet condemned all his reasons for doing so. That I had still managed to form a bond with Smithy despite Burrich's watchfulness convinced him of my deceitful nature. Repeatedly, he came back to my wayward childhood as the root of all my problems in finding my Old Blood magic. Again, he reminded me of Galen disparaging the Bastard for trying to master the Skill, the magic of kings. Among a folk where I had thought finally to find acceptance, I discovered that yet again I was neither fish nor fowl. If I complained to Nighteyes at how he treated us, Rolf would snarl at me to stop whimpering to my wolf and apply myself to learning better ways."

Nighteyes learned more easily and often the wolf was the one to convey finally to me what Rolf had failed to rattle into me. Nighteyes also sensed more strongly than I did how much Rolf pitied him. The wolf did not react well to that, for Rolf's pity was based on the notion that I did not treat Nighteyes as well as I should. He took it amiss that I had been almost a grown man and Nighteyes little more than a cub at the time of our bonding. Over and over, Rolf rebuked me for treating Nighteyes as less than an equal, a distinction that both of us disputed.

The first time Rolf and I butted heads over it was in the fashioning of our winter home. We selected a site convenient to Rolf and Holly's home, yet isolated enough that we would not intrude on one another. That first day, I began to build a cabin, while Nighteyes went hunting. When Rolf dropped by, he rebuked me for forcing Nighteyes to live in a dwelling that was entirely human. The structure of his own home incorporated a natural cave in the hillside, and was designed to be as much bear den as man house. He insisted that Nighteyes should dig a den into the hill face, and that I must then build my hut to incorporate it. When I conferred on this with Nighteyes, he replied that he had been accustomed to human dwellings since he was a pup, and he saw no reason why I should not do all the work to make a comfortable place for both of us. When I conveyed this to Rolf, he vented his temper at both of us explosively, telling Nighteyes he found nothing humorous in his surrendering his nature for the selfish comfort of his partner. It was so far from what either of us felt about the situation that we very nearly left Crowsneck right then. Nighteyes was the one who decided we must stay and learn. We followed Rolf's directions, and Nighteyes laboriously excavated a den for himself and I built my hut around the mouth of it. The wolf spent very little time in the den, preferring the warmth of my fireside, but Rolf never discovered that.

Many of my disagreements with Rolf shared those same roots. He saw Nighteyes as too humanized, and shook his head at how little of wolf there was in me. Yet at the same time he warned us both that we had twined ourselves too tightly together, that he could find no place where he could sense one of us and not the other. Perhaps the most valuable thing Rolf taught us was how to separate from one another. Through me, he conveyed to Nighteyes the need that each of us had for privacy in matters such as mating or grieving. I had never been able to convince the wolf that the need for such a sundering existed. Again, Nighteyes learned it more swiftly and better than I did. When he so desired, he could vanish completely from my senses. I did not enjoy the sensation of being isolated from him. I felt halved by it, and sometimes as less than a half, and yet we both saw the wisdom of it, and strove to perfect our abilities in that area. Yet no matter how satisfied we were with our progress, Rolf remained adamant that even in our separations, we still shared a unity so basic that neither of us were even aware of it anymore. When I tried to shrug it off as inconsequential, he became almost incensed.

"And when one of you dies, what then? Death comes to all of us, sooner or later, and it cannot be cheated. Two souls can not long abide in one body before one takes control and the other becomes but a shadow. It is a cruelty, no matter which becomes the stronger. Hence, all Old Blood traditions shun such greedy snatching at life." Here Rolf frowned at me most severely. Did he suspect I had already sidestepped my death once by such a ruse? He could not, I promised myself. I returned his gaze guilelessly.

He knit his dark brows ominously. "When a creature's life is over, it is over. It perverts all nature to extend it. Yet Old Blood alone knows the true depth of agony when two souls that have been joined are parted by death. So it must be. You must be able to separate into yourselves when that time comes." He beetled his heavy brows at us as he spoke. Nighteyes and I both grew still of thought, considering it. Even Rolf finally seemed to sense how much it distressed us. His voice grew gruffer, yet kinder. "Our custom is not cruel, at least no crueler than it must be. There is a way to keep a remembrance of all that has been shared. A way to keep the voice of the other's wisdom and the love of the other's heart."

"So one partner could go on living within the other?" I asked, confused.

Rolf shot me a disgusted look. "No. I have just told you, we do not do that. When your time comes to die, you should separate yourself from your partner and die, not seek to leech onto his life."

Nighteyes made a brief whistle of whine. He was as confused as I was. Rolf seemed to concede that he was teaching a difficult concept, for he stopped and scratched his beard noisily. "It's like this. My mother is long dead and gone. But I can recall still the sound of her voice singing me a lullaby, and hear the warnings she would give when I tried to do something foolish. Right?"

"I suppose so," I conceded. This was another sore spot between Rolf and me. He had never accepted that I had no memories of my natural mother, although I had spent the first six years of my life with her. At my lukewarm response, he narrowed his eyes.

"As can most folks," he went on more loudly, as if sound alone could persuade me. "And that is what you can have when Nighteyes is gone. Or what he can keep of you."

"Memories," I agreed quietly, nodding. Even discussing Nighteyes' death was unsettling.

"No!" Rolf exclaimed. "Not just memories. Anyone can have memories. But what a bonded one leaves behind for his partner is deeper and richer than memories. It's a presence. Not living on in the other's mind, not sharing thoughts, decisions, and experiences. But just—being there. Standing by. So now you understand," he informed me heavily.

No, I started to say, but Nighteyes leaned heavily against my leg, so I simply made a sound that might have been agreement. And over the next month, Rolf instructed us in his dogged way, bidding us separate, and then allowing us to come back together, but only in a thin, insubstantial way. I found it completely unsatisfactory. I was convinced we were doing something wrong, that this could not be the comfort and "being" that Rolf had spoken about. When I expressed my doubts to Rolf, he surprised me by agreeing with me, but then went on to declare that we were still far too intertwined, that the wolf and I must separate even more. And we gave heed to him and sincerely tried, but held our own counsel as to what we would actually do when death came for one of us.

We never voiced our obstinacy, but I am sure Rolf was aware of it. He took great pains to "prove" to us the error of our ways, and the examples he showed us were truly wrenching. A careless Old Blood family had let swallows nest in their eaves where their infant son could not only hear their familial twitterings but watch their comings and goings. And that was all he did, even now as a grown man of about thirty. In Buckkeep Town, folk would have called him simple, and so he was, but when Rolf bade us reach toward him more discriminatingly with the Wit, the reason was clear to us both. The boy had bonded, not just to a swallow, but to all swallows. In his mind he was a bird, and his dabbling in mud and fluttering hands and snapping after insects were the work of his bird's mind.

"And that's what comes of bonding too young," Rolf told us darkly.

There was one other pair he showed us, but only from a distance. On an early morning when mist lay heavy in the vales, we lay on our bellies on the lip of a dell and made no sound or thought amongst ourselves. A white hind drifted through the fog toward a pond, walking not with a deer's true caution but with a woman's languid grace. I knew her partner must be close by, concealed in the mist. The deer lowered her muzzle to the water and drank long slow draughts of the coolness. Then she slowly lifted her head. Her large ears swiveled forward. I felt the tentative brush of her questing. I blinked, trying to focus on her, while the wolf made a small, questioning whine in the back of his throat.

Rolf rose abruptly, showing himself disdainfully. He coldly refused the contact. I sensed his disgust as he strode away, but we remained, staring down at her. Perhaps she sensed ambivalence, for she watched us with a very undeer-like boldness. An odd moment of vertigo washed over me. I squinted, trying to make the shape before me resolve into the two that my Wit told me were there.

When I was Chade's apprentice, he used several exercises to teach me to see what my eyes truly beheld, not what my mind expected to see. Most were simple drills, to look at a tangle of line and decide if it were knotted or merely flung down, or to glance at a jumble of gloves and know which ones lacked mates. A more peculiar trick he showed me was to write the name of a color in a mismatched ink, the word *red* painted in bright blue letters. To read a list of such colors, correctly saying the printed word rather than the color of the inked letters, took more concentration than I had expected it would.

And so I rubbed my eyes and looked again and saw only

a deer. The woman had been an expectation of my mind, based on my Wit. Physically, she was not there. Her presence inside the hind distorted my Wit-sense of the deer. I shuddered away from the wrongness of it. Rolf had left us behind. In confusion, Nighteyes and I hastened after Rolf as he strode away from the sheltered dell and the quiet pool. Some time and distance later, "What was that?" I asked him.

He rounded on me, affronted by my ignorance. "What was that? That was you, a dozen years hence, if you do not mend your ways. You saw her eyes! That was no deer down there, but a woman in the skin of a hind. It's what I wanted you to see. The wrongness of it. The complete perversion of what should have been shared trust."

I looked at him quietly, waiting. I think he had expected me to concur with his judgment, for he made a deep noise in his throat. "That was Delayna, who slipped through the ice into Marple Pond and drowned two winters ago. She ought to have died right then, but no, she clung to Parela. The hind either hadn't the heart or the strength to oppose her. Now there they are, a deer with the mind and heart of a woman, and Parela with scarcely a thought to call her own. It goes against all nature, it does. Ones like Delayna are at the root of all the evil talk the un-Blooded wag on about us. She's what makes them want to hang us and burn us over water. She deserves such treatment."

I looked away from his vehemence. I'd come too close to that fate myself to believe anyone could deserve it. My body had lain cold in my grave for days while I'd shared Nighteyes' flesh and life. I was certain then that Rolf suspected as much of me. I wondered then, if he so despised me, why he taught me at all. As if he had caught some whiff of my thought, he added gruffly, "Anyone untaught can do a wrong thing. But after he's been taught, there's no excuse to repeat it. None at all."

He turned and strode off down the path. We trailed after him. Nighteyes' tail stuck out straight behind him. Rolf muttered to himself as he stumped along. "Delayna's greed destroyed them both. Parela's got no life as a deer. No mate, no young, when she dies, she'll just stop, and Delayna with her. Delayna couldn't accept death as a woman, but she won't accept life as a deer, either. When the bucks call, she won't let Parela answer them. She probably thinks she's being faithful to her husband or some such nonsense. When Parela dies and Delayna with her, what will either of them have gained, save a few years of existence that neither of them could call complete?"

I could not argue with him. The wrongness I had sensed still crawled along my spine. "Yet." I struggled to make myself admit this to the Fool. "Yet privately I wondered if any save those two could fully understand the decision that had been made. If perhaps, despite how it appeared to us, it felt right to them."

I paused for a time in my telling. The story of those two always disturbed me. If Burrich had not been able to call me back from the wolf and into my own body, would we have become as they did? If the Fool had not been nearby today, would Nighteyes and I dwell in one body even now? I did not speak the thought aloud. I knew the Fool would have already made that leap. I cleared my throat.

"Rolf taught us a great deal in the year we were there, but even as we learned the techniques of the magic we shared, Nighteyes and I stopped short of accepting all the customs of the Old Blood folk. The secrets we learned, I felt we had a right to, simply by virtue of what we were, but I did not feel bound to accept the rules Rolf attempted to impose on us. Perhaps I would have been wiser to dissemble, but I was tired to death of deception, and the layers of lies that must be woven to protect it. So I held myself back from that world, and Nighteyes consented to be held back with me. So it was that we observed their community, but never engaged fully in the lives of the Old Blood folk."

"And Nighteyes too held back from them?" The Fool's question was gentle. I tried not to think that there might be a hidden rebuke in it, a questioning as to whether I was the one who had held him back for my own selfish reasons.

"He felt as I did. The knowledge of the magic that is in us by our blood: this was something they owed to us. And when Rolf dangled it over us as a reward to be given only when we accepted the yoke of his rules—well, that is a form of exclusion, my friend." I glanced over at the gray wolf curled in my blankets. He slept deeply, paying the price of my interference with his body.

"Did no one extend a simple friend's hand to you there?" The Fool's question drew me back to my story. I considered it.

"Holly tried to. I think she pitied me. She was shy and solitary by nature; it was something we had in common. Sleet and his mate had a nest in a great tree on the hillside above Rolf's house, and Holly herself was wont to spend hours perched on a woven platform not far below Sleet's nest. She was never talkative to me, but showed me many small kindnesses, including the gift of a feather bed, a side-product of Sleet's kills."

I smiled to myself. "And she taught me the many skills of living on my own, all I had never learned while I lived in Buckkeep Castle and others saw to my needs. There is a genuine pleasure to making leavened bread, and she taught me to cook, beyond Burrich's traveling stews and porridges. I was ragged and worn when I first arrived there. She demanded all my clothes, not to mend, but to teach me the proper care of them. I sat by her fire, and learned to darn socks without lumping them, how to turn the hems on cuffs before they frayed hopelessly . . ." I shook my head, smiling at the memories.

"And no doubt Rolf was pleased to see your heads bent together so cozily and so often?" The Fool's tone asked the other question. Had I given Rolf reason to be jealous and spiteful?

I drank the last of the lukewarm elfbark tea and leaned back in my chair. The familiar melancholy of the herb was stealing over me. "It was never like that, Fool. You can laugh if you wish, but it was more like finding a mother. Not that she was that much older than I, but the gentleness and acceptance and the wishing me well. But"—I cleared my throat—"you are right. Rolf was jealous, though he never put it into words. He would come in from the cold, to find Nighteyes sprawled on his hearth, and my hands full of yarn from some project of Holly's needles, and he would immediately find some other task that she must do for him. Not that he treated her badly, but he took pains to make it clear she was his woman. Holly never spoke of it to me, but in a way I think she did it on purpose, to remind him that however many years they had been together, she still had a life and a will of her own. Not that she ever tried to raise the pitch of his jealousy.

"In fact, before the winter was over, she had made efforts to bring me into the Old Blood community. At Holly's invitation, friends came to call, and she took great pains to introduce me to all of them. Several families had marriageable daughters, and these ones seemed to visit most often when I too was invited to share a meal with Rolf and Holly. Rolf drank and laughed and became expansive when guests called, and his enjoyment of these occasions was evident. He often observed aloud that this was the merriest winter he could recall in many a year, from which I deduced that Holly did not often open her home to so many guests. Yet she never made her efforts to find me a companion too painfully evident. It was obvious that she considered Twinet my best match. She was a woman but a few years older than I, tall and dark-haired with deep blue eyes. Her companion beast was a crow, as merry and mischievous as she was. We became friends, but my heart was not ready for anything more than that. I think her father more resented my lack of ardor than Twinet did, for he made several ponderous comments to the effect that a woman would not wait forever. Twinet, I sensed, was not as interested in finding a mate as her parents supposed. We remained friends throughout the spring and into summer. Ollie, Twinet's father, gossiping to Rolf, precipitated my departure from the Old Blood community at Crowsneck. He had told his daughter that she must either stop seeing me, or press me to declare my intent. In response, Twinet had strongly expressed her own intent, which was not to marry anyone who did not suit her, let alone 'a man so much younger than myself, both in years and heart. For the sake of making grandchildren, you'd have me bed with someone raised among the un-Blooded, and carrying the taint of Farseer blood.' "

"Her words were carried back to me, not by Rolf, but by Holly. She spoke them softly to me, her eyes downcast as if shamed to utter such rumor. But when she looked up at me, so calmly and gently waiting for my denial, my ready lies died on my lips. I thanked her quietly for making me privy to Twinet's feelings about me, and told her that she had given me much to ponder. Rolf was not there. I had come to their home to borrow his splitting maul, for summer is the time to make ready winter firewood. I left without asking for the loan of it, for both Nighteyes and I immediately knew that we would not be wintering amongst the Old Blood. By the time the moon appeared, the wolf and I had once more left Buck Duchy behind us. I hoped that our abrupt departure would be seen as a man's reaction to a courtship gone bad rather than the Bastard fleeing those who had recognized him."

Silence fell. I think the Fool knew that I had spoken aloud to him my most lingering fear. The Old Blood had knowledge of my identity, of my name, and that gave them power over me. What I would never admit to Starling, I explained plainly to the Fool. Such power over a man should not reside with those who do not love him. Yet they had it, and there was nothing I could do about it. I lived alone and apart from the Old Blood folk, but not a moment passed for me that I was not distantly aware of my vulnerability to them. I thought of telling him Starling's story of the minstrel at Springfest. Later, I promised myself. Later. It was as if I wished to hide danger from myself. I felt suddenly morose and sour. I glanced up to find the Fool's eyes on my face.

"It's the elfbark," he said quietly.

"Elfbark," I conceded irritably, but could not convince myself that the hopelessness that swept through me was completely the aftereffect of the drug. Did not at least some of it stem from the pointlessness of my own life?

The Fool got up and paced the room restlessly. He went from door to hearth to window twice, and then diverted to the cupboard. He brought the brandy and two cups back to the table. It seemed as good an idea as any. I watched him pour.

I know we drank that evening and well into the night. The Fool took over the talking. I think he tried to be amusing and lighten my mood, but his own spirits seemed as damped as mine. From anecdotes of the Bingtown Traders, he launched into a wild tale of sea serpents that entered cocoons to emerge as dragons. When I demanded to know why I had not seen any of these dragons, he shook his head. "Stunted," he said sadly. "They emerge in the late spring, weak and thin, like kittens born too soon. They may yet grow to greatness, but for now the poor creatures feel shamed at their frailty. They cannot even hunt for themselves." I well recall his look of wide-eyed guilt. His golden eyes bored into me. "Could it be my fault?" he asked softly, senselessly, at the end of his tale. "Did I attach myself to the wrong person?" Then he filled his glass again and drank it down with a purposefulness that reminded me of Burrich in one of his black moods.

I don't remember going to bed that night, but I do recall lying there, my arm flung across the sleeping wolf, drowsily watching the Fool. He had taken out a funny little instrument that had but three strings. He sat before the fire and strummed it, plucking discordant notes that he smoothed with the words of a sad song in a language I had never heard. I set my fingers to my own wrist. In the darkness, I could feel him there. He did not turn to look at me, but awareness prickled between us. His voice seemed to grow truer in my ears, and I knew he sang the song of an exile longing for his homeland.

chapter IX

DEAD MAN'S REGRETS

The Skill is often said to be the hereditary magic of the Farseer line, and certainly it seems to flow most predictably in those bloodlines. It is not unknown, however, for the Skill to crop up as a latent talent almost anywhere in the Six Duchies. In earlier reigns, it was customary for the Skillmaster who served the Farseer monarch at Buckkeep to regularly seek out youngsters who showed potential for the Skill. They were brought to Buckkeep, instructed in the Skill if they showed strong talent, and encouraged to form coteries: mutually chosen groups of six that aided the reigning monarch as required. Although there is a great dearth of information on these coteries, almost as if scrolls relating to them were deliberately destroyed, oral tradition indicates that there were seldom more than two or three coteries in existence at any time, and that strong Skill-users have always been rare. The procedure Skillmasters used for locating children with latent talent is lost to time. King Bounty, father to King Shrewd, discontinued the practice of building coteries, perhaps believing that restricting knowledge of the Skill to the exclusive use of princes and princesses would increase the power of those who did possess it. Thus it was that when war came to the shores of the Six Duchies in the reign of King Shrewd, there were no Skill coteries to aid the Farseer reign in the defense of the kingdom.

I awoke in the night with a jolt. Malta. I had left the Fool's mare picketed out on the hillside. The pony would come in, and likely had even put herself within the barn, but I had left the horse out there, all day, with no water.

There was only one thing to do about it. I arose silently and left the cabin, not closing the door behind me lest the shut of it awaken the Fool. Even the wolf I left sleeping as I walked out into the dark alone. I stopped briefly at the barn. As I suspected, the pony had come in. I touched her gently with my Wit-sense. She was sleeping and I left her where she was.

I climbed the hill to where I had picketed the horse, glad that I was not walking in the true dark of a winter night. The stars and the full moon seemed very close. Even so, my familiarity with my path guided me more than my eyes. As I came up on Malta, the horse gave a rebuking snort. I untied her picket line and led her down the hill. When the stream cut our path on its way to the sea, I stopped and let her drink.

It was a beautiful summer night. The air was mild. The chirring of night insects filled the air, accompanied by the sound of the horse sucking water. I let my gaze wander, filling myself with the night. Dark stole the colors of the grass and trees, but somehow their stark shades of black and gray made the landscape seem more intricate. The moisture in the cooler air awoke all the summer scents that had dozed by day. I opened my mouth and drew in a deep breath, tasting the night more fully. I gave myself up to my senses, letting go of my human cares, taking this moment of now and letting it stretch eternally around me. My Wit unfurled around me and I became one with the night splendor.

There is a natural euphoria to the Wit. It is both like and unlike the Skill. With the Wit, one is aware of all the life that surrounds one. It was not just the warmth of the mare nearby that I sensed. I knew the scintillant forms of the myriad insects that populated the grasses, and felt even the shadowy life force of the great oak that lifted its limbs between the moon and me. Just up the hillside, a rabbit crouched motionless in the summer grasses. I felt its indistinct presence, not as a piece of life located in a certain place, but as one sometimes hears a single voice's note within a market's roar. But above all, I felt a physical kinship with all that lived in the world. I had a right to be here. I was as much a part of this summer night as the insects or the water purling past my feet. I think that old magic draws much of its strength from that acknowledgment: that we are a part of that world, no more, but certainly no less than the rabbit.

That rightness of unity washed through me, laving away the nastiness of the Skill greed that had earlier befouled my soul. I took a deeper breath, and then breathed it out as if it were my last, willing myself to be part of this good, clean night.

My vision wavered, doubled, and then cleared. For a pent breath of time, I was not myself, was not on the summer hillside near my cabin, and I was not alone.

I was a boy again, escaped from confining stone walls and tangling bedclothes. I ran lightshod through a sheep pasture dotted with tufts of ungrazed weeds, trying vainly to keep up with my companion. She was as beautiful as the star-dotted night, her tawny coat spangled with darkness. She moved as unobtrusively as night herself did. I followed her, not with human eyes, but with the Wit-bond that joined us. I was drunk with love of her and love of this night, intoxicated with the heady rush of this wild freedom. I knew I had to go back before the sun rose. She knew, just as strongly, that we did not, that there was no better time than now to make our escape.

And in my next breath, that knowing was gone. The night still bloomed and beckoned around me, but I was a grown man, not a boy lost in the wonder of his first Wit-bond. I did not know who my senses had brushed, or where they were, nor why we had meshed our awarenesses so completely. I wondered if he had been as cognizant of me as I was of him. It did not matter. Wherever they were, whoever they were, I wished them well in their night's hunting. I hoped their bond would last long and be deep as their bones.

I felt a questioning tug at the lead rope. Malta had quenched her thirst and had no wish to stand still while the insects feasted on her. I became aware that my own warm body had attracted a swarm of little bloodsuckers as well. She swished her tail and I waved my hand about my head before we set off down the hill once more. I stabled her, and slipped softly back into the cabin, to seek out my own bed for the rest of the night. Nighteyes had stretched out, leaving me less than half the bed, but I did not mind. I stretched out beside him, and set my hand lightly on his ribs. The beating of his heart and the movement of his breath were more soothing than any lullaby. As I closed my eyes, I felt more at peace than I had in weeks.

I awoke easily and early the next morning. My interlude on the hillside seemed to have rested me more than sleep. The wolf had not fared so well. He still slept heavily, a healing sleep. I felt a twinge of conscience over that, but pushed it aside. Whatever I had done to his heart seemed to tax the resources of the rest of his body, but surely that was better than letting him die. I surrendered the bed to him and left him sleeping.

The Fool was not about, but the door was left standing open, a fair indication that he had gone out. I set a small fire, put on the kettle, and then took some time with washing up and shaving. I had just smoothed my hair back behind my ears when I heard the Fool's footsteps on the porch. He entered with a basket of eggs on his arm. When I looked up from drying my face, he stopped in his tracks. A wide grin spread slowly over his face.

"Why, it's Fitz! A bit older, a bit more worn, but Fitz all the same. I had wondered what you looked like under that thatch."

I glanced back into the mirror. "I suppose I don't take much pains with my appearance anymore." I grimaced at myself, then dabbed at a spot of blood. As usual, I had nicked myself where the old scar from my time in Buckkeep's dungeons seamed my face. Thank you, Regal. "Starling told me that I look far older than my years. That I could return to Buckkeep Town and never fear that anyone would recognize me."

The Fool made a small sound of disgust as he set the eggs on the table. "Starling is, as usual, wrong on both counts. For the number of years and lives you have lived, you look remarkably young. It's true that experience and time have changed your features; folk recalling the boy Fitz would not see him grown to a man in you. Yet, some of us, my friend, would recognize you even if you were flayed and set afire."

"Now there's a comforting thought." I set the mirror down and turned to the task of making breakfast. "Your color has changed," I observed a moment later as I broke eggs into a bowl. "But you yourself don't look a day older than the last time I saw you."

The Fool was filling the teapot with steaming water. "It's the way of my kind," he said quietly. "Our lives are longer, so we progress through them more slowly. I've changed, Fitz, even if all you see is the color of my flesh. When last you saw me, I was just approaching adulthood. All sorts of new feelings and ideas were blossoming in me, so many that I scarce could keep my mind on the tasks at hand. When I recall how I behaved, well, even I am scandalized. Now, I assure you, I am far more mature. I know that there is a time and place for everything, and that what I am destined to do must take full precedent over anything I might long to do for myself."

I poured the beaten eggs into a pan and set them at the fire's edge. I spoke slowly. "When you speak in riddles, it exasperates me. Yet when you try to speak clearly of yourself, it frightens me."

"All the more reason why I should not speak of myself at all," he exclaimed with false heartiness. "Now. What be our tasks for the day?"

I thought it out as I stirred the setting eggs and pushed them closer to the fire. "I don't know," I said quietly.

He looked startled at the sudden change in my voice. "Fitz? Are you all right?"

I myself could not explain the sudden lurch in my spirits. "Suddenly, it all seems so pointless. When I knew Hap was going to be here for the winter, I always took care to provide for us both. My garden was a quarter that size when the boy first came to me, and Nighteyes and I hunted day to day for our meat. If we did not hunt well and went empty for a day or so, it did not seem of much consequence. Now, I look at all I have already set by and think, If the boy is not here, if Hap is wintering with a master while he starts to learn his trade, why, then, I already have plenty for both Nighteyes and me. Sometimes it seems that there's no point to it. And then I wonder if there's any point left to my life at all."

A frown divided the Fool's brows. "How melancholy you sound. Or is this the elfbark I'm hearing?"

"No." I took up the shirred eggs and brought them to the table. It was almost a relief to speak the thoughts I'd been denying. "I think it was why Starling brought Hap to me. I think she saw how aimless my life had become, and brought me someone to give shape to my days."

The Fool set down plates with a clatter, and dished food onto them in disgusted splats. "I think you give her credit for thinking of something beyond her own needs. I suspect she picked up the boy on an impulse, and dumped him here when she wearied of him. It was just lucky for both of you that you helped each other."

I said nothing. His vehemence in his dislike for Starling surprised me. I sat down at the table and began eating. But he had not finished.

"If Starling meant for anyone to give shape to your days, it was herself. I doubt that she ever imagined you might need anyone's companionship other than hers."

I had an uncomfortable suspicion he was right, especially when I recalled how she had spoken of Nighteyes and Hap on her last visit.

"Well. What she thought or didn't think scarcely matters now. One way or another, I'm determined to see Hap apprenticed well. But once I do—"

"Once you do, you'll be free to take up your own life again. I've a feeling it will call you back to Buckkeep."

"You've 'a feeling'?" I asked him dryly. "Is this a Fool's feeling, or a White Prophet's feeling?"

"As you never seemed to give credence to any of my prophecies, why should you care?" He smiled archly at me and began eating his eggs.

"A time or three, it did seem as if what you predicted came true. Though your predictions were always so nebulous, it seemed to me that you could make them mean anything."

He swallowed. "It was not my prophecies that were nebulous, but your understanding of them. When I arrived, I warned you that I had come back into your life because I must, not because I wanted to. Not that I didn't want to see you again. I mean only that if I could spare you somehow from all we must do, I would."

"And what is it, exactly, that we must do?"

"Exactly?" he queried with a raised eyebrow.

"Exactly. And precisely," I challenged him.

"Oh, very well, then. Exactly and precisely what we must do. We must save the world, you and I. Again." He leaned back, tipping his chair onto its back legs. His pale brows shot toward his hairline as he widened his eyes at me.

I lowered my brow into my hands. But he was grinning like a maniac and I could not contain my own smile. "Again? I don't recall that we did it the first time."

"Of course we did. You're alive, aren't you? And there is an heir to the Farseer throne. Hence, we changed the course of all time. In the rutted path of fate, you were a rock, my dear Fitz. And you have shifted the grinding wheel out of its rut and into a new track. Now, of course, we must see that it remains there. That may be the most difficult part of all."

"And what, exactly and precisely, must we do to ensure that?" I knew his words were bait for mockery, but as ever, I could not resist the question.

"It's quite simple." He ate a bite of eggs, enjoying my suspense. "Very simple, really." He pushed the eggs around on his plate, scooped up a bite, then set his spoon down. He looked up at me, and his smile faded. When he spoke, his voice was solemn. "I must see that you survive. Again. And you must see that the Farseer heir inherits the throne."

"And the thought of my survival makes you sad?" I demanded in perplexity.

"Oh, no. Never that. The thought of what you must go through to survive fills me with foreboding."

I pushed my plate away, my appetite fled. "I still don't understand you," I replied irritably.

"Yes you do," he contradicted me implacably. "I suppose you say you don't because it is easier that way, for both of us. But this time, my friend, I will lay it cold before you. Think back on the last time we were together. Were there not times when death would have been easier and less painful than life?"

His words were shards of ice in my belly, but I am nothing if not stubborn. "Well. And when is that ever not true?" I demanded of him.

There have been very few times in my life when I have been able to shock the Fool into silence. That was one of them. He stared at me, his strange eyes getting wider and wider. Then a grin broke over his face. He stood so suddenly he nearly overset his chair, and then lunged at me to seize me in a wild hug. He drew a deep breath as if something that had constricted him had suddenly sprung free. "Of course that is true," he whispered by my ear. And then, in a shout that near deafened me, "Of course it is!"

Before I could shrug free of his strangling embrace, he sprang apart from me. He cut a caper that made motley of his ordinary clothes, and then sprang lightly to my tabletop. He flung his arms wide as if he once more performed for all of King Shrewd's court rather than an audience of one. "Death is always less painful and easier than life! You speak true. And yet we do not, day to day, choose death. Because ultimately, death is not the opposite of life, but the opposite of choice. Death is what you get when there are no choices left to make. Am I right?"

Infectious as his fey mood was, I still managed to shake my head. "I have no idea if you are right or wrong."

"Then take my word for it. I am right. For am I not the White Prophet? And are not you my Catalyst, who comes to change the course of all time? Look at you. Not the hero, no. The Changer. The one who, by his existence, enables others to be heroes. Ah, Fitz, Fitz, we are who we are and who we ever must be. And when I am discouraged, when I lose heart to the point of saying, 'But why cannot I leave him here, to find what peace he may?,' then, lo and behold, you speak with the voice of the Catalyst, and change my perception of all that I do. And enable me to be once more what I must be. The White Prophet."

I sat looking up at him. Despite my efforts, a smile twisted my mouth. "I thought I enabled other people to be heroes. Not prophets."

"Ah, well." He leapt lightly to the floor. "Some of us must be both, I fear." He gave himself a shake, and tugged his jerkin straight. Some of the wildness went out of him. "So. To return to my original question. What are our tasks today? My turn to give you the answer. Our first task today is to give no thought to the morrow."

I took his advice, for that day at least. I did things I had not been giving myself permission to do, for they were not the serious tasks that provided against the morrow, but the simple work that brought me pleasure. I worked on my inks, not to take to market and sell for coin, but to try to create a true purple for my own pleasure. It yielded no success that day; all my purples turned to brown as they dried, but it was a work I enjoyed. As for the Fool, he amused himself by carving on my furniture. I glanced up at the sound of my kitchen knife scraping across wood. The movement caught his eye. "Sorry," he apologized at once. He held the knife up between two fingers to show me, and then carefully set it down. He got up from his chair and wandered over to his saddle pack. After a moment of digging, he tugged out a roll of fine bladed tools. Humming to himself, he went back to the table and set to on the chairs. He went bare-fingered to his task, tugging off the fine glove that usually masked his Skill hand. As the day progressed, my simple chairs gained leafy vines twining up their backs, and occasional little faces peeping out of the foliage.

When I looked up from my work in mid-afternoon, I saw him come in with chunks of seasoned wood from my woodpile. I leaned back from my desk to watch him as he turned and considered each one, studying them and tracing their grain with his Skill fingers as if he could read their secrets hidden to my eyes. At length he selected one with a knee in it and started in on it. He hummed to himself as he worked, and I left him to it.

Nighteyes woke once during the day. He clumped down from my bed with a sigh and tottered outside. I offered him food when he returned but he turned his nose up at it. He had drunk deeply, all the water he could hold, and he lay himself down with a sigh on the cool floor of the cabin. He slept again, but not as deeply.

And so I passed that day in pleasure, which is to say, in the sort of work I wanted to do rather than the work that I thought I ought to be doing. Chade came often to my mind that day. I wondered, as I seldom had before, at how the old assassin had passed his long hours and days up in his isolated tower before I had come to be his apprentice. Then I sniffed disdainfully at that image of him. Long before I had arrived, Chade had been the royal assassin, bearing the King's Justice in the form of quiet work wherever it needed to go. The sizable library of scrolls in his apartments and his endless experiments with poisons and deadly artifice were proof that he had known how to occupy his days. And he had had the welfare of the Farseer reign to give him a purpose in life.

Once, I too had shared that purpose. I had shrugged free of it to have a life of my own. Odd, that in the process I had somehow wrenched myself free of the very life I had thought to have to myself. To gain the freedom to enjoy my life, I had severed all connections with that old life. I had lost contact with all who had loved me and all I had loved.

That wasn't the complete truth, but it suited my mood. An instant later, I realized I was wallowing in self-pity. My last three attempts at a purple ink were drying to brown, though one did have a very nice shade of rose to the brown. I set aside that scrap of paper, after making notes on it as to how I had gotten the color. It would be good ink for botanical illustrations, I thought.

I unfolded my legs from my chair and rose, stretching. The Fool looked up from his work. "Hungry?" I asked him.

He considered a moment. "I could eat. Let me cook. The food you make fills the stomach but does little more than that."

He set aside the figurine he was working on. He saw me glance at it, and covered it, almost jealously. "When I'm finished," he promised, and began a purposeful ransacking of my cupboards. While he was tsking over my lack of any interesting spices, I wandered outside. I crossed the stream, which could have led me gently down to the beach. Idly I walked up the hill, past both horse and pony grazing freely. At the crest of the hill I walked more slowly until I reached my bench. I sat down on it. Only a few steps away, the grassy hill gave way to sudden slate cliffs and the rocky beach below them. Seated on my bench, all I could see was the wide vista of ocean spread out before me. Restlessness walked through my bones again. I thought of my dream of the boy and the hunting cat out in the night and smiled to myself. Run away from it all, the cat had urged the boy, and the thought had all my sympathy.

Yet, years ago, that was what I had done, and this was what it had brought me. A life of peace and self-sufficiency, a life that should have satisfied me; yet, here I sat.

A time later, the Fool joined me. Nighteyes too came at his heels, to lie down at my feet with a martyred sigh. "Is it the Skill-hunger?" the Fool asked with quiet sympathy.

"No," I replied, and almost laughed. The hunger he had unknowingly waked in me yesterday was temporarily crippled by the elfbark I had consumed. I might long to Skill, but right now my mind was numbed to that ability.

"I've put dinner to cook slowly over a little fire, to keep from driving us out of the house. We've plenty of time." He paused, and then asked carefully, "And after you left the Old Blood folk, where did you go?"

I sighed. The wolf was right. Talking to the Fool did help me to think. But perhaps he made me think too much. I looked back through the years and gathered up the threads of my tale.

"Everywhere. When we left there, we had no destination. So we wandered." I stared out across the water. "For four years, we wandered, all through the Six Duchies. I've seen Tilth in winter, when snow but a few inches deep blows across the wide plains but the cold seems to go down to the earth's very bones. I crossed all of Farrow to reach Rippon, and then walked on to the coast. Sometimes I took work as a man, and bought bread, and sometimes the two of us hunted as wolves and ate our meat dripping."

I glanced over at the Fool. He listened, his golden eyes intent on my story. If he judged me, his face gave no sign of it.

"When we reached the coast, we took ship north, although Nighteyes did not enjoy it. I visited Bearns Duchy in the depth of one winter."

"Bearns?" He considered that. "Once, you were promised to Lady Celerity of Bearns Duchy." The question was in his face but not his voice.

"That was not of my will, as you recall. I did not go there to seek out Celerity. But I did glimpse Lady Faith, Duchess of Bearns, as she rode through the streets on her way to Ripplekeep Castle. She did not see me, and if she had, I am sure she would not have recognized the ragged wanderer as Lord FitzChivalry. I hear that Celerity married rich in both love and lands, and is now the Lady of Ice Towers near Ice Town."

"I am glad for her," the Fool said gravely.

"And I. I never loved her, but I admired her spirit, and liked her well enough. I am glad of her good fortune."

"And then?"

"I went to the Near Islands. From there, I wished to make the long crossing to the Out Islands, to see for myself the land of the folk who had raided and made us miserable for so long, but the wolf refused to even consider such a long sea journey.

"So we returned to the mainland, and traveled south. We went mostly by foot though we took ship past Buckkeep and did not pause there. We journeyed down the coast of Rippon and Shoaks, and on beyond the Six Duchies. I didn't like Chalced. We took ship from there just to get away from it."

"How far did you go?" the Fool prompted when I fell silent.

I felt my mouth twist in a grin as I bragged, "All the way to Bingtown."

"Did you?" His interest heightened. "And what did you think of it?"

"Lively. Prosperous. It put me in mind of Tradeford. The elegant people and their ornate houses, with glass in every window. They sell books in street booths there, and in one street of their market, every shop has its own sort of magic. Just to walk down that way dizzied me. I could not tell you what kind of magic it was, but it pressed against my senses, giddying me like too-strong perfume . . ." I shook my head. "I felt like a backward foreigner, and no doubt so they thought me, in my rough clothes with a wolf at my side. Yet, despite all I saw there, the city couldn't live up to the legend. What did we used to say? That if a man could imagine a thing, he could find it for sale in Bingtown. Well, I saw much there that was far beyond my imagining, but that didn't mean it was something I'd want to buy. I saw great ugliness there, too. Slaves coming off a ship, with great cankers on their ankles from the chains. We saw one of their talking ships, too. I had always thought them just a tale." I grew silent for a moment, wondering how to convey what Nighteyes and I had sensed about that grim magic. "It wasn't a magic I'd ever be comfortable around," I said at last.

The sheer humanity of the city had overwhelmed the wolf, and he was happy to leave as soon as I suggested it. I felt smaller after my visit there. I appreciated anew the wildness and isolation of Buck's coast, and the rough militancy of Buckkeep. I had once thought Buckkeep the heart of all civilization, but in Bingtown they spoke of us as barbaric and rude. The comments I overheard stung, and yet I could not deny them. I left Bingtown a humbled man, resolved to add to my education and better discover the true width of the world. I shook my head at that recollection. Had I ever lived up to my resolve?

"We didn't have the money for ship passage, even if Nighteyes could have faced it. We decided to journey up the coast on foot."

The Fool turned an incredulous face to me. "But you can't do that!"

"That's what everyone warned us. I thought it was city talk, a warning from folk who had never traveled hard and rough. But they were right."

Against all counsel, we attempted to travel by foot up the coastline. In the wild lands outside of Bingtown, we found strangeness that near surpassed what we had discovered beyond the Mountain Kingdom. Well is that coast called the Cursed Shores. I was tormented by half-formed dreams, and sometimes my conscious imaginings were giddy and threatening. It distressed the wolf that I walked on the edges of madness. I can offer no reason for this. I suffered no fevers or any of the other symptoms of the illnesses that can unseat a man's mind, yet I was not myself as we passed through that rough and inhospitable country. Vivid dreams of Verity and our dragons came back to haunt me. Even awake, I tormented myself endlessly with the foolishness of past decisions, and thought often of ending my own life. Only the companionship of the wolf kept me from such an act. Looking back, I recall, not days and nights, but a succession of lucid and disturbing dreams. Not since I had first traveled on the Skill-road had I suffered such a contortion of my own thoughts. It is not an experience I would willingly repeat.

Never, before or since, had I seen a stretch of coast as devoid of humanity. Even the animals that lived there rang sharp and odd against my Wit-sense. The physical aspects of this coast were as foreign to us as the savor of it. There were bogs that steamed and stank and burned our nostrils, and lush marshes where all the plant life seemed twisted and deformed despite its rank and luxuriant growth. We reached the Rain River, which the folk of Bingtown call the Rain Wild River. I cannot say what distorted whim persuaded me to follow it inland, but I attempted it. The swampy shores, rank growth, and strange dreams of the place soon turned us back. Something in the soil ate at Nighteyes' pads and weakened the tough leather boots I wore until they were little more than tatters. We admitted ourselves defeated, but then added a greater error to our wayward quest when we cut young trees to fashion a raft. Nighteyes' nose had warned us against drinking any of the river water, but I had not fully appreciated what a danger it presented to us. Our makeshift raft barely lasted to carry us back to the mouth of the river, and we both incurred ulcerating sores from the touch of the water. We were relieved to get back to good honest saltwater. Despite the sting of it, it proved most healing to our sores.

Although Chalced has long claimed rightful domain of the land up to the Rain River, and has frequently asserted that Bingtown too lies within its reign, we saw no signs of any settlements on that coast. Nighteyes and I traveled a long and inhospitable way north. Three days past the Rain River, we seemed to leave the strangeness behind, but we journeyed another ten days before we encountered a human settlement. By then, regular washing in brine had healed many of our sores, and my thoughts seemed more my own, but we presented the aspect of a weary beggar and his mangy dog. Folk were not welcoming to us.

My footsore journey north through Chalced persuaded me that folk there are the most inimical in the world. I enjoyed Chalced fully as much as Burrich had led me to believe I would. Even its magnificent cities could not move me. The wonders of its architecture and the heights of its civilization are built on a foundation of human misery. The reality of widespread slavery appalled me.

I paused in my tale to glance at the freedom earring that hung from the Fool's ear. It had been Burrich's grandmother's hard-won prize, the mark of a slave who had won freedom. The Fool lifted a hand to touch it with a finger. It hung next to several others carved of wood, and its silver network caught the eye.

"Burrich," the Fool said quietly. "And Molly. I ask you directly this time. Did you ever seek them out?"

I hung my head for a moment. "Yes," I admitted after a time. "I did. It is odd you should ask now, for it was as I crossed Chalced that I was suddenly seized with the urge to see them."

One evening as we camped well away from the road, I felt my sleep seized by a powerful dream. Perhaps the images came to me because in some corner of her heart, Molly still kept a place for me. Yet I did not dream of Molly as a lover dreams of his beloved. I dreamed of myself, I thought, small and hot and deathly ill. It was a black dream, a dream all of sensations without images. I lay curled tight against Burrich's chest, and his presence and smell were the only comforts I knew in my misery. Then unbearably cool hands touched my fevered skin. They tried to lift me away, but I wiggled and cried out, clinging to him. Burrich's strong arm closed around me again. "Leave her be," he commanded hoarsely.

I heard Molly's voice from a distance, wavering and distorted. "Burrich, you're as sick as she is. You can't take care of her. Let me have her while you rest."

"No. Leave her beside me. You take care of Chiv and yourself."

"Your son is fine. Neither of us is ill. Only you and Nettle. Let me take her, Burrich."

"No," he groaned. His hand settled on me protectively. "This is how the Blood Plague began, when I was a boy. It killed everyone I loved. Molly. I couldn't bear it if you took her away from me and she died. Please. Leave her beside me."

"So you can die together?" she demanded, her weary voice going shrill.

There was terrible resignation in his voice. "If we must. Death is colder when it finds you alone. I will hold her to the last."

He was not rational, and I felt both Molly's anger and her fear for him. She brought him water, and I fussed when she half-sat him up to drink it. I tried to drink from the cup she held to my mouth, but my lips were cracked and sore, my head hurt too badly, and the light was too bright. When I pushed it away, the water slopped on my chest, icy cold, and I shrieked and began to wail. "Nettle, Nettle, hush," she bade me, but her hands were cold when she touched me. I wanted nothing of my mother just then, and knew an echo of Nettle's jealousy that another child claimed the throne of Molly's lap now. I clutched at Burrich's shirt and he held me close again and hummed softly in his deep voice. I pushed my face against him where the light could not touch my eyes, and tried to sleep.

I tried so desperately to sleep that I pushed myself into wakefulness. I opened my eyes to my breath rasping in and out of my lungs. Sweat cloaked me, but I could not forget the tightness of my hot, dry skin in the Skill-dream. I had wrapped my cloak about me when I lay down to sleep; now I fought clear of its confines. We had chosen to sleep away the deep of the night on a creek bank; I staggered to the water and drank deeply. When I lifted my face from the water, I found the wolf sitting very straight and watching me. His tail neatly wrapped all four of his feet.

"He already knew I had to go to them. We set out that night."

"And you knew where to go, to find them?"

I shook my head. "No. I knew nothing, other than that when they first left Buckkeep, they had settled near a town called Capelin Beach. And I knew the, well, the 'feel' of where they lived then. With no more than that, we set out.

"After years of wandering, it was odd to have a destination, and especially to hurry toward it. I did not think about what we did, or how foolish it was. A part of me admitted it was senseless. We were too far away. I'd never get there in time. By the time I arrived, they would be either dead or recovered. Yet having begun that journey, I could not deviate from it. After years of fleeing any who might recognize me, I was suddenly willing to hurl myself back into their lives again? I refused to consider any of it. I simply went."

The Fool nodded sympathetically to my account. I feared he guessed far more than I willingly told him.

After years of denying and refusing the lures of the Skill, I immersed myself in it. The addiction clutched at me and I embraced it in return. It was disconcerting to have it come back upon me with such force. But I did not fight it. Despite the blinding headaches that still followed my efforts, I reached toward Molly and Burrich almost every evening. The results were not encouraging. There is nothing like the heady rush of two Skill-trained minds meeting. But Skill-seeing is another matter entirely. I had never been instructed in that application of the Skill; I had only the knowledge I had gained by groping. My father had sealed off Burrich to the Skill, lest anyone try to use his friend against him. Molly had no aptitude for it that I knew. In Skill-seeing them, there could be no true connection of minds, but only the frustration of watching them, unable to make them aware of me. I soon found that I could not achieve even that reliably. Disused, my abilities had rusted. Even a short effort left me exhausted and debilitated by pain, and yet I could not resist trying. I strove for those brief connections and mined them for information. A glimpse of hills behind their home, the smell of the sea, black-faced sheep pastured on a distant hill—I treasured every hint of their surroundings, and hoped they would be enough to guide me to them. I could not control my seeing. Often I found myself watching the homeliest of tasks, the daily labor of a tub of laundry to be washed and hung, herbs to be harvested and dried, and yes, beehives to tend. Glimpses of a baby Molly called Chiv whose face reflected Burrich's features cut me with both jealousy and wonder.

Eventually I found a village called Capelin Beach. I found the deserted cottage where my daughter had been born. Other folk had lived here since then; no recognizable trace of them remained to my eyes, but the wolf's nose was keener. Nevertheless, Molly and Burrich were long gone from there, and I knew not where. I dared not ask direct questions in the village, for I did not want anyone to bear word to Burrich or Molly that someone was looking for them. Months had passed in my journeying. In every village I passed, I saw signs of new graves. Whatever the sickness had been, it had spread wide and taken many with it. In none of my visions had I seen Nettle; had it carried her off, as well? I spiraled out from Capelin Beach, visiting inns

and taverns in nearby villages. I became a slightly daft traveler, obsessed with beekeeping and professing to know all
there was to know on the topic. I started arguments so others would correct me and speak of beekeepers they had
known. Yet all my efforts to hear the slightest rumor of
Molly were fruitless until late one afternoon I followed a
narrow road to the crest of the hill, and suddenly recognized a stand of oak trees.

All my courage vanished in that instant. I left the road
and skulked through the forested hills that flanked it. The
wolf came with me, unquestioning, not even letting his
thoughts intrude on mine as I stalked my old life. By early
evening, we were on a hillside looking down on their cottage. It was a tidy and prosperous stead, with chickens
scratching in the side yard and three straw hives in the
meadow behind it. There was a well-tended vegetable garden. Behind the cottage were a barn, obviously a newer
structure, and several small paddocks built of skinned logs. I
smelled horse. Burrich had done well for them. I sat in the
dark and watched the single window glow yellow with candlelight, and then wink to blackness. The wolf hunted
alone that night as I kept my vigil. I could not approach and
I could not leave. I was caught where I was, a leaf on the
edge of their eddy. I suddenly understood all the legends of
ghosts doomed to forever haunt some spot. No matter how
far I roamed, some part of me would always be chained here.

As dawn broke, Burrich emerged from the cottage
door. His limp was more pronounced than I recalled it, as
was the streak of white in his hair. He lifted his face to the
dawning day and took a great breath, and for one wolfish
instant, I feared he would scent me there. But he only
walked to the well and drew up a bucket of water. He carried it inside, then returned a moment later to throw some
grain to the chickens. The smoke of an awakened fire rose
from the chimney. So. Molly was up and about also. Burrich
went out to the barn. As clear as if I were walking beside

him, I knew his routine. After he had checked every animal, he would come outside. He did, and drew water, packing bucket after bucket into the barn.

My words choked me for an instant. Then I laughed aloud. My eyes swam with tears but I ignored them. "I swear, Fool, that is when I came closest to going down to him. It seemed as unnatural a thing as I had ever done, to watch Burrich work and not toil alongside him."

The Fool nodded, silent and rapt beside me.

"When he came out, he was leading a roan stallion. It astonished me. 'Buckkeep's best,' shouted every line of his body. His spirit was in the arch of his neck, his power in his shoulders and haunches. My heart swelled in me just to see such a horse, and to know he was in Burrich's keeping rejoiced me. He turned the horse loose in a paddock, and then hauled yet more water to the trough there.

"When he next led Ruddy out, much of the mystery was cleared for me. I did not know, then, that Starling had hunted him down and seen to it that both his horse and Sooty's colt were given over to him. It was just good to see man and horse together again. Ruddy looked to have settled into good-natured stability; even so, Burrich did not paddock him next to the other stud, but put him as far away as possible. He hauled more water for Ruddy, then gave him a friendly thump and went back into the cottage.

"Then Molly came out."

I took another breath and held it. I stared out at the ocean, but that was not what I saw. The image of she who had been my woman moved before my eyes. Her dark hair, once wild and blowing to the wind, was braided and pinned sedately to her head, a matron's crown. A little boy toddled unsteadily after her. Basket on her arm, she moved with placid grace toward the garden. Her white apron draped her swelling pregnancy. The swift and slender girl was gone, but I found this woman no less attractive. My heart yearned after her and all she represented: the cozy hearth and the settled home, the companionship of the years to come as she filled her man's home with children and warmth.

"I whispered her name. It was so strange. She lifted her head suddenly, and for one sharp moment I thought she was aware of me. But instead of looking up to the hill, she laughed aloud, and exclaimed, 'Chivalry, no! Not good to eat.' She stooped slightly, to pull a handful of pea flowers from the child's mouth. She lifted him, and I saw the effort it cost her. She called back to the cottage, 'My love, come fetch your son before he pulls the whole garden up. Tell Nettle to come and pull some turnips for me.'

"Then I heard Burrich call back, 'A moment!' An instant later, he stood in the doorway. He called over his shoulder, 'We'll finish the washing-up later. Come help your mother.' I watched him cross the yard in a few strides and snatch up his son. He swung him high, and the child gave a whoop of delight as Burrich landed him on his shoulder. Molly set a hand atop her belly and laughed with them, looking up at them both with delight in her eyes."

I stopped speaking. I could no longer see the ocean. Tears blinded me like a fog.

I felt the Fool's hand on my shoulder. "You never went down to them, did you?"

I shook my head mutely.

I had fled. I had fled the sudden gnawing envy I felt, and I fled lest I glimpse my own child and have to go to her. There was no place down there for me, not even on the edges of their world. I knew that. I had known it since first I knew they would marry. If I walked down to that door, I would carry destruction and misery with me.

I am no better than any other man. There was bitterness in me, and anger at both of them, and the stark awareness of how fate had betrayed us all. I could not blame them for turning to each other. Neither did I blame myself for the anguish I felt that by that act, they had excluded me forever from their lives. It was done and over, and regrets were useless. The dead, I told myself, have no right to regret. The most I can claim for myself is that I did walk away. I did not let my pain poison their happiness, or compromise my daughter's home. That much strength, I found.

I drew a long breath and found my voice again. "And that is the end of my tale, Fool. Next winter caught us here. We found this hut and settled into it. And here we have been ever since." I blew out a breath and thought over my own words. Suddenly none of it seemed admirable.

His next words rattled me. "And your other child?" he asked quietly.

"What?"

"Dutiful. Have you seen him? Is not he your son, just as much as Nettle is your daughter?"

"I . . . no. No, he is not. And I have never seen him. He is Kettricken's son and Verity's heir. So Kettricken recalls it, I am sure." I felt myself reddening, embarrassed that the Fool had brought this up. I set my hand to his shoulder. "My friend, only you and I know of how Verity used me . . . my body. When he asked my permission, I misunderstood his request. I myself have no memory of how Dutiful was conceived. You must recall; I was with you, trapped in Verity's misused flesh. My King did what he did to get himself an heir. I do not begrudge it, but neither do I wish to remember it."

"Starling does not know? Nor even Kettricken?"

"Starling slept that night. I am sure that if she even suspected, she would have spoken of it by now. A minstrel could not leave such a song unsung, however unwise it might be. As for Kettricken, well, Verity burned with the Skill like a bonfire. She saw only her King in her bed that night. I am certain that if it had been otherwise . . ." I sighed suddenly and admitted, "I feel shamed to have been a party to that deception. I know it is not my place to question Verity's will in this, but still . . ." My words trickled away. Not even to the Fool could I admit the curiosity I felt about Dutiful. A son, mine and not mine. And as my father had chosen with me, so had I with him. To not know him, for the sake of protecting him.

The Fool set his hand on top of mine and squeezed it firmly. "I have spoken of this to no one. Nor shall I." He took a deep breath. "So. Then you came to this place, to settle yourself in peace. That is truly the end of your tale?"

It was. Since the last time I had bidden the Fool farewell, I had spent most of my days either running or hiding. This cottage was my selfish retreat. I said as much.

"I doubt that Hap would see it that way," he returned mildly. "And most folks would find saving the world once in their lifetime a sufficient credit and would not think to do more than that. Still, as your heart seems set on it, I will do all I can to drag you through it again." He quirked an eyebrow at me invitingly.

I laughed, but not easily. "I don't need to be a hero, Fool. I'd settle for feeling that what I did every day had significance to someone besides myself."

He leaned back on my bench and considered me gravely for a moment. Then he shrugged one shoulder. "That's easily done, then. Once Hap is settled in his apprenticeship, come find me at Buckkeep. I promise, you'll be significant."

"Or dead, if I'm recognized. Have not you heard how strong feelings run against the Witted these days?"

"No. I had not. But it does not surprise me, no, not at all. But recognized? You spoke of that worry before, but in a different light. I find myself forced to agree with Starling. I think few would remark you. You look very little like the FitzChivalry Farseer that folk would recall from fifteen years ago. Your face bears the tracks of the Farseer bloodline, if one knows to look for them, but the court is an inbred place. Many a noble carries a trace of that same heritage. Who would a chance beholder compare you to, a faded portrait in a darkened hall? You are the only grown man of your line still alive. Shrewd wasted away years ago, your father retired to Withywoods before he was killed, and Verity was an old man before his time. I know who you are, and hence I see the resemblance. I do not think you are in danger from the casual glance of a Buckkeep courtier." He paused, then asked me earnestly, "So? I will see you in Buckkeep before snow flies?"

"Perhaps," I hedged. I doubted it, but knew better than to waste breath arguing with the Fool.

"I shall," he decided resolutely. Then he clapped me on the shoulder. "Let's go back. Supper should be ready. And I want to finish my carving."

chapter X

A SWORD AND A
SUMMONS

*Perhaps every kingdom has its tales of a secret and powerful
protector, one that will rise to the land's defense if the need be
great enough and the entreaty sincere enough. In the Out
Islands, they speak of Icefyre, a creature who dwells deep in the
heart of the glacier that cloaks the heart of Island Aslevjal. They
swear that when earthquakes shake their island home, it is
Icefyre rolling restlessly in his chill dreams deep within his ice-
bound lair. The Six Duchies legends always referred to the
Elderlings, an ancient and powerful race who dwelt somewhere
beyond the Mountain Kingdom and were our allies in times of
old. Only a king as desperate as King-in-Waiting Verity Farseer
would have given such legends not only credence, but enough
importance that he left his legacy in the care of his ailing father
and foreign Queen while he made a quest to seek the aid of the
Elderlings. Perhaps it was that desperate faith that gave him the
power not only to wake the Elderling-carved stone dragons and
rally them to the Six Duchies' aid, but also to carve for himself
a dragon body and lead them to defend his land.*

The Fool stayed on, but in the days that followed, he stu-
diously avoided any serious topics or tasks. I fear I followed
his example. Telling him of my quiet years seemed to settle
those old ghosts. I should have been content to slip back
into my old routines but instead a different sort of restlessness itched. A changing time, and a time to change.
Changer. The Catalyst. The words and the thoughts that
went with them wound through my days and tangled my
dreams at night. I was no longer tormented by my past so

much as taunted by the future. Looking back over what I had made of my own youth, I suddenly found myself much concerned for how Hap would spend his years. It suddenly seemed to me that I had wasted all the years when I should have been preparing the lad to face a life on his own. He was a good-hearted young man, and I had no qualms about his character. My worry was that I had given him only the most basic knowledge of making his way in the world. He had no specialized skills to build on. He knew all that he needed to know to live in an isolated cottage and farm and hunt for his basic needs. But it was the wide world I was sending him into; how would he make his way there? The need to apprentice him well began to keep me awake at night.

If the Fool was aware of this, he gave no sign of it. His busy tools wandered through my cabin, sending vinework crawling across my mantelpiece. Lizards peered down from the door lintel. Odd little faces leered at me from the corners of cupboard doors and the edge of the porch steps. If it was made of wood, it was not safe from his sharp tools and clever fingers. The activities of the water sprites on my rain barrel would have made a guardsman blush.

I chose quiet work for myself as well, and toiled indoors as much as out despite the fine weather. Part of it was that I felt I needed a thoughtful time, but the greater share was that the wolf was slow to recover his strength. I knew that my watching over him would not hasten his healing, but I could not chase away my anxiety for him. When I reached for him with the Wit, there was a somber quality to his silence, most unlike my old companion. Sometimes I would look up from my work to find him watching me, his deep eyes pensive. I did not ask him what he was thinking; if he had wanted to share it, his mind would have been accessible to mine.

Gradually, he regained his old activities, but some of the spring had gone out of him. He moved with a care for his body, never challenging himself. He did not follow me about my chores, but lay on the porch and watched my comings and goings. We hunted together still in the evening, but we went more slowly, both pretending to be hampered by the Fool. Nighteyes was as often content to point out the game and wait for my arrow rather than spring to the kill himself. These changes troubled me, but I did my best to keep my concerns to myself. All he needed was time to heal, I told myself, and recalled that the hot days of summer had never been his best time. When autumn came, he would recover his old vigor.

The three of us were settling into a comfortable routine. There were tales and stories in the evening, an accounting of the lesser events in our lives. Eventually we ran out of brandy, but the talk still flowed as smooth and warming as the liquor had. I told the Fool what Hap had seen at Hardin's Spit, and of the talk about the Witted in the market. I shared, too, Starling's account of the minstrels at Springfest, and Chade's assessment of Prince Dutiful and what he had asked of me. All these stories, the Fool seemed to take into himself as a weaver takes up divergent threads to create from them a tapestry.

We tried the rooster feathers in the crown one evening, but the shafts of the feathers were too thin for the sockets, so the feathers sprawled in all directions. We both knew without speaking that they were completely wrong. Another evening, the Fool set out the crown on my table, and selected brushes and inks from my stores. I took a chair to one side to watch him. He arranged all carefully before him, dipped a brush in blue ink, and then paused, thinking. We sat still and silent so long that I became aware of the sounds of the fire burning. Then he set down the brush. "No," he said quietly. "It feels wrong. Not yet." He rewrapped the crown and put it back in his pack. Then one evening, while I was still wiping tears of laughter from my eyes at the end of a ribald song, the Fool set aside his harp and announced, "I must leave tomorrow."

"No!" I protested in disbelief at his abruptness, and then, "Why?"

"Oh, you know," he replied airily. "It is the life of a White Prophet. I must be about predicting the future, saving the world—all those minor chores. Besides, you've run out of furniture for me to carve on."

"No, really," I protested. "Cannot you stay at least a few more days? At least, stay until Hap returns. Meet the boy."

He sighed. "Actually, I have stayed far longer than I should. Especially since you insist you cannot go with me when I leave. Unless?" He sat up hopefully. "You have changed your mind?"

I shook my head. "You know I have not. I can scarcely go off and abandon my home. I must be here when Hap comes back."

"Ah, yes." He sagged back into his chair. "His apprenticeship. And you do have chickens to care for."

The mockery in his voice stung. "It may not seem much of a life to you, but it's mine," I pointed out sourly.

He grinned at having needled me. "I am not Starling, my dear. I do not disparage any man's life. Consider my own, and tell me what height I look down from. No. I go to my own tasks, as dull as they must seem to one who has a whole flock of chickens to tend and rows of beans to hoe. My own tasks are just as weighty. I've a flock of rumors to share with Chade, and rows of new acquaintances to cultivate at Buckkeep."

I felt a twinge of envy. "I expect they will all be glad to see you again."

He shrugged. "Some, I suppose. Others were just as glad to see me go. And most will not recall me at all. Most, verging on all, if I am clever." He rose abruptly. "I wish I could just stay here," he confessed quietly. "I wish I could believe, as you seem to, that my life is my own to dispose of. Unfortunately, I know that is not true for either of us." He walked to the open door and looked out into the warm summer evening. He took a breath as if to speak, then sighed it out. A time longer he stared. Then he squared his shoulders as if making a resolve and turned back to me. There was a grim smile on his face. "No, it is best I leave tomorrow. You'll follow me soon enough."

"Don't count on that," I warned him.

"Ah, but I must," he rejoined. "The times demand it. Of both of us."

"Oh, let someone else save the world this time. Surely there is another White Prophet somewhere." I spoke lightly, intending my words as jest. The Fool's eyes widened at them, and I heard a shudder as he drew breath.

"Do not even mention that future. It bodes ill for me that there is even the seed of that thought in your mind. For truly, there is another who would love to claim the mantle of the White Prophet, and set the world into the course that she envisions. From the beginning, I have struggled against her pull. Yet in this turning of the world, her strength waxes. Now you know what I hesitated to speak of more openly. I shall *need* your strength, my friend. The two of us, together, might be enough. After all, sometimes all it takes is a small stone in a rut for a wheel to lurch out of its track."

"Mm. It does not sound like a good experience for the stone, however."

He turned his eyes to mine. Where once they had been pale, they now glowed golden and the lamplight danced in them. There was both warmth and weariness in his voice. "Oh, never fear, you shall survive it. For I know you must. And hence I bend all my strength toward that goal. That you will live."

I feigned dismay. "And you tell me not to fear?"

He nodded, and his face was too solemn. I sought to turn the talk. "Who is this woman you speak of? Do I know her?"

He came back into the room and sat down once more at the table. "No, you do not know her. But I knew her, of old. Or rather I should say, I knew of her, though she was a woman grown and gone while I was just a child . . ." He glanced back at me. "A long time ago, I told you something of myself. Do you remember?" He did not wait for an answer. "I was born far, far to the south, of ordinary folk. As much as any folk are truly ordinary . . . I had a loving mother, and my fathers were two brothers, as is the custom of that place. But from the moment I emerged from my mother's womb, it was plain that the ancient lineage had spoken in me. In some distant past, a White had mingled his blood with my family lines, and I was born to take up the tasks of that ancient folk.

"As much as my parents loved and cherished me, they knew it was not my destiny to stay in their home, nor to be raised in any of their trades. Instead, I was sent away to a place where I could be educated and prepared for my fate. They treated me well there, and more than well. They too, in their own way, cherished me. Each morning I was questioned as to what I had dreamed, and all I could recall was written down for wise men to ponder. As I grew older and waking dreams overtook me, I was taught the art of the quill, that I might record my visions myself, for no hand is so clear as the one that belongs to the eye that has seen." He laughed self-deprecatingly and shook his head. "Such a way to raise a child! My slightest utterances were cherished as wisdom. But despite my blood, I was no better than any other child. I made mischief where I would, telling wild tales of flying boars and shadows that carried royal bloodlines. Each wild story I told was larger than the last, and yet I discovered a strange thing. No matter how I might try to foil my tongue, truth always hid in my utterances."

He cast his glance briefly toward me, as if expecting me to disagree. I kept silence.

He looked down. "I suppose I have only myself to blame that when finally the biggest truth of all blossomed in me and would not be denied, no one would believe me. The day I proclaimed myself the White Prophet that this age had awaited, my masters shushed me. 'Calm your wild ambitions,' they told me. As if anyone would ever desire to take on such a destiny! Another, they told me, already wore that mantle. She had gone forth before me, to shape the future of the world as her visions prompted her. To each age, there is only one White Prophet. All know that. Even I knew that was so. So what was I? I demanded of them. And they could not answer what I was, yet they were sure of what I was not. I was not the White Prophet. Her they had already prepared and sent forth."

He took a breath and fell silent for what seemed a long time. Then he shrugged.

"I knew they were wrong. I knew the trueness of their error as deeply as I knew what I myself was. They tried to make me content with my life there. I do not think they ever dreamed I would defy them. But I did. I ran away. And I came north, through ways and times I cannot even describe to you. Yet north and north I made my way, until I came to the court of King Shrewd Farseer. To him I sold myself, in much the same way you did. My loyalty for his protection. And scarce a season had I been there before the rumor of your coming rattled that court. A bastard. A child unexpected, a Farseer unacknowledged. Oh, so surprised they all were. All save me. For I had already dreamed your face and I knew I must find you, even though everyone had assured me that you did not and could not exist."

He leaned over suddenly and set his gloved hand to my wrist. He gripped my wrist for only an instant, and our skin did not touch, but in that moment I felt a flash of binding. I can describe it no other way. It was not the Skill; it was not the Wit. It was not magic at all, as I know magic. It was like that moment of double recognition that sometimes overtakes one in a strange place. I had the sense that we had sat together like this, spoken these words before, and that each time we had done so, the words had been sealed with that brief touch. I glanced away from him, only to encounter the wolf's dark eyes burning into mine.

I cleared my throat and tried to find a different subject. "You said you knew her. Has she a name, then?"

"Not one you would have ever heard. Yet you have

heard of her. Recall that during the Red Ship War, we knew their leader only as Kebal Rawbread?"

I bobbed my head in agreement. He had been a tribal leader of the Outislanders, one who had risen to sudden, bloody prominence, and just as swiftly fallen from power with the waking of our dragons. Some tales said Verity's dragon had devoured him, others that he had drowned.

"Did you ever hear that he had someone who advised him? A Pale Woman?"

The words rang oddly familiar in my mind. I frowned, trying to recall them. Yes. There had been a rumor, but no more than that. Again I nodded.

"Well." The Fool leaned back. He spoke almost lightly. "That was she. And I will tell you one more thing. As surely as she believes that she is the White Prophet, so she believes that Kebal Rawbread is her Catalyst."

"Her one who comes to enable others to be heroes?"

He shook his head. "Not that one. Her Catalyst comes to dismantle heroes. To enable men to be less than what they should be. For where I would build, she would destroy. Where I would unite, she would divide." He shook his head. "She believes all must end before it can begin anew."

I waited for him to balance his statement, but he fell silent. Finally I nudged him toward it. "And what do you believe?"

A slow smile spread over his face. "I believe in you. You are my new beginning."

I could think of nothing to say to that, and a stillness grew up in the room.

He reached slowly up to his ear. "I've been wearing this since the last time I left you. But I think I should give it back to you now. Where I go, I cannot wear it. It is too unique. Folk might remember seeing an earring like this on you. Or on Burrich. Or on your father. It might tickle memories I wish to leave undisturbed."

I watched him struggle with the catch. The earring was a silver net with a blue gemstone captured inside it. Burrich had given it to my father. I had been next to wear it. In my turn, I had entrusted it to the Fool, bidding him give it to Molly after my death as a sign I had never forgotten her. In his wisdom, he had kept it. And now?

"Wait," I bade him suddenly, and then, "Don't."

He looked at me, mystified.

"Disguise it if you must. But wear it. Please."

Slowly he lowered his hands. "Are you sure?" he asked incredulously.

"Yes," I said, and I was.

❧   ❧   ❧

When I rose the next morning, I found the Fool up and washed and dressed before me. His pack waited on the table. Glancing about the room, I saw none of his possessions. Once more he was attired nobly. His garb contrasted oddly with the humble task of stirring the porridge.

"You are leaving, then?" I asked stupidly.

"Right after we eat," he said quietly.

We should go with him.

It was the most direct thought the wolf had shared with me in days. It startled me, and I looked toward him, as did the Fool. "But what of Hap?" I asked him.

Nighteyes only looked at me in reply, as if I should already know his answer. I did not. "I have to stay here," I said to both of them. Neither one looked convinced. It made me feel sedate and staid to refuse them both, and I did not care for either sensation. "I have responsibilities here," I said, almost angrily. "I cannot simply go off and allow the boy to come back to an empty home."

"No, you cannot," the Fool agreed quickly, yet even his agreement stung, as if he said it only to mollify me. I found myself suddenly in a surly mood. Breakfast was grim and when we rose from the table, I suddenly hated the sticky bowls and porridge pot. The reminders of my daily, mundane chores suddenly seemed intolerable.

"I'll saddle your horse," I told the Fool sullenly. "No sense in getting your fine clothes dirty."

He said nothing as I rose abruptly from the table and went out of the door.

Malta seemed to sense the excitement of the journey to come, for she was restive, though not difficult. I found myself taking my time with her, so that when she was ready, her coat gleamed as did her tack. I almost soothed myself, but as I led her out, I saw the Fool standing by the porch, one hand on Nighteyes' back. Discontent washed through me again, and childishly I blamed him for it. If he had not come to see me, I would never have recalled how much I missed him. I would have continued to pine for the past, but I would not have begun to long for a future.

I felt soured and old as he came to embrace me. Knowing there was nothing admirable about my attitude did nothing to improve it. I stood stiffly in his farewell clasp, barely returning it. I thought he would tolerate it, but when his mouth was by my ear, he muttered mawkishly, "Farewell, Beloved."

Despite my irritation, I had to smile. I gave him a hug and released him. "Go safely, Fool," I said gruffly.

"And you," he replied gravely as he swung onto the saddle. I stared up at him. The aristocratic young man on the horse bore no resemblance to the Fool I had known as a lad. Only when his gaze met mine did I see my old friend there. For a time we stood looking at one another, not speaking. Then, with a touch of the rein and a shift of his weight, he wheeled his horse. With a toss of her head, Malta asked for a free rein. He gave it to her, and she sprang forward eagerly into a canter. Her silky tail floated on the wind of her passage like a pennant. I watched him go, and even when he was out of sight, I watched the dust hanging in the lane.

When I finally went back into the cabin, I found he had cleaned all the dishes and the pot and put them away. In the center of my table, where his pack had concealed it, a

Farseer buck was graven deep, his antlers lowered to charge. I ran my fingers over the carved figure and my heart sank in me. "What do you want of me?" I asked of the stillness.

🐎 🐎 🐎

Days followed that one, and time passed for me, but not easily. Each day seemed possessed of a dull sameness, and the evenings stretched endless before me. There was work to fill the time, and I did it, but I also marked that work only seemed to beget more work. A meal cooked meant only dishes to clean, and a seed planted only meant weeding and watering in the days to follow. Satisfaction in my simple life seemed to elude me.

I missed the Fool, and realized that all those years I had missed him as well. It was like an old injury wakened to new complaint. The wolf was no help in enduring it. A deep thoughtfulness had come upon him, and evenings often found us trapped in our individual ponderings. Once, as I sat mending a shirt by candlelight, Nighteyes came to me and rested his head on my knee with a sigh. I reached down to fondle his ears and then scratch behind them. "Are you all right?" I asked him.

It would not be good for you to be alone. I'm glad the Scentless One returned to us. I'm glad that you know where to find him.

Then, with a groan, he lifted his chin from my knee and went to curl on the cool earth by the front porch.

The final heat of summer closed down on us like a smothering blanket. I sweltered as I hauled water for the garden twice a day. The chickens stopped laying. All seemed too hot and too dull to survive it. Then, in the midst of my discontent, Hap returned. I had not expected to see him again until the month of full harvest was over, but one evening, Nighteyes lifted his head abruptly. He arose stiffly and went to the door, to stare down the lane.

After a moment I set aside the knife I was sharpening and went to stand beside him. "What is it?" I asked him.

The boy returns.

So soon? But as I framed the thought, I knew it was not soon at all. The months he had spent with Starling had devoured the spring. He'd shared high summer with me, but been gone all the month of early harvest and part of full harvest. Only a moon and a half had passed, and yet it still seemed horribly long. I caught a glimpse of a figure at the far end of the lane. Both Nighteyes and I hastened to meet him. When he saw us coming, he broke into a weary trot to meet us halfway. When I caught him in my arms in a hug, I knew at once that he had grown taller and lost weight. And when I let him go and held him at arm's length to look at him, I saw both shame and defeat in his eyes. "Welcome home," I told him, but he only gave a rueful shrug.

"I've come home with my tail between my legs," he confessed, and then dropped down to hug Nighteyes. "He's gone all to bone!" Hap exclaimed in dismay.

"He was sick for a while, but he's on the mend now," I told him. I tried to make my voice hearty and ignore the jolt of worry I felt. "The same could be said of you," I added. "There's meat on the platter and bread on the board. Come eat, and then you can tell us how you fared out in the wide world."

"I can tell you now as we go, in few words," he returned as we trudged back to the cabin. His voice was deep as a man's and the bitterness was a man's, also. "Not well. The harvest was good, but wherever I went, I was last hired, for always they wanted to hire their cousin first, or their cousin's friends. Always I was the stranger, put to the dirtiest and heaviest of the labor. I worked like a man, Tom, but they paid me like a mouse, with crumbs and cut coins. And they were suspicious of me, too. They didn't want me sleeping within their barns, no, nor talking to their daughters. And between jobs, well, I had to eat, and all cost far more than I thought it should. I've come home with only a handful more of coins than when I left. I was a fool to leave. I would have done as well to stay home and sell chickens and salt fish."

The hard words rattled out of him. I said nothing, but let him get all of them said. By then we were at the door. He doused his head in the water barrel I had filled for the garden while I went inside to set out food on the table. He came into the cabin, and as he glanced around, I knew without his saying it that it had grown smaller in his eyes. "It's good to be home," he said. And in the next breath, he went on, "But I don't know what I'm going to do for an apprentice fee. Hire out another year, I suppose. But by then, some might think me too old to learn well. Already one man I met on the road told me that he had never met a master craftsman who hadn't begun his training before he was twelve. Is that honey?"

"It is." I put the pot on the table with the bread and the cold meat, and Hap fell to as if he had not eaten for days. I made tea for us, and then sat across the table from my boy, watching him eat. Ravenous as he was, he still fed bits of his meat to the wolf beside his chair. And Nighteyes ate, not with appetite, but both to please the boy and for the sake of sharing meat with a pack member. When the fowl was down to bones with not even enough meat left to make soup, he sat back in his chair with a sigh. Then he leaned forward abruptly, his eager fingers tracing the charging buck on the tabletop. "This is beautiful! When did you learn to carve like this?"

"I didn't. An old friend came by and spent part of his visit decorating the cabin." I smiled to myself. "When you've a moment, take a look at the rain barrel."

"An old friend? I didn't think you had any save Starling."

He did not mean the observation to sting, but it did. His fingers traced again the emblem. Once, FitzChivalry

Farseer had worn that charging buck as an embroidered crest. "Oh, I've a few. I just don't hear from them often."

"Ah. What about new friends? Did Jinna stop in on her way to Buckkeep?"

"She did. She left us a charm to make our garden grow better, as thanks for a night's shelter."

He gave me a sideways glance. "She stayed the night, then. She's nice, isn't she?"

"Yes, she is." He waited for me to say more but I refused. He ducked his head and tried to smother a grin in his hand. I reached across the table and cuffed him affectionately. He fended off the mock blow, then suddenly caught my hand in his. His grin ran away from his face to be replaced by anxiety. "Tom, Tom, what am I going to do? I thought it would be easy and it wasn't. And I was willing to work hard for a fair wage, and I was civil and put in a fair day, and still they all treated me poorly. What am I going to do? I can't live here at the edge of nowhere for all my life. I can't!"

"No. You can't." And in that moment I perceived two things. First, that my isolated lifestyle had ill prepared the boy to make his own way, and second, that this was what Chade must have felt when I had declared that I would not be an assassin anymore. It is strange to think that when you gave a boy what you thought was the best of yourself you actually crippled him. His frantic glance left me feeling small and shamed. I should have done better by him. I would do better by him. I heard myself speak the words before I even knew I had thought them. "I do have old friends at Buckkeep. I can borrow the money for your apprenticeship fee." My heart lurched at the thought of what form the interest on such a loan might take, but I steeled myself. I would go to Chade first, and if what he asked of me in return was too dear, I would seek out the Fool. It would not be easy to humbly ask to borrow money, but—

"You'd do that? For me? But I'm not even really your son." Hap looked incredulous.

I gripped his hand. "I would do that. Because you're as close to a son as I'm ever likely to get."

"I'll help you pay the debt, I swear."

"No you won't. It will be my debt, taken on freely. I'll expect you to pay close attention to your master and devote yourself to learning your trade well."

"I will, Tom. I will. And I swear, in your old age, you shall lack for nothing." He spoke the words with the devout ardency of guileless youth. I took them as he intended them, and ignored the glowing amusement in Nighteyes' gaze.

See how edifying it is when someone sees you as tottering toward death?

I never said you were at your grave's edge.

No. You just treat me as if I were brittle as old chicken bones. Aren't you?

No. My strength returns. Wait for the falling of the leaves and cooler weather. I'll be able to walk you until you drop. Just as I always have.

But what if I have to journey before then?

The wolf lowered his head to his outstretched forepaws with a sigh. *And what if you jump for a buck's throat and miss? There's no point to worrying about it until it happens.*

"Are you thinking what I am?" Hap anxiously broke the seeming silence of the room.

I met his worried gaze. "Perhaps. What were you thinking?"

He spoke hesitantly. "That the sooner you speak to your friends at Buckkeep, the sooner we will know what to expect for the winter."

I replied slowly. "Another winter here would not suit you, would it?"

"No." His natural honesty made him reply quickly. Then he softened it with, "It isn't that I don't like it here with you and Nighteyes. It's just that . . ." He floundered for a moment. "Have you ever felt as if you could actually feel time flowing away from you? As if life were passing you by and you were caught in a backwater with the dead fish and old sticks?"

You can be the dead fish. I'll be the old stick.

I ignored Nighteyes. "I seem to recall I've had such a feeling, a time or two." I glanced at Verity's incomplete map of the Six Duchies. I let out my breath and tried not to make it a sigh. "I'll set out as soon as possible."

"I could be ready by tomorrow morning. A good night's sleep and I'll be—"

"No." I cut him off firmly but kindly. I started to say that the people I must see, I must see alone. I caught myself before I could leave him wondering. Instead, I tipped a nod toward Nighteyes. "There are things here that will want looking after while I am gone. I leave them in your care."

Instantly he looked crestfallen, but to his credit he took a breath, squared his shoulders, and nodded.

Beside the table, Nighteyes rolled to his side, and then onto his back. *Here's the dead wolf. Might as well bury him, all he's fit for is to lie about in a dusty yard and watch chickens he's not permitted to kill.* He paddled his paws vaguely at the air.

Idiot. The chickens are why I'm asking the boy to stay, not you.

Oh? So, if you woke up tomorrow and they were all dead, there would be no reason we could not set out together?

You had better not, I warned him.

He opened his mouth and let his tongue hang to one side. The boy smiled down at him fondly. "I always think he looks as if he's laughing when he does that."

I didn't leave the next morning. I was up long before the boy was. I pulled out my good clothes, musty from disuse, and hung them out to air. The linen of the shirt had yellowed with age. It had been a gift from Starling, long ago. I think I had worn it once on the day she gave it to me. I looked at it ruefully, thinking that it would appall Chade and amuse the Fool. Well, like so many other things, it could not be helped.

There was also a box, built years ago and stored up in the rafters of my workshop. I wrestled it down, and opened it. Despite the oily rags that had wrapped it, Verity's sword was tarnished with disuse. I put on the belt and scabbard, noting that I'd have to punch a new notch in the belt for it to hang comfortably. I sucked in a breath and buckled it as it was. I wiped an oily rag down the blade, and then sheathed the sword at my hip. When I drew it, it weighed heavy in my hand, yet balanced as beautifully as ever. I debated the wisdom of wearing it. I'd feel a fool if someone recognized it and asked difficult questions. I would feel even stupider, however, if my throat were cut for lack of a weapon at my side.

I compromised by wrapping the jeweled grip with leather strips. The sheath itself was battered but serviceable. It looked appropriate to my station. I drew it again, and made a lunge, stretching muscles no longer accustomed to that reach. I resumed my stance and made a few cuts at the air.

Amusement. *Better take an axe.*

I don't have one anymore. Verity himself had given me this sword. But both he and Burrich had advised me that my style of fighting was more suited to the crudity of an axe than this graceful and elegant weapon. I tried another cut at the air. My mind remembered all Hod had taught me, but my body was having difficulty performing the moves.

You chop wood with one.

That's not a battle-axe. I'd look a fool carrying that about with me. I sheathed the sword and turned to look at him.

Nighteyes sat in the doorway of the workshop, his tail neatly curled about his feet. Amusement glinted in his dark eyes. He turned his head to stare innocently into the distance. *I think one of the chickens died in the night. Sad. Poor old thing. Death comes for all of us eventually.*

He was lying, but he had the satisfaction of seeing me sheathe the sword and hurry to see if it were so. All six of my biddies clucked and dusted themselves in the sun. The rooster, perched on a fencepost, kept a watchful eye on his wives.

How odd. I would have sworn that fat white hen looked poorly yesterday. I'll just lie out here in the shade and keep an eye on her. He suited his actions to his thought, sprawling in the dappling shade of the birches while staring at the chickens intently. I ignored him and went back into the cabin.

I was boring a new hole in the sword belt when Hap woke up. He came sleepily to the table to watch me. He came awake when his eyes fell on the sword waiting in its sheath. "I've never seen that before."

"I've had it for a long time."

"I've never seen you wear it when we went to market. All you ever carried before was your sheath-knife."

"A trip to Buckkeep is a bit different from a trip to market." His question made me look at my own motives for taking the blade. When last I had seen Buckkeep, a number of people there wished me dead. If I encountered any of them and they recognized me, I wanted to be ready. "A city like that has a lot more rogues and scoundrels than a simple country market."

I finished boring the new belt notch and tried it on again. Better. I drew the sword and heard Hap's indrawn breath. Even with the handle wrapped in plain leather, there was no mistaking it for a cheap blade. This was a weapon created by a master.

"Can I try it?"

I nodded permission and he picked it up gingerly. He adjusted his grip for the heft of it, and then fell into an awkward imitation of a swordsman's stance. I had never taught Hap to fight. I wondered for an instant if that omission had been a bad decision. I had hoped he would never need the skills of a fighter. But not teaching them to him was no protection against someone challenging him.

Rather like refusing to teach Dutiful about the Skill.

I pushed that thought aside and said nothing as Hap swung the blade at the air. In a few moments he had tired himself. The hard muscles of a farm hand were not what a man used to swing a blade. The endurance to wield such a weapon demanded both training and constant practice. He set it down and looked at me without speaking.

"I'll be leaving for Buckkeep tomorrow morning at dawn. I still need to clean this blade, grease my boots, pack some clothing and food—"

"And cut your hair," Hap interjected quietly.

"Hm." I crossed the room and took out our small looking glass. Usually, when Starling came to visit me, she cut my hair for me. For a moment I stared at how long it had grown. Then, as I had not in years, I pulled it to the back of my head and fastened it into a warrior's tail. Hap looked at me with his brows raised, but said nothing about my martial aspect.

Long before dusk, I was ready to travel. I turned my attention to my smallholding. I busied myself and the boy with making sure all would go well for him while I was gone. By the time we sat down to our evening meal, we were ahead on every chore I could think of. He promised he would keep the garden watered and harvest the rest of the peas. He would split the last of the firewood and stack it. I caught myself telling him things he knew, things he had known for years, and finally stopped my tongue. He smiled at my concerns.

"I survived on my own out on the roads, Tom. I'll be fine here at home. I only wish I were going with you."

"If all works out, when I return, we will make a trip to Buckkeep together."

Nighteyes sat up abruptly, pricking his ears. *Horses.*

I went to the door with the wolf at my side. A few moments later, the hoofbeats reached my ears. The animals were coming at a steady trot. I stepped to where I could see around the bend in our narrow lane, and glimpsed the horseman. It was not, as I had hoped, the Fool. This was a stranger. He rode a rangy roan horse and led another. Dust mottled the sweat streaks on his horse's withers. As I watched them come, a sense of foreboding rose in me. The wolf shared my trepidation. His hackles bristled down his spine and the deep growl that rose from him brought Hap to the door as well. "What is it?"

"I'm not sure. But it's no random wanderer or peddler."

At the sight of me, the stranger reined in his horse. He lifted a hand in greeting, then came forward more slowly. I saw both horses prick their ears at the scent of the wolf, and felt their anxiety as well as their eagerness for the water they could also smell.

"Are you lost, stranger?" I greeted the man from a safe distance.

He made no reply but rode closer to us. The wolf's growl reached a crescendo. The rider seemed unaware of the rising warning.

Wait, I bade him.

We stood our ground as the man rode closer. The horse he led was saddled and bridled. I wondered if he had lost a companion, or stolen it from someone.

"That's close enough," I warned him suddenly. "What do you seek here?"

He had been watching me intently. He did not pause at my words, but made a gesture at first his ears, and then his mouth as he rode closer. I held out a hand. "Stop there," I warned him, and he understood my motion and obeyed it. Without dismounting, he reached into a messenger's pouch that was slung across his chest. He drew out a scroll and proffered it to me.

Stay ready, I warned Nighteyes as I stepped forward to take it. Then I recognized the seal on it. In thick red wax, my own charging buck was imprinted. A different sort of trepidation swept through me. I stared at the missive in my hand, then with a gesture gave the deaf-mute permission to dismount. I took a breath and spoke to Hap with a steady voice. "Take him inside and provide him food and drink. The same for his horses. Please."

And to Nighteyes, *Keep an eye on him, my brother, while I see what this scroll says.*

Nighteyes ceased his rumbling growl at my thought, but followed the messenger very closely as a puzzled Hap gestured him toward our cabin. The weary horses stood where he had left them. A few moments later, Hap emerged to lead them off to water. Alone I stood in the dooryard and stared at the coiled scroll in my hand. I broke the seal at last and studied Chade's slanting letters in the fading daylight.

Dear Cousin,

Family matters at home require your attention. Do not delay your return. You know I would not summon you thus unless the need was urgent.

The signature that followed this brief missive was indecipherable. It was not Chade's name. The real message had been in the seal itself. He never would have used it unless the need *was* urgent. I rerolled the scroll and looked up toward the sinking sun.

When I entered the house, the messenger stood up immediately. Still chewing, he wiped his mouth on the back of his hand, and indicated he was ready to leave at once. I suspected his orders from Chade had been very specific. There was no time to lose in sleep or rest for man or beast. I gestured him back to his food. I was glad my rucksack was already packed.

"I unsaddled the horses and wiped them down a bit," Hap told me as he came in the door. "They look as if they've come a long way today."

I took a breath. "Put their saddles back on. As soon as our friend has eaten, we'll be leaving."

For a moment, the boy was thunderstruck. Then he asked in a small voice, "Where are you going?"

I tried to make my smile convincing. "Buckkeep, lad.

And faster than I expected." I considered the matter. There was no way to estimate when I might be back. Or even if I would come back. A missive like this from Chade would definitely mean danger of some kind. I was amazed at how easily I decided. "I want you and the wolf to follow at first light. Use the pony and cart, so if he gets weary, he can ride."

Hap stared at me as if I had gone mad. "What about the chickens? And the chores I was to do while you were gone?"

"The chickens will have to fend for themselves. No. They wouldn't last a week before a weasel had them. Take them to Baylor. He'll feed and watch them for the sake of their eggs. Take a day or so, and close the house up tight. We may both be gone a while." I turned away from the incomprehension on Hap's face.

"But . . ." The fear in his voice made me turn back to him. He stared at me as if I were suddenly a stranger. "Where should I go when I get to Buckkeep Town? Will you meet me there?" I heard an echo of the abandoned boy in his voice.

I reached back in my memory fifteen years and tried to summon up the name of a decent inn. Before I could dredge one out, he hopefully put in, "I know where Jinna and her niece live. Jinna said I could find her there, when next I came to Buckkeep. Her house has a hedge-witch sign on it, a hand with lines on the palm. I could meet you there."

"That will be it, then."

Relief showed on his face. He knew where he was going. I was glad he had that security. I myself did not. But despite all my uneasiness, a strange elation filled me. Chade's old spell fell over me again. Secrets and adventures. I felt the wolf nudge against me.

A time of change. Then, gruffly: *I could try to keep pace with the horses. Buckkeep is not so far.*

I do not know what this means, my brother. And until I do, I would just as soon that you stayed by Hap's side.

Is that supposed to salve my pride?

No. It's supposed to ease my fears.

I will bring him safely to Buckkeep Town, then. But after that, I am at your side.

Of course. Always.

Before the sun kissed the horizon good night, I was mounted on the nondescript gray horse. Verity's disguised sword hung at my hip, and my pack was fastened tightly to the back of my saddle. I followed my silent companion as he hastened us down the road to Buckkeep.

chapter XI

CHADE'S TOWER

Between the Six Duchies and the Out Islands as much blood has been shared as has been shed. Despite the enmity of the Red Ship War, and the years of sporadic raiding that preceded it, almost every family in the Coastal Duchies will acknowledge having "a cousin in the Out Islands." All acknowledge that the folk of the Coastal Duchies are of those mingled bloodlines. It is well documented that the first rulers of the Farseer line were likely raiders from the Out Islands who came to raid and settled instead.

Just as the history of the Six Duchies has been shaped by geography, so too has the chronicle of the Out Islands. Theirs is a harsher land than ours. Ice rules their mountainous islands year round. Deep fjords slash their islands and rough water divides them. We consider their islands immense, yet the domination of glaciers grants men only the edges of those islands as dwelling places. What arable land they have along the coasts of their islands is stingy and thin in its yield. Thus no large cities can be supported there, and few towns. Barriers and isolation are the hallmark of that land, and so the folk dwell in fiercely independent villages and town-states. In times past, they were raiders by necessity as well as by inclination, and robbed one another as often as they ventured across the seas to harry the Six Duchies coastline. It is true that during the Red Ship War, Kebal Rawbread was able to force a brief alliance among the island folk, and from that alliance, he hammered together a powerful raiding fleet. Only the devastation of the Six Duchies dragons was sufficient to shatter his merciless hold over his own people.

Having once seen the strength of such an alliance, the

*individual headmen of the Out Island villages realized that
such power could be used for more than war. In the years of
recovery that followed the end of the Red Ship War, the
Hetgurd was formed. This alliance of Out Island headmen
was an uneasy one. At first, they sought only to replace
interisland raiding with trading treaties between individual
headmen. Arkon Bloodblade was the first headman to point
out to the others that the Hetgurd could use its unified
strength to normalize trade relations with the Six Duchies.*

BRAWNKENNER, "THE OUT ISLAND CHRONICLES"

As always, Chade had planned well. His silent messenger
seemed very familiar with his ways. Before noon the next
day, we had changed our exhausted horses for two others at
a decrepit farmhouse. We traveled across brown hillsides
seared by summer, and left those two horses at a fisherman's
hut. A small boat was waiting and the surly crew took us
swiftly up the coast. We put in at a landing at a tiny trading
port, where two more horses awaited us at a run-down inn.
I stayed as silent as my guide, and no one questioned me
about anything. If coin was exchanged, I never saw it. It is
always best not to see what is meant to be concealed. The
horses carried us to yet another waiting boat, this one with
a scaly deck that smelled much of fish. It struck me that we
were approaching Buckkeep not by the swiftest possible
path, but by the least likely one. If anyone watched the
roads into Buckkeep for us, they were doomed to disappointment.

Buckkeep Castle is built on an inhospitable strip of
coast. It stands, tall and black, atop the cliffs, but it commands a fine view of the Buck River mouth. Whoever controls that castle controls trade on the Buck River. For that
reason was it built there. The vagaries of history have made
it the ruling seat of the Farseer family. Buckkeep Town
clings to the cliffs below the castle like lichens to rock. Half
of it is built out on docks and piers. As a boy, I had thought

the town had grown as large as it could, given its geography, but on the afternoon that we sailed into it, I saw that I had been wrong. Human ingenuity had prevailed over nature's harshness. Suspended pathways now vined across the face of the cliffs, and tiny houses and shops found purchase to cling there. The houses reminded me of mud-swallows' nests, and I wondered what pounding they took during the winter storms. Pilings had been driven into the black sand and rock of the beaches where I had once run and played with Molly and the other children. Warehouses and inns squatted on these perches, and at high tide, one could tie up right at their doorsteps. This our fishing boat did, and I followed my mute guide "ashore" onto a wooden walkway.

As the small boat cast off and left us there, I gawked about us, a country farmer come to town. The increase in structures and the lively boat commerce indicated that Buckkeep prospered, yet I could take no joy in it. Here was the final evidence of my childhood erased. The place I had both dreaded and longed to return to was gone, swallowed by this thriving port. When I glanced about for my mute guide, he had vanished. I loitered where he had left me a bit longer, already suspecting he would not return. He had brought me back to Buckkeep Town. From here, I needed no guide. Chade never liked any of his contacts to know every link of the convoluted paths that led to him. I shouldered my small rucksack and headed toward home.

Perhaps, I thought as I wended my way through Buckkeep's steep and narrow streets, Chade had even known that I would prefer to make this part of my journey alone. I did not hurry. I knew I could not contact Chade until after nightfall. As I explored the once-familiar streets and byways, I found nothing that was completely familiar. It seemed that every structure that could sprout a second story had, and on some of the narrower streets the balconies almost met overhead, so that one walked in a perpetual twilight. I found inns I had frequented and stores where I had traded, and even glimpsed the faces of old acquaintances overlaid with fifteen years of experience. Yet no one exclaimed with surprise or delight to see me; as a stranger I was visible only to the boys hawking hot pies in the street. I bought one for a copper and ate it as I walked. The taste of the peppery gravy and the chunks of river fish in it were the taste of Buckkeep Town itself.

The chandlery that had once belonged to Molly's father was now a tailor's shop. I did not go inside. I went instead to the tavern we had once frequented. It was as dark, as smoky, and as crowded as I recalled. The heavy table in the corner still bore the marks of Kerry's idle whittling. The boy who brought my beer was too young ever to have known me, but I knew who had fathered him by the line of his brow and was glad the business had remained in the same family. One beer became two, and then three, and the fourth was gone before twilight began to venture through the streets of the town. No one had uttered a word to the dour-faced stranger drinking alone, but I listened all the same. But whatever desperate business had led Chade to call on me, it was not common knowledge. I heard only gossip of the Prince's betrothal, complaints about Bingtown's war with Chalced disrupting trade, and the local mutterings about the very strange weather. Out of a clear and peaceful night sky, lightning had struck an unused storage hut in the outer keep of the castle and blown the roof right off. I shook my head at that tale. I left an extra copper for the boy, and shouldered my pack once more.

The last time I had left Buckkeep it had been as a dead man in a coffin. I could scarcely reenter the same way, and yet I feared to approach the main gate. Once I had been a familiar face in the guardroom. Changed I might be, but I would not take the chance of being recognized. Instead, I went to a place both Chade and I knew, a secret exit from the castle grounds that Nighteyes had discovered when he was just a cub. Through that small gap in Buckkeep's defenses, Queen Kettricken and the Fool had once fled Prince Regal's plot. Tonight, I would return by that route.

But when I got there, I found that the fault in the walls that guarded Buckkeep had been repaired a long time ago. A heavy growth of thistles cloaked where it had been. A short distance from the thistles, sitting cross-legged on a large embroidered cushion, a golden-haired youth of obvious nobility played a pennywhistle with consummate skill. As I approached, he ended his tune with a final scattering of notes and set his instrument aside.

"Fool," I greeted him fondly and with no great surprise.

He cocked his head and made a mouth at me. "Beloved," he drawled in response. Then he grinned, sprang to his feet, and slipped his whistle inside his ribboned shirt. He indicated his cushion. "I'm glad I brought that. I had a feeling you might linger a time in Buckkeep Town, but I didn't expect to wait this long."

"It's changed," I said lamely.

"Haven't we all?" he replied, and for a moment there was an echo of pathos in his voice. But in an instant it was gone. He tidied his gleaming hair fussily and picked a leaf from his stocking. He pointed at his cushion again. "Pick that up and follow me. Hurry along. We are expected." His air of petulant command mimed perfectly that of a foppish dandy of the noble class. He plucked a handkerchief from his sleeve and patted at his upper lip, erasing imaginary perspiration.

I had to smile. He assumed the role so deftly and effortlessly. "How are we going in?"

"By the front gate, of course. Have no fear. I've put word about that Lord Golden is very dissatisfied with the quality of servants he has found in Buckkeep Town. None have suited me, and so today I went to meet a ship bringing to me a fine fellow, if a bit rustic, recommended to me by my second cousin's first valet. By name, one Tom Badgerlock."

He proceeded ahead of me. I picked up his cushion and followed. "So. I'm to be your servant?" I asked in wry amusement.

"Of course. It's the perfect guise. You'll be virtually invisible to all the nobility of Buckkeep. Only the other servants will speak to you, and as I intend that you will be a downtrodden, overworked, poorly dressed lackey of a supercilious, overbearing, and insufferable young lord, you will have little time to socialize at all." He suddenly halted and looked back. One slender, long-fingered hand clasped his chin as he looked down his nose at me. His fair brows knit and his amber eyes narrowed as he snapped, "And do not dare to meet my eyes, sirrah! I will tolerate no impertinence. Stand up straight, keep your place, and speak no word without my leave. Are you clear on these instructions?"

"Perfectly." I grinned at him.

He continued to glare at me. Then suddenly the glare was replaced by a look of exasperation. "FitzChivalry, the game is up if you cannot play this role and play it to the hilt. Not just when we stand in the Great Hall of Buckkeep, but every moment of every day when there is the remotest chance that we might be seen. I have been Lord Golden since I arrived, but I am still a newcomer to the Queen's court, and folk will stare. Chade and Queen Kettricken have done all they could to help me in this ruse, Chade because he perceived how useful I might be, and the Queen because she feels I truly deserve to be treated as a lord."

"And no one recognized you?" I broke in incredulously.

He cocked his head. "What would they recognize, Fitz? My dead-white skin and colorless eyes? My jester's motley and painted face? My capers and cavorting and daring witticisms?"

"I knew you the moment I saw you," I reminded him.

He smiled warmly. "Just as I knew you, and would know you when first I met you a dozen lives hence. But few others do. Chade with his assassin's eyes picked me out, and arranged a private audience at which I made myself known to the Queen. A few others have given me curious glances from time to time, but no one would dare to accost Lord Golden and ask him if fifteen years ago he had been King

Shrewd's jester at this selfsame court. My age appears wrong to them, as does my coloring, as does my demeanor, as does my wealth."

"How can they be so blind?"

He shook his head and smiled at my ignorance. "Fitz, Fitz. They never even saw me in the first place. They saw only a jester and a freak. I deliberately took no name when first I arrived here. To most of the lords and ladies of Buckkeep, I was just the fool. They heard my jokes and saw my capers, but they never really saw *me*." He gave a small sigh. Then he gave me a considering look. "You made it a name. The Fool. And you saw me. You met my eyes when others looked aside, disconcerted." I saw the tip of his tongue for a second. "Did you never guess how you frightened me? That all my ruses were useless against the eyes of a small boy?"

"You were just a child yourself," I pointed out uneasily.

He hesitated. I noticed he did not agree or disagree with me when he went on. "Become my faithful servant, Fitz. Be Tom Badgerlock, every second of every day that you are at Buckkeep. It is the only way you can protect both of us. And the only guise in which you can aid Chade."

"What, exactly, does Chade need of me?"

"That would be better heard from his lips than mine. Come. It grows dark. Buckkeep Town has grown and changed, as has Buckkeep itself. If we try to enter after dark, we may well be turned away."

It had grown later as we talked and the long summer day was fading around us. He led and I followed as he took me roundabout to the steep road that led to Buckkeep Castle's main gate. He lingered in the trees to let a wine merchant round a bend before we ourselves stepped out on the road. Then Lord Golden led and his humble servant Tom Badgerlock trudged behind him, bearing his embroidered cushion.

At the gate he was admitted without question and I followed at his heels, unnoticed. The guard on the gate wore Buckkeep's blue and their jerkins were embroidered with the Farseer leaping buck. Small things like that twisted my heart unexpectedly. I blinked and then coughed and rubbed my eyes. The Fool had the kindness not to look back at me.

Buckkeep had changed as much as the town that clung to the cliffs below it. Overall, the changes were ones I approved. We passed a new and larger stable. Paving stones had been laid where once muddy tracks had run. Although more folk thronged the castle than I recalled, it seemed cleaner and better maintained. I wondered if this was Kettricken's Mountain discipline applied to the keep, or simply the result of peace in the land. All the years that I had lived in Buckkeep had been years of the Outislander raids and eventually outright war. Relative peace had brought a resumption of trade, and not just with the countries to the south of the Six Duchies. Our history of trading with the Out Islands was as long as our history of fighting with them. I had seen the Outislander ships, both oared and sailed, in Buckkeep's harbor when I arrived.

We entered through the Great Hall, Lord Golden striding imperiously along while I hastened, eyes down, at his heels. Two ladies detained him briefly with greetings. I think it was hardest then for me to keep my guise of servingman in place. Where once the Fool had inspired unease or outright distaste, Lord Golden was greeted with fluttering fans and eyelashes. He charmed them both with a score of elegantly woven compliments on their dresses, their hair, and the scents they wore. They parted with him reluctantly, and he assured them he was as loath to leave them, but he had a servant to be shown his duties, and certainly they knew the drudgery of that. One simply could not get good servants anymore, and although this one came with a high recommendation, he had already proven to be a bit slow-witted and woefully countrified. Well, one had to make do with what one could get these days, and he hoped to enjoy their company on the morrow. He planned to stroll through the thyme gardens after breakfast, if they cared to join him?

They would, of course, with great delight, and after several more rounds of exchanged pleasantries, we were allowed to go our way. Lord Golden had been given apartments on the west side of the keep. In King Shrewd's day, these had been considered the less desirable rooms, for they faced the hills behind the keep and the sunset, rather than the water and the sunrise. In those days, they had been furnished more simply, and were considered suitable for lesser nobility.

Either the status of the rooms had improved, or the Fool had been very lavish with his own money. I opened a heavy oak door for him at his gesture, and then followed him into chambers where both taste and quality had been indulged in equal measure. Deep greens and rich browns predominated in the thick rugs underfoot and the opulently cushioned chairs. Through a door I glimpsed an immense bed, fat with pillows and feather bed, and so heavily draped that even in Buck's coldest winter, no draft would find the occupant. For the summer weather, the heavy curtains had been roped back with tasseled cords, and a fall of lace sufficed to keep all flying insects at bay. Carved chests and wardrobes stood casually ajar, the volume of garments within threatening to cascade out into the room. There was an air of rich and pleasant disorder, completely unlike the Fool's ascetic tower room that I recalled of old.

Lord Golden flung himself into a chair as I closed the door quietly behind us. A last slice of sunlight from the westering sun came in the tall window and fell across him as if by accident. He steepled his graceful hands before him and lolled his head back against the cushions, and suddenly I perceived the deliberate artifice of the chair's position and his pose. This entire rich room was a setting for his golden beauty. Every color chosen, every placement of furniture was done to achieve this end. In this place and time, he glowed in the honey light of the sunset. I lifted my eyes to consider the arrangement of the candles, the angles of the chairs.

"You take your place like a figure stepping into a carefully composed portrait," I observed quietly.

He smiled, his obvious pleasure in the compliment a confirmation of my words. Then he came to his feet as effortlessly as a cat. His arm and hand twined through a motion to point at each door off the room. "My bedchamber. The privy room. My private room." This door was closed, as was the last one. "And your chamber, Tom Badgerlock."

I did not ask him about his private room. I knew his need for solitude of old. I crossed the room and tugged open the door to my quarters. I peered inside the small, dark room. It had no window. As my eyes adjusted, I could make out a narrow cot in the corner, a washstand, and a small chest. There was a single candle in a holder on the washstand. That was all. I turned back to the Fool with a quizzical look.

"Lord Golden," he said with a wry smile, "is a shallow, venal fellow. He is witty and quick-tongued, and very charming to his fellows, and completely unaware of those of lesser stations. So. Your chamber reflects that."

"No window? No fireplace?"

"No different from most of the servants' chambers on this floor. It has, however, one singularly remarkable advantage that most of the others lack."

I glanced back into the room. "Whatever it is, I don't see it."

"And that is exactly what is intended. Come."

Taking my arm, he accompanied me into the dark little room. He shut the door firmly behind us. We were instantly plunged into complete darkness. Speaking quietly next to me, he observed, "Always remember that the door must be shut for this to work. Over here. Give me your hand."

I complied, and he guided my hand over the rough stone of the outer wall adjacent to the door. "Why must we do this in the dark?" I demanded.

"It was faster than kindling candles. Besides, what I am showing you cannot be seen, only felt. There. Feel that?"

"I think so." It was a very slight unevenness in the stone.

"Measure it off with your hand, or whatever you want to do to learn where it is."

I obliged him, discovering that it was about six of my handspans from the corner of the room, and at the height of my chin. "Now what?"

"Push. Gently. It does not take much."

I obeyed and felt the stone shift very slightly beneath my hand. A small click sounded, but not from the wall before me. Instead, it came from behind me.

"This way," the Fool told me, and in the darkness led me to the opposite wall of the small chamber. Again, he set my hand to the wall and told me to push. The darkness gave way on oiled hinges, the seeming stone no more than a façade that swung away at my touch. "Very quiet," the Fool observed approvingly. "He must have greased it."

I blinked as my eyes adjusted to a subtle light leaking down from high above. In a moment I could see a very narrow staircase leading up. It paralleled the wall of the room. A corridor, equally narrow, snaked away into darkness, following the wall. "I believe you are expected," the Fool told me in his aristocratic sneer. "As is Lord Golden, but in far different company. I will excuse you from your duties as my valet, at least for tonight. You are dismissed, Tom Badgerlock."

"Thank you, master," I replied snidely. I craned my neck to peer up the stairs. They were stone, obviously built into the wall when the castle was first constructed. The gray quality of the light that seeped down suggested daylight rather than lamplight.

The Fool's hand settled briefly on my shoulder, delaying me. In a far different voice he said, "I'll leave a candle burning in the room for you." The hand squeezed affectionately. "And welcome home, FitzChivalry Farseer."

I turned to look back at him. "Thank you, Fool." We nodded to one another, an oddly formal farewell, and I began to climb the stair. On the third stair, I heard a snick behind me, and looked back. The door had closed.

I climbed for quite a distance. Then the staircase turned, and I perceived the source of the light. Narrow openings, not even as wide as arrow slits, permitted the setting sun to finger in. The light was growing dimmer, and I suddenly perceived that when the sun set, I would be plunged into absolute darkness. I came to a junction in the corridor at that time. Truly, Chade's rat warren of tunnels, stairs, and corridors within Buckkeep Castle were far more extensive than I had ever imagined. I closed my eyes for a moment and imagined the layout of the castle. After a brief hesitation, I chose a path and went on. As I traveled, from time to time I became aware of voices. Tiny peepholes gave me access to bedchambers and parlors as well as providing slivers of light in long dark stretches of corridor. A wooden stool, dusty with disuse, sat in one alcove. I sat down on it and peered through a slit into a private audience chamber that I recognized from my service with King Shrewd. Evidently the magnificent woodwork that framed the hearth furnished this spy post. Having taken my bearings from this, I hastened on.

At last, I saw a yellowish glow in the secret passageway far ahead of me. Hurrying toward it, I found a bend in the corridor, and a fat candle burning in a glass. Far down another stretch, I glimpsed a second candle. From that point on, the tiny lights led me forward, until I climbed a very steep stair and suddenly found myself standing in a small stone room with a narrow door. The door swung open at my touch, and I found myself stepping out from behind the wine rack into Chade's tower room.

I looked about the chamber with new eyes. It was uninhabited at the moment, but a small fire crackling on the hearth and a laden table told me I was, indeed, expected. The great bedstead was overladen with comforters, cushions, and furs as it had always been, yet an elaborate spiderweb constructed amidst the dusty hangings spoke of disuse. Chade used this room still, but he no longer slept here.

I ventured down to the workroom end of the chamber, past the scroll-laden racks and the shelves of arcane equipment. Sometimes, when one goes back to the scene of one's childhood, things seem smaller. What was mysterious and the sole province of adults suddenly seems commonplace and mundane when viewed with mature eyes.

Such was not the case with Chade's workroom. The little pots carefully labeled in his decisive hand, the blackened kettles and stained pestles, the spilled herbs and the lingering odors still worked their spell on me. The Wit and the Skill were mine, but the strange chemistries that Chade practiced here were a magic I had never mastered. Here I was still an apprentice, knowing only the basics of my master's sophisticated lore.

My travels had taught me a bit. A shallow gleaming bowl, draped with a cloth, was a scrying basin. I'd seen them used by fortune-tellers in Chalcedean towns. I thought of the night that Chade had wakened me from a drunken stupor to tell me that Neat Bay was under attack from Red Ship raiders. There had been no time, that night, to demand how he knew. I had always assumed it had been a messenger bird. Now I wondered.

The work hearth was cold, but tidier than I recalled. I wondered who his new apprentice was, and if I would meet the lad. Then my musings were cut short by the sound of a door closing softly. I turned to see Chade Fallstar standing near a scroll rack. For the first time, I realized that there were no obvious doors in the chamber. Even here, all was still deception. He greeted me with a warm if weary smile. "And here you are at last. When I saw Lord Golden enter the Great Hall smiling, I knew you would be awaiting me. Oh, Fitz, you have no idea how relieved I am to see you."

I grinned at him. "In all our years together, I can't recall a more ominous greeting from you."

"It's an ominous time, my boy. Come, sit down, eat. We've always reasoned best over food. I've so much to tell you, and you may as well hear it with a full belly."

"Your messenger did not tell me much," I admitted, taking a place at the small lavishly spread table. There were cheeses, pastries, cold meats, fruit that was fragrantly ripe, and spicy breads. There was both wine and brandy, but Chade began with tea from an earthenware pot warm at the edge of the fire. When I reached for the pot, a gesture of his hand warded me off.

"I'll put on more water," he offered, and hung a kettle to boil. I watched the set of his mouth as he sipped the dark brew in his cup. He did not seem to relish it, yet he sank back in his chair with a sigh. I kept my thoughts to myself.

As I began to heap my plate, Chade noted, "My messenger told you as much as he knew, which was nothing. One of my greatest tasks has been to keep this private. Ah, where do I begin? It is hard to decide, for I don't know what precipitated this crisis."

I swallowed a mouthful of bread and ham. "Tell me the heart of it, and we can work backward from there."

His green eyes were troubled. "Very well." He took breath, then hesitated. He poured us both brandy. As he set mine before me he said, "Prince Dutiful is missing. We think he might have run on his own. If he did, he likely had help. It is possible that he was taken against his will, but neither the Queen nor I think that likely. There." He sat back in his chair and watched for my reaction.

It took me a moment to marshal my thoughts. "How could it happen? Whom do you suspect? How long has he been gone?"

He held up a hand to halt my flow of questions. "Six days and seven nights, counting tonight. I doubt he will reappear before morning, though nothing would please me better. How did it happen? Well. I do not criticize my Queen, but her Mountain ways are often difficult for me to accept. The Prince has come and gone as he pleased from both castle and keep since he was thirteen. She seemed to think it best that he get to know his people on a common footing. There have been times when I thought that was wise, for it has made the folk fond of him. I myself have felt that it was time he had a guard of his own to accompany him, or at the least a tutor of the well-muscled sort. But Kettricken, as you may recall, can be as unbending as stone. In that, she had her way. He came and went as he wished, and the guards had their orders to let him do so."

The water was boiling. Chade still kept teas where he always had, and he made no comment as I rose to make my tea. He seemed to be gathering his thoughts, and I let him, for my own thoughts were milling in every direction like a panicky flock of sheep. "He could already be dead," I heard myself say aloud, and then could have bitten my tongue out at the stricken look on Chade's face.

"He could," the old man admitted. "He is a hearty, healthy boy, unlikely to turn away from a challenge. This absence need not be a plot; an ordinary accident could be at the base of it. I thought of that. I've a discreet man or two at my beck, and they've searched the base of the sea cliffs, and the more dangerous ravines where he likes to hunt. But I think that if he were injured, his little hunting cat might still have come back to the castle. Though it is hard to say with cats. A dog would, I think, but a cat might just revert to being wild. In any case, unpleasant as the idea is, I have thought to look for a body. None has been discovered."

A hunting cat. I ignored my jabbing thought to ask, "You said run away, or possibly taken. What would make you think either one likely?"

"The first, because he's a boy trying to learn to be a man in a court that makes neither easy for him. The second, because he's a prince, newly betrothed to a foreign princess, and rumored to be possessed of the Wit. That gives several factions any number of reasons to either control him or destroy him."

He gave me several silent minutes to digest that. Several

days would not have been enough. I must have looked as sick as I felt, for Chade finally said, softly, "We think that even if he has been taken, he is most valuable to his kidnappers alive."

I found a breath and spoke through a dry mouth. "Has anyone claimed to have him? Demanded ransom?"

"No."

I cursed myself for not staying abreast of politics in the Six Duchies. But had not I sworn never to become involved in it again? It suddenly seemed a child's foolish resolve never to get caught in the rain again. I spoke quietly, for I felt ashamed. "You are going to have to educate me, Chade, and swiftly. What factions? How does it benefit their interests to have control of the Prince? What foreign princess? And"—and this last question near choked me—"why would anyone think Prince Dutiful was Witted?"

"Because you were," Chade said shortly. He reached again for his teapot and replenished his cup. It poured even blacker this time, and I caught a whiff of a treacly yet bitter-edged aroma. He gulped down a mouthful, and swiftly followed it with a toss of brandy. He swallowed. His green eyes met mine and he waited. I said nothing. Some secrets still belonged to me alone. At least, I hoped they did.

"You were Witted," he resumed. "Some say it must have come from your mother, whoever she was, and Eda forgive me, I've encouraged that thinking. But others point back a time, to the Piebald Prince and several other odd-lings in the Farseer line, to say, 'No, the taint is there, down in the roots, and Prince Dutiful is a shoot from that line.'"

"But the Piebald Prince died without issue; Dutiful is not of his line. What made folk think that the Prince might be Witted?"

Chade narrowed his eyes at me. "Do you play cat and mouse with me, boy?" He set his hands on the edge of the table. Veins and tendons stood up ropily on their backs as he leaned toward me to demand, "Do you think I'm losing my faculties, Fitz? Because I can assure you, I'm not. I may be getting old, boy, but I'm as acute as ever. I promise you that!"

Until that moment, I had not doubted it. This outburst was so uncharacteristic of Chade that I found myself leaning back in my chair and regarding him with apprehension. He must have interpreted the look in my eyes, for he sat back in his chair as well and dropped his hands into his lap. When he spoke again, it was my mentor of old that I heard. "Starling told you of the minstrel at Springfest. You know of the unrest in the land among the Witted, yes, and you know of those who call themselves the Piebalds. There is an unkinder name for them. The Cult of the Bastard." He gave me a baleful look, but gave me no time to absorb that information. He waved a hand, dismissing my shock. "Whatever they call themselves, they have recently taken up a new weapon. They expose families tainted by the Wit. I do not know if they seek to prove how widespread the Wit is, or if their aim is the destruction of their fellows who will not ally with them. Posts appear in public places. 'Gere the Tanner's son is Witted; his beast is a yellow hound.' 'Lady Winsome is Witted; her beast is her merlin.' Each post is signed with their emblem, a piebald horse. Who is Witted and who is not has become Court gossip these days. Some deny the rumors; others flee, to country estates if they are landed, to a distant village and a new name if they are not. If those posts are true, there are far more who possess the Beast Magic than even you might suppose. Or"—and he cocked his head at me—"do you know far more of all this than I do?"

"No," I replied mildly. "I do not." I cleared my throat. "Nor was I aware how completely Starling reported to you."

He steepled his hands under his chin. "I've offended you."

"No," I lied. "It's not that, it's that—"

"Damn me. I've become a testy old man despite all I've done to avoid it! And I offend you and you lie to me about it and when only you can aid me I drive you away from me. My judgment fails me just when I need it most."

His eyes suddenly met mine and horror stood in his gaze. Before me, the old man dwindled. His voice became an uncertain whisper. "Fitz, I am terrified for the boy. Terrified. The accusation was not posted publicly. It was sent in a sealed note. It was not signed at all, not even with the Piebalds' sigil. 'Do what is right,' it said, 'and no one else ever need know. Ignore this warning, and we will take action of our own.' But they didn't say what they wanted of us, not specifically, so what could we do? We didn't ignore it; we simply waited to hear more. And then he is gone. The Queen fears . . . the Queen fears too many things to list. She fears most that they will kill him. But what I fear is worse than that. Not just that they will kill him, but that they will reduce him to . . . to what you were when Burrich and I first pulled you from that false grave. A beast in a man's body."

He rose suddenly and walked away from the table. I do not know if he felt shamed that his love for the boy could reduce him to such terror, or if he sought to spare me the recollection of what I had been. He need not have bothered. I had become adept at refusing those memories. He stared unseeing at a tapestry for a time, then cleared his throat. When he went on, it was the Queen's advisor who spoke. "The Farseer Throne would not stand before that, FitzChivalry. We have needed a king for too long. If the boy were proven Witted, even that I think I could manage to set in a different light. But if he were shown to his dukes as a beast, all would come undone, and the Six Duchies will never become the Seven Duchies, but will instead be reduced to squabbling city-states and lands between that know no rule. Kettricken and I have come such a long and weary road, my boy, in the years that you have been gone. Neither she nor I can really muster the unquestionable authority that a true Farseer-born king could wield. Through the years, we have sailed a shifting sea of alliances with first these dukes, then those ones, always netting a majority that allowed us to survive another season. We are so close now, so close. In two more years, Prince Dutiful will be Prince no more, but take the title of King-in-Waiting. One year of that, and I think I could persuade the dukes to recognize him as a full king. Then, I think, we might feel secure for a time. When King Eyod of the Mountains dies, Dutiful inherits his mantle as well. We will have the Mountains at our back, and if this marriage alliance Kettricken has negotiated with the Out Islands Hetgurd prospers, we will have friendship in the seas to the north."

"Hetgurd?"

"An alliance of nobles. They have no king there, no high ruler. Kebal Rawbread was an anomaly for them. But this Hetgurd has a number of powerful men in it, and one of them, Arkon Bloodblade, has a daughter. Messages have gone back and forth. His daughter and Dutiful seem to be suitable for one another. The Hetgurd has sent a delegation to formally recognize their betrothal. It will be here soon. If Prince Dutiful meets their expectations, the affiancing will be recognized at a ceremony at the next new moon." He turned back to me, shaking his head. "I fear it is too soon for such an alliance. Bearns does not like it, nor Rippon. They would probably profit from the renewed trade, but the wounds are still too fresh. Better, I would think, to wait another five years, let the trade swell slowly between the countries, let Dutiful take up the reins of the Six Duchies, and then propose an alliance. Not with my Prince, but with a lesser offering. A daughter of one of the dukes, perhaps a younger son . . . but that is only my advice. I am not the Queen, and the Queen has made her will known. She will have peace in her lifetime, she proclaims. I think she attempts too much: to meld the Mountain Kingdom into the Six Duchies as a seventh, and to put an Outislander woman on our throne as Queen. It is too much, too soon. . . ."

It was almost as if he had forgotten I was there. He thought aloud before me, with a carelessness that he had never displayed in the years when Shrewd was on the throne. In those years, he would never have spoken a word of doubt on any of the King's decisions. I wonder if he regarded our foreign-born Queen as more fallible, or if he deemed me now mature enough to hear his misgivings. He took his chair across from me and again our eyes met.

In that moment, cold walked up my spine as I realized what I confronted. Chade was not the man he had been. He had aged, and despite his denials, the keen mind fought to shine past the fluttering curtains of his years. Only the structure of his spy-web, built so painstakingly through the years, sustained his power now. Whatever drugs he brewed in his teapot were not quite enough to firm the façade. To realize that was like missing a step on a dark steep stair. I suddenly grasped just how far and how swiftly we all could fall.

I reached across the table to set my hand atop his. I swear, I strove to will strength into him. I gripped his eyes with mine and sought to give him confidence. "Begin the night before he disappeared," I suggested quietly. "And tell me all that you know."

"After all these years, I should report to you, and let you draw the conclusions?" I thought I had affronted him, but then his smile dawned. "Ah, Fitz, thank you. Thank you, boy. After this long while, it is so good to have you back at my side. So good to have someone I can trust. The night before Prince Dutiful vanished. Well. Let me see, then."

For a time, those green eyes looked far afield. I feared for a moment that I had sent his mind wandering, but then he suddenly looked back at me, and his glance was keen. "I'll go back a bit further than that. We had quarreled that morning, the Prince and I. Well, not quarreled exactly. Dutiful is too mannered to quarrel with an elder. But I had lectured him, and he had sulked, much as you used to. I declare, sometimes it is a wonder to me how much that boy can put me in mind of you." He huffed out a brief sigh.

"Anyway. We had had a little confrontation. He came

to me for his morning Skill lesson, but he could not keep his mind on it. There were circles under his eyes, and I knew he had been out late again with that hunting cat of his. And I warned him, sharply, that if he could not regulate himself so as to arrive refreshed and ready for lessons, it could be done for him. The cat could be put out in the stables with the other coursing beasts to assure that my Prince would get a good sleep every night.

"That, of course, ill suited him. He and that cat have been inseparable ever since the beast was given to him. But he did not speak of the cat or his late-night excursions, possibly because he thinks I am less well informed of them than I truly am. Instead he attacked the lessons, and his tutor, as being at fault. He told me that he had no head for the Skill and never would no matter how much sleep he got. I told him not to be ridiculous, that he was a Farseer and the Skill was in his blood. He had the nerve to tell me that I was the one being ridiculous, for I had but to look in the mirror to see a Farseer who had no Skill."

Chade cleared his throat and sat back in his chair. It took me a moment to realize that he was amused, not annoyed. "He can be an insolent pup," he growled, but in his complaint I heard a fondness, and a pride in the boy's spirit. It amused me in a different way. A much milder remark from me at that age would have earned me a good rap on the head. The old man had mellowed. I hoped his tolerance for the boy's insolence would not ruin him. Princes, I thought, needed more discipline than other boys, not less.

I offered a distraction of my own. "Then you've begun teaching him the Skill." I put no judgment in my voice.

"I've begun trying," Chade growled, and there was concession in his. "I feel like a mole telling an owl about the sun. I've read the scrolls, Fitz, and I've attempted the meditations and the exercises they suggest. And sometimes I almost feel . . . something. But I don't know if it's what I'm meant to feel or only an old man's wistful imagining."

"I told you," I said, and I kept my voice gentle. "It can't

be learned, nor taught, from a scroll. The meditation can ready you for it, but then someone has to show it to you."

"That's why I sent for you," he replied, too quickly. "Because you are not just the only one who can properly teach the Skill to the Prince. You are also the only one who can use it to find him."

I sighed. "Chade, the Skill doesn't work that way. It—"

"Say rather that you were never taught to use the Skill that way. It's in the scrolls, Fitz. It says that two who have been joined by the Skill can find one another with it, if they need to. All my other efforts to find the Prince have failed. Dogs put on his scent ran well for half the morning, and then raced in circles, whimpering in confusion. My best spies have nothing to tell me, bribes have bought me nothing. The Skill is all that is left, I tell you."

I thrust aside my piqued curiosity. I did not want to see the scrolls. "Even if the scrolls claim it can be done, you say it happens between two who have been joined by the Skill. The Prince and I have no such—"

"I think you do."

There is a certain tone of voice Chade has that stops one from speaking. It warns that he knows far more than you think he does, and cautions you against telling him lies. It was extremely effective when I was a small boy. It was a bit of a shock to find it was no less effective now that I was a man. I slowly drew breath into my lungs but before I could ask, he answered me.

"Certain dreams the Prince has recounted to me first woke my suspicions. They started with occasional dreams when he was very small. He dreamed of a wolf bringing down a doe, and a man rushing up to cut her throat. In the dream, he was the man, and yet he could also see the man. That first dream excited him. For a day and a half, he spoke of little else. He told it as if it were something he had done himself." He paused. "Dutiful was only five at the time. The detail of his dream far exceeded his own experience."

I still said nothing.

"It was years before he had another such dream. Or, perhaps I should say it was years before he spoke to me of one. He dreamed of a man fording a river. The water threatened to sweep him away, but at the last he managed to cross it. He was too wet and too cold to build a fire to warm himself, but he lay down in the shelter of a fallen tree. A wolf came to lie beside him and warm him. And again, the Prince told me this dream as something that he himself had done. 'I love it,' he told me. 'It is almost as if there is another life that belongs to me, one that is far away and free of being a prince. A life that belongs to me alone, where I have a friend who is as close as my own skin.' It was then that I suspected he had had other such Skill-dreams, but had not shared them with me."

He waited, and this time I had to break my silence.

I took a breath. "If I shared those moments of my life with the Prince, I was unaware of it. But, yes, those are true events." I halted, suddenly wondering what else he had shared. I recalled Verity's complaint that I did not guard my thoughts well, and that my dreams and experiences sometimes intruded on his. I thought of my trysts with Starling and prayed I would not blush. It had been a very long time since I had bothered to set Skill-walls round myself. Plainly, I must do so again. Another thought came in the wake of that. Obviously, my Skill-talent had not degraded as much as I believed. A surge of exhilaration came with that thought. It was probably, I told myself viciously, much the same as what a drunk felt on discovering a forgotten bottle beneath the bed.

"And you have shared moments of the Prince's life?" Chade pressed me.

"Perhaps. I suspect so. I often have vivid dreams, and to dream of being a boy in Buckkeep is not so foreign from my own experience. But—" I took a breath and forced myself on. "The important thing here is the cat, Chade. How long has he had it? Do you think he is Witted? Is he bonded to the cat?"

I felt like a liar, asking questions when I already knew the answers. My mind was rapidly shuffling through my dreams of the last fifteen years, sorting out those that came with the peculiar clarity that lingered after waking. Some could have been episodes from the Prince's life. Others—I halted at the recollection of my fever dream of Burrich—Nettle, too? Dream-sharing with Nettle? This new insight reordered my memory of the dream. I had not just witnessed those events from Nettle's perspective. I had been Skill-sharing her life. It was possible that, as with Dutiful, the flow of Skill-sharing had gone both ways. What had seemed a cherished glimpse into her life, a tiny window on Molly and Burrich, was now revealed as her vulnerability before my carelessness. I winced away from the thought and resolved a stronger wall about my thoughts. How could I have been so incautious? How many of my secrets had I spilled before those most vulnerable to them?

"How would I know if the boy was Witted?" Chade replied testily. "I never knew you were, until you told me. Even then, I didn't know what you were telling me at first."

I was suddenly weary, too tired to lie. Whom was I trying to protect with deceit? I knew too well that lies did not shield for long, that in the end they became the largest chinks in any man's armor. "I suspect he is. And bonded to the cat. From dreams I've had."

Before my eyes, the man aged. He shook his head wordlessly, and poured more brandy for both of us. I drank mine off while he drank his in long, considering sips. When he finally spoke, he said, "I hate irony. It is a manacle that ties our dreams to our fears. I had hoped you had a dream bond with the boy, a tie that would let you use the Skill to find him. And indeed you do, but with it you reveal my greatest fear for Dutiful is real. The Wit. Oh, Fitz. I wish I could go back and make my fears foolish instead of real."

"Who gave him the cat?"

"One of the nobles. It was a gift. He receives far too

many gifts. All try to curry favor with him. Kettricken tries
to turn aside those of the more valuable sort. She worries it
will spoil the boy. But it was only a little hunting cat . . . yet
it may be the gift that spoils him for his life."

"Who gave it to him?" I pressed.

"I will have to look back in my journals," Chade confessed. He gave me a dark look. "You can't expect an old
man to have a young man's memory. I do the best I can,
Fitz." His reproachful look spoke volumes. If I had returned
to Buckkeep, resumed my tasks at his side, I would know
these vital answers. The thought brought a new question to
my mind.

"Where is your new apprentice in all this?"

He watched me speculatively. After a moment he said,
"Not ready for tasks such as these."

I met his gaze squarely. "Is he, perhaps, recovering
from, well, from a lightning strike from a clear sky? One
that exploded an unused storage shed?"

He blinked, but kept control of his face. Even his
voice remained steady as he ignored my thrust. "No,
FitzChivalry, this task belongs to you. Only you have the
unique abilities needed."

"What, exactly, do you want of me?" The question was
as good as surrender. I had already hastened to his side at his
call. He knew I was still his. So did I.

"Find the Prince. Return him to us, discreetly, and Eda
save us, unharmed. And do it while my excuses for his absence are still believable. Get him home safely to us before
the Outislander delegation arrives to formalize the betrothal to their Princess."

"How soon is that?"

He shrugged helplessly. "It depends on the winds and the
waves and the strength of their oarsmen. They have already
departed the Out Islands. We had a bird tell us so. The formality is scheduled for the new moon. If they arrive before
that and the Prince is not here, I could, perhaps, fabricate

something about his meditating alone before such a serious event in his life. But it would be a thin façade, one that would crumble if he did not appear for the ceremony."

I reckoned it quickly in my head. "That's more than a fortnight away. Plenty of time for a recalcitrant boy to change his mind and run home again."

Chade looked at me somberly. "Yet if the Prince has been taken, and we do not yet know by whom or why, let alone how we will recover him, then sixteen days seems but a pittance of time."

I put my head in my hands for a moment. When I looked up, my old mentor was still regarding me hopefully. Trusting me to see a solution that eluded him. I wanted to flee; I wanted never to have known any of this. I took a steadying breath. Then I ordered his mind as he had once disciplined mine. "I need information," I announced. "Don't assume I know anything about the situation, because it is likely I don't. I need to know, first of all, who gave him the cat. And how that person feels about the Wit, and the Prince's betrothal. Expand the circle from there. Who rivals the gift-giver, who allies with him? Who at Court most strongly persecutes those with the Wit, who most directly opposes the Prince's betrothal, who supports it? Which nobles have most recently been accused of having the Wit in their families? Who could have helped Dutiful run, if run he did? If he was taken, who had the opportunity? Who knew his midnight habits?" Each question I formulated seemed to beget another, yet in the face of that volley, Chade seemed to grow steadier. These were questions he could answer, and his ability to answer them strengthened his belief that together we might prevail. I paused for breath.

"And I still need to report to you the events of those days. However, you seem to be forgetting that the Skill might save us hours of talk. Let me show you the scrolls, and see if they make more sense to you than they do to me."

I looked around me, but he shook his head. "I do not

bring the Prince here. This part of the castle remains a secret from him. I keep the Skill-scrolls in Verity's old tower, and it is there that the boy has his lessons. I keep the tower room well secured, and a trusted guard is always before the door."

"Then how am I to have access to them?"

He cocked his head at me. "There is a way to them, from here to Verity's tower. It's a winding and narrow way, with many steps, but you're a young man. You can manage them. Finish eating. Then I will show you the way."

chapter XII

CHARMS

*Kettricken of the Mountains was wed to King-in-Waiting
Verity of the Six Duchies before she had reached her
twentieth year. Their marriage was a political expedient,
part of a larger negotiation to cement an alliance of trade
and protection between the Six Duchies and the Mountain
Kingdom. The death of her older brother on the eve of her
wedding bestowed an unexpected benefit on the Six
Duchies: any heir she now bore would inherit the Mountain
crown as well as that of the Six Duchies.*

*Her transition from Mountain princess to Six Duchies
queen was not an easy one, yet she faced it with the
acceptance of duty that is the stamp of the Mountain rulers.
She came to Buckkeep alone, without so much as a lady's
maid to sustain her. She brought to Buckkeep her personal
standards that required her to be ever ready to sacrifice
herself in any way that her new station might demand of
her. For in the Mountains, that is the accepted role of the
ruler: The king is Sacrifice for his people.*

— BEDEL'S "MOUNTAIN QUEEN"

Night was ebbing toward morning before I made my way
down the hidden stairs to seek my own bed. My head was
stuffed full of facts, few of which seemed useful to my puzzle.
I'd go to sleep, I decided. Somehow, when I awoke, my
mind would have sorted it all out.

I reached the panel that would lead back into my bedchamber and paused. Chade had already taught me all his

cautions for using these passages. Breath pent, I peered through the tiny slit in the stone. It afforded me a very narrow view of the room. I could see a candle guttering on a small table set in the center of the room. That was all. I listened, but heard nothing. I silently eased a lever that set unseen counterweights into motion. The door swung open and I slipped back into my room. A nudge from me sent the door back into place. I stared at the wall. The portal was as invisible as ever.

Lord Golden had thoughtfully provided a couple of scratchy wool blankets for the narrow cot in the stuffy little room. Tired as I was, it still looked remarkably uninviting. I could, I reminded myself, return to the tower room and sleep in Chade's magnificent bed. He no longer used it. But that prospect was uninviting in a different way. Recently used or not, that bed was Chade's bed. The tower room, the maps and the scroll racks, the arcane laboratory and the two hearths: all of that was Chade's, and I had no desire to make it mine by using it. This was better. The hard bed and the stuffy room were comforting reminders that my stay here was to be very brief. After a single evening of secrets and machinations, I was already weary of Buckkeep politics.

My pack and Verity's sword were on the bed. I threw the pack to the floor, leaned Verity's sword in a corner, kicked my discarded clothing under the table, blew out the candle, and groped my way to bed. I thrust Dutiful and the Wit and all the attendant threads resolutely aside. I expected to fall asleep immediately. Instead I stared open-eyed into the dark room. More personal worries found me and chewed on me. My boy and my wolf would be on the road to Buckkeep tonight. It was unsettling to realize I was now counting on Hap to care for the old wolf that had always been his protector. He had his bow, and he was good with it. They'd be fine. Unless they were set on by highwaymen. Even then, Hap would probably eliminate one or two before they were captured. Which would probably anger the rest of them. Nighteyes would fight to the death before he'd let Hap be taken. Which left me with the pleasant image of my wolf dead in the road and my son captured by angered highwaymen. And I'd be too far away to do anything for them.

Wool blankets itch even more when you sweat. I rolled over to stare at a different patch of darkness. I wouldn't think about Hap just now. There was no point to worrying about disasters that hadn't happened yet. Unwillingly, I let my mind wander back to Chade's Skill-scrolls and the present crisis. I had expected three or four scrolls. What he had shown me were several chests of scrolls, in various degrees of preservation. Even he had not been through all of them, though he thought he had them somewhat sorted into topics and levels of difficulty. He had presented me with a large table with three scrolls unrolled on it. My heart sank. The lettering on two of the scrolls was so archaic I could barely decipher it. The other seemed more recent, but almost immediately I encountered words and phrases that made no sense to me. It recommended an "anticula trance" and suggested a helpful infusion made from an herb called "Shepherd's Wort." I'd never heard of it. The scroll further cautioned me to beware of "dividing my partner's self-barrier" as I might then "diffuse his anma." I looked up to Chade in bewilderment. He instantly divined my problem.

"I thought you would know what it meant," he said defeatedly.

I shook my head. "If Galen ever knew what these words and terms meant, he never divulged them to me."

Chade gave a snort of contempt. "I doubt our 'Skillmaster' could even read these characters." He sighed. "Half of any trade is understanding the vocabulary and idiom that the practitioners use. With time, we might piece it together with clues from the other scrolls. But we have precious little time. With every passing moment, the Prince may be carried farther from Buckkeep."

"Or he may never even have left the town. Chade, you have cautioned me many times not to take action simply for the sake of taking action. If we rush forth, we may be rushing in the wrong direction. First think, then act."

It had felt so strange to remind my master of his own wisdom. I had watched him grudgingly nod to it. While he pored over the archaic lettering, muttering as his pen flowed a clear translation onto paper, I had carefully read the more accessible scroll. Then I had read it again, hoping it would make more sense. On my third attempt, I found myself nodding off over the old, blurred lettering. Chade had leaned across the table to clasp my wrist gently. "Go to bed, boy," he ordered me gruffly. "Lack of sleep makes a man stupid, and this will demand your best wits." I had conceded and left him there, still hunched over his pen and paper.

I shifted onto my back. I ached from all the stairs I had climbed today. Well, as long as I could not sleep, I might as well see what good I could do. I closed my eyes to the pressing darkness and composed myself. I emptied my mind of my concerns, and tried only to recall the last dream I had had of the boy and the cat. I conjured up their exhilaration at the night and the hunt. I summoned my recollection of the scents that had flavored the air, and reached for the indefinable aura of a dream not my own. Almost I could enter that dream, but that was not what I sought. I tried to recall a tenuous Skill-link I had not been aware of at the time I experienced it.

Prince Dutiful. The son of my body. These titles in my mind had no impressions attached to them, yet oddly they interfered with what I was trying to do. My preconceived notions of Dutiful, my possessive idealizations of what my natural son would be like, stood between me and the frail threads of the Skill-link I sought to untangle. From somewhere in the keep, the stone bones of the castle carried a stray bit of music to my ears. It distracted me. I blinked at the dark before me. I had lost all sense of time; night stretched eternally around me. I hated this windowless room, shut off from the natural world. I hated the confinement I had to endure. I had lived with the wolf too long to find it tolerable.

In frustration, I abandoned the Skill and reached out with the Wit for my companion. He still had up the guard he had so often employed of late. I could sense him sleeping, and as I leaned against his walls, I felt the dull thunder of pain in his hips and back. I withdrew quickly when I sensed that my focusing on his pain was bringing it to the forefront of his mind. I had sensed no fear or foreboding in him, only weariness and aching joints. I wrapped him in my thoughts, drawing gratefully on his senses.

I'm sleeping, he grumpily informed me. Then, *You're worried about something?*

It's nothing. I just wanted to know you were fine.

Oh, yes, we're fine. We've had a lovely day of walking down a dry, dusty road. Now we're sleeping at the edge of it. Then, more kindly, he added, *Don't worry about things you can't change. I'll be with you soon.*

Watch Hap for me.

Of course. Go to sleep.

I could smell damp grass and the waning smoke of the campfire, and even Hap's salty sweat as he lay nearby. It reassured me. All was well in my world, then. I let go of all save those simple sensations and finally spiraled down into sleep.

      ❧   ❧   ❧

"Might I remind you that you are to serve as my valet, not the reverse?"

The words that jolted me from sleep were spoken with Lord Golden's arrogant sneer, but the smile on the Fool's face was entirely his own. A set of clothing hung over his arm, and I could smell warm, scented water. He was already faultlessly dressed in garb that was even more elegantly understated than what he had worn yesterday. His colors today were cream and forest green, with a thin edging of gilt at his cuffs and collar. He wore a new earring, a filigreed golden orb. I knew what was inside it. He looked fresh and alert. I sat up and then cradled my aching head in my hands.

"Skill-headache?" he asked sympathetically.

I shook my head and the pain rattled inside it. "I only wish it were," I muttered. I glanced up at him. "I'm just tired."

"I thought perhaps you would sleep in the tower."

"It didn't feel right." I rose and tried to stretch but my back kinked in protest. The Fool set the clothing across the foot of the bed, and then sat down on my rumpled blankets. "So. Any thoughts on where our Prince might be?"

"Too many. Anywhere in Buck Duchy, or even beyond the borders by now. There are too many nobles who might want to take him. If he ran on his own, that only increases the number of places he might have gone." The wash water was still steaming. A few leaves of lemon balm floated fragrantly on the surface of the plain pottery bowl. I plunged my face into it gratefully and came up rubbing my hands over my face. I felt more awake and aware of the world. "I need a bath. Are the steam baths behind the guard barracks still there?"

"Yes, but servants don't use them. You'll have to be wary of falling back into old habits. Personal servants, generally speaking, get the second use of their master's or mistress's bathwater. Or they haul their own from the kitchens."

I gave him a look. "I'll haul my own tonight." I proceeded to make the best use I could of the handbasin while he sat and silently watched me. While I was shaving, he observed quietly, "You'll have to get up earlier tomorrow. All the kitchen staff know that I'm an early riser."

I looked at him in consternation. "And?"

"And they'll be expecting my servant to come down for my breakfast tray."

The sense sank in slowly. He was right. I needed to do a better job of stepping into my role if I was to find out anything useful. "I'll go now," I offered.

He shook his head. "Not looking like that. Lord Golden is a proud and temperamental man. He would not keep such a rough-thatched servant as you show yourself now. We must make you look your part. Come here and sit down."

I followed him out into the light and air of the master chamber. He had set out comb, brush, and shears on his table, and propped a large mirror on it. I steeled myself to endure this. I crossed to the door to be sure it was securely bolted against untimely intrusion. Then I sat in a chair and waited for him to lop my hair into a servant's short cut. I freed my hair from its tail as Lord Golden took up the shears. When I looked into his ornately framed mirror, I saw a man I scarcely recognized. There is something about a large glass and seeing oneself all at once. Starling was right, I decided. I did look much older than my years. When I leaned back from the mirror and regarded my face, I was surprised to see how my scar had faded. It was still there as a seam, but it was not as remarkable as it had been on a young man's unlined face. The Fool let me look at myself for a time in silence. Then he gathered my hair into his hands. I glanced up at his face in the mirror. His lower lip was caught in his teeth in an agony of indecision. Abruptly he clacked the shears back onto the table. "No," he said emphatically. "I can't bring myself to do it, and I don't think we need to." He took a breath, then rapidly curried my hair back into its warrior tail. "Try the clothing," he urged me. "I had to guess at size, but no one expects a servant's clothing to be well tailored."

I went back to the small chamber and looked at the garments draped across the foot of my cot. They were cut from the familiar blue homespun that servants at Buckkeep had always worn. It was not all that different from the clothing I had worn as a child. But as I put it on, it felt different. I was donning the garments that marked me to all eyes as a servingman. A disguise, I told myself. I was not truly anyone's servant. But with a sudden pang, I wondered how Molly had felt the first time she had donned the blue dress of a servinggirl. Bastard or not, I was the son of a prince. I had never expected to wear the garments of a servant. In place of my Farseer charging buck, there was an embroidery of Lord Golden's golden cock pheasant. Yet the garments fit me well, and, "Actually, these are the best quality clothes I've worn in years," I ruefully admitted. The Fool leaned round the door to look at me, and for a second I thought I saw anxiety in his eyes. But at the sight of me, he grinned, then made a show of walking a slow circle of inspection around me.

"You'll do, Tom Badgerlock. There are boots by the door, made a good three finger-widths longer than my foot, and wider, too. Best you put your things away in the chest, so that if anyone does become curious to look about our rooms, there will be nothing to arouse suspicion."

This I did hastily while the Fool quickly tidied his own chamber. Verity's sword went under the clothing in my chest. There were scarcely enough garments to cover it. The boots fit as well as new boots usually did. Time would make them comfortable.

"I'm sure you remember the way to the kitchens. I always eat my breakfast on a tray in my room; the kitchen boys will be glad to see you're taking on the task of bringing it to me. It may give you an opening for gossip." He paused. "Tell them I ate little last night and hence am ravenous this morning. Then bring up enough for both of us."

It was strange to have him direct me so minutely, but, I reminded myself, I had best get used to it. So I bobbed a bow at him and essayed a "Yes, sir," before I went out of the door of the chamber. He started to smile, caught himself, and inclined a slow nod to me.

Outside the chamber, the castle was well awake. Other servants were busy, replenishing candles and sweeping soiled rushes away or scurrying about with fresh linens or buckets of wash water. Perhaps it was my new perspective, but it seemed to me that there were far more servants in Buckkeep than I recalled. It was not the only aspect that had changed. Queen Kettricken's Mountain ways were more in evidence than ever. In her years of residence, the inside of the castle had been raised to a new standard of cleanliness. A sparse simplicity characterized the rooms I passed, replacing decades of ornate clutter that had once filled them. The tapestries and banners that remained were clean and free of cobwebs.

But in the kitchens, Cook Sara still reigned. I stepped into the steam and smells and it was like stepping through a doorway back into my boyhood. As Chade had told me, the old cook was ensconced on a chair rather than bustling from hearth to table to hearth, but clearly food was cooked in Buckkeep kitchens as it had always been cooked. I wrenched my eyes from Sara's ample form, lest she catch my gaze and somehow know me. I humbly tugged at the sleeve of a servingboy to make Lord Golden's breakfast wishes known to him. The boy pointed out the trays, dishes, and cutlery and then gestured wide at the cooking hearths. "Yer his servant, not me," he pointed out snippily, and went back to chopping turnips. I scowled at him, but was inwardly grateful. I had soon served up enough for two very ample breakfasts onto the tray. I whisked it and myself out of the kitchen.

I was halfway up the stairs when I heard a familiar voice in conversation. I halted and then leaned on the balustrade to look down. Unbidden, a smile came to my face. Queen Kettricken strode through the hall below, a half-dozen ladies struggling valiantly to keep pace with her. I knew none of her ladies; they were all young, none much past twenty. They had been children when last I was at Buckkeep. One looked vaguely familiar, but perhaps I had known her mother. My gaze fixed on the Queen.

Kettricken's shining hair, still gloriously golden, was looped and pinned about her head in a crown of braids. She wore a simple circlet of silver atop her head. She was dressed in russet brown with an embroidered yellow kirtle, and her skirts rustled as she walked. Her ladies emulated her simple style without being able to capture it, for it was Kettricken's innate grace that lent elegance to her unpretentious garb. Despite the years that had passed, her posture and stride were still upright and unfettered. She walked with purpose, but I saw a stillness captured in her face. Some part of her was constantly aware of her missing son, and yet she still moved through the court as a queen. My heart stood still at the sight of her. I thought how proud Verity would be of this woman and, "Oh, my Queen," I breathed to myself.

She halted in mid-stride and I almost heard the intake of her breath. She glanced about and then up, her eyes meeting mine across the distance. In the shadow of the Great Hall, I could not see her blue gaze, but somehow I felt it. For an instant our eyes locked, but her face held puzzlement, not recognition.

I felt the sudden thwack of fingers against the side of my head. I turned to my attacker, too amazed to be angry. A gentleman of the Court, taller than I, looked down on me in sharp disapproval. His words were clipped. "You are obviously new to Buckkeep, oaf. Here, the servants are not permitted to stare so brazenly at the Queen. Be about your business. After this, remember your place, or soon you will have no place to remember."

I looked down at the tray of food I gripped, struggling to control my face. Anger filled me. I knew that my face had darkened with blood. It took every bit of my will to avert my eyes and bob my head. "Your pardon, sir. I will remember." I hoped he took my strangled voice for crushed humiliation rather than rage. Gripping the sides of the tray tightly, I continued my journey up the stairs as he went down and did not allow myself to glance over the balustrade to see if my Queen watched me go.

A servant. A servant. I am a loyal, well-trained manservant. I am newly come from the country, but well recommended, so I am a mannered servant, accustomed to discipline. Accustomed to humiliation. Or was I? When I had followed Lord Golden into Buckkeep, Verity's blade in its plain scabbard had hung at my side. Surely, some would have marked that. My complexion and the scars on my hands marked me as a man who lived more out-of-doors than in. If I was to play this role, then it must be believable. It must be a role I could endure, as well as one I could act convincingly.

At Lord Golden's door, I knocked, paused discreetly to allow my master to expect me, then entered. The Fool was at the casement looking out. I carefully closed the door behind me, latched it, and then set down the tray on the table. As I began to lay out the meal, I spoke to his back. "I am Tom Badgerlock, your servant. I was recommended to you as a fellow who was educated above his station by an indulgent master, but kept more for his blade than his manners. You chose me because you wanted a manservant capable of being your bodyguard as well as your valet. You have heard that I am moody and occasionally quick-tempered, but you are willing to try me to see if I will serve your purpose. I am . . . forty-two years old. The scars I bear I took defending my last master from an attack by three—no, six—highwaymen. I killed them all. I am not a man to be provoked lightly. When my last master died, he left me a small bequest that enabled me to live simply. But now my son has come of age, and I wished to apprentice him in Buckkeep Town. You persuaded me to return to service as a way to defray my expenses."

Lord Golden had turned from the window. His aristocratic hands clasped one another as he listened to my soliloquy. When I had finished, he nodded. "I like it, Tom Badgerlock. Such a coup for Lord Golden, to have a manservant who is just a tiny bit dangerous to keep about. Such an air shall I put on over having hired such a man! You will do, Tom. You will do well."

He advanced to the table, and I drew his chair out for

him. He seated himself, and looked over the setting and dishes I had prepared for him. "Excellent. This is exactly to my liking. Tom, keep this up, and I shall have to raise your wages." He lifted his gaze to meet mine. "Sit down and eat with me," the Fool suggested.

I shook my head. "Best I practice my manners, sir. Tea?"

For an instant the Fool looked horrified. Then Lord Golden lifted a napkin and patted at his lips. "Please."

I poured for him.

"This son of yours, Tom. I have not met him. He's in Buckkeep Town, is he?"

"I told him to follow me here, sir." I suddenly realized I had told Hap little more than that. He would arrive with a weary old pony pulling a rickety cart with an aging wolf in it. I had not gone to Jinna's niece, to ask her to expect him. What if she took affront at my assumption that my boy could come there? Like a wave breaking over me, my other life caught up with me. I'd made no provisions for him. He knew no one else in Buckkeep Town, save Starling, and I did not even know if she was currently in residence here. Besides, with relations strained between us, Hap was unlikely to turn to her for aid.

I suddenly knew I had to seek out the hedge-witch and be sure my boy would be accepted there. I'd leave a message for Hap with her. And I had to approach Chade immediately about making provisions for him. Given what I knew now, it seemed a cold bargain and my heart shrank within me at the thought of it. I could always borrow the money from the Fool. I winced at the thought. Just what are my wages? I prompted myself to ask. But the words could not find their way to my tongue.

Lord Golden pushed back from his table. "You are quiet, Tom Badgerlock. When your son does arrive, I expect you to present him to me. For now, I think I shall let you have this first morning to yourself. Tidy up here, get to know the castle and the grounds." He looked me over critically. "Fetch me paper, quill, and ink. I will write you a letter of credit to Scrandon the tailor. I expect you will find his shop easily enough. You knew it of old. You need to be measured for more clothing, some for everyday, and some for when I want you to show well. If you are bodyguard as well as valet, then I think it fitting that you stand behind my chair at formal dinners and accompany me when I ride. And go also to Croy's. He has a weapons stall down near the smithy's lane. Look through his used swords and find yourself a serviceable blade."

I nodded to each of his orders. I went to a small desk in the corner to set out pen and ink for my master. Behind me, the Fool spoke quietly. "Both Hod's work and Verity's blade are likely to be too well remembered here at Buckkeep Castle. I'd advise you to keep that blade in Chade's old tower room."

I did not look at him as I replied. "I shall. And I shall also be speaking to the Weaponsmaster, to ask him to provide me a practice partner. I shall tell him my skills are a bit rusty and you want me to sharpen them. Who was Prince Dutiful's drill partner?"

The Fool knew. He always knew things like that. He spoke as he took his seat at the writing desk. "Cresswell was his instructor, but he paired him most often with a young woman named Delleree. But you can't very well ask for her by name . . . hmm. Tell him you'd like to work with someone who fights with two swords, to sharpen your defense skills. I believe that is her specialty."

"I shall. Thank you."

A few moments passed as his pen scratched busily across the paper. Once or twice he looked up, regarding me with a speculative look that made me uneasy. I wandered over to his window and looked out of it. It was a lovely day. I wished it belonged solely to me. I smelled melting wax and turned around to see Lord Golden applying his seal to his missives. He let the wax cool a bit, then held them out to me.

"Off you go, to tailor and weapons dealer. As for me, I think I shall stroll for a bit in the gardens, and then I have been invited to the Queen's parlor for—"

"I saw her. Kettricken." I choked on a bitter laugh. "It seems so long ago: us waking the stone dragons, and all. And then something will happen and it seems like yesterday. The last time I saw Kettricken, she sat astride Verity-as-Dragon and bade us all farewell. Now, today, I saw her and it suddenly all came real for me. She has reigned here as Queen for well over a decade.

"I stepped aside from all this to heal, and because I thought I could no longer be a part of it. Now, I've returned and I look around me and think, I've missed my life. While I was off and alone, it went on here, without me, and I'm forever doomed to be a stranger in my own home."

"Regrets are useless," the Fool replied. "All you can do is start from where you are. And who knows? Perhaps what you bring back from your self-imposed exile may prove to be just what is needed."

"And time flies by us, even as we speak."

"Quite so," Lord Golden replied. He gestured at his wardrobe. "My coat, Badgerlock. The green one."

I opened the wardrobe doors and extracted the required garment from its many brethren, then closed the panels as best I could upon the bulging excess. I held his coat for him as so often I had seen Charim hold a coat for Verity, and assisted him into it. He held out his wrists to me, and I adjusted the cuffs and tugged the skirts of it straight. A flicker of amusement passed through his eyes. "Very good, Badgerlock," he murmured. He preceded me to the door and then waited while I opened it for him.

Once he was gone, I latched it, and quickly finished the rest of the cooling breakfast. I stacked the dishes back on the tray. I looked at the entry to the Fool's private room. Then I kindled a candle, entered my small chamber, and shut the door firmly behind me. But for the candle, the darkness would have been absolute. It took me a few moments to find the trigger that released the catch, and then two tries before I pressed the right spot on the wall. Despite the protest in my aching legs, I carried Verity's sword up the multitude of stairs to Chade's tower and leaned it in the corner by the mantel.

Once I was back in the Fool's room, I cleared the table. When I glanced into the looking glass, the breakfast things in my hands, I saw a Buckkeep servingman. I gave a short sigh, reminded myself to keep my eyes lowered, and left the room.

Had I feared that on my return to Buckkeep Castle, all would instantly recognize me? The reality was that no one even saw me. A glance at my servant's clothing and lowered eyes and I was dismissed from the mind. I did receive sidelong looks from my fellow servants, but for the most part they were occupied with their own tasks. A few offered hasty greetings, and I accepted their welcome amiably. I would cultivate the servants, for little happens in any great house that the servants do not know about. I returned the dishes to the kitchen and left the castle. The guards passed me through with scarcely a word. I soon found myself on the steep road that led down to the town. It was a fine day and the road was well traveled. Summer seemed determined to linger a time yet. I fell in behind a group of ladies' maids going down to the town with baskets on their arms. They glanced warily back at me twice, and then ignored me. The rest of the way down the hill, I listened hungrily to their gossip, but found no hints there. They were speaking of the festivities that would accompany the Prince's betrothal, and what their mistresses would wear. Somehow the Queen and Chade had been able to disguise the Prince's absence.

In the town, I quickly went about Lord Golden's errands but kept my ears pricked for any word that might pertain to Dutiful. I found the tailor's shop with no difficulty.

As Lord Golden had told me, I knew it of old, when it was Molly's chandlery. It was strange to enter that place. The tailor took my letter of credit with no hesitation, but clucked over Golden's command for haste in the sewing. "Still, he has paid me well enough to make it worth my sleep tonight. Your clothes will be ready by tomorrow." I gathered from his other comments that Lord Golden had patronized him before. I stood silently on a low stool and was measured. No questions were asked of me, for Lord Golden had specified in his note how he wished his servant dressed. I was free to stand silent and wonder if I could still catch the scents of beeswax and scented herbs, or if I deceived myself. Before I departed, I asked the man if he knew of any hedge-witches in Buckkeep. I wanted to ask one if my new position boded well for me. He shook his head at my low-born superstition, but told me to ask about it near the smithy's lane.

This suited me well, for my next errand took me to Croy's. I wondered that Lord Golden knew this man's shop at all, for it was a jackdaw's nest of battered weapons and armor. But again the proprietor took Lord Golden's note without question. I took my time finding a blade I could live with. I wanted a simple, well-made weapon, but of course that is what any true man-at-arms chooses, so that was what Croy had fewest of. After trying to interest me in several remarkable swords that had elaborate guards and nondescript blades, he gave up on me and left me to sort through his collection. I did so, but kept up a constant stream of observations at how Buckkeep had changed since I was last there. It was not hard to get him gossiping, and then to turn his tongue to omens and portents and those who dealt in them. I did not have to mention Jinna by name to hear of her. At length I selected a blade truly worthy of my rusty skills. Croy tutted over it. "Your master has gold and to spare, good man. Choose yourself something with a bit of a sparkle on it, or some style to the basket."

I shook my head. "No, no, I want nothing that will catch in a man's clothes when the fighting is close and hot. This is the one I'll have. But I'll take a knife to go with it."

This was soon found and I left his shop. I walked through the loud clanging and gusting heat that marked the smithy's lane. The hammers of competing smithies were a stunning counterpoint to the sun's beat. I had forgotten how constant the noise of a city was. I searched my memory as I walked, trying to recall if anything I had said to Jinna would conflict with my newly modified life history. At length, I decided it would have to do. If something did not make sense to her, well, she would just have to believe me a liar. I frowned at how much that disturbed me.

Croy had described a dark green sign with a white hand painted on it. The lines on the hand were all done in red, quite skillfully. From the low eaves of her roof several of her charms tinkled and turned in the sunlight. Luckily for me, none seemed to be against predators. It took me but a moment's pause to guess at their purpose. Welcome. They attracted me to the house and the door. It took a time for anyone to reply to my knock, but then the top half of the door opened and Jinna herself greeted me.

"Badgerlock!" she exclaimed, peering at me, and it was pleasant that neither my warrior's tail nor my new clothes had kept her from knowing me. She instantly swung the lower door open. "Come in! Welcome to Buckkeep Town. Will you let me repay the debt of hospitality I owe you? Do come in."

There is little in life so reassuring as a genuine welcome. She took my hand and drew me into the cool dimness of her home as if I were an expected guest. The ceiling was low and the furnishings modest. There was a round table with several chairs set about it. Nearby shelves held the tools of her trade, including an assortment of draped charms. Dishes and food were on the table; I had interrupted her meal. I halted, feeling awkward. "I did not mean to intrude."

"Not at all. Sit down and share." She took a seat at the table as she spoke and I could scarcely do otherwise. "Now. Tell me what brings you to Buckkeep." She pushed the platter toward me. It held several jam tarts and smoked fish and cheese. I took a tart to give myself time to think. She must have noticed that I wore servant's garb, but left it to me to tell her what it meant. I liked that.

"I've taken a position at Buckkeep as a manservant to Lord Golden." Even knowing it was false, it was still hard to say those words. I had never realized what a proud fellow I was until I had to masquerade as the Fool's servant. "When I left home, I told Hap to join me when he could. At that time, I was not sure of my plans. I think that when he gets to Buckkeep Town, he may seek you out. May I leave word for him with you, so you can send him on to me?"

I braced myself for all the inevitable questions. Why had I suddenly taken this employment, why hadn't I simply brought Hap with me, how did I know Lord Golden? Instead, her eyes brightened and she exclaimed, "With great pleasure! But what I propose is simpler. When Hap arrives, I'll keep him here and send word up to the keep. There's a little room in the back he can use; it was my nephew's before he grew up and married away. Let the boy have a day or so in Buckkeep Town; he seemed to enjoy it so at Springfest, and your new duties will probably not allow you time to show him about yourself."

"I know he would love that," I found myself saying. It would be far easier for me to maintain my role as Lord Golden's servant if I did not have Hap in the midst of it. "My hope is that here in Buckkeep I'll be able to earn the coin to purchase him a good apprenticeship."

Coming up. A large tawny cat announced this to me at the same moment that he effortlessly elevated onto my lap. I stared at him in surprise. Never had an animal spoken so clearly to me via the Wit save for my own bond-animals. Nor had I ever been so completely ignored by an animal that had just spoken mind to mind with me. The cat stood, hind legs on my lap, front paws on the table, and surveyed the food. A plumy tail waved before my face.

"Fennel! Shame on you, stop that. Come here." Jinna leaned across the table to scoop the cat from my lap. She picked up the conversation as she did so. "Yes, Hap's told me of his ambitions, and it's a fine thing to see a young man with dreams and hopes."

"He's a good boy," I fervently agreed with her. "And he deserves a good chance at making something of himself. I'd do anything for him."

Fennel now stood on Jinna's lap and stared at me across the table. *She likes me better than you.* He stole a piece of fish from the edge of her plate.

Do all cats speak so rudely to strangers? I rebuked him.

He leaned back to bump his head possessively against Jinna's chest. His yellow-eyed stare was daunting. *All cats talk however they want. To whomever they want. But only a rude human speaks out of turn. Be quiet. I told you. She likes me better than you.* He twisted his head to look up at Jinna's face. *More fish?*

"That's plain," she agreed. I tried to remember what I had said to her as I watched her give the cat a bit of fish at the edge of the table. I knew Jinna was not Witted. I wondered if the cat was lying to me about all cats talking. I knew little of cats. Burrich had never kept them in the stables. We'd had rat dogs to keep the vermin down.

Jinna misinterpreted my preoccupation. A touch of sympathy came into her eyes as she added, "Still, it must be hard to leave your own home and being your own master to come to town and serve, no matter how fine a man Lord Golden may be. I hope he's as openhanded at paying you as he is when he comes down to Buckkeep Town to trade."

I forced a smile to my face. "You know of Lord Golden, then?"

She bobbed a nod at me. "By coincidence, he was right here in this very room just last month. He wanted a charm to keep moths from his wardrobe. I told him I had never made such a thing before, but that I could attempt one. So gracious he was for such a noble man. He paid me for it, just on my word that I would make one. And then he insisted on looking at every charm I had in my shop, and bought no less than six of them. Six! One for sweet dreams, one for light spirits, another to attract birds—oh, and he seemed quite entranced with that one, almost as if he were a bird himself. But when I asked to see his hands, to tune the charms to him, he told me they were all intended as gifts. I told him he might send each recipient to me, to have the charms tuned if they wished, but as yet none of them have come. Still, they will work well enough as I built them. I do like to tune the charms, though. It's all the difference between a charm built by rote, and one created by a master. And I do regard myself as a master, thank you very much!"

These last words she offered with a hint of laughter in her voice in response to my raised brows. We laughed together, and I had no right to feel as comfortable with her as I did at that moment. "You've put my mind at rest," I declared. "I know Hap is a good lad, and little in need of my care anymore. Yet I'm afraid I'm always imagining the worst befalling him."

Don't ignore me! Fennel threatened. He hopped up onto the table. Jinna put him on the floor. He floated back onto her lap. She petted him absently.

"That's just a part of being a father," she assured me. "Or a friend." A strange look came over her face. "I'm not above foolish worries myself. Even when they're none of my business." She gave me a frankly speculative look that evaporated all the ease in my body. "I'm going to speak plainly," she warned me.

"Please," I invited her but every bone in my body wished she would not.

"You're Witted," she said. It was not an accusation. It was more as if she commented on a disfiguring disease. "I travel quite a bit in my trade, more perhaps than you have in the last few years. The mood of the folk has changed toward Witted ones, Tom. It's become ugly everywhere I've been recently. I didn't see it myself, but I heard that in a town in Farrow they displayed the dismembered bodies of the Witted ones they'd killed, with each piece in a separate cage to prevent them coming back to life."

I kept my face still but I felt as if ice were creeping up my spine. Prince Dutiful. Stolen or run away, but in either case vulnerable. Outside the protective walls of Buckkeep where people were capable of such monstrosities, the young Prince was at risk.

"I'm a hedge-witch," Jinna said softly. "I know what it is to be born with magic already inside you. It's not something you can change, even if you want to. More, I know what it's like to have a sister who was born empty of it. She seemed so free to me sometimes. She could look at a charm my father had made, and to her it was just sticks and beads. It never whispered and nagged at her. The hours I spent beside my father, learning his skills, were hours she spent with my mother in the kitchen. When we were growing up, the envy went both ways. But we were a family and we could be taught tolerance of our differences." She smiled at her memories, then shook her head, and her face grew graver. "Out in the wide world, it's different. Folk may not threaten to tear me apart or burn me, but I've seen hatred and jealousy in more than one set of eyes. Folk think either that it isn't fair that I've got something they can never have, or they fear that somehow I'll use what I've got to hurt them. They never stop to think they've got talents of their own that I'll never master. They might be rude to me, jostle me on the street, or try to squeeze me out of my market space, but they won't kill me. You don't have that comfort. The smallest slip could be your death. And if someone provokes your temper . . . Well. You become a different man altogether. I confess it's been bothering me since the last time I saw you. So, well . . . to put my own mind at rest, I made you something."

I swallowed. "Oh. Thank you." I could not even find the

courage to ask what she had made me. Sweat was leaking down my spine despite the coolness of the dim room. She had not intended to threaten me, but her words reminded me how vulnerable I was to her. My assassin's training went deep, I discovered. Kill her, suggested that part of me. She knows your secret and that makes her a threat. Kill her.

I folded my hands on the table before me.

"You must think me strange," she murmured as she rose and went to a cupboard. "To be interfering in your life so when we have only met once or twice." I could tell she was embarrassed, yet determined to give me the gift she had made.

"I think you are kind," I said awkwardly.

Her rising had displaced Fennel. He sat on the floor, wrapped his tail around his feet and glared up at me. *There goes the lap! All your fault.*

She had taken a box from the cupboard. She brought it back to the table and opened it. Inside was an arrangement of beads and rods on leather thongs. She lifted it and gave it a shake and it became a necklace. I stared at it, but felt nothing. "What does it do?" I asked.

She laughed lightly. "Very little, I am afraid. I cannot make you seem un-Witted, nor can I make you invulnerable to attack. I cannot even give you something that will help you master your temper. I tried to make something that would warn you of ill feelings toward you, but it became so bulky and large, it was more like a war harness than a charm. You will forgive my saying that my first impression of you was that you were a rather forbidding fellow. It took me a while to warm to you, and if Hap had not spoken so well of you, I would not have given you a moment of my time. I would have thought you a dangerous man. So did many appraise you as they passed us in the market that day. And so, bluntly, did you later show yourself to be. A dangerous man, but not a wicked one, if you will excuse my judging you. Yet the set of your face, by habit, shows folk that darker aspect of yourself. And now, with a blade at your hip and your hair in a warrior's tail, well, it does not give you a friendly demeanor. And it is easiest to hate a man whom you first fear. So. This is a variation on a very old love charm. I have made it, not to attract lovers, but to make people well disposed toward you, if it works as I hope it will. When you try to create a variation on a standard theme, it often lacks strength. Sit still, now."

She walked behind my chair with the dangling necklace. I watched her lower it past my face, and without being told, I bowed my head so she could fasten it at the nape of my neck. The charm made me feel no different, but her cool fingers against my skin sent a prickling chill over me. Her voice came from behind me. "I flatter myself that I got this fit right. It must not be too loose or it will dangle, nor so tight it chokes. Let me see it on you now. Turn around."

I did as I was bid, twisting in my chair. She looked at the necklace, looked at my face, and then grinned broadly. "Oh, yes, that will do. Though you are taller than I recalled. I should have used a narrower bead for that . . . Well, it will do. I had thought it might take some adjusting, but I fear if I tinker with it, I will take it back to its origin. Now, wear it with your collar pulled up, like so, so just a slice of it shows. There. If you are in a situation where you feel it might be useful, find an excuse to loosen your collar. Let it be seen, and folk will find you a more persuasive talker. Like so. Even your silences will seem charming."

She looked down into my face as she tugged my collar more open about the charm. I looked up at her and felt a sudden blush heat my face. Our eyes locked.

"It works very well, indeed," she observed, and unabashedly lowered her face to offer me her mouth. Not to kiss her was unthinkable. She pressed her mouth to mine. Her lips were warm.

We sprang apart guiltily as the door handle rattled. The door scraped open, and a woman's silhouette was outlined against the day's brightness. Then she came inside, pushing the door shut behind her. "Whew. It's cooler in here, thank Eda. Oh. Beg pardon. Were you doing a reading?"

She had the same scattering of freckles on her nose and forearms. Clearly, this was Jinna's niece. She looked about twenty or so, and carried a basketful of fresh fish on her arm.

Fennel ran to greet her, wrapping around her ankles. *You love me best. You know you do. Pick me up.*

"Not a reading. Testing a charm. It seems to work." Jinna's voice invited me to share her amusement. Her niece glanced from Jinna to me, knowing she had been excluded from some joke, but taking it genially. She picked up Fennel and he rubbed his face against her, marking his possession.

"And I should be going. I'm afraid I have several other errands to do before I am required back at the keep." I wasn't sure that I wanted to leave. But how interested I was in staying did not fit in at all with what I was supposed to be doing in Buckkeep. Most of all, I felt I needed a bit of time alone to decide what had just happened, and what it meant to me.

"Must you go so right away?" Jinna's niece asked me. She seemed genuinely disappointed at seeing me rise from my chair. "There's plenty of fish, if you'd care to stay and eat with us."

Her impromptu invitation took me aback, as did the interest in her eyes.

My fish. I'll eat it soon. Fennel leaned down to look at the food fondly.

"The charm seems to work very well, indeed," Jinna observed in an aside. I found myself tugging my collar near closed.

"I really must go, I'm afraid. I've work to do, and I'm expected back at the keep. But thank you for the invitation."

"Perhaps another time, then," the niece offered, and Jinna added, "Certainly another time, my dear. Before he leaves, let me introduce Tom Badgerlock. He has asked me to keep watch for his son, a young friend of mine named Hap. When Hap arrives, he may stay with us for a day or so. And Tom will certainly have supper with us then. Tom Badgerlock, my niece, Miskya."

"Miskya, a pleasure," I assured her. I lingered long enough to exchange parting pleasantries, and then hurried out into the sunlight and noise of the city. As I hastened back to Buckkeep, I watched the reactions of folk whom I met. It did seem that more smiled at me than usually did, but I realized that might simply be their reaction to my meeting their eyes. I usually looked aside from strangers on the street. A man unnoticed is a man unremembered, and that is the best that an assassin can hope for. Then I reminded myself that I was no longer an assassin. Nonetheless, I decided that I would remove the necklace as soon as I got home. I found that having strangers regard me benevolently for no reason was more unnerving than having them distrust me on sight.

I made my steep way up to the keep gate and was admitted by the guardsmen there. The sun was high, the sky blue and clear, and if any of the passing folk were aware that the sole heir to the Farseer crown had vanished, they showed no sign of it. They moved about their ordinary tasks with no more than the concerns of a working day to vex them. By the stable, several tall boys had converged on a plump young man. I knew him for a dullard by his flat face and small ears and the way his tongue peeped out of his mouth. Slow fear showed in his small eyes as the boys spread to encircle him. One of the older stablehands looked toward them irritably.

No, no, no.

I turned, seeking the source of the floating thought, but of course that availed me nothing. A faint snatch of music distracted me. A stableboy, sent hurrying about his tasks, jolted into me, then, at my startled look, begged my pardon most abjectly. Without thinking, I had allowed my hand to ride my sword hilt. "No harm done," I assured him, and added, "Tell me, where would I find the Weaponsmaster this time of day?"

The boy stopped suddenly, looked more closely at me, and smiled. "Down at the practice courts, man. They're just past the new granary." He pointed the way.

I thanked him, and as I turned away, I tugged my collar closed.

chapter XIII

BARGAINS

*Hunting cats are not entirely unknown within Buck Duchy,
but they have remained for years an anomaly. Not only is
the terrain of Buck more suited to hound-hunting, but also
hounds are more suited to the larger game that is usually the
prey of mounted hunters. A lively pack of hounds, boiling
and baying, is a fine accompaniment for a royal hunt. The
cat, when it is employed, is usually seen as more fittingly the
dainty hunting companion of a lady, suitable for the taking
of rabbits or birds. King Shrewd's first queen, Queen
Constance, kept a little hunting cat, but more for pleasure
and companionship than sport. Her name was Hisspit.*

     SULINGA'S "A HISTORY OF COURSING BEASTS"

"The Queen wishes to see you."

"When?" I asked, startled. It was hardly the greeting I
had expected from Chade. I had opened the panel that admitted me to his tower to find him sitting in his chair before
the hearth, waiting for me. He immediately stood.

"Now, of course. She wants to know what progress we
have made, and is naturally anxious to hear from you as
soon as possible."

"But I haven't made any progress," I protested. I had
not even reported my day's work to Chade yet. I probably
stank of sweat from the weapons court.

"Then she'll want to hear that," he replied relentlessly.
"Come. Follow me." He triggered the door and we left the
tower chamber.

It was evening. I had spent my afternoon doing as the Fool had advised me, playing the role of a servant learning his way about a new place. As such, I'd talked to quite a number of my fellow servitors, introduced myself to Weaponsmaster Cresswell, and successfully arranged it that he would suggest I freshen my blade skills against Delleree. She proved to be a formidable swordswoman, nearly as tall as I was, and both energetic and light-footed. I was pleased she could not get past my guard, but I was soon panting with the effort of maintaining it. Trying to penetrate her defenses was not yet an option for me. The weapons training Hod had enforced on me long ago stood me in good stead, but my body simply could not react as swiftly as my mind. Knowing what to do under an attack is not the same thing as being able to do it.

Twice I begged leave for breathing space and she granted it to me with the satisfaction of the insufferably young. Yet my leading questions about the Prince availed me little, until at my third rest interlude I loosened my collar and opened my shirt wide to the cool air. I almost felt guilty doing it, yet I will not deny that I wanted to test if the charm would coax her to be more loquacious with me.

It worked. Leaning on the wall in the shade of the weapons shed, I caught my breath, and then looked up into her face. As our gazes met, her brown eyes widened, in the way that a person's eyes widen at the sight of something pleasantly anticipated. Like a rapier rushing to its target, I thrust my question past her guard. "Tell me, do you press Prince Dutiful so hard when he practices with you?"

She smiled. "No, I fear I do not, for I am usually more occupied with maintaining my own defenses against him. He is a skilled swordsman, creative and unpredictable in his tactics. No sooner do I devise a new trick to use against him than he learns it and tries it against me."

"Then he loves his blade-work, as good fighters usually do."

She paused. "No. I do not think that is it. He is a youth who makes no half-measures in anything he does. He strives to be perfect in all he attempts."

"Competitive, is he?" I tried to make my query casual. I busied my hands in smoothing my wayward hair back into its tail.

Again she considered. "No. Not in the usual sense. There are some I practice with who think only of beating their opponents. That preoccupation can be used against them. But I do not think the Prince cares if he wins our matches, only that he fights each one perfectly. It is not the same thing as competing with my skills . . ." Her voice trailed away as she pondered it.

"He competes with himself, against an ideal he imagines."

My prompting seemed to startle her for an instant. Then, grinning, "That is it, exactly. You've met him, then?"

"Not yet," I assured her. "But I've heard a great deal about him, and look forward to meeting him."

"Oh, that won't be soon," she informed me guilelessly. "He has his mother's Mountain ways in some things. Often he goes apart from the whole court for a time, to spend time just thinking. He isolates himself in a tower. Some say he fasts, but I have never seen signs of it when he returns to his routine."

"So what does he do?" I asked in hearty puzzlement.

"I've no idea."

"You've never asked him?"

She gave me an odd look, and when she spoke, her voice had cooled. "I am only his training partner, not his confidante. I am a guardsman and he is a prince. I would not presume to question my Prince on his private time alone. He is, as all know, a private person, with a great need for solitude."

Necklace or not, I knew I had pushed her too hard. I smiled, I hoped disarmingly, and straightened up with a groan. "Well, as a training partner, you're the equal of any I've ever had. The Prince is fortunate to have someone such as you to sharpen his skills against. As am I."

"You are welcome. And I hope we can measure ourselves against one another again."

I left it at that. I had as much success with the other servants. My queries, whether direct or indirect, yielded little information. It was not that the servants refused to gossip; they were as willing to chatter about Lord Golden or Lady Elegance as one could wish, but on the topic of the Prince, they simply seemed to know nothing. The picture I formed of Dutiful was of a boy who was not disliked, but was isolated not only by his rank but by his nature. It did not encourage me. I feared that if he had run, he had divulged his plans to no one. His solitary habits would have left him singularly vulnerable to kidnappers, as well.

My mind went back to the note the Queen had received. It had told her that the Prince was Witted and demanded she take suitable action. What had the writer intended as "suitable action"? Revealing his Wit and proclaiming that the Witted must be accepted? Or purifying the Farseer line with his demise? Had the writer contacted the Prince, too?

Chade's old workbench had yielded me the lock-picks I needed for my dinner-hour adventure. The Prince had Prince Regal's former grand chambers. That lock and I were old friends and I anticipated that I could slip it easily. While the rest of the keep was at table, I approached the Prince's rooms. Here again I saw his mother's influence, for there was not only no guard at his door, but it was not locked. I slipped silently within, closing it softly behind me. Then I stared about me in perplexity. I had expected the same clutter and disorder that Hap tended to leave in his wake. Instead the Prince's sparse possessions were all stored in such an orderly fashion that the spacious room looked nearly empty. Perhaps he had a fanatical valet, I mused.

Then, recalling Kettricken's upbringing, I wondered if the Prince had any body servants at all. Personal servants were not a Mountain custom.

It took me very little time to explore his rooms. I found a modest assortment of clothing in his chests. I could not determine if any were missing. His riding boots were still there, but Chade had already told me that the Prince's horse was still in his stall. He possessed a neat array of brush, comb, washbasin, and looking glass, all precisely aligned in a row. In the room where he pursued his studies, the ink was tightly stoppered and the tabletop had never suffered any blots or spills. No scrolls had been left out. His sword was on the wall, but there were empty pegs where other weapons might have hung. There were no personal papers, no ribbons or locks of hair tucked into the corner of his clothing chest, not even a sticky wineglass or an idly tossed shirt under his bed. In short, it did not strike me as a boy's bedchamber at all.

There was a large cushion in a sturdy basket near the hearth. The hair that clung to it was short, yet fine. The stoutly woven basket bore the marks of errant claws. I did not need the wolf's nose to smell cat in the room. I lifted the cushion, and found playthings beneath it: a rabbitskin tied to a length of heavy twine, and a canvas toy stuffed with catmint. I raised my eyebrows to that, wondering if hunting cats were affected by it as mousing cats were.

The room yielded me little else: no hidden journal of princely thoughts, no defiant runaway's final note to his mother, nothing to suggest that the Prince had been spirited away against his will. I retreated quietly from his rooms, leaving all as I had found it.

My route took me past the door of my old boyhood room. I paused, tempted. Who stayed there now? The hallway was empty and I yielded to the impulse. The lock on the door was the one I had devised, and it demanded my rusty skills to get past it. It was so stiff I was persuaded it had not turned in some time. I shut the door behind me and stood still, smelling dust.

The tall window was shuttered, but the shutters were, as they had always been, a poor fit. Daylight leaked past them, and after a few moments, my eyes adjusted to the dusky light. I looked around. There, my bedstead, with cobwebs embroidering the familiar hangings. The cedar clothing chest at the foot of it was thick with dust. The hearth, empty, black, and cold. And above it, the faded tapestry of King Wisdom treating with the Elderlings. I stared at it. When I was a boy of nine, it had given me nightmares. Time had not changed my opinion of the oddly elongated forms. The golden Elderlings stared down on the lifeless and empty room.

I suddenly felt as if I had disturbed a grave. As silently as I had entered the chamber, I left it, locking the door behind me.

I had thought to find Lord Golden in his chambers, but he was not there. "Lord Golden?" I inquired, and then advanced to tap lightly at the door of his private chamber. I swear I did not touch the catch, but it swung open at my touch.

Light flooded out. The small chamber had a window, and the setting sun filled it with gold. It was a pleasant, open room that smelled of wood shavings and paint. In the corner, a plant in a tub climbed a trellis. Hanging on the walls, I recognized charms such as Jinna made. On the worktable in the middle of the room, amongst the scattered tools and paint pots, there were pieces of rod, string, and beads, as if he had disassembled a charm. I found I had taken a step into the room. There was a scroll weighted flat on the table, with several charms drawn on it. They were unlike anything I had seen in Jinna's shop. Even at a glance, the sketches were oddly unsettling. I remember that, I thought, and then, when I looked closer, I was absolutely certain I had never seen the like before. A shiver ran down my back. The little beads had faces; the rods were carved with spinning spirals. The longer I stared, the more they disturbed me. I felt as if I could not quite get my breath, as if they were pulling me into them. "Come away." The Fool spoke softly from behind me. I could not reply.

I felt his hand on my shoulder and it broke the spell. I turned at his touch. "I'm sorry," I said instantly. "The door was ajar and I—"

"I did not expect you back so soon, or it would have been latched."

That was all he said, and then he drew me from the room and shut the door firmly behind us.

I felt as if he had pulled me back from a precipice. I drew a shaky breath. "What were those?"

"An experiment. What you told me of Jinna's charms made me curious, so when I reached Buckkeep Town, I resolved to see them for myself. Once I had, I wanted to know how they worked. I wanted to know if the charm could only be made by a hedge-witch, or if the magic was in the way they were assembled. And I wanted to know if I could make them work better." His voice was neutral.

"How can you stand to be around them?" I demanded. Even now, the hair on the back of my neck was standing.

"They are tuned to humans. You forget that I am a White."

The statement left me as speechless as the insidious little sketches had. I looked at the Fool and for one blink I could see him as if for the first time. As attractive as his coloring was, I had never seen any other person with it. There were other differences, the way his wrists attached his hands to his arms, the airiness of his hair . . . but when our eyes met, I was looking at my old friend again. It was like jolting back to the earth after a fall. I suddenly recalled what I had done. "I'm sorry. I didn't intend to . . . I know you need your privacy—" I felt shamed and hot blood rushed to my face.

He was silent for a moment. Then he said justly,

"When I came to your home, you hid nothing from me." I sensed that the statement reflected his idea of what was fair rather than his emotions on the topic.

"I won't go in there again," I promised fervently.

That brought a small smile to his face. "I doubt that you would."

I suddenly wanted to change the subject, but the only thought that came to me was, "I saw Jinna today. She made this for me." I opened the collar of my shirt.

He stared, first at the charm, then up at my face. He seemed struck dumb. Then a wide and fatuous grin spread over his face.

"It's supposed to make people feel kindly toward me," I explained. "To counteract my grim appearance, I think, though she was not so unkind as to say that directly."

He took a breath. "Cover it," he begged, laughing, and as I did so, he turned away from it. He walked almost hastily to the chamber window and looked out. "They are not tuned to my bloodlines, but that does not mean I am completely impervious against them. You often remind me that in some ways I am still very human."

I unfastened it from my throat and held it out to him. "You can take it and study it if you like. I'm not entirely sure I like wearing it. I think I'd rather know what people honestly think of me."

"Somehow I doubt that," he muttered, but he returned to take the charm from my hand. He held it out in the air between us, studied it, and then glanced at me. "Tuned to you?" he guessed.

I nodded.

"Intriguing. I would like to keep it, for a day or so. I promise not to take it apart. But after that, I think you should wear it. Always."

"I'll think about it," I promised, but felt no inclination to don it again.

"Chade wanted to see you as soon as you came in," he suddenly said, as if he had only then remembered it.

And there we had left it, and I felt that I was, if not excused, at least forgiven for going where I had no business being.

Now as I followed Chade through the narrow passageway, I asked him, "How was all this built? How can a labyrinth like this that winds all through the castle be kept secret?"

He carried a candle and walked before me. He spoke over his shoulder, softly. "Some was built into the bones of the keep. Our ancestors were never trusting folk. Part of it was intended as a system of bolt-holes. Some of it has always been used for spying. Some of it used to be servants' stairs, incorporated into the secret passages during a phase of intense reconstruction following a fire. And some was created deliberately, in your lifetime. When you were small, do you remember when Shrewd ordered that the hearth in the guardroom be rebuilt?"

"Vaguely. I did not pay much attention at the time."

"No one did. You may have noticed that a wooden façade was added to two walls."

"The cupboard wall? I thought it was built so that Cook had a bigger larder, one that kept rats out. It made the room smaller, but warmer as well."

"And above the cupboards, there is a passageway, and several viewing slits. Shrewd liked to know what his guards were thinking of him, what they feared, what they hoped."

"But the men who built it would have known of it."

"Different craftsmen were brought in to do different parts of the job. I myself added the viewing slits. If any of them thought it odd that the ceilings of the cupboards were so sturdily built, they said nothing. And here we are. Hush."

He lifted a tiny leather flap on the wall and peered into the revealed hole. After a moment, he whispered, "Come."

The silent door admitted us into a privy chamber. There we paused again, while Chade again peered through a peephole, then tapped lightly at the door. "Enter," Kettricken responded quietly.

I followed Chade into a small sitting room off the Queen's bedchamber. The connecting door to the bed-chamber was closed and a bolt in place. The room was dec-orated sparsely in the Mountains' severe but restful way. Fat scented candles gave us light in the windowless chamber. The table and chairs were of bare pale wood. The woven mat on the floor and the wall hangings were made of grass worked into a scene of waterfalls tumbling down a moun-tainside. I recognized Kettricken's own handiwork. Other than that, the chamber was bare. All this I noticed periph-erally, for my Queen stood in the center of the room.

She was waiting for us. She wore a simple gown of Buck blue, with a white and gold kirtle. Her gold hair was dressed close to her head, and crowned only with a simple band of silver. She was empty-handed. Another woman would have brought her needlework or had set out a platter of food, but not our Queen. She was waiting for us but I did not sense impatience or anxiety. I suspected she had been meditating, for an aura of stillness still clung to her. Our eyes met, and the small lines at the corners of her mouth and eyes seemed lies, for in the gaze we shared no time had passed at all. The courage I had always admired still shone there, and her self-discipline was like an armor she wore. Yet, "Oh, Fitz!" she cried low on seeing me, and in her voice there was warm welcome and relief.

I bowed low to her, and then sank on one knee. "My Queen!" I greeted her.

She stepped forward and touched my head, her hand a benediction. "Please rise," she said quietly. "You have been at my side through too many trials for me ever to want to see you on your knees before me. And as I recall, you once called me Kettricken."

"That was many years ago, my lady," I reminded her as I rose.

She took both my hands in hers. We were nearly of a height, and her blue eyes looked deep into mine. "Far too many, for which I fault you, FitzChivalry. But Chade told me, long ago, that you might choose solitude and rest for yourself. When you did, I did not begrudge it to you. You had sacrificed everything to your duty, and if solitude was the only reward you wished, then I was glad to grant it to you. Yet I confess I am more glad to see you return, especially at such a time of crisis."

"If you have need of me, then I am glad to be here," I replied, almost without reservations.

"I am saddened that you walk among the folk of Buckkeep, and none know what sacrifices you have made for them. You should have been accorded a hero's welcome. Instead, you walk unknown among them in the guise of a servant." Her earnest blue eyes searched my own.

I found myself smiling. "Perhaps I spent too long in the Mountains, where all know that the true ruler of that kingdom is the servant of all."

For a moment her blue eyes widened. Then the genuine smile that broke forth on her face was like the sun breaking through storm clouds, despite the sudden tears that stood in her eyes. "Oh, Fitz, to hear you say such words is balm to my heart. Truly, you have been Sacrifice for your people, and I admire you for it. But to hear from your lips that you understand that it has been your duty, and took satisfaction in that, brings me joy."

I did not think that was exactly what I had said, and yet I will not deny that her praise eased some of the ancient hurt in me. I pulled back from looking at that too closely.

"Dutiful," I said suddenly. "He is why I am here, and much pleasure as I take in this reunion, I would take even more in discovering what has become of him."

My Queen kept possession of one of my hands and held it tightly as she drew me toward the table. "Oh, you were ever my friend, even before I came as a stranger to this court. And now your heart goes with mine in this matter."

She drew a deep breath, and the fears and worries of a mother broke past the control in the monarch's voice as she said, "No matter how I dissemble before the court— and it grieves me that I must deceive my own people this way—my son is never out of my thoughts for a moment. FitzChivalry, I put the blame for this at my own feet, yet I do not know if my fault was too much discipline for him, or too little, or if I demanded too much of the prince and not enough of the boy, or—"

"My Queen, you cannot approach this problem from that direction. We must begin from where we are; no good will come of trying to apportion blame. I will tell you bluntly that in my brief time here, I have discovered nothing. Those whom I have questioned speak well of the Prince. No one has divulged to me that he was unhappy or discontented in any way."

"Then you think he was taken?" she broke in.

This interruption was so uncharacteristic of Kettricken that I finally grasped the depth of her anguish. I drew out a chair for her, and as she sat, I looked down into her face and said with all the calm I could muster, "I do not think anything yet. I do not have enough facts to form an opinion."

At an impatient sign from her, both Chade and I were seated at the table. "But what of your Skill?" she demanded. "Does it tell you nothing of him? Chade told me that he suspected you and the boy were somehow linked in your dreams. I do not understand how that could be so, but if it is, surely it must tell you something. What has he dreamed these last few nights?"

"You will not like my answer, my Queen, any more than you liked my answer all those years ago when we searched for Verity. My talent now is as it was then: erratic and unreliable. From what Chade has told me, it is possible that I have occasionally shared a dream with Prince Dutiful. But if it is so, I was not cognizant of it at the time. Nor can I break into his dreams at will. If he has dreamed these last few nights, he dreamed alone."

"Or perhaps he did not dream at all," Kettricken mourned. "Perhaps he is dead already, or tormented so that he cannot sleep and dream."

"My Queen, you imagine the worst, and when you do, your mind stops at the problem and does not consider the solution." Chade's voice was almost severe. Knowing how distraught he was over the boy's absence, his sternness surprised me, until I saw the Queen's reaction. Kettricken took strength from his firmness.

"Of course. You are right." She took a breath. "But what can our solution be? We have discovered nothing, and neither has FitzChivalry. You have counseled me to keep his disappearance a secret, lest we panic the people and precipitate rash decisions. But there have been no demands for ransom. Perhaps we should make public that the Prince is missing. Someone, somewhere, must know something. I think we must announce it and ask the people to help."

"Not yet," I heard myself say. "For you are right in saying that someone, somewhere, must know something. And if they are aware the Prince is absent from Buckkeep, and they have not come forward, then they have a reason. And I should like to know what it is."

"Then what do you suggest?" Kettricken demanded of me. "What is left to us?"

I knew it would chafe her, yet I still suggested it. "Give me a little more time. A day, at most two. Let me ask more questions and sniff about some more."

"But anything could have happened to him by then!"

"Anything could have happened to him by now," I pointed out levelly. I spoke calmly the cruel words. "Kettricken. If someone took him to kill him, they have done it by now. If they took him to use him, they are still awaiting our move in this game. If he ran away, then he may yet run home again. While we keep his absence a secret, the next move belongs to us. Let it be known, and others will make that move for us. You will have nobles tearing up the countryside, looking for him, and not all will have his best interests at heart. Some will want to 'rescue' him to curry favor, and others may think to seize a prize from another weasel's jaws."

She closed her eyes but nodded reluctantly to my words. When she spoke, her voice was strained. "But you know that time runs out for us. Chade has told you that an Outislander contingent comes to formalize Prince Dutiful's affiance? When they arrive a fortnight from now, I must be able to produce him or I risk not only embarrassment but also insult and an end to a carefully wrought truce that I hope to make an alliance."

"Bought with your son." The words leapt out of my mouth before I knew I had thought them.

She opened her eyes and gazed at me directly. "Yes. As the Mountain alliance with the Six Duchies was bought with me." She cocked her head at me. "Do you consider it a poor transaction?"

I deserved rebuke. I bowed my head to it. "No, my Queen. I think it was the best bargain that the Six Duchies ever made."

She nodded to my compliment and a faint blush rosed her cheeks. "I shall listen to your counsel, Fitz. Two more days will we seek Dutiful on our own, before we reveal his absence to our people. In those days, we will use every means at our disposal to discover what may have become of him. Chade has opened to you the concealed maze within the walls of Buckkeep. I little like what it says of us, that we furtively spy on our own folk, but I grant the freedom of it to you, FitzChivalry. I know you will not abuse it. Use it as seems wise to you."

"Thank you, my Queen," I replied awkwardly. I did not truly welcome this gift, the access to every lord's and lady's small and grubby flaws. I did not glance at Chade. What had it cost him to be privy not just to the massive secrets of the throne, but the dirty and shameful sins of the folk of the keep? What vices had he inadvertently witnessed, what painful shortcomings had he glimpsed, and how did he meet the eyes of those folk every day in the broad and well-lit chambers of the keep?

". . . and whatever you must do."

My mind had been wandering, but my Queen was look-ing at me, waiting. I made the only possible response. "Yes, my Queen."

She gave a great sigh as if she had feared my refusal. Or as if she dreaded what she next must say. "Then do so, FitzChivalry, ever friend. I would not spend you this way if it could be avoided. Safeguard your health. Be wary of the drugs and herbs, for as thorough as your old master is, no translation should ever be absolutely trusted." She took a breath, then added in a different tone, "If either Chade or I press you too hard, tell us so. Your head must stand guard against my mother's heart. Do not . . . do not let me shame myself in this, by asking more of you than you can . . ." Her voice trailed away. I think she trusted me to take her mean-ing. She drew another breath. She turned her head and looked away from me, as if that would keep me from know-ing that tears stood in her eyes. "You will begin tonight?" she asked in an unnaturally high voice.

I knew what I had just agreed to. I knew then that I stood at the lip of the abyss.

I flung myself off into it. "Yes, my Queen."

ᨒ   ᨒ   ᨒ

How shall I describe that long climb up the stairs to the tower? Chade led the way through the secret places of the keep and I followed his uncertain lamplight. Dread and an-ticipation warred inside me. I felt I had left my stomach far behind me, and yet I longed for him to hurry up the steps. Excitement coursed through me as we approached that in-dulgence so long denied to me. My hopes and focus should have been on recovering the Prince, but the prospect of drowning myself in Skill dominated all my thoughts. It ter-rified and tantalized me. My skin felt taut and alive, and my senses seemed to strain against the confines of my flesh. Music seemed to move through the air at the edges of my hearing.

Chade triggered the door's opening, and then gestured for me to precede him. As I edged past him, he observed, "You look nervous as a bridegroom, boy."

I cleared my throat. "It seems strange to rush headlong into that which I have tried to school myself to avoid."

He shut the door behind us as I glanced about the room. A small fire burned on the grate. Even in the height of summer, the thick stone walls of the keep seemed to whisper a chill into the room. Verity's sword leaned up against the hearth where I had left it, but someone had removed the leather on the hilt. "You recognized Verity's blade," I observed.

"How could I not? I am glad you kept it safe."

I laughed. "More like, it kept me safe. Well. What exactly do you propose?"

"I suggest you make yourself comfortable and that you attempt to Skill out after the Prince. That is all."

I looked around for a place to sit. Not on the hearthstones. Yet, as it ever had been, there was only one comfortable chair near the fire. "And the drugs and herbs the Queen mentioned?"

Chade gave me a sidelong glance. I thought I detected some wariness in the look. "I do not think we will need them. She refers to several scrolls within the Skill collection. There are teas and tinctures that are suggested for Skill students who seem to have difficulty attaining a receptive state. We had considered using them on Prince Dutiful but had decided to postpone it until we were sure they are necessary."

"Galen never used any herbs when he was instructing us." I brought a tall stool from the workbench and set it opposite Chade's chair. I perched on it. He settled in his chair, but then had to look up at me. I suspect it annoyed him. He sounded peevish when he spoke.

"Galen never used any herbs when he was instructing *you*. Did you never suspect that perhaps the others in your Skill coterie received special attentions that you were not privy to? I did. Of course, we will never be certain of that."

I shrugged my shoulders to that. What else could I do? It was years ago and they were all dead, several of them at my hands. What did it matter now? But the thoughts had stirred my old aversion to the Skill. From anticipation, I had shifted suddenly to dread. I changed the subject. "Did you find out for me who gave the cat to the Prince?"

Chade looked startled at my abrupt shift. "I—yes, of course. Lady Bresinga of Galeton and her son Civil. It was a birthday gift. The cat was presented to him in a little jeweled harness with a leash. The animal was about two years old, a long-legged stripy creature with a rather flat face and a tail as long as the rest of it. I understand those cats cannot be bred, that a kitten must be taken from a wild den before its eyes have opened if anything is to be made of it. It is an exotic coursing animal, suited to solitary hunting. The Prince took to it immediately."

"Who took the kitten from the den?" I asked.

"I have no idea. Their Huntsman, I imagine."

"Did the cat like the Prince?"

Chade frowned. "I had not really concerned myself with that. As I recall, they approached the dais, with Lady Bresinga holding the end of the cat's leash and her son actually carrying the animal. It seemed almost dazed by all the light and noise of the festivities. I wondered myself if they had drugged it lest it panic and struggle to escape. But when they had made their courtesies to the Prince, the lady put the end of the leash in his hand and Civil, her son, set the cat at Dutiful's feet."

"Did it try to get away? Did it test the leash?"

"No. As I said, it seemed quite calm, almost unnaturally so. I believe it looked at the Prince for a time, and then bumped its head against his knee." Chade's eyes had gone distant, and I saw his trained mind recalling the scene in detail. "He reached down to stroke it, and it cowered away. Then it sniffed his hand. Then it did this strange thing, opening its mouth wide and breathing near his hand, as if it could taste his scent from the air. After that, it seemed to accept him. It rubbed its head up and down his leg, just as a little cat does. When a servant tried to lead it away, it would not go, so it was allowed to remain near the Prince's chair for the rest of the evening. He seemed very well pleased with it."

"How soon did he begin hunting it?"

"I believe he and Civil took it out the next day. Civil and the Prince are nearly of an age, and the Prince was eager to try the cat, as any boy would be. Civil and his mother stayed on at court the rest of the week, and I think that Civil and the Prince took out the cat every morning. It was his chance to learn how to hunt with it, you see, from people familiar with the sport."

"And did they hunt well together?"

"Oh, I suppose so. It is not for large game of course, but they brought back, oh, birds, I think, and hares."

"And it always slept in his room?"

"As I understand it, it has to be kept close to a human to keep it tamed. And of course, the hounds in the stable would not have left it in peace. So, yes, it slept in his room and followed him about the keep. Fitz, what do you suspect?"

I answered him honestly. "The same thing that you do. That our Witted Prince has vanished with his hunting cat companion. And that none of this is a coincidence. Not the gift of the animal, not the bonding, not the disappearance. Someone planned this."

Chade frowned, not wanting to admit what he believed. "The cat could have been killed when the Prince was taken. Or she could have run off."

"So you've said. But if the Prince is Witted, and the cat is bonded to him, she would not have run off when he was taken." The stool was uncomfortable but I stubbornly remained perched on it. I closed my eyes for a moment.

Sometimes, when the body is weary, the mind takes flight. I let my thoughts skip where they would. "I've bonded thrice, you know. The first time to Nosy, the puppy that Burrich took from me. And again, to Smithy when I was still a boy. The last time, to Nighteyes. Each time, there was that instant sense of connection. With Nosy, I bonded before I was even aware I was doing it. I suspect it happened because I was lonely. Because when Smithy offered love, I accepted it with no discrimination. And when the wolf's anger and hatred of his cage so exactly matched mine, I could not distinguish between us." I opened my eyes briefly and met Chade's startled stare. "I had no walls, you see." I looked away from him, down at the dwindling fire. "From what I've been told, in Witted families, the children are protected from doing that. They are taught to have walls when they are young. Then, when they are of an age, they are sent out to find suitable partners, almost like seeking a suitable marriage partner."

"What are you suggesting?" Chade asked quietly.

I followed the thought where it led me. "The Queen has chosen a bride for Prince Dutiful for the sake of a political alliance. What if an Old Blood family has done the same?"

A lengthy silence followed my words. I looked back at Chade. His eyes were on the fire, and I could almost see his mind working frantically to sort out all the implications of what I had said. "An Old Blood family deliberately selects an animal for the Prince to bond with. Assumptions, then: that Lady Bresinga is Witted, that indeed her whole line is, as you put it, Old Blood. That they somehow knew or suspected the Prince is also Witted." He paused, pursed his mouth, and considered. "Perhaps they were the source of the note claiming the Prince was Witted . . . I still do not grasp what they would profit from it."

"What do we profit from marrying Dutiful to some Outislander girl? An alliance, Chade."

He scowled at me. "The cat somehow is part of the

Bresinga family and retains ties to it? The cat can somehow influence the Prince's political actions?"

The way he said it made it seem ridiculous. "I haven't got it completely worked out yet," I admitted. "But I think there is something there. Even if their only goal is to prove that the Prince himself is Witted, and hence that other Witted folk should not be chopped up and burned for being the way they are. Or to gain the Prince's sympathy toward Witted folk, and through him, the Queen's."

Chade gave me a sidelong glance. "Now *that* is a motive I can concede. There is also possible blackmail there. Once they have bonded the Prince to an animal, they can hold out for political favors under the threat that they will tell others he is Witted." He looked aside from me. "Or attempt to reduce him to the level of an animal, if we do not comply with their political wishes."

As always, Chade's mind was capable of far more convolutions than mine was. It was almost a relief to have him refine my ideas. I did not want my mentor to be failing in mind or body. In so many ways, he still stood as shield between me and the world. I nodded to his suggestions.

He stood up suddenly. "So all the more reason we should proceed as we had planned. Come, take my chair. You look like a parrot perched up there; you can't possibly be comfortable. One thing all the basic scrolls stress is that a practitioner of the Skill should find a comfortable starting place, one in which the body is relaxed and unobtrusive to the mind."

I opened my mouth to say that was the opposite of what Galen had done to us. On the contrary, when he was teaching us, he had made us so miserable in body that the mind became our only escape. I shut my mouth, the words unsaid. Useless to protest or ponder what Galen had done. The twisted, pleasureless man had tormented us all, and those he had succeeded in training, he had warped into a mindlessly loyal coterie for Prince Regal. Perhaps that had had something to do with it; perhaps he had wanted to break down the body's resistance and the mind's judgment before he could shape them into the coterie he desired.

I sat down in Chade's chair. It retained his warmth and the imprint of his body. It felt strange to sit there in his presence. It was as if I were becoming him. He assumed my perch on the stool and looked down on me from that towering height. He crossed his arms on his chest and leaned forward to smirk down at me.

"Comfortable?" he asked me.

"No," I admitted.

"Serves you right," he muttered. Then, with a laugh, he got off the stool. "Tell me what I can do to help you with this process."

"You want me to just sit here and Skill out, hoping to find the Prince?"

"Is that so hard?" It was a genuine question.

"I tried for several hours last night. Nothing happened except that I got a headache."

"Oh." For a moment he looked discouraged. Then he announced firmly, "We will simply have to try again." In a lower voice he muttered, "For what else can we do?"

I could think of no answer to that. I leaned back in his chair and tried to relax my body. I stared at his mantelpiece, only to have my attention stick on a fruit knife driven into the wood. I had done that, years ago. Now was not the time to dwell on that incident. Yet I found myself saying, "I crept into my old room today. It looks as if it has not been used since last I slept there."

"It hasn't. Castle tradition says it is haunted."

"You're joking!"

"No. Think about it. The Witted Bastard slept there, and he was taken to his death in the castle dungeons. It's a fine basis for a ghost tale. Besides, flickering blue lights have been seen through its shutters at night, and once a stable-boy said he saw the Pocked Man staring down from that window on a moonlit night."

"You kept it empty."

"I am not entirely devoid of sentiment. And for a long time, I hoped you would someday return to that room. But, enough of this. We have a task."

I drew a breath. "The Queen did not mention the note about the Prince being Witted."

"No. She did not."

"Do you know why?"

He hesitated. "Perhaps some things are so frightening that even our good Queen cannot bring herself to consider them."

"I'd like to see the note."

"Then you shall. Later." He paused, then asked me heavily, "Fitz? Are you going to settle down and do this thing or keep procrastinating?"

I took a deliberate breath, blew it out slowly, and fixed my gaze on the dwindling fire. I looked into its heart as I gradually unfastened my mind from my thoughts. I opened myself to the Skill.

My mind began to unfold. I have, over the years, given much thought to how one could describe Skilling. No metaphor really does it justice. Like a folded piece of silk, the mind opens, and opens, and opens again, becoming larger and yet somehow thinner. That is one image. Another is that the Skill is like a great unseen river that flows at all times. When one consciously pays attention to it, one can be seized in its current and drawn out to flow with it. In its wild waters, minds can touch and merge.

Yet no words or similes do it justice, any more than words can explain the smell of fresh bread or the color yellow. The Skill is the Skill. It is the hereditary magic of the Farseers, yet it does not belong to kings alone. Many folk in the Six Duchies have a touch of it. In some it burns strong enough that a Skilled one can hear their thoughts. Sometimes, I can even influence what a Skill-touched person thinks. Far more rare are those who can reach out with the

Skill. That ability is usually no more than a feeble groping unless the talent is trained. I opened myself to it, and let my consciousness expand but with no expectations of reaching anyone.

Threads of thought tangled against me like waterweed. "I hate the way she looks at my beau." "I wish I could say one last word to you, Papa." "Please hurry home, I feel so ill." "You are so beautiful. Please, please, turn around, see me, at least give me that." Those who flung the thoughts out with such urgency were, for the most part, ignorant of their own strength. None of them were aware of me sharing their thoughts, nor could I make my own thoughts known to them. Each cried out in their deafness with voices they believed were mute. None was Prince Dutiful. From some distant part of the keep, music reached my ears, temporarily distracting me. I pushed it aside and strove on.

I do not know how long I prowled amongst those unwary minds, nor how far I reached in my search. The range of the Skill is determined by strength of ability, not distance. I had no measure of my strength and time does not exist when one is in the grip of the Skill. I trod again that narrow measure, clinging to my awareness of my own body despite the temptation to let the Skill sweep me free of my body forever.

"Fitz," I murmured, in response to something, and then, "FitzChivalry," I said aloud to myself. A fresh log crashed down onto the embers of the fire, scattering the glowing heart into individual coals. For a time I stared at it, trying to make sense of what I was seeing. Then I blinked, and became aware of Chade's hand resting on my shoulder. I smelled hot food, and slowly turned my head. A platter rested on a low table near the chair. I stared at it, wondering how it had come to be there.

"Fitz?" Chade said again, and I tried to recall his question.

"What?"

"Did you find Prince Dutiful?"

Each word gradually made sense to me until I perceived his query. "No," I said as a wave of weariness rolled over me. "No, nothing." In the wake of the fatigue, my hands began to tremble and my head to pound. I closed my eyes, but found no relief. Even with my eyes closed, snakes of light trembled across the dark. When I opened my eyes, they were superimposed on the room before me. I felt as if too much light were getting inside my head. The waves of pain tumbled me in a surf of disorientation.

"Here. Drink this."

Chade put a warm mug into my hands and I lifted it gratefully to my mouth. I took a mouthful, then nearly spat it out. It was not elfbark tea to soothe my headache, but only beef broth. I swallowed it without enthusiasm. "Elfbark tea," I reminded him. "That is what I need right now. Not food."

"No, Fitz. Recall what you yourself told me. Elfbark stunts the Skill ability, and numbs you to your talent. That is something we cannot risk just now. Eat something. It will restore your strength."

Obediently I looked at the tray. Sliced fruit floated in cream next to fresh-baked bread. There was a glass of wine and pink slices of baked river fish. I carefully set the mug of broth down next to the revolting stuff and turned my gaze away. The fire was rekindling itself, dancing licks of flame, too bright. I lowered my face into my hands, seeking darkness, but even there the lights still danced before my eyes. I spoke into my hands. "I need some elfbark. It has not been this bad in years, not since Verity was alive, not since Shrewd took strength from me. Please, Chade. I cannot even think."

He went away. I sat counting my heartbeats until he came back. Each thud of my heart was a flare of pain in my temples. I heard the scuff of his steps and lifted my head.

"Here," he said gruffly, and set a cool wet cloth to my

forehead. The shock of it made me catch my breath. I held it to my brow and felt the thudding ease somewhat. It smelled of lavender.

I looked at him through a haze of pain. His hands were empty. "The elfbark tea?" I reminded him.

"No, Fitz."

"Chade. Please. It hurts so bad I can't see." Each word was an effort. My own voice was too loud.

"I know," he said quietly. "I know, my boy. But you will just have to bear it. The scrolls say that sometimes the use of the Skill brings this pain, but that, with time and repeated effort, you will learn to master it. Again, my understanding of it is imperfect, but it seems to have to do with the split effort you make, both to reach out from yourself and to hold tight to yourself. Given time, you will learn how to reconcile those tensions and then—"

"Chade!" I did not mean to bellow but I did. "I just need the damned elfbark tea. Please!" I took sudden control of myself. "Please," I added softly, contritely. "Please, just the tea. Just help me ease this pain, and then I could listen to you."

"No, Fitz."

"Chade." I spoke my hidden fear. "Pain such as this could push me into a seizure."

I saw a brief flicker of uncertainty in his eyes. But then, "I don't think it will. Besides, I'm here beside you, boy. I'll take care of you. You have to try to get through this without the drug. For Dutiful's sake. For the Six Duchies."

His refusal stunned me into silence. Hurt and defiance tore me. "Fine." I bit off the word. "I have some in my pack in my room." I tried to find the will to stand.

A moment of silence. Then, unwillingly he admitted, "You had some in your pack in your room. It is gone. As is the carryme that was with it."

I took the rag from my forehead and glared at him. My anger built on the foundation of my pain. "You have no right. How dare you?"

He took a breath. "I dare as much as my need demands. And my need is great." His green-eyed gaze met mine challengingly. "The throne needs the talent that only you possess. I will allow nothing that diminishes your Skill."

He did not look away from me, but I could scarcely keep my eyes on him. Light was flaring all around him, stabbing into my brain. The barest edge of control kept me from throwing the compress at him. As if he guessed that, he took it from me, offering me a freshly cooled one in its place. It was a pitiful comfort, but I put it on my brow and leaned back in the chair. I wanted to weep with frustration and anguish. From behind the compress, I told him, "Pain. That's what being a Farseer means to me. Pain and being used."

He made no reply. That had always been his greatest rebuke, the silence that forced me to hear my own words over and over. When I took the cloth from my forehead, he was ready with another one. As I pressed it to my eyes, he said mildly, "Pain and being used. I've known my share of that as a Farseer. As did Verity, and Chivalry, and Shrewd before them. But you know there is more to that. If there weren't, you wouldn't be here."

"Perhaps," I conceded grudgingly. The fatigue was winning. I just wanted to curl up around the pain and sleep but I fought it. "Perhaps, but it isn't enough. Not for going through this."

"And what more would you ask, Fitz? Why are you here?"

I knew he meant it to be a rhetorical question but the anxiety had been with me for too long. The answer was too close to my lips, and the pain made me speak without thought. I lifted a corner of the cloth to peer at him. "I do this because I want a future. Not for myself, but for my boy. For Hap. Chade, I've done it all wrong. I haven't taught him a thing, not how to fight, nor how to make a living. I need to find him an apprenticeship with a good master. Gindast. That's who he wishes to teach him. He wants to be a joiner, and I should have seen that this would come and saved my money, but I didn't. And here he is, of an age to learn and I haven't a thing to give him. The coins I've saved aren't enough to—"

"I can arrange that." Chade spoke quietly. Then, almost angrily, he demanded, "Did you think I wouldn't?" Something in my face betrayed me, for he leaned closer, brows furrowed, as he exclaimed, "You thought you'd have to do this in order to ask my help, didn't you?" The damp cloth was still in his hand. It slapped the stone flags when he flung it in a temper. "Fitz, you—" he began, then words failed him. He stood up and walked away from me. I thought he would leave entirely. Instead he went down to the workbench and the unused hearth at the other end of the chamber. He walked around the table slowly, looking at it and at the scroll racks and utensils as if seeking for something he had misplaced. I refolded the second cloth and held it to my forehead, but surreptitiously I watched him from under my hand. Neither of us said anything for a time.

When he came back to me, he looked calmer but somehow older. He took a fresh cloth from a pottery dish, wrung it out, folded it, and offered it to me. As we exchanged the compresses, he said softly, "I'll see that Hap gets his apprenticeship. You could simply have asked me to do that when I visited you. Or years ago, you could have brought the lad to Buckkeep and we'd have seen him decently educated."

"He can read and write and figure," I said defensively. "I saw to that."

"Good." His reply was chill. "I'm glad to hear you retained that much common sense."

There seemed no rejoinder to that. Both pain and weariness were overcoming me. I knew I had hurt him but I didn't feel it was my fault. How could I have known he'd be so willing to help me? Nevertheless, I apologized. "Chade, I'm sorry. I should have known that you would help me."

"Yes," he agreed mercilessly. "You should have. And you're sorry. I don't doubt you're sincere. Yet I seem to recall warning you, years ago, that those words will only work so often, and then they ring hollow. Fitz, it hurts me to see you this way."

"It's starting to ease," I lied.

"Not your head, you stupid ass. It hurts me to see that you are still . . . as you've always been since . . . damn. Since you were taken from your mother. Wary and isolated and mistrustful. Despite all I've . . . After all these years, have you given your trust to no one?"

I was silent for a time, pondering his words. I had loved Molly, but I had never trusted her with my secrets. My bond with Chade was as essential as my bones, but no, I had not believed that he would do all he could for Hap, simply for the sake of what we shared. Burrich. Verity. Kettricken. Lady Patience. Starling. In every instance, I had held back. "I trust the Fool," I said, and then wondered if I truly did. I did, I assured myself. There was almost nothing about me that he didn't know. That was trust, wasn't it?

After a moment, Chade said heavily, "Well, that's good. That you trust someone." He turned away from me and spoke to the fire. "You should force yourself to eat something. Your body may rebel, but you know that you need the food. Recall how we had to press food on Verity when he Skilled."

The neutrality in his voice was almost painful. I realized then that he had hoped I would insist that I did trust him. It would not have been true, and I would not lie to him. I rummaged about in my mind for something else to give him. I spoke the words without thinking. "Chade, I do love you. It's just that—"

He turned to me almost abruptly. "Stop, boy. Say no more." His voice was almost pleading as he said, "That's enough for me." He set his hand to my shoulder and squeezed nearly painfully. "I won't ask of you that which you can't give. You are what life has made you. And what I made you, Eda be merciful. Now pay attention to me. Eat something. Force yourself if you must."

It would have been useless to tell him that the sight and smell of the food was enough to make me gag. I took a breath, and quaffed down the beef broth, not breathing until it was gone. The fruit in cream felt slimy in my mouth, the fish reeked, and the bread near choked me, but I forced myself to swallow it half-chewed. I took a deep breath, and drank the wine. When I set the cup down, my stomach churned and my head reeled. The wine was a more potent vintage than I had thought. I lifted my eyes to Chade's. His mouth hung ajar in dismay. "I didn't mean like that," he muttered.

I lifted a hand at him in a gesture of futility. I feared to open my mouth to reply.

"You'd best go to bed," he suggested humbly.

I nodded in reply and levered myself to my feet. He opened the door for me, gave me a candle, and then stood at the top of the passage holding a light until my path carried me out of his view. My room seemed impossibly distant, but eventually I arrived at the entry. Queasy as I was, I extinguished my light before I approached and carefully peered through the peephole before I triggered the access to my dark room. No candle burned there tonight. It didn't matter. I stumbled into the stuffy darkness and thrust the door shut behind me. A few steps carried me to my bed and I dropped onto it. I was too hot and my clothes bound me uncomfortably, but I was too tired to do anything about it. The black was so absolute I could not tell if my eyes were open or shut. At least the lights under my eyelids had been quenched. I stared up into the darkness and longed for the cool peace of the forest.

The thick walls of the room muffled all sound, and sealed me off from the night. It was like being sealed in a tomb. I closed my eyes to the blackness and listened to my headache thump with the beat of my heart. My stomach gurgled unhappily. I drew a deep breath, and "Forest," I said quietly to myself. "Night. Trees. Meadow." I reached for the comforting familiarity of the natural world. I painted in the details for myself. A light wind stirring in the treetops. Stars flickering through rags of moving clouds. Coolness, and the rich scents of the earth. Tension eased away from me, taking my pain with it. I drifted with my imagination. The packed earth of a game trail beneath my feet, and I was moving softly through darkness, following my companion.

She went more quietly than night itself, each step sure and swift. Try as I might, I could not keep up with her. I could not even catch a glimpse of her. I knew of her passage by her scent hanging in the night air, or by the still-rustling bushes just ahead of me. My cat followed her, but I was not swift enough. "Wait!" I called to them.

Wait? she mocked me. *Wait for you to ruin the night's hunting? No. I shall not wait. You shall make haste, and do so silently. Have you learned nothing of me? Lightfoot am I and Nightfriend and Shadowstalker. Be you so, and come, come, come to share the night with me.*

I hurried after her, drunk with the night and her presence, drawn as irresistibly as a moth is drawn to a candle. Her eyes were green, I knew, for she had told me, and her long tresses were black. I longed to touch her, but she was elusive and taunting, always ahead of me, never revealing herself to my eyes let alone my touch. I could only run after her through the night, the breath rasping in my chest as she flew before me. I did not complain. I would prove myself worthy of her and win her.

But my heart was thundering and my breath burning in my lungs. I crested the top of a hill and stopped for breath. Before me spread the vista of the river valley. The moon hovered round and yellow. Had we come so far, in one night's hunting? Far below me, the walls of Galeton were a dark huddle of stone on the riverbank. A few isolated lights still shone yellow in the windows of the keep. I wondered who burned candles while the rest of the household slumbered.

Do you long to sleep in a stuffy room mounded with blankets? Is that how you would squander a night such as this? Save sleep for when the sunlight can warm you, save sleep for when the game is hidden in den or burrow. Hunt now, my clumsy one. Hunt with me! Prove yourself. Learn to be one with me, think as I do, move as I do, or lose me forever.

I started to go after her. My thoughts snagged on something, delaying me. There was something I must do, right now. Something I must tell someone, right now. Startled, I halted where I stood. The thought divided me. Part of me had to go, had to hunt at her heels before she left me behind. But another part of me stood still. I must tell him now. Right now. I peeled myself free, separating while holding on to the knowledge I had gained. It flickered in my grasp, threatening to become the nonsense of a fading dream. I gripped the thought, letting all else fade. Hold it. Say it out loud. Cling to the word, cling tight to the thought. Don't let it go, don't let it melt away with the dream.

"Galeton!"

I said the word aloud, sitting upright in my bed in the stifling darkness. My shirt stuck to me with sweat and the Skill-headache had returned with clanging bells attached to it. It didn't matter. I lurched from my bed and began a patting search of the invisible walls. "Galeton," I said aloud, lest the word slip from my grasp. "Prince Dutiful hunts near Galeton."

chapter XIV

LAUREL

There is a certain black stone, often finely veined with white or silver threading, that was extensively used by the Elderlings in their architecture. At least one quarry for this stone exists in the wild lands beyond the Mountain Kingdom, but it is almost certain that other sources for it exist, for it is difficult to even imagine how it might otherwise have been used in such large buildings in so many far-flung locations. It was used, not only in the construction of their buildings, but also in the monoliths they raised at certain crossroads. Due to several odd qualities of the roads that the Elderlings designed, it can be deduced that a ground or graveled form of the stone was also instrumental in their creation. Wherever the Elderlings built, this stone was a favored instrument, and even in the places that they seemed to have visited only sporadically, monuments of this stone are found. A close scrutiny of the Witness Stones of Buckkeep will convince the examiner that, although defaced by harsh weather or perhaps intentionally vandalized by men in ages past, the stone is of the same type. Some have suggested that the Witness Stones of Buckkeep and other "oath stones" throughout the Six Duchies were originally raised by the Elderlings for a very different purpose.

I awoke in Chade's great four-poster bed in the tower chamber. I knew a few moments of disorientation before deciding this was not another dream. I was truly awake. I did not recall going to sleep, only sitting down on the side of the bed for a few moments. I was still dressed in yesterday's clothing.

I sat up cautiously; the hammers and anvils in my head

had subsided to a monotonous drumming. The room appeared empty, but someone had been there recently. Wash water steamed near the hearth, and a small covered dish of porridge kept warm near it. As soon as I discovered these items, I put them to good use. My stomach was still reluctant to accept food, but I ate stoically, knowing it was for the best. I washed, put on a kettle for tea, and then wandered down to the worktable. A large map of Buck was unfurled across it. The corners were weighted with a mortar and two pestles and a teacup. An inverted wineglass rested on the map itself. When I lifted it, I found Galeton underneath it. It was on a tributary of the Buck River, northwest of Buck and on the other side of the river from Buckkeep. I had never been there. I tried to recall what I knew of Galeton and swiftly did so. Absolutely nothing.

My Wit alerted me to Chade's presence, and I turned as the hidden door swung open. He entered briskly. The tops of his cheeks were pink with the morning, and his white hair gleamed silver. Nothing invigorated the old man so much as fresh intrigue. "Ah, you're up. Excellent," he greeted me. "I managed to arrange an early breakfast with Lord Golden, despite the absence of his servingman. He assured me that he could be ready to travel in a few hours. He's already concocted an excuse for the trip."

"What?" I asked him, befuddled.

Chade laughed aloud. "Bird feathers, of all things. Lord Golden has a number of interesting hobbies, but his most current fascination is feathers. The larger and brighter the better. Galeton borders on a wooded upland, and has a reputation for pheasants, grouse, and whiptails. The latter have rather extravagant plumage, especially their tail feathers. He's already sent a runner on ahead to Lady Bresinga of Galeton, entreating hospitality from her while on his quest. It won't be refused. Lord Golden is the most popular novelty that Buckkeep Court has seen in a decade. Having him guest at her manor will be a social coup for her."

He paused, but it was I who took a breath. I shook my

head as if it would settle my brains and enable me to catch up with him. "The Fool is going to Galeton to find Dutiful?"

"Ah-ah!" Chade cautioned me. "Lord Golden is going to Galeton to hunt birds. His manservant, Tom Badgerlock, will of course accompany him. I hope that in the course of running down birds, you'll pick up the trail of the Prince. But that, of course, is our private errand."

"So I'm going with him."

"Of course." Chade peered at me. "Are you all right, Fitz? You seem wool-witted this morning."

"I am. It seems that all is happening so fast." I didn't say to him that I had become accustomed to ordering my own life and journeys. It felt strange to revert to living each day as another person decreed. I swallowed my protests. What had I expected? If we were to regain Prince Dutiful, this was how it must be. I struggled to find new footing for my thoughts. "Does Lady Bresinga have a daughter?"

Chade considered. "No. Only the son, Civil. I believe she fostered a girl cousin for a time. That would have been Fillip Bresinga. She is, let me see, I think she would be nearly thirteen now. She has returned home since spring."

I shook my head, both in denial and in wonder. Chade had obviously refreshed his information on the Bresinga family since last night. "I sensed a woman, not a child. An . . . attractive woman." I had nearly said "seductive." When I thought back to my experience of the night before, the dream became mine, and I recalled only too well how she had stirred my blood. Tantalizing. Challenging. I glanced back at Chade. He was watching my face with undisguised dismay. I asked the next question. "Has Dutiful expressed an interest in a woman? Might they have run away together?"

"Eda forbid," Chade exclaimed fervently. "No." He denied it almost desperately. "There is no woman in Dutiful's life, not even a girl he finds attractive. We have been very careful not to allow him the opportunity to develop such a bond. Kettricken and I decided long ago that it would be for the best." More quietly, he added, "She did not want to see her son torn as you were, between heart and duty. Have you never wondered how different things might have been if you had not loved Molly, if you had accepted your match with Lady Celerity?"

"I have. But I will never regret loving Molly."

I think the vehemence in my voice persuaded Chade to change tack. "There is no such love in Dutiful's life," he declared with finality.

"There wasn't. There may be now," I contradicted him.

"Then I pray it is a youthful infatuation, one that can be swiftly—" He searched for a word. "Terminated," he said at last, and winced at his own choice. "The boy is already promised. Don't look at me like that, Fitz."

Obediently, I looked away. "I do not think he has known her long. Part of her allure was her mystery."

"Then we must endeavor to recover him swiftly, with little damage done."

The next question was my own, asked for me. "What if he does not wish to be recovered?" I asked in a low voice.

Chade was silent for a moment. Then he said heartily, "You must do as you think best."

My shock must have been apparent on my face, for he laughed aloud. "For there is little use in my pretending that you will do otherwise, is there?" He drew a breath and sighed it out. "Fitz. I ask only this. Think in large terms. A boy's heart is a precious thing, as is a man's life. But the well-being of all the people of the Six Duchies and the Out Islands is even more precious. So, do what you think best. But be sure you truly have given it thought."

"I can't believe you are allowing me that much leeway!" I exclaimed.

"Can't you? Well, perhaps I know you better than you think I do."

"Perhaps," I conceded. But I wondered if he knew me as well as he thought he did.

"Well, you arrived only a few days ago, and here I am

sending you off again," Chade abruptly observed. He clapped me on the shoulder but his smile seemed a bit forced. "Think you can be ready to leave in an hour or so?"

"I've not much to pack. But I'll need to make a trip down to Buckkeep Town, to leave a message for Hap with Jinna."

"I can take care of that for you," Chade offered.

I shook my head. "She doesn't read, and if I am to be Tom Badgerlock, then I wouldn't have folk running errands for me. I'll take care of it." I didn't tell him that I wanted to do it myself.

"As you wish," he replied. "Let me prepare a note for the boy to present to Master Gindast when he goes to him about his apprenticeship. The rest will be done subtly, I promise you. The joiner will believe he takes Hap on as a favor to one of his most affluent customers." Chade paused a moment. "You know, all we can offer the boy is a chance to prove himself. I can't force the man to keep him on if Hap is clumsy or lazy." At my outraged look, Chade grinned. "But I am sure he is not. Just allow me a moment to compose my note for Hap to carry."

It took more than a moment, of course. When I finally had it in hand, I found myself hurrying after the fleeing morning. I encountered Lord Golden in his chambers when I emerged from my own dark little cell. He clucked over the state of my slept-in clothes and commanded that I pick up my new garments from the tailor so that I would have appropriate garb for our journey. He informed me that we would travel alone and swiftly. Lord Golden had already established a reputation for both eccentricity and adventurousness. No one would look askance at this expedition. He also told me that he had himself selected a horse for me, and was having her freshly shod. I could pick her up from a smithy. He assumed I would wish to select my own tack, and gave me a letter of credit for that as well before sending me on my way. At no time did he vary from his Lord Golden manners, and I maintained my demeanor as Tom

Badgerlock. These were roles we had to settle into as swiftly as possible. No errors could be made once we began to move in public. By the time I finally set out for Buckkeep Town, I was laden with errands and the sun was moving far too swiftly across the sky.

The tailor sought to delay me with a final fitting and adjustment of my new clothes. I refused, and did not even open the bundled garments to inspect them. I could tell Scrandon was accustomed to making a ceremony of delivering his finished goods, but I told him bluntly that Lord Golden had commanded me to make the greatest haste. At that he sniffed, and said he would take no responsibility then if the garments did not suit. I assured him that I would make no complaints and hastened out of his shop with an annoyingly bulky parcel.

I next went to Jinna's shop, but there I met disappointment. She was not home, and her niece had no idea when she would be back. Fennel came to greet me. *You love me. You know you do. Pick me up.*

It seemed pointless to disobey. I picked him up. He sank his claws into my shoulder as he diligently marked my jerkin with his brow.

"Jinna went up into the hills yesterday evening, and spent the night there, so that she could gather mushrooms first thing in the morning. She might be back in a moment, she might not return until the night falls," Miskya told me. "Oh, Fennel, stop being a pest. Come here." She took the cat from my arms, tsking over the coating of tawny hair that clung to my jerkin.

"No matter that, I assure you. But, oh, this is awkward," I apologized, and told her that my master had suddenly decided to take a journey and I must accompany him. I left with her the letter Chade had written for Hap, along with a note from me to my boy. Nighteyes would not be pleased to reach the city and find me gone. Nor would he relish lingering there, waiting for me. I belatedly realized I was leaving Jinna not just my son, but a wolf, a pony, and a cart to tend until my return. I wondered if Chade could be of any help with that. I had no coin to leave for their keep, only my greatest thanks and deepest assurances that I would make good any expenses she encountered on their behalf.

"So you've told me, Tom Badgerlock." Miskya smiled at me in gentle rebuke, obviously humoring my worry. Fennel tucked his head under her chin and regarded me severely. "Three times now you've told me that you'll be back soon and pay us well. Rest comfortable, your son will be in good hands and welcome here, pay or not. I doubt you asked coin of my aunt when you welcomed her to your home."

At Miskya's words, I realized I had been clucking on like an apprehensive hen. With an effort, I stopped myself from explaining again just how sudden and urgent my errand was. By the time I had conveyed my awkward thanks, I felt completely disorganized and befuddled. Scattered, as if parts of me were at my abandoned home and with Nighteyes and Hap, and even in the tower room at Buckkeep. I felt vulnerable and exposed. "Well, goodbye," I offered Miskya.

Sleeping in the sun is nicer. Take a nap with the cat, Fennel suggested as Miskya told me, "Travel well."

As I walked away from Jinna's house, guilt gnawed at me. I was leaving my responsibilities for strangers to deal with. I rigorously denied my disappointment at not seeing Jinna again before I left. The single kiss she had given me hung waiting, like a conversation unconcluded, but I refused to contemplate where it might lead. As complicated as things were, adding another tangle to my life was the last thing I should consider. Yet I had looked forward to seeing her again, and being denied that dimmed my excitement at the journey.

For I was excited to be on my way. The guilt that I felt at leaving Hap's welfare to someone else was an odd reflection of how freed I felt by this undertaking. In a short time the Fool and I would ride off together into El knew what, with only ourselves to look after. It promised to be a pleasant ride in fair weather with a good companion. There was more of holiday to it than errand. My fears for Prince Dutiful had been largely laid to rest by last night's dream. The boy had been in no physical danger. Intoxicated with the night and the woman he pursued, the only danger was to his young heart, and no one could shield him from that. Truth to tell, I did not see my task as particularly difficult. We knew where to look for the lad, and with or without my wolf, I had always been a good tracker. If Lord Golden and I did not immediately flush the young Prince from Gale-keep, then I would track him down in the surrounding hills. Doubtless we would not be gone long. With that reassuring thought, I salved my conscience and went on to the smithy.

I had not expected much of a horse. Almost, I had feared that the Fool's sense of humor would express itself through Lord Golden's selection of horseflesh. I found the smith's girl cooling herself with water from the rain barrel and told her I had come to fetch the horse Lord Golden had left for shoeing. She bobbed her head in understanding, and I waited where she left me standing. The day was warm enough. I had no desire to enter the inferno of noise and heat that was the blacksmith's shop.

The girl was back soon enough, leading a rangy black mare. I walked around her once and looked up to find she was regarding me with the same wary gaze I was giving her. She appeared sound and unscarred by misuse. I quested lightly toward her. She snorted and would not look at me, refusing the contact. She had no interest in being friends with a human.

"She was a nasty bit to shoe," the smith informed me loudly as he came sweating from his shop. "No manners about lifting her feet for a man to handle. And she'll kick if she gets the chance, so mind that. Tried to take a nip out of my girl, too. But it was only while we were shoeing her. The rest of the time, she minded her manners well enough."

I thanked him for his warnings and gave him the promised purse from Lord Golden. "Has she a name that you know?" I asked him.

The smith pursed his lips and shook his head. "Never saw her afore this morning. If she had a name, she likely lost it in the horse-trade. Call her what you will; likely she'll ignore it." I set the issue of her name aside. Her worn halter went with her, and by that I led her down to a saddler. I purchased plain, serviceable tack, and despite my best bargaining efforts, I was still outraged at what they charged for it. The man's expression plainly said he thought me unreasonable. As I went outside with the tack I had selected, I wondered if I truly were. I had never had to purchase tack before; perhaps Burrich's obsession with repairing tack had been founded on how much the stuff cost.

The mare had been restive as I had tried several saddles on her, and when I tried to mount her, danced sideways. Once I was up, she answered the reins and my knees, but sloppily. I scowled at that but schooled myself to patience with her. Perhaps after we had taken one another's measure she would serve me better. And if she did not, well, patience was required to unteach any horse's bad habits. I had best accustom myself to that now. As I rode her carefully up the steep streets of Buckkeep Town, I reflected that perhaps I had been far more spoiled in my youth than I had ever known. Excellent horses, good tack, fine weapons, decent clothing, plentiful food: I had taken so much for granted.

A horse? I could teach a horse whatever it needs learning. Why do you need a horse?

Nighteyes had slipped into my mind so easily I'd scarce been aware of him sharing my thoughts. *I have to go somewhere. With the scentless one.*

Must it be on horseback? He didn't allow me time to reply. I sensed his annoyance. *Wait for me. I'm nearly there.*

Nighteyes, no, don't come to me. Stay with the boy. I'll be back soon enough.

But he was gone, and my own thought was left hanging

unanswered. I quested toward him but found only fog. He wouldn't argue with me. He simply wouldn't hear me telling him to stay with Hap.

The guards at the gate scarcely gave me a glance. I frowned and resolved to speak about that to Chade. Just because I was wearing blue clothing did not mean I had legitimate business in the castle. I rode up to the stable doors, dismounted, and then halted, heart hammering. From inside the stable came the voice of a man genially instructing someone in how to correctly clean a horse's hooves. Years had deepened the voice, but I still recognized it. Hands, my boyhood friend and now the Stablemaster at Buckkeep, was just inside the open doors. My mouth went dry. The last time he had seen me, he had regarded me as either a ghost or a demon, and run shouting for the guards. That had been years ago. I was much changed, I told myself, but could put no faith in the years as my sole disguise. I took refuge in becoming Tom Badgerlock.

"Here, boy," I summoned a lad loitering outside the stable. "Put this horse up for me. She belongs to Lord Golden, so see she is well treated."

"Yes, sir," he replied. "He sent us word to watch for Tom Badgerlock and a black mare, and to saddle up his own horse as soon as you returned. He said to tell you that you're wanted up in his rooms as soon as you show." With that, he took my mare away without another word. I breathed out, relieved at how easily I had passed that hurdle, and turned away from the stable. Before I had gone a dozen steps, a man hurried past me, evidently on an errand of his own. As he passed me he gave me not a glance. I stared after Hands. He had put on girth with the years, but then, so had I. His dark hair was thinning on his head, but bristled thicker than ever on his brawny arms. In a moment he turned a corner and was out of sight. I stood gaping after him, feeling as if I truly were a ghost, invisible in his world. Then I took a breath and hurried on my own way. In time, I reflected, he would catch a glimpse of Tom Badgerlock here and there about the keep, and by the time we stood face-to-face, I would have assumed that name and identity so completely that he would not question it.

I felt my life as Fitz was like footprints on a dusty floor, already being swept aside and overtrodden by others. It did not help that as I passed the Great Hall, I heard Lord Golden's voice lifted in sudden summons. "Ah, there you are, Tom Badgerlock! Excuse me, ladies, here is my good man now. Farewell, fare well all in my absence!"

I watched him detach himself from a gaggle of noble ladies. They let him go reluctantly, fluttering fans and eyelashes after him, one making a pretty mouth of disappointment. Lord Golden smiled fondly on them all, waving a languid valediction with a graceful hand as he strode up to me. "Errands done? Excellent. Then we shall complete our preparations and be on our way while the sun is still high."

He swept past me and I followed behind at a discreet distance, nodding to his words as he instructed me in how he wished his things packed. Yet when we reached his rooms and I closed the door behind us, I saw his well-stuffed traveling bags already waiting on the chair. I turned to the sound of him latching the door behind us. He gestured at my room just as the door of it opened and Chade emerged into our midst.

"There you are and not a moment too soon. The Queen has received your tidings, and commands that you depart immediately. I do not think she will be completely at ease until the boy is under this roof again. Well, and neither will I." He bit his lower lip briefly and then announced, more to Lord Golden than to me, "The Queen has decided that Huntswoman Laurel will go with you. She readies herself now."

"We don't need her," Lord Golden exclaimed in annoyance. "The fewer who know of this business, the better."

"She is the Queen's own Huntswoman, and in her confidence in many things. Her mother's family lives less than a day's ride from Galeton. She claims to know the area well from childhood times spent there, so that may be a help to you. Besides, Kettricken is determined you will take her. Well do I know the futility of arguing with the Queen when she has made up her mind to something."

"I recall something of that myself," Lord Golden replied, but there was much of the Fool in that rueful voice. I felt a smile crook the corner of my own mouth. I too knew what it was to quail before the blue determination of my Queen's gaze. I wondered who this Laurel was, and what she had done to win the Queen's confidence. Did I feel a prick of envy that someone had replaced me as Kettricken's confidante at Court? Well, it had been fifteen years since I had filled that role. Had I expected her to take no one in my place?

Lord Golden's displeased resignation broke into my thoughts. "Well, so be it, then, if it must. She can come, but I'll not wait upon her. Tom, are not you packed yet?"

"Close enough," I rejoined and recalled myself enough to add, "my lord. I shall be but a moment. I've little enough to pack."

"Excellent. See that you bring Scrandon's wares, for I will have you dressed appropriately to serve me in Galekeep."

"As you will, sir," I replied, and left them to step into my chamber. I put the bundle of new garments into the new saddle pack I found there. It was marked with Lord Golden's cock pheasant. I added a few of my old garments for the night work I expected to be doing in Galeton, and then looked about the room. I already wore my serviceable sword. There was nothing else to add to the pack. No poisons, no cunningly made small weapons to smuggle along. I abruptly felt strangely naked despite having gone without them for years.

As I emerged with my packed bags slung over my shoulder, Chade stopped me with a lifted hand. "One more small item," he offered sheepishly, and held out a leather roll without meeting my eyes. As I took it into my hands, I knew the contents without having to check it. Picks for locks, and other subtle tools of the assassin's trade. Lord Golden looked aside as I slipped the roll inside my pack. Of old, my clothing had featured hidden pockets for such things. Well, I hoped I would not have to be at this long enough to make such concerns necessary again.

Our farewells were hurried and odd. Lord Golden bade Chade a formal farewell, as if there were an entire audience of strangers watching them. Thinking I should emulate their example, I offered Chade a servant's bow, but he seized me by the arms and embraced me hastily. "Thank you, my boy," he muttered by my ear. "Go in haste and bring Dutiful back to us. And go easy on the boy. This is as much my fault as his."

Emboldened, I replied, "Watch over my boy for me, then. And Nighteyes. I hadn't thought I'd be burdening Jinna with him, let alone a pony and cart."

"I'll see they come to no harm," he offered, and I know he saw the gratitude in my eyes. Then I hastened to unlatch the door for Lord Golden, and followed at his heels carrying our bags as he strode through Buckkeep. Many called out farewells to him, and he acknowledged them warmly but briefly.

If Lord Golden had sincerely hoped to leave Laurel behind, she disappointed him. She was standing at the stable door, holding all our horses and waiting for us with every evidence of impatience. I placed her in her middle to late twenties. She was strongly built, not unlike Kettricken herself, long-boned and muscled, yet still womanly in form. She was not from Buck, for our women tend to be small and dark, and Laurel was neither. She was not fair like Kettricken, but her eyes were blue. Her brown hair was sunstreaked with blond, and bleached near white at her temples. Sun had browned her face and hands. She had a narrow straight nose above a strong mouth and determined chin. She wore the leathers of a hunter, and her horse was one of those small, wiry ones that leap like a terrier over any barrier and can race like a weasel through the most tangling brush. He was a homely little gelding, and his eyes shone with his spirit. Her small baggage roll was secured behind her saddle. As we approached, Malta lifted her head and whickered eagerly to her master. My black stood by disinterestedly. It was oddly humiliating.

"Huntswoman Laurel. Ready to go, I see," Lord Golden greeted her.

"Yes, my lord. Waiting only for you to be ready."

At this, they both glanced at me. Recalling abruptly that I was Lord Golden's servant, I took Malta's reins from Laurel and held her while Lord Golden mounted. I fastened both our saddle packs onto my black, a process she did not much approve of. As I took my reins from Laurel, she smiled at me and proffered a hand. "Laurel of the Downs family near Pitbank. I am Her Majesty's Huntswoman."

"Tom Badgerlock. Lord Golden's man," I replied as I bowed over her hand.

Lord Golden had already set his horse in motion with a noble disregard for the doings of servants. We both hastily mounted and set off after him. "And where is your family from, Tom?" Laurel asked.

"Um. Near Forge. On Bramble Creek." Bramble Creek was what Hap and I called it. If the creek near our cottage had any other name, I had never heard it. But the impromptu pedigree seemed to satisfy Laurel. The black was annoying me by tugging at her bit and trying to move up. Evidently she was not used to following another horse. Her stride was longer than Malta's as well. I held her in place, but it was a near constant battle of wills.

Laurel gave me a sympathetic look. "New mount?"

"I've had her less than the day. Discovering her temperament on a journey may not be the best way to get to know her."

She grinned at me. "No, but it may be the quickest. Besides, what choice do you have?"

We left the castle by the west gate. In my boyhood at Buckkeep, this gate had been kept secured at most times,

and the road that led from it had been little more than a
goat path. Now it stood open, with a small manned guard-
house next to it. We were passed out with scarcely a pause,
and found ourselves on a well-traveled road that traversed
the hills behind Buck Castle before winding down to the
riverside. The steepest bits of the old path had been
rerouted, and the whole way widened. Tracks told me that
carts used this meandering path, and as it carried us on our
wandering way down to the river, I caught glimpses of
wharves below, and the roofs of warehouses. I was still
shocked when I began to catch glimpses of cottages back
beneath the trees.

"Folk did not used to live there," I said. I bit my tongue
before I added that Prince Verity had loved to hunt these
hills. I doubted they offered much game anymore. Trees had
been cleared to allow small gardens to be cultivated. Don-
keys and ponies grazed in brushy pastures.

Laurel nodded to my surprise, but added, "Then you
have not been here since the Red Ship War ended. All this
has sprung up in the last ten years or so. When trade improved, more folk wanted to live near Buckkeep, and yet did
not want to be too far from the castle lest the raids resume."

I could think of no sensible reply to her words, but the
new stretch of town still surprised me. There was even a
tavern as we got closer to the docks, and a hiring hall for
rivermen. We rode past a row of warehouses that fronted
onto the docks. Donkey carts seemed the favored trans-
portation. Blunt-nosed river craft were tied up to the docks,
unloading cargo from Farrow and Tilth. We passed another
tavern, and then several cheap rooming houses such as
sailors seem to favor. The road followed the river upstream.
Sometimes it was wide and sandy; in other places timbers
had been laid in a sort of boardwalk over boggy stretches.
The other horses seemed to take no notice of the change,
but at every one we traversed, my black slowed her pace
and set back her ears. She did not like the drumming of her
hooves on the timber. I set my hand to her withers and

quested toward her, offering reassurance. She turned her head to roll an eye at me, but remained as distant as ever. She probably would have refused to go on if there had not been two other horses to follow. She was plainly far more interested in her own kind than in any companionship I might offer.

I shook my head at the difference between her and the amiable horses in Burrich's stable, and wondered if his Wit had made the difference. Whenever a mare birthed a foal, Burrich was at her side, and the baby knew the touch of his hand almost as soon as it knew the lick of its mother's tongue. Was it merely the early presence of a human that had made the beasts in his stable so accepting, or was it his own Wit, suppressed but still present, that had made them so receptive to me?

The afternoon sun beat down on us, and the sun bounced off the river's wide and gleaming surface. The thudding hooves of the three horses were a pleasant counterpoint to my thoughts as I pondered. Burrich had seen the Wit as a dark and low magic, a temptation to let the beast in my nature overwhelm me. Common lore agreed with him and went further; the Wit was a tool for evil, a shameful magic that led its practitioners into degradation and wickedness. Death and dismemberment was the only recognized cure for the Wit. My equanimity over Dutiful's absence was suddenly threatened. True, the boy had not been kidnapped. But although the Skill had let me find him, it was undoubtedly the Wit the boy was employing in his night hunts. If he betrayed himself to anyone, he might be put to death. Perhaps not even his status as a prince would be enough to protect him from that fate. After all, the Wit had been enough to tumble me from the favor of the coastal dukes straight into Regal's dungeons.

No wonder Burrich had given up all use of the Wit. No wonder he had so often threatened to beat it out of me. Yet I could not regret having it. Curse or blessing, it had saved my life more often than it had endangered it. And I could not help but believe that my deep sense of kinship with all life enhanced my days. I drew a deep breath and cautiously let my Wit unfold into a general sensing of the day around me. My awareness of both Malta and the Huntswoman's horse sharpened, as did their acknowledgment of me. I sensed Laurel, not as another rider beside me, but as a large and healthy creature. Lord Golden was as unknowable to my Wit as the Fool ever was. From even that sense, he rippled aside, and yet his very mystery was a familiar one to me. Birds in the trees overhead were bright startles of life amongst the leaves. From the largest of the trees we passed, I sensed a deep green flow of being, a welling of existence that was unlike an animal's awareness and yet was life all the same. It was as if my sense of touch expanded beyond my skin to make contact with all other forms of life around me. All the world shimmered with life, and I was a part of that network. Regret this oneness? Deny this expanded tactility?

"You're a quiet one," Laurel observed. With a start I became aware of her as a person again. My thoughts had run so deep, I had almost forgotten the woman riding beside me. She was smiling at me. Her eyes were pale blue, but with rings of darker blue at the edges. One iris, I noted, had an odd streak of green in it, radiating out from the center. I could think of no reply so I simply shrugged and nodded. Her smile grew wider.

"Have you been Huntswoman for the Queen long?" I asked, simply to be saying something.

Laurel's eyes grew thoughtful as she toted up the years. "Seven years now," she said quietly.

"Ah. Then you know her well," I rejoined, wondering how much she truly knew of our present errand.

"Well enough," Laurel replied, and I could almost see her wondering the same about me.

I cleared my throat. "Lord Golden visits Galeton in search of gamebirds. He has a passion for collecting feathers, you know." I did not directly ask any question.

She looked at me from the corner of her eye. "Lord Golden has many passions, it is said," she observed in a low voice. "And the funds to indulge them all." She gave me another glance, as if to ask if I would defend my master, but if there was an insult, I did not take its meaning. She looked ahead and spoke on. "As for me, I but travel along to scout the hunting for my Queen. She likes to go after game birds in the autumn. I have hopes that in Galeton woods we may find the kind that she likes best."

"So do we all hope," I agreed. I liked her caution. We would get along well enough, I decided.

"Have you known Lord Golden long?" she asked me.

"Not directly," I hedged. "I had heard he was looking for a man, and I was glad when an acquaintance recommended me."

"Then you've done this kind of work before?"

"Not for some time. For the past ten years or so I've lived quietly, just my boy and me. But he's of an age to apprentice out, and that takes hard coin. This is the fastest way I know to earn it."

"And his mother?" she asked lightly. "Won't she be lonely with both of you away?"

"She's gone many years," I said. Then, realizing that Hap might sometime venture up to Buckkeep, I decided to keep as close to the truth as I could. "He's a fosterling I took in. I never knew his mother. But I think of him as my son."

"You're not married, then?"

The question surprised me. "No, I'm not."

"Neither am I." She gave me a small smile as if to say this gave us much in common. "So, how do you like Buckkeep so far?"

"Well enough. I lived close by when I was a boy. It's changed a great deal since then."

"I'm from Tilth myself. Up on the Branedee Downs is where I grew up, though my mother was from Buck. Her family lived not far from Galeton; I know the area, for I ranged there as a child. But mostly we lived near the Downs, where my father was Huntsman for Lord Sitswell. My father taught both my brothers and me the skills of being a Huntsman. When he died, my older brother took his position. My younger brother returned to live amongst my mother's people. I stayed on, mostly training the coursing horses in Lord Sitswell's stable. But when the Queen and her party came hunting there years ago, I turned out to help, for the party was so large. The Queen took a liking to me, and"—she grinned proudly—"I've been her Huntswoman ever since."

I was trying to think of something more to say when Lord Golden beckoned us both to come closer.

I urged the black forward, and when we were close, he announced, "Those were the last of the houses for a way. I did not want folks saying that we rode in great haste, but neither do I wish to miss this evening's only ferry from Lampcross. So now, good people, we ride. And Badgerlock, we'll see if that black is truly as fleet as the horse seller said. Keep up as best you can. I'll hold the ferry for us all." So saying, he touched his heels to Malta and let out her reins. It was all the permission she required. She sprang forward, showing us her heels.

"My Whitecap can match her any day!" Laurel proclaimed, and gave her horse his head.

Catch them! I suggested to the black, and was almost shocked at her competitive response. From a walk, she all but leapt into a run. The smaller horses had the lead on us. Packed mud flew up from their hooves, and Malta led only by virtue of the narrowing trail. My black's longer stride diminished their lead until we were close behind them, getting the full benefit of the mud they threw. The sound of us at their heels spurred them to greater effort and once more they pulled ahead of us. But I could feel that my black had not yet hit her peak. There was still unrealized reach in her stride, and the tempo of her gait said that she had not reached her hardest gallop. I tried to hold her back where the flying clods would not shower us so heartily, but she paid no heed to the rein. The moment the trail widened, she surged forward into the gap, and in a few strides she passed them both. I heard them both cry out to their horses, and I thought they would overtake us. But like a lengthening wolfhound on the scent, my black reached out to seize even longer strides of the path and fling it behind us. I glanced back at them once, to see both their faces alight with the challenge.

Faster, I suggested to my black. I did not really think she had more speed in her, but as a flame roars up a dry tree, she again surged forward. I laughed aloud at the pure joy of it, and saw her ears flicker in response. She did not reach toward my mind with any thought, but I felt a tentative glimmer of her approval. We would do well enough together.

We were first to reach Lampcross Ferry.

chapter XV

GALETON

Since the time of the Piebald Prince, the scouring of the Witted has been accepted within the Six Duchies as matter-of-factly as enforced labor for bad debt or flogging for thieves. It was the normal way of the world, and unquestioned. In the years following the Red Ship War, it was natural that the purging should begin in earnest. The Cleansing of Buck had freed the land of the Red Ship Raiders and the Forged ones they had created. Honest folk hoped to purify the Six Duchies of unnatural taints completely. Some were, perhaps, too swift to punish on little evidence. For a time, accusations of being Witted were enough to make any man, guilty or not, tremble for fear of his life.

    The self-styled Piebalds took advantage of this climate of suspicion and violence. While not revealing themselves, they publicly exposed well-known figures who were possessed of the Wit but never spoke out against the persecution of their more vulnerable fellows. It was the first attempt by the Witted as a group to wield any sort of political power. Yet it was not the effort of a people to defend themselves against unjust persecution, but the underhanded tactic of a duplicitous faction determined to seize power for themselves by any available means. They had no more loyalty to themselves than a pack of dogs.

    ❧ DELVIN'S "THE POLITICS OF THE PIEBALD CABAL"

As it turned out, my race to the ferry landing was of small use. The ferry was there and tied up, and so it would remain, the captain told me, until an expected cargo of two wagons of sea salt arrived. When Lord Golden and Laurel arrived, which, to speak fairly, was not so much longer after I did, the captain remained adamant. Lord Golden offered him a substantial purse to leave without the wagons, but the captain shook his head with a smile. "I'd have your coins once, and nice as they might clink, I could only spend them once. I wait for the wagons at Lady Bresinga's request. Her coins come to me every week, and I'll not do anything to risk her ill will. You'll have to wait, good sir, begging your pardon."

Lord Golden was little pleased with this, but there was nothing he could do. He told me to remain there with the horses, and took himself off to the landing inn where he could have a mug of ale in comfort while he waited. It was in keeping with our roles, and I harbored no resentment. I told myself this several times. If Laurel had not been with us, perhaps he would have found a way for us to share some time without compromising our public roles. I had looked forward to a companionable journey with him and time in which we did not have to maintain our façade of master and servant but I resigned myself to what was necessary. Still, something of my regret must have showed in my face, for Laurel came to keep pace with me as I walked the horses about in a field near the ferry landing. "Is something troubling you?" she asked me.

I glanced at her in some surprise at the sympathy in her voice. "Just missing an old friend," I replied honestly.

"I see," she answered, and when I offered no more on the topic, she observed, "You've a good master. He held no grudge against you that you beat him in our race. Many's the master who would have found a way to make you regret your victory over him."

The idea startled me, not as Tom Badgerlock but as Fitz. It had never occurred to me that the Fool might resent a race fairly won. Plainly I was not fully settled into my role. "That's true, I suppose. But the victory was his as much as mine. He chose the horse, and at first I was not much impressed with the beast. But she can run, and in running she showed a spirit I didn't suspect she had. I think I can make a good mount of her yet."

Laurel stepped back to run a critical eye over my black. "She seems a good mount to me. What made you doubt her?"

"Oh." I searched for words that would not make me sound Witted. "She seemed to lack a certain willingness. Some horses want to please. Your Whitecap is one, and Malta another. My black seems to lack that. But as we get to know one another, perhaps it will come."

"Myblack? That's her name?"

I shrugged and smiled. "I suppose. I hadn't given her one, but, yes, I suppose that's what I've been calling her."

She gave me a sideways glance. "Well, it's a little better than Blacky or Queenie."

I grinned at her disapproval. "I know what you mean. Well, she may yet show me a name that fits her more truly, but for now she's Myblack."

For a time we walked in silence. She kept glancing up the roads that led down to the ferry landing. "I wish those wagons would come. I don't even see them."

"Well, the land rises and falls a good deal along here. They may crest a hill anytime and come into view for us."

"I hope so. I'd like to be on our way. I'd hoped to reach Galeton before full dark. I'd like to get up in the hills as soon as possible and take a look around."

"For the Queen's quarry," I supplied.

"Yes." She glanced aside from me for a time. Then, as if making sure I understood that she did not break a confidence, she said bluntly, "Queen Kettricken told me that both you and Lord Golden are to be trusted. That I need hold nothing back from either of you."

I bowed my head to that. "The Queen's confidence honors me."

"Why?"

"Why?" I was startled. "Well, such confidence from such a great lady to one like me is—"

"Unbelievable. Especially when you arrived in Buck-keep Castle but a few days ago." Her eyes met mine squarely.

Kettricken had chosen her confidante well. Yet her very intelligence could be a threat to me. I licked my lips, debating my answer. A small piece of truth, I decided. Truth was easiest to keep straight in later conversations. "I have known Queen Kettricken of old. I served her in several confidential ways during the time of the Red Ship War."

"Then it was for her that you came to Buckkeep rather than Lord Golden?"

"I think it is fair to say I came for myself."

Silence ensued. Together we led our horses to the river and allowed them to drink. Myblack showed no caution of the water, wading out to drink deep. I wondered how she would react to boarding the ferry. She was big and the river was wide. If she decided to give trouble, it could be an unpleasant crossing for me. I dipped a kerchief in the cold water and wiped my face with it.

"Do you think the Prince just ran away?"

I dropped the kerchief from my eyes to stare at her in surprise. This woman was blunt. She did not look away from me. I glanced about to be sure no one could hear us. "I don't know," I said as bluntly. "I suspect he may have been lured rather than taken by force. But I do think others were involved in his leaving." Then I bit my tongue and chided myself for being too open. How would I back up that opinion? By revealing I was Witted? Better to listen than to talk.

"Then we may be opposed in recovering him."

"It's possible."

"Why do you think they lured him away?"

"Oh, I don't know." I was beginning to sound vapid and I knew it.

She met my eyes squarely. "Well. I also think he was lured away, if not taken outright. I speculate that those who took him did not approve of the Queen's plan for marrying him to the Outislander narcheska." She glanced away and added, "Nor do I."

Those words gave me pause. It was the first hint that she was not unquestioning in her loyalty to the Queen. All Chade's old training came to the fore, as I sought to see how deep her disagreement ran. Could she have had something to do with the Prince's disappearance? "I am not sure that I agree with it myself," I replied, inviting her to say more.

"The Prince is too young to be pledged to anyone," Laurel said forthrightly. "I have no confidence that the Out Islands are our best allies, let alone that they will remain true. How can they? They are little more than city-states scattered along the coast of a forbidding land. No one lord holds true power there, and they squabble constantly. Any alliance we make there is as like to draw us into one of their petty wars as to benefit us in trade."

I was taken aback. She had obviously given this a great deal of thought, and in a depth I would not have expected of a Huntswoman. "What would you favor, then?"

"Were the decision mine—and well I know it is not—I would hold him back, in reserve as it were, until I saw surely what was happening, not just in the Out Islands but to the south, as well, in Chalced and Bingtown and the lands beyond. There has been talk of war down there, and other wild tales. Dragons have been seen, they do say. Not that I believe all I hear, but dragons did come to the Six Duchies during the Red Ship War. I've heard those tales too often to set them aside. Perhaps they are attracted to war and the prey it offers them."

To enlighten her in that regard would have required hours. I merely asked, "Then you would marry our Prince off to a Chalcedean noblewoman, or a Bingtown Trader's daughter?"

"Perhaps it would be best for him to marry within the Six Duchies. There are some who mutter that the Queen is foreign-born, and that a second generation of a foreign queen might not be good."

"And you agree?"

She gave me a look. "Do you forget I am the Queen's

Huntswoman? Better a foreigner like her than some of the Farrow noblewomen I've had to serve in the past."

Our talk died there for a time. We led the horses away from the river. I removed bits and let the animals graze. I was hungry myself. As if she could read my thoughts, Laurel dug into her saddlebag and came up with apples for us both. "I always carry food with me," she said as she offered one to me. "Some of the folk I've hunted for think no more of the comfort of their hunters than they do of their horses or dogs."

I bit back a response that would have defended Lord Golden from such a charge. Best to let the Fool decide how he wished to present himself. I thanked her and bit into the apple. It was both tart and sweet. Myblack lifted her head suddenly.

Share? I offered her.

She flicked her ears at me disdainfully and went back to grazing.

A few days without me and he's consorting with horses. I might have known. The wolf used the Wit without subtlety, startling me and spooking all three horses.

"Nighteyes!" I exclaimed in surprise. I looked around for him.

"Beg pardon?"

"My . . . dog. He's followed me from home."

Laurel looked at me as if I were mad. "Your dog? Where?"

Luckily for me, the great wolf had just come into view, slipping out of the shelter of the trees. He was panting, and he headed straight for the river to drink. Laurel stared. "That's a wolf."

"He does look a great deal like a wolf," I conceded. I clapped my hands and whistled. "Here, Nighteyes. Here, boy."

I'm drinking, you idiot. I'm thirsty. As you might be if you had trotted all the way here instead of riding a horse.

"No," Laurel replied evenly. "That is *not* a dog that looks like a wolf. That is a wolf."

"I adopted him when he was very small." Nighteyes was still lapping. "He's been a very good companion to me."

"Lady Bresinga may not welcome a wolf into her home."

Nighteyes lifted his head suddenly, looked about, and then without a glance at me, slunk back into the woods. *Tonight,* he promised me in parting.

I'll be on the other side of the river by tonight.

So will I. Trust me. Tonight.

Myblack had caught Nighteyes' scent and was staring after him. She whickered uneasily. I looked back at Laurel and found her regarding me curiously.

"I must have been mistaken. That was, indeed, a wolf. Looked a great deal like my dog, though."

You've made me look like an idiot.

That wasn't hard.

"It was a very peculiar way for a wolf to behave," Laurel observed. She was still staring after him. "It's been years since I've seen a wolf in these parts."

I offered Myblack the apple core. She accepted it, and left a coating of green slime on my palm in return. Silence seemed the wisest choice.

"Badgerlock! Huntswoman!" Lord Golden summoned us from the roadside. In great relief, I led the horses over to him.

Laurel trailed us. As we approached him across the meadow, she made a small sound of approval in her throat. I glanced back at her in consternation. Her eyes were fixed on Lord Golden, but at my questioning glance, she quirked a small smile at me. I looked back at him.

Aware of our scrutiny, he all but struck a pose. I knew the Fool too well to be fooled by Lord Golden's careless artifice. He knew how the wind off the river toyed with his golden locks. He had chosen his colors well, blues and white, and his elegant clothing was cut to complement his slender figure. He looked like a creature of sun and sky. Even carrying food bundled in a white linen napkin and a jug, he still managed to look elegantly aristocratic.

"I've brought you a meal and drink so you'll not be tempted to leave the horses untended," he told me. He handed me the napkin and the moisture-beaded jug. Then he ran his eyes over Laurel and gave her an approving smile. "If the Huntswoman would enjoy it, I would be pleased to share a meal with her while we await those cursed wagons."

The fleeting glance Laurel sent my way was laden with meaning. She begged my pardon for deserting me even as she was certain I could see this was too rare an opportunity for her to miss.

"I am certain I would enjoy it, Lord Golden," she replied, inclining her head. I took Whitecap's reins before she could think to ask me. Lord Golden offered her his arm as if she were a lady. With only the slightest hesitation, she set her sun-browned fingers on the pale blue of his sleeve. He immediately covered her hand with his long, elegant fingers. Before they were three steps away from me, they were in deep conversation about game birds and seasons and feathers.

I closed my mouth, which had been hanging just slightly ajar. Reality reordered itself around me. Lord Golden, I suddenly realized, was every bit as complete and real a person as the Fool had been. The Fool had been a colorless little freak, jeering and sharp-tongued, who tended either to rouse unquestioning affection or abhorrence and fear in those who knew him. I had been among those who had befriended King Shrewd's jester, and had valued his friendship as the truest bond two boys could share. Those who had feared his wickedly barbed jests and been repulsed by his pallid skin and colorless eyes had been the vast majority of the castle folk. But just now an intelligent and, I must admit, very attractive young woman had chosen Lord Golden's companionship over mine.

"There's no accounting for tastes," I told Whitecap, who was looking after his departing mistress with an aggrieved air.

What's in the napkin?

I didn't think you'd go far. A moment.

I put the horses to graze with makeshift picket lines and went over to where the field met the edge of a forested bramble. There was a great mossy river boulder there, and I spread the napkin out atop it. When I unstoppered the jug, I found it held sweet cider. Within the napkin were two meat pasties.

One for me.

Nighteyes did not come all the way out of the bramble. I tossed one of the pasties to him and immediately bit into my own. It was still warm from cooking and the meat and gravy were brown and savory. One of the lovely things about the Wit is that one can carry on a conversation while eating without choking. *So. How did you find me, and why?* I asked him.

I found you just as I'd find any fleabite. Why? What else was I to do? You could not have expected me to stay in Buckkeep Town. With a cat? Please. Bad enough that you reek of that creature. I could not have abided sharing space with him.

Hap will worry about you when he discovers you are missing.

Perhaps, but I doubt it. He was so excited to come back to Buckkeep Town. Why a boy would find it enticing, I do not know. There is nothing but noise and dust, no game worth speaking of, and far too many humans crammed into one space.

Then you came after me solely to spare yourself that aggravation. It had nothing to do with being concerned for me or missing me?

If you and the Scentless One hunt, then I should hunt with you. That is only sense. Hap is a good boy, but he is not the best hunter. Better to leave him safe in town.

But we are on horseback, and, my friend, you are not as fleet as you used to be, nor do you have the endurance of a young wolf. Best you go back to Buckkeep Town and keep watch over the boy.

Or maybe you could just dig a hole right here and bury me.

"What?" His bitterness startled the word out of me. I did choke on the cider I was drinking.

Little brother, do not treat me as if I am already dead, or dying. If you see me that way, then I would rather truly be dead. You steal the now of my life away, when you constantly fear that tomorrow will bring my death. Your fears clutch cold at me and snatch all my pleasure in the day's warmth from me.

As he had not in a long time, the wolf dropped all the barriers between us. I suddenly perceived what I had been hiding from myself. The recent reticence between us was not entirely Nighteyes' doing. Half of it was mine, my retreat from him for fear that his death would be unbearably painful for me. I was the one who had set him at a distance; I was the one who had been hoarding my thoughts from him. Yet enough of my feelings had reached past that wall that he was wounded by them. I had been on the verge of abandoning him. My slow pulling away from him had been my resignation to his mortality. Truly, since the day I had pulled him back from death, I had not seen him as fully alive.

I sat for a time feeling shabby and small. I did not need to tell him I felt ashamed. The Wit forms a bond that makes many explanations unnecessary. I spoke my apology aloud. "Hap is really old enough to take care of himself. From now on, we belong together, come what may."

I felt his concurrence. *So. What is it we hunt?*

A boy and a cat. Prince Dutiful.

Ah. The boy and the cat from your dream. Well, at least we shall know them when we find them. It was a bit disconcerting that he made that leap of connection so effortlessly, and that he acknowledged so easily what I had balked at. We had shared thoughts with those two, and more than once. I pushed that uneasiness aside.

But how will you cross the river? And how will you keep up with the horses?

Don't let it trouble you, little brother. And don't betray me by gawking.

I sensed that it amused him to leave me wondering, and so left it at that with no nagging. I finished my meal and leaned my back against the boulder that had been my table. It had soaked up the warmth of the day. I had had little sleep of late and I felt my eyelids growing heavy.

Go ahead and nap. I'll keep watch on the horses for you.

Thank you. It was such a relief to close my eyes and welcome sleep without wariness. My wolf watched over me. The deep connection between us flowed unimpeded again. It brought me more peace than a full belly and sunshine.

✍   ✍   ✍

They come.

I opened my eyes. The horses still grazed peaceably but their shadows had lengthened on the meadow grass. Lord Golden and Laurel stood at the edge of the field. I lifted a hand in recognition of them, then came reluctantly to my feet. My posture had kinked my back, and yet I would gladly have gone back to sleep. Later, I promised myself. I could see the freight wagons approaching the ferry ramp.

Both Whitecap and Malta came to my chirrup. Only Myblack went out to the end of the picket line and had to be drawn in. Once I had her reins, she surrendered and came with me as if she had never contemplated anything else. I led them to meet the oncoming wagons. When I noticed a set of gray wolf legs beneath one of the wagons, I looked aside.

The ferry was a large, flat vessel of splintery timbers, secured by a heavy line to each shore. Teams of horses drew it back and forth, but there were crewmen with push-poles manning it, as well. They loaded Lady Bresinga's wagons first, then passengers and their mounts. I was the last aboard. Myblack balked at boarding the ferry. In the end, I think she came aboard for the sake of the other horses' company rather than any of my coaxing and praise. The ferry cast off from its dock and began its ponderous crossing of the Buck River. The river lapped and gurgled at the edge of the laden barge.

It was full dark before we reached the north shore of the Buck. We were first off the ferry, but then waited for the wagons to unload. Lord Golden decreed that, rather than wait out the night at the inn, we would follow the wagons to Lady Bresinga's manor at Galeton. The wagoneers knew the way by heart. They kindled lanterns and hung them from the sideboards, and so we followed them well enough.

The round moon shone down on us. We followed well back, and yet the dust of the wagons still hung in the air and stuck to my skin. I was far more tired than I had expected to be. The ache in my back was sharpest around the old arrow scar. I longed suddenly to have a quiet talk with the Fool, to somehow connect again to the healthy young man I had once been. But, I reminded myself, neither Fitz nor the Fool were here. Only Lord Golden and his man Badgerlock. The sooner I fixed that in my mind, the better for both of us. Laurel and Lord Golden carried on a quiet conversation. His attention flattered her, and she did not attempt to disguise the pleasure she took in it. They did not exclude me and yet I would not have felt comfortable sharing it.

We came at length to Galeton. We had crested several rocky hills and crossed the oak valleys between, and then as we reached the top of yet another rolling hill, the winking lights of a small town shone out below us. Galeton fronted onto a small tributary of the Buck called Antler River. It was too small a body of water to be navigable by large boats. Most of the goods that came to Galeton made the last stretch of their journey by wagon. The Antler furnished water for the cattle and the fields, and fish for the folk that lived alongside it. The Bresinga manor was on a small rise that overlooked the little town. In the dark it was impossible to see the extent of the great house, but the spacing of the candlelit windows convinced me it was substantial. The wagons entered through the gate of a long stone wall and we followed unchallenged. When the drivers pulled up in the wagonyard beside the manor, men with torches came out to meet them. I noted the absence of barking dogs, and thought it odd. Lord Golden led Laurel and me on to the main entrance of the manor itself. Before we had even alighted, the door opened for us, and servants poured out to greet us.

We were expected. A messenger had preceded us on the morning ferry. Lady Bresinga herself appeared to greet us and welcome us to her home. Servants led our horses away, and bore our baggage for us as I followed Lord Golden and the Queen's Huntswoman into the spacious entry hall of Bresinga Manor. Of oak and river stone was this imposing house built. Thick timbers and massive stonework commanded the eye, dwarfing the folk who filled the chamber.

Lord Golden was the center of their attention. Lady Bresinga had taken his arm in welcome. Short and plump, the woman looked up at him approvingly as she chatted. Her smile crinkled the corners of her eyes and stretched her upper lip tightly above her teeth. The lanky boy who stood at her side was likely Civil Bresinga. He was taller than Hap, yet about his age, and wore his dark hair brushed straight back above his forehead, revealing a pronounced widow's peak. He gave me an odd glance in passing, then directed his attention back to his mother and Lord Golden. An odd little shiver of awareness danced across my skin. The Wit. Someone here was Old Blood, and concealing it with consummate skill. I breathed a thought of warning to the wolf. *Be small.* His acknowledgment was more subtle than the scent of night flowers when day comes, yet I saw Lady Bresinga turn her head slightly, as if to catch a distant sound. Too soon to be certain, yet I felt that Chade's and my suspicions were well founded.

The Huntswoman of the Queen had her own circle of admirers courting her favor. The Bresinga Huntsman was at Laurel's elbow already, telling her that as soon as she arose in the morning, he'd be pleased to show her the best uplands for game birds. His assistants stood alertly at his elbow. Later, he would escort her into a late dinner with Lady Bresinga and Lord Golden. When hunting was planned, those two could expect to share table and wine with their betters.

In the midst of the hubbub of welcoming, little attention was paid to me. I stood, as any good servant did, awaiting my next command. A servingwoman hastened up to me. "I'll show you the chambers we've prepared for Lord Golden so that you may arrange them to his taste. Will he want a bath this evening?"

"Undoubtedly," I replied to the young woman as I followed her. "And a light repast in his rooms. Sometimes he is taken with an appetite late at night." This was a fabrication on my part to be sure that I did not have to go hungry. It was expected that I would see to my master's comfort first, and then my own.

Lord Golden's unexpected visit had commanded a fine chamber as large as my entire cottage. An immense bed dominated the room. It was mounded with feather beds and fat pillows. Enormous bouquets of cut roses scented the chamber, and a veritable forest of beeswax tapers added both light and their delicate scent. By daylight, the room would look over the river and across the valley, but tonight the windows were shuttered. I opened one "for air," and then assured the maid that I could unpack my master's garments if she would see to bathwater. A small antechamber opened off Lord Golden's for my own use. It was small, but better furnished than many servants' chambers that I'd seen.

It took me longer to unpack Lord Golden's clothing than I had expected. I was amazed at how much he had managed to fit into his packs. Not only clothing and boots, but jewelry, perfumes, scarves, combs, and brushes emerged from the compact bags. I put it all in place as best I could imagine. I tried to recall Charim, Prince Verity's serving-man and valet. Standing in his shoes suddenly put all he had done in a different perspective. That good man had always been present, and always engaged in some task for Verity's comfort or convenience. Unobtrusive, yet ever ready for his master's command. I tried to think what he would do in my place.

I kindled a small fire in the hearth so that my master would be comfortable while he was drying after his bath. I turned down Lord Golden's bed and set his nightshirt out atop the linen. Then, smirking, I retreated to my own chamber, wondering what the Fool would have made of all this.

I had expected my own unpacking to be simple and it was until I got to the package of clothing from the tailor. I untied the string, and the garments seemed to burst from their confines like a blossom unfurling. The Fool had reneged on Lord Golden's promise to keep me poorly dressed. The clothing the tailor had sewn was the best quality I had ever possessed in my life. There was a set of servant's blues, better tailored than what I now wore, and of a finer weave. Two snowy shirts of linen were more elegant than what most servants wore. There was a doublet of rich blue, with dark hose with a gray stripe in it, and another in deep green. I held the green doublet up against me. The doublet's skirt came almost to my knees, longer than I was accustomed to, and yellow embroidery ran riot over it. Yellow leggings. I shook my head. There was a wide leather belt to fasten about it. Lord Golden's golden cock pheasant was embroidered on the breast of the jerkin. I rolled my eyes at my reflection. Truly, the Fool had expressed himself in these clothes for me. Dutifully I put them away. No doubt he would soon find an excuse to make me wear them.

I had scarcely finished my unpacking before I heard a step in the hallway. A knock at the door announced that Lord Golden's tub had arrived. Two servingboys carried it in, followed by three others bearing buckets of both hot and cold water. It was expected that I would mix these to achieve Lord Golden's preference in his bath. Then another lad arrived carrying a tray of scented oils that he might choose from, and yet another with a towering stack of towels. Two men arrived carrying the painted screens that would protect him from drafts while he was enjoying his ablutions. I have not always been swift at appraising social situations, yet dim as I was, I was awakening to Lord Golden's social stature. A welcome this effusive was more likely to be accorded to royalty rather than to a landless noble of dubious origin. Obviously, his popularity at court far exceeded my initial regard of it. It chagrined me that I had not previously perceived it. Then, with unerring certainty, I knew the reason for it.

I knew who he was. I knew his past, or far more of it than any of his admirers did. To me, he was not the exotic and fabulously wealthy nobleman of some distant Jamaillian family. To me, he was the Fool in the midst of one of his elaborate pranks, and I was still expecting that at any moment he would cease his juggling and let all his flying illusions come clattering to the ground. But there was no moment of revelation awaiting. Lord Golden was real, as real as the Fool had been to me. I stood stock-still a moment, reeling in that unveiling thought. Lord Golden was as real as the Fool. And hence, the Fool had been as real as Lord Golden.

So who was this man that I had known for most of my life?

A hint of presence, more a scent than a thought, carried me to the window. I looked, not out over the river, but down into the bushes outside the window. Nighteyes' mind brushed softly against mine, cautioning me to control our Wit-bond. A pair of deep eyes looked up and met mine. *Cat*, his delicate touch confirmed before I had even thought to ask it. *Cat-piss stink on the corners of the stable, and on the underside of the bushes behind it. Cat scat buried in the rose garden. Cats everywhere.*

More than one? Dutiful's cat was a gift from this family. Perhaps they favor them as coursing animals.

That is a certainty. The stink of them is pervasive. It makes me uneasy. I have little desire to meet one in the flesh. All I have known of them I have learned since this afternoon, when Hap proposed that I should be friendly with one. I did no more than put my nose into the door when that orange fury flew at me, all claws and spitting.

I know no more of them than you do. Burrich never kept cats about the stable.

He was wiser than either of us knew.

A door closed softly behind me. I whirled to the sound, but it was only Lord Golden come into the room. Whether Fool or Golden, he was still one of the few in the world who could take me by surprise. I recalled my role, straightened, and bowed to him. "Master, I have seen to arranging your things. Your bath awaits."

"Well done, Badgerlock. And the night air is refreshing. Is the view pleasant?"

"Excellent, sir. The room commands a wide view of the river valley. And the night is fine, with a near full moon that would set most wolves howling."

"Is it?" He crossed swiftly to the window and looked down on Nighteyes. The smile that lit his face was genuine. He drew a deep breath of satisfaction, as if savoring the air. "A good night, indeed. Doubtless many night creatures are abroad hunting tonight. May our hunting tomorrow go as well as theirs does by moonlight. Unfortunate, indeed, that I must put off my hunting until tomorrow. Tonight, I am invited to sup late with Lady Bresinga and her son Civil. But they have excused me for a bit that I might refresh myself. You will, of course, attend me at the dinner."

"Of course, master," I concurred with a sinking heart. In reality I had hoped to slip out of the open window and do a bit of reconnaissance with Nighteyes.

It's nothing that I cannot manage better on my own. I shall snuff and range outside. See that you do the same inside. The sooner we are finished with the errand, the sooner we are for home again.

That's true, I agreed, but I wondered at the slight sinking of my heart at the thought. Didn't I want to leave Buckkeep and resume my own life as soon as possible? Or was I coming to relish my role as a servingman to a wealthy fop? I asked myself sarcastically.

I took Lord Golden's coat for him, and then eased him from his boots. As I had so often seen Charim do without paying any heed, I brushed and hung the jacket, and gave the boots a hasty dusting before setting them aside. When Lord Golden offered me his wrists, I undid the fastenings of the lacy cuffs of his shirt and set the glittering gauds aside. He leaned back in his chair. "I shall wear my blue doublet tonight. And the linen shirt with the fine blue stripe in it. Dark blue hose, I think, and the shoes with the trimming of silver chain. Lay it all out for me. Then pour the buckets, Badgerlock, and be generous with the rose oil. Then set the screens and leave me to my thoughts for a bit. Oh, and please, take some of this water into your chambers and avail yourself of it. When we dine, I shall want to smell the food, not you standing behind me. Oh. And wear the dark blue tonight. I think it will set off my own garb the better. One other thing. Put this on as well, but I counsel you to keep it covered unless you truly need it."

From his pocket he drew forth Jinna's charm. It coiled into my extended hand.

All this he announced with an air of genial good cheer. Lord Golden was a man well pleased with himself, looking forward to an evening of pleasant talk and hearty viands. I did as I was bade, and then gratefully retreated to my own room with washwater and a bit of apple-scented oil. Shortly I heard Lord Golden splashing luxuriously while humming a tune I did not know. My own washing-up was a bit more restrained but just as welcome to me. I hurried, knowing that my services would soon be required again.

I struggled with my doublet, finding that it had been

tailored far more close-fitting than I was accustomed to. There was scarcely room to conceal Chade's roll of tools let alone the small knife that I decided I would carry. I could scarcely wear a sword into the dining room on a social occasion, but I found I did not wish to go completely unarmed. The wolf's secretive approach to the Wit tonight had infected me with wariness. I cinched the belt that secured the doublet and then pulled my hair back into its warrior tail. Some of the apple-scented oil persuaded my hair to lie flatter. I realized I had not heard splashing for some moments, and hastened back into Lord Golden's chamber.

"Lord Golden, do you require my assistance?"

"Scarcely." A shadow of the Fool was in Golden's drawled sarcasm. He emerged from behind the screen, fully dressed, and adjusting the fall of lace at his cuffs. A small smile of pleasure at surprising me was playing about his mouth as he lifted his eyes to me. Abruptly, the smile faded. For a time he simply stared at me, mouth slightly ajar. Then his eyes lit. As he advanced to me, satisfaction shone in his face. "It's perfect," he breathed. "Exactly as I had hoped. Oh, Fitz, I always imagined that, had I the chance, I could show you off as befitted you. And look at you."

His use of my name was as astonishing as the way he gripped my shoulders and propelled me toward the immense mirror. For a moment I looked only at the reflection of his face over my shoulder, alight with pride and satisfaction. Then I shifted my gaze and stared at a man I scarcely recognized.

His directions to the tailor must have been very complete. The doublet encased my shoulders and chest. The white of the shirt showed at the collar and the sleeves. The blue of the doublet was Buck blue, my family color, and even if I now wore it as a servant, the cut of the doublet was not that of servant but of soldier. The tailoring made my shoulders look broad and my belly flat. The white of the shirt contrasted with my dark skin and eyes and hair. I gazed at my own face in consternation. The sharpness of my scars had faded with my youth. There were lines on my brow and starting at the corners of my eyes, and somehow these lessened the severity of the scar's passage down my face. I had long ago accepted the modification of my broken nose. The streak of white in my hair was more noticeable with my hair drawn back in a warrior's tail. The man who looked back at me from the mirror put me somewhat in mind of Verity, but even more of the portrait of King-in-Waiting Chivalry that still hung in the hall at Buckkeep.

"I look like my father," I said quietly. The prospect of that both pleased and alarmed me.

"Only to someone seeking that resemblance," the Fool replied. "Only someone knowing enough to peer past your scars would see the Farseer in you. Mostly, my friend, you look like yourself, only more so. You look like the FitzChivalry that was always there, but kept hidden by Chade's wisdom and subterfuge. Did you never wonder at how your clothes were cut, simply and almost rough, to make you look more stablehand and soldier than prince's bastard? Mistress Hasty the seamstress always thought the orders came from Shrewd. Even when she was allowed to indulge in her fripperies and fashion, it was only the ones that drew attention to themselves and her sewing skills and away from you. But this, Fitz, this is how I have always seen you. And how you have never seen yourself."

I looked back at the glass. I think I speak truth when I say that I have never been a vain man. It took a moment for me to accept that, while I had aged, the change was one of maturity rather than of degeneration. "I don't look that bad," I conceded.

The Fool's smile went broader. "Ah, my friend, I have been places where women would have fought one another with knives over you." He lifted a slender hand and rubbed his chin thoughtfully. "And now, I fear I must wonder if my fancy has succeeded too well. You will not pass without remark. But perhaps that is for the best. Flirt a bit with the kitchen maids, and who knows what they will tell you?"

I rolled my eyes at his mockery. His gaze met mine in the mirror. "Nothing finer than we two has dined in these halls before," he decided emphatically. He squeezed my shoulder, and then stood straight, abruptly Lord Golden again.

"Badgerlock. The door. We are expected."

I jumped to obey my master. Somehow, those few moments with the Fool had restored my tolerance for this new charade of ours. I even found my interest warming to it. If Prince Dutiful were here at Galeton, as I suspected he was, we would find him out before the night was through. Lord Golden preceded me through the door and I followed two steps behind him and to his left.

chapter XVI

CLAWS

The depredations of the Red Ship War took their heaviest tolls on the Coastal Duchies. Old fortunes were decimated, family lines failed, and once-proud holdings were reduced to ashy ruins and weedy courtyards. Yet in the wake of the war, just as seedlings sprout in the spring after a lightning fire, so too did many of the minor nobility find their fortunes swelling. Many of the humbler holdings had escaped the raiders' attention. Flocks and crops survived, and what would once have seemed secondary properties, came to be seen as places of plenty. The lesser lords and ladies of these lands suddenly found themselves seen as desirable matches for the heirs of older but suddenly less wealthy family lines. Thus the widowed lord of the Bresinga holdings near Galeton took a much younger and wealthier bride from amongst the Earwood family of Lesser Tor in Buck. The Earwood family was an old and noble line that had dwindled in both standing and wealth. Yet in the years of the Red Ship War, their sheltered valley prospered and shared harvest with the devastated folk of the Bresinga holdings that bordered them. This kindness bore fruit for the Earwood family when Jaglea Earwood became Lady Bresinga. She bore her elderly lord an heir, Civil Bresinga, shortly before his death from a fever.

    🐾 SCRIBE DUVLEN, "A HISTORY OF THE EARWOOD LINE"

Lord Golden moved with the grace and certainty that is supposedly bone-bred in the nobility. Unerringly he led me to an elegant antechamber where his hostess and her son awaited him. Laurel was there, attired in a simple gown of soft cream trimmed with lace. She was deep in conversation with the Bresinga Huntsman. I thought that the gown did not suit her as well as her simple tunic and riding breeches had, for her tanned arms and face seemed to make the dainty lace at the collar and belled sleeves incongruous on her. Lady Bresinga was elaborately flounced and draped for dinner, the abundance of her garments swelling the proportions of her bust and hips. There were three other guests: a married couple and their daughter of about seventeen, obviously local gentry. All had been waiting for Lord Golden.

Their reaction when we entered was everything the Fool had claimed it would be. Lady Bresinga turned to greet her guest, smiling. Her eyes swept over him, widening with pleasure. "Our honored guest is here," she announced. Lord Golden turned his head slightly to one side, tucking his chin in with an innocent air as if he were unaware of his own beauty. Laurel stared at him in frank admiration as Lady Bresinga introduced Lord Golden to Lord and Lady Grayling of Cotterhills and their daughter Sydel. Their names were unfamiliar but I seemed to recall Cotterhills as a tiny holding in the foothills of Farrow. Sydel's cheeks grew pink and she appeared almost flustered at being included in Lord Golden's bow, and after that, the young gentlewoman's gaze appeared fixed on him. Her mother's eyes had wandered over to me and were frankly appraising me in a way that should have made her blush. I glanced away only to find Laurel looking at me with a bemused smile, as if she had forgotten she knew me. I could almost feel Lord Golden's radiant satisfaction in how he had turned their heads.

He offered his arm to Lady Bresinga, and her son Civil escorted Sydel. Lord and Lady Grayling followed and then came the Huntmasters. I followed my betters into the dining room and took up my post behind Lord Golden's chair. My position proclaimed me bodyguard as well as servant. Lady Bresinga glanced at me questioningly but I did not meet her eyes. If she thought that Lord Golden had breached her hospitality by having me accompany him, she did not comment on it. Young Civil simply stared for a moment or two, and then shrugged off my presence with a quiet aside to his companion. And after that, I became invisible.

I think it was the most curious vantage point I'd ever held in my spying career. It was not comfortable. I was hungry, and Lady Bresinga's board was loaded with dishes both savory and sweet. The servants who brought and cleared away the repast passed right before me. I was also weary and aching from the long day's ride, yet I forced myself to stand as still as possible, with no restless shifting, and to keep my eyes and my ears open.

All the talk at the table had to do with game and hunting. Lord Grayling and his lady and daughter were avid hunters, and evidently had been invited for this reason. Almost immediately, another common thread emerged. They hunted, not with hounds, but with cats. Lord Golden professed himself a complete novice at this sort of sport and begged them to enlighten him. They were only too pleased to do so, and the conversation soon bogged down into intricate arguments as to which breed of hunting cat did better on birds, with various tales exchanged to illustrate the different breeds' prowess. The Bresingas were vocal in support of a short-tailed breed called ealynx, while Lord Grayling vociferously offered heavy wagers that his gruepards would take the day regardless of whether they sought birds or hares.

Lord Golden was a most flattering listener, asking avid questions and expressing amazement and fascination at the replies. The cats, he learned for both of us, were not coursing beasts, at least not in the same manner as hounds. Each hunter took a single feline, and it rode to the hunt on a special cushion, secured just behind its master's saddle. The larger gruepards could be loosed against game up to the size of young deer. They relied on a burst of speed to catch their prey, and then suffocated it to death with a throat hold.

The smaller ealynex was more often set loose in tall grassy meadows or underbrush, where it stalked its prey until it could leap upon it. It preferred to stun with a blow from a swift paw, or to break the neck or back with a single bite. It was sport, we learned, to loose such beasts upon a flock of tame pigeons or doves, to see how many they could bat to the ground before the whole flock took flight. Often these smaller, bobtailed cats were matched against one another in bird-batting competitions, with sizable wagers riding on the favorites. The Bresingas boasted no less than twenty-two cats of both types in their hunting stables. The Graylings had only the gruepards, and but six of them in their clowder, but Lady Bresinga assured Lord Golden that her friend was fortunate in possessing some of the best breeding lines she had ever seen.

"Then they are bred, these hunting cats? I was told that they had to be captured, that they would not breed if tamed." Lord Golden fastened his attention on the Bresingas' Huntmaster.

"Oh, the gruepards will breed, but only if they are allowed to carry out their mating battles and harsh courtship without interference. The enclosure Lord Grayling has devoted to this purpose is quite large, and no human must ever enter it. We are quite fortunate that his efforts in that regard have been successful. Prior to this, as you perhaps know, all gruepards were brought in from either Chalced or the Sandsedge regions of Farrow, all at great expense, of course. They were quite rare in this area when I was a boy, but the moment I saw one, I knew that was the hunting beast for me. And I hope I don't sound a braggart in saying that, since the gruepards were so expensive, I was one of the first who thought of trying to tame our native ealynex to the same task. Hunting with the ealynex was quite unknown in Buck until my uncle and I first caught two of them. The ealynex are the cats that must be taken as adults, usually in pit-traps, and schooled to hunt as companions."

This all spouted from the Bresinga Huntsman, a tall fellow who hunched forward earnestly as he spoke. Avoin was his name. The topic was plainly his passion.

Lord Golden flattered him with his unwavering attention. "Fascinating. I must hear how such deadly little creatures are brought to heel. Nor was I aware there were so many names for hunting cats. I had assumed there was but one breed. So. Let me see. I was told that Prince Dutiful's hunting animal had to be taken from the den as a kitten. It must be a gruepard, then?"

Avoin exchanged a glance with his mistress, almost as if he asked permission before he spoke. "Ah, well. The Prince's cat is neither ealynex nor gruepard, Lord Golden. It is a rarer creature than either of those. Most know it as the mistcat. It ranges much higher into the mountains than our cats do, and is known for hunting amidst the branches of the trees as well as on the ground." Avoin had dropped into the lecturing tone of the expert. Once he had begun to share his expertise, he would continue until his listeners' eyes glazed over. "For its size, it takes game substantially larger than itself, dropping down on both deer and wild goats to either ride them to exhaustion, or to break the neck with a bite. On the ground, it is neither as swift as the gruepard nor as stealthy as the ealynex, but combines the techniques of both with good success against small game. But of the mistcat, you heard true. It must be taken from its home den before its eyes are opened if it is to be tamed at all. Even then, it may have an uneven temperament, but those who are taken and trained correctly become the truest companions that any hunter could desire. They will only hunt for one master, however. Of mistcats it is said, 'from the den to the heart, never to part.' Meaning, of course, that only he who is sly enough to find the mistcat's den will ever possess one. It is quite a feat, to have a mistcat. When you see a hunter with a mistcat, you know you're seeing a master of cat-hunting."

Avoin's voice suddenly faltered. If some sign had passed

between him and his mistress, I had not seen it. Was the Huntsman involved, then, in the circumstances that had brought such a cat to the Prince?

Lord Golden, however, blithely ignored the implications of what he had heard. "A sumptuous gift for our Prince, indeed," he enthused. "But it quite dashes my hopes of having a mistcat as my hunting creature tomorrow. At least, shall I have the prospect of seeing one set loose?"

"I fear not, Lord Golden," Lady Bresinga replied graciously. "We have none in our hunting pack. They are quite rare. To see a mistcat hunt, you will have to ask the Prince himself to take you along on one of his outings. I am sure he would be delighted to do so."

Lord Golden shook his head merrily, tucking his chin in as if taken aback. "Oh, no, dear lady, for I have heard that our illustrious Prince hunts afoot with his cat, at night, regardless of the weather. Much too physical an endeavor for me, I fear. Not at all to my taste, not at all!" Chuckles tumbled from him like spinning pins in a juggler's hands. All around the table, the others joined in his mirth.

Climb.

I felt the prickle of tiny claws and glanced down. From somewhere, a small striped kitten had materialized. She stood on her hind legs, her front feet securely attached to my leggings by her embedded claws. Her yellow-green eyes looked up earnestly at mine. *Coming up!*

I refused the touch of her mind without, I hoped, seeming to. At the table, Lord Golden had led the conversation to what types of cats they might use tomorrow, and whether or not they would damage the plumage on the game. Feathers, he reminded them all, were what he sought, though he did enjoy game bird pie.

I shifted my leg, hoping to dislodge the young bramblefoot. It did not work. *Climbing!* she insisted, and hopped up another notch. Now she hung from me from all four paws, her claws having penetrated my leggings to hook in my flesh. I reacted, I hoped, as any other servant might. I winced and then unobtrusively bent to pry the creature free, one thorny foot at a time. My action might have escaped attention if she had not mewled piteously at being thus thwarted. I had hoped to set her gently back on the floor, but Lord Golden's amused voice with, "Well, Badgerlock, and what have you caught?" directed all eyes to me.

"Just a kitten, sir. She seemed determined to climb my leg." She was like a puff of dandelion fuzz in my hand. The deceptive depth of her fluffy coat was belied by the tiny rib cage in my hand. She opened her little red mouth and miaowed for her mother.

"Oh, there you are!" Lord Grayling's daughter exclaimed, leaping up from the table. Heedless of any decorum, Sydel rushed to take the squirming kitten from my hand. With both hands she cradled the kitten under her chin. "Oh, thank you for finding her." She walked back to her place at the table, speaking as she went. "I could not bear to leave her alone at home, and yet she must have slipped out of my room just after breakfast, for I haven't seen her all day."

"And is this, then, the kit of a hunting cat?" Lord Golden asked as the daughter seated herself.

Sydel leapt at the chance to address Lord Golden. "Oh, no, Lord Golden, this is my own sweet pet, my little pillow-cat, Tibbits. She is such a mischief, aren't you, lovey? And yet I cannot bear to be parted from her. How you have worried me this afternoon!" She kissed the kitten on the top of her head and then settled the creature in her lap. No one at the table seemed to regard her behavior as unusual. As the meal and conversation resumed, I saw the little tabby head pop up at the edge of the table. *Fish!* the kit thought delightedly. A few moments later, Civil offered her a sliver of fish. I decided it meant little; it could be coincidence, or even the unconscious reaction that those without the Wit sometimes make to the wishes of animals they know well. The kit swiped a paw to claim possession of the morsel, and then took it into her owner's lap to devour it.

Servants entered the hall to clear dishes and platters away, while a second rank of servants followed with sweet dishes and berry wines. Lord Golden had seized control of all conversation. The hunting tales he told were either fabulous concoctions or indicated that his life during the last ten years or so had been far different from what I had imagined. When he spoke of spearing sea mammals from a skin boat drawn by harnessed dolphins, even Sydel looked slightly incredulous. But as is ever the case, if a story is well told, the listeners will stay with it to the end, and so they did this time. Lord Golden finished his recital with a flourish and a wicked gleam in his eye that suggested that if he were embellishing his adventure, he would never admit it.

Lady Bresinga called for brandy to be brought, and the table was cleared again. The brandy appeared with yet another assortment of small items to tempt already-satiated guests. Eyes went from sparkling with wine and merriment to the deep gleam of contentment that good brandy brings forth after a fine meal. My legs and lower back ached abominably. I was hungry, as well, and tired enough that if I had been free to lie down on the flagged floor, I would instantly have been asleep. I scraped my nails against the inside of my palms, pricking myself back to alertness. This was the hour when tongues were loosest and talk most expansive. Despite the way Lord Golden leaned back in his chair, I doubted that he was as intoxicated as he seemed. The subject had rounded back to cats and hunting again. I felt I had learned as much as I needed to know about the topic.

The kitten had managed, after six thwarted efforts, to gain the top of the table. She had curled up and briefly napped, but now was wending her way amongst the bottles and glasses, threatening to topple them as she rubbed against each. *Mine. And mine. This is mine too. And mine.* With the total confidence of the very young, she claimed every item on the table as her own. When Civil reached for the brandy carafe to refill his glass and that of his companion, the kitten arched her little back and bounced toward him on her toes, intent on making good on her claims. *Mine!*

"No. Mine," he told her affably, and fended her off with the back of his wrist. Sydel laughed at the exchange. A slow excitement uncoiled within me but I kept my dulled stare apparently fixed on my master's shoulder. Witted. Both of them. I was sure of it now. And as it tended to be inherited in families . . .

"So. Who did catch the mistcat for the Prince's gift?" Lord Golden suddenly asked. The question almost followed from the conversation, yet it was pointed enough to turn all heads at the table. Lord Golden gave a small hiccup that bordered on being a discreet belch. It was enough of a distraction to combine with his slightly goggled stare to take the edge from his query. "I'll wager it was you, Huntsman." His graceful hand made his words a compliment to Avoin.

"No, not I." Avoin shook his head but oddly volunteered no more information.

Lord Golden leaned back, tapping his forefinger on his lips as if it were a guessing game. He rolled his gaze about the table, then chortled sagely and pointed at Civil. "Then it was you, young man. For I heard it was you who carried the cat up to Prince Dutiful to present him."

The boy's eyes flickered once to his mother's before he gravely shook his head. "Not I, Lord Golden," he demurred. And again, that unusual silence of information withheld followed his words. A united front, I decided. The question would not be answered.

Lord Golden lolled his head back against his chair, and took a long noisy breath and sighed it out. "Damned fine gift," he observed liberally. "Love to have one myself, from all I've heard. But hearing's no substitute for seeing. B'lieve I will ask Prince Dutiful to allow me to 'company him some night." He sighed again and let his head wag to one side. "If he ever comes back from his meditation retreat. Not natural, if you ask me, for a boy that age to spend so much time

alone. Not natural a'tall." Lord Golden's enunciation was
giving way rapidly.

Lady Bresinga's diction was quite clear as she asked,
"So our Prince has retired again from the public eye, to follow his own thoughts for a time?"

"Yes, indeed," Lord Golden affirmed. "And been a long
time gone this time. 'Course, he has a good deal to think
about these days. Betrothal coming up and all, Outislander
delegation coming. A lot for a young man to handle. I
mean, how would you take to it, young sir?" He wagged a
finger in Civil's general direction. "How'd you like to be betrothed to a woman you've never met . . . well, she isn't
even a woman yet, if rumor runs true. More like a girl on
the cusp. She's what, eleven? So young. Terribly young,
don't you think? And I don't understand the advantages of
the match. That I do not."

His words were indiscreet, verging on direct criticism
of the Queen's decision. Looks were exchanged around the
table. Plainly Lord Golden had taken more brandy than he
handled well, and yet he was pouring more. His words hung
unchallenged in the air. Perhaps Avoin thought he was
turning conversation into a safer channel when he asked,
"The Prince often retreats to meditate, then?"

"It's the Mountain way," Lord Golden confirmed. "Or
so I am told. Wha' do I know? Only that it's not the Jamaillian way. The young nobles of my fair home are more
worldly-minded. And that is encouraged, mind you, for
where better will a young nobleman learn the manners and
ways of the world than t'be out in the midst of it? Your
Prince Dutiful might do better t'mingle more with his
court. Yes, and to look closer to home for a suitable con-
sort." A Jamaillian accent had begun to flavor Lord
Golden's softening words, as if intoxication took him back
to the speech habits of his erstwhile home. He sipped from
his glass and then set it back upon the table so awkwardly
that a tiny amber wave leapt over the edge. He rubbed his

mouth and chin as if to massage away the brandy's numbing effect. I suspected that he had done little more than hold the brimming glass against his lip.

No one had replied to his comments, but Lord Golden appeared not to notice.

"And this time has marked his longest absence of all!" he enlarged. "That's all we hear at the Court these days. 'Where is Prince Dutiful? What, still in seclusion? When will he return? What, no one can say?' Very dampening t'spirits at the Court for our young ruler t'be absent so long. Wager that his cat hates it, too. What d'you think, Avoin? Does a hunting cat pine when his master's away for long?"

Avoin appeared to consider it. "One devoted to his cat would not leave it long alone. A cat's loyalty is not a thing to be taken for granted, but courted day by day."

Avoin drew breath to continue but Lady Bresinga smoothly interrupted. "Well, our cats hunt best while dawn is still on the land. So if we are to show Lord Golden our beauties at their prime, we had all best retire so we may arise early." At a small sign from her, a servant moved forward to draw back her chair. Everyone else came to his or her feet, though Lord Golden did so with a small lurch. I thought I heard a small titter of amusement from the Graylings' daughter, but Sydel was none too steady herself. Knowing my role, I moved forward to offer Lord Golden a firm arm. He loftily disdained it, waving me aside and scowling at my impertinence. I stood stolidly by as the nobility offered good-nights to one another, and then followed Lord Golden to his chambers.

I opened the door for him and saw him through it. Following him, I perceived that the household servants had been at work in our chambers. The bath things were tidied away, fresh candles filled the holders, and the window was shut. A tray of cold meats, fruit, and pastries rested on the table. My first act after closing the door was to open the window. It simply felt wrong to have a solid barrier between Nighteyes and me. I glanced out, but saw no sign of the wolf. Doubtless he was doing his own prowl of the premises, and I would not risk questing out toward him. I made a swift circuit of our rooms, checking for any signs of a search, and then looking under beds and within wardrobes for possible spies. The Bresinga household and its guests had been wary tonight. Either they knew why we had come, or they were expecting someone like us to come seeking the Prince. But I found no spies in the bedclothes, nor any sign that my carelessly hung garments had been disturbed. I never left a room in perfect order. It is easy to return a searched room to perfect order, more difficult to recall exactly how both sleeves of the garment flung across the chair touched the floor.

I completed a similar perusal of Lord Golden's chamber while he waited in silence. When I was finished, I turned back to my master. He dropped heavily into a chair and puffed out an immense sigh. His eyes drooped as his chin dropped to his chest. All of his features sagged with drink. I made a small sound of dismay. How could he have been so careless as to get drunk? As I watched him, he kicked out his feet one after the other so that his heels clonked against the floor. Obediently I went to draw his boots off and set them to one side. "Can you stand?" I asked him.

"Whsay?"

I glanced up from where I crouched by his feet. "I said, can you stand?"

He opened his eyes a slit, and then a slow smile stretched his mouth. "I am so good," he congratulated himself in a whisper. "And you are such a satisfactory audience, Fitz. Do you know how draining it can be, to strike poses when no one knows they are poses, to assume a whole different character when there is no one to appreciate how well I do it?" A glint of the old Fool's mischief shone in his golden eyes. Then it faded and his mouth became serious. He spoke very softly. "Of course I can stand. And dance and leap, if need be. But tonight is not for that. Tonight, you must go to the kitchens and complain of how hungry you are. Fetching as you look, I don't doubt you will be fed. And see where you can lead the conversation. Go ahead, go now, I am perfectly capable of getting myself to bed. Do you wish the window left open?"

"I would prefer it so," I hedged.

And I. The confirming thought from Nighteyes was softer than a breath.

"Then it shall be so," Lord Golden decreed.

The kitchen was still full of servants, for the end of the meal is not the end of the serving of it. Indeed, few folk work harder or longer hours than those who feed a keep, for usually just as the tidying and washing is done from the evening meal it is nearly time to set the bread rising for the next. This was as true at Galeton as it was at Buckkeep Castle. I came to the door and ventured to lean in with an inquisitive and hopeful look on my face.

Almost immediately one of the kitchen women took pity on me. I recognized her as one of the women who had waited on the table. Lady Bresinga had addressed her as Lebven. "You must be ravenous. There they all sat, eating and drinking, and treated you as if you were made of wood. Well, come in. As much as they ate, there is still plenty and to spare."

In a short time, I was perched on a tall stool at a corner of the floury and scarred bread table. Lebven set out an array of dishes within arm's reach of me, and true to her telling, there was plenty and to spare. Slices of cold smoked venison still half filled a platter artfully ringed with little pickled apples. Sweetened apricots were fat golden cushions in little pastry squares so rich they crumbled away at one bite. Scores of tiny bird livers marinated with bits of garlic in an oily bath did not appeal to me, but beside those there were dark breasts of duck garnished with syrupy slices of sweet gingerroot. I wallowed in culinary indulgence. There was good brown bread and a slab of butter to grease it down as well. Lebven brought a mug of cold ale and a pitcher to refill it. When she had set it down to my nodded thanks, she stood at the table across from me, sprinkled flour generously, and turned out onto it a risen sponge of bread. She commenced to thump and turn it, adding handfuls of flour as she worked at the dough until it was satiny.

For a time I simply ate and watched and listened. It was the usual kitchen talk, gossip and minor rivalries between servants, one spat over a bucket of milk left out to sour, and talk of the work to prepare for the morrow. The grand folk of the house would be up early, but they would expect the food to be ready when they were, and as lavish as tonight's dinner. They'd want saddle-food to carry along as well, and this must charm the eye as much as fill the gut. I watched Lebven as she flattened the dough, spread it with butter, folded it, and then flattened it again, only to butter and fold it again. She became aware of me watching her and looked up with a smile. "It makes lots of layers in the rolls this way, all flaky and crisp. But it's a lot of work for something that they'll eat down in less than a minute."

Behind her, a servant placed a covered basket on the counter. He opened it, spread a linen napkin to line it, and then began to place food in it: fresh rolls, a small pot of butter, a dish with slices of meat in it, and some of the pickled apples. I watched him from the corner of my eye, while nodding and replying to Lebven's words. "It's odd. Most of them don't give half a thought to how much work goes into our making them comfortable."

There was more than one muttered assent in the kitchen. "Well, look at you," Lebven returned the sympathy. "Kept on guard all through dinner, like someone might do your master harm in a house where he's guesting. Ridiculous Jamaillian way of thinking. But for that, you could have had a meal and some time to yourself tonight."

"I would have welcomed that," I returned honestly. "I'd have liked a look around. I've never been in a place where they kept cats instead of dogs."

The other servant took the basket to the back door. A man waiting there took it from his hands. Something furry swung limp from his other hand. I only had a glimpse before the door was closed again. I longed to leap up and follow that food, but Lebven was still speaking.

"Well. That's only been in the last ten years or so, since the old master died. Before that, we had hounds for the most part, and only a cat or two for my lady's hunting. But the young master prefers the cats to the dogs, and so he's let the hounds die out. Not that I miss their barking and yammer, nor having them underfoot! The big cats are kept to their pens, save when they're hunting. And as for the small ones, why, they're darlings and no mistake. Not a river rat dares put his nose into this kitchen anymore." She cast a fond look at a particolored house cat on the hearth. Despite the mild evening, he was toasting himself by the dwindling cook fire. She finally gave off her folding, and commenced beating the layered dough until it began to blister. It made conversation difficult and my departure more graceful. I went to the door of the kitchen and opened it. The man with the food was out of sight.

Lebven called to me, "If you're seeking the backhouse, it's out the other door and around the side. Just before you get to the rabbit hutches."

I thanked her and obediently went out of the other door. A long look around showed me no other folk moving. I went around the side of the house, but another wing thwarted my view. The moonlight showed me rows of rabbit hutches between the house and the stable. So that had been what the man carried, a rabbit, its neck freshly wrung. The perfect late meal for a hunting cat. But there was no sign of the man and I dared not reach out toward Nighteyes, nor be gone from the kitchen too long. I growled to myself in frustration, certain that the packed meal had been for the Prince and his cat. I'd missed a chance. I returned to the warmth and light of the kitchen.

The kitchen had grown quieter. The washing-up was mostly done, and the chore boys and girls escaped to their beds. Only Lebven remained beating the dough, and a morose man who was tending a pot of simmering meat. I resumed my seat and poured the last of the ale into my mug. Doubtless the others would get what sleep they could before they had to rise and prepare the next meal. The mottled cat abruptly stretched, rose, and came to investigate me. I feigned ignoring him as he sniffed at my shoes and then my calf. The tom turned his head and opened his mouth wide as if expressing disgust, but I suspected he was only savoring my scent.

Smells like that dog outside. A disdainful curl of thought from him. Effortlessly, he floated up to land on the table beside me and thrust his nose toward the platter of venison. I fended him off with the back of my wrist. He took neither offense nor notice, but stepped over my arm to seize the slice he desired.

"Oh, Tups, such manners in front of our guest. Don't you mind him, Tom, he's as spoiled as they come." She picked him up with floury hands. He kept possession of his meat as she set him on the floor then hunkered down over it, turning his head sideways to shear off mouthfuls. He gave Lebven one reproachful look. *Shouldn't feed the dogs at the table, woman.* It was hard not to imagine malevolence in his yellow-eyed stare. Childishly, I stared right back, knowing well that most animals hate that. He muttered a threat in his throat, seized his meat, and whisked himself out of sight under the table.

I drank the last of my ale slowly. The cat knew. Did that mean the whole household knew of my connection to Nighteyes? Despite Avoin's monologues all evening, I still knew too little of the hunting cats. Would they regard Nighteyes as an intruder, or would they ignore his scent in the courtyard? Would they think the information significant enough to communicate to the Witted humans? Not all Wit-bonds were as intimate as the one I shared with Nighteyes. His concern with the human aspects of my life had distressed Black Rolf almost to the point of disgusting him. Perhaps these cats only bonded with humans for the joy of the hunt. It was not impossible. Unlikely, but not impossible.

Well, I had not learned much more than what we had already suspected, but I'd had a more than ample meal. Sleep seemed the only other thing I could accomplish tonight. I offered Lebven my thanks and good-night, and despite her insistence that she would do it, cleared my things from the table. The keep was quiet as I made my way softly back to my room. Only a dim light shone from under the door. I set my hand to it, expecting to find it latched. It was not. Every nerve suddenly ajangle, I eased it silently open on the darkened room. Then I caught my breath and stood motionless.

Laurel wore a long dark cloak over her nightgown. Her hair was loose and spilling down her back. Lord Golden wore an embroidered dressing gown over his nightshirt. The light from the tiny fire in the hearth glinted off the burnished thread of the birds embroidered on the back and sleeves of his dressing gown, and picked up the lighter streaks in Laurel's flowing hair. He wore lacy gloves on his hands. They stood very close together by the fire, their heads bent together. I stood silent as a shocked child, wondering if I had interrupted an embrace. Lord Golden glanced over Laurel's shoulder at me, and then made a small motion for me to come in and shut the door. As Laurel turned to see me, her eyes seemed very large.

"I thought you were asleep in your chamber," she said quietly. Was she disappointed?

"I was down in the kitchen, eating," I explained to her. I expected her to reply to my words, but she merely looked at me. I felt a sudden desire to be elsewhere. "But I am extremely tired. I think I shall be going to bed immediately. Good night." I turned toward my servant's room, but Lord Golden's voice halted me.

"Tom. Did you learn anything?"

I shrugged. "Small details of the servants' lives. Nothing that seems useful." I was still not certain of how freely I should speak before Laurel.

"Well. Laurel seems to have done better." He turned to her, inviting her to speak. Any woman would have been flattered by his golden focus.

"Prince Dutiful has been here," Laurel announced in a breathless whisper. "Before I retired to sleep, I asked Avoin to show me the stables and the cattery. I wanted to see how the animals were housed."

"His mistcat was there?" I guessed incredulously.

"No. Nothing that obvious. But the Prince has always insisted on tending to the cat's needs himself. Dutiful has certain odd little habits, ways of folding things or hanging tack. He is very fussy about such things. There was an empty enclosure in the cattery. On the shelf by it were brushes and such, arranged just so. It was the Prince's doing. I know it."

I recalled the Prince's chamber at Buckkeep, and suspected she was right. And yet— "Do you think the Prince would have let his precious cat be housed down there? In Buckkeep, the creature sleeps in his rooms."

"There is everything for a cat's comfort there: things to claw, the herbs they fancy, fresh greens growing in a tub, toys for exercise, even live prey for their meals. The Bresingas keep hutch upon hutch of rabbits, so that their cats need never eat cold meat. The cats are truly pampered royalty."

It seemed to me that my next question followed logically. "Might the Prince have stayed down in the stables to be closer to his cat?" Perhaps the basket had not had too long a journey to make.

Laurel raised one brow at me. "The Prince stay in the cattery?"

"He seemed to be very fond of the animal. I thought he might do that rather than be parted from it." I had nearly betrayed my conclusion: that the Prince was Witted and would not be parted from his bond-animal. There was a small silence. Lord Golden broke it. His mellow voice carried no farther than the two of us. "Well, at least we have discovered that the Prince was here, even if he is not here now. And tomorrow may yield us more information. The Bresingas play cat and mouse with us. They know the Prince has left the Court with his cat. They may suspect that we have come seeking him. But we shall stay in our roles, and graciously dance after whatever they dangle for us. We must not betray what we know."

"I hate this sort of thing," Laurel declared flatly. "I hate the deceit, and the polite faces we must wear. I wish I could simply go and shake that woman awake and demand to know where Dutiful is. When I think of the anguish that she has caused our Queen . . . I wish I had asked to see the cattery before dinner. I would have asked different questions, I assure you. But I brought you the news as soon as I could. The Bresingas had furnished me with a maid who insisted on helping me prepare for bed, and then I did not dare slip from my room until I was sure most of the keep was asleep."

"Asking blunt questions will not serve us, nor shaking the truth out of noble ladies. The Queen wants Dutiful returned quietly. We must all keep that in mind." Lord Golden included me in his instruction.

"I will try," Laurel replied with quiet resignation.

"Good. And now we must all try to get what rest we can before tomorrow's hunt. Good night, Tom."

"Good night, Lord Golden, Huntswoman Laurel."

After a moment or two of silence, I realized something. I had been expecting Laurel to leave so that I could secure the door behind her. I had wanted to tell the Fool about the basket and the dead rabbit. But Laurel and Lord Golden were waiting for me to leave. She was studying a tapestry on a wall with an intensity it did not merit, while Lord Golden contentedly contemplated the gleaming fall of Laurel's hair.

I wondered if I should lock the outer door for them, then decided that would be an oafish act. If Lord Golden wanted it locked, he would do it. "Good night," I repeated, trying to sound sleepy and not awkward. I took a candle and went to my own chamber, shutting the connecting door gently behind me. I undressed and got into bed, refusing to let my mind wander beyond that closed door. I felt no envy, I told myself, only the sharper bite of my loneliness in contrast to what they might be sharing. I told myself I was selfish. The Fool had endured years of loneliness and isolation. Would I begrudge him the gentle touch of a woman's hand now that he was Lord Golden?

Nighteyes? I floated the thought, light as a dry leaf on the wind.

The brush of his mind against mine was a comfort. I sensed oak trees and fresh wind blowing past his fur. I was not alone. *Sleep, little brother. I hunt our prey, but I think nothing new will we learn until dawn.*

He was wrong.

chapter XVII

THE HUNT

Among the Old Blood, there are teaching tales that are
intended as guides for the very young. They are simple
stories that instruct a child in virtues by telling of the
animals that exemplify an admirable quality. Those not of
Old Blood might be surprised to hear the Wolf praised for his
dedication to his family, or the Mouse for her wisdom in
providing for the cold winter months ahead. The Gander
who keeps watch while the rest of the flock feeds is praised
for his unselfishness and the Porcupine for his forbearance in
only injuring those who attack him first. The Cat's attribute
is independence. A tale is told of a woman who seeks to
bond with a cat. The cat offers to try her companionship for
a day or two, if the woman will seek to perform well the
tasks given her. The tale relates the duties the cat tries the
woman at, stroking her fur, amusing her with string,
fetching her cream, and so on. The woman complies
cheerfully with each request and does each one well. At the
end of that time, the Witted woman again proposes that they
bond, for she felt they were obviously well suited to one
another. The cat refuses, saying, "If I bonded with you, you
would be the poorer, for you would lose that which you love
best about me, for it is that I do not need you, yet I tolerate
your company." It is, the Old Blood say, a cautionary
fable, meant to warn a child not to seek a bond-beast who
cannot take as much from the relationship as it gives.

⟜ BADGERLOCK'S "OLD BLOOD TALES"

Let me just see you.
    You have. I have shown myself to you. Stop nagging me for

*that, and pay attention. You said you would learn this for me.
You promised it to me. It is why I have brought you here, where
there are no distractions. Be the cat.*

It's too hard. Let me see you with my eyes. Please.

*When you are ready. When you can be the cat as easily as
you are yourself. Then you will be ready to know me.*

She was ahead of me. I toiled up the hill behind her,
every bush scratching me, every dip and every stone catching at my feet. My mouth was dry. The night was cool, but
as I pushed my way through the brush, dust and pollen rose
to choke me. *Wait!*

*Prey does not wait. A cat does not cry out "wait" to the one
she hunts. Be the cat.*

For an instant, I almost caught a glimpse of her. Then
the tall grass closed around her and she was gone. Nothing
stirred, I heard no sound. I was no longer sure which way to
go. The night was deep beneath the golden moon, the
lights of Galeton lost behind me in the rolling hills. I took
a breath, and then closed my mouth, resolving to breathe
silently if it choked me. I moved forward, a single gliding
step at a time. I did not push branches out of my way, but
swayed around them. I eased through the grass, striving to
part it with my stride rather than push through it. I eased
my weight from one carefully set footstep to the next. What
had she bade me? *"Be the night. Not the wind that stirs the
trees, not even the soundless owl a-wing or the tiny mouse
crouched motionless. Be the night that flows over all, touching
without being felt. For night is a cat."* Very well, then. I was
night, sleek and black and soundless. I halted under the
sheltering branches of an oak. Its leaves were still. I opened
my eyes as wide as they would go, striving to capture every
bit of light I could. Slowly I turned my head. I flared my
nostrils and then took in a deep silent breath through my
mouth, trying to taste her on the air. Where was she, which
way had she gone?

I felt a sudden weight, as if a brawny man had clapped
both his hands to my shoulders and then sprung back from

me. I spun around, but it was only Cat. She had dropped on me like a falling leaf, and then let herself drop to the ground. Now she crouched in the dry grass and ancient leaves under the tree. Belly to the ground, she looked up at me and then away. I crouched down beside her. "Which way, Cat? Which way did she go?"

Here. She is here. She is always here, with me.

After my love's deep throaty voice, Cat's thought in my mind was a reedy purr. I was fond of her, but to have her thoughts touch mine when I was longing instead for my love was almost intolerable. Gently I put her aside from me. I tried to ignore her injured protest that I should do so.

"Here," I breathed. "I know she is close. But where?"

Closer than you know. But you shall never know me as long as you set the cat aside. Open to the cat. Be the cat. Prove yourself to me.

Cat flowed soundlessly away from me. I could not see where she had gone. She was night flowing into night, and it was like trying to discern the water you had poured into a stream. I drew a soundless breath and poised myself to follow, not just with my feet but with my heart. I pushed fear aside and opened myself to the cat.

Cat was back suddenly, easing out of the darkness to become a richer shadow. She pressed close against my legs. *Hunted.*

"Yes. We hunt, we hunt for the woman, my love."

No. We are hunted. Something scents us, something follows Cat-and-Boy through the night. Up. Climb.

She suited her words to her thoughts, flowing up the oak tree. *Tree to tree. He cannot track us up here. Follow tree to tree.* I knew that was what she was doing, and she expected me to follow. I tried. I flung myself at the oak, but the trunk was too large for me to shinny up and yet not coarse enough for my clawless fingers to find purchase. For an instant, I clung, but I could not climb. I slid back, nails bending and clothing snagging as the tree refused me. I could hear the predator coming now. It was a new sensa-

tion, one I did not like, to be hunted thus. I'd find a better
tree. I turned and ran, sacrificing stealth for speed, but finding neither.

I chose to go uphill. Some predators, such as bears,
could not run well on an uphill slope. If it was a bear, I
could outdistance him. I could not think what else it might
be that dared to hunt us. Another oak, younger and with
lower branches, beckoned me. I ran, I leapt and caught the
lowest branch. But even as I pulled myself up, my pursuer
reached the bottom of the tree below me. And I had chosen
foolishly. There were no other trees close by that I could
leap to. The few that touched branches with mine were
slender, unreliable things. I was treed.

Snarling, I looked down at my stalker. I looked into my
own eyes looking into my own eyes looking into my own
eyes—

I sat bolt upright, flung from sleep. Sweat sheathed me
and my mouth was dry as dust. I rolled out of bed and stood,
disoriented. Where was the window, where was the door?
And then I recalled that I was not in my own cottage, but
in a strange room. I blundered through the darkness to a
washstand. I lifted the pitcher there and drank the tepid
water in it. I dipped my hand in what little was left and
rubbed it around on my face. Work, mind, I bade my struggling brain. It came to me. Nighteyes had Prince Dutiful
treed somewhere in the hills behind Galeton. While I had
slept, my wolf had found the Prince. But I feared that the
Prince had discovered us, as well. How much did he know
of the Skill? Was he aware that we had been linked? Then
all wondering was pushed aside. As the lowering storm is
suddenly loosed by a bolt of lightning, so did the flash of
light that seemed to fill my eyes herald the clanging of the
Skill-headache that dropped me to my knees. And I had
not a scrap of elfbark with me.

But the Fool might.

It was the only thought that could have brought me to
my feet again. My groping hands found the door and I

stumbled out into his chamber. The only light came from a small nest of dying coals in the hearth and the uncertain light of the night torches burning on the grounds outside the open window. I staggered toward his bed. "Fool?" I called out softly, hoarsely. "Fool, Nighteyes has Dutiful treed. And . . ."

The words died on my lips. The dream had forced the earlier events of the night from my mind. What if that huddled shape beneath the blankets were not one body but two? An arm flung back a coverlet to reveal only one form occupying the great bed. He rolled to face me and then sat up. Concern furrowed his brow. "Fitz? Are you hurt?"

I sat down heavily on the edge of his bed, set one hand to each side of my head and pushed, trying to hold my skull together. "No. Yes. It's the Skill, but we haven't time for that. I know where the Prince is. I dreamed him. He was night-hunting with a cat in the hills behind Galeton. Then something was hunting us, and the cat went up one tree and I . . . the Prince went up another. And then he looked down and he saw Nighteyes under the tree. The wolf has him treed somewhere in those hills. If we go now, we can take him."

"No we can't. Use your common sense."

"I can't. My head is cracking like an eggshell." I hunched forward, elbows on my knees, head in my hands. "Why can't we go get him?" I asked piteously.

"Walk your thoughts through it, my friend. We dress and creep out of this room, get past the stable folk to take our horses out, ride through unfamiliar country by night until we come to where the Prince is up a tree with a wolf at the foot of it. One of us climbs the tree and forces the Prince down. Then we coax him to come back with us. Lord Golden miraculously appears at breakfast with, I imagine, a very disgruntled Prince Dutiful, or Lord Golden and his man simply disappear from Lady Bresinga's hospitality without a word of explanation. In any case, in a few days a lot of very uncomfortable questions are going to be asked about Lord Golden and his man Tom Badgerlock, not to mention Prince Dutiful."

He was right. We already suspected the Bresingas were involved in the Prince's "disappearance." Bringing him back to Galekeep would be foolish. We had to recover him in such a way that we could take him straight back to Buckkeep and no one the wiser. I pressed my fingers to my eyeballs. It felt as if the pressure inside my skull would force them out of their sockets. "What do we do, then?" I asked thickly. I didn't even really want to know. I wanted to fall over on my side and huddle into a miserable ball.

"The wolf keeps track of the Prince. Tomorrow, during our hunt, I will send you back for something I've forgotten. Once you are on your own, you will go to where the Prince is and persuade him to return to Buckkeep. I chose you a big horse. Take him with you immediately and return him to Buckkeep. I'll find a way to explain your absence."

"How?"

"I haven't thought of it yet, but I will. Don't be concerned about it. Whatever tale I tell, the Bresingas will have to accept for fear of offending me."

I picked at the next largest hole in the plan. It was hard to keep my thoughts in order. "I . . . persuade him to come back to Buckkeep?"

"You can do it," the Fool replied with great confidence. "You will know what to say."

I doubted it, but had run out of strength to object. There were painfully bright lights behind my closed eyes. Knuckling them made them worse. I opened my eyes to the dim room, but zigzags of light still danced before my vision, sharding it. "Elfbark," I pleaded quietly. "I need it."

"No."

My mind could not encompass that he had refused me. "Please." I pushed the word out. "The pain is worse than I can explain." Sometimes I could tell when a seizure was coming on. I hadn't had one in a long time. Was I imagining that odd tension in my neck and back?

"Fitz, I can't. Chade made me promise." In a lower voice, as if he feared it was too little to offer, he added, "I'll be here with you."

Pain tumbled me in a wave. Fear mingled with it.

Should I come?

No. "Stay where you are. Watch him." I heard myself say the words out loud as I thought them. There was something I was supposed to worry about in that. I recalled it. "I need elfbark tea," I managed to say. "Or I can't hold the limits. On the Wit. They'll know I'm here."

The bed moved under me as the Fool clambered out of it, a terrible jostling that pounded my brain against the inside of my skull. I heard him go to the washstand. A moment later, he was back, damp cloth in hand. "Lie back," he told me.

"Can't," I muttered. Any movement hurt. I wanted to get back to my own room, but could not. If I was going to have a fit, I didn't want to do it in front of the Fool.

The cold cloth on my brow was like a shock. I retched with it, then took short panting breaths to get my stomach under control. I more felt than saw the Fool crouch down before me as I sat on the edge of the bed. He took my hand in gloved ones and his fingers fumbled over mine. An instant later, they bit down, pinching hard between the bones of my hand. I gave an inarticulate cry and tried to pull free of him, but as ever he was stronger than I expected.

"Just for a moment," he muttered as if reassuring me. The pain in my hand became a racing numbness. A moment later, he seized my arm just above my elbow in both his hands, and again his fingers sought and then pinched down hard.

"Please," I begged him, and tried to move away from him. He moved with me and the pain in my head was such I couldn't escape. Why was he hurting me?

"Don't struggle," he begged me. "Trust me. I think I can help. Trust me." Again his hands moved, this time to my shoulder, and again those relentless fingers jabbed down hard. I gasped, and then his hands were on either side of my neck, his fingers pressing in and up as if he wished to detach my head. I grasped his wrists but could find no strength in my hands. "A moment," he begged me again. "Fitz, Fitz, trust me. Trust me."

Then something went out of me. My head dropped forward on my chest, lolling on my neck. The pain was not gone, but it was much diminished. I fell over on my side and he rolled me onto my back. "There. There," he said, and for a moment I stared into blessed darkness. Then the gloved hands were back, thumbs on my brow, spread fingertips seeking spots on my temples and the sides of my face, and then they pressed mercilessly, his smallest fingers digging in at the hinge of my jaw.

"Take a breath, Fitz," I heard him tell me, and I then realized that I was not breathing. I gasped for air, and everything suddenly eased. I wanted to weep for relief. Instead, I sank instantly into a bottomless sleep. I dreamed a strange dream. I dreamed I was safe.

I came to a hazy wakefulness before dawn. I took a deep breath, and realized I was in the Fool's bed. I think he had just arisen. He was moving quietly about the room, selecting clothing for himself. I think he felt me watching him, for he came back to the bedside. He touched my brow, pushing my head back onto the pillow. "Go back to sleep. You have a little more time to rest, and I think you need it." Two gloved fingers traced twin lines from the top of my head to the bridge of my nose. I slept again.

When next I woke, it was because he was gently shaking me. My servant-blue clothing was laid out on the bed beside me. He was already fully dressed. "Time to hunt," he told me when he saw I was awake. "I'm afraid you'll have to hurry."

I moved my head cautiously. I ached all along my spine and neck. I sat up stiffly. I felt as if I had been in a fistfight . . .

or had a seizure. There was a sore spot inside my cheek as if I'd bitten it. I looked away from him as I asked, "Did I have a fit last night?"

A small silence preceded his words. He kept his voice casual. "A small one, perhaps. You tossed your head about and trembled for a time in your sleep. I held you still. It passed." He did not want to speak of it any more than I did.

I dressed slowly. My whole body ached. My left arm bore the marks of the Fool's fingers, small dark circles of bruising. So I had not imagined the strength of his grip. He saw me inspecting my arm, and winced sympathetically. "It leaves bruises, but sometimes it seems to work," was all he offered by way of explanation.

Hunt mornings at Galekeep were very similar to hunt mornings at Buckkeep Castle. Suppressed excitement was tingling in the air. Breakfast was a hurried affair, taken standing in the courtyard, and the painstaking efforts of the kitchen folk were scarcely noticed. I had only a mug of beer for I dared face no more than that. I did, however, have the foresight to do as Laurel had noted, and store some food in my saddle pack and make sure my waterskin was freshly filled. I glimpsed Laurel in the hubbub of folk, but she was very busy, talking to at least four people at once. Lord Golden strolled through the crowd, greeting each person with a warm smile. Lord Grayling's daughter was always at his elbow. Sydel's smile and chatter were constant, and Lord Golden replied with attentive courtesy. Did young Civil look a bit irritated with that?

The horses were brought, saddled and gleaming, from the stables. Myblack seemed unimpressed with the excitement in the air, and again I wondered at her seeming lack of spirit. The gathering seemed oddly muted to me, and then I smiled to myself. There was no excited baying to lift the heart and infect the horses with excitement. I missed hounds. The hunters and their attendants mounted, and then the cats were brought forth on their leads.

The cats were sleek, short-coated creatures, with elongated bodies. Their heads appeared small to me at first glance. Their coats were tawny, but in certain angles of the light, subdued dappling could be distinguished. Each cat's long, graceful tail seemed to harbor an independent life. They padded through the thronging horses as calmly as dogs among sheep. These were the gruepards, and they knew very well what the milling, mounted folk meant. With little guidance each cat sought out its mounted master. I watched in stunned surprise as leads were loosed, and each cat leapt nimbly into place. I watched Lady Bresinga turn in her saddle to mutter fond words to her cat, while Civil's gruepard put a heavy paw on his shoulder and pulled the boy back so the cat could bump faces with him. I waited in vain for some manifestation of the Wit. I was almost certain both the Bresingas possessed it, but it was controlled to an extent I had not imagined possible. Under the circumstances, no matter how I longed for the touch, I dared not quest out toward Nighteyes. His silence to me was so absolute it was like an absence. Soon, I promised myself, soon.

We set out for the hills where Avoin promised us good groundbirds and much sport in the taking of them. I rode in back with the other attendants, breathing dust. Despite the early hour, the day already promised to be unseasonably warm. The fine dust of our passing hung thick in the still air. The soil of the hills was strange stuff, for once the thin surface turf was broken by a trail, it became a track of fine powdery soil. I soon wished for a kerchief to cover my mouth and nose, and the hanging dust discouraged conversation. The hooves of the horses were muffled by the stuff, and with the absence of baying dogs, I felt that we rode in near silence. Soon we left the riverside and the trail behind us and rode across the face of the sun-drenched hill through crisping gray-green brush. We wended our way through rolling hills and draws that all looked deceptively alike.

The hunters were well ahead of us and moving steadily when we crested a hill. I think the flock of birds we rousted there surprised even Avoin, but everyone reacted quickly. I was too far back to see if a signal released the cats, or if the beasts simply reacted to the game. These were large, heavy-bodied birds that ran, wings open and beating, before they could lift from the ground. Several never made it into the air, and I saw at least two brought down on the wing by the leaping gruepards. The speed of the cats was heart-stopping. They flowed from their cushions, leaping to the ground impactlessly and shooting after the fleeing birds with a speed like a striking snake. One cat actually brought down two birds, seizing one in her jaws even as her clutching paws clasped one to her breast. I had noticed four or five boys on ponies riding behind us. They came forward now, game bags open, to take up the prey. Only one gruepard was reluctant to relinquish her kill, and I understood that she was a young hunter, her training still incomplete.

The birds were shown to Lord Golden before they were bagged. Sydel, who had been riding beside him, pushed her horse closer to see the trophies and exclaim over them. He took tail feathers from several of the birds, and then summoned me to his side. As I accepted the trophy feathers from him, he instructed me, "Put them in the case right away, so they are not marred."

"The case?"

"The feather case. I showed it to you when we were packing at Buckkeep . . . Sa's Breath, man, you have not left it behind, have you? Ah! Well, you shall have to go back for it. You know the one, of tooled red leather with a felted-wool lining. It is most likely amongst my things at Galekeep, unless you have left it at Buckkeep. Here, give Huntswoman Laurel the feathers to carry until you return. Make haste now, Tom Badgerlock. I need that case!" Lord Golden did not disguise his irritation at his servant's inept-ness. There was, indeed, such a case amongst Lord Golden's belongings, but he had never told me it was a feather case, nor told me to bring it. I managed to look suitably chas-tened at my negligence as I bobbed my head to his orders.

So simply was I cut free from the hunt. Obedient to my

master, I wheeled Myblack and touched heels to her. I put two rolling hills between the hunting party and us before I reached out cautiously to Nighteyes. *I come.*

Better late than never, I suppose, was the grudging reply.

I pulled in my horse and sat still. Wrongness flooded me. I closed my eyes, and saw through the wolf's. It was a nondescript area, just like every hill and dale I had ridden through that morning. Oak trees in the draws and dusty scrub brush and yellow grass on the hillsides. But I knew where he was somehow and how to get to where he was. It was as Nighteyes described it: I knew where I itched before I scratched. I also knew, without his telling me, that there was a reason for his stillness. I quested toward him no more, but simply put heels to Myblack and leaned forward to urge her on. She was a runner for level terrain, not these rolling hills, but she did well enough. I soon looked down on the dale where I knew Nighteyes waited.

I longed to rush straight down to him. His stillness was as ominous as flies buzzing around blood. I forced myself to cut a wide path around the dale and go slowly, reading the ground and breathing deep for any scents that might linger. I found the tracks of two shod horses, and a moment later cut the same tracks going in the opposite direction. Horses had come and gone from the copse of oak trees, and not long ago. I could restrain myself no longer. I rode into the welcoming shade of the trees as if I were running my head into a snare. *Nighteyes.*

Here. Hush.

He lay, panting heavily, in the dry shade of the oaks. Old leaves were stuck to the bloody gashes on his muzzle and flank. I flung myself from my horse and ran to him. I set my hands to his coat and his thoughts flowed silently into mine in the quietest possible sharing of the Wit.

They worked together against me.

The boy and the cat? I was surprised that he was surprised at that. The boy and the cat were Wit-bonded. Of course they would act together.

The cat and the horseman who brought the horses. I was watching the boy up the tree the whole while. I sensed nothing from him, not even that he called to the cat for help. But just after dawn broke, the damned cat attacked me. Dropped right out of a tree onto me, and I hadn't even known she was coming. She must have traveled tree to tree like a squirrel. She clung like a burr. I thought I was winning when I flung her to the ground, but she wrapped her front paws around me and tried to disembowel me with her hind claws. Nearly succeeded, too. Just then, the man came up with the horses. The boy climbed down into the saddle, and then like a flash the cat was on the horse behind him. They galloped off and left me here.

Let me see your belly.

Water, first, before you poke at me.

Myblack annoyed me by dancing away from me twice before I caught her reins. I tied her securely to a bush after that, and then brought both water and food to Nighteyes. I let him drink from my cupped hands, and then we shared the food between us. I wanted to wash the blood from the gashes I could see, but I knew he wouldn't allow it. *Leave them to close themselves. I've already licked them clean.*

At least let me see the ones on your belly.

He was not happy about it, but he complied. The damage was much worse there, for the cat had obviously pulled him close, and his belly lacked the thick fur that had somewhat protected his back. They were not clean slashes, but jagged tears that were already festering. The only good aspect was that the claws had not penetrated the wall of his belly. I had feared to see bulging entrails; all I saw was lacerated flesh. I cursed myself for not having any salve to comfort the wounds. It had been too long since I had had to worry about things such as this; I had grown careless in the precautions I took.

Why didn't you call for me to come and help you?

*You were too far away to get here in time. And—*uneasiness tinged his thoughts—*I thought they wanted me to call* *you. The man on the big horse and the cat. They listened, as if my call to you were game they sought to beat out of hiding.*

Not the Prince.

No. My brother, there is something very strange here. He was surprised when the horseman came with the extra mount. Yet I sensed the cat was not, the cat expected the man and the horses. The Prince does not perceive all that his bond-partner does. He goes blindly into his bond. It is . . . uneven. One commits and the other accepts the commitment, but does not return it in full. And the cat is . . . wrong.

He could make it no clearer than that to me. I sat for a time, my fingers buried deep in his coat, pondering what to do next. The Prince was gone. Someone he had not summoned had arrived to carry him away from Nighteyes, at precisely the moment that the cat was diverting the wolf. Carry him away to where?

I chased them for a time. But it is as you said. I cannot keep up with a running horse anymore.

You never could.

Well. Neither could you. You couldn't even keep up with a running wolf for long.

True. That's very true. I smoothed his coat, and tried to pluck a dead leaf from one of his scabs.

Leave that alone! I'll bite your hand off! And he could have. Fast as a snake, he seized my wrist in his jaws. He squeezed it, then let me go. *It isn't bleeding, so leave it alone. Stop picking at me and go after them.*

And do what?

Begin by killing the cat. It was a vindictive suggestion with no heart in it. He knew as well as I did what it would do to the Prince if we killed his bond-animal.

I do. A pity he does not share your scruples about killing your bond-brother.

He doesn't know you are bonded to me.

They knew I was bonded to somebody, and would have liked to discover just whom. That knowledge did not dissuade them from hurting me. I sensed his thoughts racing ahead of mine, pondering a situation I had not deciphered yet. *Be careful, Changer. I recognize this pattern of old. You think this is a game of some kind, with limits and rules. You seek to bring the Prince back as a mother carries an errant cub back to the den. You have not even considered that you might have to injure him, or kill the cat, to do so. Even farther from your thoughts is that they might kill you to prevent you from taking the Prince back. So I change my advice to you. Do not go after them now, alone. Give me until this evening to get past my soreness. And when we track them, let us take the Scentless One with us. He is clever, in a human sort of way.*

Do you think the Prince has that in him? To kill me before letting me take him back to Buckkeep? The thought appalled me. Yet, I had been younger than Prince Dutiful when I first killed on Chade's orders. I had not especially enjoyed it, but I had not deeply pondered the right or wrong of it. Chade was my conscience then, and I had trusted his discretion. I wondered. Was there such a person in the Prince's life, someone whose counsel was enough to make him suspend his own judgment?

Stop thinking that you are dealing with a young prince. You are not. Nor is it the cat we must fear. This is something deeper and stranger, my brother, and we are best to go very, very carefully.

He drank the rest of my water. Then I left him there under the oaks, though I did not like to. I did not attempt to follow their trail, but returned to the Bresinga manor at Galeton, found the feather case, and rode back to the hunt. They had moved on, but it was easy enough to track them. When I presented the case to Lord Golden, he observed, "You were a long time bringing it, Badgerlock." He looked round at his hunting companions and added, "Well, at least it is not as I had feared. I almost thought you had taken my words to mean that you must bring the case, even if you had to go all the way to Buckkeep Castle for it." There was a general laugh at my supposed dullness.

I bobbed my head in docile agreement. "My apologies, master, for the delay in finding it. It was not where I expected it to be."

He accepted my apology with a nod, then handed me the case again. "Collect the feathers from Huntswoman Laurel. See that you put them in carefully."

Laurel had a substantial handful of feathers. The red case opened like a book. Within, the case was lined with felted wool to cushion the feathers against hurts. I held the case while she carefully arranged each feather in its place. The other hunters rode on, seeming to pay no attention to us. "The cats hunt well?" I asked as she positioned feathers.

"Very well. They are amazing to watch. I had seen the Prince's mistcat hunt before, but this is my first experience of gruepards. They have set the cats twice on birds and once on hares since you left us."

"Think you they will hunt much longer?"

"I doubt it. Lord Golden confided that the midday sun is too harsh on his skin and may give him a headache. I think they will turn back soon."

"That would suit me well, also." The others were now a distance away from us, talking amongst themselves. She closed the feather case and handed it back to me. We rode side by side until we caught up with the hunting party. She turned in her saddle to look at me and met my eyes as she said, "Last night, Tom Badgerlock, you looked a different man. You should take more care with your daily appearance. The effect is well worth your effort."

Her words left me speechless. She smiled to see me struck dumb, then left me behind with the other attendants as she spurred her horse forward to ride at Lord Golden's stirrup. I do not know what words, if any, passed between them, only that soon the hunting party decided to return to Galekeep. The game bags were heavy, the beat of the sun overhead was becoming oppressive, and the cats seemed irritable and less interested in the hunt.

This being so, the nobles turned their horses and set

spurs to them, hastening back to the welcome cool of Galekeep's thick stone walls. The rest of us followed as best we might. Myblack easily kept their pace, though I had to ride in their dust.

The nobility retired to their chambers to wash the dust away and don fresh clothing while others cared for their sweated horses and cranky cats. I followed Lord Golden as he strode ebulliently through the halls. I hastened to open the door for him, and then to shut it behind us after he had passed through. I fastened the latch quietly.

I turned to find him already laving the dust from his face and hands. "What happened?" he asked me.

I told him.

"Will he be all right?" he asked anxiously.

"The Prince? I hardly know."

"Nighteyes," the Fool clarified impatiently.

"As well as he may be. I'll take him more water and meat when I return. He was in pain but not like to die of his injuries." Though I had not liked the look of the inflamed scratches. The Fool almost seemed to answer my thoughts.

"I've a salve that may soothe his hurts, if he will let you use it."

I had to smile. "I doubt that he will, but I will be glad to take it all the same."

"Well. There but remains for me to manufacture a reason for the three of us to depart Galekeep immediately after lunch. We dare not let his trail grow cold. Nor do I think it likely that we will be returning here." As he spoke, he was changing his jacket, brushing dust from his trousers, and wiping a cloth over his boots. He considered his reflection in the mirror, then hastily ran a brush through his fine hair. The pale strands floated after the brush and clung to it. The shorter pieces at his temples stood out like a cat's whiskers. He exclaimed in annoyance, and refastened the heavy silver clip that he used to secure his hair at the base of his neck. "There. That will have to do. Pack us up, Tom Badgerlock.

Be prepared to leave by the time I return from my meal."
And he was gone.

There was fruit and cheese and bread on the table from
the night before. The bread was a bit stale but I was hungry
enough that it did not matter. I ate as I hastily packed my
own things. Lord Golden's wardrobe presented me with
more problems. I could not recall how he had fit so much
clothing into such a small bag. At length, I managed to
cram it all in, though I wondered what the fine shirts would
look like when they emerged again.

The midday meal was still in progress when I finished. I
took advantage of that and slipped down to the kitchen for
cold beer and spicy sausages. My old skills served me in
good stead, for when I left several thick slices off a cold
joint were concealed in the breast of my servant's tunic.

I returned to our rooms and spent the early afternoon
impatiently awaiting Lord Golden's return. I longed to
reach for the wolf, and dared not. Every passing moment
might be carrying the Prince farther away. The afternoon
was flowing away from me. I flung myself down on my bed
to wait. Despite my anxiety, I must have dozed off.

I awoke to Lord Golden opening the door. I rolled from
the bed to my feet, feeling sodden with sleep yet eager to
leave. He shut the door behind him and in response to my
look, replied grimly, "It is proving socially difficult to extri-
cate us. There were guests at today's luncheon, and not just
those we hunted with. The Bresingas seem determined to
exhibit me to all their wealthy neighbors. They have
planned dinners and teas and more hunts with half the
countryside in attendance. I have been unable to invent a
pressing enough reason for us to leave. This is damnably in-
convenient. Would that I could go back to my motley and a
more honest form of juggling and rope-walking."

"We're not leaving yet," I observed stupidly.

"No. There is a large dinner in my honor this evening.
For us to abruptly leave before that would be insult. And

when I hinted that I might have to cut my visit short and leave tomorrow morning, I was told that Lord Crias from across the river had planned a morning hunt for me, and an afternoon repast at his manor."

"They delay you on purpose. The Bresingas are involved in the Prince's disappearance. I am sure they provided food for him and the cat last night. And Nighteyes is certain that the cat who attacked him is aware he is bonded to someone. They tried to flush me out."

"Perhaps. But even if we were sure, I could scarcely fling accusations about. And we are not positive. Perhaps they but seek social advancement at Court, or to show me their various marriageable daughters. I gather that is why the girl was at dinner last night."

"I thought she was Civil's companion."

"She was at great pains during the hunt to tell me that they were childhood friends with absolutely no romantic interest in one another." He sighed and sat down at the small table. "She told me that she too collects feathers. Tonight after dinner she wishes to show me her collection. I am certain it is an invention to spend more time with me."

Had my own needs not been so pressing, I would have smiled at his dismay.

"Well, I shall have to deal with it as best I may. And perhaps it can even be turned to our advantage, now that I think of it. Oh, I've an errand for you. It seems that while we were hunting today, I lost a silver chain. At lunch I noticed it was missing. It is one of my favorites. You will have to retrace our steps and see if you can find it. Take your time."

As he spoke, he drew a necklace from his pocket, wrapped it in his kerchief, and handed it to me. I pocketed it. He opened his clothing case, shot me an accusing look at the compressed jumble inside it, and then fished about until he discovered the pot of salve. He handed it to me.

"Shall I lay out your clothing for dinner before I go?"

He rolled his eyes mockingly at me as he drew a crumpled shirt from his clothing bag. "I think you've already done enough for me, Badgerlock. Just go." As I moved toward the door, his voice stopped me. "Does the horse suit you?"

"The black is fine," I assured him. "A good healthy beast and fleet, as we proved. You chose a good horse."

"But you would rather have chosen your own mount."

I nearly said yes. But then, as I considered it, I realized that was not true. If I had been choosing the horse, I would have sought for a companion to bear me through the years. It would have taken me weeks, if not months, to select one. And now that I was reluctantly confronting the wolf's mortality, I felt a strange hesitance to offer that much of myself to an animal. "No," I replied honestly. "It was much better that you chose one for me. She's a good horse. You chose well."

"Thank you," he said quietly. It seemed to matter to him a great deal. If the wolf had not been waiting, it would have given me pause.

chapter XVIII

FOOL'S KISS

*Many are the tales told of Witted taking on their beasts'
shapes to wreak havoc upon their neighbors. The bloodier
legends are of Witted in wolves' skins, who in that guise
rend their neighbors' families as well as their flocks. Less
sanguine are the tales that depict Witted suitors taking on
the shapes of birds, or cats, or even dancing bears to gain
access to a bedchamber in the course of a seduction.*

*All such tales are imaginative nonsense, perpetuated
by those who seek to fuel hatred of the Witted. Although a
Witted person can share the mind of his beast and, hence,
its physical perceptions, he cannot metamorphose his human
form into that of an animal. It is true that some Witted who
have been long in a partnership with their animal sometimes
take on some of their habits of posture, diet, and
mannerisms. But a man who eats, dens, scavenges, and
smells like a bear does not become a bear. If that myth of
shapechanging could be vanquished, it would go far to
reestablishing trust between the Witted and un-Witted.*

       BADGERLOCK'S "OLD BLOOD TALES"

The wolf was not where I had left him. It rattled me, and I
took some few moments convincing myself that I had not
mistaken the spot. But there were the spatters of his blood
where he had sprawled on last year's leaves, and here were
the spatters in the dust where he had lapped water from my
hands. He had been here and now he was not.

It is one thing to track two shod horses with riders. It is
another to follow the spoor of a wolf over dry ground. He

had left no trace of his passage, and I feared to reach out toward him. I followed the tracks of the horses, believing that he would have done the same. As I trailed them through the sun-drenched hills, their tracks went down into a draw and crossed a small stream. They had stopped here to let the horses water. And there in the muddy bank was a wolf's pawprint atop the horse's hoofmark. So. He was tracking them.

Three hills later, I caught up with him. He knew I was coming. He did not pause to wait for me, but moved on. That gait caught my eyes. It was not his purposeful trot. He walked. Myblack was not especially pleased to approach the wolf, but she didn't fight me. As I drew closer, he stopped in the shelter of some trees and awaited me.

"I brought meat," I told him as I dismounted.

I felt his awareness of me, but he sent no thought toward me. It was eerie. I took the meat out of my shirt and gave it to him. He gulped it down and then came to sit down beside me. I took the salve out of my pouch. He sighed and lay down.

The claw swipes down his belly were livid ridges of lacerated flesh, and hot to the touch. When I applied the salve, the pain became an edged thing between us. I was as gentle as I could be and still be thorough. He tolerated it, but not gladly. I sat for a time beside him, my hand resting on his ruff. He sniffed at the salve I had applied. *Honey and bear grease*, I told him. He licked the long scratch and I let him. His tongue would push the ointment deeper into the wound and do him no harm. Besides, there was no way I could have stopped him. He already knew that I would have to go back to Galekeep.

It would be wisest for me to keep following them, even if I don't go swiftly. The longer you are delayed, the colder the trail will be. Easier for you to come to me than to try to follow fading tracks.

There is no arguing with that. I gave no voice to my worries that he could neither hunt nor defend himself just now. He knew it, I knew it, and he had made his decision. *I'll catch up with you as soon as I can.* He knew that too, but I could not refrain from the promise.

My brother. Be careful what you dream tonight.

I won't seek to dream with them.

I fear they may seek you.

Apprehension smoked through my mind, but again there was nothing to say. I wished, vainly, that I had been brought up knowing more of the Wit. Perhaps if I had understood Old Blood better, I would know what I was dealing with now.

No. I think not. What you do, how you link to him, that is not just Skill. It is the crossing of your magic. You open the door with one and travel with the other. As when I attacked Justin after he had bridged into you with Skill. His Skill made the bridge, but I used my bond with you to run across it.

He had deliberately shared that thought with me, acknowledging a worry that had been growing in me for some time. Dog-magic, Justin had called my Wit, and told me that my use of the Skill stank of it. Verity had never complained of that. But Verity, I admitted unwillingly, shared my truncated education in the Skill. Perhaps he had not detected a staining of the Wit in my use of the Skill, or perhaps he had been too kind to ever rebuke me with it. Now I worried for my wolf. *Do not follow them too closely. Try not to let them know that we track them.*

What did you fear? That I would attack a cat and a boy on horseback? No. That battle belongs to you. I will trail this game; it is up to you to bring it to bay and down it.

His thought created unpleasant images in my mind all the way back to Galekeep. I had entered into this to track down a boy, runaway or perhaps kidnapped. Now I was facing not only a boy who did not wish to be returned to Buckkeep, but his confederates. How far would I go in my efforts to return him to the Queen, and what limits would he set in his determination to have his own way?

Would those with him have any constraints as to what they would do to keep him?

I knew Lord Golden was wise to continue our play. Much as I longed to drop all pretense and simply hunt down the Prince and drag him back to Buckkeep, I could see the consequences of that. If the Bresingas were convinced that we pursued him, they would certainly get a warning to him. He would flee faster and hide deeper. Worse, they might directly interfere with our pursuit of him. I had no wish to meet with an untimely "accident" as we tracked Prince Dutiful. As matters stood, we could still hope to move secretly to regain the Prince and discreetly convey him back to Buckkeep. He had fled Galekeep at our arrival, yet not gone far at first. Now he was on the move again, but still had no reason to connect Lord Golden to any pursuit. If the Fool could pry us loose of Lady Bresinga's hospitality without arousing any suspicion, we could follow him unobtrusively and have a better chance of catching up with him.

I returned to Galekeep hot and dusty and parched. It still seemed odd to surrender my horse to a stableman. I found Lord Golden napping in his chambers. The curtains were drawn against the heat and light, putting the room in twilight. I went quietly past him to my own room to wash most of the dust and sweat away. I hung my shirt on the bedpost to dry and air and slung my fresh one over my shoulder.

Servants had replenished the bowl of fruit in Lord Golden's chamber. I helped myself to a plum and ate it by the window, peering around the curtain at the garden outside. I felt both tired and restless. I could think of nothing constructive to do, and no way to pass the time. Frustration and worry chafed me.

"Did you find my chain, Badgerlock?" It was Lord Golden's aristocratic tone that interrupted my thought.

"Yes, my lord. Just where you thought you'd lost it."

I drew the delicate jewelry from my pocket and carried it over to where he lounged on his bed. He accepted it as gratefully as if he were truly a nobleman and it had truly been lost. I lowered my voice. "Nighteyes follows the trail for us. When we can leave, we can go straight to the wolf."

"How is he?"

"Stiff. Sore. But I think he will recover."

"Excellent." He sat up, and swung his legs over the side of the bed. "I've selected evening clothing for us, and laid it out in your room. Really, Badgerlock, you must learn to handle my garments more carefully."

"I'll try, my lord," I muttered, but I could not get my heart back into the game. I was suddenly tired of the whole charade. "Have you thought of a discreet way for us to leave?"

"No." He strolled to the table. Wine had been left there for him. He poured a glass and drank it, then poured another. "But I've thought of an indiscreet one, and already laid the groundwork for it this afternoon. Not without regrets—I'll be compromising Lord Golden's reputation somewhat, but what is a nobleman without a bit of scandal to his name? It will probably just increase my popularity at court. Everyone will want to know my side of it, and will speculate on what truly happened." He sipped from his glass. "I think that if I succeed at this, it will convince Lady Bresinga that her fears that we are seeking the Prince are groundless. No proper emissary of the Queen would behave as I intend." He gave me a sickly smile.

"What have you done?"

"Nothing, just yet. But I fancy that by morning, our leaving will be facilitated as swiftly as we could wish." He drank again. "Sometimes I don't care for the things that I must do," he observed, and there was a plaintive note in his voice. He finished the glass of wine as if girding himself for a task.

Not another word would he divulge to me. He arrayed himself carefully for dinner, and I had to suffer the indignity of the green jerkin and yellow leggings. "Perhaps it is a shade too bright," he conceded in response to my incensed gaze. His grin was too broad for me to believe any apology

in his words. I did not know if it was the wine or one of his
fey humors. "Stop glowering, Badgerlock," he rebuked me
as he adjusted the cuffs of a muted green coat. "I expect my
servants to maintain a pleasant demeanor. Besides, the
color does set off the darkness of your eyes and skin and
hair—all of you. It rather reminds me of an exotic parrot.
You may not appreciate such a show of yourself, but the
ladies will."

Obeying him taxed all my ability to dissemble. I walked
behind him to where the nobility had gathered before dinner. This was a larger group than the night before, for Lady
Bresinga had extended her hospitality to those who had
hunted with her earlier. They might have been invisible for
all the notice Lord Golden gave them. Sydel was seated at a
low table with young Civil. An assortment of feathers was
spread out before her on a cloth, and they seemed to be discussing them. She had obviously been watching the door,
for the moment Lord Golden entered, her face was transfig-
ured. She gleamed like a lantern in the darkness. Young
Civil also underwent a transformation, but it was not so
pleasant. He could not very well sneer at a guest in his
mother's home, but his features went very still and cold.
Dismay clutched at my belly. No. I wanted no part of this.

But Lord Golden, smiling and charming, made directly
for the pair. His greetings to everyone else in the chamber
were brief to the point of neglect. Without even a pretense
of subtlety, he seated himself between them, obliging Civil
to move over to make room for him. From that moment on,
he virtually ignored everyone else in the room as he focused
all of his allure on the girl. Their heads bent together over
the feathers. His every movement was a seduction. His long
fingers stroked the gaudy feathers on the cloth. He selected
one, and touched its softness to his own cheek, and then
leaned forward to draw it gently down the length of Sydel's
arm. She giggled nervously and drew back from the touch.
He smiled. She blushed. He set the feather back on the
cloth and shook a reproachful finger at it as if it were at

fault. Then he selected another one. Boldly he held it against the sleeve of her gown, murmuring some comparison of color. He gathered others from the cloth, arranged them in a sort of feather bouquet. With the tip of one forefinger, he turned her face to look at his, and then, by a trick I could not see, fastened the feathers into her hair so that they hung down and followed the line of her cheek.

Civil rose abruptly and stalked away. His mother spoke to a woman at her side, who moved swiftly to intercept him before he left the chamber. There were low-voiced words between them, and the young man's tone was not calm. I could not follow what he said, for Lord Golden's words rose over the general conversation to proclaim, "Would that I had a looking glass to show you, but you must be content to see how well this ornament becomes you by looking into my eyes."

Earlier in the day, I had been appalled at how brazenly she had stalked Lord Golden and how willing she had been to throw over her young suitor for the strange nobleman. Now I almost pitied Sydel. One hears of birds charmed by snakes, though I have never seen such a thing. What I witnessed now was more like a flower leaning toward light. She absorbed his attention and blossomed in its warmth. In the space of a few moments, her girlish infatuation with his age and wealth and fine ways had been transformed into a more womanly warmth and fascination with him. I knew with crawling certainty that she was his to bed, if he chose. Should he tap at her chamber door tonight, she would admit him without hesitation.

"He goes too far." Laurel's breathless whisper was tinged with horror as she strolled past me.

"He excels at that," I murmured in reply. I shifted my shoulders in the confines of my gaudy jacket. My pretense at being Lord Golden's bodyguard might become real tonight. Certainly the look Civil shot him promised murder.

When Lady Bresinga announced that it was time to dine, Civil made the foolish mistake of hesitating. Before he had even the chance to churlishly refuse to escort Sydel to the table, his rival had offered his arm and the girl had taken it. This left Civil duty-bound to escort his slighted mother as they followed their esteemed guest and his prey into the dining hall.

I tried to rein my emotions in and be a stoic observer of that dinner. Lord Golden's tactic revealed much to me. Sydel's parents were obviously torn between courtesy to Lady Bresinga and her son, and the enticing prospect of their daughter winning the attention of this extremely wealthy nobleman. Lord Golden was a far more desirable catch than young Civil, yet they were not unmindful of the danger to their young daughter. To catch a nobleman's eye is not the same as to have the pledge of one. There was a danger that he might toy with her and ruin her for future marriage. It was a dangerous line for a young girl to walk, and in the way that Lady Grayling picked her bread to pieces I plainly saw her mother's doubts that Sydel could toe it.

Avoin and Laurel tried desperately to kindle a conversation about the day's hunt, and the talk lurched along, but Lord Golden and Sydel were too deeply engrossed in their own quiet talk to pay any attention. Civil, seated to the other side of Sydel, was ignored by both of them. Avoin was holding forth on the uses of rue in training cats, for all knew that a cat would avoid anything marked with the essence of the herb. Laurel said that onion was sometimes used for the same purpose. Lord Golden offered Sydel a tidbit from his plate, and then stared in rapt fascination as the girl ate it. He was drinking heavily tonight, glass after glass, and it appeared as if he was actually pouring it down his throat. I felt anxiety. The Fool, drunk, had always been both unpredictable and volatile. Would Lord Golden have more restraint when in his cups?

Civil's anger must have flared, for I felt a querying Wit-echo from something. I could not catch the thought, only the emotion that accompanied it. Something was fully willing to rend Lord Golden to shreds on Civil's behalf. I did not doubt that his hunting cat was his Wit-beast. For that unguarded moment of fury, the connection between them sang with bloodlust. It was quenched in an instant, but there was no mistaking what it was. The boy was Witted. And Lady Bresinga? I looked past her, watching her without seeming to. I felt no trace of the Wit from her, but she radiated maternal disapproval of her son's lapse. Because he had betrayed his Old Blood to any who might be aware of such things? Or because his displeasure showed so plainly on his face? Betraying one's emotions so blatantly was not genteel.

I stood, as I had the previous night, behind Lord Golden's chair all through the meal. I learned little from the words exchanged that night, but much from the glances. Lord Golden's scandalous behavior both fascinated and horrified the other guests. Quiet words were exchanged, as were shocked glances. Lord Grayling, at one point, sat breathing through his white-pinched nostrils for several moments while his wife spoke frantically to him in an undertone. She appeared willing to gamble the Bresingas' good will for the possible benefit of a better match. Through all this interplay, I sifted expressions and exchanges, looking for some sign of who was Witted. It was not information I could quantify, but before the dinner was over, I was satisfied that both Civil and Lady Bresinga were. I was equally certain their Huntsman was not. Of the other guests at their table, there were two I suspected of the Wit. A certain Lady Jerrit had something of the cat in her mannerisms. She was perhaps unaware of how she breathed in the scent of every dish before she ventured to taste it. Her spouse, a hale and hearty man, had a trick of turning his head sideways to the leg of fowl he was devouring, as if he had sharper teeth there with which to scissor the meat free. Small habits, but telling. As the Prince had fled Buckkeep to Galekeep, so he might, when driven from Galekeep, go to another Wit-friendly holding. These two lived to the south. The Prince's trail led north, but that did not mean he would not circle back.

I noticed another thing, as well. Lady Bresinga's eyes came often to settle on me, and I did not think she was admiring my gaudy garments. She looked like a woman trying to recall something. I was almost certain I had never met her in my other life as FitzChivalry. But to be almost certain of something means that there is always a squirming of doubt in the back of the mind. For a time, I kept my head slightly lowered and my eyes cast to one side. Only after I observed the others did I realize what a wolflike attitude that was. When next she looked at me, I met her eyes squarely and stared back. I was not so bold as to smile at her, but I deliberately widened my eyes, feigning an interest in her. Her affront at Lord Golden's insolent servant was plain. Catlike, she unfocused her eyes and looked through me. In that glance, I was finally sure of her. Old Blood.

I wondered if she was the woman who had captivated my Prince's fancy. Certainly, she was attractive. Her full lips hinted at sensuality. Dutiful would not be the first young man to fall victim to a knowledgeable older woman. Had that been her aim in giving the cat to him? To seduce him and win his young heart, so that no matter where he was wed, she would always keep a piece of his soul? It would explain why he had come here when he had fled Buckkeep. But, I reflected, it would not explain his unfulfilled passion. No. If she had intended to seduce the Prince, she would have moved swiftly to entangle him as deeply as possible. There was something else here, something strange, as the wolf had said.

A brief flip of Lord Golden's hand at the end of the meal dismissed me. I went, but reluctantly. I wanted to witness whatever reactions his abominable behavior might bring. The diners would move on to other amusements now; music, games of chance, and conversation. I went to the kitchen, and again was offered a choice of the feast's remains. There had been a piglet tonight, cooked whole, and plenty of tender meat and crisp skin lay scattered among the bones on the platter. A sauce of sour apples and berries had accompanied it. This, with bread and soft white cheese and several mugs of ale, made a more than adequate meal. It might have been more enjoyable if Lord Golden's man had not been taken to task over his master's behavior.

Civil and Sydel, I was informed sternly by Lebven, had been affianced almost from birth. Well, if not formally, at least it was common knowledge among all the folk of both households that the two were intended for one another. His mother's house and Lord Grayling's family had always been on the best of terms, and the two estates were adjacent to one another. Why should not Lord Grayling's daughter benefit from Lady Bresinga's rapid rise in the world? Old friends should help one another. What was my master thinking, to come between them? Could his intentions be honorable? Would he steal young Civil's bride from him, to bear her off to court and wealth beyond her station? Did he womanize at Buckkeep, was he but toying with her affections? Was he good with a sword? For it was well known that Civil had a temper, and hospitality or no, the boy might challenge him over Sydel.

To all of this I professed ignorance. I was newly come to Lord Golden's service, and to the court at Buckkeep. I knew little of my master's ways or temperament yet. I was as curious as they were as to what would befall them all. The excitement that Lord Golden had stirred was such that I could not steer the conversation to Dutiful or Old Blood or any useful topic. I lingered only long enough to purloin a large chunk of meat. Then I pleaded my duties and departed the kitchen for my room, frustrated of knowledge and deeply concerned for Lord Golden's welfare. As soon as I was in our rooms, I changed back into my humbler blue clothing. The green jerkin had rather suffered from concealing the meat. Then I sat down to await my master's return. Anxiety roiled through me. If he carried this role too far, he might indeed find himself facing young Civil's blade.

I doubted that Lord Golden was any better with a blade than the Fool had been. It would, of course, be scandalous if it came to bloodshed, but young men in Civil's position were not inclined to worry about such niceties.

The depths of the night had passed and we were venturing toward the shallows of dawn when there was a tap at the door. A dour-faced maid informed me that my master required my assistance. Heart in mouth, I followed her, to discover Lord Golden senseless with drink on a bench in a parlor. He sprawled there like a cast-off garment. If other folk had witnessed his collapse, they had left. Even the maid gave a small toss of her head as she abandoned me to tend to him. As soon as she left, I half expected him to rouse and tip me a wink that this was all a sham. He did not.

I hauled him to his feet but even that did not stir him. I could either drag him or carry him. I resorted to the undignified expediency of slinging him over my shoulder and toting him back to his chamber like a sack of grain. I dumped him unceremoniously onto the bed, and fastened the door behind us. Then I dragged off his boots and shook him out of his jacket. As he fell back onto the bed, he said, "Well, I did it. I'm certain of it. I'll apologize tomorrow, most abjectly, to Lady Bresinga. Then we'll leave immediately. And all will be relieved to see us go. No one will follow us, no one will suspect we track the Prince." His voice wavered toward the end of this speech. He still had not opened his eyes. Then, in a strained voice he added, "I think I'm going to vomit."

I brought him the washbasin and set it on the bed next to him. He crooked an arm around it as if it were a doll. "What, exactly, did you do?" I demanded.

"Oh, Eda, make it all stand still." He clenched his eyes tightly and spoke. "I kissed him. I knew that would do it."

"You kissed Sydel? Civil's intended?"

"No," he groaned, and I knew a short-lived moment of relief. "I kissed Civil."

"What?"

"I had gone to piss. When I came back, he was waiting for me outside the parlor where the others were gaming. He grabbed my arm and all but dragged me into a sitting room where he confronted me. What were my intentions toward Sydel? Did not I grasp that they had an understanding?"

"What did you say?"

"I said—" He paused abruptly and his eyes grew round. He leaned toward the basin, but after a moment he only burped gassily and lay back. He groaned, then continued: "I said I understood their understanding, and hoped that perhaps we could come to an understanding of our own. I clasped his hand in mine. I said I saw no difficulty. That Sydel was a lovely girl, as lovely a girl as he was a boy, and that I hoped we might all become close and loving friends."

"And then you kissed him?" I was incredulous.

Lord Golden screwed his eyes shut. "He seemed a bit naïve. I wanted to be sure he took the fullness of my meaning."

"Eda and El in a tangle," I swore. I stood up and he groaned as the bed moved beneath him. I walked to the window and stared out. "How could you?" I demanded of him.

He took a breath and strained mockery crept into his voice. "Oh, please, Beloved. You needn't be jealous. It was the most brief and chaste kiss you can imagine."

"Oh, Fool," I rebuked him. How could he make a jest of something like this?

"It wasn't even on the mouth. Just a warm press of my lips to the palm of his hand, a single flick of my tongue." He smiled feebly. "He snatched it away as if I had branded him." Suddenly he hiccuped loudly and then made a sour face. "You're dismissed. To your room, Badgerlock. I've no more need of you tonight."

"Are you certain?"

He nodded, a short vehement nod. "Go away," he said plainly. "If I'm going to puke, I don't want you watching me."

I understood his need to preserve that much dignity. He had little enough left. I retreated to my room and shut the door. I busied myself with packing my things. A short time later, when I heard the sounds of his misery, I did not go to him. Some things a man should do alone.

I did not sleep well. I longed to touch minds with my wolf, but dared not allow myself that comfort. Necessary they might be, yet I still felt dirtied by the Fool's political manipulations. I longed to live the direct and clean life of a wolf. Toward dawn, I came out of a doze to the sound of the Fool moving about in his chamber. I found him sitting at the small table looking haggard. Somehow the fresh clothing he had donned only made him look the more rumpled. Even his hair looked sweaty and disheveled. He had a little box in front of him and a mirror. As I watched, puzzled, he dipped his finger in something and wiped it under his eye. The shadow there deepened to a pouch. Then he sighed. "I hate what I did last night."

I did not need him to explain. I tried to ease his conscience. "Perhaps it was a kindness. Perhaps it is better they discovered, before they wed, that Sydel's heart is not as constant as Civil believed."

He shook his head, refusing the comfort. "If I had not led, she would not have followed in that dance. Her first sallies were but a girl's coquetry. I think it as instinctive for a girl to flirt as it is for boys to show off their muscles and daring. Girls of her age are like little kittens pouncing at grass to practice their hunting skills. They do not yet know the meaning of the motions they make." He sighed, and went back to his little box of colored powders.

Silently I watched as he not only made himself look more ill, but added a decade to his years by delineating the lines in his face.

"Do you think that's necessary?" I asked him as he snapped the little box shut and handed it to me. I tucked it back into his case, which was, I noted, already neatly packed for our journey.

"I do. I wish to be sure that the glamour I put over Sydel is completely broken before I depart. Let her see me as

substantially older than she is, and dissolute. She will wonder what she was thinking, and flee back to Civil. I hope he
will have her. It would be better than her pining after me."
He gave a melodramatic sigh, but I knew his ridicule was for
himself. This morning, Lord Golden's façade was fractured
and the Fool shone forth from the cracks.

"A glamour?" I asked skeptically.

"Of course. No one is invulnerable to me if I choose to
enchant them. No one but you, that is." He rolled his eyes
at me dolorously. "But there is no time for me to mourn
that. Now you must go forth and make it known that I wish
a private moment with Lady Bresinga. Then go and tap at
Laurel's door and let her know that we ride soon."

By the time I returned from the second half of my errand, Lord Golden had departed the room to his meeting
with Lady Bresinga. It was a very brief meeting, and when
he returned, he indicated that I should take our bags down
immediately. He did not stop to eat anything, but I had already purloined all the fruit that had been in our room. We
would survive, and he was probably wiser to avoid food for
a time yet.

Our horses were brought around. Lady Bresinga descended to wish us a chill farewell. Not even the servants
deigned to notice our departure. Lord Golden offered yet
another apology, attributing much of his behavior to the
fine quality of her wines. If this flattery was meant to appease her, it failed. We rode slowly from her courtyard, Lord
Golden setting a very easy pace for us. At the foot of the
hill, we turned toward the ferry. Only when the line of trees
along the road hid us from the manor's view did he halt and
ask me, "Which way?"

Laurel had been riding in a mortified silence. She had
said nothing, but I gathered that in humiliating himself,
Lord Golden had daubed her with the same brush. Now she
looked shocked as I said, "This way," and turned Myblack
off the road and into the sun-dappled forest.

"Don't wait for us," he told me brusquely. "Go as swiftly

as you can to close the gap. We'll catch up as we may, though my poor head may hold us back a bit. The worry now is that we may lose his trail. I am certain Laurel can follow yours. Go now."

I wanted no more than that. I saw the purpose of his order at once. It would allow me to be alone when I overtook Nighteyes and to confer with him privately. I nodded once and set my heels to Myblack. She sprang forward willingly, and I let my heart lead us. I did not bother looping back to where I had last seen the wolf, but reined her north and east to where I knew he was today. I let a tiny thread of my awareness tug at him to let him know I was coming and felt the twitch of his response. I urged Myblack to greater speed.

Nighteyes had covered a surprising amount of ground. I did not let myself worry about whether or not Laurel could easily track me. My drive now was to rejoin my wolf, see that he was well, and then push on in pursuit of the Prince. My uneasiness for him had been steadily swelling.

The day was hot, summer's last sprawl across the land, and the sun beat down on us even through the thin shade of the trees. The dry air seemed laden with dust that sucked the moisture from my mouth and clung to my eyelashes. I did not bother trying to find trails but pushed Myblack through the forested hills and down into the dales between them. Lusher vegetation showed where creeks sometimes ran, but their waters seeped under the surface now. Twice we crossed streams, and each time I stopped to let Myblack water and to drink deeply myself. Then we pushed on.

By early afternoon, I had an indefinable conviction that Nighteyes was near. Before I saw him or scented him, I began to get the strange feeling that I had seen this terrain before, that something about those trees ahead was oddly familiar. I pulled in the horse and slowly scanned the hills around me, only to have him step out from a patch of alder brush scarce a stone's throw away. Myblack flinched and then focused her full attention on him. I set a hand to her neck. *Calm. No need to fear. Calm.*

Too tired and not hungry enough to chase you, Nighteyes added helpfully.

"I brought you meat."

I know. I smell it.

I had scarcely unwrapped it before it was gone. I wanted to look at his injuries, but knew better than to bother him with that while he was eating. And as soon as he had finished eating, he gave himself a shake. *Let's go.*

Let me look at—

No. Maybe tonight. But while they have light, they travel, and so must we. They already have a good start on us, and the dry soil holds their scents poorly. Let's go.

He was right about tracking them. The dry ground resisted both print and scent. Before the afternoon was over, we had twice been stymied, and had only rediscovered their trail by casting for it in a wide circle. The shadows were growing long when Lord Golden and Laurel caught up with us. "I see your dog has found us again," she observed wryly, and I could think of nothing to say in reply.

"Lord Golden tells me that you track the Prince, that a servinggirl told you the Prince had fled north?" There was question in her voice, and her mouth was flat with disapproval. I did not know if she hoped to catch Lord Golden in a lie, or if I was supposed to have seduced someone for the information.

"She didn't know he was the Prince. She simply called him a lad with a hunting cat." I tried to think of something that would divert her from more questions. "The trail is poor. Any help you could give me would be welcome."

My ruse worked. She proved an able tracker. As the light went out of the day, she picked up small signs that I might have missed, and thus we kept following them long past the hour when I would have said the light was too poor. We came to a creek where they had stopped to water. The spoor of two men, two horses, and the cat were all plain in the damp soil at the water's edge. There we decided to make camp for the night. "It's better to stop tracking while we know we are on the right trail than to wait until we are not certain, and have confused things with our own tracks. Early tomorrow we will start again," Laurel announced.

We made a bare camp, little more than a tiny fire and our blankets beside it. Food was in short supply, but at least we had plenty of water. The fruit I had taken from our room was warm and bruised but welcome. Laurel carried, from habit, some twists of dried meat and travel bread. There was precious little of it, and she unwittingly bought much good favor from me when she announced, "We don't need the meat as much as the dog does. We have both fruit and bread." Another woman, I thought, might have ignored the wolf's hunger and hoarded the meat for the next day. Nighteyes, for his part, deigned to take it from her hand. And afterward, when I insisted on looking at his scratches, he did not snarl when she joined me, though she was wise enough not to attempt to touch him. As I had suspected, he had licked most of the unguent away. The scratches were scabbed closed and the flesh beside them did not look too angry. I decided against putting more ointment on them. As I put the unused pot away, Laurel nodded her head in quiet agreement. "Better dry and sealed than greased too well and the scab softened too much."

Lord Golden had already stretched out on his blanket. I surmised that neither his head nor his belly were yet calm. He had spoken little throughout our camp-making and sparse meal. In the gathering dark, I could not tell if his eyes were closed or if he stared up at the sky.

"Well. I suppose he has the right of it," I said, gesturing at him. "Early to bed, and an early start tomorrow. Perhaps, with luck, we'll overtake them."

I think Laurel assumed Lord Golden was already asleep. She lowered her voice. "It will take some hard riding, as well as a measure of luck. They ride assuredly, knowing where they are bound, while we must go carefully lest we lose them." Laurel cocked her head and studied me across the small fire. "How did you know when to leave the road to find their trail?"

I took a breath and chose a lie at random. "Luck," I replied quietly. "I had a feeling they would be going in this direction, and when I struck their trail, we followed it."

"And your dog had the same feeling, which is why he had gone ahead of you?"

I just looked at her. The words rose to my tongue without my volition. "Maybe I'm Witted."

"Oh, yes," she replied sarcastically. "And that is why the Queen trusts you to go after her son. Because you are one of those she most fears. You are not Witted, Tom Badgerlock. I've known Witted folk before; I've endured their disdain and snubs for folks who do not share their magic. Where I grew up, there were plenty of them, and in that place and time, they did little to conceal it. You are no more Witted than I am, though you are one of the best trackers I've ever ridden with."

I did not thank her for the compliment. "Tell me about the Witted folk you grew up with," I suggested. I smoothed a wrinkle out of my blanket and lay back on top of it. I closed my eyes almost all the way, as if I were only mildly interested in her words. The moon, a paring less than full, looked down at us through the trees. At the edge of the fire's light, Nighteyes was diligently licking himself. Laurel fussed for a moment with her own blanket, tossing small stones out from under it. Then she smoothed it to the earth and lay back on it. She was silent for a moment or two and I did not think she was going to answer me.

Then, "Oh, they were not so bad. Not like the tales folk tell. They did not turn into bears or deer or seals at the light of the full moon, nor did they eat raw meat and steal children. Still, they were bad enough."

"How?"

"Oh." She hesitated. "It just was not fair," she said at last, with a sigh. "Imagine never being sure that you were alone, for some little bird or lurking fox might carry the eyes and ears of your neighbor. They took full advantage of their Wit, for their animal partners forever told them where the hunting was best or the berries first ripened."

"Were they that open that they were Witted? Never have I heard of such a village."

"It was not that they were open about what they were, so much as that I was excluded for what I was not. Children are not subtle."

The bitterness of her words shocked me. I recalled, abruptly, how the rest of Galen's coterie had treated me with disdain when I could not seem to master the Skill. I tried to imagine growing up amidst such snubbing. Then a thought intruded. "I thought your father was Huntsman for Lord Sitswell. Did not you grow up on his estate, then?" I wanted to know where this place was, where Witted ones were so common their children had come to expect it of their playmates.

"Oh. Well, but that came later, you see."

I was not sure if she lied then, or if she had lied earlier, only that the untruth hung almost palpably between us. It made an uncomfortable silence. My mind darted amongst the possibilities. That she was Witted, that she was an un-Witted child in a family with Witted siblings or parents, that she had made the whole tale up, that all of Lord Sitswell's manor was riddled with Witted servants. Perhaps Lord Sitswell himself was of the Old Blood. Such speculation was not entirely useless. It prepared the mind to sort whatever other information she might toss my way into the appropriate possibilities. I harkened back to an earlier conversation we had had, and found a chance remark that put a chill down my back. She had said she would know these hills well, having spent time not far from Galeton, amongst her other folk. Chade too had mentioned something of that. I tried to find a way to renew the conversation.

"So. You sound as if you do not share the currently fashionable hatred of the Witted. That perhaps you do not wish to see them all burned and cut up."

"It's a filthy habit," she said, and the way she said it made me feel as if fire and blade were too small a cure for it. "I think that parents who teach their children to indulge it should be whipped. Those that choose to practice it should not marry nor have children. They already have a beast to share their homes and lives. Why should they cheat a woman or a man by taking a spouse? Those who are Witted should have to choose, early in their lives, which they will bind to, an animal or another human. That's all."

Her voice had risen on the vehemence of her reply. At her last words, it dropped away, as if she suddenly recalled that Lord Golden was sleeping. "Good night, Tom Badgerlock," she added belatedly. She tried to soften her tone, perhaps, but it still plainly told me that our talk was over. As if to emphasize it, she rolled on her blanket to put her back to me.

Nighteyes rose with a groan and came stiffly to me. He lay down beside me with a sigh. I let my hand come to rest on his ruff. Our shared thoughts flowed as secretly as our blood.

She knows.

Then you think she is Witted? I asked him.

I think she knows that you are Witted, and I don't think she likes it much.

For a time, I lay silently mulling that. *But she fed you.*

Oh, well, I think she likes me. It's you she's not sure about. Go to sleep.

Are you going to reach after them tonight?

I didn't want to. If I succeeded, it would give me a terrible headache. The mere thought of the pain made me nauseous. Yet if I could touch the Prince, I might gain information that could help us catch up sooner. *I should try.*

I felt his resignation. *Go ahead, then. I'll be right here.*

Nighteyes. When I Skill and afterward . . . do you share the pain?

Not exactly. Though it is hard for me to remain apart from it, I can. It just feels cowardly when I do.

It's not cowardly at all. What is the point of both of us suffering?

He made no answer to me, but I sensed that he reserved some thought on that for himself. Something about my question almost amused him. I lifted my hand from his fur and set it on my chest. Then I closed my eyes, centered myself, and tried for a Skill-trance. Dread of pain kept intruding on my thoughts, pushing awry my carefully constructed peace. Finally, I managed to find a balancing point and held myself there, somewhere between dreaming and waking. I reached forth into the night.

That night I felt, as I had not in years, the sweetness of the pure connection of the Skill. I reached out and it was as if someone reached back and clasped both my hands in welcome. It was a simple, sweet joining, as comforting as homecoming after a long journey. There was the linking of the Skill, and someone drowsing in a soft bed in a loft under the eaves of a thatched roof. The homely smells of a cottage surrounded me, the lingering smell of a good stew cooked that night, and the honey-tang of a beeswax candle burning late somewhere below. I could hear a man and a woman talking, their voices muted as if they did not want to disturb my rest. I could not make out their words, but I knew I was home and safe and that nothing could harm me there. As our Skill-link faded, I sank deeply into the most peaceful sleep I had known in many a year.

chapter XIX

THE INN

During the years of the Red Ship War, when Prince Regal the Pretender wrongfully claimed to be King of the Six Duchies, he introduced a system of justice he called the King's Circle. Trial by arms was not unknown in the Six Duchies. It is said that if two men fight before the Witness Stones, the gods themselves look down and reward victory to him whose cause is just. Regal took this idea one step further. In his arenas, accused criminals faced either his King's Champions or wild beasts. Those who survived were judged to be innocent of the charges against them. Many Witted met their ends in those Circles. Yet those who died in these bloody trials were but half of the evil done there. For what was born in those same contests was a public tolerance of violence and mayhem that swiftly became a hunger. These trials became spectacle and amusement as much as judgment. Although one of Kettricken's first acts as Queen and Regent for young Dutiful was to put an end to such trials and have the Circles dismantled, no royal decision could quench the bloodlust that Regal's spectacles had awakened.

I awoke very early the next morning with a sense of well-being and peace. An early-morning fog was in the process of burning off. Dew glimmered on my blanket. For a time I gazed unthinking at the sky through the oak branches overhead. I was in a state of mind in which the black pattern against the blue was all that I needed to satisfy me. After a while, when my mind insisted on recognizing the sight before me as tree branches against the sky, I came back to myself and where I was and what I must do.

I had no headache. I could cheerfully have rolled over and slept most of the day away, but I could not decide if I was truly tired or simply wanted to return to the safety of my dreams. I forced myself to sit up.

Nighteyes was gone. The others still slept. I poked up the embers of the fire and fed it before it occurred to me that we had nothing to cook over it. We'd have to tighten our belts and follow the Prince and his companion. With luck, something edible would cross our path.

I drank from the stream and washed my face in the cool water. The day was already warming. As I was drinking, the wolf came back.

Meat? I asked hopefully.

A nest of mice. I didn't save you any.

That's all right. I wasn't that hungry. Yet.

He lapped alongside me for a time, then lifted his muzzle. *Where did you go last night?*

I knew what he meant. *I'm not sure. But it felt safe.*

It was nice. I'm glad you can get to a place like that.

There was wistfulness in his thought. I looked at him more closely. For an instant, I saw him as another might. He was an aging wolf, gray on his muzzle, flesh sunken on his flanks. His recent encounter with the cat still hindered him. He ignored my concern to stare into the stream. *Fish?*

I let my annoyance seep into my thought. "Not a sign of one," I muttered aloud. "And there should be. Plenty of plants, midges buzzing. There should be fish here. But there aren't."

I felt his mental shrug at how life was. *Wake the others. We need to get moving.*

He did not want my worry. It was a useless burden to him, an anxiety not to be indulged. When I returned to camp, the others were already stirring. There was little to say. Lord Golden seemed to have recovered from his excesses. No one spoke about the lack of food. Dwelling on it would not change it. Instead, in a remarkably short time, we were in our saddles again and following the Prince's fading trail. He was moving steadily north. At noon, we found a campfire, the ashes gone cold. The area around the fire was well trampled, as if folk had camped there for several days. The mystery was easily solved. Two trees bore the mark of a picket line. Someone had waited here. When the Prince, the cat, and their companion arrived, they had departed together. North. Laurel and I debated the number of horses in the other party, and finally settled on four. They had picked up two more companions here.

We pressed on, increasing our pace as the multiple tracks were easier to follow. A high overcast came in, and then thickened into clouds. I blessed the dimming of the sun's harshness, but Nighteyes still panted as he kept pace with us. I watched him with growing concern. I longed to link more tightly with him, to be sure that he did not press on in spite of pain, but while Laurel rode with us, I dared not.

As shadows lengthened and the day began to cool, we came out of the forest and looked down at a wide yellow road crossing our path. From the crest of a hill, we stared down at it with dismay. If the Prince and his fellows had chosen to follow it, tracking might become very difficult.

We reached the edge of the road. Their tracks merged with it. The wolf made a show of casting about, but without much enthusiasm. The Prince's trail mingled in the thick dry dust with old wagon tracks and softened hoofprints. Neither imprint nor scent would linger long. An afternoon breeze could erase all trace of their passage.

"Well," Lord Golden observed helpfully. He lifted one eyebrow at me.

I knew what he suggested. Was not this why Chade had sent me? I shut my eyes and took a breath, then I threw myself wide to the Skill without any thought for protecting myself. *Where are you?* I demanded of the rushing world around me. There might have been a twitch of response but I had no assurance that it was the Prince. After last night, I knew there was something else out there that reacted to my Skill-reaching, something that was not the Prince. I could set my hand to it, almost. I forced myself to shift my attention away from that beckoning harbor and to reach out again for the Prince. But he and the cat eluded me. I do not know how long I sat on Myblack and extended myself to the wide world. Time stands still in such a reaching. I could almost feel the Fool waiting for me; no, I *did* feel him. A shimmering thread of Skill let me know how he contained his impatience. I sighed and pulled myself back from both the peaceful invitation and my fruitless reaching after the Prince. I had no tidings to give Lord Golden.

I opened my eyes. "They were going north. Let's follow it north."

"The road is more northeast than north," Lord Golden pointed out.

I shrugged. "The other option is southwest," I replied.

"Northeast it is," he concurred, and touched his heels to Malta. I followed him, and then glanced back to see what was keeping Laurel. She had a puzzled look on her face and was looking from me to Lord Golden as if perplexed. After a moment, she came after us. I reviewed my most recent interchange with my master and could have kicked both of us. I hadn't even remembered to call him "Lord," let alone kept the proper tone of a servant to his master. Our direction had obviously been my decision. I decided the best course of action was to say nothing at all about it, and hope to make it up with future subservience though my heart sank at that thought, and I admitted to myself just how much I longed for unguarded conversation and companionship.

We rode on through the remainder of the daylight. Lord Golden ostensibly led us, but in reality we followed the road. As the light faded, I began to look for a likely camping spot. Nighteyes seemed to pluck the thought from the air, for he surged ahead of our horses to crest a low rise in the road. When he disappeared over it, I knew he wanted us to follow. "Let's go just a bit farther," I suggested despite the gathering darkness. And at the top of the hill, we were rewarded with the sparse lights of a little village in the folds of the valley before us. A river wound past it; I could smell it, and the smoke of cook fires. My stomach awoke from its resignation and growled loudly.

"There will be an inn down there, I'll wager," Lord Golden announced enthusiastically. "Real beds. And we can get provisions for tomorrow."

"Dare we ask for word of the Prince?" Laurel asked. Our weary horses seemed to sense there might be something better than grass and creek water for them tonight. They picked up their pace as they went down the hill. I saw no sign of Nighteyes, but I had not expected to.

"I'll make some quiet inquiries," I volunteered. I imagined that Nighteyes already was doing that. If they had passed through the village and paused at all, the cat would have left some sign.

With unerring instinct, Lord Golden led us to an inn. It was a grand building for such a small town, built of black stone and boasting a second story. The hanging signboard chilled my heart. It was the Piebald Prince, neatly divided into his head and four quarters. It was not the first time I had seen him depicted that way; in fact, it was the commonest way to see him, but a sense of foreboding hung over me. If either Lord Golden or Laurel were given pause by the sign, they did not betray it. Light spilled wide from the inn's open door, and talk and good cheer flowed out with it. I smelled cooking food and Smoke and beer. The level of the laughter and shouted conversation was a pleasant roar. Lord Golden dismounted and told me to take the horses to the hostler. Laurel accompanied him into the noisy common room as I led the animals around to the darkened back of the inn. In a few moments, a door was flung open, and light stabbed out into the dusty innyard. The hostler appeared, wiping his interrupted meal from his lips, and bearing a lantern. He took the horses from me and led them off to the stable. I more felt than saw Nighteyes in the deeper darkness at the corner of the inn. As I approached the inn door, a shadow detached itself and brushed past me. In that brief touch, I knew his thoughts.

They were here. Be cautious. I smell man's blood in the street in front of this place. And dogs. Usually dogs are here, but not tonight.

He blurred into the night before I could ask him any details. I went in through the back door with an uneasy heart and an empty belly. Inside, the innkeeper informed me that my master had already commanded his finest room, and I was to bring all the bags up. Wearily I turned back to the stables. While I appreciated Lord Golden's ruse to let me have a good look inside the stables, I was suddenly afflicted with a weariness that could barely be suppressed. Food and sleep. I didn't even need a bed. I would have been happy to drop where I stood.

The hostler was still putting grain into our horses' feed bins. Perhaps because I was there, they got a more generous shake of oats. I saw nothing unusual in the stables. There were three plug horses of the kind such a place usually kept for hire, and a battered cart. A cow in a byre probably provided the milk for the guests' porridge. I disapproved of the chickens roosting in the rafters. Their droppings would foul the horses' food and water, but there was little I could do about it. There were only two other horses stabled there, not enough to be the mounts of those we followed. There were no hunting cats tethered in empty stalls. Well, nothing was ever easy. The hostler was competent at his work, but not talkative, nor even curious. His clothing was pungent with Smoke; I suspected the herbs had mellowed him past caring much about anything. I got our bags and, heavily laden, made my way back to the inn.

The finest room was up a flight of worn wooden steps. The climb taxed me more than it should have. I knocked at the door, then managed to open it for myself. It was the finest room in the sense that it was the best sitting room at the inn. Lord Golden was enthroned in a cushioned chair at the head of a scarred table. Laurel sat at his right hand. There were mugs in front of them and a large earthenware pitcher. I smelled ale. I managed to set the bags down inside the door instead of just dropping them. Lord Golden deigned to notice me. "I've ordered food, Tom Badgerlock. And arranged rooms for us. As soon as they've made the beds up, they'll show you where to take the bags. Until then, do be seated, my good man. You've well earned your keep today. There's a mug for you."

He nodded to a seat at his left, and I took it. Someone had already poured the ale for me. I'm afraid I drained off that first mug without any other thought than that it was sustenance after a long day. It was neither the best nor the worst brew I'd ever tasted, but few draughts had been as welcome as that one. I set the empty mug down on the table and Lord Golden nodded permission at the pitcher. As I refilled our mugs, the food arrived. There was a roast fowl, a large bowl of buttered peas, a meal pudding with treacle and cream, crisp trout on a platter, bread, butter, and more ale. Before the servingboy left, Lord Golden added another request. He had badly bruised his shoulder that morning; would the boy bring him a slab of raw meat from the kitchen to draw the soreness from the swelling? Laurel served Lord Golden and herself and then passed the dishes on to me. We ate in near silence, all of us very intent on the food. In a short time, the fowl and fish had been reduced to bones on the platters. Lord Golden rang for the inn servants to clear away. They brought a berry pie with clotted cream for a sweet, and more ale. The slab of raw meat came with it. As soon as the servant was gone, Lord Golden neatly wrapped it in his napkin and handed it to me. I wondered with weary gratitude if anyone would notice its disappearance. A short time later I became aware that I had eaten more than I should have done, and drunk more than was wise. I had that sodden, overly full feeling that is so miserable after one has been hungry all day. Lassitude crept over me. I tried to hide my yawns behind my hand and pay attention to the hushed conversation between Lord Golden and Laurel. Their voices seemed distant, as if a noisy river rushed between them and me.

"One of us should have a quiet look around," Laurel was insisting. "Perhaps some questions asked downstairs would discover where they were going, or if they are known around here. It could be they are close by."

"Tom?" Lord Golden prodded me.

"I already have," I said softly. "They were here. But they either moved on already, or are at a different inn. If a town this size has more than one inn." I leaned back in my chair.

"Tom?" Lord Golden asked me with some annoyance. In an aside to Laurel he observed, "It's probably the Smoke. He's never had any head for it. Just walking through the fumes puts him into a fog."

I pried open my eyes. "Beg pardon?" I asked. My own voice sounded thick and distant in my ears.

"How do you know they were here?" Laurel demanded. Had she asked that before?

I was too tired to think of a good answer. "I just do," I replied shortly, and then directed my words to Lord Golden as if we had been interrupted. "There's also been blood spilled in the street outside the inn. We should go carefully around here."

He nodded sagely. "I think our wisest course is an early bed and an earlier start tomorrow." Without letting Laurel voice any objections, he rang the servants' bell again. He was told that his rooms were, indeed, ready. Laurel had a tiny room to herself up at the end of the hall. Lord Golden had a more substantial chamber, with room for a cot for his man in it. The maidservant who had come at the bell insisted that she would carry Laurel's bag up to her chamber for her, so we said good night there. I avoided her eyes. I was suddenly tremendously weary, too weary to even attempt our roles. It was all I could do to shoulder a share of our bags and follow the servant to Lord Golden's rooms. He stayed behind, chatting with the innkeeper about replenishing our travel supplies before we left in the morning.

Our room was at the back of the inn, on the ground floor. I dragged our baggage inside, closed the door behind the departing servant, and opened wide the window. I found a nightshirt for Lord Golden and laid it out on his turned-down bed. I put the meat inside my shirt, to take to Nighteyes later. Then I sat down on my bed to await Lord Golden's return.

I awoke to someone shaking my shoulder gently. "Fitz? Are you all right?"

I came up slowly out of my dream. It took a moment or two to recall who I was. In my dream, I had been in another city, a populous, well-lit city. There had been music and many torches and lights. A celebration. I had not been a servant, but was— "It's gone," I told the Fool sleepily.

I heard an odd scrabbling noise and then a thump as Nighteyes heaved himself over the windowsill and then dropped into the room. He thrust his nose into my face. I petted him absently. I felt so drowsy. My ears buzzed.

The Fool shook me again. "Fitz. Stay awake and talk to me. What's wrong? Is it the Smoke?"

"Nothing. It's just so peaceful. I want to go back to sleep." Sleep pulled at me like a retreating tide. I longed to recede with it. Nighteyes poked me again.

Stupid. It's the black stone, like the Elderling road. You're getting lost in it again. Come outside.

I forced my eyes open wider. I looked up into the Fool's concerned face, and then dazedly gazed at the walls that surrounded me. Black stone. Veined with silver. And when I looked at it, I recognized it for what it was, stone scavenged from a much older building. The stones of the inner wall of the room fitted almost seamlessly together, but the outer wall was built more roughly. No, I suddenly knew, that wasn't completely right. The building predated the town, but it had been a ruin, rebuilt from the same ancient stone. And that ancient stone was memory stone, worked by Elderling hands.

I do not know what the Fool thought as I tottered to my feet. "Stones. Memory stone," I told him thickly as I groped my way toward the fresh air. I heard his astonished cry when I threw myself out of the window into the dusty innyard. The wolf landed more softly beside me. An instant later, Nighteyes faded into the shadows as someone leaned out of a window and demanded, "What goes on there?"

"It's my idiot servingman!" Lord Golden retorted in disgust. "So drunk he has fallen out the window trying to close it for me. Well, let him lie there. Serves the sodden oaf right."

I lay still in the dust of the innyard and felt the plucking dreams recede. In a moment or two, I would stand and walk farther from the stone walls. I just needed a moment or two.

The terrible tiredness that had been burdening me all evening gradually eased. I floated in relief. I stared up into the night sky and felt as if I could rise right up into it. Somewhere a couple was arguing. He was miserable but she was insistent. It was too much trouble to focus on their words, but then they came closer, and I could not avoid overhearing them.

"I should go home," he said. He sounded very young. "I should go back to my mother. If I had not left her, none of this would have happened. Arno would still be alive. And those others."

She inserted her head under his arm, and then rested it on his chest. *That's true. And we would be apart, you forever given to another. Is that truly what you want?*

They had drifted closer. With him, I breathed the sweet scent of her, musky and wild. He held her close. The wind blew through my dream of them, tattering the edges. He stroked her fur; her long dark hair threaded through his fingers. "It isn't what I want. But perhaps it is my duty."

Your duty is to your people. And to me. She wrapped her hand around his forearm. Her fingernails pressed against his flesh like claws. She tugged at him with them. *Come on. It is time to get up again. We cannot tarry, we must ride.*

He looked down into her green eyes. "My love, I must go back. I would be more useful to all of us there. I could speak out, I could press for change. I could—"

We would be apart. Could you stand that?

"I would find a way for us to be together."

No! She cuffed his cheek, and her palm rasped against his skin. There was a hint of claws in the gesture. *No. They would not understand. They would force us apart. They would kill me, and perhaps you, too. Recall the tale of the Piebald Prince. His royal blood was not enough to protect him. Yours would be no shield to you.* A pause, then: *I am the only one who truly cares about you. Only I can save you. But I dare not come to you completely until you have proven you are one of us. Always you hold back. Are you ashamed of your Old Blood?*

No. Never that.

Then open yourself. Be what you know you are.

He was silent for a long time. "I have a duty," he said softly. Infinite regret was in his voice.

"Get him up!" The man's voice came from behind me. "There's no time for delay. We need to gain some distance." I twisted on the ground to see who spoke but saw no one.

Green eyes stared into his. I could have fallen forever into those eyes. *Trust me,* she begged him, and he had to do as she requested. *Later you can think of these things. Later you can think of duty. For now, think of living. And of me. Get up.*

The Fool took my arm and draped it across his shoulders. "Up you come," he said persuasively, and heaved me to my feet. He was dressed all in black. More time must have passed than I had thought. Laughter and talk still spilled from the common room of the inn along with light. Once I was up, I found I could walk, but the Fool still insisted on keeping my arm as he guided me to a dark corner of the innyard. I leaned against the rough wood of the stable wall and collected myself.

"Are you going to be all right?" the Fool asked me again.

"I think so." The cobwebs were clearing from my mind. But the feel of these cobwebs was more familiar. I felt the familiar twinges of a Skill-headache, but they were less determined than usual. I drew a deep breath. "I'll be all right. But I don't think I should try to sleep in the inn tonight. It's built from memory stone, Fool, like the black road. Like the stone in the quarry."

"Like the dragon Verity carved," he filled in.

I took a deep breath. My head was clearing rapidly. "It's full of memories. That's so strange, to find stone like that here in Buck. I never supposed the Elderlings had come this far."

"Of course they had. Think about it. What do you think the old Witness Stones are, if not Elderling handiwork?"

His words shocked me. Then, it was so obvious that I didn't waste time agreeing. "Yes, but standing stones are one thing. That inn is the rebuilt remains of an Elderling structure. I had never expected to see that here in Buck."

He was silent for a time. As my eyes adjusted to the deeper darkness where we sheltered, I could see that he was actually chewing at the corner of his thumbnail. After a moment, he realized I was looking at him and snatched his hand away from his mouth. "Sometimes I get so caught up in the immediate puzzle that I overlook the pieces of the larger question that are all around us," he said as if confessing a fault. "So. You are all right now?"

"I think I'll be fine. I'll find an empty stall in the stable and sleep there. If the hostler asks, I'll tell him I'm in disgrace." I turned to go, then thought to ask, "Will you be able to get back into the inn, dressed like that?"

"Just because I sometimes wear the clothes of a nobleman, don't think I've forgotten all the tricks of a tumbler."

He sounded almost offended. "I'll get back in the way I got out: through the window."

"Good. I may take a walk about the town, to 'clear my head.' And to see what I can discover. If you can make the opportunity, go to the common room. Stir the gossip pot and see if you hear anything of strangers with a hunting cat passing through here yesterday." I started to add something about bloodshed in the street, but stopped myself. There was little chance it directly related to us.

"Very well. Fitz. Go carefully."

"There's no need to remind me of that."

I started to step away from him but he suddenly caught at my arm. "Don't go just yet. I've wanted to talk to you all day." He abruptly let go of me and crossed his arms on his chest. He took a ragged breath. "I did not think this would be so hard. I've played so many roles in my life. I thought it would be easy, that it might even be fun to play master to your man. It's not."

"No. It's hard. But I think it's wise."

"We've blundered too many times with Laurel."

I shrugged helplessly. "That is as it is. She knows we were both chosen by the Queen. Perhaps we can leave her in confusion and let her draw her own conclusions. They might be more convincing than anything we could fabricate."

He cocked his head and smiled. "Yes. That tactic pleases me. For now, we shall discover what we can tonight, and plan an early start in the morning."

We separated at those words. He withdrew into the darkness, vanishing as adeptly as Nighteyes could. I watched for him to cross the innyard but did not see him. I caught one brief glimpse of him as he vaulted back through the darkened window. I did not hear a sound.

Nighteyes pressed heavily against my leg.

What news? I asked him. Our Wit was as silent as the warmth of his body against me.

Bad news. Keep silent and follow.

He took me, not through the main streets of town, but away from its center. I wondered where we were going, but dared not reach forth to touch minds with him. I curbed my Wit, though it dulled my senses not to share the wolf's awareness. We ended up in a rocky field near the river's edge. He took me to the edge of it, where large trees grew. The tall dry grasses had been tramped down flat there. I caught a whiff of cooked meat and cold ashes. Then my eyes pieced together the length of rope still hanging from a tree, and the burned-out fire beneath it. I stood very still. The night wind off the river stirred the ashes and suddenly the smell of cooked meat sickened me. I put my hand over the extinguished coals. They were sodden and cold. A fire deliberately set and deliberately drowned. I poked at them, and felt the telltale greasiness of dripping fat. They had been more than thorough. Hung, cut in quarters, burned, and the remains thrown in the river.

I moved well away from the fire to the shelter of the trees. I sat down on a big rock there. The wolf came and sat beside me. After a time, I remembered his meat and gave it to him. He ate it without ceremony. I sat with my hand over my mouth, wondering. Coldness moved through me where blood had once flowed. Townsmen had done this, and now they ate and laughed and sang songs at the inn. They had done this to someone just like me. Perhaps to the son of my body.

No. The blood does not smell right. It was not him.

It was a small comfort. It only meant that he had not died today. Did the townsfolk hold him somewhere? Was the lively night at the inn an anticipation of more blood sport on the morrow?

I became aware of someone coming softly through the night toward us. She came from the direction of the town lights, but did not walk on the road. She came through the trees at the edge of the road, moving near soundlessly.

Huntingwoman.

Laurel stepped from the shadow of the trees. I watched

her as she moved purposefully toward the burned patch. As I had earlier, she crouched over it, sniffing, and then touching the ashes.

I stood, making just enough sound to let her know I was there. She flinched, spinning to confront us.

"How long ago?" I asked the night.

Laurel sighed out a small breath as she recognized us. Then, "Just this afternoon," she answered quietly. "My maid told me about it. Bragged, actually, of how the lad she is to marry was right in the thick of it, getting rid of the Piebald. That's what they call them in this valley. Piebalds."

The river wind blew between us. "So you came out here . . . ?"

"To see what was left to be seen. Which isn't much. I feared it might be our Prince, but—"

"No." Nighteyes was leaning heavily against me, and I shared what we both suspected. "But I think it was one of his companions."

"If you know that much, then you know the others fled."

I hadn't known that, but I was shamefully relieved to hear it. "Were they pursued?"

"Yes. And the men who chased them off have not returned yet. Some chased, some stayed to kill the one they had caught. It is planned that the ones who did this"—and she indicated the rope and the fire circle with a disdainful kick—"will ride out in the morning. There is some anxiety that their friends have not returned yet. Tonight they'll drink, and build up both their courage and anger. Tomorrow they'll ride."

"Then we had best ride out before them, and swifter."

"Yes." Her glance traveled from me to Nighteyes and back again. We both looked around at the trampled ground and the dangling rope and the burned-out place. It seemed as if there should have been something for us to do, some gesture to make, but if there was, it escaped me.

We walked back to the inn together in near silence. I

marked her dark garments and the soft-soled boots she wore, and once again I thought that Queen Kettricken had chosen well. I dirtied the night with a question whose answer I dreaded. "Did she tell you many details? How or why they were attacked, if the boy and the cat were with them?"

Laurel drew a deep breath. "The one they killed was not a stranger. He was one of their own, and they had suspected him of Beast Magic for a long time. The usual stupid stories . . . that when other lambs died of the scours, his survived. That a man angered him, and after that, the man's chickens died off. He came to town today with strangers, one a big man on a warhorse, one with a cat riding behind him. The others with him were also known to these folk, boys who had grown up on outlying farms. There are usually dogs at the inn. The innkeeper's son keeps rabbit hounds, and he had just returned from the hunt. The dogs were still excited. At the sight of the cat, the dogs went mad. They surrounded the horse, leaping and snapping. The man with the cat—our Prince, most likely—drew his blade to defend the cat, and slashed at the hounds, cutting an ear off one. But that was not all he did. He opened his mouth wide, and snarled, hissing like a cat.

"At the commotion, other men boiled out of the inn. Someone shouted 'Piebald!' Another cried for a rope and a torch. The man on the warhorse laughed at them, and put his horse to kicking out at both dogs and men. One man was kicked to the ground by the horse. The mob responded with rocks and curses, and more men came out of the tavern. The Piebalds broke the circle and tried to ride off, but a lucky stone caught one of the riders on the temple and knocked him from his saddle. The mob closed on him, and he yelled at the others to ride. The girl made them all out to be cowards for fleeing, but I suspect that the one they caught delayed the mob so his companions could escape."

"He bought the Prince's life with his own."

"So it would seem."

I was silent for a moment, tallying my facts. They had

not denied what they were. None of them had attempted to placate the mob. It was confrontational behavior, a harbinger of things to come. And one of their company had sacrificed himself, and the others had accepted it as necessary and right. That indicated not only the value they placed on the Prince, but deep loyalty to an organized cause. Had Dutiful been won completely to their side? I wondered what role these "Piebalds" had assigned to the Prince, and if he concurred in it. Had Dutiful accepted that the man should die for him? When he rode on, did he know then that the man they left behind faced an agonizing death? I would have given much to know that. "But Dutiful was not recognized as the Prince?"

She shook her head. The night was growing darker around us and I felt more than saw the movement.

"So. If the others caught up with him, they would not hesitate to kill him."

"Even knowing he was the Prince would not delay them. The hatred of the Old Blood runs deep here. They would think they were cleansing the royal line, not destroying it."

Some small part of me marked that she called them "Old Blood" now. I did not think I had heard her use the phrase before. "Well. I think time becomes even more precious."

"We should ride on tonight."

The very thought made me ache. I no longer had the resilience of youth. In the past fifteen years, I had grown used to regular meals and rest every night. I was tired and sick with dread of what must come when we caught up with the Prince. And my wolf was weary beyond weariness. I knew it was a false strength that moved his limbs now. Soon, his body would demand rest, no matter how hard the circumstances. He needed food and healing time, not to be dragged on tonight.

I'll keep up. Or you'll leave me behind and do what you must.

The fatalism in the thought shamed me. The sacrifice was too close to what a man had done today for a prince. The inarguable truth was that once more I spent all our strength for a king and a cause. The wolf yielded up the days of his life to me for an allegiance he understood only in terms of his love for me. Black Rolf had been right all those years ago. It was wrong of me to use him so. I made a child's promise to myself that when this was over, I would make it up to him somehow. We would go somewhere he wanted to go, and do something he longed to do.

Our cabin and the fireside. That would be enough for me.

It is yours.

I know.

We returned to the inn by a roundabout path, avoiding the better traveled roads of the village. In the dark of the innyard, she put her mouth close to my ear. "I'll slip up to my room to pack my things. You wake Lord Golden and let him know that we must ride."

She disappeared into the shadows near the back door. I made my own entrance through the front, presenting the scowling face of a chastised servant as I hastened through the main room. The hour was late now and the mood more one of brooding than celebration. No one took notice of me. I made my way to our room. Outside the door, the sounds of argument reached me. Lord Golden's voice was raised in aristocratic fury. "Bedbugs, sir! Thick as swarming bees. I've most delicate skin. I cannot stay where such vermin thrives!"

Our landlord, garbed in nightshirt and cap and clutching a candle, sounded horrified. "Please, Lord Golden, I've other bedding, if you would—"

"No. I shall not spend the night here. Prepare an accounting immediately."

I knocked on the door. At my entrance, Lord Golden transferred his temper to me. "There you are, you worthless scoundrel! Out carousing, I don't doubt, while I've had to pack my own things and yours, as well. Well, make yourself useful in some way! Run and knock on Huntswoman Laurel's door and tell her we must leave immediately. Then roust the hostler and have our horses made ready. I cannot spend the night at an inn infested with vermin!"

I hastened away from the innkeeper's insistence that he ran a good, clean inn. In a surprisingly short time, we found ourselves outside and ready to ride. I'd saddled our mounts myself; the hostler had not responded to my efforts to roust him. The innkeeper had followed Lord Golden out into the yard, remonstrating that we would find no other inn tonight, but the noble was adamant. He mounted, and without a word to us, stirred Malta to a walk. Laurel and I followed.

For a time, we kept our sedate pace. The moon had risen, but the crowding houses thwarted her light, and the occasional lamplight leaking through shutters made more shadows than illumination for us. Lord Golden's voice carried softly to both of us. "I heard the gossip in the taproom and judged it best we leave immediately. They fled on the road."

"By going in the dark, we take a large chance on missing their trail," I pointed out.

"I know. But by waiting, we might arrive too late to do anything but bury him. Besides, none of us could sleep, and this way we go ahead of those who will ride out tomorrow."

Nighteyes ghosted up to join us. I quested toward him, and as we joined, the night seemed lighter around us. He snorted at our dust, then trotted up to lead the way. Linked by the Wit, he could not hide from me the effort that cost him. I winced but accepted his decision. I nudged Myblack to keep pace with him.

"Our saddle packs seem bulkier than when we first arrived," I observed to the night as Myblack came abreast of Malta.

Lord Golden lifted one shoulder in a careless shrug. "Blankets. Candles. Anything else that I thought might prove useful to us. I ghosted the kitchens, once I knew that we'd have to be on the road swiftly, so there is bread in that sack, as well. And apples. If I'd taken much more than that, it would have been noticed. Try not to crush the loaves."

"One would think you two had done this sort of thing before, Lord Golden." There was an edge to Laurel's tone, and just enough query on the honorific to sober us both. When neither of us came up with words, she added, "I don't think it quite fair that I share the risks of this venture, but still go blindfolded between you."

Lord Golden spoke in his best aristocratic tone. "You're right, Huntswoman. It is not fair, yet that is how it must remain for a time. For unless I am mistaken, we need to put on some speed. As our Prince left this town at a gallop, so shall we."

He acted as he spoke, setting his heels to Malta, who sprang forward joyously to challenge Myblack for the lead. Laurel was at his side in an instant. *Later, my brother.* I felt Nighteyes part himself from me, both mentally and physically. He knew he could not keep up with the running horses. He would follow at his own pace and on his own path. That sundering wrenched me, even as I knew it was his choice and the wisest course of action. Naked of him, stripped of his night vision, I rode on, letting Myblack choose her path as we cantered three abreast past the huddled houses.

The village was small. We reached the outskirts swiftly. The moon's light spilled down the ribbon of road. Malta broke into a gallop, and both the other horses bolted forward to keep up with her. We passed farmsteads, and fields both harvested and standing. I tried to keep watch for the tracks of running horses leaving the road, but saw nothing. We let the horses run until they wanted to slow down and breathe. As soon as Malta tugged at her bit, Lord Golden let her have her head and we were off again. The two were more of one mind than I had realized. It was his complete trust that gave her such cheeky confidence. We rode through what remained of the night, and Lord Golden set our pace.

As dawn grayed the skies, Laurel spoke my thoughts aloud. "At least we have a good start on those who intended to ride out at dawn to see what luck their fellows had in hunting Piebalds. And clearer heads."

She left unspoken a fear I knew we all shared; that we had lost the Prince's trail in our haste to follow him. As the strengthening day hid the moon from us, we rode on. Sometimes one has to trust to luck, or to believe in fate as the Fool did.

chapter XX

STONES

There are techniques a man can use to deal with torture.
One is to learn to divorce the mind from the body. Half the
anguish that a skilled torturer inflicts is not the physical
pain, but the victim's knowledge of the level of damage
done. The torturer must walk a fine line if he wishes his
victim to talk. If he takes his destruction past what the
victim knows can heal, then the victim loses all incentive to
talk. He but wishes to plunge more swiftly into death. But if
he can hold the torment short of that line, then the torturer
can make the victim an accomplice in his own torment.
Suspended in pain, the anguish for the victim is wondering
how long he can maintain his silence without pushing his
tormentor over the line into irrevocable damage. As long as
the victim refuses to talk, then the torturer proceeds,
venturing closer, ever closer to damage the body cannot
repair.

    Once a man has been broken by pain, he remains
forever a victim. He cannot ever forget that place he has
visited, the moment when he decided that he would
surrender everything rather than endure more pain. It is a
shame no man ever completely recovers from. Some try to
drown it by becoming the perpetrator of similar pain, and
creating a new victim to bear for them that shame. Cruelty
is a skill taught not only by example but by experience of it.

    ❧ FROM THE SCROLL "VERSAAY'S USES OF PAIN"

As the sun rose, we rode on. Farmsteads, cultivated fields,
and pastures became less common, and then vanished to be
replaced by rocky hillsides and open forest. My anxiety was

divided between fear for my wolf and for my young Prince.
All in all, I had greater faith in my four-legged companion's
ability to take care of himself than I did in Dutiful. With a
resolution Nighteyes would have approved, I set him out of
my thoughts and concentrated on the road beside me. The
increasing heat of the day was exacerbated by the thickness
of the air. I could feel a storm brewing. A heavy rainfall
might take all trace of their trail from the road. Tension
chewed at me.

Without speaking of it, Laurel rode close to the left-
hand side of the road and I the right. We looked for any
sign of horses leaving the road; specifically, we looked for
sign of at least three horses, galloping in flight. I knew that
if I were fleeing mounted pursuers my first thought would
have been to get off the road and take to the woods where
there was a better chance of losing them. I assumed the
Prince and his companions would do the same.

My fears that we had missed their trail in the dark built,
but suddenly Laurel cried out that she had them. I no
sooner looked at the marks than I was sure she was right.
Here were a plentitude of shod hooves leaving the road,
and all in haste. The wide tracks of the great warhorse were
unmistakable. I was certain we had discovered where the
Prince had left the road with his companions, and where
the mob had pursued them.

As the others left the road and followed, I paused and
dismounted briefly on the pretense of securing our baggage
better to Myblack's saddle. I used the opportunity to relieve
myself at the side of the road, knowing Nighteyes would be
seeking sign of my passage.

Mounted again, I swiftly caught up with the others. A
darkness gathered at the far horizon. We heard several long
rumbling threats of thunder in the distance. The trampled
path of the pursuit was easy to follow, and we urged our
weary beasts to a canter as we followed it. Over two open
hills of grass and scrub we followed them. As we ascended
the third hill, a forest of oak and alder came down to meet

us. There we caught up with the pursuers. There were half a dozen of them, sprawled in the tall grass in the shadows of the trees.

Their ambushers had killed their mounts and the dogs, as well. It was a wise thing to do; riderless horses returning to the village would have brought out the pursuit much sooner. Yet the act sickened me, the more so because it had been done by those of Old Blood. It seemed ruthless in a way that frightened me. The animals had done nothing to deserve death. What sort of folk were these that the Prince rode with now?

Laurel covered her mouth and nose with her hand and held it there. She did not dismount. Lord Golden looked tired and sickened, but he dismounted alongside me. Together we moved among the dead, inspecting them. They were all young men, just at the age to be caught up in such madness. Yesterday afternoon, they had leapt onto their horses and ridden off to kill some Piebalds. Yesterday evening, they had died. Lying there, they did not look cruel or vicious or even stupid. Only dead.

"There were archers in those trees," I decided. "And they were waiting here. I think the Prince's party rode through, relying on folk that already were in position here to protect them." I had found but one broken arrow, cast aside. The others had been frugally and coolly recovered from the bodies.

"That is not the mark of an arrow." Lord Golden pointed out a body that lay apart from the others. There were deep puncture wounds in his throat. Powerful clawed hind legs had disemboweled him. His guts buzzed and clustering flies covered the look of horror in his eyes.

"Look at the dogs. Cats attacked them, as well. All the Piebalds rounded and stood together here, and killed those who followed."

"And then they rode on."

"Yes." Had the Prince's cat killed this man? Had their minds been joined as the cat killed?

"How many do you think we follow now?"

Laurel had ridden a little way ahead. I suspected she did so to be away from the bloating bodies as much as to study the trail. I didn't blame her. Now she called back in a low voice, "I make it at least eight that we follow now."

"And follow we must," Lord Golden said. "Immediately."

Laurel nodded. "There will be others from the village riding out by now, wondering why these men have not returned. When they find these bodies, their fury will drive them mad. The Prince must be extricated before these two groups clash."

Her words made it sound so simple. I went back to Myblack, who annoyed me by sidling away twice before I could catch her reins. She wanted schooling but now was not the time for it. I reminded myself that blood will unnerve the calmest animal, and that patience with her now would pay great dividends later. "A different rider would give you a fist between the ears for that," I told her mildly after I was mounted.

Her shiver of apprehension surprised me. Evidently she was more aware of me than I supposed. "Don't worry. I don't do things like that," I reassured her. Horselike, she ignored my calming remark. Thunder rolled again in the distance and she laid her ears back flat.

I think it bothered all of us to ride away and leave those bodies swelling in the heat. Realistically, it was the wise thing to do. Their fellows would find them soon enough, and to them should fall the burying. The delay it would cause them would work to our good.

Wise or not, it felt wrong.

The tracks we followed now were the deep cuts of hard-ridden horses. The soil under the forest roof was moister and held the trail better. At first, they had ridden for distance and speed, and a child could have followed their marks. But after a time, the trail descended into a ravine and followed a twisting stream. I rode with my eyes on the trees overhead, trusting Myblack to follow Malta's lead as I watched for possible ambush. An unspoken concern occupied my mind. The Piebalds the Prince rode with seemed very organized, almost to a military level. This was the second group of men who had waited for the Prince, and then ridden on with him. At least one member of the party had not hesitated to sacrifice his life for the others, nor had they scrupled at slaughtering all those who followed them. Their readiness and ruthlessness bespoke a great determination to keep the Prince and bear him on to whatever destination they had in mind. Retrieving him was very likely beyond our abilities, yet I could discover no alternatives save to follow them. Sending Laurel back to Buckkeep to fetch the guard was not feasible. By the time she returned, it would be too late. We would lose not only time, but the secrecy of our mission.

The ravine widened and became a narrow valley. Our quarry left the stream. Before we departed it, we paused briefly to refill waterskins and share out a bit of the Fool's purloined bread and some apples. I bought a bit of Myblack's favor with the apple core. Then we were up and off again. The long afternoon wore on. None of us had spoken much. There was little to say unless we worried out loud. Danger rode behind us, as well. In either direction we were outnumbered, and I badly missed my wolf at my side.

The trail left the valley floor and wound up into the hills. The trees thinned and the terrain became rocky. The hard earth made tracking more difficult, and we went more slowly. We passed the stony foundations of a small village, long abandoned. We rode past odd hummocky formations that jutted from the boulder-strewn hillside. Lord Golden saw me looking at them and said quietly, "Graves."

"Too big," I protested.

"Not for those folk. They built stone chambers to hold their dead, and often entire families were interred in them as they died."

I looked curiously back at them. Tall dead grass waved

on the mounds. If there was stone beneath that sod, it was well covered. "How do you know such things?" I demanded of him.

He didn't meet my eyes. "I just do, Badgerlock. Put it down to the advantages of an aristocratic education."

"I've heard tales of these sorts of places," Laurel put in, her voice hushed. "They say tall thin ghosts rise from those mounds sometimes, to capture straying children and . . . Oh, Eda save us. Look. The standing stone from the same tales."

I lifted my eyes to follow her pointing finger. A shiver walked up my back.

Black and gleaming, the stone stood twice as tall as a man did. Silver veined it. No moss clung to it. The inland breezes had been kinder to it than the salt-heavy storm winds that had weathered the Witness Stones near Buck-keep. At this distance, I could not see what signs were carved into its sides, but I knew they would be there. This stone pillar was kin to the Witness Stones and to the black pillar that had once transported me to the Elderling city. I stared at it, and knew it had been cut from the same quarry that had birthed Verity's dragon. Had magic or muscle borne it so far from that place to this?

"Do the graves go with the stone?" I asked Lord Golden.

"Things that are next to each other are not always re-lated to one another," he observed smoothly, and I knew he evaded my question. I turned slightly in the saddle to ask Laurel, "What does the legend say about the stone?"

She shrugged one shoulder and smiled, but I think the intensity of my question made her uneasy. "There are lots of tales, but most have the same spine." She drew a breath. "A straying child or an idle shepherd or lovers who have run away from forbidding parents come to the mounds. In most tales they sit down beside them to rest, or to find a bit of shade on a hot day. Then the ghosts rise from the mounds, and lead them to the standing stone. And they follow the ghost inside, to a different world. Some say they never come back. Some say they come back aged and old after being gone but a night, but others say the opposite: that a hundred years later, the lovers came back, hand in hand, as young as ever, to find their quarreling parents long dead and that they are free to wed."

I had my own opinion of such tales, but did not voice them. Once I had stepped through such a pillar, to find myself in a distant dead city. Once the black stone walls of that long-dead city had spoken to me, and the city had sprung to life around me. Monoliths and cities of black stone were the work of the Elderlings, long perished from the world. I had believed the Elderlings had been denizens of a far realm, deep in the mountains behind Kettricken's Mountain Kingdom. Twice now I had seen evidence that they had walked these Six Duchies hills, as well. But how many summers ago?

I tried to catch Lord Golden's eye, but he stared straight ahead and it seemed to me that he hastened his horse on. I knew by the set of his mouth that any question I asked him would be answered with another question or with an evasion. I focused my efforts on Laurel.

"It seems odd that you would hear tales of this place in Farrow."

She gave that small shrug again. "The tales I heard were of a similar place in Farrow. And I told you. My mother's family came from a place not far from the Bresinga holdings. We often visited, when she was still alive. But I'd wager that the folk around here tell the same sort of tales about those mounds and that pillar. If any folk do live around here."

That seemed unlikely as the day wore on. The farther we rode on, the wilder the country became. The horizon darkened and the storm muttered threats but came no nearer. If these valleys had ever known the plow, or these hills ever nurtured pasturing kine, they had forgotten it these many years. The earth was dry, stones thrusting out amongst the clots of dried-up grasses and scrubby brush.

Chirring insects and birdcalls were the only signs of animal life. The trail became more difficult to follow and perforce we went more slowly. Often I glanced back behind us. Our tracks atop the tracks we followed would make it easier for our pursuers to catch up with us, but I could think of no alternative.

The constant hum of the insects suddenly hushed off to our left. I turned toward it, my heart in my mouth, but an instant later I felt my brother's presence. Two breaths, and I could see him. As always I marveled at how well the wolf could hide himself even in the scantiest of cover. As he drew closer, my gladness at seeing him turned to dismay. He trotted determinedly, head down, and his tongue hung nearly to his knees. Without a word to the others, I pulled up Myblack and dismounted, taking down my waterskin. He came to me, to drink water from my cupped hands.

How did you catch up so swiftly?

You follow tracks, going slowly to find your way. I followed my heart. Where your path has wound through these hills, mine brought me straight to you, over terrain a horse would not relish.

Oh, my brother.

No time to pity me. I came to bring you warning. You are followed. I passed those who come behind you. They stopped at the bodies. They were enraged, shouting to the skies. Their anger will delay them for a time, but when they come on, they will ride fast and furious.

Can you keep up?

I can hide, far more easily than you can. Instead of thinking of what I will do, you should think of what you should do.

There was little enough we could do. I remounted, kicked Myblack, and caught up with the others. "We should try for more speed."

Laurel gave me a look, but said nothing. Only a shift in Lord Golden's posture betrayed he had heard me, but in answer Malta sprang forward. Myblack suddenly decided she would not be outdone. She leapt forward, and in four strides we led the way. I kept my eyes on the ground as we hurried along. It looked as if the Prince and his fellows had made for the shelter of some trees; I applauded their decision. I looked forward to gaining the cover. I urged a bit more speed from Myblack and led us all directly into the ambush.

A mental shout from Nighteyes prompted me to rein to one side. Laurel took the arrow, dropping to the earth with a cry. The shot had been intended for me. Fury and horror blazed up in me and I rode Myblack straight at the stand of trees. My luck was that there was only one archer, and he had not had time to nock another arrow. As we passed under the downsweeping branches, I stood up in my stirrups, miraculously caught a firm hold, and pulled myself up on the branch. The archer was trying to swing his arm to bring the arrow to bear on me, but the intervening small branches were hampering him. There was no time to think about consequences. I launched myself at him, springing like a wolf. We fell in a tangle of two men and the bow. A projecting branch nearly broke my shoulder without breaking our fall. It turned us in the air. We landed with the young archer on top of me.

The impact slammed the air out of me. I could think but not act. Nighteyes saved me the need. He dashed in, a rush of claws and teeth that swept the youth off my body. I felt our attacker's surprised attempt at a *repel* against Nighteyes. I think he was too shocked to put much strength into it. I lay on the earth as they fought beside me, trying frantically to pull air into my lungs. He swung a fist but Nighteyes dodged and seized his passing wrist. The archer shrieked and launched a wild kick at the wolf. I felt its stunning impact. Nighteyes kept his hold but lost the strength in it. As the man wrenched his torn wrist from the wolf's jaws, I found enough breath to act.

From where I lay, I kicked the archer in the head. I flung myself on top of the man. My hands found his throat as Nighteyes seized his right calf in his jaws and hung on. The man flopped wildly between us but could not escape.

Nighteyes worried his leg. I squeezed his throat and held on until I felt his struggles cease. Even then, I kept a grip on his throat with one hand as my other found my belt knife. The entire world had shrunk to a reddened circle that was my vision of his face.

". . . kill him! Don't kill him! Don't kill him!"

Lord Golden's shouts penetrated my mind finally as I held the knife to our attacker's throat. I had never been less inclined to listen. Yet as the red haze of battle faded from my vision, I found myself looking down at a boy little older than Hap. His blue eyes stood out in their sockets, both in horror of death and for lack of air. Something in our fall had scraped the side of his face and blood stood out in fine rows on his cheek. I loosened my grip and Nighteyes dropped his leg. But still I straddled his chest and held my knife to his throat. I was not at all sentimental as to the innocence of young boys. We'd already seen this one's bow-work. He would as soon kill me as not. I kept my gaze on him as I asked the Fool, "Is Laurel dead?"

"Scarcely!" The incensed voice was female. Laurel staggered over to us. A glance showed me her hand clamped tight to the point of her shoulder. Blood was leaking through her fingers. She had already pulled the arrow out.

"Did you get the head out?" I asked quickly.

"I would not have pulled it out if I hadn't been sure I could get the whole thing," she replied waspishly. Pain did not improve her temperament. She was pale but two bright spots of color stood on her cheeks. She looked down at the boy I straddled and her eyes went very wide. I heard her take a ragged breath.

Nighteyes stood beside me, panting heavily. *We should get out of here.* The thought was sluggish with pain. *Others may come. Those who follow or those who went ahead.* I saw the boy's brow furrow.

I glanced at Laurel. "Can you ride as you are? Because we must leave here. We need to question him, but this isn't the time. We don't want to be caught by those who follow, or by his friends coming back for him."

I could tell by her eyes that she didn't know the answer to my question but she lied bravely. "I can ride. Let's go. I too have questions I'd like to ask this one." The archer stared at her, horror-stricken at the venom in her voice. He suddenly bucked under me, trying to escape. I backhanded him with my free hand. "Don't try that again. It's much easier for me to kill you than drag you along."

He knew I spoke truth. His eyes went to Lord Golden and then to Laurel before his gaze came back to me. He peered up at me, blood leaking from his nose, and I recognized his shocked look. This was a young man who had killed, but never before been in imminent danger of being killed. I felt oddly qualified to introduce him to the sensation. No doubt I had once worn that same expression.

"On your feet." Fifteen years ago, I would have backed up the command by hauling him upright. Now I kept a grip on his shirtfront but let him stand up himself. I was short of breath after our tussle, and not inclined to spend my reserves on a show of strength. Nighteyes lay down on the moss beneath the tree, unabashedly panting.

Disappear, I suggested to him.

In a moment.

The archer stared from me to my wolf and back again, confusion growing in his eyes. I refused to meet his gaze. Instead, I cut the leather thong that fastened the collar of his shirt. He flinched as my knife blade tugged through it. I jerked the leather loose, and roughly turned him. "Your hands," I demanded, and without quibbling, he put them behind him. The fight seemed to have gone out of him. The teeth marks in his wrist were still bleeding. I tied his wrists tightly together. I completed my task and glanced up to find Laurel glowering at my prisoner. Obviously, she was taking the attack personally. Perhaps no one had ever tried to kill her before. The first time is always a memorable experience.

Lord Golden assisted Laurel into the saddle. I knew she wanted to refuse his help, but didn't dare. Missing her mount would be more humiliating than accepting his support. That left Myblack to carry my captive and me. Neither my horse nor I were happy with it. I picked up the archer's bow, and after a moment's hesitation, flung it up into the tree where it snagged and hung. With luck, no one passing here would happen to glance up and see it. From the way he stared after it, I knew it had been precious to him.

I took up Myblack's reins. "I'm going to mount," I told my captive. "Then I'm going to reach down and pull you up behind me. If you don't cooperate, I'm going to knock you cold and leave you for those others. You know the ones I mean. The ones you thought we were, the killers from the village."

He moistened his lips. The whole side of his face had started to puff and darken. For the first time, he spoke. "You aren't with them?"

I stared at him coldly. "Did you even wonder about that before you shot at me?" I demanded. I mounted my horse.

"You were following our trail," he pointed out. He looked over at the woman he had shot and his expression was almost stricken. "I thought you were the villagers coming to kill us. Truly."

I rode Myblack over to him and reached down. After an instant's hesitation, he hitched his shoulder up toward me. I got a firm grip on his upper arm. Myblack snorted and turned in a circle, but after two hops, he managed to get a leg over her. I gave him a moment to settle behind me, and then told him, "Sit tight. She's a tall horse. Throw yourself off her, you'll likely break a shoulder."

I glanced back the way we had come. There was still no sign of pursuit, but I had a sense of our luck running out. I looked around. The trail of the Witted led uphill, but I didn't want to follow them farther until I had wrung from this boy whatever he knew. My eyes plotted out a possible ruse. We could go downhill to where a stream probably flowed in winter. The moister soil at the bottom of the hill would take our tracks well. We could follow the old streambed for a time, then leave it. Then up the opposite side and across a rocky hillside and back into cover. It might work. Our tracks would be fresher, but they might just assume they were catching up. We might draw the pursuers off the Prince.

"This way," I announced, and put my plan into action. My horse was not pleased with her double burden. She stepped out awkwardly as if determined to show me this was a bad idea.

"But the trail . . ." Laurel protested as we abandoned the faint tracks we had followed all day.

"We don't need their tracks. We've got him. He'll know where they're headed."

I felt him draw a breath. Then he said, through gritted teeth, "I won't tell."

"Of course you will," I assured him. I kicked Myblack at the same time that I asserted to her that she *would* obey me. Startled, she stepped out, and despite the added weight, she bore us both well. She was a strong and swift horse, but one accustomed to using those traits only as she pleased. We would have to come to terms about that.

I made her move fast down the hill and then pushed her along the stream until we came to a dry watercourse that met it. It was stony and that pleased me. We diverged there, and when I came to a rock-scrabble slope, we went up it. Behind me, the archer hung on with his knees. Myblack seemed to handle the challenge without too much effort. I hoped I was not setting too difficult a pace and course for Laurel. I urged Myblack up the gravelly hill at a steep angle. If I had lured the village mob into following us, I hoped this would present them with some nasty tracking.

At the top of the hill, I paused for the others to catch up. Nighteyes had vanished. I knew he rested now, gathering his strength to come after us. I wanted my wolf at my side, yet I knew he was in less danger by himself than in my company. I scanned the surrounding terrain. Night would be coming on soon, and I wanted us out of sight and in a defensible location, one that overlooked other approaches. Up, I decided. The hill we were on was part of a ridgeline hummocking through the land. Its sister was both higher and steeper, the rocks of her bones showing more clearly.

"This way," I told the others, as if I knew what I was doing, and led them on. We descended briefly into a scantily wooded draw, and then I led them up again, following a dry streambed. Chance and good fortune blessed us. On the next hillside, I encountered a narrow game trail, obviously made by something smaller and more agile than horses. We followed it. For a large horse, Myblack managed well, but I heard my captive catch his breath several times as the trail edged across the hill's steep face. I knew Malta would make nothing of this. I dared not look back to see how Laurel was faring. I had to trust Whitecap to bear his mistress along.

My captive dared to speak to me. "I am Old Blood." He whispered it insistently, as if it should mean something to me.

"Are you?" I replied in sarcastic surprise.

"But you are—"

"Shut up!" I cut his words off fiercely. "Your magic matters nothing to me. You're a traitor. Speak again, and I'll throw you off the horse right now."

He resumed a stunned silence.

As the path led up and up, I wondered if I had chosen well. The few trees we passed were twisted and gaunt, the leaves hanging limp in the hovering storm's aura. The flesh of the earth gave way to bony stones. I knew my refuge when I saw it. It was not a true cave, but was more a deep undercut in a cliff. We had to dismount to coax our horses the rest of the way up to it. I led Myblack in. It was cooler beneath the undercut and water oozed from the rock face at the back. Perhaps at some times of the year it had been responsible for carving the undercut, but now it did little more than leave a damp, green streak on the cave floor before it dribbled away down the hillside. There was no feed for the horses. It could not be helped. It offered us the best shelter and it looked defensible.

"We'll spend the night here," I announced quietly. I wiped sweat from my brow and neck. The storm was lowering and the air thick with the threat of rain. I pointed to a spot near the back of the cavern. "Get down and sit there," I told my prisoner. He spoke not a word, but sat, staring down at me. I gave him no second chance. I reached up, seized the front of his shirt, and jerked him off the horse. Anger has always multiplied my strength. I let him almost stand, then flung him hard from me, so that he hit the back wall of the cave and then slid down it to sit flat on the floor, half-stunned. "There's worse to come," I promised him harshly.

Laurel stared, white-faced and wide-eyed, probably shocked at my taking command. I took her horse from her and Lord Golden helped her ease herself down. My captive showed no inclination to try to flee, and so I ignored him as I unsaddled the horses and set up our makeshift camp. My black lipped and then sucked at the traces of water. I scraped away sand to deepen the depression at the bottom of the wall and, gratifyingly, water began to pool there. Lord Golden was seeing to Laurel's shoulder. Deft as the Fool had always been, he had cut and peeled the clothing back from the injury. Now he held a dampened cloth to it. The blood on the cloth looked dark rather than bright. Their heads were bowed together over it in quiet talk. I drew closer. "How bad is it?" I asked quietly.

"Bad enough," Lord Golden replied succinctly, but it was Laurel's glance that shocked me. She stared at me as if I were a rabid beast. It was far more than the affront she might take at one who had rudely interrupted a private conversation. I withdrew, wondering if the baring of her shoulder before me was what bothered her. Yet she seemed to have no qualms about Lord Golden touching her. Well, I had other things to tend, and would intrude no further.

I considered the small supply of food that remained to us. Bread and apples made up most of it. There was little enough for three, and not enough for four. I coldly decided our prisoner could do without. Like as not, he'd had his own provisions, and had probably eaten better today than we had. Thinking of him made me decide to check on him. He was sitting awkwardly, his hands still bound behind him, considering his lacerated leg. I glanced at it, but offered no sympathy. I stood silently over him until he spoke.

"Can I have some water?"

"Turn around," I ordered him and was impassive as he struggled to obey. I untied his wrists. He made a small sound as I jerked the leather thong free of the clotted blood there. Slowly he moved his hands around in front of him. "You can get water over there, when the horses are satisfied."

He nodded slowly. I knew well how badly his shoulders ached by now. My own was still throbbing from striking the tree branch. His scraped face had darkened and scabbed from the damage taken in our fall. One blue eye was shot with blood. Somehow, his injuries made him look even younger. He studied the wrist the wolf had mangled. By the set of his jaw, I knew he was afraid even to touch his injury. Slowly he lifted his eyes to me, and then looked past me.

"Where is your wolf?" he asked me.

I nearly backhanded him. He flinched at my aborted gesture. "You don't ask questions," I told him coldly. "You answer them. Where are they taking the Prince?"

He looked at me blankly and I cursed my own clumsiness. Perhaps he had not known the Prince's identity. Well, too late to call the words back. I'd probably have to kill him anyway. I recognized that thought as Chade's and set it aside. "The boy who rides with the cat," I clarified. "Where are they taking him?"

He swallowed dryly. "I don't know," he lied sullenly.

I wanted to throttle the truth out of him. He threatened me in too many ways. I stood up abruptly before I could give in to my temper. "Yes you do. I'll give you some time to think about all the ways that I could make you tell me. Then I'll be back." I walked a few steps away from him before I forced a grin onto my face and turned. "Oh. And if you think this is a good time to make a run for it . . . well, two or three steps outside, and you'd no longer be wondering where my wolf is."

A white blast of light suddenly flared into our shelter. The horses screamed, and two heartbeats later, thunder shook the earth. I blinked, momentarily blinded, and then outside the mouth of the cave, the rain came down as if someone had overturned a bucket. Abruptly, it was dark outside. A puff of wind carried rain into our cave mouth, and then shifted away. The warmth of the day departed.

I took food over to Lord Golden and Laurel. She looked a bit dazed. He had dragged one of the saddles and a blanket over to make a backrest for her. She pushed her straggling hair back from her face with her left hand. Her right lay in her lap. She had bled more than I thought, for blood had trickled down to clot between her fingers and outline her nails. Lord Golden accepted the bread and apples for both of them.

I glanced at the downpour outside the cave's mouth and shook my head. "This storm will wash every bit of trail away. The good of that is that perhaps the villagers will just take their dead and go home. The bad is that we lose the Prince's trail, too. Making our ambusher talk is our only hope of finding the Prince now. I'll tend to that when I get back." I unbuckled my sword belt and held it out. When neither reached for it, I drew the blade and set it on the ground beside them. I lowered my voice.

"You might have to use it. If you do, don't hesitate. Kill him. If he gets away and manages to warn his friends, we'll have no chance of recovering the Prince. I'm letting him think for a bit. Then I'll get the truth out of him. Meanwhile, I'm going out to get a bit of firewood while there's any still dry. And I'll check to see if anyone is following our trail."

Laurel lifted her good hand to cover her mouth. She suddenly looked sick. Lord Golden's glance went to the prisoner, and then met mine. His eyes were troubled, but surely he knew I had to look for Nighteyes. "Take my cloak," he suggested.

"It would only get as wet as the rest of me. I'll change into dry things when I get back."

He didn't tell me to be careful, but it was in his look. I nodded to it, steeled myself, and walked out into the pouring rain. It was every bit as cold and unpleasant as I expected it to be. I stood, eyes squinted and shoulders hunched to it, peering out through the gray downpour. Then I took a breath and resolutely changed my expectations. As Black Rolf had once shown me, much discomfort was based on human expectations. As a man, I expected to be warm and dry when I chose to be. Animals did not harbor any such beliefs. So it was raining. That part of me that was wolf could accept that. Rain meant being cold and wet. Once I acknowledged that and stopped comparing it to what I wished it to be, the conditions were far more tolerable. I set out.

The rain had turned the pathway up to the cave into a milky stream. The footing was treacherous as I went down it. Even knowing that our tracks were there, I had a hard time seeing them. I allowed myself to hope that rain, dark, and the lack of a trail to follow would send our pursuers back to town. Some would have undoubtedly turned back to the village to bear the tidings of the deaths. Did I dare to hope they all had, bearing the bodies with them?

At the foot of the hill, I paused. Cautiously, I quested out. *Where are you?*

There was no answer. Lightning cracked in the distance, and thunder rumbled a few moments later. The fury of the rain renewed itself in a roar. I thought of my wolf as I had last seen him, battered and tired and old. I threw aside all caution and howled my fear to the sky. *Nighteyes!*

Be quiet. I'm coming. He was as disgusted with me as if I

were a yelping cub. I closed down my Wit, but still sighed in deep relief. If he could be that irritated with me, then he was not in as bad a way as I had feared.

I watched for wood, and found some that was almost dry in the shelter of a long-fallen tree. I took handfuls of the pithy wood from the rotting trunk, and broke dead branches into manageable length. I pulled off my shirt and bundled my tinder and fuel into it in the hopes of keeping it marginally drier. As I toiled back up the hill to the cavern, the rain ceased as abruptly as it had begun. The pattering of secondhand drops from the tree branches and the trickling sounds of water seeking to soak into the earth filled the evening. Somewhere in the near distance, a night bird sang a cautious two notes.

"It's me," I said quietly as I approached the overhang of stone. Myblack snorted a soft reply. I could barely see the others within, but after a few moments, my eyes adjusted. Lord Golden had set out my flint box for me. Luck was with me, and in a few moments, I had a tiny fire kindled in the back of the cave. The smoke crawled along the stony roof until it found its way out. I stepped outside to check that it was not too visible from the hillside below. Satisfied, I returned, to build the fire to a respectable size.

Laurel sat up and then scooted closer to the friendly light. She looked a bit better, but her pain was still evident on her face. I watched her steal a sidelong glance at the archer. There was accusation in her eyes, but also misplaced pity. I hoped she wouldn't try to interfere in what I had to do.

Lord Golden was already muttering through his pack. A moment later, he pulled out one of my blue servant shirts and offered it to me. "Thanks," I muttered. At the edge of the firelight, my prisoner sat with his shoulders hunched. I noticed the neat bandaging on his leg and wrist and recognized the Fool's knots. Well, I had not told him to leave the man alone; I should have known he would tend to him. I dropped my sodden shirt to the floor. As I shook out the dry shirt, Laurel spoke softly from the shadows.

"That's quite a scar."

"Which one?" I asked without thinking.

"Center of your back," she replied as quietly.

"Oh. That one." I tried to keep my voice light. "That was an arrow whose head didn't come out with the shaft."

"So that was your concern earlier. Thank you." She smiled at me.

It was almost an apology. I could think of no reply. Her words and gentle smile had made me self-conscious. Then I became aware of Jinna's charm exposed at my throat. Ah. I finished putting on the dry shirt. Then I took the leggings that Lord Golden handed me and stepped into the shadows behind the horses to change. The dribble of water down the inside wall had swelled to a steady trickle, and a tiny stream was now venturing past the horses and out the mouth of the cave. Well, at least they would have water tonight, if not grass. I tasted a scooped handful. It was earthy but not foul.

Back by the fire, Lord Golden solemnly offered me a hunk of bread and an apple. I had not realized how hungry I was until I took the first bite. All of it would not have filled me, but I ate only the apple and half the bread. Unfortunately, by the last bite, I still felt just as hungry. I ignored that as I had the rain earlier. It was another human-based assumption, that one had the right to a full belly at regular intervals. It was a comforting idea, but not truly necessary to survival. I repeated that several times to myself. I looked up from the flames to find Lord Golden eyeing me. Laurel had tugged a blanket over herself and dozed off. I spoke quietly. "Did he say anything while you were bandaging him?"

Lord Golden considered. Then a smile broke through the façade. "Ouch?" the Fool offered.

I grinned back, then forced myself to face the eventuality. Despite Laurel's shut eyes, I lowered my voice, pitching it only for the Fool's ears. "I have to know everything he knows about their plans. They're organized and they're ruthless. There's more to this than Witted folk helping a runaway boy. I have to make him tell us where they've taken the Prince."

The smile faded from the Fool's face, but Lord Golden's hauteur did not replace it. "How?" he asked in dread.

"However I must," I replied coldly. I felt a sick anger that he would make this harder for me. The Prince and his well-being were what mattered. Not his squeamishness, nor the life of the Old Blood boy who sat by the cavern wall. Not even my own feelings mattered in this. I was doing this for Chade, for my Queen, for the Farseer line, for the Prince himself. This dirty little task was what I had been schooled to do; it was all part of the "quiet work" of an assassin's training. My guts clenched inside me. I pulled my eyes away from the Fool's anxious gaze and stood up. Get it over with. Make him talk. Then kill him. I dared not let him go and we certainly couldn't be hindered by taking him with us. It wouldn't be the first time I'd killed for the Farseers. I'd never had to beat information out of my victim first, but I knew how to do that too. I'd learned those lessons firsthand in Regal's dungeon. I only wished the circumstances had left me another choice.

I turned away from the light and walked into the darkness where the young man waited. He was sitting on the ground, his back to the cavern wall. For a time, I just stood over him, looking down on him. I hoped his dread of this encounter was as great as mine. When he finally gave in and looked up at me, I growled, "Where are they taking him?"

"I don't know," he said, but the words had no strength in them.

I kicked him hard, the toe of my boot catching him under his ribs. I'd gauged it to drive the air from his lungs without doing permanent damage. It wasn't time for that yet. He yelped and curled over his injury. Before he could recover at all, I reached down, grabbed him by the shirt-front, and jerked him to his feet. I had the advantage of height, so I gritted my teeth and held him on his toes. His hands caught at my wrists and tugged feebly. He was still gasping for air.

"Where?" I demanded flatly. Outside, the rain resumed in a sudden hissing roar.

"They . . . didn't . . . say," he wheezed, and all Eda's mercy made me long to believe him. I dared not. I slammed him hard against the cavern wall, so that the back of his head bounced off it. The impact made my bruised shoulder shout at me. I saw him bite his lip against his own pain. Behind me, I heard a muffled sound from Laurel but didn't turn to it.

"You can tell me now or you can tell me later," I warned him as I held him hard against the wall. I hated what I was doing, yet somehow his stupid resistance was fueling my anger toward him. I drew on it, trying to build the will I needed to continue. Quickest was kindest; harshest was actually most merciful. The sooner he talked, the sooner it would be over. He had chosen the path that led him to this. He was a traitor in league with those who had lured Kettricken's son from her side. The heir to the Six Duchies throne might even now be in mortal danger, and what this man knew could let me rescue him. Whatever I did to him now, he had brought upon himself.

Something like a boy's sob shook him. He caught a breath. "Please," he said quietly.

I hardened my heart and drew back my fist.

But you promised. Never again. No more of the killing that brings no meat and Forges the heart. Nighteyes was aghast.

Stay out of this, my brother. I have to do this.

No. You don't. I come. I come as swift as I can. Wait for me, my brother, please. Wait.

I broke free of the wolf's thoughts. Time to end this. Break him. But the stubborn traitor looked very much like a boy fighting desperately to keep his secret. Tears cut clean streaks down his cheeks. The wolf's thoughts had stolen my determination. I found I had set him back on his feet. I had never had any passion for this sort of thing. Some men, I knew well, took pleasure in breaking another man's spirit, but the torture I had endured in Regal's dungeon had locked me forever into the role of victim. Whatever I did to this young man, I would feel. Worse, I would see myself through his eyes, as I became to him what Bolt had been to me. I looked aside before he could see the weakness in my eyes, but it did me no good, for the Fool stood but an arm's length away, and all the horror I tried to suppress was in his gaze. The pity mixed with his horror stung me. He saw. He saw, despite all the years, the beaten boy that still huddled within me, and always would. Somewhere I forever cowered, somewhere I was endlessly unmanned by what had been done to me. It was intolerable that anyone should know that. Even my Fool. Perhaps especially him.

"Don't interfere," I told him harshly, in a voice I had not known I owned. "Go tend to the Huntswoman."

It was as if I had struck him. His mouth opened but no sound came out. I set my own jaw. I made myself cold. I tightened my grip slowly on my captive's collar. He struggled to swallow and then his breath wheezed in his throat. His blue eyes flickered over my scar and broken nose. It was not the face of a merciful, civilized man. Traitor, I reminded myself as I gazed at him. You betray your Prince, just as Regal betrayed Verity. How often had I fantasized about what I would have done to Regal, had I ever been given a chance for vengeance? This boy deserved it just as richly. He would bring the Farseer line to an end if I let him keep his secret. I breathed slowly, staring at him, letting those thoughts come to the front of my mind. I felt them change the set of my mouth and my eyes. My resolve firmed. Time to end this, one way or another. "Last chance," I warned harshly as I took out my knife. I watched my hands as if they belonged to someone else. I put the tip of the bared blade just below his left eye. I let it dig into the skin there. He clenched the eye shut, but we both knew that would not protect it. "Where?"

"Stop him," Laurel pleaded in a shaking voice. "Please, Lord Golden, make him stop." At her words, I felt the man in my grip start to tremble. How frightening for him, that even my companions dreaded what I would do to him. A smile took over my face and froze it in a rictus.

"Tom Badgerlock!" Lord Golden addressed me imperiously. I didn't even turn to his words. He had dragged me into this just as much as Chade and Kettricken had. It was all inevitable now. Let him watch and see where the road led. If he didn't like it, he could avert his eyes. I couldn't. I'd have to live it.

No. You don't. And I refuse to. I won't be bonded to that. I won't allow it.

I felt him before I saw him. A moment later, the faint reach of the firelight picked out his silhouette, and then my wolf tottered in. Water dripped from him; the guard hairs of his coat had gone to downward points. He came a few steps farther into the cave, and then paused to shake himself. The touch of his mind on mine was like a firm hand on my shoulder. He turned my thoughts to him, and to us, pushing aside all other concerns. *My brother. Changer. I am so weary. I am cold and wet. Please. I need your help.* He ventured closer still, and then he leaned against my leg, asking quietly, *Food?* With the physical touch, he pushed aside a darkness that I had not known lived within me, to fill me with his wolfness and the now.

I let go of my prisoner and he sagged away from me. He tried to stand, but his knees gave out and he sat down heavily on the floor. His head fell forward and I thought I heard a muffled sob. He didn't matter right now. I pushed that FitzChivalry Farseer away to become the wolf's partner.

I took a breath. I felt weak with relief at seeing Nighteyes. I clutched at his presence and felt it sustain me. *I saved you some bread.*

Better than nothing. He pressed his shaking body against my leg as he led me back to the fire and its welcome warmth. He waited patiently while I found the chunk of bread for him. I sat down close beside him, heedless of his wet fur, and handed him the bread a bit at a time. When he had finished eating, I smoothed my hand along his back. My touch slicked away rain. The wet had not penetrated his coat, but I could sense his pain and his weariness. Yet his vast love for me was what wrapped me and made me myself again.

I found a thought worth sharing. *How are those scratches healing?*

Slowly.

I slipped my hand down to the flesh of his belly. Mud had spattered on it and contaminated the wounds. He was cold, but the swollen scratches were hot. They were festering. Lord Golden's pot of unguent was still in my saddle pack. I fetched it and, amazingly, Nighteyes let me apply it to the long, raised welts. Honey, I knew, was a drawing thing. It might suck the heat from his wounds. I glanced up, suddenly aware of the Fool beside us. He knelt down and put both his hands on the wolf's head like a benediction. He looked deep into Nighteyes' eyes as he said, "I am so relieved to see you, old friend." I heard the edge of tears in his words. Wariness haunted his voice as he cautiously asked me, "When you are finished with the ointment, might I have some for Laurel's shoulder?"

"Of course," I said quietly. I dabbed a last bit onto Nighteyes, then gave the pot to the Fool. As he leaned closer to take it, he whispered softly, "I have never been so frightened in my life. And there was nothing I could do. I think only he could have called you back."

As he stood, the back of his hand brushed my cheek. I didn't know if he sought to reassure himself or me. I felt an instant of misery for both of us. It was not ended, only put off.

With a sigh, Nighteyes suddenly stretched out beside me. He rested his head on my leg. He stared out toward the mouth of the cave. *No. It is ended. I forbid it, Changer.*

I have to find the Prince. He knows where he is. I have no choice.

I am your choice. Believe in me. I'll track the Prince for you. I doubt this storm has left any trail to follow.

Trust me. I'll find him for you. I promise. Only do not do this thing.

Nighteyes, I can't let him live. He knows too much.

He ignored that thought, or seemed to. Instead, he bade me, *Before you kill him, think of what you take from him. Remember what it is to be alive.*

Before I could reply, he trapped me in his senses and swept me into his wolf's "now." FitzChivalry Farseer and all his concerns were banished. We stared out into the black night outside the cave mouth. The falling rain had wakened all the scents of the hills and he read them for me. The rain was a steady hiss against the ground, masking all other sounds. Beside us, the fire was subsiding. I was peripherally aware of the Fool tending it, feeding it bits of firewood to keep it alive but hoarding our supply against the long night to come. I smelled the smoke, the horses, the other humans . . .

His intent was to take me away from being a man with a man's cares and back to being a wolf. In that, he succeeded better than he planned. Perhaps Nighteyes was wearier than he knew, or perhaps the hissing rain lulled us both into the closeness of puppies that set no boundaries. I drifted into him, into his mind and spirit and then into his body.

Slowly I came to awareness of the flesh that enclosed him. He had no reserves left. The weariness that filled him pushed out all else. He was dwindling, like the fire, taking in sustenance but, nonetheless, growing ever smaller.

Life is a balance. We tend to forget that as we go blithely from day to day. We eat and drink and sleep and assume that we will always rise up the next day, that meals and rest will always replenish us. Injuries we expect to heal, and pain to lessen as times goes by. Even when we are faced with wounds that heal more slowly, with pain that lessens by day only to return in full force at nightfall, even when sleep does not leave us rested, we still expect that somehow tomorrow all will come back into balance and that we will go on. At some point, the exquisite balance has tipped, and despite all our flailing efforts, we begin the slow fall from the body that maintains itself to the body that struggles, nails clawing, to cling to what it used to be.

I stared at the darkness before us. It suddenly seemed that each of the wolf's exhalations was longer than the breaths he drew in. Like a foundering ship, he sank each day deeper into an acceptance of routine pain and decreased vitality.

He slept heavily now, all wariness forgotten, his broad-skulled head on my lap. I drew a stealthy breath and then gently set my hand to his brow.

As a lad, I had been a source of strength for Verity. He had set his hand to my shoulder, and by his Skill, drawn off the strength he desperately needed to fight the Red Ships. I thought back to the day on the riverbank, and what I had done to the wolf then. I had reached him with the Wit, but mended him with the Skill. I had known for some time that the two magics could mingle. I had even feared that my use of the Skill must always be contaminated by the Wit. Now that fear became a hope that I could use the two magics together for my wolf. For one could not just take strength with the Skill; one could lend it.

I closed my eyes and steadied my breathing. The wolf's barriers were down, my Farseer concerns pushed from my mind. Only Nighteyes mattered. I opened myself and willed my strength, my vitality, the days of my life into him. It was like a long exhalation of breath, a flow of life leaving my body and seeping into his. I felt dizzied, yet I sensed him growing steadier, like a wick given a fresh supply of oil. I sent another exhalation of life into him, feeling fatigue seep through me as I did so. It did not matter. What I had given him had steadied him but not restored him; he needed more of my strength. I could eat and sleep and regain my vitality later. Right now, his need was greater.

Then his awareness flared up like a leaping flame, and,

no! He forbade it, jerking his body away from mine. He separated himself from me, throwing up walls that nearly sealed me out. Then his thoughts blasted my mind. *If ever you attempt that again, I will leave you. Completely and forever. You will not see my body, you will not touch my thoughts, and you will not even catch my scent near your trails. Do you understand me?*

I felt like a puppy, shaken and flung aside. The abruptness of the severing left me disoriented. The world swung around me. "Why?" I asked shakily.

Why? He seemed amazed that I could ask.

At that moment, I heard a furtive footfall grating sand. I turned to catch sight of my prisoner darting out the mouth of the cave. I sprang to my feet and leapt after him. In the darkness and rain, I collided with him, and then we were rolling over and over down the rocky hillside in front of the cave. He yelped once as we fell. Then I seized him, and did not let go until we skidded to a halt in the brush and scree at the foot of the slope. Bruised and shaken, we lay panting together as loosened stones bounced past us. My knife was under me, the hilt digging into my hip. I seized the archer by the throat.

"I should kill you right now," I snarled at him. From above, in the darkness, I heard questioning voices. "Be quiet!" I roared at them, and they ceased. "Get up," I told my prisoner savagely.

"I can't." His voice shook.

"Get up!" I demanded. I staggered upright without letting go of him, and then half hauled him to his feet. "Move!" I told him. "Up the hill, back to the cave. Try to run again, and I'll pound you bloody."

He believed me. The reality was that my efforts with Nighteyes had drained me. I could barely keep pace with him as we clambered back up the rain-slick slope. As we scrabbled and slid, a Skill-headache painted bolts of lightning on my eyelids. We were both caked with mud before we regained the cave. Once inside, I ignored Lord Golden's anxious expression and Laurel's questions while I securely trussed my prisoner's wrists behind his back and bound his ankles together. I handled him viciously, the pounding pain in my skull spurring me on. I could feel Laurel and the Fool watching me. It made me feel both angry and ashamed of what I did. "Sleep well," I hissed at him when I was finished. I stepped back from him and drew my knife from its sheath. I heard Laurel's gasp and the prisoner gave a sudden sob. But I only walked to the trickle of water to clean the mud from the hilt and sheath. I sloshed mud off my hands and then rubbed my face with cold water. I'd wrenched my back in the struggle. Nighteyes whined low in his throat, a worried sound at my pain. I clenched my teeth and tried to block it away from him. As I stood up, my prisoner spoke. "You're a traitor to your own kind." Fear of death gave the boy a false courage. He flung his words at me, but I wouldn't even look at him. His voice rose in shrill accusation. "What did they pay you to betray us? What reward is there for you and your wolf if you bring back the Prince? Do they hold a hostage? A mother? Your sister? Do they swear that if you do this, they'll let you and your family live? They lie, you know. They always lie." His shaking voice was gaining volume. "Old Blood hunts Old Blood, and for what? So the Farseers can deny that the blood of the Piebald Prince runs in their line? Or do you work for those who hate the Queen and her son? Will you take him back so that he can be denounced as Old Blood, and the Farseers brought down by those who think they could rule better than they?"

I should have been focused on what he was saying about the Farseers. Instead I heard only his denunciation of what I was. He spoke with certainty. He knew. I tried to brush his words aside. "Your wild accusations mean nothing. I am sworn to the Farseers. I serve my Queen," I replied, though I knew it was stupid to be baited into talking to him. "I will rescue the Prince, regardless of who holds him, or what they are to me—"

"Rescue? Ha! Return him to slavery, you mean." The

archer had transferred his glare to Laurel as if to convince her. "The boy with the cat rides with us to safety, not as a prisoner, but as one coming home to his own kind. Better a free Piebald than a prince in a cage. So you betray him doubly, for he is a Farseer whom you are sworn to serve, and Old Blood kin as truly as you are. Will you drag him back to be hanged and quartered and burned, as so many of us have been? As they killed my brother but two nights ago?" His voice was suddenly choked. "Arno was only seventeen. He had not even the magic, himself. But he was kin to Old Blood, and chose to stand with us, even to giving up his life for us. He declared himself a Piebald and rode with us. Because he knew he was one of us, even if the magic did not work for him." He looked back at me. "Yet there you stand, as Old Blood as I am, you and your Wit-wolf beside you, and you would hunt us to the death. Lie all you wish, for you only shame yourself. Do you think I cannot sense you speaking to him?"

I stared at him. My throbbing head calculated what he had just done to me. By betraying me in front of Laurel, he had not only endangered me; he had taken Buckkeep from me once more. I could not return there now; not with Laurel knowing what I was. Horror had drained all color from her face. She looked as if she would be ill. I saw a shifting in her eyes when I glanced at her, a rearranging of her opinion of me. The Fool's face was very still. It was as if he struggled to conceal so many emotions that he was left wearing no expression at all. Had he already discerned what I must do? It was like a spreading poison. They knew I was Witted. Now it was not just the archer I'd have to kill, but Laurel, as well. If I didn't, I'd always be vulnerable.

Yet if I did, it would destroy all that was between the Fool and me. The assassin's conclusion to that was to kill him, too, so that he would never look at me with those deaths in his eyes.

And then you could kill me, and then you could kill your-

*self, and no one would ever know of all we had shared. It would
remain our shameful secret, taken to the grave with both of us.
Kill us all, rather than admit to anyone what we are.*

As unerring as a cold pointing finger, the thought
jabbed me in the terrible division that had plagued me
since we had captured the archer . . . no, since I had first realized that, for the sake of my Farseer oath, I must set myself
against the Old Blood and against the Prince's wishes for
himself.

"Are you Witted?" Laurel asked me slowly. Her voice
was quiet but the question rang in my ears.

The others were still staring at me. I reached for the lie,
but could not utter it. To speak it would be to deny the wolf.
I was alienated from the Old Blood, yet there was still a kinship that went deeper than emotion or learned loyalties. I
might not live as Old Blood, but the threats that hovered
over their heads menaced me, too.

But I was sworn to the Farseers, and that too was my
bloodline.

What must I do?

*What is right. Be what you are, Farseer and Old Blood
both. Even if it kills us, it will be easier than these endless denials. I'd rather die being true to ourselves.*

It was like pulling my soul out of a morass.

The pain of my Skill-headache abruptly lessened, as if
finding my own decision had freed me of something. I
found my tongue. "I am Witted," I admitted quietly and
soberly. "And I am sworn to the Farseer line. I serve my
Queen. And my Prince, though he may not yet recognize it.
I will do whatever I must to keep my oath of loyalty to
them." I stared at the boy with wolf-eyes, and spoke what
we both knew. "The Old Bloods have not taken him out of
any loyalty or love for him. They do not seek to 'free' him.
They have taken him in an effort to claim him. Then they
will use him. They will be as ruthless in that as they have
been in taking him. But I will not allow that to befall him.

No matter what I must do to assure that he is saved from that, I will do it. I will find where they have taken him and I will take him home. Regardless of what it may cost me."

I saw the archer blanch. "I am a Piebald," he declared shakily. "Do you know what that means? It means I refuse to be ashamed of my Old Blood. That I will declare myself and assert my right to use my magic. And I will not betray my own kind. Even if it means facing my death." Did he say those words to show his determination equaled mine? Then he was mistaken. Obviously he had taken my words as a threat. Another mistake . . . I didn't care. I didn't bother to correct his misapprehension. One night spent in fear would not kill him, and perhaps he might, by morning, be ready to tell me where they were taking the Prince. If not, my wolf and I would find him.

"Shut up," I told him. "Sleep while you can." I glanced at the others, who were watching our exchange closely. Laurel was staring at me with loathing and disbelief. The set lines in the Fool's face aged him. His mouth was small and still, his silence an accusation. I closed my heart against it. "We should all sleep while we can."

And suddenly fatigue was a tide rising around me. Nighteyes had come to sit beside me. He leaned against me, and the bone-weariness he felt was suddenly mine, too. I sat down, muddy and wet as I was, on the sandy floor of the cave. I was cold, but then, it was a night when one should expect to be cold. And my brother was beside me, and between us we had warmth to share. I lay down, put my arm over him, and sighed out. I meant to lie still for just a moment before I rose to take the first watch. But in that instant, the wolf drew me down and wrapped me in his sleep.

chapter XXI

DUTIFUL

In Chaky, there was an old woman who was most skilled at weaving. She could weave in a day what it took others a week to do, and all of the finest work. Never a stitch that she took went awry, and the thread she spun for her best tapestries was so strong that it could not be snipped with the teeth but must be cut with a blade. She lived alone and apart, and though the coins came in stacks to her for her work, she lived simply. When she missed the week's market for the second time, a gentlewoman who had been waiting for the cloak the weaver had promised her rode out to her hut to see if aught was wrong. There was the old woman, sitting at her loom, her head bent over her work, but her hands were still and she did not stir to the woman's knock at her doorjamb. So the gentlewoman's manservant went in to tap on her shoulder, for surely she dozed. But when he did, the old woman tumbled back, dead as a stone, to sprawl at his feet. And from her bosom leapt out a fine fat spider, big as a man's fist, and it scampered over the loom, trailing a thick thread of web. So all then knew the trick of her weaving. Her body they cut in four pieces and burned, and with her they burned all the work known to come from her loom, and then her cottage and loom itself.

        🙵 BADGERLOCK'S "OLD BLOOD TALES"

I awoke before dawn, with the terrible sensation of having forgotten something. I lay still for a time in the darkness, piecing together my uneasiness. Sleepily I tried to recall what had wakened me. Through the tattering veils of a headache, I forced my mind to function. Threads of a tangling nightmare came back to me slowly. They were unnerving; I had been a cat. It was like the worst of the old Wit-tales, in which the Witted one was gradually dominated by his beast until one day he awoke as a shapechanger, doomed to take on the form of his beast and forever prey to his beast's worst impulses. In my dream, I had been the cat, but in a human body. Yet there had been a woman there also, sharing my awareness with the cat, mingled so thoroughly that I could not determine where one began and the other left off. Disturbing. The dream had caught at me, snagged me with its claws, and held me under. Yet some part of me had heard . . . what? Whispers? The soft jingle of harness, the grit of boots and hooves on sand?

I sat up and glared around at the darkness. The fire was no more than a dark red smudge on the earth nearby. I could not see, but I was already certain that my prisoner was gone. Somehow he had wriggled loose, and now he had gone ahead to warn the others that we followed. I gave my head a shake to clear it. He had probably taken my damn horse, as well. Myblack was the only one of the horses dumb enough to allow herself to be stolen without a sound.

I found my voice. "Lord Golden! Awake. Our prisoner has escaped."

I heard him sit up in his blankets, no more than an arm's length away. I heard him scrabble in the darkness, then a handful of wood bits was thrown on the fire. They glowed, and then a small flame of true fire leapt up. It only flared briefly, but what it showed was enough to confound me. Not only our prisoner was missing, but Laurel and Whitecap were gone.

"She went after him," I guessed stupidly.

"They went together." The Fool pointed out the more likely scenario. Alone with me, he completely abandoned Lord Golden's voice and posture. In the fading flare of the fire, he sat up on his blanket, his knees tucked under his chin and his arms wrapped around his legs as he expostulated. He shook his head at his own stupidity. "When you fell asleep, she insisted she would take first watch. She promised to wake me when her duty was over. If I had not been so concerned over your behavior, I might have seen how peculiar that offer was." His wounded look was almost an accusation. "She loosed him, and then they left deliberately and quietly. So quietly that not even Nighteyes heard them go."

There was a question in his words if not his voice. "He isn't feeling well," I said, and bit down on any other explanation. Had the wolf intentionally held me deep in sleep while he allowed them to leave? He still slept heavily by my side, the sodden sleep of exhaustion and sickness. "Why would she go with him?"

The silence lasted too long. Then, unwillingly, the Fool guessed, "Perhaps she thought you would kill him, and she didn't want it to come to that."

"I wouldn't have killed him," I replied irritably.

"Oh? Well, then, I suppose it is good that at least one of us is sure of that. Because frankly, the same fear had crossed my mind." He peered at me through the dimness, and then spoke with disarming directness. "You frightened me last night, Fitz. No. You terrified me. I almost wondered if I knew you at all."

I didn't want to discuss that. "Do you think he could have freed himself and then forced Laurel to go with him?"

He was quiet for a time, then accepted my change of subject. "That is possible, but only just. Laurel is . . . very resourceful. She would have found some way to make a noise. Nor can I imagine why he would do so." He frowned. "Did you think they looked at one another oddly? Almost as if they shared a secret?"

Had he seen something I had not? I tried to think that through, then gave it up as a hopeless task. Reluctantly, I pushed my blanket completely away. I spoke quietly, still not wishing to wake the wolf. "We have to go after them. Now." My wet, muddy clothes from the night before were clammy and stiff on my body. Well, at least I didn't have to get dressed. I stood up. I refastened my sword belt a notch closer to its old setting. Then I stopped, staring at the blanket.

"I covered you," the Fool admitted quietly. He added, "Let Nighteyes sleep, at least until dawn. We will need some light to find their trail." He paused, then asked, "You say we should follow them because you think . . . what? That he will go to wherever the Prince has gone? Do you think he would take Laurel there with him?"

I bit a torn corner off my thumbnail. "I don't know what I think," I admitted.

For a time we both pondered in silence and darkness. I drew a breath. "We must go after the Prince. Nothing must distract us from that. We should go back to where we left his trail yesterday and try to discover it again, if the rains have left anything for us to discover. That is the only path that we are absolutely certain will lead to Dutiful. If that fails us, then we will fall back on trying to follow Laurel and the Piebald and hope that that trail also leads to the Prince."

"Agreed," the Fool replied softly.

I felt oddly guilty because I felt relief. Not just that he had agreed with me, not just that the Piebald had been put out of my reach, but relief that with Laurel and the prisoner gone, we could drop pretenses and just be ourselves. "I've missed you," I said quietly, knowing that he would know what I meant.

"So have I." His voice came from a new direction. In the dark, he was up and moving silently and gracefully as a cat. That thought brought my dream back to me abruptly. I grasped at the tattered fragments of it. "I think the Prince might be in danger," I admitted.

"You're only now concluding that?"

"A different type of danger from what I expected. I suspected the Witted ones of luring him away from Kettricken and the Court, of bribing him with a cat to be his Wit-partner so that they could take him off and make him one of their own. But last night, I dreamed, and . . . it was an evil dream, Fool. Of the Prince displaced from himself, of the cat exerting so much influence over their bonding that he could scarcely recall who or what he was."

"That could happen?"

"I wish I knew for certain. The whole thing was so peculiar. It was his cat, and yet it was not. There was a woman, but I never saw her. When I was the Prince, I loved her. And the cat, I loved the cat, too. I think the cat loved me, but it was hard to tell. The woman was almost . . . between us."

"When you were the Prince." I could tell that he could not even decide how to phrase the question.

The mouth of the cave was a lighter bit of darkness now. The wolf slumbered on. I fumbled through an explanation. "Sometimes, at night . . . it's not exactly Skilling. Nor is it completely the Wit. I think that even in my magic, I am a bastard cross of two lines, Fool. Perhaps that is why Skilling sometimes hurts so much. Perhaps I never learned to do it properly at all. Maybe Galen was right about me, all the time—"

"When you were the Prince," he reminded me firmly.

"In the dreams, I become him. Sometimes I recall who I truly am. Sometimes I simply become him and know where he is and what he is doing. I share his thoughts, but he is not aware of me, nor can I speak to him. Or perhaps I can. I've never tried. In the dreams, it never occurs to me to try. I simply become him, and ride along."

He made a small sound, like breathing out thoughtfully. Dawn came in the way it does at the change of the seasons, going from dark to pearly gray all in an instant. And in the moment, I smelled that summer was over, that the thunderstorm last night had drowned it and washed it away, and the days of autumn were undeniably upon us. There was a smell in the air of leaves soon to fall, and plants abandoning their greenery to sink back into their roots, and even of seeds on the wing seeking desperately for a place to settle and sink before the frosts of winter found them.

I turned away from the mouth of our cave and found the Fool, already dressed in clean clothes, putting the final touch on our packing. "There's just a bit of bread and an apple left," he told me. "And I don't think Nighteyes would fancy the apple."

He tossed me the bread for the wolf. As the light of day reached his face, Nighteyes stirred. He carefully thought nothing at all as he rose, cautiously stretched, and then went to lap water from the pool at the back of the cave. When he came back, he dropped down beside me and accepted the bread as I broke it into pieces.

So. How long have they been gone? I asked him.

You know I let them go. Why do you even ask me that?

I was silent for a time. *I had changed my mind. Couldn't you feel that? I had decided I wouldn't even hurt him, let alone kill him.*

Changer. Last night you bore us both too close to a very dangerous place. Neither one of us truly knew what you would do. I chose to let them go rather than find out. Did I choose wrong?

I didn't know. That was the frightening part, that I didn't know. I wouldn't ask him to help me track Laurel and the archer. Instead I asked, *Think we can pick up the Prince's trail?*

I promised you I would, didn't I? Let us simply do what we must do and then go home.

I bowed my head. It sounded good to me.

The Fool had been juggling the apple in one hand. Once Nighteyes had finished eating, he stopped, gripped the apple in both hands, and then gave it a sudden twist. It broke smoothly into two halves, and he tossed one to me. I caught it, and shook my head at him, grinning. "Every time I think I know all your tricks—"

"You find out how wrong you are," he finished. He ate his half rapidly, saving the core for Malta, and I did the same for Myblack. The hungry horses were not enthusiastic about the day ahead. I smoothed their ragged coats a bit be-

fore I saddled them and fastened our saddle packs to Myblack. Then we led them out and down the gravelly slope,
now slippery with mud. The wolf limped along behind us.

As so often happens after a good thunderstorm, the sky
was blue and clear. The scents of the day were strong as the
rising sun warmed the wet earth. Birds sang. Overhead, a
flock of ducks headed south in the morning light. At the
bottom of the hill, we mounted. *Can you keep up?* I asked
Nighteyes worriedly.

*You'd better hope so. Because without me, you haven't a
chance of trailing the Prince.*

A single set of horse tracks led back the way we had
come. Heavy imprints. They were riding double, as fast as
Whitecap could carry them. Where were they going, and
why? Then I put Laurel and the Piebald out of my head. It
was the Prince we sought.

Whitecap's hoofprints returned to where we had been
ambushed the day before. I noted, in passing, that the
Piebald had retrieved his bow. Then they had ridden back
toward the road. Whitecap's tracks were still pushed deep
in the damp soil. They had gone on together, then.

Theirs were not the only fresh tracks under the tree.
Two other horses had come and gone there since the night's
rain. Their tracks overcut those of the heavily burdened
Whitecap. I frowned over that. These were not the tracks
of the pursuers from the village. They had not come this far;
at least not yet. I decided to hope that the deaths of their
friends and the horrid weather had turned them back.
These fresh tracks came from the northwest, then turned,
and went back that way. I pondered for a time, then the obvious hammered me: "Of course. The archer had no horse.
The Piebalds sent someone back for their sentry." I grinned
ruefully. "At least they've left us a clear trail to follow."

I glanced over but the Fool's face was still. He did not
share my elation.

"What's wrong?"

He gave a sickly smile. "I was imagining how we would feel now if you had killed that boy last night, beating their destination out of him."

I did not want to follow that thought. I said nothing and concentrated on the tracks in the earth. Nighteyes and I led, and the Fool followed. The horses were hungry, and Myblack in particular fractious because of it. She snatched at yellow-veined willow leaves and clumps of dry grass whenever she could, and I felt too much sympathy to correct her. Had I been able to satisfy my belly that way, I would have snatched a handful of leaves myself.

As we pushed on, I saw signs of the rider's haste as he raced back to warn his party that their sentry had been taken. The tracks followed the obvious routes now, the easiest way up a hill, the clearest path through a tongue of woods. The day was still young when we found the remnants of a camp under the spread of an oak grove.

"They must have had a wet, wild night of it," the Fool guessed, and I nodded. The fire spot showed the remains of charred logs extinguished by the downpour and never rekindled. A woven blanket had left its imprint on the sodden ground; whoever had slept there had slept wet. The ground was churned with tracks. Had other Piebalds awaited them here? The departing tracks overcut one another. There was no point in wasting time trying to puzzle it out.

"If we had pressed on yesterday after we encountered the archer, we would have caught them up here," I said remorsefully. "I should have guessed that. They put him in place, knowing that they would not go much farther. He had no horse. It's so obvious now. Damn, Fool, the Prince was within our grasp yesterday."

"Then likely he is today, also. This is better, Fitz. Fate has played into our hands. Today we go unencumbered, and we yet may hope to surprise them."

I frowned as I studied the tracks. "There is no sign that Laurel and the ambusher came this way. So a man was sent back to pick up their sentry and returned alone, with the news that he'd been taken. What they will make of that is hard to say, but they definitely left in a hurry, without their archer. We should assume they'll be on their guard now."

I took a breath. "They will fight us when we try to take the Prince." I bit my lip, then added, "We'd best assume that the Prince will fight us, also. Even if he doesn't, he's going to be of little help to us. He was so vague last night . . ." I shook my head and discarded my concerns.

"So our plan is?"

"Surprise them if we can, hit them hard, take what we want, and get out fast. And ride for Buckkeep as swiftly as we can, because we won't be safe until we are there."

He followed the thought further than I had been willing to. "Myblack is swift and strong. You may have to leave Malta and me behind once you have the Prince. Don't hesitate."

And me.

The Fool glanced at Nighteyes as if he had heard him.

"I don't think I can do that," I said carefully.

Don't fear. I'll protect him for you.

I felt a terrible sinking in my heart. I kept severely to myself the worry, *But who will protect you?* I would not let it come to that, I promised myself. I would not leave either of them. "I'm hungry," the Fool noted. It was not a complaint, merely an observation, but I wished he had not said it. Some things are easier to ignore than acknowledge.

We rode on, the trail much plainer now in the rain-dampened earth. They had cut their losses and pushed on without the archer, just as they had left one of their own behind to die when they had fled the village. Such cold determination spoke loudly to me of how valuable the Prince was to them. They would be willing to fight to the death. They might even kill the Prince rather than let us take him. The fact that we knew so little of their motives would force me to be totally ruthless. I discarded the idea of attempting to talk to them first. I suspected their answer would be the same greeting that their archer had had for us yesterday.

I thought longingly of a time when I would have sent Nighteyes ahead to spy out the way for us. Now, with the trail so clear, the panting wolf was holding us back. I knew the moment when he realized it, for he abruptly sat down beside the trail. I pulled in Myblack, and the Fool halted also.

My brother?

Go on without me. The hunt belongs to the swift and keen.

Shall I go on without my eyes and nose, then?

And without your brain, too, alas. Be on your way, little brother, and save your flattery for someone who might believe it. A cat, perhaps. He came to his feet, and despite his weariness, in a few steps he had melted into the surrounding brush in his deceptively effortless way. The Fool looked askance at me.

"We go on without him," I said quietly. I glanced away from the troubled look in his eyes. I nudged Myblack and we went on, but faster now. We pushed our horses and the tracks before us grew fresher. At a stream, we stopped to let the horses water and to refill our skins. There were late blackberries there, sour and hard, the ones that had turned color but in the shade, without the direct heat of the sun to sweeten them. We ate handfuls of them anyway, glad of anything we could chew and swallow. Reluctantly, we left fruit on the bushes, mounting as soon as the horses had fairly slaked their thirsts. We pushed on.

"I make out six of them," the Fool observed as we rode.

I nodded. "At least. There were cat tracks near the water. Two different sizes."

"We know one rode a warhorse. Should we expect at least one large warrior?"

I shrugged reluctantly. "I think we should expect anything. Including more than six opposing us. They ride toward safety of some kind, Fool. Perhaps an Old Blood settlement, or a Piebald stronghold. And perhaps we are watched even now as we follow." I glanced up. I had not noticed any birds paying us undue attention, but that did not mean there weren't any. With the folk we pursued now, a bird in the air or a fox in a bush could be a spy. We could take nothing for granted.

"How long has it been happening to you?" the Fool asked as we rode.

"The shared dreams with the Prince?" I had not the energy to try to dissemble with him. "Oh, for some time."

"Even before that night you dreamed he was at Galekeep?"

I answered reluctantly. "I'd had a few odd dreams before then. I didn't realize they were the Prince's."

"You hadn't told me of them, only that you'd dreamed of Molly and Burrich and Nettle." He cleared his throat and added, "But Chade had mentioned some of his suspicions to me."

"Did he?" I was not pleased to hear that. I did not like to think of Chade and the Fool discussing me behind my back.

"Was it always the Prince, or only the Prince? Or are there other dreams?" The Fool tried to conceal the depth of his interest, but I had known him too long.

"Besides the dreams you already know about?" I deferred. I debated swiftly, not whether to lie to him, but how much of the truth I wished to share. Lying to the Fool was wasted effort. He had always known when I lied to him, and managed to deduce the truth from it. Limiting his knowledge was the better tactic. And I felt no scruples about it, for it was the device he most often employed against me. "You know that I dreamed of you. And, as I told you, once I dreamed clearly of Burrich, clear enough that I nearly went to him. Those, I would say, are the same types of dreams as those I have had about the Prince."

"You do not, then, dream of dragons?"

I thought I knew what he meant. "Of Verity-as-Dragon? No." I looked away from his keen yellow glance. I mourned my King still. "Even when I touched the stone that had held him, I felt no trace of him. Only that distant

Wit-humming, like a beehive far under the earth. No. Even in my dreams, I do not reach him."

"Then you have no dragon-dreams?" he pressed me.

I sighed. "Probably no more than you do. Or anyone who lived through that summer and watched them fly through the skies over the Six Duchies. What man could have seen that sight, and never dream of it again?" And what Skill-addicted bastard could have watched Verity carve his dragon and enter into it, and not have dreamed of ending that way himself? Flowing into the stone, and taking it on as flesh, and rising into the sky to soar over the world. Of course, I dreamed sometimes of being a dragon. I suspected, nay, I knew, that when old age found me, I would make a futile trek into the Mountains and back to that quarry. But like Verity, I would have no coterie to assist me in the carving of my dragon. Somehow it did not matter that I knew I could not succeed. I could imagine no other death than one devoted to the attempt to carve a dragon.

I rode on, distracted, and tried to ignore the odd looks the Fool cast my way from time to time. I did not deserve the next bolt of luck that struck me, but I was glad of it all the same. As we came to the lip of a small valley, a trick of the terrain provided me with a single glimpse of those we pursued. The narrow valley was forested, but divided by a noisy watercourse swollen by last night's storm. Those we followed were in the midst of fording it. They would have had to turn in their saddles and look up to see us. I reined in, motioning the Fool to do likewise, and silently watched the party below. Seven horses, one riderless. There were two women and three men, one on an immense horse. There were three cats, not two, though in fairness to my tracking skills, two were similar in size. All three cats rode behind their owners' saddles. The smallest cat rode behind a boy, dark haired in a voluminous cloak of Buckkeep blue. The Prince. Dutiful.

His cat's distaste for the water they crossed was evident in her tense posture and the set of her claws. I saw them for but an instant, and felt an odd giddiness at the sight. Then tree branches cloaked them. As I watched, the final rider and her mount lurched from the rocky streambed and up the slick clay bank beyond it. As she vanished into the forest, I wondered if she was the Prince's ladylove.

"That was a big man on the big horse," the Fool observed reluctantly.

"Yes. And they will fight as one. They were bonded, those two."

"How could you tell?" he demanded curiously.

"I don't know," I replied honestly. "It is the same as seeing an old married couple in the market. No one has to tell you. You can just see it, in how they move together and how they speak to one another."

"A horse. Well, that may present some challenges I hadn't expected." It was my turn to give him a puzzled look, but he glanced away from it.

We followed, but more cautiously. We wanted to catch glimpses of them without being seen ourselves. As we did not know where they were going, we could not race ahead to intercept them, even if the rough and wild terrain had offered us that possibility. "Our best option may be to wait until they've settled for the night, and then go in after the Prince," the Fool suggested.

"Two flaws," I replied. "By nightfall, we may reach wherever it is they're going. If we do, we may find them in a fortified location, or with many more companions. The second is that if they camp again, they will post sentries, just as they did before. We'd have to get past them first."

"So your plan is?"

"Wait until they camp tonight," I admitted gloomily. "Unless we see a better opportunity before then."

My premonition of disaster grew as the afternoon passed. The trail we followed showed signs of use by more than deer and rabbits. Other people used this path; it led to somewhere, a town or village, or at the least, a meeting place. I dared not wait for nightfall and their camp.

We ghosted closer than we had before. The unevenness of the terrain we crossed favored us, for as soon as they began their descent of the ridge, we could venture closer. Several times we had to leave the trodden path to keep hidden below the ridgeline, but those we followed seemed confident that they were now in safer territory. They did not often look back. I studied their marching order as trees hid and then revealed them. The man on the big horse led the way, followed by the two women. The second woman led the riderless horse. Our Prince came fourth, with his cat behind him on the saddle. Following him were the two other men and their cats. They rode like folk determined to cover ground before nightfall.

"He looks like you did as a boy," the Fool observed as we once more watched them wend out of sight.

"He looks like Verity to me," I disagreed. It was true. The boy did look like Verity, but he looked even more like my father's portrait. I could not say if he looked like me at that age. I had had little to do with looking glasses then. He had dark, thick hair, as unruly as Verity's and mine. I wondered, briefly, if my father had ever struggled to get a comb through his. His portrait was my only image of him, and in that he was faultlessly groomed. Like my father, the young Prince was long of limb, rangier than stocky Verity, but he might fill out as he got older. He sat his horse well. And just as I had noted with the man on the large horse, I could see his bond with the cat that rode behind him. Dutiful held his head tipped back, as if to be aware always of the cat behind him. The cat was smallest of the three, yet larger than I had expected her to be. She was long legged and tawny, with a rippling pattern of pale and darker stripes. Sitting on her saddle cushion, her claws well dug in, the top of her head came to the nape of the Prince's neck. Her head turned from side to side as they rode, taking in all that they passed. Her posture said that she was weary of riding, that she would have preferred to cross this ground on her own.

Getting rid of her might be the trickiest part of the

whole "rescue." Yet not for an instant did I consider taking her back to Buckkeep with the Prince. For his own good, he would have to be separated from his bond-beast, just as Burrich had once forced Nosey and I to part.

"It just isn't a sound bond. It feels not so much that he has bonded as that he has been captured. Or captivated, I suppose. The cat dominates him. Yet . . . it is not the cat. One of those women is involved in this, perhaps a Witmentor as Black Rolf was to me, encouraging him to plunge into his Wit-bond with an unnatural intensity. And the Prince is so infatuated that he has suspended all his own judgment. That is what worries me."

I looked at the Fool. I had spoken the thought aloud, with no preamble, but as often seemed with us, his mind had followed the same track. "So. Will it be easier to unseat the cat and take both Prince and horse, or snatch the Prince and hold him on Myblack with you?"

I shook my head. "I'll let you know after we've done it."

It was agonizing to shadow after them, hoping for an opportunity that might not come. I was tired and hungry, and my headache from the night before had never completely abated. I hoped that Nighteyes had managed to catch some food for himself and was resting. I longed to reach out to him, but dared not, lest I make the Piebalds aware of me.

Our route had taken us up into the rugged foothills. The gentle plain of the Buck River was far behind us now. As the late afternoon stole the strength of the sun from the day, I saw what might be our only chance. The Piebald party rode silhouetted against a ridgeline. Their trail led to a precipitous path that slashed steeply down and across the face of a sheer and rocky hill. Standing in my stirrups and staring through the thickening light, I decided the horses would have to go in single file. I pointed this out to the Fool.

"We need to catch them up before the Prince begins the descent," I told him. It would be close. We had let them get almost too far ahead of us in an effort to remain hidden from them. Now I put my heels to Myblack, and she sprang forward, with little Malta right behind us.

Some horses are fleet only on a level, straight stretch. Myblack proved herself as able on broken terrain. The Piebalds had taken the easiest route, following the ridgelines. A steep-sided gorge, thick with brush and trees, sliced between them and us. We could cut off a huge loop of trail by plunging down the slope to reach the next ascending jog in the trail. I kneed Myblack and she crashed down through the brushy slope, splashed through the creek at the bottom, and then fought her way up the other side through mossy turf that gave way under her hooves. I did not look back to see how Malta and the Fool were faring. Instead, I rode low to her back, avoiding the branches that would have swept me from the saddle.

They heard us coming. Doubtless we sounded more like a herd of elk or a whole troop of guardsmen than a single horseman bent on catching up with them. In response to the sound of our pursuit, they fled. We caught them at the last possible moment. Three of their party had already ventured out onto the steep, narrow trail across the hill face. The lead horse had just begun the descent. The three horses remaining carried cats as well as riders. The last one wheeled to meet my charge with a shout, while the second-to-last chivied the Prince along as if to hurry him out onto the escarpment.

I crashed into the one who had turned to confront us, more by accident than by any battle plan. The footing on the mountainous path was treacherous with small rolling stones. As Myblack slammed shoulder to shoulder with the smaller horse, the cat leapt from its cushion yowling a threat, landed downhill from us, and slid and scrabbled away from the plunging hooves of the struggling horses.

I had drawn my sword. I urged Myblack forward, and she easily shouldered the smaller horse off the path. As I passed, I plunged my sword once into a man who was still attempting to draw a wicked toothed knife. He cried out, and the cat echoed his cry. He began a slow topple from his saddle. No time for regrets or second thoughts, for as we pressed past him, the second rider turned to meet us. I could hear confused shouts from women, and overhead a crow circled, cawing wildly. The narrow passage had a sheer rock face above it, and a slippery scree slope below it. The man on the big horse was shouting questions that no one was answering, interspersed with demands that the others back up and get out of his way so he could fight. The path was too confined for him to wheel his horse. I had a glimpse of his warhorse trying to back along the cramped trail while the women on the smaller horses behind him were trying to ride forward and escape the battle behind them. The riderless horse was between the women and the Prince. A woman screamed to Prince Dutiful to hurry up at the same moment that the man on the big horse demanded that they both back up and give him room. His horse obviously shared his opinion. His massive hindquarters were crowding the far smaller horse behind him. Someone would have to give way, and the likeliest direction was down.

"Prince Dutiful!" I bellowed as Myblack chested the rump of the next horse. As Dutiful turned toward me, the cat on the horse between us opened its mouth in a yowling snarl and struck out at Myblack's head. Myblack, both insulted and alarmed, reared. I barely avoided her head as she threw it back. As we came down, she clattered her front hooves against the other horse's hindquarters. It did little physical damage, but it unnerved the cat, who sprang from her cushion. The rider had turned to confront us, but could not reach me with his short sword. The Prince's horse, blocked in front, had halted half on the narrowing trail. The riderless horse in front of him was trying to back up, but the Prince had no room to yield to him. Dutiful's cat was snarling angrily but had nowhere to vent her rage. I looked at her, and felt an odd doubling of vision. All the while, the man on the great horse was bellowing and cursing, demanding furiously that the others get out of his way. They could scarcely obey him.

The rider I had engaged managed to wheel his horse on the meager apron of earth that led to the narrow path across the hill face, but he nearly trampled his cat in doing so. The beast hissed and made a wild swipe at Myblack, but she danced clear of the menacing claws. The cat seemed daunted; I was sure my horse and I were far larger than any game he might normally pursue. I took advantage of that hesitation, kicking Myblack forward. The cat retreated right under the hooves of her partner's horse. The horse, reluctant to trample the familiar creature, in turn backed up, crowding the Prince's horse forward.

On the slender ledge of the path, a horse screamed in sudden panic, echoed by the owner's cry as it went down in an effort to avoid being pushed off the ledge by the warhorse that was backing determinedly toward us. The young woman on the horse kicked free of the stirrups and scrambled to stand, her back pressed against the ledge as the panicky animal, in a frantic bid to regain its footing, stumbled to one side and then slid off the edge. The woman's horse slid down the steep slope, slowly at first, its churning efforts to halt its fall only loosening more stone to cascade with it. Spindly saplings that had found a footing in the sparse soil and cracked rock were snapped off as the horse crashed through them. The animal screamed horribly as one sapling, stouter than the others, stabbed deep into it and arrested its fall briefly before its struggles tore it loose to slide again.

Behind me, there were other sounds. I gathered without looking that the Fool had arrived, and that he and Malta were busying the other cat. His partner, I trusted, would still be down. My sword thrust had gone deep.

Ruthlessness soared in me. I could not reach the cat's owner with my blade, but the spitting cat menacing Myblack was within range. Leaning down, I slashed at him. The creature leapt wildly aside, but I had scored a long, shallow gash across his flank. Cries of anger and pain from both him and his human partner were my reward. The man reeled with his cat's pain, and I experienced an odd moment of knowing the Wit-curses they flung at me. I closed my mind to them, kicked Myblack, and we slammed together, horse to horse. I stabbed at the rider and when he tried to evade my blade, he tumbled from his saddle. Riderless and panicky, his horse was only too glad to flee the moment Myblack gave it room to get past her. In her turn, the Prince's horse backed away from the struggle before her and off the steep trail onto the small apron of land that approached it.

The cat that rode behind the Prince had bristled her fur to full extension and now confronted me with an angry snarl. There was something wrong with her, something misshapen that appalled me. Even as I struggled to grasp what was awry, the Prince turned his horse and I came face-to-face with young Dutiful.

I have heard people describe instances when all time seemed to pause for them. Would that it had been so for me. I was confronted suddenly with a young man who, until this moment, had been to me little more than a name coupled with an idea.

He wore my face. He wore my face to the extent that I knew the spot under his chin where the hair grew in an odd direction and would be hard to shave, when he was old enough to shave. He had my jaw, and the nose I had had as a boy, before Regal had broken it. His teeth, like mine, were bared in a battle rictus. Verity's soul had planted the seed in his young wife to conceive this boy, but his flesh had been shaped from my flesh. I looked into the face of the son I had never seen or claimed, and a connection suddenly formed like the cold snap of a manacle.

If time had stood still for me, then I would have been ready for the great cut of his sword as he swung it toward me. But my son did not share my moment of stunned recognition. Dutiful attacked like seven kinds of demons, and his battle cry was a cat's ululating cry. I all but fell out of my saddle leaning back to avoid his blade. Even so, it still sliced the fabric of my shirt and left a stinging thread of pain in its wake. As I sat up, his cat sprang at me, screaming like a woman. I turned to his onslaught, and caught the creature in mid-flight with the back of my elbow and arm. I yelled in revulsion as he struck me. Before he could lock onto me, I twisted violently, throwing him in the face of the cat-rider I had just unseated. She yowled as they collided, and they fell together. She gave a sharp screech as he landed on top of her, then clawed her way out from under him, only to scrabble limpingly back from Myblack's trampling hooves. The Prince's gaze followed his cat, a look of horror on his face. It was all the opening I needed. I struck his sword from his unready grip.

Dutiful had expected me to fight him. He was not prepared for me to seize his reins and take control of his horse's head. I kneed Myblack, and for a wonder she answered, wheeling. I kicked her and she sprang to a gallop. The Prince's horse came eagerly. She was anxious to escape the noise and fighting, and following another horse suited her perfectly. I think I shouted to the Fool to flee. In some manner that I did not recognize, he seemed to be holding the clawed Piebald at bay. The man on the warhorse bellowed that we were stealing the Prince, but the cluster of struggling people, horses, and cats could do nothing. My sword still in my hand, I fled. I could not afford to look back and see if the Fool followed. Myblack set a pace that kept the other horse's neck stretched. The Prince's horse could not keep up with Myblack's best speed, but I forced her to go as fast as she possibly could. I reined Myblack from the trail and led Dutiful's mount at breakneck speed down a steep hill and then cross-country. We rode through slapping brush, and clattered up steep rocky hills, and then down terrain where a sane man would have dismounted and led his horse. It would have been suicide for the Prince to leap from his horse. My sole plan was to put as much distance between Dutiful's companions and us as I could.

The first time I spared a glance back at him, Dutiful was hanging on grimly, his mouth set in a snarling grimace and his eyes distant. Somewhere, I sensed, an angry cat followed us. As we came down one steep hillside in a series of leaps and slides, I heard a crashing in the brush behind and above us. I heard a shout of encouragement, and recognized the Fool's voice as he urged Malta to greater speed. My heart leapt with relief that he still followed us. At the bottom of the hill, I pulled Myblack in for an instant. The Prince's horse was already lathered, the white foam dripping from her bit. Behind her, the Fool reined Malta in.

"You're all in one piece?" I asked hastily.

"So it appears," he agreed. He tugged his shirt collar straight and fastened it at the throat. "And the Prince?"

We both looked at Dutiful. I expected anger and defiance. Instead, he reeled in his saddle, his eyes unfocused. His gaze swung from the Fool to me and back again. His eyes wandered over my face, and his brow furrowed as if he saw a puzzle there. "My Prince?" the Fool asked him worriedly, and for that instant, his tone was that of Lord Golden. "Are you well?"

For a moment, he just gazed at both of us. Then, life returned to his face and, "I must go back!" he suddenly shouted wildly. He started to pull his foot free of the stirrup. I kicked Myblack, and in that instant we were off again. I heard his cry of dismay, and looked back to see him clutching frantically at his saddle as he tried to regain his seat. With the Fool at our heels, we fled on.

chapter XXII

CHOICES

The legends of the Catalyst and the White Prophet are not Six Duchies' legends. Although the writings and lore of that tradition are known to some scholars in the Six Duchies, it has its roots in the lands far to the south, beyond even the reaches of Jamaillia and the Spice Islands. It is not properly a religion, but is more a concept both of history and philosophy. According to those who believe such things, all of time is a great wheel that turns in a track of predetermined events. Left to itself, time turns endlessly, and all the world is doomed to repeat the cycle of events that lead us all ever deeper into darkness and degradation. Those who follow the White Prophet believe that to each age is born one who has the vision to redirect time and history into a better path. This one is known by his white skin and colorless eyes. It is said that the blood of the ancient lines of the Whites finds voice again in the White Prophet. To each White Prophet there is a Catalyst. Only the White Prophet of that particular age can divine who the Catalyst is. The Catalyst is one who is born in a unique position to alter, however slightly, predetermined events, which in turn cascade time into other paths with possibilities that diverge ever wider. In partnership with this Catalyst, the White Prophet labors to divert the turning of time into a better path.

                               ❦ CATERHILL'S "PHILOSOPHIES"

We could not keep up the pace forever, of course. Long before I felt safe, the condition of the horses forced us to breathe them. The sounds of pursuit had faded behind us; a warhorse is not a courser. As the evening approached true dark around us, we walked the horses down a winding streambed. The Prince's horse could barely hold her head up. As soon as the heat was walked off her, we would have to stop for a time. I rode crouched in my saddle to avoid the sweeping branches of the willows that lined the stream. The others followed. When we had first slowed the horses, I had feared that the Prince would try a leaping escape. But he had not. Instead he sat his horse in sullen silence as I led her on.

"Mind this branch," I warned Dutiful and Lord Golden as a low limb snagged on me when Myblack pushed her way under it. I tried not to let it snap back in the Prince's face.

"Who are you?" the Prince suddenly demanded in a low voice.

"You do not recognize me, my lord?" Lord Golden asked him anxiously. I recognized his effort to distract the Prince's attention from me.

"Not you. Him. Who is he? And why have you assaulted me and my friends in this way?" There was an amazing depth of accusation in his voice. Abruptly he sat up straighter in his saddle as if he were just discovering his anger.

"Duck," I warned him as I released another branch. He did.

Lord Golden spoke. "That is my servant, Tom Badgerlock. We've come to take you home to Buckkeep, Prince Dutiful. The Queen, your mother, has been most worried about you."

"I do not wish to go." With every sentence, the young man was recovering himself. There was dignity in his voice as he spoke these words. I waited for Lord Golden to reply, but the splashing thuds of the horses' hooves in the stream and the swish and crackle of the branches we passed through were the only sounds. To our right, a meadow suddenly opened out. A few blackened, snaggly stumps in it were reminders of a forest fire in this area years ago. Tall grasses of browned seedheads vied against fireweed with sprung and fluffy seedpods. I turned the horses out of the stream and onto the grass. When I looked up at the sky, it was dark enough to show a pricking of early stars. The dwindling moon would not show herself until night was deep. Even now, the gathering darkness was leaching color from the day, making the surrounding forest an impenetrable tangle of blackness.

I led them out to the center of the meadow, well away from the forest edge, before I reined in. Any attackers would have to cross open ground before they reached us. "Best we rest until moonrise," I observed to Lord Golden. "It will be difficult enough to make our way then."

"Is it safe to stop?" he asked me.

I shrugged my shoulders. "Safe or not, I think we must. The horses are nearly spent, and it's getting dark. I think we've gained a good lead. That warhorse is strong, but not swift or nimble. The terrain we've covered will daunt him. And the Piebalds must either abandon their wounded, splitting their party, or come after us more slowly. We have a little breathing space."

I looked back at the Prince before I dismounted. He sat, shoulders slumped, but the anger in his eyes proclaimed him far from defeated. I waited until he swung his dark eyes to meet mine, and then spoke to him. "It's up to you. We can treat you well and simply return you to Buckkeep. Or you can behave like a willful child and try to run away back to your Witted friends. In which case I will hunt you down, and take you back to Buckkeep with your hands bound behind you. Choose now."

He stared at me, a flat, challenging stare, the rudest thing one animal can do to another. He didn't speak. It offended me on so many levels that I could scarcely keep my temper.

"Answer me!" I commanded.

He narrowed his eyes. "And who are you?" His tone made the repeated question an insult.

In all the years I'd had the care and raising of Hap, he had never provoked me to the level of temper that this youth had instantly roused in me. I wheeled Myblack. I was taller than the lad to begin with and the differences in our mounts made me tower over him. I crowded both him and his horse, leaning over him to look down on him like a wolf asserting authority over a cub. "I'm the man who's taking you back to Buckkeep. One way or another. Accept it."

"Badgerlo—" Lord Golden began warningly, but it was too late. Dutiful made a move, a tiny flexing of muscle that warned me. Without considering anything, I launched at him from Myblack's back. My spring carried us both off our horses and onto the ground. We landed in deep grass, luckily for Dutiful, for I fell atop him, pinning him as neatly as if I had intended it. Both our horses snorted and shied away, but they were too weary to run. Myblack trotted a few paces, knees high, snorted a second rebuke at me, and then dropped her head to the grass. The Prince's horse, having followed her so far today, copied her example.

I sat up, straddling the Prince's chest while pinning both his arms down. I heard the sound of Lord Golden dismounting, but did not even turn my head. I stared down at Dutiful silently. I knew by the laboring of his chest that I had knocked the wind out of him, but he refused to make a sound. Nor would he meet my eyes, not even when I took his knife from him and flung it disdainfully into the forest. He looked past me at the sky until I seized his chin and forced him to look me in the face.

"Choose," I told him again.

He met my eyes, looked away, then met them again. When he looked away a second time, I felt some of the fight go out of him. Then his face twisted with misery as he stared past me. "But I have to go back to her," he gasped out. He drew breath raggedly, and tried to explain. "I don't expect you to understand. You're nothing but a hound sent to track me down and drag me back. Doing your duty is all you know. But I have to go after her. She is my life, the

breath in my body . . . she completes me. We have to be together."

Well. You won't be. I came a knife's edge away from
saying those words, but I did not. Matter-of-factly, I told
him, "I do understand. But that doesn't change what I have
to do. It doesn't even change what you have to do."

I got off him as Lord Golden approached. "Badgerlock,
that is Prince Dutiful, heir to the Farseer Throne," he reminded me sharply.

I decided to play the role he'd left open for me. "And
that's why he's still got all his teeth, my lord. Most boys who
draw knives on me are lucky to keep any." I tried to sound
both surly and truculent. Let the lad think Lord Golden
had me on a short leash. Let him worry that I wasn't completely under the lord's control. It would give me an edge of
mastery over him.

"I'll tend the horses," I announced, and stalked away
from them into the darkness. I kept one eye and one ear on
the shapes of the Fool and the Prince as I dragged off saddles, slipped bits, and wiped the horses down with handfuls
of grass. Dutiful got slowly to his feet, disdaining Lord
Golden's offered hand. He brushed himself off, and when
Golden asked if he had taken any harm, replied with stiff
courtesy that he was as well as could be expected. Lord
Golden retreated a short way, to consider the night and allow the lad to collect his shattered dignity. In a short time,
the horses were grazing as greedily as if they had never seen
grass before. I had put the saddles in a row. I removed bedding from Myblack's saddle packs and began to make it into
pallets near them. If possible, I'd steal an hour of sleep. The
Prince watched me. After a moment he asked, "Aren't you
going to build a fire?"

"And make it easier for your friends to find us? No."

"But—"

"It's not that cold. And there's no food to cook anyway." I shook out the last blanket, then asked him, "Do you
have any bedding in your saddle pack?"

"No," he admitted unhappily. I divided the blankets to make three pallets instead of two. I saw him pondering something. Then he added, "I do have food. And wine." He took a breath, then said, "It seems a fair trade for a blanket." I kept a wary eye on him as he approached and began to open his saddle packs.

"My Prince, you misjudge us. We would not think of making you sleep on the bare earth," Lord Golden protested in horror.

"You might not, Lord Golden. But *he* would." He cast me a baleful glance and added, "He does not even accord me the courtesy one man gives to another, let alone the respect a servant should have for his sovereign."

"He is a rough man, my Prince, but a good servant all the same." Lord Golden gave me a warning look.

I made a show of lowering my eyes, but muttered, "Respect a sovereign? Perhaps. But not a runaway boy fleeing his duty."

Dutiful took a breath as if he would reply in fury. Then he let it out as a hiss, but leashed his anger. "You know nothing of what you speak about," he said coldly. "I did not run away."

Lord Golden's tone was much gentler than mine had been. "Forgive me, my lord, but that is how it must appear to us. The Queen feared at first that you had been kidnapped. But no notes of ransom arrived. She did not wish to alarm her nobles, or to offend the Outislander delegation soon to arrive for your betrothal agreement. Surely you have not forgotten that in nine more nights, the new moon brings your betrothal? For you to be absent at such a time goes beyond mere discourtesy to insult. She doubted that was your intent. Even so, she did not turn out the guards after you, as she might have done. Preferring to be subtle, she asked me to locate you and bring you safely home. And that is our only aim."

"I did not run away," he repeated adamantly, and I saw that the accusation had stung him more sharply than I had suspected. Nonetheless, he stubbornly added, "But I have no intention of returning to Buckkeep." He had taken a bottle of wine from his pack. Now he pulled out food. Smoked fish wrapped in linen, several slabs of hard-crusted honey cake, and two apples; hardly traveling rations, but the toothsome repast that loyal companions would supply for a prince's enjoyment. He unfolded the linen on the grass, and began to divide the food into three portions. Dainty as a cat, he arranged the food. I thought it was well done, a show of a gracious nature by a boy in an uncomfortable situation. He uncorked the wine and set it in the middle. With a gesture he invited us, and we were not slow to respond. Little as there was, it was very welcome. The honey cake was heavy, suety, and thick with raisins. I filled my mouth with half my slab and tried to chew it slowly. I was fiercely hungry. Yet even as we attacked the food, the Prince, less hungry, spoke seriously.

"If you try to force me to return with you, you will only get hurt. My friends will come for me, you know. She will not surrender me so easily, nor I her. And I have no desire to see you get hurt. Not even you," he added, meeting my stare. I had thought he intended his words as a threat. Instead, he seemed sincere as he explained, "I must go with her. I am not a boy running away from his duty, nor even a man fleeing an arranged marriage. I do not run away from unpleasantness. Instead, I join myself where I most belong . . . where I was born to belong." His careful unfolding of words put me in mind of Verity. His eyes traveled slowly from me to Lord Golden and back again. He seemed to be seeking an ally, or at least a sympathetic ear. He licked his lips as if taking a risk. Very quietly, he asked, "Have you ever heard the tale of the Piebald Prince?"

We were both silent. I swallowed food gone tasteless. Was Dutiful mad? Then Lord Golden nodded, once, slowly.

"I am of that line. As sometimes happens in the Farseer line, I was born with the Wit."

I did not know whether to admire his honesty, or be horrified at his naïve assumption that he had not just condemned himself to death. I kept my features motionless and did not let my eyes betray my thoughts. Desperately I wondered if he had admitted this to others at Buckkeep.

I think our lack of reaction unnerved him more than anything else we could have done. We both sat quietly, watching him. He took a gambler's breath. "So you see now why it would be best for everyone if you let me go. The Six Duchies will not follow a Witted king, nor can I forsake what my blood makes me. I will not deny what I am. That would be cowardice, and false to my friends. If I returned, it would only be a matter of time before all knew of my Wit. If you drag me back, it can only lead to strife and division amongst the nobles. You should let me go, and tell my mother you could not find me. That way is best for all."

I looked down at the last of my portion of fish. Quietly I asked, "What if we decided it was best for all if we killed you? Hung you and cut you in quarters and burned the parts near running water? And then told the Queen we had not found you?" I looked away from the wild fear in his eyes, shamed by what I had done and yet knowing he must be taught caution. After a space: "Know men before you share your deepest secrets with them," I counseled him.

Or your kill. He came up on me as quietly as a shadow, his thought light as the wind against my skin. Nighteyes dropped a rabbit, a bit the worse for wear, on the ground beside me. He had already eaten the guts. Casually, he lifted the smoked fish from my hands, gulped it down, and then lay down beside me with a heavy sigh. He dropped his head onto his forepaws. *That rabbit started up right under me. Easiest kill I've ever made.*

The Prince's eyes opened so wide I could see white all around them. His gaze darted from the wolf to me and back again. I don't think he had overheard our shared thought, but he knew all the same. He leapt to his feet with an angry cry. "You should understand! How can you tear me from not just my bond-beast but the woman who shares that Old Blood kinship with me? How can you betray one of your own?"

I had more important questions of my own. *How did you cover that much ground so quickly?*

The same way his cat will, and for much the same reason. A wolf can go straight where a horse must go around. Are you ready for them to find you? With my hand resting on his back, I could feel the weariness thrumming through him. He shuddered away my concern as if it were flies on his coat. *I'm not that decrepit. I brought you meat,* he pointed out.

You should have eaten it all yourself.

A trace of humor. *I did. The first one. You don't think I'd be foolish enough to follow you all this way on an empty belly? That one is for you and the Scentless One. And this cub, if you so will it.*

I doubt he will eat it raw.

I doubt there is sense to avoiding a fire. Come they will, and they need no light to guide them. The boy calls to her; it is like breath sighing in and out of him. He yowls it like a mating call.

I am not aware of it.

Your nose is not the only sense that you have that is not as keen as mine.

I stood up, then nudged the eviscerated rabbit with my foot. "I'll make a fire and cook this." The Prince was staring at me silently. He was well aware I'd been having a conversation that excluded him.

"What about drawing pursuit to us?" Lord Golden asked. Despite his question, I knew he was hoping for the comfort of a fire and hot meat.

"He's already doing that." I gestured at the Prince with my chin. "Having a fire long enough to have some hot food will not make it any worse."

"How can you betray your own kind?" Dutiful demanded again.

I had already puzzled out the answer to that the night

before. "There are levels of loyalty here, my Prince. And my highest loyalty is to the Farseers. As yours should be." He was more my own kind than I had the heart to tell him, and I ached for him. Yet my actions did not feel like a betrayal to me. Rather, I imposed safe boundaries on him. As Burrich had once done for me, I thought ruefully.

"What gives you the right to tell me where my loyalty should be?" he demanded. The anger in his voice let me know that I had touched that very question within him.

"You're correct. It's not my right, Prince Dutiful. It's my duty. To remind you of what you seem to have forgotten. I'll find some firewood. You might ponder what will become of the Farseer Throne if you simply refuse your duty and vanish."

Despite his weariness, the wolf heaved himself to his feet and followed me. We went back to the stream's edge, to look for dead wood carried by higher waters and left to dry all summer. We drank first, and then I dabbed my chest with water where the Prince's blade had scored me. Another day, another scar. Or perhaps not. It had not even bled very much. I turned from that to looking for dry wood. Nighteyes' keener night vision helped my lesser senses, and I soon had an armload. *He's very like you,* the wolf observed as we made our way back.

Family resemblance. He's Verity's heir.

Only because you refused to be. He's our blood, little brother. Yours and mine.

That struck me into silence for a time. Then I pointed out, *You are much more aware of human concerns than you used to be. Time was when you took no notice of such things.*

True. And Black Rolf warned us both that we have twined too deeply, and that I am more man than a wolf should be, and you more wolf. We'll pay for it, little brother. Not that we could have helped it, but that does not change it. We will suffer for how deeply our natures have meshed.

What are you trying to tell me?

You already know.

And I did. Like myself, the Prince had been brought up amongst folk who did not use the Wit. And as I had, unguided, he seemed to have not only fallen into his magic, but to be wallowing in it. Untaught, I had bonded far too deeply. In my case, I had first bonded to a dog when we were both young, and far too immature to consider the implications of such a joining. Burrich had forcibly separated us. At the time, I had hated him for it, a hate that lasted years. Now I looked at the Prince, in the full throes of his obsession with the cat, and counted myself lucky that when I had bonded, there had only been the puppy involved. Somehow, his attachment to his cat had grown to include a young woman of Old Blood. When I took him back to Buckkeep, he would lose not only his companion, but also a woman he believed he loved.

What woman?

He speaks of a woman, one of Old Blood. Probably one of those women who rode with him.

He speaks of a woman, but he does not smell of a woman. Does not that strike you odd?

I pondered that on my way back to camp. I dropped the wood in a small tumble. As I set my fuel and then shaved a dry stick for tinder, I watched the boy. He had tidied away the linen napkin but left out the bottle of wine. Now he sat morosely on a blanket, his knees drawn up to his chin, staring out at the deepening night.

I dropped all my guards and quested toward him. The wolf was right. He keened for his Wit-partner, but I was not sure if he was even aware of doing it. It was a sad little seeking he sent forth, like a lost pup whimpering for its mother. It grated on my nerves, once I was aware of it. It was not just that he would call his friends down on us; it was the whining aspect of it that appalled me. It made me want to cuff him. Instead, as I worked with my tinder and flint, I asked callously, "Thinking of your girl?"

He swiveled toward me, startled. Lord Golden flinched at the directness of my question. I bent deeper to puff gen-

tly at the tiny spark I had conjured up. It glowed, then became a pale, licking flame.

The Prince reached for a measure of dignity. "I am always thinking of her," he said softly.

I tented several skinny sticks over my tiny fire. "So.
What's she look like?" I spoke with a soldier's crude interest, the inflection learned from many a meal with the
guardsmen at Buckkeep. "Is she . . ."—I made the unmistakable, universal gesture—"any good?"

"Shut up!" He spat the words savagely.

I leered at Lord Golden knowingly. "Ah, we both know
what that means. It means he don't know. At least, not
firsthand. Or maybe it's only his hand that knows." I leaned
back and smirked at him challengingly.

"Badgerlock!" Lord Golden rebuked me. I think I had
truly scandalized him.

I didn't take the hint. "Well, that's always how it is,
isn't it? He's just a moony boy for her. Bet he's never even
kissed her, let alone . . ." I repeated the gesture.

The taunting had the desired effect. As I added larger
sticks to the flames, the Prince stood up indignantly. The
firelight revealed that his color was high and his nostrils
pinched with anger. "It isn't like that!" he grated. "She isn't
some . . . Not that I expect you to understand anything
other than whores! She's a woman worth waiting for, and
when we come together, it will be a higher and sweeter
thing than you can imagine. Hers is a love to be earned,
and I will prove myself worthy of her."

Inside, I bled for him. They were a boy's words, taken
from minstrel tellings, a lad's imaginings of something he
had never experienced. The innocence of his passion
blazed in him, and his idealistic expectations shone in his
eyes. I tried to summon some withering crudity worthy of
the role I had chosen, but could not force it past my lips.
The Fool saved me.

"Badgerlock!" Lord Golden snapped. "Enough of this.
Just cook the meat."

"My lord," I acknowledged gruffly. I gave Dutiful a side-long sneer that he refused to see. As I picked up the stiff rabbit and the knife, Lord Golden spoke more gently to the Prince.

"Does she have a name, this lady you so admire? Have I met her at court?" Lord Golden was courteously curious. Somehow the warmth in his voice made it flattering that he would care to ask such a question. Dutiful was instantly charmed, not only despite his earlier irritation with me, but perhaps because of it. Here was a chance for him to prove himself a well-bred gentleman, to ignore my crass interest and reply as politely as if I did not exist.

He smiled as he looked down at his hands, the smile of a boy with a secret sweetheart. "Oh, you will not have met her at Court, Lord Golden. Her kind is not to be found there. She is a lady of the wild woods, a huntress and a forester. She does not hem handkerchiefs in a garden on a summer's day, nor huddle within walls by a hearth when the wind begins to blow. She is free to the open world, her hair blowing in the wind, her eyes full of the night's mysteries."

"I see." Lord Golden's voice was warm with a worldly man's tolerance for a youth's first romance. He came to sit on his saddle, next to the boy and yet slightly above him. "And does this paragon of the forest have a name? Or a family?" he asked paternally.

Dutiful looked up at him and shook his head wearily. "There, you see what you ask? That is why I am so weary of the Court. As if I cared whether she has family or fortune! It is her whom I love."

"But she must have a name," Lord Golden protested tolerantly as I slid my knife blade under the rabbit's hide and loosened it. "Else what do you whisper to the stars at night when you dream of her?" I peeled the hide from the rabbit as Lord Golden stripped the layers of secrets from the boy's romance. "Come. How did you meet her?" Lord Golden picked up the wine bottle, drank delicately from it, and then handed it to the Prince.

The lad turned it in his hands thoughtfully, glanced up at Golden's smile, and drank. Then he sat, the bottle held loosely in his hands, the neck of it pointed toward the small fire that limned his features against the night. "My cat took me to her," he confided at last. He took another sip of the wine. "I had slipped out one night to go hunting with her. Sometimes, I just have to get away on my own. You know what it is like at court. If I say I will ride at dawn, I arise and there are six gentlemen ready to accompany me, and a dozen ladies to bid us farewell. If I say I will walk in the gardens after dinner, I cannot turn a corner in the path without finding a lady writing poetry beneath a tree, or encountering some noble who wishes me to have a word with the Queen on his behalf. It's stifling, Lord Golden. In truth, I do not know why so many choose to come to court when they do not have to. Had I the privilege of freedom, I would leave it." He drew himself up suddenly and looked all around at the night. "I *have* left it," he declared abruptly, almost as if it surprised him. "I'm here, away from all that pretense and manipulation. And I'm happy. Or I *was* happy, until you came to drag me back." And he glared at me, as if it were all my doing, and Lord Golden an innocent bystander.

"So. You went out hunting with your cat one night, and this lady . . . ?" Lord Golden deftly picked up the threads that had interested him.

"I went out hunting with my cat and—"

The cat's name? Nighteyes pressed with sudden urgency.

I grunted mockingly. "Sounds to me as if the cat and the lady got the same name. 'Neverspeakit.'" I skewered the rabbit on my sword. I didn't like to cook on the end of my blade; it was bad for the tempering. But to get a green branch I would have had to leave the conversation and go to the forest's edge and I wanted to hear what he had to say.

The Prince replied scathingly to my comment. "I would think that you, as a Piebald, would know that beasts have their own names, which they reveal to you at a time they think is proper. My cat has not shared her true name with me yet. When I am worthy of that confidence, I will have it."

"I'm not a 'Piebald,'" I asserted gruffly.

Dutiful ignored me. He took a breath and spoke earnestly to Lord Golden. "And the same is true of my lady. I do not need to know her name when it is her essence that I love."

"Of course, of course," Lord Golden comforted him. He hitched himself closer to the Prince and went on. "But I would hear of your first meeting with the fair one. For I confess that at heart, I am as soft a romantic as any court lady weeping at a minstrel's tale." He spoke as if what Dutiful had said was of no consequence. But a profound sense of wrongness washed through me. It was true that Nighteyes had not immediately shared his true name with me, but the cat and the Prince had been together for months. I turned the sword, but the rabbit flopped around on the blade, its body cavity a loose fit, the seared side turning back to the flames. Grumbling, I pulled it out of the fire and burnt my fingers jamming it more firmly onto the weapon. I thrust it back over the flames and held it there.

"Our first meeting," Dutiful mused. A rueful smile curved his mouth. "I fear that has yet to happen. In some ways. In all the important ways, I have met her. The cat showed her to me, or rather, she revealed herself to me through the cat."

Lord Golden cocked his head and gave the boy an interested, if confused, look. The lad's smile widened.

"It is hard to explain to someone with no experience of the Wit. But I will try. Through my magic, I can share thoughts with the cat. Her senses enhance my own. Sometimes, I can lie abed at night, and surrender my mind to hers, and become one with her. I see what she sees, feel what she feels. It's wonderful, Lord Golden. Not debased and bestial as others would have you believe. It brought the world to life around me. If there was some way I could share the experience with you, I would, just so that you could understand it."

The boy was so earnest in his proselytizing. I glimpsed the quick flash of amusement through Lord Golden's eyes, but I am sure the Prince saw only his sympathetic warmth. "I shall have to imagine it," he murmured.

Prince Dutiful shook his head. "Ah, but you cannot. No one can, who is not born with this magic. That is why all persecute us. Because, lacking this magic, they become filled with envy and it turns to hatred."

"I think fear might have something to do with it," I muttered, but the Fool shot me a glance that bade me shut up. Chastened, I turned away from them and rotated the smoking rabbit.

"I think I can imagine your communion with the cat. How wondrous it must be to share the thoughts of such a noble creature! How rich to experience the night and the hunt with one so attuned to the natural world! But I confess, I do not understand how she could reveal this wondrous lady to you . . . unless she guided you to her?"

How pleasant to feel her filthy claws raking your belly!
Shush.
Cats noble creatures? Spitting, carrion-breathed sneaks.

With difficulty, I ignored Nighteyes' asides and focused on the conversation while appearing to be engrossed with the rabbit. The Prince was smiling and shaking his head at Lord Golden, totally enraptured now with speaking of his love. Had I ever been that young?

"It was not like that. One night, as the cat and I moved through a forest of black trees, lit to silver by the moon's radiance, I perceived we were not alone. It was not that uncomfortable sensation of being watched. This was more like . . . Imagine if the wind was the breath of a woman on the back of your neck, if the scent of the forest was her perfume, the chuckling of a brook her amusement. There was nothing there I had not seen or heard or felt a hundred times, and yet that night it was more than it had ever been before. At first, I thought I was imagining it, and then, through the cat, I began to know more of her. I felt her watching us as we hunted together, and I knew that she approved of me. When I shared fresh meat with the cat from her kill, I sensed that the woman shared its savor. The cat's senses sharpen my own, I told you that. But suddenly I was seeing things, not as the cat or as myself, but as she saw things. I saw how the tumbled gap in a stone wall framed a struggling sapling, I saw the infinite pattern in the ripple of moonlight on a stream's rapids, I saw . . . I saw the night world as her poetry."

Prince Dutiful sighed slowly. He was lost in his romance, but the slow suspicion forming in my mind sent a chill up my back. I could feel the perk of the wolf's ears and the readiness in his muscles as he shared my foreboding.

"That was how it began. As shared glimpses of the beauty of the world. I was so foolish. At first, I thought she must be near us, watching us from a hiding place. I kept asking the cat to take me to her. And she did, but not in the manner I had expected. It was like approaching a castle through a fog. Layer after layer of mist lifted like veils. The closer I came to her, the more I longed to behold her in the flesh. Yet she taught me it would be nobler to wait for that. First, I must complete my lessons in the Wit. I must learn to surrender my human boundaries and self, and let the cat possess me. When I let the cat inside me, when I become the cat completely, then am I most aware of my lady. For we are both bonded to the same creature."

Can that happen? The wolf's question was incredulous and sharp.

I don't know, I admitted. Then, more strongly, *But I don't think so.*

"It doesn't work that way," I said aloud. I tried to say it in an unthreatening way, but I wanted the Fool to know that immediately. Nevertheless, the Prince bristled at me.

"I said that it did. Do you call me a liar?"

I slumped back into my thuggish personality. "If I

wanted to call you a liar," I greased my threatening words, "I would have said, 'You're a liar.' I didn't. I said, 'It doesn't work that way.'" I smiled, showing my teeth. "Why don't you take it that I think that you don't know what you're talking about? That you're just spilling out what someone else has filled you full of."

"For the last time, Badgerlock, be silent. You are interrupting a fascinating tale, and neither the Prince nor I particularly care if you believe it. I simply want to hear how it ends. So. When you finally did meet?" Lord Golden's tone implied he was on the edge of his seat.

The warm romanticism of Dutiful's voice suddenly crashed into heartsick desperation. "We haven't. Not yet. That was where I was going. She called me to her, and I left Buckkeep. She promised she would send folk to help me on my path to her. And she did. She promised that as I learned my magic, as my bond with the cat deepened and became truer, I would know more and more of her. I would have to prove myself worthy, of course. My love would be tested, as would my true willingness to be one with my Old Blood. I would have to learn to drop all barriers between the cat and myself. She told me it would be arduous, she warned me that I would have to change the way I thought about things. But, when I was ready," and despite the darkness, I could see the flush rise to the Prince's cheeks, "she promised we would be joined, in a way that would be more compelling and true than anything I could imagine." His young voice went husky on those last words.

A slow anger began to build in me. I knew what he was imagining, and I was almost certain that what she was offering him had nothing to do with that. He thought he would be consummating their relationship. I feared he was about to be consumed by it.

"I understand," said Lord Golden, and there was compassion in his voice. For my part, I was certain that he did not understand at all.

Hope flamed in the boy. "So now you understand why

you must let me go? I have to go back. I do not ask that you take me back to my guides. I know they will be furious and a danger to you. All I ask is that you give me my horse and let me go. It is easy for you to do. Go back to Buckkeep; say you never found me. No one will know any better."

"I would," I pointed out sweetly as I took the rabbit from the fire. "The meat's cooked," I added.

Charred to the bone.

The look the Prince gave me was venomous. I almost felt the clear solution flash through his mind. *Kill the servant. Silence him.* I would wager that Kettricken's son had not been schooled in such ruthlessness before the Piebalds taught him. Yet it was an idea truly worthy of his Farseer forebears. I met his gaze, and let my mouth curl slightly, daring him. I saw his chest swell, and then I saw him master himself. He glanced away, veiling his hatred. Admirable self-control. I wondered if he'd try to kill me in my sleep.

I kept my gaze on him, challenging him to meet my eyes as I tore the rabbit into smoking pieces. The grease and soot coated my fingers. I passed a portion to Lord Golden, who took it with genteel distaste. Knowing how ravenous the Fool had been earlier in the day, I recognized it was but a show.

"Meat, my Prince?" Lord Golden asked him.

"No. Thank you." His voice was cold. .He was too proud to accept anything from me, for I had mocked him.

The wolf declined a share of the well-cooked meat, so Lord Golden and I silently devoured it down to the bones. The Prince sat apart from us as we ate, staring off into the darkness. After a time, he lay down on his blanket. I sensed his Wit-keening grow in volume.

Lord Golden broke the leg bone he held, sucked a bit of marrow from it, and tossed it into the embers of the fire. In its fading light, he looked at me with the Fool's eyes. That gaze held such a mixture of sympathy and rebuke that I did not know how to react to it. We both looked over at the lad. He appeared to be asleep.

"I'll check on the horses," I offered.

"I want to check on Malta myself," he replied. We both rose. My back clenched for a moment as I got up, and then eased. I was no longer accustomed to this type of life.

I'll watch him, the wolf volunteered wearily. With a sigh he got up from where he lay, and walked stiffly over to the blankets, saddles, and sleeping Prince. Unerringly he chose the blanket I had put out for myself. He scuffed it up to suit himself and then lay down on it. He blinked his eyes at me, and then transferred his gaze to the boy.

The horses were in fine shape, considering how badly we'd treated them. Malta went to the Fool eagerly, rubbing her head against his shoulder as he petted her. Myblack, without apparently ever noticing me, still managed to sidle away whenever I tried to approach her. The Prince's horse was neutral, neither welcoming nor shy about my touching her. After I'd petted her for a few moments, Myblack was suddenly behind me. She gave me a nudge, and when I turned to her, she allowed me to stroke her. The Fool spoke quietly, to Malta rather than to me.

"It must be hard for you, meeting him for the first time like this."

I wasn't going to reply. There seemed nothing to say. Then I surprised myself by saying, "He isn't really mine that way. He's Verity's heir, and Kettricken's son. My body was there, but not me. Verity wore my body."

I tried to rein my mind away from that memory. When Verity had told me that there was a way to wake his dragon, that my life and passion were the key, I had thought my King was asking me to give him my life. In my loyalty and my misery, I would have been glad to surrender it. Instead he had used the Skill to take the use of my body, leaving me trapped in the shambling wreckage of his while he went in to his young wife and conceived an heir with her. I had no memories of their hours together. Instead, I recalled a long evening spent as an old man. Not even Kettricken was completely aware of what had happened. Only the Fool shared my knowledge of Dutiful's conception. Now his voice jolted me from my painful musing.

"He looks so like you at that age that it makes my heart ache."

I knew there was nothing to say to that.

"He makes me want to hold him tight and keep him safe. Protect him from all the terrible things that were done to you in the name of the Farseer reign." The Fool paused. "I lie," he admitted. "I would protect him from all the terrible things that were done to you because I used you as my Catalyst."

The night was too black and our enemies were too near for me to want to hear any more of that. "You should sleep near him, near the fire. The wolf will stay there, too. Keep your sword handy."

"And you?" he said after a moment. Was he disappointed that I had turned the conversation so firmly?

I tossed my head toward the row of trees along the streambed. "I'm going to climb one of those and keep watch. You should get a few hours of sleep. If they try to fall on us, they'll have to cross the whole meadow. I'll see them against the firelight in time to take action."

"What action?"

I shrugged. "If there's a few, we fight. If there's many, we run."

"Complex strategy. Chade taught you well."

"Rest while you can. We ride at moonrise."

And we parted. I had the nagging sense that something had been left unspoken between us, something important. Well. There would be a better time later.

Anyone who thinks it is easy to find a good climbing tree in the dark has never tried it. On my third try, I found one that had a limb broad enough to sit on that still afforded me an unencumbered view of our campsite. I could have sat and pondered the vagaries of fate that had made me the father of two children and the parent of neither. Instead, I decided to worry about Hap. I knew Chade would keep his word, but could Hap hold up his end of the bargain? Had I taught him how to work well enough, would he have enough care for what he did, would he listen well and endure correction humbly?

The darkness was pitch-black. I looked in vain for the waning moon to rise. She and her dwindling light would not appear until the dead of night. Against the black-red smear of our campfire, I could just make out the shapes of Lord Golden and the boy in their blankets. Time passed. A friendly branch stub nudged against the small of my back and prevented me from getting too comfortable.

Come down.

I had dozed. I could not see the wolf, but I knew that he was in the shadows at the base of my tree. *Something's wrong?*

Come down. Be silent.

I came down, but not as quietly as I had hoped. I hung by my hands and then dropped, only to discover there was a hollow beneath the tree and the fall was greater than I had expected. The jar clacked my teeth together and jolted my spine against the base of my skull. *I'm too old to do this sort of thing anymore.*

No. You only wish you were. Come.

I followed him, my teeth gritted. He took me silently back to the campsite. The Fool sat up noiselessly as I drew near. Even in the dark, I could make out his questioning look. I made a small motion for silence and watched.

The wolf went to where the Prince was curled like a kitten in his blankets. He put his muzzle close to Dutiful's ear. I gestured at him not to wake the boy, but he ignored me. In fact, he levered his nose under the Prince's cheek and nudged him. The boy's head gave limply to his touch, lolling like a dead man's. My heart stood still, and then I heard the rasp of his sleeping breath. The wolf nudged him again. He still didn't wake.

I met the Fool's wide-eyed stare, then I went to kneel by the boy. Nighteyes looked up into my face.

He was questing for them, questing and reaching, and then suddenly, he was just gone. I can't feel him. Nighteyes was anxious.

He's gone far and deep. I considered a moment. *This is not the Wit.*

"Watch over us," I bade the Fool. Then I lay down beside Dutiful. I closed my eyes. As if I were steeling myself to dive into deep water, I measured each breath I drew into myself. I matched the rhythm to the boy's breathing. *Verity*, I thought, for no reason at all save that it seemed to center me. I hesitated, then I groped for and found the boy's hand. I held it in mine, and it pleased me unreasonably that his palm was callused with work. I drew a final breath and plunged into the flow of the Skill. Skin to skin, I found him immediately.

I attached my consciousness to his and flowed with him. This, I suddenly knew, was how Galen's coterie had spied on King Shrewd all those years ago. Then I had despised that leeching of knowledge. Now I seized onto it relentlessly and followed my Prince.

There had been a shock of recognition, a jolt of kinship, when I had first seen the boy. It did not compare to what I experienced now. I knew this boy's wild seeking, his artless and fearless Skilling. It was as my own had been, a wild reaching with no knowledge of how I did it or the dangers it posed. He quested with his Wit and did not know that he Skilled out as well. For a daunting moment, I realized that like my own Skill magic, his was tainted with the Wit. Having taught himself to Skill this way, could he ever learn to use the Skill magic purely?

Then that consideration was pushed completely aside. Cloaked within the Skill, I witnessed his Wit magic, and I was appalled.

Prince Dutiful was the cat. He was not merely bonded

with the animal; he flowed completely into it, reserving nothing of himself. I knew that the wolf and I had interwoven our consciousness to a deep and dangerous level, but it was superficial compared to the Prince's complete surrender to his bond.

Worse was the creature's complete acceptance of the boy's subservience. Then, as if I had blinked, I perceived it was not a cat at all. The cat was but a thin layer. It was a woman.

I swirled in confusion, and nearly lost my grip on the Prince. The Wit did not go from human to human. That was the province of the Skill. Did he Skill to this woman, then? No. This joining was not the Skill. I tried to sort it out and could not. I could not separate the woman from the cat, and Dutiful was submerged in both of them. It did not make sense. The woman was plumbing the boy's mind. No. She was here, pooling into his body like cold thick water. I felt her flowing through him, exploring the shape of his flesh around her. It was still foreign to her. There was a strange eroticism to that chilling internal touch. Their joining in the cat was not yet complete enough, but soon, soon, she promised him, soon he would know her completely. They were coming for him, she assured him, and she knew where he was. I witnessed how he poured forth to her everything he knew about Lord Golden and me, the stamina and condition of our horses, the wolf that followed me, and I sensed her fury and revulsion for an Old Blood who betrayed his own kind.

They were coming. I saw with the cat's eyes, and recognized the Piebalds we had battled earlier in the day. Limping, she led them. The big man came slowly, on foot, leading his massive horse as they forced their way through the dark forest. The two women rode slowly behind him. The scratched man with the injured cat came last of all. They led two riderless horses now, so we had either killed or severely injured one of their party. *We come, my love. And a bird has been sent, summoning others to your aid. Soon you will be with us again,* she promised. *We will take no chances of losing you. When the others are near, we will close in and free you.*

Will you kill Lord Golden and his servant? the Prince asked anxiously.

Yes.

I wish you wouldn't kill Lord Golden.

It is necessary. I regret it, but it must be, for Lord Golden has come too far into our territory. He has seen the faces of our folk, and ridden our paths. He has to die.

Can you not let him go? He is sympathetic to our cause. Shown our strength, he might simply go back to the Queen and say he had never found—

Where is your loyalty? How can you trust him so quickly? Have you forgotten how many of our own folk have been killed by the Farseer reign? Or do you wish to see me and all our people die?

This question was like the snap of a whip and it pained me to feel Dutiful cower before it. *My heart is with you, my love, with you,* he assured her.

Good. That's good. Then trust only me, and let me do what I must do. There is no need for you to dwell on it. You need not feel responsible for what people bring down upon themselves. It is none of your doing. You tried to leave quietly. They are the ones who pursued you and attacked us. Put it from your mind.

Then she wrapped him in love, in a surging wave of warm affection that overpowered any thought of his own that he might have. But she seemed to be only at the edges of that flow. It was cat-love, the fierce claws-and-teeth love of a feline. The emotion drenched me and, despite my wariness, I near succumbed to it myself. I felt the Prince accept that she would do what she must do. She only did it so that they could be together. Was any price too high to pay for that?

She's dead.

The wolf's thought was like a voice in the room of a sleeping man. For a moment, I incorporated it into my dreams. Then the sense of it struck me like a punch to the belly. *Of course. She's dead. She rides the cat.*

And in that foolish moment of my sharing with the wolf, she was aware of me.

What is this? Her fear and outrage were nothing compared to her utter shock. She had never experienced anything like this. It was outside her magic completely, and in the rawness of her astonishment, she betrayed much of her self.

I wrenched free of all contact before she could know any more than that someone had been there, watching her, just as I felt her make surer her grip upon him. It reminded me of a great cat seizing a mouse in her jaws and paralyzing it with a bite. I got that same sense of both possession and devouring. For one clear moment, I hoped that the Prince perceived her as clearly as I did. He was a toy for her, a possession and a tool. She felt no love for him.

But the cat does, Nighteyes pointed out to me.

And in that twisting disparity, I came back to myself.

It reminded me of my jolting leap from the tree. Slammed back into my own flesh, I sat up, gasping for air and space. Beside me, the Prince remained inert, but Nighteyes was instantly with me, thrusting his great head under my arm. *Are you all right, little brother? Did she hurt you?*

I tried to answer, but instead rocked forward, moaning as a Skill-headache exploded in my skull. I was literally blinded, isolated in a black night riven by lightning bolts of blazing white across my vision. I blinked, then knuckled my eyes, trying to make the glaring light go away. It burst into colors that sickened me. I hunched my shoulders and curled up against the pain.

A moment later, I felt a cold cloth laid across the back of my neck. I sensed the Fool beside me, blessedly silent. I swallowed and drew several deep breaths and then spoke into my hands. "They're coming. The Piebalds we fought today, and others. They know where we are from the Prince. He's like a beacon fire. We can't hide, and they're too many for us to fight and survive. Running is our only chance. We can't wait for moonrise. Nighteyes will lead us."

The Fool spoke very softly as if he guessed at my pain. "Shall I wake the Prince?"

"Don't bother trying. He's far and deep, and I don't think she'll let him come back to his body right now. We'll have to take him as a dead weight. Saddle the horses, will you?"

"I will. Fitz, can you ride as you are?"

I opened my eyes. Floating jags of light still divided my vision, but now I could see the darkened meadow beyond them. I forced a smile to my face. "I'll have to ride, just as my wolf will have to run. And you may have to fight. Not what any of us would choose, but there it is. Nighteyes. Go now. Choose a path for us, and get as far ahead of us as you can. I don't know from which direction the other attackers are coming. Spy ahead for us."

You think to send me out of harm's way. The thought was almost reproachful.

I would if I could, my brother, but the truth is that I may be sending you directly into danger. Scout for us. Go now.

He rose stiffly and stretched. He gave himself a shake, and then set out, not at a lope, but at his distance-devouring trot. Almost immediately, he became invisible to me, the gray wolf gone into the gray meadow. *Go carefully, my heart,* I wished after him, but softly, softly, lest he know how much I feared for him.

I rose, moving very carefully, as if my head were an overfull glass. I did not actually believe my brains would spill out of the top of my skull if I were careless, but I almost hoped it. I took the Fool's wet handkerchief off the back of my neck and held it to my brow and eyes for a time. When I looked down on the Prince, he hadn't moved. If anything, his body was curled more tightly. I heard the Fool come up behind me leading the horses and I turned cautiously to look at him.

"Can you explain?" he asked softly, and I realized how

little he knew. It was all the more amazing that he so unquestioningly acted on my requests.

I drew a breath. "He's using the Skill and the Wit. And he hasn't been trained in either, so he's vulnerable, very vulnerable. He's too young to understand just how much at risk he is. Right now, his consciousness rides with the cat. For all intents, he is the cat."

"But he will awaken and come back to his body?"

I shrugged. "I don't know. I hope so. Fool, there is more. There is someone else joined to the cat. I, that is, we, Nighteyes and I, suspect that she is the cat's former owner."

"Former? I thought Witted ones bonded to their animals for life?"

"They do. She would be dead now. But her consciousness is within the cat, using the cat."

"But I thought the Prince—"

"Yes. The Prince is there, too. I do not think he realizes that this woman he loves does not exist as a woman anymore. I know he has no concept of how much power she has over him. And over the cat."

"What can we do?"

The throbbing in my head was making me sick to my stomach. I spoke more harshly than I intended. "Forcibly separate the boy from the cat. Kill the cat, and hope the boy doesn't die."

"Oh, Fitz!" He was appalled.

I didn't have time to care.

"Saddle just two of the horses, Malta and Myblack. I'll put the boy in front of me. And then we have to ride."

I did nothing while the Fool prepared the horses. I didn't pack up anything, for I didn't intend to take anything with us. Instead I just sat still and tried to persuade my head to ease. It was made the more difficult in that I was still Skill-twined with the boy. I felt more his absence than his presence. I sensed that there was pressure upon him, but it was a Wit-pushing. I could not decide if she reached trying to know more of me, or if she reached trying to possess the boy's body. I did not wish to respond to it; they already knew enough of me from that earlier glancing touch. So I sat, head in hands, and looked at Kettricken's son. As Verity had taught me so long ago, I carefully set my Skill-walls. This time, I set them to include the boy at my feet. I did not consider what I was trying to hold out. Instead, I focused on keeping open the space that was his mind, reserving it for him to return to.

"Ready," the Fool said quietly, and I stood up again. I mounted Myblack, who was amazingly steady under me as the Fool hoisted the boy up into my arms. As always, the strength of the slender man surprised me. I arranged the Prince before me so that I had one arm to hold on to him, and one hand for the reins. It would have to do. In an instant, the Fool was mounted on Malta beside me. "Which way?" he asked.

Nighteyes? I kept the questing as small and secret as I could. They might sense our Wit, but I doubted they could use that to follow us.

My brother. His reply was as discreet. I nudged Myblack and we moved off. I could not have told anyone where Nighteyes was, but I knew that I moved toward him. The Prince was a swaying weight in my arms. It was already uncomfortable. Giving in to my frustration with my pain and his dead weight, I gave him a rough shake. He made a faint sound of protest, but it might have been just air moving out of his lungs. For a time we traveled through forest, ducking swoops of branches and pressing through tangles of underbrush. The Prince's horse, stripped of harness, followed us. We did not go swiftly. The footing was treacherous for the weary horses and the trees dense. I followed the wolf's elusive presence down into a ravine. The horses clattered along through a rushing stream over slippery wet rocks. The ravine became a vale, then spread wide and we rode under moonlight through a meadow. Startled deer bounded away from us. Into the forest again, our hooves thudded on deep layers of packed ancient leaves. Then we came to a steep place I did not recognize, but when we completed our scrabbling mount of that hill, the night spilled us out onto the road. The wolf's route had cut the rough country and put us back on the same road we had traveled that morning. I pulled in Myblack and let her breathe. Ahead of us, on the next rise, the stingy light of the quarter-moon showed me the silhouette of a wolf waiting for us to appear. As soon as he saw us, he turned, and trotted down the next hill and out of sight. *All is clear. Come swiftly.*

"Now we ride," I warned the Fool in a low voice. I leaned forward, spoke a word to Myblack as my knees urged her on. When she was sluggish to respond, I suggested with my predator's Wit, *Pursuit is just behind us. They come swiftly.*

Her ears flicked back once. I think she was a bit skeptical, but she gathered herself. As Malta threatened to pass us, I felt her powerful muscles bunch and then she stretched under me and we galloped. Encumbered by our double weight and weary from her day's work, she ran heavily. Malta gamely kept the pace, her presence pushing Myblack on. The Prince's horse was left behind. The wolf ran before us, and I fastened my eyes to him as to my final hope. It seemed he had somehow discarded his years; he ran like a yearling, bounding ahead of us.

To our left, the horizon appeared as dawn began its timid creep toward day. I welcomed the light that made our footing surer even as I cursed how it would reveal us to our enemies. We pressed on, varying our pace as the morning grew stronger, trying to ration our mounts' endurance. The last two days had been hard on both horses. To run them to dropping would not help our situation.

"When will it be safe to stop?" the Fool asked me during a period when we had slowed to let the horses breathe.

"When we reach Buckkeep Castle. Perhaps." I did not add that the Prince would not be safe until I had turned back and killed the cat. We had only his body in our keeping. The Piebalds still had his soul.

At mid-morning, we passed the tree where their archer had ambushed us. It made me realize how much I was trusting the wolf to choose our path. He had decided this way was safe and I was following him unquestioningly.

Are we not pack? Of course you must follow your leader. The tease in his thought could not quite mask his weariness.

We were all tired; men, wolf, and horses. A sustained trot was the best I could wring from Myblack now. Dutiful was a lolling weight in my arms as we jolted along. The pain in my back and shoulders from supporting his weight vied with the dull throbbing in my head. The Fool still sat his horse well but made no attempt at conversation of any kind. He had offered once to take the Prince on Malta with him, but I had declined. It was not that I thought that he or his horse lacked the strength. I could not define exactly why I felt I must keep possession of Dutiful's body. I worried that he had been so long insensible. Somewhere, I knew his mind worked, that he saw with the cat's eyes, felt with the cat's body. Sooner or later, he would realize—

The Prince stirred in my arms. I kept silent. It took him some little while to come back to himself. As he regained his senses, he twitched unpleasantly in my arms, reminding me of my own seizures. Then he sat up with a sudden hoarse gasp of breath. Breath after breath he took, as he turned his head wildly from side to side, trying to make sense of his situation. I heard him swallow. In a dry and cracked voice he asked, "Where are we?"

Useless to lie. Above us on the hill, Laurel's mysterious standing stones cast their shadows. He would surely recognize them. I didn't bother to answer him at all. Lord Golden rode closer to us.

"My Prince, are you well? You have been long unconscious."

"I am—well. Where are you taking me?"

They come!

In a breath, our situation had changed. I saw the wolf fleeing back toward us. On the road behind him, horsemen had suddenly appeared. I made them five at a quick count. Two hounds, Wit-beasts both, ran alongside them. I swiveled in my saddle. Two rises back, other riders were cresting a hill. I saw one lift an arm, waving a triumphant greeting to the other group of riders.

"They've caught us," I said calmly to the Fool.

He looked ill.

"Up the hill. We'll put one of those barrows at our back." I reined Myblack from the road, and my companions followed.

"Let me go!" my Prince commanded me. He struggled in my arms, but his long insensibility had left him weak. It was not easy to keep my grip on him, but we had not far to go. As we came abreast of the barrow and the adjacent standing stone, I reined in Myblack. My dismount was not graceful, but I pulled the Prince down with me. Myblack stepped wearily away from us, and then turned to give me a look of rebuke. In an instant the Fool was beside us. I sidestepped Dutiful's swing at me, caught his wrist and stepped behind him with it. I caught his other shoulder and held him firmly, one arm twisted high behind his back. I was no rougher than I had to be, but he did not give in easily. "Breaking your arm or dislocating your shoulder wouldn't kill you," I pointed out to him harshly. "But it would keep you from being a nuisance for a time."

He subsided, grunting with pain. The wolf was a gray streak pouring himself up the hill toward us. "Now what?" the Fool asked me as he stared around us wide-eyed.

"Now we make a stand," I said. The riders below us were already spreading wide. The barrow at our backs would be a poor barrier against attack from behind, blinding us as much as it shielded us. The wolf stood with us, panting.

"You'll die here," the Prince pointed out through gritted teeth. I still held him quite firmly.

"That seems very likely," I conceded.

"You'll die, and I'll go with them." His voice was strained

with pain. "So why be stupid? Release me now. I'll go to them. You can run. I promise I'll ask them to let you go."

My eyes met the Fool's over the boy's head. I knew what my answer to that would be, but then I knew what I'd be sending the Prince to face. It might buy us an opportunity to come after him again, but I doubted it. The woman-cat would see to it that they hunted us down and killed us. Death standing and waiting, or death after flight? I didn't want to choose how my friends would die.

I'm too tired to flee. I'm dying here.

The Fool's eyes wavered to Nighteyes. I do not know if he grasped that flicker of thought, or if he simply saw the wolf's weariness. "Stand and fight," he said faintly.

He drew his sword from its sheath. I knew he had never fought in his life. As he lifted his blade, he looked very uncertain. Then he took a breath, and set his face in the lines of Lord Golden's expression. He squared his shoulders and an expression of cold competence came into his eyes.

He can't fight. Don't be stupid.

The riders were closing in. They walked their horses up the hill toward us, unhurried, letting us watch our deaths come. *You have an alternative?*

"You can't hold me and fight!" Dutiful's voice was elated. He obviously believed that they had already won. "The moment you let go, I'll run. You'll die for nothing! Let me go now, let me talk to them. Maybe I can bargain for your life."

Do not let her have him. Kill him before you let them take him.

I felt a great coward, but shared the thought anyway. *I do not know if I can do that.*

You must. We both know what they intend. If you cannot kill him then . . . then take him into the pillar. The boy can Skill, and you were linked with the Scentless One once. It may be enough. Go into the pillar. Take them with you.

The riders below conferred with one another briefly, then fanned out to flank us as they came. As the woman had promised, they would take no chances. They were grinning and shouting to one another. Like the Prince, they believed they had us trapped.

It won't work. Don't you remember what it was like? It took all my strength to hold you together in that passage, and we were tightly linked. I might be able to hold the boy together through the journey, or you, but not both of you. I do not know if I could even pull the Fool in with me. Our Skill-link is old and thin. I might lose you all.

You don't have to choose. I cannot go with you. I'm too tired, my brother. But I will stay here and hold them back for as long as I can, while you escape.

"No," I groaned, even as the Fool suddenly said, "The pillar. You said the boy was Skilling. Could not you—?"

"No!" I cried out. "I will not leave Nighteyes to die alone! How can you suggest it?"

"Alone?" The Fool looked puzzled. A very odd smile twisted his mouth. "But he will not be alone. I will be here with him. And"—he drew himself up, squaring his shoulders—"I will die before I allow them to kill him."

Ah, that would be so much better. Every hackle on Nighteyes' body was standing as he watched the advancing line of men and horses, but his eyes glinted merriment at me.

"Send the lad down to us!" a tall man shouted. We ignored him.

"Do you think that makes it better for me?" I demanded of the Fool. They were mad, both of them. "I might be able to go through the pillar. I might even be able to drag the boy through, though I wonder if his mind would come through intact. But I doubt that I can take you with me, Fool. And Nighteyes refuses to go."

"Go where?" Dutiful demanded. He tried to shake off my grip and I twisted his arm tighter. He subsided.

"For the last time, will you yield?" the tall horseman shouted up at us.

"I seek to reason with him!" Lord Golden called back. "Give me time, man!" He put a note of panic in his voice.

"My friend." The Fool set his hand on my shoulder. He pushed me softly, backward toward the stone. I gave ground and took Dutiful with me. The Fool's eyes never left mine. He spoke softly and carefully, as if we were alone and had all the time in the world. "I know I can't go with you. It grieves me that the wolf will not. But I still tell you that you must go and take the boy. Don't you understand? This is what you were born for, why you have stayed alive despite all the odds against you all these years. Why I have forced you to stay alive, despite all that was done to you. There must be a Farseer heir. If you keep him alive and restore him to Buckkeep, that is all that matters. We keep the future on the path I have set for it, even if it must go on without me. But if we fail, if he dies . . ."

"What are you talking about?" the Prince demanded angrily.

The Fool's voice faded. He stared down the hill at the steadily advancing men, but his gaze seemed to go farther than that. My back was nearly touching the monolith. Dutiful was suddenly quiescent in my grip, as if spelled by the Fool's soft voice. "If we all die here," he said faintly. "Then . . . it ends. For us. But he is not the only change we have wrought . . . time must seek to flow as it always has, washing all obstacles away. So . . . fate finds her. In all times, fate battles against a Farseer surviving. Here and now, we guard Dutiful. But if we all fall, if Nettle becomes the lone focus of that battle . . ." He blinked his eyes a number of times, then he drew a ragged breath before he turned back to me. He seemed to be returning from a far journey. He spoke softly, breaking ill tidings to me gently. "I can find no future in which Nettle survives after the Prince has died." His face went sallow and his eyes were old as he admitted, "There are not even any swift, kind ends for her." He drew a deep breath. "If you care anything at all for me, do this thing. Take the boy. Keep him alive."

Every hair on my body stood up in horror. "But—" I choked. All the sacrifices I had made to keep her safe? All for nothing? My mind completed the picture. Burrich, Molly, and their sons would stand beside her, would fall with her. I could not get my breath.

"Please go," the Fool begged me.

I could not tell what the boy made of our talk. He was a weight I grasped, firmly immobilizing him as my mind raced furiously. I knew there was no escape from this maze fate had set us. The wolf formed my thought for me. *If you stay, we all still die. If the boy does not die, the Witted take him, and use him to their own ends. Dying would be kinder. You cannot save us, but you can save the boy.*

I cannot leave you here. We cannot end like this, you and I. Tears blinded me just when I needed to see most clearly.

We not only can, we must. The pack does not die if the cub survives. Be a wolf, my brother. Things are clearer so. Leave us to fight while you save the cub. Save Nettle, too. Live well, for both of us, and someday, tell Nettle tales of me.

And then there was no more time. "Too late now!" a man shouted up at us. The line of men and horses had curved to surround us. "Send us the lad, and we'll end you quick! If not—" And he laughed aloud.

Don't fear for us. I'll force them to kill us quickly.

The Fool rolled his shoulders. He lifted his sword in a two-handed grip. He swung it once, experimentally, then held it aloft. "Go quickly, Beloved." Poised, he looked more a dancer than a warrior.

I could either draw my sword or keep a grip on the Prince. The standing stone was right behind me. I gave it one hasty glance over my shoulder. I could not identify the wind-eroded symbol carved in this face of it. Wherever it took me would have to be good enough. I did not recognize my voice as I demanded of the world, "How can the hardest thing I have ever done in my life also be the most cowardly?"

"What are you doing?" the boy demanded. He sensed something was about to happen, and though he could not have guessed what it was, he began to struggle wildly. "Help me!" he cried to the encircling Piebalds. "Free me now!"

The thunder of charging horses was his answer.

Inspiration struck me. As I tightened my grip on the struggling boy, I spoke to the Fool. "I'll come back. I'll take him through and come back."

"Don't risk the Prince!" The Fool was horrified. "Stay with him and guard him. If you came back for us and were killed, he'd be alone in . . . wherever. Go! Now!" The last smile he gave me was his old Fool's smile, tremulous and yet mocking the world's ability to hurt him. There was a wildness in his golden eyes that was not fear of death, but acceptance of it. I could not bear to look at it. The closing circle of horsemen engulfed us. The Fool swung his sword and it cut a gleaming arc in the blue day. Then a Piebald charged between us, swinging his blade and yelling. I dragged the Prince back with me.

I caught a last glimpse of the Fool standing over the wolf, a sword in his hands. It was the first time I had ever seen him hold a weapon as if he actually intended to use it. I heard the clash of metal on metal and the wolf's rising snarl as he sprang for a horseman's leg.

The Prince yelled wildly, a wordless cry of fury that was more cat than human. A rider charged straight at us, blade lifted high. But the towering black stone was at my back. "I'll return!" I promised them. Then I tightened one arm around Dutiful, clasping him to my chest. I spoke right by his ear. "Hold tight to who you are!" It was the only warning I could give him. Then I twisted, and pressed my hand against the stone's graven symbol.

chapter XXIII

THE BEACH

The Skill is infinitely large, and yet intimately small. It is as large as the world and the sky above it, and as small as a man's secret heart. The way the Skill flows means that one can ride it, or experience its passage, or encompass the whole of it within one's self. The same sense of immediacy pervades all.

This is why, to master the Skill, one must first master the self.

         HAILFIRE, SKILLMASTER TO QUEEN FRUGAL

I had expected darkness and disorientation. I had expected the Skill pulling at me, and a struggle to hold the Prince and myself together. I forced myself to be aware of both of us, and to keep him intact. Holding on to him within my Skill-barriers was much like clutching a handful of salt in a deluge. There was the same sensation that if I relaxed my grip at all, he would trickle away from me. There was all that, and an illogical sensation that we fell upward. I clutched Dutiful to me, promising myself that it would soon be over. I was not prepared to fall from the pillar into icy seawater.

Saltwater flooded my mouth and nose as I gasped in shock. We tumbled together in the water. My shoulder struck something. Dutiful struggled wildly, and I nearly lost my grip on him. The water sucked at us, and then, just as I saw light through a layer of murky green and deduced which way was up, a wave gathered us and flung us against a rocky beach.

The impact broke my grip on the Prince. The wave rolled us on the rocky shore without letting us reach air. The mussel-and-barnacle-encrusted rocks tore at me. Then, as the wave retreated, my body snagged on the rocks, hooking my sword belt, and the water stranded me there. I lifted my head, choking and gagging out water and sand. I blinked, trying to see Dutiful, and spotted him still in the water. He was belly-down on the beach, scrabbling to catch hold of rocks as the outgoing wave sucked at him. He slid backward toward deeper water, then managed to find a grip and lay still, gasping. I found a breath.

"Get up!" I yelled. It came out as a hoarse caw. "Before the next wave. Get up."

He looked at me without comprehension. I staggered upright and flung myself toward him. Catching the back of his collar, I dragged him over the shredding barnacles and up the rocky beach toward the higher shoreline. A wave still caught us and flung me to my knees, but the water was not powerful enough to drag us out again. The next time the wave went out, Dutiful managed to get to his feet. Holding on to one another, we staggered up past the toothy rocks and into a belt of black sand festooned with squelching strands of tangled kelp. When we reached the loose dry sand, I let go of Prince Dutiful. He took perhaps three more steps and then dropped to the ground. For a time he just lay on his side, breathing. Then he sat up, spat out sand, and wiped his nose on his wet sleeve. He looked all around us with no comprehension, and when his eyes came back to me, his expression was that of a confused child.

"What happened?"

The sand in my teeth gritted whenever I moved my mouth. I spat. "We came through a Skill-pillar." I spat again.

"A what?"

"A Skill-pillar," I repeated. I looked back to point it out to him.

There was nothing out there but ocean. Another wave rushed in, reaching higher up the beach. Scummy white foam laced the sand as the water retreated. I came awkwardly to my feet and stared out over the incoming tide. Just water. Moving waves. Crying gulls above the waves. No Skill-pillar of black stone broke that heaving green surface. There was not even a clue as to where it had deposited us out offshore.

No way back.

I had left my friends to die. Regardless of what the Fool had said, I had resolved to return immediately via the pillar. Otherwise, I would not have gone. I would not have done it if I had thought I was not going back to them. Telling myself that did not make me feel a shard less cowardly.

Nighteyes! I quested desperately, flinging the call with all my strength.

No one answered.

"Fool!" The word ripped out of me, a futile scream of Wit and Skill and voice. Distant gulls seemed to echo it mockingly. My hope faded with their dwindling cries over the windswept sea.

Unmoving, I stared out over the water until an incoming wave lapped against my feet. The Prince had not moved, except to fall back onto his side on the wet sand. He lay, staring blankly and shivering. I slowly turned away from the surf and surveyed the land. Black cliffs rose up before us. The tide was coming in. My mind put the pieces together.

"Get up. We have to move before the tide traps us."

To the south, the rocky cliffs gave way to a half-moon of black sand. A grassy tableland backed it. I reached down and seized the Prince's arm. "Up," I repeated. "Unless you want to drown here."

The lad lurched to his feet without protest. We trudged

down the shore as the waves reached ever higher toward us. Desolation was a cold weight inside me. I dared not look at what I had just done. It was too monstrous to consider. While I walked down this beach, did their blood flow down swords? I stopped my mind. As if I were setting walls against an intrusive mind, I blocked all feelings from myself. I stopped all thoughts and became a wolf, concerned only with the "now."

"What was that?" Dutiful demanded suddenly. "That . . . feeling. That pulling . . ." Words failed him. "Was that the Skill?"

"Part of it," I answered brusquely. He seemed entirely too interested in what he had just experienced. Had it called to him that strongly? The Skill's attraction was a terrible trap for the unwary.

"I . . . he tried to teach me, but he couldn't tell me what it felt like. I couldn't tell if I was doing it or not, and neither could he. But that!"

He expected a response to his excitement. I gave him none. The Skill was the last thing I wanted to talk about just now. I didn't want to speak at all. I did not want to break the numbness that wrapped me.

When we reached the beach, I kept Prince Dutiful walking. His wet clothes flapped around his body, and he hugged himself against the chill. I listened to his shivering breaths. A greenish sheen on the sand proved to be the flow of a freshwater stream over the beach to the sea. I walked him upstream, away from the sandy beach and into a field of coarse sedge grasses until I reached a place where the trickle was deep enough for me to cup handfuls of it. I washed out my mouth several times and then drank. I was splashing water on my face to get sand out of my eyes and ears when the Prince spoke again.

"What about Lord Golden and the wolf? Where are they, what happened to them?" He looked out over the water as if he expected to see them there.

"They couldn't come. By now, I imagine your friends have killed them."

It amazed me that I could speak the words so flatly. No choking tears, no gasping breath. It was a thought too terrible to be real. I could not allow myself to consider it. Instead, I flung the words at him, hoping to see him flinch from them. But he just shook his head, as if my words made no sense, then asked numbly, "Where are we?"

"We are here," I replied, and laughed. I had never known that anger and despair could make a man laugh. It was not a pleasant sound, and the Prince cowered away from me for an instant. Then in the next, he stood up very straight and pointed an accusing finger at me. "Who are you?" he demanded, as if he had suddenly discovered the one mystery that underlay all his questions.

I looked up from where I still crouched by the water. I drank another handful before I answered. "Tom Badgerlock." I slicked my hair back with my wet hands. "For this. I was born with this white streak at my temple, and so my parents named me."

"Liar." He spoke the word with flat contempt. "You're a Farseer. You may not have the looks of a Farseer, but you have the Skill of one. Who are you? A distant cousin? Someone's by-blow?"

I'd been called a bastard many times in my life, but never by someone I might call a son. I looked up at Dutiful, Verity's and Kettricken's heir from the seed of my body. Well, if I'm a bastard, I wonder what that makes you? What I said instead was, "Does it matter?"

While he was still struggling to find an answer to that, I scanned our surroundings. I was stuck in this place with him, at least until the tide went out. If I was fortunate, it would bare the pillar that brought us here, and I could use it to return. If I was unfortunate, the water wouldn't retreat that far, and then I'd have to discover just where we truly were and how to get back to Buckkeep.

The Prince spoke angrily to mask his sudden uncertainty. "We can't be that far. It only took us a moment to arrive."

"Magic such as we used makes little of distance. We may not even be in the Six Duchies anymore." I abruptly decided he needed to know no more than that. Whatever I told him, the woman would likely know, as well. The less said, the better.

Slowly he sat down on the ground. "But—" he said, and then fell silent. The look on his face was that of an apprehensive child reaching out desperately for something familiar. But my heart did not go out to him. Instead, I repressed an urge to give him a firm whack on the back of the head. For this whimpering, self-obsessed juvenile, I'd traded the lives of my wolf and my friend. It seemed the poorest bargain I'd ever made. Nettle, I reminded myself. Keeping him alive might keep her safe. Farseer heir or not, it was the only value that I could see in him just then.

I am disappointed in my son.

I examined that thought, and reasserted to myself that Dutiful was not my son, and since I had never accepted any responsibility for his rearing, I had no right to be either disappointed or pleased by him. I walked away from him. I let the wolf in me have ascendancy, and he spoke to me of the need for immediate creature comfort. The wind along the beach was constant and chill, slapping my wet garments against my body. Find wood, get a fire going if I could. Dry out. Look for food at the same time. There was no point to agonizing about what had become of Nighteyes and the Fool. The tide was still coming in. That meant that the next low tide would probably come in the dark of night. The following low tide would be sometime the next morning. I had to be resigned that my next opportunity to return to my friends was nearly a full day away. So, for now, gather strength and rest.

I looked across the grassy tableland at the forest that backed it. The trees here were the green of summer still, yet somehow it impressed me as an unfriendly and lifeless place. I decided that there was no point in hiking across the meadow and hunting under the trees. I had no heart for a chase and a kill. The small creatures of the beach would suffice.

It was a poor decision to make during an incoming tide. There was driftwood to gather for a fire, flung high by a previous storm tide, out of reach of today's water. The blue mussels and other shellfish were already underwater, however. I chose a place where the cliffs subsided into the table-land, a spot somewhat sheltered from the wind, and kindled a small fire. Once I had it going, I took off my boots and socks and shirt, and wrung as much water from everything as I could. I propped the garments on driftwood sticks to dry near the fire, and put my boots upside down on two stakes to drain. I sat by the fire, hugging myself against the chill of the fading day. Expecting nothing, I still ventured to quest again. *Nighteyes?*

There was no response. It meant nothing, I told myself. If he and the Fool had managed to escape, then he would not reach out toward me for fear of being detected by the Piebalds. It might mean only that he was choosing to be silent. Or it might mean he was dead. I wrapped my own arms around myself and held tight. I must not think such thoughts or grief would tear me apart. The Fool had asked me to keep Prince Dutiful alive. I'd do that. And the Piebalds would not dare to kill my friends. They would want to know what had become of the Prince, how he could have vanished before their eyes.

What would they do to the Fool to wring answers from him?

Don't think such things.

Reluctantly, I rose to seek out the Prince.

The boy had not moved from where I had left him. I walked up behind him, and when he did not even turn toward me, I nudged him rudely with my foot. "I've a fire," I said gruffly.

He didn't respond.

"Prince Dutiful?" I could not keep the sneer from my voice. He did not flinch.

I crouched down next to him and set a hand on his shoulder. "Dutiful." I leaned around him to look into his face.

He wasn't there.

His expression was slack, his eyes dull. His mouth hung slightly ajar. I groped toward our tenuous Skill-bond. It was like tugging at a broken fishing line. There was no resistance, no sense that anyone had ever been at the other side of that bond.

A terrible echo of a long-ago lesson came to me. "If you give in to the Skill, if you do not hold firm against its attraction, then the Skill can tatter you away and you will become as a great drooling babe, seeing nothing, hearing nothing . . ." The hair stood up on the back of my neck. I shook the Prince, but his head just lolled and nodded on his neck. "Damn me!" I roared to the sky. I should have foreseen he would try to reach the cat, I should have known this could happen.

I tried to force calmness on myself. Stooping, I lifted his arm and set it across my shoulders. I set my arm around his waist and drew him to his feet. As I hauled him down the beach, his toes dragged in the sand. When I reached the fire, I put him down beside it. He sprawled over on his side.

I spent several minutes replenishing the blaze with nearby driftwood. I built it large and hot, not caring who or what it might draw. My hunger and my weariness were forgotten. I dragged the Prince's boots from his feet, emptied them of water, and set them upside down to dry. My own shirt was steaming warm now. I peeled Dutiful's wet shirt from his back and hung it out. I spoke to him the whole time, rebuking him and taunting him at first, but before long I was pleading with him. He made no response at all. His skin was chill. I wrestled his arms into the sleeves and dragged my warmed shirt onto him. I chafed his arms, but his stillness seemed to invite the cold to fill him. With every passing moment, his body seemed to have less life in it. It was not that his breathing labored or that his heart beat more slowly, but more that my Wit-sense of his presence was fading, exactly as if he were traveling away from me.

Finally, I sat down behind him. I pulled him back against me, his back to my chest, and put my arms around him in a vain effort to warm him. "Dutiful," I said by his ear. "Come back, boy. Come back. You've a throne to inherit, and a kingdom to rule. You can't go like this. Come back, lad. It can't all have been for nothing. Not the Fool and Nighteyes both spent for nothing. What will I say to Kettricken? What will Chade say to me? Gods, gods, what would Verity say to me now?"

It was not so much what Verity would have said to me as what Verity would have done for me. I held his son close to me, and then placed my face next to his beardless cheek. I took a deep breath and dropped all my walls. I closed my eyes, and slipped into the Skill in search of him.

I nearly lost myself.

There have been times when I could scarcely reach the flow of Skill, and in other times and places, I have experienced the Skill as a flowing river of power, incredibly swift and powerful. As a boy, I had nearly lost myself in that river, sustained and rescued only by Verity's intervention. I had grown in strength and control since then. Or so I had thought. This sensation was like diving into a racing current of Skill. Never before had I felt it so strong and seductive. In my present frame of mind, it seemed to offer the complete and perfect answer to me. Just let go. Stop being this person Fitz trapped in a battle-scarred body. Stop bleeding sorrow for the death of my closest friends. Just let go. The Skill offered me existence without thought. It was not the suicide's temptation to die and make the world stop for him. This was far more enticing. Change the shape of your being and leave all those considerations behind. Merge.

If I had had only myself to think of, I know I would

have yielded to it. But the Fool had charged me with seeing that he did not die in vain, and my wolf had bade me live and tell Nettle of him. Kettricken had asked me to bring her son back to her. Chade was depending on me. And Hap. So I found myself in that seething current of streaming sensations, and I fought to remain who I was. I don't know how long it took me to do that. Time has no meaning in that place. That alone is one of the Skill's dangers. Some part of me knew I was burning my body's strength, but when one is immersed in the Skill it is hard to care about physical things.

When I was sure of myself, I cautiously reached out in search of Dutiful.

I had thought it would be easy to find him. The night before, it had been effortless. I had but clasped his hand then, and found him within the Skill. Tonight, though I knew that somewhere I cradled his chilling body, I could not discover him. It is difficult to describe how I sought him. The Skill is not truly a place or a time. Sometimes I think it can be described as being without the boundaries of self. At other times, that defining seems too narrow, for "self" is not the only boundary we set to how we experience being.

I opened myself to the Skill and let it stream through me like water through a sieve, and still I found no trace of the Prince. I stretched myself beneath the flow of the Skill like a hillside full of tiny grasses under sunlight and let it touch each blade of me, and still I could not sense him. I wove myself throughout the Skill, twining over it like ivy, and still I could not separate the lad from its flow.

He had left a sense of himself in the Skill, but like a bootmark in fine dust on a windy day that trace was crumbling to meaningless grains flowing with the Skill. I gathered what I could of him, but it was no more Prince Dutiful than the scent of a flower is the flower. Nevertheless, I took to myself the bits that I recognized and held them fiercely. It was becoming more difficult for me to recall what exactly was the essence of the Prince. I had never known him well, and the body that my body held was rapidly losing its connection to him.

In an effort to find the boy, I engaged completely with the Skill. I did not surrender myself, but I stepped free of all the safety holds that always before I had clung to. It was an eerie feeling. I was a kite cut free and flying, a tiny boat with no hand on the tiller. I had not lost my sense of self, but I had given up the absolute certainty that I could find my way back to my body. Yet it put me no closer to finding Dutiful. It only made me more aware of the vastness that surrounded me and the hopelessness of my task. It would have been easier to net the smoke from an extinguished fire than to gather the boy together again.

And all the while the Skill plucked at me, whispering promises. It was only cold and rushing so long as I resisted it. If I gave in, I knew it would become all warmth and comfort and belonging. If I surrendered to it, I would subside into peaceful existence without individual awareness. What would be so terrible about that? Nighteyes and the Fool were gone. I'd failed in my mission to bring Dutiful back to Kettricken. Molly did not wait for me; she had a life and a love. Hap, I told myself, trying to stir some sense of responsibility. What about Hap? But I knew that Chade would see to Hap's needs, at first out of a sense of duty to me, but before long for the sake of the boy himself.

But Nettle. What of Nettle?

The answer was terrible. I had already failed her. I knew I could not recover Dutiful, and without him, she was doomed. Did I wish to return and witness that? Could I be aware of it and stay sane? Then a worse thought came to me. In this timeless place, it had all already happened. Even now, she had perished.

That decided me. I let go of the bits of Dutiful and they streamed away from me. How to describe that? As if I stood on a sunny hillside and released a rainbow I had imprisoned in my hand. As he flowed away, I realized that those traces of him had become tangled with my own essence. My being

flowed with his. It didn't matter. FitzChivalry Farseer ribboned away from me, the thread of myself snagged and now
unraveling in the streaming Skill.

Once, I had put memories into a stone dragon. I had
gratefully thrust away pain and hopeless love and a dozen
other experiences. I had given away that part of my life
so that the dragon would have enough essence to come to
life. This felt different. Imagine bleeding that feels pleasur-
able and yet is still just as deadly. I passively witnessed the
draining.

Now stop that. Warm feminine amusement in the voice
that filled my mind. I was helpless to prevent it as she
wound the thread of my being around me as if she were
gathering yarn back into a skein. *I had forgotten how passion-
ately dramatic humans can be at their silliest. No wonder we enjoyed you so. Such ardent little pets as you were.*

Who? I could refine the thought no more than that.
Her presence left me limp with happiness.

*And this is yours too I suppose. No, wait, this is a different
one. Two of you here, at once, and coming all apart! Are you
lost, then?*

Lost. I repeated the thought to her, unable to frame any
concept of my own. I was a dandled infant, adored for my
mere presence, and it left me helpless with delight. Her
love transfused me with warmth. It was something I had
never even been able to imagine before: I was loved
enough, and valued enough, and I needed nothing more
than what I presently had. This enough was more bountiful
than plenty, more rich than a king's gleaming hoard. Never
in my life had I experienced this sensation.

*Back you go. Be more careful next time. Most of the others
would not even notice that they had attracted you.*

Like plucking a burr off herself, I thought with dim dismay. While she held me, I was too giddy with pleasure to
oppose her, even though I knew she was about to do the unthinkable. *Wait wait wait,* I managed, but the thought was

.weightless and she gave me no heed. For less than a blink I was aware of Dutiful close beside me.

Then I was back in the horrid confines of my miserable little body. It ached, it was cold and damaged, old damage, new damage, it had never worked that well in the first place, and worst of all, it did not have enough of anything. It was riddled with wants and great gaping needs. In here, I had never had, I would never have, enough love or regard or—

I flung myself out of it again.

All that happened was that my body gave a great twitch and fell over on the sand. I could not get out of it. I was cramped and stifling in the ill-fitting flesh that coated and confined me, and I could not find a way out. The discomfort was acute and alarming, akin to having a limb twisted or being choked. The more I struggled, the more I sank into the thrashing limbs of my flesh, until I was hopelessly embedded in my sweating, shaking self. I subsided, feeling the misery of having a physical self. Cold. Sand in the wet waistband of my leggings, sand at the corner of one eye and up my nose. Thirsty. Hungry. Bruised and cut.

Unloved.

I sat up slowly. The fire was nearly out; I'd been gone for quite a time. I got up stiffly and tossed the last piece of wood onto it. The world fell into place around me. My losses engulfed me as completely as the night that surrounded me. I stood perfectly still, mourning the Fool and Nighteyes, but devastated even beyond those losses by my abandonment by . . . by whatever she had been. It was not like waking from a dream. Rather, it was the opposite. In her, there had been truth and immediacy and the simplicity of being. Plunged back into this world, I sensed it as a tangling web of distractions and annoyances, illusions and tricks. I was cold and my shoulder hurt and the fire was going out, and all those discomforts plucked at me. Larger loomed the problem of Prince Dutiful and how we would get back to Buck and what had become of Nighteyes and the Fool. Yet even those things now seemed but diversions danced before my eyes to keep my attention from the immense reality beyond them. All of this existence was composed of trivial pains and searing agonies, and each of them was yet another mask between me and the face of the eternal.

Yet the layers of masks were back in place, and must be recognized. My body shivered. The tide was going out again. I could not see anything beyond the ring of our firelight, but I could hear the waters retreat in the rhythm of the falling waves. The unmistakable smell of low tide, of bared kelp and shellfish, was in the air.

The Prince lay on his back staring up at the sky. I looked down at him and thought at first that he was unconscious. In the fickle light of my dying fire, I saw only black cavities where his eyes should be. Then he spoke. "I had a dream." There was wonder and uncertainty in his voice.

"How nice." It was a neutral sneer. I was incredibly relieved that he was back in his body and could speak. To an equal degree, I hated that I was trapped inside my own body again and had to listen to him.

He seemed immune to my nastiness. The edges of his voice were soft. "I've never had a dream like that. I could feel . . . everything. I dreamed my father held me together and told me that I was going to be fine. That was all. But the strangest part was, that was enough." Dutiful smiled up at me. It was a luminous smile, wise and young. It made him look like Kettricken.

"I have to find more firewood," I said at last. I turned from the light and the fire and the smiling boy and walked away into the darkness.

I didn't look for wood. The retreating waves had left the sand wet and packed under my bare feet. A fading slice of moon had risen. I looked at it, then up at the sky, and felt my stomach drop. According to the stars, we were substantially south of the Six Duchies. My previous experience with Skill-pillars was that they could save a few days of travel time. This evidence of their power was not reassuring. If tomorrow's low tide did not bare the stone, we faced a long journey home, with no resources to aid us. The moon reminded me too that our time was dwindling. In eight nights, the new moon would herald Prince Dutiful's betrothal ceremony. Would the Prince stand at the narcheska's side? It was hard to make the question seem important.

There are times when not thinking requires all of one's concentration. I don't know how far I walked before I stepped on it. It shifted in the wet sand beneath my foot, and for an instant I thought I had stepped on a knife blade lying flat on the sand. In the darkness, I stooped and located it by touch. I picked it up. It was about the length of the blade of a butcher's knife, and somewhat shaped the same. It was hard and cold, stone or metal, I could not tell which. But it was not a knife. I ran my fingers over it cautiously. There was no sharpened edge. A rib ran up the center of it, and then the object was finely striated in parallel rows at an angle to the rib on both sides. It culminated in a sort of tube at one end. It was heavy, yet not as heavy as it seemed it should have been. I stood holding it in the darkness, feeling sure I knew what it was, but unable to summon up that knowledge. It was familiar in an eerie way, as if I picked up something that had been mine a long time ago.

The puzzle of the object was a welcome distraction from my own thoughts. I held it in my hand as I continued down the beach. I hadn't gone a dozen steps before I stepped on another one. I picked it up. By touch I compared the two. They were not quite identical, one being slightly longer. I held them, weighing them in my hands.

When I stepped on the third one, I was almost expecting it. I lifted it from the sand and wiped the wet grit from it. Then I stood still where I was. I had a strange sense of something waiting for me. It hovered, unable to take shape without my volition. I had the strangest sensation of standing on the edge of a cliff. One more step, and I would either plummet to my death, or discover I could fly.

I stepped back from it. I turned around and walked

back toward the dying campfire on the beach. As I watched, I saw Dutiful's silhouette pass before the flames, and the sparks leapt up into the night as he dropped more wood on the fire. Well, at least he could do that much for himself.

It was hard to go back to the circle of that light. I didn't want to face him, didn't want his questions or his accusations. I did not want to pick up the reins of my life. But by the time I reached the fire, Dutiful was stretched out beside it, feigning sleep. He wore his own shirt, and mine had been draped on the stakes to warm and dry. I put it on silently. As I tugged up the collar, my fingers encountered Jinna's charm. Ah. Well, that explained his smile and kindly words. I lay down on my side of the fire.

Before I closed my eyes, I examined the objects I had found. They were feathers. Of stone or metal, I still could not say. In the fire's deceptive light, they were dark gray. I instantly knew where they belonged. I doubted they would ever be there. I put them on the ground beside me and closed my eyes, fleeing into sleep.

chapter XXIV

CONFRONTATIONS

So up strides Jack and stands before the Other, so bold that he rocked from his heels to his toes and back again. "Oh, ho," says he, and he holds up the bag of red pebbles that he'd gathered. "So all that rests on this beach is yours? Well, I say that what I've gathered is mine, and he who wants what is mine will not get it without me taking a piece of his flesh in exchange." And Jack showed the Other his every tooth, from white in the front to black in the back, and his fist too doubled up like a tree knot. "I'll slam you," he says, "and I'll rip your ears from the sides of your head." And it's certain that he would have that very moment, save that Others have no more ears than a toad, as any child knows.

But all the same, the Other knew he would not take the sack of red pebbles without a fight. So all in a moment, he shimmered and shook. He reeked of dead fish no longer then, but gave off the scent of every flower that blooms in high summer. He shivered his skin so he sparkled and to Jack's eyes there was suddenly a maiden standing there, naked as a new leaf and licking her lips as if she tasted honey there.

    ~ *"TEN VOYAGES WITH JACK, VOYAGE THE FOURTH"*

I think that for a time I slept dreamlessly. Certainly I was weary enough. Far too much had happened to me, far too swiftly. Sleep was as much a respite from thought as it was rest. Yet after a time, dreams claimed me and tumbled me. I climbed the steps to Verity's tower. He was sitting at the window, Skilling. My heart leapt joyfully at first sight of him, but when he turned to me, his face was grieved. "You did not teach my son, Fitz. I'll have to take your daughter for that." Both Nettle and Dutiful were stones on a game cloth, and with a single sweep of his hand, he exchanged their positions. "It's your move," he said. But before I could do anything, Jinna came to brush all the stones from the cloth into her hand. "I'll make a charm of these," she promised me. "One to protect all of the Six Duchies."

"Put it away," I begged her, for I was the wolf and the charm was one against predators. It sickened and cowed me just to behold it. It was potent, far more potent than any of the other charms she had shown me. It was magic stripped to its most basic form, all human sentiment abraded from it. It was magic of an older time and place, magic that cared nothing for people. It was as implacable as the Skill. It was sharp as knives and burning as poison. "Put it away!"

He couldn't hear me. He had never been able to hear me. The Scentless One wore it around his throat, and he had opened his collar wide to bare it. It was all I could do to force myself to stand still and guard his back. Even behind him, I could feel its harsh radiance. I could smell blood, his and my own. I still felt the warm slow seep of my blood down my flank, and my strength dripping away with it.

A man with a whining dog stood guard over us, scowling. Behind him, a fire burned, and Piebalds slept around it. Beyond them was the open mouth of the shelter, and an edge of dawn in the sky. It seemed horribly far away. Our guard's face was contorted, not just with anger but with fear and frustration. He longed to hurt us, but dared come no closer. It was not a dream. It was the Wit and I was with Nighteyes and he lived. The surge of joy I felt amused him but only for an instant. *Your witnessing this will not make it easier for either of us. You should have stayed away from this.*

"Cover that damned thing!" the guard growled at him.

"Make me!" the Scentless One suggested. I heard the Fool's lilting reply with the wolf's ears. The whip-snap of his old mockery capered in his words. Some part of him relished this defiance. His sword was gone, taken from him when they had been captured, but he sat defiantly straight, throat bared to show a charm that burned with cold magic. He had placed himself between the wolf and those who would torment him.

Nighteyes showed me a chamber, walls of stone, floor of earth. A cave, perhaps. He and the Fool were in a corner of it. Blood had sheeted down the side of the Fool's tawny face. Dried, it had cracked so that he looked like a badly glazed pot. Nighteyes and the Fool were prisoners, violently taken but kept alive, the Fool because he might know where the Prince had gone and how, and the wolf because of his link to me.

They puzzled that out, that we are linked?

I'm afraid it was obvious to all.

From out of the shadows, the cat appeared. She stalked stiffly toward us. Her whiskers vibrated and her intent stare fixed on Nighteyes. When the guard's dog turned to look at her, she spat and slashed at him. He leapt back with a yipe and the guard's scowl deepened, but both he and his dog gave ground to her. She prowled back and forth, padding stiff-legged and casting sidelong glances up at the Fool while rumbling a threat in her throat. Her tail floated behind her.

The charm holds her at bay?

Yes. But not for long, I fear. The wolf's next thought surprised me. *The cat is a miserable creature, honeycombed with the woman as a sick deer is riddled with parasites. She stalks about with a human looking out of her eyes. She does not even move like a true cat anymore.*

The cat halted suddenly and opened her mouth wide as if taking our scent. Then she suddenly spun about and trotted purposefully away.

You should not have come. She senses you are with me. She has gone to find the big man. He is bonded to a horse. The charm does not bother prey, nor those who bond with them.

The wolf's thought rang with contempt for grass-eaters,

but there was an element of dread behind it. I pondered it. The Fool's charm was a charm against predators; it was logical it would not bother the man bonded to the warhorse.

Before I could follow that thought further, the cat returned with the man behind her. She sat down at his side, insufferably pleased with herself, and fixed us with a very uncatlike stare. The big man stared too, not at the defiant Fool, but past him at my wolf.

"There you are. We've been waiting for you," he said slowly.

Nighteyes would not meet his gaze, but the big man's words fell on his ears and came to me. "I have your friends, you treacherous coward. Will you betray them as you've betrayed your Old Blood? I know you're somewhere with the Prince. I don't know how you vanished, nor do I care. I say only this to you. Bring him back, or they die slowly."

The Fool stood up between the man and my wolf. I knew he spoke to me when he said, "Don't listen. Stay away. Keep him safe."

I could not see past the Fool, but the shadow of the big man loomed suddenly larger. "Your hedge-witch charm means nothing to me, Lord Golden."

Then the Fool's flying body crashed suddenly into my battered wolf, and my Wit-bond to him vanished.

I jolted awake. I leapt to my feet, but all I saw was the graying of dawn and the empty beach. I heard only the cries of seabirds wheeling overhead. In my sleep, I had drawn my body up into a ball for warmth, but now I shook with something that was not cold. Sweat sheathed me and I was breathing hard. Sleep had fled completely. I stared out over the sea, my dream still vivid in my mind. I did not doubt the reality of it. I took a long, shuddering breath. The tide was rising again, but had not quite peaked. I sought in vain for some sign of a Skill-pillar thrusting up from the waves. I would have to wait until afternoon, when the water would be at full ebb. I dared not wonder what would happen to the

Fool and Nighteyes in the intervening hours. If luck sided with me, the retreating waves would bare the pillar that had brought us here, and I would go back to them. The Prince would have to manage here on his own until I could return for him.

If the retreating water did not reveal the pillar— I refused to consider what that might mean. Instead, I focused on the problems I could solve right now. Find food and eat it. Keep up my strength. And break the woman's hold on the Prince. I turned to the still-sleeping boy and nudged him firmly with my foot. "Get up!" I grated at him.

I knew that waking him would not necessarily break his Wit-link with the cat, but it would make it more difficult for him to focus on it exclusively. When I was a lad, I had spent my sleeping hours "dreaming" of hunts with Nighteyes. Awake, I was still aware of the wolf, but not in such an immediate way. When Dutiful groaned, and rolled away from me, stubbornly clinging to his Wit-dreams, I bent over him, seized him by the collar, and stood him on his feet. "Wake up!"

"Leave me alone, you ugly bastard," he rasped at me. Catlike he glowered at me, head canted, mouth ajar. I almost expected him to hiss and claw at me. Then my temper got the better of me. I gave him a violent shake, then thrust him from me, so that he stumbled back, lost his footing, and nearly fell into the embers of the fire.

"Don't call me that," I warned him. "Don't you ever call me that!"

He wound up sitting on the sand, staring up at me in astonishment. I doubted that anyone had ever spoken to him that way in his life, let alone given him a shaking. It shamed me that I was the first. I turned away from him and spoke over my shoulder. "Build up the fire. I'm going to see if the tide has bared anything for us to eat, before it covers it up again." I strode away without looking back at him. Within three strides, I wanted to go back for my boots, but

I would not. I didn't want to face him again just yet. My temper with him was still too high, my thwarted fury at the Piebalds too strong.

The tide had not quite reached the sand of the beach. On the bared black rock I stepped gingerly, trying to avoid barnacles. I gathered black mussels, and seaweed to steam them in. I found one fat green crab wedged under an outcropping of rock. He attempted to defend himself by clamping onto my finger. He bruised me but I captured him and pouched him in my shirt with the mussels. My gathering carried me some little way down the beach. The chill of the day and the simplicity of collecting food cooled my anger toward the Prince. Dutiful was being used, I reminded myself, by folk who should know better. The ugliness of what the woman was doing should prove that the folk who conspired had no ethics. I should not blame the boy. He was young, not stupid or evil. Well, perhaps young and stupid, but had not I been the same once?

I was returning to the fire when I stepped on the fourth feather. As I stooped to pick it up, I saw the fifth one glinting in the sunlight, not a dozen paces away. The fifth one shone with extraordinary colors, dazzling to the eyes, but when I reached it, I decided it had been a trick of the sunlight and damp, for it was as flat a gray as its brethren.

The Prince was not by the fire when I returned, though he had built it up before he left. I set the two feathers with the three I had found the night before. I glanced about for the lad and saw him walking back toward me. He had evidently visited the stream, for his face was damp and his hair washed back from his brow. When he reached the fire, he stood over me for a time, watching me as I killed the crab and wrapped it and the mussels in the flat fronds of seaweed. With a stick I nudged some of the burning wood aside and then gingerly placed the packet on the bared coals. It sizzled. He watched me pushing other coals up around it. When he spoke, his voice was even, as if he commented on the weather.

"I've a message for you. If you do not bring me back before sunset, they will kill them both, the man and the wolf."

I did not even betray that I had heard his words. I kept my eyes on the food, edging the coals closer to it. When I finally spoke, my words were just as cold. "Perhaps, if they do not free the man and the wolf before noon, I will kill you." I lifted my face to look into his, and showed him my assassin's eyes. He took a step back.

"But I am the Prince!" he cried. An instant later, I saw how he despised those words. But he could not call them back. They hung quivering in the air between us.

"That would only matter if you acted like the Prince," I observed callously. "But you don't. You're a tool, and you don't even know it. Worse, you're a tool used against not just your mother, but the whole of the Six Duchies." I looked aside from him as I spoke the words I must. "You don't even know that the woman you worship doesn't exist. Not as a woman, at any rate. She's dead, Prince Dutiful. But when she died, instead of letting go, she pushed into her cat's mind, to live there. She rides the cat, a shameful thing for any Old Blood one to do. And she has used the cat to lure you in and deceive you with words of love. I do not know what she intends in the end, but it will not be good for any of you. And it will cost my friends' lives."

I should have known that she was with him. I should have known that that was the one thing that she would not permit me to tell him. He hissed like a cat from his open mouth as he sprang, and the tiny sound gave me an instant of warning. I leaned to one side as he threw himself at me. I turned to his passage, caught him by the back of his shirt, and jerked him back toward me. I pinioned him in a hug. He threw his head back in an effort to smash my face, but got only the side of my jaw. I had long been wise to that trick, as it was one of my own favorites.

It was not much of a fight, as fights go. He was at that lanky stage of his growth when bones and muscles do not yet match one another, and he fought with the heedless frenzy of youth. I had long been comfortable in my body, and I had a man's weight and years of experience to back it. With his arms tightly pinioned, he could do little more than toss his head about and kick at me with his feet. I recognized abruptly that no one had ever grappled with him this way. Of course. A prince would be trained with a blade, not with fists. Nor had he had brothers or a father for rough play. He did not know what to make of being manhandled this way. He *repelled* at me, the Wit equivalent of a mental shove. As Burrich had so long ago with me, I deflected it back at him. I felt his shock at that. In the next moment, he redoubled his struggle. I felt the fury that coursed through him. It was like fighting myself, and I knew he set no limits to what he would do in an attempt to injure me. His mindless savagery was limited only by his inexperience. He tried to fling us both to the ground, but I had his balance too well. His efforts to wriggle out of my embrace only made me tighten my grip. His face was bright red before his head suddenly drooped. For a moment he hung limp and gasping in my arms. Then he whispered in a sullen voice, "Enough. You win."

I let go, expecting him to drop to the sand. Instead, he spun, my knife in his hand, and thrust it into my belly. At least, that was his intent. The buckle of my sword belt deflected it, the blade skidded across the leather of the belt, and then plunged past me, wrapping in my shirt as it went. The blade so near my flesh woke my anger. I caught his wrist, snapped it sharply back, and the knife went flying. A blow from my fist to the side of his neck hammered him to his knees. He yowled in fury as he fell, and the sound stood my hair on end. The glaring glance he turned on me was not the Prince's, but some awful combination of cat, boy, and a woman who would master them both. Her will was the one that brought him up off his knees and springing toward me.

I tried to catch his charge and control him, but he fought like a mad thing, clawing and spitting and ripping at my hair. I hit him hard in the center of his chest, a blow that should have at least slowed him, but he came back at me, his fury doubled. I knew then that she had full control of him, and that she would care nothing about pain I dealt him. I'd have to damage him if I wanted to stop him, and even at that moment, I could not bring myself to do that. So I flung myself to meet his charge, wrapped him in my arms, and used my weight to bear him down. We came down very near the fire, but I was on top, and resolved to stay there. Our faces were inches apart as I made good my hold on him. He twisted his head about wildly, and tried to strike me in the face with his brow. The eyes that met mine were not the Prince's. She spat up at me and cursed me. I lifted him and slammed him back against the earth. I saw his head bounce off the ground. He should have been near stunned, but he darted his mouth at my arm as if to bite me. I felt a surge of fury that started somewhere so deep it was outside me.

"Dutiful!" I roared. "Stop fighting me!"

He went limp in my arms. The woman-cat glared at me furiously, but slowly she faded from his eyes. Prince Dutiful goggled up at me in terror. Then even that faded from his eyes. He stared like a dead man. Blood outlined his teeth. It was his own, leaking from his nose and over his mouth. He lay very still. I felt sickened. I peeled myself away from him and stood slowly, chest heaving. "Eda and El, mercy," I prayed as I seldom did, but the gods were not interested in undoing what I had done.

I knew what I had done. I had done it before, coldly and deliberately. I had used the Skill to forcefully imprint on my uncle, Prince Regal, that he would suddenly become adamantly loyal to Queen Kettricken, and the child she carried. I had intended that Skill imprint to be permanent, and it had been, though Prince Regal's untimely death but a few months later had prevented me from ever knowing how long such an imposed command would remain in force.

This time I had acted in anger, with no thought beyond

the moment. The furious command I had given him had printed itself onto his mind with the full strength of my Skill behind it. He had not decided to stop fighting me. Part of him doubtless wished to kill me still. His baffled look told me that he had no comprehension of what I had done to him. Neither did I, really.

"Can you get up?" I asked him guardedly.

"Can I get up?" He echoed my words eerily. His diction was blurred. His eyes rolled about as he seemed to seek an answer in himself, then his gaze came back to me.

"You can get up," I ventured fearfully.

And at my words, he could.

He came to his feet unsteadily, reeling as if I had knocked him cold. The force of my command seemed to have driven the woman's control away. Yet to have supplanted that with my own will over him was no victory for me. He stood, shoulders slightly hunched, as if investigating a pain in himself. After a time, he lifted his eyes to look at me. "I hate you," he told me, in a voice devoid of rancor.

"That's understandable," I heard myself reply. I sometimes shared that sentiment.

I couldn't look at him. I found my knife on the sand and returned it to its sheath. The Prince lurched around the fire, then sat down on the opposite side. I watched him surreptitiously. He wiped his hand across his mouth and then looked at his bloody palm. Mouth slightly ajar, he ran his tongue past his teeth. I feared he would spit some out, but he did not. He made no complaint at all. Instead, he looked like a man trying desperately to recall something. Humiliated and confused, he stared at the fire. I wondered what he pondered.

For a time I sat, feeling all the new little pains he had given me. Many of them were not physical. I doubted they equaled what I had done to him. I could think of nothing to say to him, so I poked at the food in the fire. The seaweed I'd wrapped it in had shrunken and dried in the heat and was beginning to char. I poked the packet out from the coals. Inside, the mussels had opened, and the crab's flesh had gone from opaque to white. Close enough to cooked to satisfy me, I decided.

"There's food here," I announced.

"I'm not hungry," the Prince replied. Voice and eyes were distant.

"Eat it anyway, while there's food to eat." My words came out as a callous command.

Whether it was my Skill-hold upon him, or his own common sense, I couldn't tell. But after I had taken my share of the food from the seaweed packet, he came cautiously around the fire to claim his share. In some ways, he reminded me of Nighteyes when he had first come to me. The cub had been wary and defiant, yet pragmatic enough to realize he had to depend on me to provide for him. Perhaps the Prince knew that without me, he had no hopes of returning easily to Buck.

Or perhaps my Skill-command had burned so deep that even a suggestion from me must be obeyed.

The silence lasted as long as the food did, and a bit longer. I broke it. "I looked at the stars last night."

The Prince nodded. After a time, "We're a long way from home," he admitted grudgingly.

"We may face a long journey home with few resources. Do you know how to live off the land at all?"

Again, a silence followed my words. He did not want to speak to me, but I had knowledge he desperately needed. His question came grudgingly.

"What about the way we came here? Can't we go back that way?" A frown divided his brows as he asked, "How did you learn to do that magic? Is it the Skill?"

I broke a little piece of the truth off and gave it to him. "King Verity taught me to Skill. A long time ago." Before he could ask another question, I announced, "I'm going to walk down the beach and climb up those cliffs. It could be there's a town nearby." If I had to leave the boy here alone, I'd do my best to leave him in a safe place. And if the Skill-pillar did not emerge from the water, then I'd best prepare for a long walk home. My will was iron in that regard. I'd return to Buck if I had to crawl there. And once there, I'd hunt down every one of those Piebalds and kill them slowly. The promise gave purpose to my motions. I began to pull on my socks and boots. The feathers still lay on the sand. A flick of my fingers slid them up my sleeve. I'd secure them better later. I did not wish to discuss them with the Prince. Dutiful made no reply to my words, but when I stood up and walked away from the fire, he followed me. I stopped at the fresh-water stream, to wash my hands and face and to drink, as well. The Prince watched me, and when I was finished, he walked upstream to drink himself. While he was occupied, a strip from my shirt secured the feathers to my forearm. By the time he looked up from washing the blood from his face, my sleeve once more concealed them. Together we walked on. The silence felt like a heavy thing we carried between us. I could feel him mulling over what I had told him about the woman. I wanted to lecture him, to batter him with words until he understood exactly what the woman was trying to do. I wanted to ask if she was still in his mind with him. Instead I bit my tongue and held back my words. He wasn't stupid, I told myself. I'd told him the truth. Now I had to let him work out what it meant to him. We kept walking.

To my relief, we found no more feathers on the sand. We found little of anything useful, though the beach seemed to have more than its share of flotsam. There were bits of rotting rope, and worm-bored lengths of ship timbers. The remains of a dead-eye lay not far from a thole. As we walked, the black cliff gradually loomed larger, until it towered above us and promised a good vantage of the land around it. As we drew closer, I saw that its face was pocked with holes. In a sand cliff, I would have thought them swallows' nests, but not in black stone. The holes seemed too regular and too evenly spaced to be the work of natural forces. The sun striking them seemed to wake glints in some of them. Curiosity beckoned me.

The reality was stranger than anything I could have imagined. When we reached the foot of the cliff, the holes were revealed as alcoves, of graduated sizes. Not all, but many of them held an object. Wordless with wonder, the Prince and I strolled along looking at the lowest levels of alcoves. The variety of objects put me in mind of some mad king's treasure hoard. One held a jeweled goblet, the next a porcelain cup of amazing delicacy. In a large alcove was something that looked like a wooden helmet for a horse, save that a horse's eyes are set on the sides of its head, not the front. A net of gold chain studded with tiny blue gems had been draped over a stone about the size of a woman's head. A tiny box of gleaming wood with images of flowers on it, a lamp carved from some lustrous green stone, a sheet of metal with odd characters graven into it, a delicate stone flower in a vase—treasure after treasure after treasure was displayed there.

Wonder wrapped me. Who would so display such wealth, on an isolated cliff where the wind and waves could batter it? Each item shone as a cherished gem. No tarnish marred the metal, no coating of salt dimmed the wood. To whom did all this belong, and how and why was it here? I looked behind me down the beach, but saw no sign of any inhabitants. No footprints save our own marred the sand. All these marvels were left unguarded. Tempted beyond my control, I reached a finger to touch the flower in the vase, only to encounter resistance. It was as if a soft glass covered the opening of the alcove. Foolishly curious, I pressed my hand against the pliable surface. The harder I pressed, the more unyielding the invisible barrier became. I managed to touch one finger to the flower; it moved and a delicate chiming from its petals just reached my ears. Yet it would have taken a stronger man than I to press a hand in deep enough to grasp that flower. I drew my hand back, and as my flesh left the alcove, my fingers tingled unpleasantly. It reminded me of brushing a nettle, save that it did not last as long.

The Prince had watched me. "Thief," he observed quietly.

I felt like a child caught in some reckless act. "I did not intend to take it. I but wished to touch it."

"Certainly," he observed sarcastically.

"Have it as you will," I replied. I turned my eyes from the distraction of the treasures and looked up the cliff. I realized then that one series of vertical holes was a ladder rather than a succession of alcoves. I said not a word to the Prince as I approached them. Studying them, I decided they had been cut for a man taller than myself, but that I could probably manage.

Dutiful watched me curiously, but I decided he deserved no explanation. I began my climb. Each handhold was a bit of a stretch for me, and placing my feet demanded that I lift each foot uncomfortably high. I was about a third of the way up the cliff before I realized just how much work the whole climb was going to be. The new bruises the Prince had given me throbbed dully. If I had been by myself, I probably would have backed down.

I kept climbing, though the old injury in my back began to shriek in protest each time I reached for the next handhold. By the time I reached the top, my shirt was stuck to my back with sweat. I hauled myself over the lip of the cliff on my belly, and then lay still for a moment or two, catching my breath. The wind was freer here, and colder. I stood up slowly and surveyed my surroundings.

Lots of water. The shores beyond the point I stood on were rocky and abrupt. No beaches. Behind me I saw forest. Beyond the tableland that fronted our beach was more forest. We were either on an island or a peninsula. I saw no sign of human habitation, no ships on the sea, not even a tendril of smoke rising anywhere. If we had to leave our beach on foot, we'd have to go through the forest. The thought sent a surge of unease through me.

After a time, I became aware of a thin sound. I walked to the cliff's edge and looked down. Prince Dutiful looked up at me and shouted a question, but the inflection of his words was all that reached my ears. I made a vague hand motion at him, feeling annoyed. If he wanted so badly to know what I saw, let him climb up here himself. My mind was busy with other concerns. Someone had made those alcoves and gathered those treasures. I should see some sign of human occupation somewhere. Logic demanded it. At last I discovered what might be a footpath far down the beach. It led through the tableland and toward the forest. It did not look well used. It might be no more than a game trail, I thought, but I fixed it in my mind in case we had to resort to it.

Then I looked out over the retreating water, searching for anything that might indicate worked stone. Nothing was exposed yet, but one area looked promising. As each wave fell back, I had glimpses of what might be several large black stones with straight edges. They were still under a shallow layer of water. I hoped it was not a geological quirk. There was a tangle of driftwood on the beach, with a seaweed-festooned branch that pointed toward the rocks. I noted it as a guide. I wasn't sure the tide would bare the rocks completely, but when it reached its full ebb, I intended to investigate them as much as I could.

Finally, with a sigh, I lay down on my belly, scrabbled my legs over the edge, and felt for the first foothold. The climb down was even more unpleasant than the journey up, for I had to grope blindly for each step as I descended. By the time I reached the ground, my legs had a tremor of weariness in them. I skipped the last two steps, dropping to the sand and nearly falling to my knees.

"Well, what did you see?" the Prince demanded.

I let him wait while I caught my breath. "Water. Rocks. Trees."

"No town? No road?"

"No."

"So what are we going to do?" He sounded annoyed, as if it were all my fault.

I knew what I would do. I was going back through the Skill-pillar, even if I had to dive to find it. But what I said to him was, "What I tell you, she knows. Isn't that true?"

That stole all his words from him. He stood for a time just staring at me. When I set off down the beach, he followed me, unaware of how much authority he had ceded to me.

The day was not warm, but hiking on sand demands more effort than walking on solid ground. I was tired from my climb and preoccupied with my own worries, so I made no effort at conversation. It was Dutiful who broke the silence. "You said she was dead," he abruptly accused me. "That's impossible. If she is dead, how does she speak to me?"

I took a breath to speak, sighed it out after a moment, and then took another. "When you are Witted, you bond to an animal. It's more than sharing thoughts, it's sharing being. After a time, you can see through the animal's eyes, experience its life as it does, perceive the world as the animal does. It isn't just—"

"I *know* all that. I am Piebald, you know." He gave a snort of contempt for my words.

I don't think an interruption had ever irritated me more. "Old Blood," I corrected him sharply. "Tell me you're Piebald again, and I'll have to beat it out of you. I've no respect for what they do with their magic. Now. How long have you known that you're Witted?" I demanded suddenly.

"I—why—" I saw him struggle to push his mind past my threat. I'd meant it and he knew it. He took a breath. "For about five months. Since the cat was given to me. Almost as soon as her leash was given over to me, I felt—"

"You felt a trap closing on you, one you've been too stupid to perceive. The cat was given to you because others knew you were Witted before you knew it yourself. So you've shown signs of it, without being aware that you were doing so. Someone noticed, someone decided to use you. So they presented you with an animal to bond with. That's not how it's supposed to be, you know. Witted parents don't just hand their child an animal and say, here, this is your partner for as long as you both live. No. Usually the child is well schooled in the Wit and its consequences before it bonds. Usually the child makes a quest of some sort, seeking a like-minded animal. When it's done right, it's like getting married. This wasn't done right. You weren't educated about the Wit by people that cared about you. A group of Witted saw an opening, and took advantage of it. The cat didn't choose you. That's bad enough. But I don't think the cat was even allowed to choose the woman. She stole it, as a kit, from the mother's den, and forced the bond. Then the woman died, but she kept on living in the cat."

His eyes were wide and dark, staring up at me. He looked slightly aside from me, and I felt the Wit working between them.

"I don't believe you. She says she can explain it all, that you're trying to confuse me." The words spilled out of him hastily, as if he tried to hide behind them.

I glanced over at the boy. Skepticism and confusion had closed his face.

I took a breath and kept my temper. "Look, lad. I don't know all the details. But I can speculate. Perhaps she knew she was dying; maybe that's why she chose such a helpless creature and forced the bond. When a bond is uneven, as that one would have been, the stronger partner can control the weaker one. She could dominate the kit, and move in and out, sharing the cat's body as she pleased. And when she died, instead of dying with her own body, she stepped over to the cat's."

I stopped walking. I waited until Dutiful met my eyes. "You're next," I said quietly.

"You're mad! She loves me!"

I shook my head. "I sense great ambition in her. She'll want a human body of her own again, not to be a cat, not to die when the cat's days are done. She'd have to find someone. It would have to be someone who was both Witted, and ignorant of the Wit. Why not someone well placed? Why not a prince?"

Conflicting expressions flickered over his face. Some part of him knew I spoke truth, and it shamed him that he had been so deceived. He struggled to disbelieve me. I tried to temper my words, so that he did not feel so foolish.

"I think she selected you. You never had any choice at all, any more than the cat did. The woman-cat is what you're bonded to, not the cat itself. And it wasn't done for love of you, any more than she loved the cat. No. Somewhere, someone has a very careful plan, and you're just a tool for it. A tool for the Piebalds."

"I don't believe you!" His voice rose on the words. "You're a liar!" On those words, his voice cracked.

I saw his shoulders heave with the breath he took. I almost felt my Skill-command hold him back from attacking me. For a time I was carefully quiet. When I judged he had mastered himself, I spoke very quietly. "You've called me a bastard, a thief, and now a liar. A prince should be more mindful of what insults he flings, unless he thinks that his title alone will protect him. So here's an insult for you, and a warning. Hide behind being a prince while calling me nasty names, and I'll call you a coward. The next time you insult me, your bloodlines won't stop my fist."

I held his gaze until he looked aside from me, a cub cowed by a wolf. I lowered my voice, forcing him to listen carefully to catch my words. "You're not stupid, Dutiful. You know I'm not a liar. She's dead, and you are being used. You don't want it to be true, but that's not the same as disbelieving me. You'll probably keep hoping and praying that something will happen to prove I'm wrong. It won't." I took a deep breath. "About the only thing I can offer you right now is that none of this is really your fault. Someone should have protected you from this. Someone should have taught you about Old Blood from the time you were small."

There was no way to admit to either of us that that someone was me. The same person who had introduced him to the Wit and all it could be, through Skill-dreams when he was four.

We walked for a long time without speaking. I kept my eyes on my seaweed-festooned snag. Once I'd left the Prince here, I could not predict how long I'd be gone. Could he care for himself? The treasures in the alcove made me uneasy. Such wealth belonged to someone, and that person might resent an intruder on his beach. Yet I could not take him back with me. He'd be a hindrance. A time alone, taking care of himself, might do him good, I decided. And if I died trying to save the Fool and Nighteyes? Well, at least the Piebalds would not have the Prince.

I set my teeth, trudged through the sand, and kept my grim thoughts to myself. We had nearly reached my snag when Dutiful spoke. His voice was very low. "You said my father taught you to Skill. Did he teach you to—"

Then he tripped on something. As he fell, the toe of his boot jerked a gold chain free of the sand that had covered it. He sat up, cursing, and then reached down to free his boot. As he dragged the looped chain clear of the sand, I gaped at it. It was an intricately woven thing, each thread of metal the thickness of a horsehair. He coiled it into his hand, a necklace-length of chain that filled his palm. He gave a final tug to free the last loop, and a figurine popped from the sand. It was fastened to the chain as a dangling charm. It was the length of Dutiful's little finger. Bright colors had been enameled onto the metal.

It was the image of a woman. We stared down at the proud face. The artist had given her black eyes and let the dark gold shine through for the tone of her skin. Her hair was painted black with a standing blue ornament crowning it. The draped garments bared one of her breasts. Bare feet of dark gold peeped from beneath the hem.

"She's beautiful," I said. He made no reply.

The Prince was engrossed by her. He turned the figurine over in his hand and traced the fall of hair down her back.

"I don't know what this is made from. It weighs scarcely anything."

We both lifted our heads at the same instant. Perhaps it was our Wit warning us of the presence of another living being, but I do not think so. I had caught the scent of something indescribably foul on the air. Yet even as I turned my head to seek the source of the stench, I almost became persuaded it was a sweet perfume. Almost.

Some things one never forgets. The insidious tendriling of mind touch is one of them. Terror spasmed through me and I slammed up the Skill-walls around my mind in a reflex I thought I had forgotten. My reward was that I perceived the full foulness of its stench as I turned to confront a nightmare creature.

It stood as tall as I did, but that was only the portion of its body that reared upright. I could not decide if it reminded me of a reptile or a sea mammal. The flat flounder eyes on the front of its face looked unnatural in their orientation. The brain bump of its skull seemed tumescently large. Its lower jaw dropped like a trapdoor as it stared at us. Its mouth could have engulfed a rabbit. A stiff, fishy tongue protruded from it briefly. As we stared, it jerked its tongue back in and closed its jaws with a snap.

To my horror, the transfixed Prince was smiling at the creature in an addled way. He swayed a step closer to it. I set my hand firmly to his shoulder and gripped hard. I set my thumb to his flesh and tried to invoke the earlier Skill-bond I had laid on him without breaching my own walls. "Come with me," I said quietly but firmly. I drew him back toward me, and if he did not actively obey at least he did not resist me.

The thing reared up even taller. Sacs at the sides of its throat puffed up as it lifted its flipperlike limbs. It suddenly spread finny hands that were large and wide. Claws like bullfish spines stood out from the ends of the digits. Then it spoke, wheezing and belching the syllables. The shock of its distorted words felt like pebbles pelting against me. "You did not come by the path. How came you?"

"We came by—"

"Silence!" I warned the Prince and gave him a rough shake. I was backing us away from the creature, but it hummocked its ungainly body over the sand toward us. Where had it come from? I glanced about wildly, fearing to see more of the creatures, but there was only the one. It made a sudden rush forward, interposing its huge body between the tableland and us. I responded by retreating toward the water. It was where I wished to go anyway, the only possible escape that I could imagine. I prayed the tide would bare the Skill-pillar.

"You must leave it!" the creature belched at us. "What the ocean washes up on the treasure beach must always remain here. Drop what you have found."

The Prince opened his hand. The figurine fell but the chain tangled on his lax fingers, to dangle from his hand like a puppet.

"Drop it!" the creature repeated more urgently.

I decided the time for subtlety was past. I drew my sword awkwardly with my left hand, for I feared to let go of the Prince. "Stay back," I warned. My feet were crunching over barnacles on the uneven rocks. I risked a glance behind me. I could see my squared-off black stones, but they barely stuck up above the water. The creature mistook my look.

"Your ship has left you here! There is nothing out there but ocean. Drop the treasure." There was a hissing quality to its speech, most unnerving. It had no more lips than a lizard, but the teeth that the opened mouth bared were multitudinous and sharp. "The treasures of this beach are not for humans! What the sea brings here is meant to be lost to humankind! You were not worthy of it."

Seaweed squelched underfoot. The Prince slipped and nearly went down. I kept my grip on his shoulder and dragged him back to his feet. Three more steps, and water lapped around my feet.

"You cannot swim far!" the creature warned us. "The beach will have your bones!"

Like a distant wind, I faintly felt the buffeting of fear that he directed at us. The Prince's mind was unshielded, and he gave a sudden cry of wild terror. "I don't want to drown!" he cried out. "Please, I don't want to drown!" When he turned to me, the whites showed all around the edges of his eyes. I did not think him a coward. I knew only too well what it was like to have another mind impose panic on my unguarded thoughts.

"Dutiful. You have to trust me. Trust me."

"I can't!" he bellowed, and I believed him. He was torn between us, my Skill-command for obedience warring with the insidious waves of fear the creature gushed at him. I tightened my grip and dragged him back with me as I retreated. The water was up to our knees. Every wave nudged against us in its passage. The wallowing creature did not hesitate to follow us. Doubtless it would be more at home in the sea. I risked another glance behind me. The Skill-pillar was close. I felt that vague confusion that the black memory stone always inflicted on me. It was strange, to push myself toward disorientation in the hopes of salvation.

"Give me the treasure!" the creature commanded, and virulent green droplets shimmered suddenly at the end of its claws. It lifted them menacingly.

In one motion, I sheathed my sword, threw my left arm around Dutiful, and flung us both backward into the water. As the creature dove toward us, I thought I saw a sudden flash of comprehension in those inhuman eyes, but it was too late. We fell full length into the cold saltwater, and my groping fingers sought and found the canted surface of the fallen pillar. I had no time to warn the Prince as it swallowed us.

We stumbled out into an almost-warm afternoon. The Prince dropped nervelessly from my grip to sprawl on a cobblestoned street in the gush of saltwater that had accompanied us. I drew a deep breath and looked around us. "Wrong face!" I had known this could happen but had been too intent on escaping the thing on the beach to consider it. Each face of a Skill-pillar was carved with a rune that told where that surface would transport you. It was a wonderful system, if one understood what the runes meant. With a jolt, I suddenly grasped how much I had just risked. What if this pillar had been buried under stone, or shattered to pieces? I dared not think what might have become of us. Shaking, I stared at the foreign landscape. We stood in the windswept ruins of an abandoned Elderling city. It looked vaguely familiar and I wondered if it was the same city that a similar pillar had once carried me to. But there was no time for exploration or speculation. All had gone wrong. My original plan had been to return alone through the pillar, to rush unhindered to the aid of my friends. But I could not leave Dutiful stunned and alone in this barren place any more than I could have left him on the hostile beach. I'd have to take him with me. "We have to go back," I told the Prince. "We have to get back to Buck exactly as we came."

"I didn't like that at all." His voice shook, and I knew instinctively that he was not speaking about the creature on the beach. Going through a pillar was a harrowing experience for an untrained mind. Regal had used the pillars recklessly in transporting his young Skill-users, little caring how many of them went mad from the process. I would not use my Prince so recklessly. Except that I had no other choice, and no time.

"I know," I said gently. "But we have to go now, before the tide comes in any deeper." He stared at me without comprehension. I weighed him keeping his sanity against what the woman might know through him. Then I threw that concern aside. He had to understand, at least a little, or I'd emerge from the pillar with a drooling idiot. "We have to go back to the pillar on the beach. We know it has a facet that will take us back to Buck. We'll have to discover which one."

The boy made a small retching sound. He hunkered down on the cobblestones, pressing the heels of his hands to his temples. "I don't think I can," he said faintly.

My heart smote me. "Waiting won't make it any better," I warned him. "I'll hold you together as best I can. But we have to go now, my Prince."

"That thing might be waiting for us!" he cried wildly, but I think he feared the passage more than any lurking creature.

I stooped and put my arms around him, and although he struggled wildly, I dragged him back into the pillar with me.

I had never used a pillar twice in such swift succession. I was unprepared for the sharp sensation of heat. As we emerged, I accidentally snuffed warm seawater up my nose. I stood up, holding Dutiful's head above water. The water around the pillar was seething with the heat from it. And the Prince had been right. As I held his lax body in my arms and shook water from my face, I heard startled grunts from the beach. Not one, but four of the ungainly creatures had congregated there. At the sight of us, they charged, hunching across the sand and into the waves. No time to think or look or choose. The Prince was limp and lolling. I clutched him to me, and risked dropping my Skill-walls to try to hold his mind intact. As an incoming wave drove me to my knees, I slapped a hand to the steaming surface of the Skill-pillar. It dragged me in.

The transit this time seemed unbearable. I swear I smelled a strange odor, oddly familiar and yet repulsive. *Dutiful. Dutiful, prince. Heir to the Farseer throne. Son of Kettricken.* I wrapped his tattering thoughts in my own and named him by every name I could think of.

Then came a moment he reached back to me. *I know*

you. That was all I sensed from him, but after that, he held on to himself and to me. There was a queer passivity to our bond, and when at length we washed out onto green grass under a lowering sky, I wondered if the Prince's mind had survived our escape from the treasure beach.

chapter XXV

RANSOM

By these signs may you know one who has the potential for the Skill:

A child who comes of Skilled parents.

A child who wins often at games of physical skill, and his opponents stumble, lose heart, or play poorly against him.

A child who possesses memories not rightfully his.

A child who dreams, and his dreams are detailed and contain knowledge beyond the child's own experience.

    ❦ DUN NEEDLESON, SKILLMASTER TO KING WIELDER

The barrow crouched on the hillside above us. It was raining, a misty but determined fall of water. The grass was deep and wet. I suddenly didn't have the strength to stand by myself, let alone support the Prince. As one, we sank down until I knelt on the wet earth. I lowered his body to the sward. His eyes were open but they stared blindly. Only the rasping of his breath showed me he was alive. We were back in Buck, but our situation was only marginally better than when we had last left here.

We were both soaking wet. After a moment, I became aware of an odd smell and realized that the pillar behind us was radiating warmth. The smell was the dampness forced out of the stone. I decided I would rather be cold than get too close to it. The figurine still dangled from the chain tangled in the Prince's fingers. I plucked it free, gathered up the chain, and put it inside my pouch. The Prince made no response to any of this. "Dutiful?" I leaned closer and looked directly into his eyes. They didn't focus on me. The rain was falling on his face and his open eyes. I tapped him lightly on the cheek. "Prince Dutiful? Do you hear me?"

He blinked slowly. It was not much of a response, but it was better than nothing.

"You'll feel better in a little while. Just rest here for a time." I wasn't sure that was true, but I left him on the wet grass and climbed up on top of the barrow. I surveyed the surrounding lands, but saw no other humans. There wasn't much of anything to see, just rolling countryside and a few copses of trees. A flock of starlings wheeled in unison, and settled again, squabbling over feed. Beyond the wild meadow, there was forest. There was nothing that looked like an immediate threat, but nothing that looked like food, drink, and shelter, either. I was fairly certain that Dutiful would benefit from all three, and feared that without them he would sink further into unresponsiveness, but what I needed was even more basic. I wanted to know if my friends lived. I wanted beyond all rationality to reach out for my wolf. I longed to howl for him, to put my whole heart into that questing. I also knew it was the most foolish and reckless thing I could do. It would not only alert any Witted ones nearby that I was here, it would also warn them that I was coming.

I forced order onto my thoughts. I needed a refuge, and quickly. It seemed likely to me that the woman and the cat would be constantly questing for the Prince. Even now, they might be coming for him. The afternoon was already venturing toward evening. Dutiful had told me the Piebalds would kill Nighteyes and the Fool at sunset if I had not returned him. Somehow, I must get the Prince to a safe place before the woman could find us, then slip off on my own to discover where the Piebalds held my friends and then free them. Before sunset. I racked my brain. The closest inn I knew of was the Piebald Prince. I doubted that Dutiful would get a fond welcome there. Yet Buckkeep was a long walk and a river-fording away. I pondered but could think of no other refuge for him. In his present condition, I could scarcely leave him here alone, and another trip through a pillar would be the end of Dutiful's mind, even if we emerged physically unscathed. I once more scanned the empty landscape. I reluctantly admitted that though I had choices, none of them were good. I abruptly decided that I would get us moving, and try to think of something better along the way.

I gave one final glance around before descending from the barrow. As I did so, my eye caught something, not a shape, but a movement beyond a cluster of trees. I crouched low and stared at it, trying to resolve what I had seen. In a few moments, the animal emerged. A horse. Black and tall. Myblack. She stared toward me. Slowly I stood again. She was too far off to go chasing after her. She must have fled when the Piebalds captured Nighteyes and the Fool. I wondered what had become of Malta. I watched her for a moment longer, but she only stood and stared back at me. I turned my back on her and descended to the Prince.

He was no more coherent, but at least had reacted to the chill rain by drawing into a ball and shivering. My apprehension for him was mixed with a guilty hope. Perhaps in his present condition, he could not use his Wit to let the Piebalds know where we were. I set my hand to his shoulder and tried to make my voice gentle as I told him, "Let's get you up and walking. It will warm both of us."

I don't know if my words made sense to him. He stared ahead blankly as I pulled him to his feet. Once up, he hunched over his crossed arms. The shivering did not abate. "Let's walk," I suggested, but he did not move until I put an arm around him and told him, "Walk with me. Now." Then he did, but it was a stumbling, staggering gait. At a snail's pace, we traversed the wet hillside.

Very gradually, I became aware of the thud of hooves behind us. A glance back showed Myblack following us, but when I stopped, she stopped also. When I let go of the Prince, he sagged toward the earth and the horse immediately became suspicious. I dragged the Prince back to his feet. As we plodded on again, I could hear her uneven hoof-beats behind us again.

I ignored Myblack until she had nearly caught up with us. Then I sat down and let Dutiful lean against me until her curiosity overcame her native wariness. I paid no attention to her until her breath was actually warm on the back of my neck. Even then I did not turn to her, but snaked a hand stealthily around to catch hold of the dangling reins.

I think she was almost glad to be caught. I stood slowly and stroked her neck. Her coat was streaked with dried lather, and all her tack was damp. She had been grazing around her bit. Mud was crusted into one side of the saddle where she had tried to roll. I led her in a slow circle and confirmed what I feared. She was lamed. Something, perhaps the Wit-hounds, had tried to run her down, but her fleetness had saved her. I was amazed that she had even stayed in the area, let alone come back to me when she saw me. Yet there would be no wild gallop to safety for any of us. The best we would do was a halting walk.

I spent some little time trying to cajole the Prince into standing and mounting the horse. It was only when I lost my patience and ordered him to get to his feet and get on the damned horse that he obeyed me. Dutiful did not respond to conversation, but he obeyed simple orders from me. Then I appreciated how deep that jolt of Skill-command had gone, and how firmly linked we remained. "Don't fight me," I had charged him, and some part of him interpreted that as "don't disobey me." Even with his cooperation, the mount was an awkward maneuver. As I heaved him up into the saddle, I feared he would topple off the other side. I didn't try to ride behind him. I doubted that Myblack would have tolerated it. Instead I led her. The Prince swayed with Myblack's hitching gait but did not fall. He looked terrible. All the maturity had been stripped from his features, leaving him a sick child, his dark-circled eyes wide, his mouth drooping. He looked as if he could die. The full impact of that possibility seized my heart in a cold grip. The Prince dead. The end of the Farseer line and the shattering of the Six Duchies. A messy and painful death for Nettle. I could not let it happen that way. We entered a strip of open woods, startling a crow who rose, cawing like a prophet of doom. It seemed an ill omen.

I found myself talking to both Prince and horse as we walked. I spoke in Burrich's soothing cadence, using his reassuring words, in a calming ritual remembered from my childhood. "Come along now, we're all going to be fine, there, there, the worst part is over, that's right, that's right."

From that I progressed to humming, and again it was some tune that Burrich had often hummed when he worked on injured horses or laboring mares. I think the familiar song calmed and settled me more than it did the horse or the Prince. After a time, I found myself talking aloud, as much to myself as to them. "Well, it looks as if Chade was right. You're going to Skill whether you're taught to or not. And I'm afraid the same holds true for the Wit. It's in your blood, lad, and unlike some, I don't think it can be beaten out of you. I don't think it should be. But it shouldn't be indulged the way you've indulged it, either. It's not that different from the Skill, really. A man has to set limits on his magic and on himself. Setting limits is part of being a man. So if we come out of this alive and intact, I'll teach you. I guess I'll teach myself as well. It's probably time for me to look into all those old Skill scrolls and find out what's really in them. It scares me, though. In the last two years, the Skill has come back on me like some sort of spreading ulcer. I don't know where it's taking me. And I fear what I don't know. That's the wolf in me, I guess. And Eda's breath, let him be safe right now, and my Fool. Don't let them be in pain or dying simply because they knew me. If anything happens to either of them . . . it's strange, isn't it, how you don't know how big a part of you someone is until they're threatened? And then you think that you can't possibly go on if something happens to them, but the most frightening part is that, actually, you will go on, you'll have to go on, with them or without them. There's just no telling what you'll become. What will I be, if Nighteyes is gone? Look at Small Ferret, all those years ago. He went on and on, even though the only thing left in his little mind was to kill—"

"What about my cat?"

His voice was soft. Relief washed through me that he had enough mind left to speak. At the same time, I hastily reviewed my thoughtless rambling and hoped he had not been paying too much attention.

"How do you feel, my Prince?"

"I can't feel my cat."

A long silence followed. I finally said, "I can't feel my wolf, either. Sometimes he needs to be separate from me."

He was silent for so long that I feared he wasn't going to reply. Then he said, "It doesn't feel like that. She's holding us apart. It feels as if I am being punished."

"Punished for what?" I kept my voice even and light, as if we discussed the weather.

"For not killing you. For not even trying to kill you. She can't understand why I don't. I can't explain why I don't. But it makes her angry with me." There was a simplicity to his heart-spoken words, as if I conversed with the person behind all the manners and artifice of society. I sensed that our journey through the Skill-pillar had stripped away many layers of protection from him. He was vulnerable right now. He spoke and reasoned as soldiers do when they are in great pain, or when ill men try to speak through a fever. All his guards were dropped. It seemed as if he trusted me, that he spoke of such things. I counseled myself not to hope for that, nor believe it. It was only the hardships he had been through that opened him to me like this. Only that. I chose my words carefully.

"Is she with you now? The woman?"

He nodded slowly. "She is always with me now. She

won't let me think alone." He swallowed and added hesitantly, "She doesn't want me to talk to you. Or listen. It's hard. She keeps pushing me."

"Do *you* want to kill me?"

Again there was that pause before he spoke. It was as if he had to digest the words, not simply hear them. When he spoke, he didn't answer my question.

"You said she was dead. It made her very angry."

"Because it is true."

"She said she would explain. Later. She said that should be enough for me." He was not looking at me, but when I gazed at him, he turned his whole head aside as if to be sure he would not see me. "Then she . . . she was me. And she attacked you with the knife. Because I . . . hadn't." I couldn't tell if he was confused or ashamed.

"*Wouldn't* kill me?" I suggested the word.

"Wouldn't," the Prince admitted. I was amazed at how grateful I was for the small piece of knowledge. He had refused to kill me. I had thought only my Skill-command had stopped him. "I wouldn't obey her. Sometimes I've disappointed her. But now she is truly angry with me."

"And they're punishing you for that disobedience. By leaving you alone."

He gave his head one slow, grave shake. "No. The cat does not care if I kill you or not. She would always be with me. But the woman . . . she is disappointed that I am not more loyal. So she . . . separates us. Me from the cat. The woman thinks that I should have been willing to show that I was worthy of her. How can they trust me if I refuse to prove my loyalty?"

"And you prove your loyalty by killing when you're told to kill?"

He was silent for a long time. It gave me time to reflect. I had killed when I was told to kill. It had been part of my loyalty to my King, part of my bargain with my grandfather. He would educate me if I would be loyal to him.

I discovered I did not want Kettricken's son to be that loyal to anyone.

He sighed. "It was . . . even more than that. She wants to make the decisions. All the decisions. Every time. Just as she told the cat what to hunt, and when, and took her kills away. When she holds us close, it feels like love. But she can also hold back from us, and yet we are still held . . ." He could see that I did not understand. After a time he added quietly, "I didn't like it when she used my body against you. Even if she hadn't been trying to kill you, I wouldn't have liked it. She pushed me to one side, just like . . ." He didn't want to admit it. I admired that he forced himself to it. "Just like I've felt her push the cat aside, when she didn't want to do cat things. When she was tired of grooming, or didn't want to play. The cat doesn't like it, either, but she doesn't know how to push back. I did. I pushed her back and she didn't like it. She didn't like that the cat felt me do it, either. I think that's the biggest reason why I'm being punished. That I pushed her back." He shook his head, baffled himself, and then said, "She's so real. How can you be sure she's dead?"

I found I could not lie to him. "I . . . feel it. So does Nighteyes. He says the cat is riddled with her, as if she were parasites worming through her flesh. He felt sorry for the cat."

"Oh." The word was very small. I glanced back at him, and thought he looked more gray than pale now. His eyes went distant and his thoughts traveled back. "When I first got her, she loved for me to groom her. I kept her coat like silk. But after we left Buckkeep . . . sometimes the cat would want to be brushed, but the woman always said there was no time for that. Cat lost weight and her fur was rough. I worried, but she always set my worry aside. She said it was just the season, that it would pass. And I believed her. Even though the cat wanted to be brushed." He looked stricken.

"I took no pleasure in telling you that."

"I suppose it doesn't matter now."

For a long time, I led the horse in silence as I tried to puzzle out what his last words meant. Didn't matter that I was sorry, or didn't matter that she was dead?

"I believed so many things she told me. But I already knew that— They're coming now. The crow has fetched them." A sudden note of remorse came into his voice. His words were halting. "They knew to watch the standing stone. From all the legends of such stones. But she wouldn't let me tell you that. Until now. When it doesn't matter. She finds it humorous, now." He suddenly sat up straight in the saddle. Life came back into his face. "Oh, cat!" he breathed.

Panic raced over me. I tried to set it aside. A quick scan of all horizons showed me no one, nothing. But he had said they were coming, and I was sure he had not lied. As long as he was with me and linked to the cat, I could not hope to hide from them. I could mount Myblack behind him, and run her to death, and we still would not escape. We were too far from Buckkeep, and I had no other safe place, no other allies. And a crow keeping watch for them. I should have guessed.

I dropped all restraint and reached out for my wolf. At least I would know he was alive.

I touched him. But the wave of pain that immersed me was scalding. I had discovered the only thing worse than not knowing his fate. He was alive and he suffered, and he still excluded me from his thoughts. I threw myself against his walls, but he had locked me out. In the fierceness of his defense, I wondered if he was even aware of me. It reminded me of a soldier clutching his sword beyond his ability to use it—or of wolves, jaws locked on each other's throats, dying together.

In the space of that moment, in the tortured drawing of a breath, the Piebalds appeared. They crested the hillside above us, and some emerged from the forest to our left. Behind us, they came across the wild meadows, perhaps six of them. The big man on the warhorse rode with them. The crow sailed over us once, and this time his caw was mocking. I looked in vain for a gap in their circle that might permit escape. There were none. By the time I mounted Myblack and charged toward an opening, the others could effortlessly close it. Death rode toward me from every direction. I halted and drew my sword. The foolish thought came to me that I would rather have died with Verity's sword in my hand instead of this guardsman's blade. I waited.

They did not race toward me. Rather, they came at a steady pace like the slow closing of a noose. Perhaps it amused them to think of me standing there, watching them come. It gave me far too much time to think. I sheathed my sword and took out my knife instead. "Get down," I said quietly. Dutiful looked down at me in vague confusion. "Get off the horse," I ordered him, and he obeyed, though I had to steady him before his second foot hit the ground. I wrapped an arm around his chest and carefully set the knife to his throat. "I'm sorry," I told him with great sincerity. Conviction was running through my veins like icy water. "But you are better dead than what the woman plans for you."

He stood quite still in my grip. I didn't know if he didn't want to risk resistance or if he didn't care to resist. "How do you know what she intends for me?" he asked me evenly.

"Because I know what I would do."

That statement wasn't quite true, I told myself. I'd never take over another person's body and mind simply for the sake of extending my life. I was too noble for that. So noble that I'd kill my Prince before I'd let him be used that way. So noble that I'd kill him, knowing my daughter must then die, as well. I didn't want to look too closely at that reasoning. So I held my knife to the throat of Verity's only heir and watched the Piebalds come. I waited until they were within shouting distance, and then I raised my voice. "Come any closer and I kill him."

The big man on the warhorse was their leader. He

lifted his hands to stop the advance of the others, but then he himself rode slowly forward as if to test my resolve. I watched him come and my grip on the Prince tightened. "It takes one motion of my hand and the Prince is dead," I warned him.

"Oh, come, you're being ridiculous," the big man replied. He continued to walk his horse toward me. Myblack snorted a query at his beast. "For what will you do if we obediently halt here? Stand in our midst and starve to death?"

"Let us go, or I'll kill him," I amended.

"Equally silly. Where's the benefit to us in that? If we can't have him, he might as well be dead." His voice was deep and resonant and it carried well. He had a dark, handsome face and sat his horse like a warrior. In another time and place, I would have looked at him and judged him a man worthy of my friendship. Now his followers laughed aloud at my pathetic efforts to defy him. He and his horse came closer still. The big horse stepped high as he came and his eyes shone with their Wit-bond. "And consider what happens if you do kill him as I advance. Once he's dead, we'll all be very annoyed with you. And you still won't have a chance of escape. I doubt that you can even make us kill you swiftly. So. That's my counteroffer. Give us the boy and I'll kill you quickly. You have my word on that."

Such a kind offer. His grave manner and careful speech convinced me he would honor it. Quick death sounded very appealing when I considered the alternatives. But I hated dying without having the last word.

"Very well," I conceded. "But he costs you more than my life. Release the wolf and the tawny man. Then I'll give you your Prince, and you can kill me."

The Prince stood motionless in the circle of my arm and knife. I scarcely felt him breathe, and yet I could feel him listening, as if my words soaked into him like water into dry earth. The fine web of Skill between us warned me that there was something else going on. He reached out

with his unholy combination of Wit and Skill to someone.
I readied my muscles lest the woman wrest control of his
body from him.

"Are you lying?" Dutiful asked me so softly that I
scarcely heard him. But was the question from Dutiful or
the cat's woman?

"I'm telling the truth," I lied sincerely. "If they release
Lord Golden and the wolf, I'll free you." To your death.
And the second throat I'd cut would be mine.

The big man on the big horse gave what might have
been a chuckle. "Too late for that, I'm afraid. They're already dead."

"No. They aren't."

"Aren't they?" He rode his horse closer.

"I'd know if the wolf died."

He no longer needed to shout for his voice to reach me.
He spoke in a confidential manner. "And that is why it is so
unnatural that you should oppose us. I confess, having you
answer that one question alone is enough to make me postpone your death." Warmth for me shone in his eyes and
genuine curiosity came into his voice. "Why, in the name
of the life and death that Eda and El encircle, do you stand
like this against your own kind? Do you like what is done to
us? The floggings, the hangings, the quartering and burning? Why do you support it?"

I let my own voice ring out to all of them. "Because
what you seek to do to this boy is wrong! What the woman
did to her cat is wrong! You take to yourself the name of
Piebalds and claim pride in your lineage, yet you go against
what Old Blood teaches. How can you condone what she
has done to her cat, let alone what she wishes to do to the
Prince?"

The light in the big man's eyes went cold. "He is a
Farseer. Can anything be done to him that he does not
merit, a thousand times over?"

At those words, the Prince stiffened in my grasp.
"Laudwine, is that truly what you believe?" The youth and

incredulity in Dutiful's voice was heartbreaking. "You spoke me fair when I rode with you. You said that eventually I could become the king who would unite all my folk under equal justice. You said—"

Laudwine shook his head in disdain for Dutiful's gullibility. "I would have said anything to have you come along quietly. I bought time with fair words, until the bond was knitted strong enough. I've had signs through the cat that the task is done. Peladine can take you anytime now. If there were not a knife at your throat just now, she'd already have you. But Peladine has no wish to die twice. Once was quite enough for her. Hers was a slow death, coughing and gasping as she grew weaker every day. Even my mother's was swifter. They hung her, true, but she was not quite dead when they cut her in quarters to feed their fire. And my father, well, I am sure that the time in which he watched Regal Farseer's soldiers dispose of my mother seemed to last years." He smiled unpleasantly at Dutiful. "So you see, my family's relationship with the Farseers is a long one. The debt is an old one, Prince Dutiful. I think the only pleasant time that Peladine had in her last year were the hours in which we spent planning this for you. It is only fitting that a Farseer should actually restore a life for the ones that have been taken from me."

And there it was. The seed of hate from which all this had sprung. Once more, the Farseers did not have to see far to know whence their ill fortune came. The Prince's pitfall was built from his uncle's arrogance and cruelty. Hatred was the legacy Regal had bequeathed to me, as well, but my heart closed against the sympathy that flared in me. The Piebalds were my enemies. Regardless of what they had suffered, they had no right to this boy. "And what was Peladine to you, Laudwine?" I asked evenly. I suspected I knew the answer, but he surprised me.

"She was my womb-sister, my twin, as like to me as woman can be to man. Bereft of her, I am the last of my line. Is that reason enough for you?"

"No. But it is for you. You would do anything to have her live again in human flesh. You'd help her steal this boy's body to house her mind. Even though that goes against every Old Blood teaching we hold dear." I let my voice ring with righteousness. If my words shocked any of his warriors, they hid it well.

Laudwine halted his horse a sword's length away from us. He leaned down to fix me with his stare. "There's more to it than a brother's grief. Break your lackey's bonds to the Farseer family and think for yourself. Think for your own kind. Forget our old customs of limiting ourselves. Old Blood is a gift from Eda, and we should use it! There is great opportunity here, for all of us who bear Old Blood. We have a chance to be heard. Let the Farseers admit to themselves what legend has long said is true; the Wit is in their blood as thick as the Skill. This boy will be king someday. We can make him ours. When he steps into power, he can end the persecution we have endured so long."

I bit my lower lip in a show of thoughtfulness. Laudwine could little imagine what decision I truly weighed. If I did as he wished, the Farseer line would still have its heir, in body at least. Nettle could live a life of her own, free of fate's entangling web. And there might be good in it, for the Old Blood and the Six Duchies. All I had to do was surrender Dutiful to a life of torment. The Fool and my wolf could go free, and Nettle could live, and perhaps the Old Blood could eventually be free of persecution. Even I could live. Give up a boy I scarcely knew to buy all that. One single life, weighed against all those others.

I made my decision.

"If I thought you spoke true—" I began, and then halted. I stared at Laudwine.

"You might come over to us?"

He believed me to be a man caught between death and compromise. I let uncertainty show in my eyes, and then gave the briefest possible nod. I reached up one-handed and tugged at my collar, loosening it. Jinna's beads peeped out at him. You like me, I begged him. Trust my words. Desire me for a friend. Then I spoke my coward's speech. "I could be useful to you, Laudwine. The Queen expects Lord Golden to bring the Prince back to her. If you kill him and the Prince goes back alone, they will wonder what became of Golden, and why. If you let us live, and we take the Prince back to them, well, I can explain away the changes in his demeanor. They'll accept him back unquestioningly."

His eyes wandered over me, deliberating. I watched him convince himself. "And Lord Golden would go along with what you said?"

I made a small sound of derision. "He has not the Wit. He has only his eyes to tell him that we have regained the Prince alive and unharmed. He will think only of his hero's welcome at Buckkeep. He will believe that I negotiated the Prince's freedom, and be glad to claim the credit for it at court. In fact, he will witness me doing it. Take us to where you hold him. Let us make a show for him. Send him on his way with my wolf, assuring him that the Prince and I will follow." I nodded sagely as if confirming the thought to myself. "Actually, it is best if he is well on his way. He should not witness the woman taking over the boy. He might wonder what was amiss with him. Let Lord Golden be gone first."

"You seem very concerned for his safety," Laudwine probed.

I shrugged. "He pays me well to do very little. And he tolerates my wolf. We are both getting on in years. Such a post is not easily found."

Laudwine grinned, but in his eyes I saw his secret contempt for my servant's ethic. I opened my collar more.

He glanced at Dutiful. The boy's eyes were fixed on his face. "A problem," Laudwine observed softly. "The boy has no benefit in our bargain. He may well betray it to Lord Golden."

I felt Dutiful draw breath to speak. I tightened my grip on him, asking for silence while I thought, but he spoke anyway. "My interest is in living," he said clearly. "However poor an existence it may become. And in my cat. For she is true to me, even if your sister is false to both of us. I will not abandon the cat to her. And if she takes my body from me, then perhaps that is the price I must pay, for letting a Piebald make a fool of me with promises of fellowship. And love." His voice was steady, and pitched to carry. Beyond Laudwine's shoulder, I saw two of his riders look aside, as if Dutiful's words pained them. But no one spoke up on his behalf.

A thin smile twisted Laudwine's mouth. "Then our pact is made." He extended his free hand toward me, as if we would seal the bargain with a touch. He smiled disarmingly at me. "Take your knife from the boy's throat."

I gave him a wolf's smile in return. "I think not, just yet. You have said this Peladine can take him at any time? Perhaps, if she does, you will think you have no need of me. You might kill me, let your sister have the boy, and then present him to Lord Golden, the hostage freed to return to court. No. We will do it my way. Besides, this lad may change his feelings about what we do. The knife helps him remember that my will is what will be." I wondered if Dutiful would hear my promise enfolded in those words. I kept my eyes fixed on Laudwine and did not vary my tone. "Let me see Lord Golden remounted and set free, with my wolf at his side. Then, when I see how you keep your word, I will surrender us both to your will."

Feeble, feeble plan. My true strategy went no further than getting them to take us to the Fool and Nighteyes. I continued to hold my smile and gaze on Laudwine but I was aware of the others edging their horses closer. My grip on the knife was steady. At some point, the Prince had reached up to grasp my wrist. I had scarcely been aware of his touch, for although it looked as if he resisted my blade, he did not. In truth, it was almost as if he held the knife steady against his own throat.

"We will do it your way," Laudwine conceded at last.

It was an awkward business to mount Myblack while

keeping my knife a threat to the Prince, but we managed it. Dutiful was almost too cooperative a victim; I feared Laudwine would see. I would have given much, just then, for the Prince to have been trained in Skilling. Our thread of joining was too fine for me to know his thoughts, nor did he know how to focus his mind toward mine. All I could sense was his anxiety and determination. Determination to do what, I could not divine. Myblack was not pleased with the doubled burden she had to carry, and my heart misgave me. Not only did I risk making her injury worse, or permanent, but if it became necessary to flee, she would already be weary and sore. Every hitch of Myblack's limp was a rebuke to me. But I had no alternatives. We rode, following Laudwine, and his companions closed in around us. They did not look well disposed toward me. I recognized a woman from our brief battle. I did not see either of the men I had fought. The Prince's former companions showed no evidence of sympathy or friendship for him now. He did not seem to see them, but rode looking forward with the point of my knife pressed high against his ribs.

We turned back and cut across the hillsides, past the barrow and toward the forest. The land we crossed hummocked oddly, and I soon decided that many years ago, a town of some sort had stood here. Meadow and woods had taken the land again, but land that has borne the plow ever after lies flatter. Moss had coated the stony walls that had once divided pastureland, and grass grew atop that, amidst the thistle and bramble that seem to love such stony places. "No one lives forever," the walls seemed to say. "Four stones stacked atop one another will outlive all your dreams and still stand when your descendants have long forgotten that you lived here."

Dutiful was silent as we rode. I kept my knife at his ribs. I do believe that if I had felt the woman take over his body, I would have pushed the blade home. His mind seemed far away. I used the time to assess our captors. There were an even dozen, including Laudwine.

We came at last to a cave cut into the side of a hill. Long ago, someone had added stone walls to extend the space. The remnants of a wooden gate hung drunkenly to one side. Sheep, I thought. It would be a good place to hold sheep at night, with the cave for shelter if rain or snow came too strong. Myblack lifted her head and gave a whinny of greeting to Malta and the three other horses tethered there. I made it fifteen of them, a respectable force to take on, even if there had been more than one of me.

I dismounted with the others and pulled the Prince down after me. He staggered as he landed on his feet and I caught him. His lips were moving as if he whispered to himself, but I heard nothing. His eyes seemed glassy and distant. I set the knife firmly to his throat. "If she tries to take him before the others are freed, I'll still kill him," I warned them. Laudwine looked surprised by my threat. Then, "Peladine!" he bellowed. In reply, a hunting cat came bounding out of the cave. She fixed me with a hateful stare. Her slow advance toward me was the angry step of a thwarted woman, not a cat's stalk.

The Prince had dropped his gaze to the cat. He said nothing, but I felt the ragged sigh of his breath as it escaped him. Laudwine advanced to the cat and then went down on one knee to speak quietly to her. "I've struck a bargain," he told her quietly. "If we let his friends go free, he gives us the Prince unscathed. More, he escorts you back to Buckkeep and helps you become accepted there."

I don't know if some sign of affirmation passed between them, or if Laudwine simply assumed her consent. When he stood, he spoke more loudly. "Inside. Your companions are there."

I was horribly reluctant to follow him into that cave. Out in the open, we had some small chance of escape. Inside, we would be cornered. The only thing I could promise myself was that they would not get Dutiful. To cut his throat would be the work of an instant. I was not so certain I could give myself a quick death, let alone Nighteyes or the Fool.

Within the cave, a small fire burned, and my stomach complained at the smell of roasting meat. A camp of sorts had been pitched there, but to my eyes it had the look of a brigands' den rather than a military encampment. The thought warned me that I should not be entirely confident that Laudwine had control of his people. Because they followed him did not mean they were subject to him. That cheery thought was entertaining me as I searched the shadowy interior of the cave while Laudwine was quietly conferring with the folk he had left on guard there. He had not placed anyone in charge of us. All eyes were on him, and I eased away from the crowd. A few noticed my movement, but no one protested it. Jinna's charm still rode outside my shirt and I smiled disarmingly. Obviously, I was going deeper into the cave, not trying to escape to the outdoors. It was another indication of how informal Laudwine's command was. My fear that the Piebalds were some sort of Witted army dissolved into a sickening suspicion that they were actually a Witted mob.

My heart found my friends before my eyes. I saw two huddled shapes on the floor in the back of the cave. I did not ask permission. With my knife at Dutiful's throat, I walked us to them.

Toward the back of the cave, the ceiling dropped and the rock walls narrowed. In that little space, they slept. Their bed was the Fool's cloak, or what remained of that fine garment. Nighteyes sprawled on his side, caught in the sleep of exhaustion. The Fool lay beside him, his body curled protectively around the wolf's. They were both filthy. The Fool had a strip of bandaging tied around his brow. The gold of his skin had gone sallow and one side of his face was marred with bruises. Someone had taken his boots, and his narrow, pale feet looked bruised and vulnerable. The wolf's throat was matted with blood and saliva, and his breathing had a whistle in it.

I wanted to drop to my knees beside them, but I feared to take my knife from Dutiful's throat.

"Wake up," I bade them, quietly. "Wake up, you two. I've come back for you."

The wolf's ears flicked, and then he opened an eye to me. He shifted, trying to lift his head and the stirring woke the Fool, as well. He opened his eyes and stared at me, unbelieving. Despair dragged at his face.

"You have to get up," I warned him quietly. "I've struck a bargain with the Piebalds, but you'll have to get up and be ready to move. Can you walk? Both of you?"

The Fool had the owlish look of a child awakened in deep night. He sat up stiffly. "I . . . what sort of a bargain?" He looked at the charm at my throat, made a small sound, and deliberately pulled his eyes away. Hastily I tugged my collar closed. Let no charm cloud his mind now, no artificial affection make him reluctant to leave when he could.

Laudwine was coming toward us, Dutiful's hunting cat at his side. He did not look pleased that I had managed to talk to his captives without him present. I spoke quickly, letting my voice carry to him. "You two go free or I kill the Prince. But once you are free, the Prince and I will follow. Trust me."

And my time to speak to them alone had gone. The wolf sat up ponderously, levering himself off the floor. When he stood, his hindquarters swayed and he staggered a step sideways before he recovered. He smelled foul, of old blood and piss and infection. I did not have a hand free to touch him. I was too busy threatening Dutiful's life. He came to lean his bloodied head against my leg, and our thoughts flowed in the contact. *Oh, Nighteyes.*

Little brother. You lie.

Yes. I lie to them all. Can you get the Scentless One back to Buckkeep for me?

Probably not.

It eases my heart to hear you say that. It's so much better than "we'll all die here."

I would rather stay and die beside you.

I would rather not witness that. It would distract me from what I must do.

What of Nettle, then?

This thought was harder to share with him. *I cannot steal the life of one for the sake of the other. I do not have that right. If we all must die, then . . .* My thoughts sputtered to a halt. I thought of the strange moments that I'd shared in the flow of the Skill with that great other presence. I groped for some sort of comfort for us. *Perhaps the Fool is wrong, and time cannot be shifted from its course. Perhaps it is all determined before we are born. Or perhaps the next White Prophet will choose a better Catalyst.*

I felt him dismiss my philosophical musing. *Give him a clean death, then.*

I will try.

It was the merest trickle of thought between us, sieved through his pain and caution. It was like rain after a drought. I cursed myself for all the years we had shared this, and I had let my soul go yearning after the Skill. The end of this sharing loomed before me, and I only now perceived the full sweetness of all we had known. My wolf was a tottering step or two from death. I would likely kill myself, or be killed, before the afternoon was over. The dilemma of what one of us would do when the other died had been snatched away from us, and replaced with the reality. Neither of us would go on forever.

The Fool had managed to stand. His golden eyes searched my face desperately but I dared show him nothing. He drew himself up and became Lord Golden when Laudwine began speaking. The Piebald leader's voice was rich and polished, his powers of persuasion like a warming cloak. Behind him, his followers fanned out to witness.

"Your friend has summed it up for you. I have proven to his satisfaction that we never intended to hurt the Prince, only to let him see for himself that those of us you call Witted are not evil beings to be torn to pieces, but simply humans with a special gift from Eda. It was all we desired, that our Prince could be shown that. We regret the depth of our misunderstanding, and that you have been injured in the process of sorting it out. But now you may take your horse and go free. The wolf also. Your friend and the Prince will come after you shortly. All of you will return to Buck-keep, where it is our earnest hope that Prince Dutiful will speak out on our behalf."

Lord Golden's eyes traveled from Laudwine to me and back again. "And the reason for the knife is?"

Laudwine's deprecatory smile spoke volumes. "Your servant has little trust in us, I fear. Despite our assurances, he feels he must threaten Prince Dutiful until he is satisfied you are freed. I commend you for having such a loyal servant."

I could have driven cattle through the gap in his logic. A slight flicker in Lord Golden's eyes told me of his doubts, but at my slow nod, he bobbed his own assent. He did not know the game, but he trusted me. Before the day was out, he would curse that trust. I closed my heart against that thought. This poor bargain was the best I could do for any of us. I forced the betrayal from my lips. "My lord, if you would take my good dog and go, I will soon follow after with the Prince."

"I doubt we shall go far or swift this day. As you can see, your dog is grievously hurt."

"No need to hurry. I shall be along to join you soon, and we can make our way home together."

Lord Golden's face remained concerned but calm. Perhaps only I was aware of all that battled within him. The situation did not make sense to him, but I obviously wanted him to take the wolf and leave. I almost *saw* him make his choice. He stooped to take up his once-rich cloak, now stained with blood and earth. He shook it out, and then swept it over his shoulders as if it were still a fine garment. "I will have my boots returned to me, of course? And my horse?" The nobleman, conscious of his superior birth, was back in his voice.

"Of course," Laudwine agreed, but I saw several scowling faces in the crowd behind him. Malta was a fine horse, a rich prize for whoever had captured Lord Golden.

"Then we shall go. Tom, I shall expect you to follow immediately."

"Of course, master," I humbly lied.

"With the Prince."

"I shall not leave until he precedes me," I promised heartily.

"Excellent," Lord Golden confirmed. He nodded to me, but the Fool's eyes shot me a troubled glance. The look he turned on Laudwine was chill. "You have treated me no better than common ruffians and highwaymen would have. I will be unable to conceal my condition from the Queen and her guard companies. You are fortunate indeed that Tom Badgerlock and I are willing to confirm to her that you have seen the error of your ways. Otherwise, I am sure she would send her troops to hunt you down like vermin."

He was perfection as the affronted nobleman, yet I nearly roared at him to shut up and get away while they could. Throughout, the mistcat watched Dutiful as a house cat watches a mousehole. I could almost feel the woman's hunger to possess him completely. I had no faith that she would be bound by Laudwine's bargain any more than his mob. If she moved to take him, if Dutiful showed any sign of her invading him, I would have to kill him whether the Fool had escaped or not. I desperately wanted them gone. I smiled, hoping it did not look too much like a snarl as Lord Golden gripped Laudwine with his eyes. Then he dared to sweep the gathered mob with that golden glance. I was not certain what they thought, but I firmly believed that he memorized every face he gazed upon. I saw anger stir in many of them at his look.

And all the while the Prince stood in the circle of my arm, my knife to his throat, ransom for my friends' lives. He stood very still, as if thinking of nothing at all. He met the cat's gaze evenly. I dared not guess what passed between them, not even when the cat glanced aside and stared resolutely past him.

Anger hardened Laudwine's features for a moment, but

then he mastered them. "Of course you must report to the Queen. But when she has heard an accounting from her son of his experiences with us, perhaps she will be more sympathetic to our position." He made a small motion with his hand, and after a pause, his followers parted. I did not envy Lord Golden his walk through that tunnel of animosity.

I looked down at Nighteyes. He leaned against my leg and pressed hard there for a moment. I focused my mind to the point of a pin. *Go to earth as soon as you may. Lead him off the road and hide as best you can.*

Such a dolorous look he gave me. Then our minds parted. Nighteyes tottered after the Fool, stiff-legged but dignified. I did not know how far he would get, but at least he would not die in this cave surrounded by hounds and hunting cats that hated him. The Fool would be beside him. That was as much comfort as I could find for myself.

The mouth of the cave was an arch of light. In that halo, I saw Malta brought to the Fool. He took her reins but did not mount her. Instead, he led her in a slow walk, one that matched the pace Nighteyes could sustain. I stared after them, a man and a horse and a wolf walking away from me. Their figures dwindled smaller, and I became aware of Dutiful standing in the circle of my arm, his breathing matching mine. Life walked away from me, and I embraced death here. "I'm so sorry," I whispered by his ear. "I'll make it fast."

He already knew. My son's reply was the barest stirring of air. "Not yet. A small corner still belongs to me. I can hold her off for a time, I think. We will let them get as far as they can."

chapter XXVI

SACRIFICE

Although it is commonly spoken of as the Mountain
Kingdom, that territory and its rulers do not at all follow the
Six Duchies' concept of what constitutes a true kingdom. A
kingdom is most often visualized as a single people in a
common territory, ruled over by a monarch. The
Mountains do not lend themselves to any of those three
defining limits. Rather than a single folk, there are the
roving hunters, the migratory herd folk, traders and
travelers with set patterns of routes, and those who choose
to eke out a living on scattered little farms throughout the
region. It is easy to understand that these folk may share
few common interests.

　　It is natural, then, that the "ruler" of these folk is not a
king in the traditional sense. Rather, the line began with a
mediator, a wise man who was adept at arbitrating the
disputes that were bound to arise between such disparate
peoples. The legends of the Chyurda "kings" abound with
tales of rulers willing to offer themselves as ransom, to risk
not only wealth but also their own lives for their people.
From this tradition comes the honorific the Mountain people
bestow on their ruler. Not King or Queen do they call their
monarch, but Sacrifice.

　　　　CHIVALRY FARSEER, "OF THE MOUNTAIN KINGDOM"

They moved in, drifting like silt, until Laudwine's folk
stood dark between the light and me. I gazed around at the
staring circle of my enemies. The daylight behind them
made it hard to distinguish their features in the dim cave,

but as my eyes adjusted, I studied each face. They were mostly young men, and among them four young women. None looked older than Laudwine. No Old Blood elders here; the Piebalds were a young man's cause. Four of the men had the same large, square teeth: brothers or at least cousins. Some seemed almost neutral, but none looked friendly. The only smiles I saw were gloatingly hostile. I loosened my collar again. If Jinna's charm made any difference, I did not perceive it. I wondered if any were related to the man I had killed at the trailhead. There were animals with them, though not so many as I would have expected. Two hounds and a cat were there, and one man had a raven on his shoulder.

I kept my silence, waiting, with no idea as to what would happen next. The Prince's cat had never moved from where she crouched on the floor before us. Several times I had seen her glance aside, but each time her eyes had eventually returned to the lad, burning with a peculiar fixation that made them seem human. Laudwine had gone to the mouth of the cave to make his false farewell to Lord Golden. Now he smiled confidently as he came back to confront us.

"I think we can dispense with your knife," Laudwine observed evenly. "I've kept my part of the bargain."

"It might not be wise," I cautioned him. Then I lied. "The boy tried to get away just a minute ago. The only thing that kept him still was the knife. Best I keep it on him until she's . . ." I sought for words. "All the way in," I finished lamely. I saw one or two faces twitch with uneasiness. Deliberately, I added, "Until Peladine takes his body as her own completely." I saw one woman swallow.

Laudwine seemed unaware that this troubled some of his followers. His affable manner never wavered. "I think not. It pains me to see you menace a throat that will soon belong to my kin. Your knife, sir. You are among your own kind here, you know. You have nothing to fear." He extended a hand for it.

Experience had taught me that those most like me presented the greatest threat to me. But I let a slow smile spread over my face and took my knife from the Prince's throat. I did not give it to Laudwine, but sheathed it at my belt. I kept one hand always on Dutiful's shoulder, holding him at my side. Here, where the cave narrowed, I could thrust him behind me if need be. I doubted that need would arise. I intended to kill him myself. Twenty years ago, Chade had drilled me repeatedly in all the ways there were to kill a man with my hands. I had learned silent ways, and swift ways, and ways that were slow. I hoped I would be as quick and accurate as I had once been. The most satisfying tactic would be to wait until the woman took the boy's body, and then kill Dutiful so quickly that the woman would die with him, unable to flee back into her little cat's body. Would I still have time to kill myself before they pulled me down? I doubted it. Best not to dwell on such thoughts.

Suddenly, the Prince spoke up for himself. "I won't struggle." He shrugged clear of my hand on his shoulder and stood as straight as the low ceiling would allow. "I've been a fool. Perhaps I deserve this for my foolishness. But I thought . . ." His gaze had been traveling the faces that surrounded us. His eyes seemed to know where to linger, and in the wake of his glance, I saw uncertainty kindle on a few faces. "I thought you genuinely believed me one of your own. Your welcome and aid seemed so real. My bond with the cat—I had never felt anything like that. And when the woman came into my mind and said that she, that she loved me—" His voice hesitated over those words, but he forced it on. "I thought I had found something real, something worth more than my crown or my family or even my own duty to my people. I was a fool. So. Her name was Peladine, was it? She never told me her name, and of course I never saw her face. Well." He folded his knees and sat cross-legged. He opened his arms to the staring cat. "Come, cat. You, at least, loved me for myself. I know you like this no better than I do. Let us both be done with this."

He glanced up at me, a swift glance fraught with a meaning I could not discern. It chilled me. "Don't despise me as a complete fool. The cat loves me, and I love the cat. That much, at least, was always true." I knew that when the creature climbed into his lap, the contact would strengthen their bond. The woman would cross into him easily. His dark eyes were steady on mine. I saw Kettricken suddenly in his features, in his calm acceptance of what would be. His words were for me. "If by doing this I would be freeing the cat of her, I would rejoice. Instead, I go to share her entrapment. We shall be two that she bonded to, simply for the use of our bodies. She never had any need for our hearts, save to use them against us."

Dutiful Farseer turned away from me, closing his eyes. He bowed his head to the advancing animal. There was not a sound, not even an indrawn breath, in the cave. All watched, all waited. Several faces were white and taut. One young man turned aside, shuddering, as the cat stalked up to him. She pressed her striped brow to the Prince's, marking him as cats do. As she swiped her face against his, her green gaze brushed mine.

Kill me now.

The sharp mind-to-mind contact was so unexpected, I could not react to it.

What had Jinna's cat told me? That all cats can speak, but that they choose when and to whom. The mind that touched mine was a cat's mind, not a woman's. I stared at the little hunting cat, unmoving. She opened her jaws wide but soundlessly, as if a twinge of pain too great to express had passed through her. Then she gave her head a shake.

Stupid brother-to-a-dog! You waste our chance. Kill me now!

These words struck my mind with the impact of a blow. "No!" cried Dutiful and belatedly I realized he had not been privy to her first words to me. He clutched at the mistcat but she launched, from the floor to Dutiful's shoulder and at me, heedless of how her claws scored him in that spring. She flew at me, claws raw and mouth wide. What is so white as a cat's teeth against her red mouth? I tried to reach my knife, but she was too fast. She landed on my chest, the curved claws of her front paws hooking securely into my flesh as her hind legs ripped at my belly. She turned her face sideways, and all I saw were teeth descending on my face as I fell backward into the corner of the cave.

Other voices shouted. "Peladine!" Laudwine roared, and I heard the Prince's agonized cry of "No, no!" but I was occupied with saving my eyes. I pushed at the cat with one hand as I dragged at my sheathed knife with the other, but her claws were well set in my flesh. I could not budge her. I twisted my face aside as we went down, inadvertently baring my throat to her fangs. She seized that opportunity quite literally, and as I felt her teeth enter my flesh, thwarted only by the beads of Jinna's charm, I managed to pull my knife free. I did not know if I fought the woman or the cat, only that the creature intended to kill me. It mattered, but not in a way that would stay my hand. It was awkward to stab her as she clung to my chest, for her spine and ribs turned my blade twice. On the third time, I finally managed to sink the metal into her. She let go of my throat to sound her death yowl, but her claws remained firmly fixed in my chest. Her hind legs had shredded my shirt. My belly was striped with fire. I pulled her body off mine, cursing, but when I would have flung it aside, Dutiful snatched it from me.

"Cat, oh, cat!" he cried, and clutched the lifeless body to his as if it were his child. "You killed her!" he cried accusingly.

"Peladine?" Laudwine asked wildly. "Peladine!"

Perhaps if his bond-animal had not just been slain, Dutiful would have had the presence of mind to pretend his body held the woman's mind. But he did not, and before I could regain my feet, I saw Laudwine's boot flying toward my head. I flung myself aside into a roll and sprang to my feet in a performance worthy of the Fool's younger self. My knife was still in the cat's body, but my sword hung at my belt. I dragged it free and charged at Laudwine.

"Run!" I bellowed at the Prince. "Get away. She bought your freedom with her life. Don't waste that!"

Laudwine was a bigger man than I, and the sword he was drawing would give him a sizable advantage in reach. I gripped my hilt two-handed and took off his forearm before his weapon cleared its sheath. He went down with a shriek, clutching at the spurting stump as if it were a cup held aloft in a toast. Shock held the mob back for an instant, barely time for me to take two steps and crowd Dutiful into the alcove behind me. He had not fled and now it was too late. Perhaps it had always been too late. He went to his knees, the cat in his arms. I swung my blade in a madman's wild arc, forcing the mob back. "Get up!" I roared at him. "Use that knife!"

I was peripherally aware of him coming to his feet behind me. I had no idea if he had the knife from the cat's body. Fleetingly, I wondered if he would put it in my back. Then the wave of men surged forward, some in the front propelled only by the push of men behind them. Two grabbed Laudwine and dragged his curled body out of my reach. Someone jumped past them to confront me. The quarters were too close for anything except butchery. My first wide cut laid open his belly and slashed the face of another man as it finished. That slowed their rush, but then they bunched toward me. The men attacking us were hampered by their own numbers. When I was forced back, I felt the Prince step aside, and suddenly both our backs were to the wall of the cave. He darted past me to stab a man who had just managed to slip inside my guard, and then spun to his right to defend himself. He screamed like a wildcat as he struck out at his man, and the man answered with a shriek of pain.

I knew we had no chance, so when the arrow flew past my ear to shatter on the wall behind me, I was not too alarmed. Some fool wasted breath sounding a horn. I ignored it, as I ignored the cries of the men falling in front of me. One was dying and I finished another on the backstroke. I swung my blade wide, and unbelievably, they gave ground before me. I roared my triumph and stepped forward into the gap. My body shielded Dutiful's now. "Come and die!" I snarled at them all. My free hand beckoned them in.

"Blades down!" someone shouted.

I swung my sword again, but those confronting me gave ground, tossing their swords to the earth. They cleared the way for an archer to advance on me. Other bowmen backed him, but his nocked arrow pointed straight at my chest. "Put it down!" he shouted again. It was the boy who had ambushed us, the one who had shot Laurel, and then fled with her. As I stood panting, wondering if I should force him to kill me, Laurel spoke behind him. She tried to speak calmingly, but her voice shook.

"Blade down, Tom Badgerlock. You're among friends."

Battle makes the world a small place, makes all life no bigger than the sweep of your sword's length. It took me a time to come back to myself, and I was fortunate that they allotted me that time. I stared about, trying to make sense of what I saw, the archer and Laurel, and the folk who stood behind her, bows drawn. These were strangers, older folk than Laudwine's band. Six men, two women. Most carried bows but a few had only staffs. Some of the arrows were pointed at Laudwine's folk. They had dropped their swords and stood as much at bay as I was. Laudwine was on the floor, rolling in their midst, still clutching at his stump. Two steps and I could finish him at least. I drew a breath. Then I felt Dutiful's hand on my upper arm. He pushed down firmly. "Blade down, Tom," he said evenly, and for a moment it was Verity's calming voice in my ear. The strength went out of my arm and I let the tip of my weapon drop to the floor. Each panting breath I took was a flow of torment down my parched throat.

"Drop it!" the archer repeated. He stepped closer, and I

heard the small sounds of a bow drawn tauter. I felt my heart begin to race again. I calculated the distance I'd have to cover.

"Hold!" Lord Golden interceded suddenly. "Give him a moment to come to himself. Battle-fury takes him and his mind is not his own." He came, pushing his way to the front of the massed archers and then stepped out between them and me with a fine disregard for the arrows that now pointed at his back. He did not even glance at the Piebalds who grudgingly parted to let him through. "Easy, Tom." He addressed me as if calming a horse. "It's done now. It's all done."

He stepped forward and set his hand on my arm, and I heard a murmur run through the crowd as if he had done something amazingly brave. At his touch, the sword fell from my grasp. Beside me, Dutiful dropped suddenly to his knees. I looked down at him. There was blood on his hand and shirtfront, but it did not seem to be his. He dropped my knife now and gathered the limp cat from the floor into his arms. He held it to his breast as if it were a child and rocked back and forth, keening. "My cat, my friend."

A look of terrible concern washed over Lord Golden's face. "My Prince," he began worriedly. He stooped to touch the lad, but I caught him and turned him aside.

"Leave him alone," I suggested quietly. "Give him his time to mourn."

Then, tottering stiffly through the crowd came my wolf. When he reached my side, it was my turn to sink down beside him.

After that, little enough attention was paid to Tom Badgerlock and his wolf. They left us where we huddled as they moved Laudwine's followers away from the Prince. That suited us both, for it gave us time to be together, and freed me to observe all around us. What we mostly watched was the Prince. The archer, one Deerkin by name, had brought an old healer with him. She set aside the bow she had carried and came to the Prince's side. She made no effort to touch him, but only sat beside him and watched him as he mourned. Nighteyes and I kept vigil on the other side of him. She looked at me once. When our eyes met, her gaze was old and tired and sick with sadness. I fear mine was the same.

The bodies of the Piebalds I had killed were dragged outside, and slung over their horses. Too late I heard the clatter of departing hooves and realized that the Piebalds had been allowed to flee. I set my teeth. I could not have stopped it from happening. Laudwine had gone last, no longer their leader, swaying in the saddle atop his frothing warhorse and steadied by a young rider behind him. That had disturbed me most of all. Not only had I snatched the Prince from him, but I had slain the animal that held his sister's soul, and maimed him, as well. I needed no more enemies than I already had, but it had been beyond my control. He had gone free, and I hoped I would not live to regret that.

The healer let the Prince hold and mourn the cat until the sun touched the horizon. Then she looked past him to me. "Take the cat's body from him," she said quietly.

It was not a task I wanted, but I did it.

It was hard to coax him to give up the cat's cooling body. I chose my words with great care. This was not a time to let the Skill-command force him to do what he was not ready to do on his own. When finally he allowed me to lift the mistcat from his lap, I was astonished at how light the creature seemed. Usually, a dead animal, lax and lolling, seems to weigh more than a live one, but with the loss of its life, the pathetic condition of the little cat was revealed. "As if she were eaten through with worms," Nighteyes had said, and he was not far off the mark. The cat was a wasted little creature, her once-sleek fur gone dry and brittle, and bumps of bone defining her spine. At her death, her fleas were leaving her, far too many for a healthy animal. As the healer took the cat from me, I saw anger flicker over her face. She spoke softly. I do not know if Dutiful heard her words, but I did. "She did not even let it keep itself as a cat would. She possessed it too completely, and tried to be a woman in a cat's fur."

Peladine had imposed a human's ways on the mistcat. She had denied her the long sleeps, the gorging to satiation, and the grooming sessions that were the natural right of a lithe little cat. Play and hunting had been denied her. It was the way of the Piebalds to use the Wit only for their own human ends. It sickened me.

The healer carried the cat's body outside and the Prince and I followed with Nighteyes walking between us. A half-built cairn awaited the little corpse. All Deerkin's people came outside to witness the interment. Their eyes were saddened, but they brimmed with respect.

Their healer spoke, for Dutiful was too numbed with grief. "She goes on without you. She died for you, to free you both. Keep within you the cat tracks she left on your soul. Let go with her the humanness that you shared with her. You are parted now."

The Prince swayed as they put the last stones on the cat, covering her death snarl. I set a hand to his shoulder to steady him, but he shrugged away my touch as if I were tainted. I did not blame him. She had commanded me to kill her, had done all she could to force me to the act, and yet I did not expect him to forgive me for having obeyed her. As soon as the cat was interred, the Old Blood healer had brought the Prince a draught. "Your share of her death," she said as she offered it to him, and he had quaffed it down before either Lord Golden or I could interfere. Then the healer gestured to me that I should take him back into the cave. There, he lay down where his cat had died, and his mourning broke loose anew.

I don't know what she gave him in that drink, but the boy's heartbroken sobs wound slowly down into the hoarse breathing of sodden sleep. There was nothing of rest in the limp way he sprawled beside me. "A little death," she had confided to me, thoroughly frightening me. "I give him a little death of his own, a time of emptiness. He died, you know, when the cat was killed. He needs this empty time to be dead. Do not try to cheat him of it."

Indeed, it plunged him into a sleep but one step shy of death. She settled him on a pallet, arranging his body as if it were a corpse. As she did so, she muttered scathingly, "Such bruises on his neck and back. How could they beat a mere boy like that?"

I was too shamed to admit I had given him those marks. I held my silence and she covered him well, shaking her head over him. Then she turned and brusquely motioned me to her side for her services. "The wolf, too. I've time for you, now that the boy's hurts are tended. His hurt was far more grievous than anything that bleeds."

With warm water she washed our wounds and salved them with a greasy unguent. Nighteyes was passive to her touch. He held himself so tightly against the pain I could scarcely feel him there. As she worked on the scratches on my chest and belly, she muttered sternly to me. I gave Jinna's charm the credit that she deigned to speak to a renegade like me at all.

But the healer's only comment on it was that my necklace had probably saved my life. "The cat meant to kill you, and no mistake about that," she observed. "But it was no will or fault of her own, I'm sure. And not the boy's fault, either. Look at him. He is a child still to our ways, far too young to bond," she lectured me severely, as if it were my fault. "He is unschooled in our ways, and look how it has hurt him. I will not tell you lies. He is like to die of this, or take a melancholy madness that will plague him to the end of his days." She tightened the bandage around my belly with a tug. "Someone should teach him Old Blood ways. Proper ways of dealing with his magic." She glared at me, but I did not reply. I only pulled what was left of my shirt back over my head. As she turned away from me, I heard her snort of contempt.

Nighteyes wearily lifted his head and set it on my knee. Salve and clotted blood smeared me. He looked at the sleeping boy. *Are you going to teach him?*

I doubt he'd wish to learn anything from me. I killed his cat. Who will, then?

I left that question hanging. I stretched out in the darkness beside the wolf. We lay between the Farseer heir and the outside world.

Not far from us, in the central part of the shelter, Deerkin sat in council with Lord Golden. Laurel sat between them. The healer had joined them, and there were two other elders present in the circle closest to the fire. I regarded them through my lashes. In the rest of the cave, the other Old Blood folk appeared casually engaged in the ordinary evening chores of a campsite. Several lounged on their blanket rolls behind Deerkin. They seemed content to let the young man speak for them, but I sensed that perhaps they were the true holders of power in the group. One was smoking a long-stemmed pipe. Another, a bearded fellow, was working a careful edge onto his sheath knife. The whetting of the blade was a monotonous undertone to the conversation. For all their casual postures, I sensed how keenly they listened to what went on. Deerkin might speak for them, but I sensed they would listen to be sure his words were what they wished said.

It was not to Tom Badgerlock that these Old Blood riders explained themselves, but to Lord Golden. What was Tom Badgerlock but a renegade to his kind, a lackey of the crown? He was worse by far than Laurel, for all knew that though she had been born to an Old Blood family, the talent was dead in her. It was expected of her that she must make her way in the world however she might, forever half-dead to all the life that blossomed and buzzed and burned about her. No shame to her that she was a Huntswoman to the Queen. I even sensed an odd pride in the Old Bloods, that one so impaired had risen so far. I had chosen my treason, however, and all the Witted folk walked a wide swath around me. One brought meat on spits and propped it over the fire. The smell was vaguely tantalizing.

Food? I asked Nighteyes.

Too tired to eat, he declined, and I agreed with him. But for me there was the added reluctance of asking food of folk who ostracized us. So we rested, ignored in the outer circle of darkness. I refused to feel hurt that the Fool had spoken so little to me. Lord Golden could not be concerned with a servant's injuries, any more than Tom Badgerlock should fret about his master's bruises. We had our roles to play still. So I feigned sleep, but from beneath lowered lashes I watched them, and listened to their talk.

The talk was general at first, and I gathered my facts in bits and by assumption. Deerkin was telling Laurel some news of an uncle they had in common. It was old news, of sons grown and wed. So. Estranged cousins, separated for years. It made sense. She had admitted she had family in this area, and as much as told me they were Witted. The rest came out in an explanation to Lord Golden. Deerkin and Arno had ridden with Laudwine's Piebalds for only a summer. They had both been sickened and angry over how the Old Blood folk were treated. When Laudwine's sister had died, he had devoted himself to his people's cause and risen as a leader. He had nothing save himself to lose, and change, he had told them, demanded sacrifice. It was time the Old Blood took the peace that was rightfully theirs. He made them feel strong and daring, these Old Blood sons and daughters rising up boldly to take what their parents feared to reach for. They would change the world. Time once more to live as a united folk in Old Blood communities, time to let their children openly acknowledge their magic. Time for change. "He made it sound so logical. And so noble. Yes, we would have to take extreme measures, but the end we sought was no more than what we were rightfully entitled to. Simple peace and acceptance. That was all. Is that so much for any man to ask?"

"It seems a righteous goal," Lord Golden murmured attentively. "Though his means to it seem . . ." He left it dangling, for them to fill in. Disgusting. Cruel. Immoral. The very lack of a description let the full baseness of it be considered.

A short silence fell. "I didn't know that Peladine was in the cat," Deerkin asserted defensively. A skeptical quiet followed his words. Deerkin looked around at the elders almost angrily. "I know you say I should have been able to sense her, but I did not. Perhaps I have not been taught as well as I should. Or perhaps she was more adept at hiding than you know. But I swear I did not know. Arno and I took the cat to the Bresingas. They knew it was an Old Blood gift, intended for Prince Dutiful, to sway him to our cause. But I swear by my Old Blood, that was all they knew. Or I. Otherwise, I would not have been a party to it."

The old healer shook her head. "So many will say of an evil thing, after the fact," she charged him. "Only this puzzles me. You know a mistcat must be taken young, and that it hunts only for the one who takes it. Did not you wonder?"

Deerkin reddened but, "I did not know Peladine was in the cat," he insisted. "Yes, I knew she had been bonded with the mistcat. But Peladine was dead. I thought the cat alone, and put her odd ways down to her mourning. What else could be done with the cat? She could not make her own way in the hills; she had never lived a wild life. And so I took her to the Bresingas, a gift fit for a prince. I thought it possible," and a hitch in his voice betrayed him, "that she might want to bond again. She had that right, if she so chose. But when the Prince came to us, I thought it was what Laudwine said it was. That he came of his own will, to learn our ways. Do you think I would have helped otherwise, do you think Arno would have sacrificed his life for such an end?"

Some, I think, must have doubted his story as much as I did. But it was not a time for such accusations. All let it pass and he continued his tale.

"Arno and I rode with Laudwine and the Piebalds, as escort for the Prince. We intended to take him to Seffers-wood, where he could live among the Piebalds and learn our ways. So Laudwine told us. When Arno was taken at Hallerby outside the Piebald Prince, we knew we had to ride for our lives. I hated to leave him, but it was what we had sworn as Piebalds: that each of us would sacrifice our life for the others as needed. My heart was full of fury when we first turned and set our ambush for the cowards that chased us. I do not regret a single one of those deaths. Arno was my brother! Then we rode on, and when next we came to a good place, Laudwine once more left me to guard the trail. 'Stop them,' he told me. 'If it takes your life to do it, so be it.' And I agreed with him."

He paused in his narrative and his eyes sought Laurel. "I swear I did not recognize you, cousin. Not even when my arrow stood in you did I know you. All I could think was to kill all those who had helped to kill Arno. Not until Bad-gerlock dragged me from the tree and I looked up at you did I realize what I had done. Shed more of my own family's blood." He swallowed and suddenly fell silent.

"I forgive you." Laurel's voice was soft but carrying. She looked at the gathered Old Bloods. "Let all here witness that. Deerkin hurt me unknowingly, and I forgive him. There is no debt of vengeance or reparation between us. At the time, I knew none of this. All I could think was that, because I lacked the magic you possessed, you had marked me as fit to kill." A laugh twisted from her throat. "Only when Badgerlock was brutalizing you did I realize that . . . that it didn't matter." She suddenly turned to look at him. Shamefaced, Deerkin still forced himself to meet her earnest gaze. "You are my cousin, and my blood," she as-serted softly. "What we share far outweighs our differences. I feared he would kill you, trying to get you to speak. And I knew that, despite what you had done, even regardless of my loyalty to the Queen, I could not let that happen. So I rose in the night while Lord Golden and his man were sleeping, and spirited my cousin away." She transferred her gaze to Lord Golden. "Earlier, you had told me I must trust you when you excluded me from the confidences you shared with Badgerlock. I decided I had the right to demand the same from you. So I left you sleeping, and did what I thought best to save my Prince."

Lord Golden bowed his head for a moment, and then nodded to her gravely.

Deerkin rubbed a hand across his eyes. He spoke as if he had not even heard her words to Lord Golden. "You are wrong, Laurel. I owe you a debt, and I will never forget it. When we were children, we were never kind to you when you came to visit your mother's kin. We always excluded you. Even your own brother called you the mole, blind and tunneling where we ran free and wise. And I had shot you. I had no right to expect any help from you. But you came to me. You saved my life."

Laurel's voice was stiff. "Arno," she said. "I did it for Arno. He was as blind and deaf as I was to this 'family' magic that excluded us. He alone was my playmate when I visited. But he loved you, always, and in the end he thought you worth his life." She shook her head. "I would not have let his death be for nothing."

Together, they had crept away from the cave that night. She had convinced him that the taking of Prince Dutiful could only bring harsh persecution down on the Old Blood, and demanded that he find elders powerful enough to demand Laudwine surrender him. Queen Kettricken, she reminded him, had already spoken out against those who lynched the Witted. Would he turn that Queen, the first who had taken their part in generations, against them? Laurel had convinced Deerkin that, as Piebalds had stolen the Prince, so the Old Blood must return him. It was the only reparation they could make.

She turned to Lord Golden. Her voice pleaded. "We returned with aid as swiftly as we could. It is not the fault of Old Blood that they must live scattered and silent. From farm to cottage we rode, gathering those of influence who were willing to speak sense to Laudwine. It was hard, for that is not the Old Blood way. Each man is supposed to rule himself, each household have its own integrity. Few wanted to stand over Laudwine and demand he do what was right." Her gaze left Lord Golden and traveled over the others gathered there. "To those of you who came, I give great thanks. And if you would let me, I would make your names known to the Queen, so she would know where her debt lies."

"And where to bring the rope and the sword?" the healer asked quietly. "Times are not yet kind enough for names to be given, Laurel. We have yours. If we need the Queen's ear, we can seek her out through you."

Those they had gathered were Old Blood folk, but they did not style themselves Piebalds, nor did they condone the latter's ways. They cleaved to the old teachings, Deerkin told Lord Golden earnestly. It shamed him that for a time he had followed Laudwine. Anger had made him do it, he swore, not a desire to master animals and turn them to his own purposes as the Piebalds did. He had seen too many of his own folk hung and quartered these last two years. It was enough to turn any man's reason, but he had seen the error of his ways, thank Eda. And thanks to Laurel, and he hoped his cousin would forgive him the cruelty of their childhood years.

The conversation lapped against me like the rhythmic washing of waves. I tried to stay awake and make sense of his words, but we were so weary, my wolf and I. Nighteyes lay beside me and I could not separate where his pain ended and mine began. I did not care. Even if pain had been all we could share anymore, I would have taken it gladly. We still had one another.

The Prince was not so fortunate. I rolled my head to look at him, but he slept on, his breath sighing in and out as if even in his dreams, he grieved.

I felt myself wavering in and out of awareness. The wolf's heavy sleep tugged at me, a pleasant lure. Sleep is the great healer, Burrich had always told me. I prayed he had been right. As if they were the notes of far-off music, I sensed Nighteyes' dreams of hunting, but I could not yet give in to my longing to share them. The Fool might be confident of Laurel and Deerkin and their fellows, but I was not. I would keep watch, I promised myself. I would keep watch.

In my seeming sleep, I shifted to observe them. I idly marked that though Laurel sat between Lord Golden and Deerkin, she sat closer to the noble than she did to her own cousin. The talk had moved closer to negotiation than explanation. I listened keenly to Lord Golden's measured and reasonable words.

"I fear you do not completely understand Queen Kettricken's position. I cannot, of course, presume to speak for her. I am but a guest at the Farseer court, a newcomer and a foreigner at that. Yet perhaps these very limitations let me see more clearly what familiarity blinds you to. The crown and the Farseer name will not shield Prince Dutiful from persecution as a Witted one. Rather they will be as oil thrown on a fire; it will immolate him. You admit Queen Kettricken has done far more than any of her predecessors to outlaw persecution of your people. But if she reveals that her son is Witted, not only may both he and she be thrown down from power, but her very efforts to shelter your folk will be seen as a suspicious attempt to shield her own blood."

"Queen Kettricken has outlawed putting us to death simply for being 'Witted,' that is true," Deerkin replied. "But it does not mean we have stopped dying. The reality is obvious. Those who seek to kill us all fabricate injuries and invent supposed wrongs we have done to them. One man lies, another swears to it, and an Old Blood father or sister is hanged and quartered and burnt. Perhaps if the Queen sees the same threat to her son that my father sees to his, she will take greater action on our behalf."

Behind Deerkin, a man gave a slow nod.

Lord Golden spread his hands gracefully. "I will do

what I can, I assure you. The Queen will hear a full accounting of all you did to save her son. Laurel too is more than a simple Huntswoman to Queen Kettricken. She is friend and confidante, as well. She will tell the Queen all you did to recover her son. More, I cannot do. I cannot make promises for Queen Kettricken."

The man who had nodded behind Deerkin leaned forward. He touched him on the shoulder, a "go on" nudge. Then he leaned back and waited. Deerkin looked uncomfortable for a moment. Then he cleared his voice and spoke. "We will be watching the Queen and listening for what she will say to her nobles. We know better than any the threat that Prince Dutiful would face, were it known that he has Old Blood in his veins. They are the dangers that our brothers and sisters face every day. We would that our own were not at jeopardy. If the Queen sees fit to stretch forth her hand and shield our folk from persecution, then Old Blood will shield her son's secret. But if she ignores our situation, if a blind eye is turned to the bloodshed . . . well . . ."

"I take your meaning," Lord Golden replied swiftly. His voice was cool but not harsh. He took a breath. "Under the circumstances, it is, perhaps, the most we could ask of you. You have already restored the Farseer heir to us. This will kindly dispose the Queen toward you."

"So we expect," Deerkin responded heavily, and the men behind him nodded gravely.

Sleep beckoned me. Nighteyes was already in a torpor. His coat was sticky with salve, as were my chest and belly. There was almost no place that we didn't hurt, but I rested my brow against the back of his neck and draped a careful arm over him. His fur stuck to my skin. The words of the conference beside the fire faded and became insignificant as I opened myself to him. I sank my consciousness past the red pain that bounded him until I found the warmth and humor of his soul.

Cats. Worse than porcupines.

Much worse.

But the boy loved the cat.

The cat loved the boy. Poor boy.

Poor cat. The woman was selfish.

Past selfish. Evil. Her own life wasn't enough for her.

That was a brave little cat. She held tight and took the woman with her.

Brave cat. A pause. *Do you think it will ever come, that Witted folk can openly declare the magic?*

I don't know. It would be good, I suppose. Look how the secrecy and evil reputation of it has shaped our lives. But . . . but it has also been good as it has been. Ours. Yours and mine.

Yes. Rest now.

Rest.

I could not sort out which thoughts were mine and which the wolf's. I didn't need to. I sank into his dreams with him and we dreamed well together. Perhaps it was Dutiful's loss that put us so much in mind of all we still possessed, and all we had had. We dreamed of a cub hunting mice beneath the rotting floor of an old outbuilding, and we dreamed of a man and a wolf pulling down a great boar between them. We dreamed of stalking one another in deep snow, tussling and yelping and shouting. Deer blood, hot in the mouth, and the rich soft liver to squabble over. And then we sank past those ancient memories into perfect rest and comfort. Healing begins in deep sleeps such as that.

He stirred first. I nearly woke as he rose, gingerly shook himself, and then stretched more bravely. His superior sense of smell told me that the edge of dawn was in the air. The weak sun had just begun to touch the dew-wet grasses, waking the smells of the earth. Game would be stirring. The hunting would be good. ·

I'm so tired, I complained. *I can't believe you're getting up. Rest for a while longer. We'll hunt later.*

You're tired? I'm so tired that rest won't ease me. Only the hunt. I felt his wet nose poke my cheek. It was cold. *Aren't you coming? I was sure you'd want to come with me.*

I do. I do. But not just yet. Give me just a bit longer.

Very well, little brother. Just a bit longer. Follow me when you will.

But my mind rode with his, as it had so many times. We left the cave, thick with man-stink, and walked past the cat's new cairn. We smelled her death, and the musk of a fox who had come to the scent, but turned aside at the smell of the campfire's smoke. Swiftly we left the camp behind. Nighteyes chose the open hillside instead of the wooded vale. The sky overhead was blue and deep, and the last star fading in the sky. The night had been colder than I had realized. Frost tipped some of the grasses still, but as the rising sun touched it, it smoked briefly and was gone. The crisp edge of the air remained, each scent as sharp as a clean knife-edge. With a wolf's nose, I scented all and knew all. The world was ours. *The turning time*, I said to him.

Exactly. Time to change, Changer.

There were fat mice hastily harvesting seedheads in the tall grass, but we passed them by. At the top of the hill, we paused. We walked the spine of the hill, smelling the morning, tasting the lip of the day to come. There would be deer in the forested creek bottoms. They would be healthy and strong and fat, a challenge to any pack let alone a single wolf. He would need me at his side to hunt those. He would have to come back for them later. Nevertheless, he halted on top of the ridge. The morning wind riffled his fur and his ears were perked as he looked down to where we knew they must be.

Good hunting. I'm going now, my brother. He spoke with great determination.

Alone? You can't bring a buck down alone! I sighed with resignation. *Wait, I'll get up and come with you.*

Wait for you? Not likely! I've always had to run ahead of you and show you the way.

Swift as thought, he slipped away from me, running down the hillside like a cloud's shadow when the wind blows. My connection to him frayed away as he went, scattering and floating like dandelion fluff in the wind. Instead of small and secret, I felt our bond go wide and open, as if he had invited all the Witted creatures in the world in to share our joining. All the web of life on the whole hillside suddenly swelled within my heart, linked and meshed and woven through with one another. It was too glorious to contain. I had to go with him; a morning this wondrous must be shared.

"Wait!" I cried, and in shouting the word, I woke myself. Nearby, the Fool sat up, his hair tousled. I blinked. My mouth was full of salve and wolf-hair, my fingers buried deep in his coat. I clutched him to me, and my grip sighed his last stilled breath out of his lungs. But Nighteyes was gone. Cold rain was cascading down past the mouth of the cave.

chapter XXVII

LESSONS

*Before the Skill can be taught, resistance to the teaching
must be eliminated. Some Skillmasters have held that they
must know each student a year and a day before teaching
can even begin. At the end of that time, the master will
know which students are ready to receive instruction. The
others, no matter how likely they seemed, are then released
back to their previous lives.*

*Other masters have held that this technique is a waste
of valuable talent and potential. They espouse a more direct
path to eliminating the student's resistance, one that does not
focus so much on trust as on compliance to the master's will.
A strict regimen of austerity becomes the basis for focusing
the student's will on pleasing his master. Tools to achieve this
humbled attitude are fasting, cold, reduced sleep, and
discipline. The use of this method is recommended in times
of need when coteries have to be trained and formed quickly
and in quantity. The quality of Skill-user created may not be
as admirable, but almost every student with any level of
talent can be forced to function this way.*

               ▸ WEMDEL, JOURNEYMAN TO
SKILLMASTER QUILO, "OBSERVATIONS"

For a day and a night, the Old Blood healer kept Prince Dutiful in a stupor. I knew it frightened Lord Golden, despite Laurel's efforts to reassure him that she had seen this before and the healer was only doing what needed to be done. For myself, I envied Dutiful. No such comfort was offered me, and very little was said to me. Perhaps part of it was ostracism; when one separates oneself from supporting a society, one loses the support of that society, as well. But I do not think it was completely callous cruelty. I was an adult as well as an outcast, and they expected me to deal with my loss in my own way. As strangers, there was very little they could say, and absolutely nothing they could do that would help me.

I was aware of the Fool's sympathy, but in a peripheral way. As Lord Golden, he could say little to me. The death of my wolf was an isolating and numbing thing. The loss of Nighteyes' companionship was cutting enough, but with him had gone my access to his keener senses. Sound seemed muted, and night darker, scent and taste dulled. It was as if the world had been robbed of its brightness. He had left me behind to dwell alone in a dimmed and stale place.

I built a funeral pyre and burned my wolf's body. This obviously distressed the Old Blood folk, but it was my way of mourning and I took it. With my knife, I cut my hair and burned it with him, thick hanks of both black and white. With him went a long, airy lock of tawny gold. As Burrich had once done for Vixen, I stayed the day by the fire, battling the rain that strove to quench it, adding wood whenever it began to die, until even the wolf's bones were ash.

On the second morning, the healer allowed the Prince to wake. She sat by him, watching him come out of his drugged stupor. I stood aside, but kept my own watch. I saw awareness come back slowly, first to his eyes and then to his face. His hands began to make a little nervous kneading motion, but the healer reached over and stilled them with one of her own. "You are not the cat. The cat died. You are a man, and you must go on living. The blessing of Old Blood is that they share their lives with us. The curse is that those lives are seldom as long as our own."

Then she rose and left him, with no more than that to ponder. In a short time, Deerkin and his fellows mounted and rode away. I noticed that he and Laurel found a time to speak privately before he left. Perhaps they mended some broken family tie. I knew that Chade would ask me what they had said, but I was too dispirited to attempt to spy on them.

The Piebalds had left several horses behind when they fled. One was given over by the Old Bloods to the Prince's use. It was a little dun creature, its spirit as dull as its hide. It suited Prince Dutiful perfectly, as did the steady drizzle of rain. Before noon, we mounted and began our journey back to Buckkeep.

I rode alongside the Prince on Myblack. She had recovered from the worst of her limp. Laurel and Lord Golden rode ahead of us. They talked to one another, but I could not seem to follow their conversation. I do not think they spoke softly and privately. Rather, it was part of the deadening of my world. I felt numbed and dazed, half-blind. I knew I was alive because my injuries hurt and the rain was cold. But all the rest of the world, all sense and sensation, was dimmed. I no longer walked fearlessly in the darkness; the wind no longer spoke to me of a rabbit on a hillside or a deer that had recently crossed the road. Food had lost all savor.

The Prince was little better. He managed his grief as graciously as I did, with surliness and silence. There was, I suppose, an unspoken wall of blame between us. But for him, my wolf would live still, or at least would have died in kindlier circumstances. I had killed his cat, right before his eyes. Somehow it was even worse that a spiderweb of Skill attached us still. I could not look at him without being aware of just how completely miserable he was. I suspect he could feel my unspoken accusation of him. I knew it was not just, but I was in too much pain to be fair. If the Prince had kept to his name and his duty, if he had stayed at Buckkeep, I reasoned, then his cat would be alive, and my wolf, as well. I never spoke the words aloud. I didn't need to.

The journey back to Buckkeep was miserable for all of us. When we reached the road, we followed it north. None of us desired to visit Hallerby and the inn of the Piebald Prince again. And despite Deerkin's assurances that Lady

Bresinga and her family had had no hand in the Piebalds' plot against the Prince, we stayed well away from their lands and keep. The rains came down. The Old Blood folk had left us what they could of supplies, but it was not much. At the first small town we came to, we spent the night in a dismal inn. There Lord Golden paid handsomely for a messenger to take a scroll by the swiftest way possible to "his cousin" in Buckkeep Town. Then we struck out cross-country, heading for the next settlement that offered a ferry across the Buck River. The detours took us two extra days. We camped in the rain, ate our scanty rations, and slept cold and wet. I knew the Fool anxiously counted the dwindling days before the new moon and the Prince's betrothal ceremony. Nonetheless, we went slowly, and I suspected that Lord Golden bought time for his messenger to reach Buckkeep and alert the Queen to the circumstances of our return. It might have been, also, that he tried to give both the Prince and me some time to deal with our bereavement before we returned to the clatter and society of Buckkeep Castle.

If a man does not die of a wound, then it heals in some fashion, and so it is with loss. From the sharp pain of immediate bereavement, both the Prince and I passed into the gray days of numb bewilderment and waiting. So grief has always seemed to me, a time of waiting not for the hurt to pass, but to become accustomed to it.

It did not help my temperament that Lord Golden and Laurel did not find the way as tedious and lonely as the Prince and I did. They rode before us, stirrup to stirrup, and though they did not laugh aloud or sing gay wayfaring songs, they conversed near continuously and seemed to take a good deal of pleasure in one another's company. I told myself that I scarcely needed a nursemaid, and that there were excellent reasons why the Fool and I should not betray the depth of our friendship to either Laurel or Dutiful. But I ached with loss and loneliness, and resentment was the least painful emotion I could feel.

Three days before the new moon, we came to Newford.

As it was named, so it was, a fording and ferry that had not existed on my last journey through this area. It had a large dockyard, and a good fleet of flat-bottomed river barges were tied there. The little town around it was new, raw as a scab with its rough timbered houses and warehouses. We did not linger but went straight to the ferry dock and waited in the rain until the evening ferry was ready to cross.

The Prince held the reins of his nondescript horse and stared silently across the water. The recent rains had swelled the river and thickened it with silt, but I could not find sufficient love of life to be scared of death. The tossing and delay as the ferrymen struggled against the current seemed but one more annoying delay. Delay? I wondered sarcastically to myself. And what did I rush toward? Home and hearth? Wife and children? I had Hap still, I reminded myself, but on the heels of that thought I knew I did not. Hap was a young man striking out on his own. For me to cling to him now and make him the focus of my life would have been the act of a leech. So who was I, when I stood alone, stripped of all others? It was a difficult question.

The ferry lurched as we scraped gravel, and then men were drawing it in tighter to the bank. We were across. Buckkeep was a day's ride away. Somewhere above the dense clouds, the sliver of old moon lingered. We would reach Buckkeep before Prince Dutiful's betrothal ceremony. We had done it. Yet I felt no sense of elation or even accomplishment. I only wanted this journey to be finished.

The rain came down in torrents as we reached the landing, and Lord Golden declared firmly that we would go no farther that night. The inn there was older than the town on the other side of the river. Rain masked the other buildings of the hamlet, but I thought I glimpsed a small livery stable, and a scatter of homes beyond it. The inn's signboard was an oar painted on an old tiller, and the lumber of its walls showed weathered gray where its whitewashing had faded. The savage night had crowded the inn near full. Lord Golden and his party were too bedraggled to invoke the assumptions of nobility. Fortunately, he had sufficient coin to buy both the respect and awe of the innkeeper. Merchant Kestrel, as he identified himself, obtained two rooms for us, although one was a small one up under the rafters. This his "sister" gamely declared would suit her admirably, and the merchant and his two servants would have the other. If the Prince had any qualms about traveling in disguise, he did not show them. Hooded and cloaked, he stood dripping on the porch with me until a servingboy came out to tell us that our master's room was ready.

As I passed through the entry, I heard a woman's clear voice lifted in song from the common room. Of course, I thought to myself. Of course. Who else could better keep watch at an inn than a minstrel? Starling sang that ancient lay of the two lovers who defied their families and ran off to leap to their deaths for love of one another. I did not even glance into the room, though I saw Laurel had paused to listen by the door. The Prince followed me listlessly up the stairs to a large but rustic chamber.

Lord Golden had preceded us. An inn boy was making up the fire while two others set up a bathing tub and draft screens in the corner. There were two large beds in the room, and a pallet near the door. There was a window at one end of the room. The Prince walked to it and morosely stared out into the night. There was a rack near the fire, and I fulfilled my role by helping Lord Golden out of his soaked and dirty cloak. I shrugged out of mine, hung them both to dry on the rack, and then pulled his wet boots off as a stream of servants moved in and out of the room, bringing buckets of hot water and a repast of meat pies, stewed fruit, bread, and ale. They all moved with such precision that they reminded me of a troop of jugglers as they swept in as a wave and then likewise receded from the room. When they had vanished out of the door once more, I shut it firmly behind them. The hot water in the tub filled the room with the aroma of bathing herbs and I suddenly longed to lean back in it and seek oblivion.

Lord Golden's words recalled me to the reality. "My Prince, your bath is ready. Do you require assistance?"

The Prince stood. He let his wet cloak fall to the floor with a slap. He looked at it for a moment, then picked it up and brought it to the drying rack. He spread it there with the air of a boy used to attending to his own needs. "No assistance. Thank you," he said quietly. He glanced at the food steaming on the table. "Do not wait for me. I do not stand on formalities. I see no sense in your going hungry while I am bathing."

"In that, you are your father's son," Lord Golden observed approvingly.

The Prince inclined his head gravely to the compliment but made no other response.

Lord Golden waited until Prince Dutiful had vanished behind the screens. From the landlord, he had secured paper, ink, and quill. He sat down at a little table with these supplies, and busied himself silently for some moments. I walked over to the hearth with a meat pie from the table. I ate it standing while the fire at my back steamed some of the wet from my clothes. Lord Golden spoke to me as his quill scratched out a final line. "Well, at least we're out of the weather for a time. I think we shall have a good sleep here, and go on tomorrow, but not too early in the morning. Does that suit you, Tom?"

"As you wish, Lord Golden," I replied as he blew on the missive, then rolled it. He tied it with a thread drawn from his once-grand cloak. He handed it to me, one eyebrow raised.

I did not mistake his meaning. "I'd rather not," I said very quietly.

He left the writing table and went to where the food was spread. He began to serve himself, deliberately clattering dishes and pots as he did so. His voice was soft as he muttered, "And I would rather you did not have to go. But I cannot. Unkempt as I am, there are still folk here that might recognize Lord Golden and mark his interest in the minstrel. I've earned enough scandal to my name on this journey. Have you forgotten my actions at Galekeep? I've all of that to explain away when I return to Buckkeep. Nor can Dutiful go, and as far as I know, Laurel is ignorant of the connection. Starling might recognize her, but would look askance at a note delivered by her. So you it must be, I fear."

I feared the same, and feared more the traitorous part of me that actually wished to go down the stairs and catch the minstrel's eye. There is a part of any man that will do anything to stave off loneliness. It is not necessarily the most cowardly part of a man's soul, but I've seen any number of men do shameful things to indulge it. Worse, I wondered if the Fool were not deliberately sending me down to her. Once before, when loneliness had threatened to devour my heart, he had told her where to find me. It had been a misguided comfort I took in her arms. I vowed I would not do so again.

But I took the tiny rolled message from his hand and slipped it up my bedraggled sleeve with the artless practice of long years of deceit. The feathers from the treasure beach still rode there, securely strapped to my forearm. That secret, at least, still remained my own, and would until I had time to share it with him privately.

Aloud, he said, "I see you're restless despite our long day. Go along, Tom. The Prince and I can fend for ourselves for an evening, and you deserve a bit of song and a quiet beer on your own. Go on now, I saw you cast a longing eye that way. We won't mind."

I wondered whom he thought to deceive. The Prince would know that my heart had no interest in anything but grief just now. In the Piebald camp, he had seen Lord Golden give way to my command and leave with the wolf. Nevertheless, I loudly thanked my master for his permission, and left the room. Perhaps it was a play we all acted for each other. I went slowly down the stairs. Laurel was coming up as I descended. She gave me a curious look. I tried to think of some words, but nothing came to me. I passed her silently, intending no slight but unable to care if she took offense. I heard her pause on the stair behind me as if she would speak to me, but I continued down.

The common room was crowded. Some had probably come for the music, for Starling's reputation was grand now, but many others looked to be folk trapped by the downpour and unable to afford a room. They would shelter here for the night, and when the music stopped, doze the storm away at the tables and benches. I managed to get both food and a mug of beer on my assurances that my master would pay for it on the morrow. Then I walked to the hearth end of the room, and crowded myself into a corner table just behind Starling's elbow. I knew it was no coincidence she was here. She had been watching for us to return, and likely she had access to a bird to pass word of us on to Buckkeep. So I was not surprised when she feigned not to notice me, and kept playing and singing.

After three more songs, she declared she needed to rest her voice and wet her pipes. The servingboy who brought her wine set it on the corner of my table. When she sat down beside me to drink, I passed her Lord Golden's note under the table. Then I tossed off the last mouthful of beer in my mug and went out to the backhouse.

She was waiting for me under the dripping eaves when I returned to the inn. "The message has been sent," she greeted me.

"I'll tell my master." I started to walk past her, but she caught my sleeve. I halted.

"Tell me," she said quietly.

Ancient caution guarded my tongue. I did not know how much information Chade had given her. "We completed our errand."

"So I guessed," she replied tartly. Then she sighed. "And I know better than to ask you what Lord Golden's errand was. But tell me of you. You look terrible . . . your hair chopped short, your clothes in rags. What happened?"

Of all I had been through, only one event was mine to share or not as I pleased. I told her. "Nighteyes is dead."

Rainfall filled her silence. Then she sighed deeply and put her arms around me. "Oh, Fitz," she said quietly. She leaned her head against my scratched chest. I could see the pale part in her dark hair, and I smelled her scent and the wine she had drunk. Her hands moved softly on my back, soothingly. "Alone again. It isn't fair. Truly it isn't. You've the saddest song of any man I've ever known." The wind gusted and rain rode it to spatter against us, but still she held me, and a small warmth gathered between us. She said nothing more for a long time. I lifted my arms and put them around her. Just as it once had, it seemed inevitable. She spoke against my chest. "I've a room to myself. It's at the river end of the inn. Come to me. Let me take your hurt away."

"I . . . thank you." That won't mend it, I wanted to tell her. If she had ever known me at all, she would know that now. But words would not make her understand it if she could not sense it on her own. I suddenly appreciated the Fool's silence and distance. He had known. No other closeness could make up for the lack of my wolf.

The rain went on falling. She loosened her hold on me and looked up into my face. A frown divided her fine brows. "You aren't going to come to me tonight, are you?" She sounded incredulous.

Strange. I had been wavering in my resolve, but the very way she phrased the question helped me to answer it correctly. I shook my head slowly. "I appreciate the invitation. But it wouldn't help."

"Are you sure of that?" She tried to make her voice light and failed. She moved, her breasts brushing against me in a way that might have been accidental but was not. I stepped a little back from her, my arms falling to my sides.

"I'm sure. I don't love you, Starling. Not that way."

"It seems to me that you told me that once before, a

long time ago. But for years, it did help. It did work." Her
eyes searched my face. She smiled confidently.

It hadn't. It had only seemed to. I could have told her
that, but it would have been an unnecessary honesty. So I
only said, "Lord Golden expects me. I have to go up to him."

She shook her head slowly. "What a grievous end to a
sad tale. And I am the only one who knows the whole of it,
and still I am not allowed to sing it. What a tragic lay it
would make. You are the son of a king, who sacrificed all for
his father's family, only to finish as the ill-used servant of an
arrogant foreign noble. He doesn't even dress you well. The
ignominy must cut you like a blade." She looked deep into
my eyes, seeking . . . what? Resentment? Outrage?

"It doesn't really bother me," I replied in some confusion. Then, as if someone had drawn a curtain open and
spilled out light, I understood. She did not know that Lord
Golden was the Fool. She truly saw me as but his servant,
passing a message to her on his behalf. For all of her minstrel cleverness, she looked at him and saw the wealthy
Jamaillian lord. I fought the smile away from my face. "I am
content with my position with him and grateful to Chade
for arranging it. I am satisfied to be Tom Badgerlock."

For a moment she looked incredulous. The look faded
into disappointment in me. Then she gave a small shake of
her head. "I should have known you would be. It's what you
always wanted, isn't it? Your own little life. To have no
responsibility for your line or for what happens at court. To
be one of the humble folk, counting for nothing in the
long run."

All my earlier efforts to spare her feelings seemed vapid
now. "I have to go," I repeated.

"Hurry along to your master." She released me. Her
voice was a trained talent, and her scorn danced in it with a
scorpion's sting.

By a vast effort of will, I said nothing in reply. I turned
and walked away from her back into the inn. I climbed the
servants' stairs to our quarters, tapped, and let myself in.

Dutiful lifted his head from the pillow to regard me. His dark hair was sleeked back, his skin flushed from his bath. The effect made him look young. The Fool's bed was empty.

"My Prince," I greeted him. Then, "Lord Golden?" I queried the screened bath.

"He left." Dutiful let his head drop back to the pillow. "Laurel tapped on the door and wished to speak with him privately."

"Ah." It almost made me smile. Wouldn't that have intrigued Starling?

"He asked me to be sure you knew we had left you the bathwater. And leave your clothes outside the door. He's arranged for a servant to wash them and return them by morning."

"Thank you, my Prince. It is most kind of you to tell me."

"Please lock the door, he said. He said he would knock and awaken you when he returned."

"As you wish, my Prince." I stepped to the door and locked it. I doubted he would be back before dawn. "Is there anything else you require before I bathe, my Prince?"

"No. And don't talk to me like that." He turned his back on me, shouldering into the bed.

I undressed. As I peeled off my shirt, I made sure the feathers went with it. I sat down for a moment on my low pallet before removing my boots. The feathers from the beach slipped from the shirt's sleeve and under the thin blanket. I removed Jinna's charm and set it on the pillow. I arose, set my clothes outside the door, locked it again, and walked to the screened tub. As I climbed into the water, Dutiful's voice followed me. "Aren't you going to ask me why?"

The water in the tub had cooled to lukewarm, but it was still far hotter than the rain outside had been. I peeled the healer's bandaging from my neck. The scratches on my belly and chest stung as I lowered myself into the water. Then they eased. I sank farther down to soak my neck, as well.

"I said, aren't you going to ask me why?"

"I suppose it's because you don't want me to call you 'my Prince,' Prince Dutiful." The salve on my injuries was melting in the water, perfuming the air with its aromatic scent. Goldenseal. Myrrh. I closed my eyes and ducked under the water. When I came up, I helped myself to the little bowl of soap that had been left for the Prince. I worked it through what was left of my hair and watched the brown suds drip into the water. I ducked again to rinse it.

"You shouldn't have to thank me and wait on me and defer to me. I know who you are. Your blood's as good as mine."

I was grateful for the screen. I splashed a bit while I tried to think, hoping he would believe I hadn't heard him.

"Chade used to tell me stories. When he first started teaching me things. Stories about another boy he had taught, how stubborn he was, and also how clever. 'When my first boy was your age,' he'd say, and then tell a story about how you'd played tricks on the washer folk, or hidden the seamstress's shears to perplex her. You had a pet weasel, didn't you?"

Slink had been Chade's weasel. I'd stolen Mistress Hasty's shears on his orders, as part of my assassin's training in theft and stealth. Surely Chade hadn't told him that, as well. My mouth was dry. I splashed loudly and waited.

"You're his son, aren't you? Chade's son and hence my—would it be a second cousin? On the wrong side of the sheets, but a cousin all the same. And I think I know who your mother was, too. She is a lady still spoken of, though none seems to know a great deal about her. Lady Thyme."

I laughed aloud, then changed it into a cough. Chade's son by Lady Thyme. Now there was an apt pedigree for me. Lady Thyme, that noxious old harpy, had been an invention of Chade's, a clever disguise for when he wished to travel unknown. I cleared my throat and nearly recovered my aplomb. "No, my Prince. I fear you are in vast error there."

He was silent as I finished washing myself. I emerged from the tub, dried myself, and stepped out from behind the screen. There was a nightshirt on the pallet. As usual, the Fool had thought of everything. As I pulled it over my wet and bristly head, the Prince observed, "You've got a lot of scars. How'd you get them?"

"Asking questions of bad-tempered folk. My Prince."

"You even sound like Chade."

An unkinder, more untrue thing had never been said of me, I was sure. I countered it with, "And when did you become so talkative?"

"Since there was no one around to spy on us. You do know Lord Golden and Laurel are spies, don't you? One for Chade and the other for my mother?"

He thought he was so clever. He'd have to learn more caution if he expected to survive at court. I turned and gave him a direct stare. "What makes you believe that I'm not a spy, as well?"

He gave a skeptical laugh. "You're too rude. You don't care if I like you; you don't try to win my confidence or my favor. You're disrespectful. You never flatter me." He laced the fingers of his hands and put them behind his head. He gave me an odd half-smile. "And you don't seem concerned that I'll have you hanged for manhandling me back on that island. Only a relative could treat someone so badly and not expect ill consequences from it." He cocked his head at me, and I saw what I most feared in his eyes. Behind his speculation was stark need. His eyes bled unbearable loneliness. Years ago, when Burrich had forcibly parted me from the first animal I had ever bonded to, I had attached myself to him. I had feared the Stablemaster and hated him, but I had needed him even more. I had needed to be connected to someone who would be constant and available to me. I've heard it said that all youngsters have such requirements. I think that mine went deeper than a child's simple need for stability. Having known the complete connection of the Wit, I could no longer abide the isolation of my own mind. I counseled myself that Dutiful's turning to me probably had more to do with Jinna's charm than with any sincere regard for me. Then I realized it still lay on my pillow.

"I report to Chade." I said the words quickly, without embellishment. I would not traffic in deceit and betrayal. I would not let him attach himself to me, believing me to be someone I was not.

"Of course you do. He sent for you. For me. You have to be the one he said he'd try to get for me. The one who could teach me the Skill better than he can."

Truly, Chade's tongue had grown loose in his old age.

He sat up in his bed and began to tick his reasoning off on his fingers. I looked at him critically as he spoke. Deprivation and grief still shadowed his eyes and hollowed his cheeks, but sometime in the last day or so, he had realized he would live. He held up his first finger. "You've a Farseer cast to your features. Your eyes, the set of your jaw . . . not your nose, I don't know where you got that from, but that's not family." He held up a second finger. "The Skill is a Farseer magic. I've felt you use it at least twice now." A third finger. "You call Chade 'Chade,' not 'Lord Chade' or 'Councillor Chade.' And once I heard you speak of my lady mother as Kettricken. Not even Queen Kettricken, but Kettricken. As if you'd been children together."

Perhaps we had. As for my nose, well, that had come from a Farseer, too. It was Regal's permanent memento to me of the days I'd spent in his dungeon.

I walked to the branch of candles on the table, and blew them all out save one. I felt Dutiful's eyes follow me as I walked back to my pallet and sat down on it. It was low and hard, placed near the door where I could guard my good masters. I lay down on it.

"Well?" he demanded.

"I'm going to sleep now." I made it the end of the conversation.

He snorted contemptuously. "A real servant would

have begged my leave to extinguish the candles. And to go to sleep. Good night, Tom Badgerlock Farseer."

"Sleep well, most gracious Prince."

Another snort from him. Then silence, save for the rain thundering on the roof and splatting on the innyard mud. Silence, save for the soft crackling of the fire, and the distant music from the common room below. Silence but for unsteady footsteps making their way past our door. But most of all, the crashing silence in my heart where for so long Nighteyes' awareness had been a steady beacon in my darkness, a warmth in my winter, a guide star in my night. My dreams were thin, illogical human things now that frayed at a moment's waking. Tears flooded warm under my closed eyelids. I opened my mouth to breathe silently through my constricted throat and lay on my back.

I heard the Prince shift in his bedding, and shift again. Very quietly, he rose from his bed and went to the window. For a time he gazed out at the rain falling in the muddy innyard. "Does it go away?" He asked the question in a very soft voice, but I knew it was for me.

I took a breath, forced steadiness into my voice. "No."

"Not ever?"

"There may be another for you someday. But you never forget the first."

He did not move from the windowsill. "How many bond-animals have you had?"

I nearly didn't answer that. Then, "Three," I said.

He turned away from the night and looked at me through the darkness. "Will there be another one for you?"

"I doubt it."

He left the window and returned to his bed. I heard him pull up his blankets and settle into them. I thought he would go to sleep, but he spoke again. "Will you teach me the Wit also?"

Someone had better teach you something, if it's only not to trust so quickly. "I haven't said I'd teach you anything."

He was silent for a time. He sounded almost sulky when he said, "Well, it were better if someone taught me something."

A long silence followed and I hoped he had gone to sleep. The uncanny way his words echoed my thought unnerved me. Rain beat against the thick whorl of glass in the window, and dark flowed into the room. I closed my eyes and centered myself. As gingerly as if I handled broken glass, I reached toward him.

He was there, still and taut as a crouching cat. I sensed him waiting and watching for me, yet unaware I stood at the borders of his mind. His rough Skill-sense was an awkward, unhoned tool. I drew back a bit and studied him from all angles, as if he were a colt I was thinking of breaking. His wariness was a mix of apprehension and aggression. It was a weapon as much as a shield that he inexpertly wielded. Nor was it pure Skill. It is a hard thing to describe, but his Skill was like a white beacon edged with green darkness. His Wit-awareness of me was what he used to focus. The Wit does not reach from a man's mind to another man's mind, but the Wit can make me aware of the animal that the man's mind inhabits. So it was with Dutiful. Bereft of the cat as a focus, his Wit was a wide-flung web, seeking a kinship. As was mine, I suddenly realized.

I recoiled from that and found myself back in my own flesh. I set my walls against the untrained fumbling of his Skill. Yet even as I did so, there were two things I could not deny. The thread of Skill that connected me to Dutiful grew stronger each time I ventured along it. And I had no idea of how to sever it, let alone remove my Skill-command from his mind.

The third piece of knowledge was as bitter as the other parts were disturbing. I quested. I had no desire to form a bond with another animal. But without Nighteyes to contain it, my Wit sprawled out like seeking roots. Like water that overbrims a vessel and must seek a place to flow, the

Wit went forth from me, silent yet reaching. Earlier I had seen need in the Prince's eyes, a desperate longing for connection and belonging. Did I radiate that same privation? I closed my heart and willed myself to stillness. Time would heal my grief. I repeated that lie until sleep claimed me.

I awoke when the light spilling in the window touched my face. I opened my eyes but lay still. The pale light filling the room after the dark of the storm was like being immersed in clear water. I felt curiously empty, as one does when one has been ill for a long time and then begins to mend. I caught at the edges of a fleeing dream, but clutched only the edges of a shining morning, the sea below me and wind in my face. Sleep had left me, but I had no inclination to rise and face the day. I felt as if I were inside a bubble of safety, and that if I remained motionless, I could cling to this moment in peace. I lay on my side, my hand and arm under the flat pillow. After a time, I became aware of the feathers under my hand.

I lifted my head, intending to look at them, but the room swung suddenly about me as if I'd had too much to drink. The realities of the day to come—the long ride to Buckkeep, the meetings with Chade and Kettricken that would follow, the resumption of my life as Tom Badgerlock—crashed down on me. I sat up slowly.

The Prince slept on in his bed. I turned and found the Fool regarding me sleepily. He lay on his side in bed, his chin propped on his fist. He looked weary, but insufferably pleased about something. The effect made him look years younger.

"I didn't expect to see you in your bed this morning," I greeted him, and then, "How did you get in? I latched that door last night."

"Did you? Interesting. But you can scarcely be more surprised to see me in my own bed than I am to see you in yours."

I let that barb go past me. I scratched the bristle on my

cheek. "I should shave," I said to myself, dreading the idea. I hadn't touched a blade to my face since we'd left Galekeep.

"Indeed you should. I'd like us to look as presentable as possible when we return to Buckkeep."

I thought of my cat-shredded shirt, but nodded acquiescence. Then I recalled the feathers. "I've something I want to show you," I began, reaching under the pillow, but just then the Prince drew a deeper breath and opened his eyes.

"Good morning, my Prince," Lord Golden greeted him.

" 'Morning," he acknowledged wearily. "Lord Golden, Tom Badgerlock." He looked and sounded marginally better than he had at the end of yesterday's ride. His formality toward me was back in place. I felt relief.

"Good morning, my Prince," I greeted him.

And so the day began. We ate in our room. Our cleaned and mended clothing arrived shortly after our breakfasts. Lord Golden looked almost restored to his former glory, and the Prince looked tidy if not exactly royal. As I had suspected, washing had done little to make my clothing more presentable. I begged a needle and thread from the servant who brought our food, saying I wished to tighten the sleeve in my mended shirt. The reality was that I required a pocket in it. Lord Golden looked at me and sighed. "Keeping you decently clothed may become the most expensive part of keeping you as a servant, Tom Badgerlock. Well, see what you can do with the rest of yourself."

I was the only one with any need to shave. Lord Golden commanded hot water and a razor and glass for me. He sat by the window, gazing out over the little landing town as I worked. I had scarcely begun my task when I became aware of the Prince's scrutiny. For a time, I ignored his intense fascination. The second time I nicked myself, I suppressed a curse, but did demand, "What? Have you never seen a man shave himself before?"

He colored slightly. "No." He looked away as he added,

"I have spent little time in the company of men. Oh, I've dined with our nobles, and hawked with them, and taken my sword lessons with the other lads of good houses. But . . ." He seemed at a loss suddenly.

Just as abruptly, Lord Golden arose from his window seat. "I've a mind to see a bit of this town before we depart it. I think I shall take a stroll about it. With my Prince's permission."

"Of course, Lord Golden. As you will."

When he left, I expected the Prince to go with him. Instead, he lingered with me. He watched me finish shaving, and when I rinsed the last of the soap from my smarting face, he asked with intense curiosity, "It hurts, then?"

"Stings some. Only if you hurry, as I always seem to do, and cut myself in the process." My mourning-shortened hair stuck up in thickets. Starling would have cut it for me, I thought, and then damned the thought and plastered it down to my head with water.

"It won't stay. Once it dries, it will just stick up again," the Prince pointed out helpfully.

"I know that. My Prince."

"Do you hate me?"

He asked it so casually, it set me completely off balance. I set aside the towel and met his earnest gaze. "No. I do not hate you."

"Because I would understand if you did. Because of your wolf and all."

"Nighteyes."

"Nighteyes." He said the name carefully. Then he looked aside from me suddenly. "I never knew my cat's name." I knew tears threatened to choke him. I sat carefully still and silent, waiting for him. After a moment, he drew a deep breath. "I don't hate you, either."

"That's good to know," I admitted. Then I added, "The cat told me to kill her." Despite my effort, the words sounded defensive.

"I know. I heard her." He sniffed a little, then tried to disguise it as a cough. "And she would have forced you to kill her. She was completely determined."

"I think I knew that," I replied ruefully, and touched the renewed bandages at my throat. The Prince actually smiled, and I found myself returning the smile.

He asked the next question quickly, as if it were important to ask, so important that he feared the answer. "Will you be staying?"

"Staying?"

"Will I see you around Buckkeep Castle?" He sat down suddenly at the table across from me and met my eyes directly with Verity's blunt stare. "Tom Badgerlock. Will you teach me?"

Chade, my old master, had asked me and I'd been able to say no. The Fool, my oldest friend, had asked me to return to Buckkeep, and I'd refused him. If the Queen herself had asked me, I could have said no. The best I could manage with this Farseer heir was, "I don't know that much to teach. What your father taught me, he taught me in secret, and he seldom had time for lessons."

He regarded me soberly. "Is there anyone who knows more of the Skill than you do?"

"No, my Prince." I did not add that I'd killed them all. I could not have said why I suddenly added his title. Only that something in his manner demanded it.

"Then you are Skillmaster now. By default."

"No." That I could answer, my tongue moving as swiftly as my thoughts. I took a breath. "I'll teach you," I said. "But it will be as your father taught me. When I can and what I can. And in secret."

Without a word, he reached his hand across the table to me, to seal the agreement with a touching of hands. Two things happened as our hands met. "The Wit and the Skill," he stipulated. As the skin of my palm touched his, the leap of Skill-spark between us sang.

Please.

His plea was sloppily done, pushed by the Wit, not the Skill. "We'll see," I said aloud. I was already regretting it. "You may change your mind. I'm neither a good teacher, nor a patient one."

"But you treat me like a man, not 'the Prince.' As if your expectations of a man were higher than those for a prince."

I didn't reply. I looked at him, waiting. He spoke hesitantly, as if the answer shamed him. "To my mother, I am a son. But I am also, always, the Prince and Sacrifice for my people. And to all others, always, I am the Prince. Always. I am no one's brother. I am no man's son. I am not anyone's best friend." He laughed, a small strangled laugh. "People treat me very well as 'my Prince.' But there is always a wall there. No one speaks to me as, well, as me." He shrugged one shoulder and his mouth twisted to one side wryly. "No one except you has ever told me I was stupid, even when I was most definitely being stupid."

I understood suddenly why he had so swiftly succumbed to the Piebalds' plot. To be loved, in a familiar, unfearing way. To be someone's best friend, even if that someone was only a cat. I could recall a time when I thought Chade was the only one in the world who would give me that. I recalled how terrifying the threat of losing that had been. I knew that any boy, prince or beggar, needed that from a man. But I wasn't sure I was a wise choice for that. Chade, why couldn't he have chosen Chade? I was still formulating an answer to that when there was a knock at the door.

I opened it to discover Laurel. Reflexively, I looked past her for Lord Golden. He wasn't there. She glanced over her own shoulder with a small frown, and then back to my face. "May I come in?" she asked pointedly.

"Of course, my lady. I just thought—"

She entered and I closed the door behind her. She considered Prince Dutiful for a moment, and something almost like relief dawned on her face as she made a courtesy to him. She smiled as she greeted him with, "Good morning, my Prince."

"Good morning, Huntswoman." His reply was solemn, but he did reply. I glanced at the boy, and realized what she saw. The Prince had come back to himself. His face was somber, his eyes shadowed, but he was with us. He no longer stared within himself to a distance no one else could see.

"It is good to see you so well recovered, my Prince. I came to inquire as to when you wished to depart for Buck-keep. The sun is climbing and the day looks fair, if cold."

"I am pleased to leave that decision to Lord Golden."

"An excellent decision, my Prince." She glanced about the room and then asked, "Lord Golden is not here?"

"He said he was going out," I replied.

My words startled her. It was almost as if a chair had spoken, and then I realized fully my error. In the presence of the Prince, a mere servant like myself would not presume to speak out. I glanced down at my feet so no one would see the chagrin in my eyes. Yet again, I resolved to focus more closely on the role I must play. Had I forgotten all of Chade's earlier training?

She glanced at Dutiful, but when he added nothing to my words, she said slowly, "I see."

"You are, of course, welcome to wait here for his return, Huntswoman." His words said one thing, his tone another. I had not heard it done so well since Shrewd was King.

"Thank you, my Prince. But if I may, I think I will seek my own room until I am sent for."

"As you wish, Huntswoman." He had turned to look out the window.

"Thank you, my Prince." She dipped a courtesy to his back. Our eyes met for a fleeting moment as she went to the door, but I read nothing there. When the door had closed behind her, the Prince turned back to me.

"There. Do you see what I mean, Tom Badgerlock?"

"She was not unkind to you, my Prince."

He motioned me to the table. As I took a chair opposite him, he said, "She was not anything to me. She treats me as they all do. 'As it please you, my Prince.' But in all the Six Duchies, I haven't a true friend."

I took a breath, then asked, "What of your companions? Your friends who ride and hunt with you?"

"I have far too many of them. I must call each one a friend, and to none of them may I show favor, lest the father of another one feel slighted. And Eda forbid that I should smile at a young woman. At my slightest attempt to form a friendship, she is whisked away, lest my attention be interpreted as courtship. No. I am alone, Tom Badgerlock. Forever alone." He sighed heavily and looked down at his hands on the table's edge. It was a bit too dramatic to befit the young man.

I spoke before I thought. "Oh, poor deprived lad." He lifted his head and glowered at me. I returned his look levelly. Then a slow smile came to his face. "Spoken like a true friend," he said.

A moment later Lord Golden came through the door. In a flicker of his long fingers, he showed me a bird's message-tube. In the next instant, it had vanished up his sleeve. Of course. He'd gone to see Starling, to see if we'd received word back from Buckkeep. And we had. No doubt Chade would have all in readiness for our return. In the next moment, his eyes took in the Prince seated at the other end of the table. If he thought it odd to find the Farseer heir sitting at table with me, watching me mend the sleeve of my shirt, he did not show it.

Not even a flick of his eyes betrayed that he had greeted me first. Instead, all his attention seemed fixed on the Prince as he addressed him. "Good day, my Prince. If it please you, we can ride as soon as we may."

The Prince drew a long breath. "It would please me, Lord Golden."

Now Lord Golden turned to me, and gave me a smile such as I had not seen on his face for days. "You have heard our Prince, Tom Badgerlock. Stir yourself to readiness and pack our things. And you can leave off mending that, my good man, at least for now. Never can it be said that I am a niggardly master, even to such a wretched servant as yourself. Put this on, lest you shame us all riding back into Buckkeep." He tossed me a bundled packet. It proved to be a shirt of homespun, far sturdier than the tattered garment in my hands. So much for a pocket up my sleeve today.

"My thanks to you, Lord Golden," I replied with humble gratitude. "I shall strive to take better care of this one than I did of the last three."

"See that you do. Put it on, and then hasten to Mistress Laurel, to let her know we'll be riding soon. And on your way down to the stables to ask that the horses be readied, stop at the kitchen and request that they pack us a luncheon, as well. A couple of cold birds and a meat pie, two bottles of wine, and some of the fresh bread I smelled baking as I entered."

"As it please you, master," I replied.

As I was pulling the new shirt on over my head, I heard the Prince ask sourly, "My Lord Golden, is it you who think I am an idiot, that you put on this show for me? Or is it the wish of Tom Badgerlock?"

I popped my head out hastily, not wishing to miss the look on Lord Golden's face. But it was the Fool who greeted me. His grin was nothing short of dazzling, as he swept a wide minstrel's bow to Dutiful, his nonexistent hat brushing his knees. As he straightened, he gave me a look of triumph. It baffled me, but I found myself answering his grin with one of my own as he replied, "Good Prince, it is neither my wish nor that of Tom Badgerlock, but of Lord Chade. He desires that we practice as much as we may, for poor actors such as ourselves need many rehearsals if we are to fool even an eye or two."

"Lord Chade. I should have known you both belonged to him." It pleased me that he did not betray I had already told him that. He was learning some discretion at least. He gave the Fool a piercing look, one with much mistrust in it.

The look shifted sideways to include me. "But who are you?" he asked in a low voice. "Who are you, the two of you?"

Without thinking, the Fool and I exchanged a look. That we conferred before we answered incensed the Prince. I could tell by the slow spots of color that rose in his cheeks. Beyond the anger, hidden in the back of his eyes, was the boy's fear that he had made a fool of himself to me. Had his trust been won by a contrived performance? Did the affection between the Fool and me preclude any friendship I would share with him? I saw his candor begin to close; I could see him retreating behind his regal wall. I reached hastily across the table, and violated every noble protocol that existed by seizing his hand. I let honesty flow through that touch, convincing him with Skill just as Verity had once won his mother's trust.

"He is a friend, my Prince. The best friend I have ever had, and like to be yours, as well." My gaze did not leave the Prince's face as I reached my free hand toward the Fool. I heard him step up beside Dutiful. An instant later, I felt him set his ungloved fingers in mine. I brought his hand to join our clasp, his long fingers closing around both our hands.

"If you will have me," the Fool offered humbly, "I will serve you as I served your father, and your grandfather before him."

chapter XXVIII

HOMECOMING

As far back as our traditions go, there has been both trade and war between the Six Duchies and the Out Islands. Like the regular ebb and flow of the tides, we have traded and intermarried, and then warred and killed our own kin. What set the Red Ship War apart in that long and bloody tradition is that for the first time, the Outislanders were united under a single war leader. Kebal Rawbread was his name. Accounts of him differ, but by most tellings, he began as a pirate and raider. As both sailor and fighter, he excelled, and the men who followed him prospered. Word of their successes and the richness of the plunder they claimed brought men of like minds to follow him. He soon commanded a fleet of raiding vessels.

Even so, he might have remained no more than a prosperous pirate, raiding wherever the wind took him. Instead, he began to take steps to force all of the Out Islands under his reign. The form of coercion he used was remarkably similar to the Forging that he later employed against the people of the Six Duchies. At about that time, he decreed that all the hulls of his raiding vessels must be painted red, and that the force of his raids would be expended only on the Six Duchies coastline. It is interesting to note that at the same time that these tactical changes were occurring in Kebal Rawbread's fleet, those in the Six Duchies first began to hear rumors of a Pale Woman at his side.

    FEDWREN'S "AN ACCOUNT OF THE RED SHIP WAR"

We reached Buckkeep Town as the afternoon faded. We could have made far better time, but the Fool deliberately delayed us. We had stopped overlong on a stretch of sandy riverbank for our late-afternoon luncheon. I believe he thought to buy the Prince one more day of quiet before he plunged into the whirl of court again. None of us had mentioned the chaos and gaiety of the betrothal ceremony that the new moon would bring. It had pleased the Prince to join in our charade, so that for the ride home he kept his mount beside Malta, as disdainful of Lord Golden's coarse servant as any well-born young man might be. He allowed Lord Golden's aristocratic talk of hunts and balls and exotic travel to amuse him while never compromising his princely demeanor. Laurel rode at Lord Golden's other stirrup, but was mostly silent. I think the Prince enjoyed his new role. I could sense his relief that we included him now. He was not a wayward boy being dragged home by his elders, but a young man returning from a misadventure, with friends. His desperate loneliness had eased. Nonetheless, I also felt his rising anxiety as we drew nearer and nearer to Buckkeep. It pulsed through the Skill-connection we shared. I wondered again if he was as aware of it as I was.

I think poor Laurel was baffled by the change in the young man. He seemed to have recovered his spirits entirely, and set behind him his misfortune among the Piebalds. I do not know if she heard the brittleness at the edges of his laughter, or marked how well Lord Golden carried the conversation during the times when the Prince could not seem to keep his mind on it. I did. I was relieved that the boy had latched on to Lord Golden so firmly. So I rode alone until, in the early afternoon, the Huntswoman dropped back to ride beside me, leaving the Prince and Lord Golden to their newfound companionship.

"He seems a different young man entirely," she observed quietly.

"He does," I agreed. I tried to keep any cynicism from my voice. With both Dutiful and Lord Golden occupied, she deigned to speak to me again. I knew I should not fault her for choosing wisely where to let her attention and fondness come to rest. For Lord Golden to honor her with his attention was no small coup for her. I wondered if she would try to continue their connection when we returned to Buckkeep Castle. She would be the envy of the ladies if she did. I even wondered how deep his affection for her went. Was my friend honestly losing his heart to her? I considered her silent profile as she rode alongside me. He could do far worse. She was healthy and young and a good hunter. I abruptly heard the echo of the wolf's values in my thoughts. I caught my breath for a moment, and then let the pain pass.

She was more astute than I had realized. "I'm sorry." She spoke softly, and her words barely reached me. "You know I do not have the Old Blood myself. Somehow it passed me, to settle on my brothers and sister instead. Nonetheless, I can guess what you suffer. I saw what my mother went through when her gander died. That bird was forty years old, and had outlived my father. . . . Truth to tell, it is why I think Old Blood as much a curse as a blessing. And I confess, when I consider the risk and the pain, I do not know why you practice this magic. How can anyone let an animal seize his heart so completely, when their lives are so short? What can you gain that is worth all the pain each time your partner dies?"

I had no answer to that. In truth, it was a rock-hard sympathy she gave me.

"I'm sorry," she said again when some little time had passed. "You must think me heartless. I know my cousin Deerkin does. But all I can say to him is what I've said to you. I do not understand. And I cannot approve. I will always think Old Blood a magic better left alone."

"If I had a choice, perhaps I would feel the same," I replied. "But I am as I was born."

"As is the Prince," she said after a long moment's consideration. "Eda save us all, and keep his secret safe."

"Amen to that," I said heavily. "And mine, as well." I gave her a sideways glance.

"I do not think Lord Golden would betray you. He values you far too highly as a servant," she replied. It was a reassurance that she never even considered I might be thinking of her tongue wagging. A moment later, she set my thoughts on a different trail when she delicately added, "And may my bloodlines not become common talk."

I replied as she had. "I am certain that as Lord Golden values you, both as a friend and as the Queen's devoted Huntswoman, he would never breathe a word that might discredit or endanger you."

She gave me a sidelong glance, then asked shyly, "As his friend? Do you think so?"

Something in her eyes and at the corners of her mouth warned me not to answer that question lightly. "So it would appear to me," I said, somewhat stiffly.

Her shoulders lifted as if I had offered her a gift. "And you have known him well and long," she embroidered my words. I refused to confirm that speculation. She looked away from me for a time, and after that we did not speak much, but she hummed as she rode. She seemed light of heart. Ahead of me, I marked that the Prince's voice had faltered to a halt. Lord Golden chatted on, but the Prince rode looking ahead, and silent.

Buckkeep Castle was a dark silhouette on the black stone cliffs against a bank of dark clouds when we reached Buckkeep Town. The Prince had pulled his hood well up over his face and dropped back to ride beside me. Laurel rode by Lord Golden now, and seemed well pleased with the change. Dutiful and I spoke little, each busy with our own thoughts. Our journey back to Buckkeep would take us up the steep path to the lesser-used West Gate. As we had left, so would we enter. We passed once more the scattering of cottages at the bottom of the climb. When I saw the first drape of greenery on a door lintel, I thought it was but an overeager celebrant. But then I saw another, and as we rode on, we eventually came to a group of workmen setting up a celebratory arch. Nearby, townsfolk busily plaited ivy with heffelwhite vines, ready to drape the arch. "A bit early, aren't you?" Lord Golden called to them congenially as we passed.

A guardsman spat and laughed aloud. "Early, milord? We're damn near too late! All thought the storms would delay the betrothal ship, but the Outislanders seemed to have used them to fly here with the wind's own wings. The treaty galleys arrived at noon with the Princess's honor guard. We've heard she'll make landfall before the sun sets, and all must be ready."

"Really?" Lord Golden enthused. "Well, I dare not be late for the festivities." He turned his smile on Laurel. "My lady, I fear we must ride as swift as we can. You lads may follow at your own pace." And with that he set his heels to Malta, and she plunged nimbly forward. Laurel matched him. The Prince and I accompanied, but at a more sedate gait. As we trailed them up the winding road to Buckkeep Castle, Lord Golden and Laurel continued up the main road and entered at the gate. But in a thicker patch of woods, I turned Myblack's head from the path and motioned for the Prince to follow. There was little more than a game trail, but I pushed Myblack through the tangles of brush, along a path I scarcely remembered, and Dutiful fell behind. We shadowed the keep wall until we came to the place the wolf had shown me so long ago. Thick thistles still covered that old breach in the wall, but I had my suspicions. In the shadow of the keep wall, we dismounted.

"What is this place?" he demanded. He pushed his hood back and looked about curiously.

"A place to wait. I will not chance taking you in either of the gates. Chade will send someone to meet us here, and I am certain he will devise a way for you to reenter the keep so it may seem that you have never left. You have seen fit to spend these days in meditation, and now you will emerge to meet your betrothed. None need be the wiser."

"I see," he replied bleakly. Overhead the clouds were

growing thicker, and the wind began to pick up. "What do we do now?" the Prince asked softly.

"We wait."

"Waiting." He sighed. "If a man can become perfect at something by practicing it, I should be perfect at waiting by now."

He sounded both tired and older than his years.

"At least you're home now," I said comfortingly.

"Yes." He did not sound glad. After a moment, he asked, "It seems a year since I was last at Buckkeep, and it is not even a full month. I remember lying on my bed and counting the days I still had before the new moon, before I had to face this. Then—for a time I thought I might never have to face it. It seemed strange, all day today, to know I was riding back to my old life, that I would pick up all the threads, all the details, and go on as if I had never left. It was overwhelming. All day, riding back here, I promised myself a quiet day or two. I wanted some time alone, to decide how much I had changed. Now . . . this very night the delegation arrives from the Out Islands to formalize my betrothal. This night my mother and the Outislander nobles set the course of the rest of my life."

I tried to smile, but I felt I was delivering him to his execution. I had come near as a knife's edge to a similar fate once. I found something to say. "You must be very excited to meet your bride."

He gave me a look. "*Apprehensive* is perhaps a better word. There is something rather dreadful about meeting the girl you will marry when you know that your own preferences have absolutely no bearing on the situation." He gave a small, sour laugh. "Not that I did so well when I thought I was choosing someone for myself." He sighed. "She's eleven. Eleven summers old." He looked away from me. "What shall I discuss with her? Dolls? Embroidery lessons?" He crossed his arms on his chest and leaned against the cold stone wall. "I do not think they even teach women to read in the Out Islands. Nor men, for that matter."

"Oh." I struggled desperately but could think of no other words. To say that fourteen was not that much older than eleven seemed a cruelty. We waited in silence.

With no warning at all, the threatened rain suddenly sluiced down on us. It began abruptly, one of those downpours that soak a man and fills his ears with the sound of falling water. I was almost grateful that it made conversation impossible. We huddled miserably, the water streaming down the horses who stood with their heads hanging.

We were both completely drenched and cold when Chade appeared to escort the Prince back into the castle. He spoke little, a hasty greeting in the cascading downpour and a promise to see me soon, and then they were gone. I grinned sourly to myself as they left me there in the wet. It was as I had expected. The old fox had not closed off this secret back door, but he was not going to show the entrance to me. I drew a deep breath. Well. My errand was done. I'd brought the Prince safely back to Buckkeep Castle in time for his betrothal. I tried on emotions. Triumph. Joy. Elation. No. Wet, tired, and hungry. Cold to my bones. Alone.

Empty.

I mounted Myblack and rode through the downpour, leading the Prince's horse. The light was fading and the horses' hooves slipped on the layers of wet leaves. I was forced to go slowly. The bushes we pushed through were laden with rain. I had not thought it was possible to get wetter, but I did. Then, as I reached the main road up to the keep, I found the way choked with men and horses and litters. I somehow doubted they were going to make way for me, or allow me to join the betrothal procession. So I sat Myblack in the rain and held the reins of the miserable dun, and watched them go by.

First came the torchbearers, holding their blazing brands aloft to show the way. They were followed by the Queen's Guards, in purple and white with the fox badge, riding white horses, very showy and dripping wet. They passed, leading the way, and then came an interesting mix of the Prince's Guard and the Outislander warriors. The Prince's Guard wore Buckkeep blue with the Farseer stag badge, and they were afoot, I suppose out of courtesy to the Outislanders. The guardians who had accompanied their narcheska were sailors and fighters, not horsemen. Their furs and leathers dripped, and I suspected the Great Hall would be rich with the stench of wet fur tonight as the warmth dried them. They strode along, rank after rank, with the rolling gait of men who had been long at sea and still expected a deck to rise to greet them at every step. They wore their weapons as their wealth, and their wealth as their weapons. Jewels glittered on sword belts, and I glimpsed axe-hafts banded with gold. I prayed no fighting would break out among the mingled guard companies tonight. There strode together veterans from both sides of the Red Ship War.

The Outislander nobles came next, riding borrowed horses, and looking singularly uncomfortable on them. I saw an assortment of Six Duchies nobles riding welcome among them. I recognized them more by their badges than by their faces. The Duke of Tilth was younger by far than I had expected him to be. There were two young women wearing Bearns insignia, and though I recognized the stamp of their bloodlines in their faces, I had never seen them before. And still the folk, both grand and martial, paraded past and I stood in the rain and watched them go by.

Then came the litter of Prince Dutiful's betrothed. It floated like a tethered cloud, immense and white, borne on the shoulders of the King's Best. The young noblemen who walked beside it bearing torches were wet and spattered with mud to the knee. The flowers and garlands that draped it looked battered by the wind and rain of the storm. It would have seemed an ominous omen, this storm-tossed litter, but for the girl inside it. The curtains of the litter were not drawn against the wind's rough kiss, but thrown wide. The three Six Duchies ladies within looked drenched and much aware of how the rain dripped from their coiffed hair and soaked their dresses. But in their midst sat a little girl reveling in the storm. Her inky black hair was long and unbound. The rain had sleeked it to her head tight as a seal's fur, and her eyes too reminded me of a seal's, immense and dark and liquid. She stared at me as they passed me, her teeth white in an excited smile. She was, as the Prince had said, a child of eleven. She was a sturdy little thing, wide cheeked and square shouldered and obviously determined not to miss a moment of her journey to the castle on the hill. Perhaps to honor her intended, she was dressed in Buck blue with an odd blue ornament in her hair, but her high-collared overblouse was of fine white leather embroidered in gold with leaping narwhals. I stared back at her, thinking I had seen her before, or met someone of her house, but before I could snag the memory, the litter was borne past me and on up the hill. And still I must wait, as the rain spattered down around me, for behind her came more ranks of her own men, and ours, to honor her.

When finally all the nobility and their guards had passed, I nudged Myblack onto the well-churned road. We joined a stream of merchants and tradesfolk heading up to the keep. Some bore their wares on their shoulders, waxcoated wheels of cheese or kegs of fine liquor, and some brought theirs in carts. I became a part of the flow and entered the main gate of Buckkeep with them, unremarked.

There were stableboys to take the horses, struggling hard to keep up with the influx of animals. I gave them the Prince's dun but I told them I wanted to care for Myblack myself, and they were glad of it. It was, perhaps, a foolish chance to take. I suppose I could have encountered Hands and he might have somehow recognized me. But in the bustle of all the strangers and extra animals to stable, I did not think it likely. The stableboys directed me to take Myblack to the "old stable" for that was the one allotted to servants' mounts now. I found it was the stable of my childhood where Burrich had reigned and I had once been his right hand. The old familiar tasks of putting the horse to rights before I left her in her stall brought an odd measure of peace to my heart. The smell of animals and hay, the muted light of the spaced lanterns, and the sounds of beasts settling for the night all soothed me. I was cold and wet and tired, but here in the Buckkeep stables, I was as close to home as I had been in a long time. All had changed in the world, but here in the stables, all was very much the same.

As I trudged across the busy yard and went in at the servants' door, the thought followed me. All had changed yet was much the same in Buckkeep. There was still the heat and clatter and chatter from the kitchens as I passed. The flagged entry to the guardroom was still muddy, and it still smelled of wet wool and spilled ale and steaming meat as I walked past the door. From the Great Hall drifted the sounds of music and laughter and eating and talk. Ladies swished past me, their maids scowling at me as if I might dare to drip on their mistresses. Outside the entrance to the Great Hall, two young lordlings were chivying a third about a girl whom he dared not speak to. The sleeves of one boy's shirt were trimmed with black-tipped ermine's tails, and another wore a collar so filigreed with silver rings that he scarcely could turn his head. I recalled how Mistress Hasty had once tormented me about my clothing, and could only pity them. The homespun on my back was coarse, but at least I could move freely in it.

Once, I would have been expected to make an appearance at such an occasion, even if I was no more than a bastard. When Verity and Kettricken had sat at the high table, I had sometimes been seated almost near them. I had dined on elaborately cooked delicacies, made conversation with noble ladies, and listened to the Six Duchies' finest musicians in my time as FitzChivalry Farseer. But tonight I was Tom Badgerlock, and I would have been the greatest fool in the world to regret that I walked unknown amongst such gaiety.

Swept up in remembering, almost I climbed the stairs that would have led to my old chamber but I caught myself in time, and made my way up to Lord Golden's rooms instead. I tapped and then entered. He was not there, but there were all the indications he had been. He had obviously bathed and donned fresh attire, and his hurry was evident. A box of jewelry was still out on the table, plundered of something and the rest left scattered across the polished wood. Four shirts had been tried on, then flung across the bed. Several pairs of disdained shoes cluttered the floor. I sighed, and put the room to rights, wedging two shirts back into his wardrobe, packing two others into a chest, and shutting the door upon the clothing and heaped shoes. I fed the hearth fire, put fresh candles in the holders against his late return, and swept up the hearth. Then I glanced about. The pleasant room seemed suddenly terribly empty. I took a deep breath and yet again explored the space in my mind where the wolf was not. Someday, I told myself, it would feel natural for that place to be empty. But just now, I did not want to be alone with myself.

I took up a candle and went into my own dark chamber. All was exactly as I had left it. I shut the door firmly behind me, worked the catch, and began the weary climb up the narrow stairs to Chade's tower.

I had half expected to find him waiting there for me, anxious for my report. Of course he was not; he must be at the festivities below. But if Chade was not there, the rooms welcomed me all the same. A tub had been left out by the hearth and a large kettle of water was steaming on the hook. Food, obviously from the same dishes the nobles shared below, waited on the table, and a bottle of wine. One plate. One glass. I could have felt sorry for myself. But I did note that a second comfortable chair now rested beside his near the hearth. On that chair was a stack of towels, and a robe of blue wool. Chade had left out lint and bandaging, as well, and a pot of smelly salve. In the midst of all he undoubtedly had to tend to, he had thought of me. I reminded myself of that, even as I knew he would not have hauled the buckets of water up here on his own. So. He had a servant, or was it his apprentice? That was still a mystery I had not solved.

I poured the steaming water into the tub, and added cold from a bucket to adjust it. I heaped a plate with food and set it with the open bottle of wine next to the tub. I shed my sodden clothing where I stood, put Jinna's charm on the table, and hid my feathers inside one of Chade's dustiest scrolls. Then I peeled off the bandaging on my neck and climbed into the tub. I eased into the water and leaned back. I ate while soaking in hot water, and drank a glass of wine, and washed myself in a desultory fashion. Slowly the cold began to seep out of my bones. The sadness that remained and weighted me seemed a tired and familiar thing. I wondered if Starling played and sang in the Great Hall. I wondered if Lord Golden led Huntswoman Laurel to the dance floor. I wondered what Prince Dutiful thought of the child bride the sea storm had washed to his doorstep. I leaned back in the tub and I drank wine from the bottle's mouth, and I suppose I dozed off.

"Fitz?"

The old man's voice was worried. It startled me awake and I sat up in the tub, sloshing water. The neck of the wine bottle was still in my hand. He caught it before I overset it and placed it on the table with a thump. "Are you all right?" he demanded.

"I must have fallen asleep." I was disoriented. I stared at him, in his court finery, with the dying firelight glinting off the jewels at his ears and throat. He seemed a stranger to me suddenly, and I was embarrassed to be caught sleeping, naked and half-drunk in a tub of cooling water. "Let me get out of this," I muttered.

"Do," he encouraged me. He built up the fire while I clambered from the tub, dried myself, and pulled on the blue robe. My hands and feet were wrinkled from the long immersion. He filled a smaller kettle and set it on the hob, and then took a teapot and cups down from the shelf. I watched him mix tea herbs from a row of cork-stoppered pots.

"How late is it?" I asked him groggily.

"So late Burrich would say it was early morning," he replied. He put a small table between the hearth chairs and arranged his teapot and cups there. He sat down in his worn chair beside the table and indicated the other chair for me. I took it and I studied Chade. He had obviously been up all night, yet he seemed not weary but energized by it. His eyes were bright and his hands steady. He folded his hands on his lap before him and for a moment he was silent, looking down on them. "I'm sorry," he said quietly. He looked up and met my gaze. "I won't pretend to completely understand your loss. He was a fine creature, your wolf. But for him, Queen Kettricken would never have escaped Buckkeep Castle all those years ago. And she has often spoken to me of how he provided meat for all of you on your journey through the Mountain Kingdom." He lifted his eyes to mine. "Have you ever thought that, if not for the wolf, neither of us would be sitting here like this?"

I didn't want to speak of Nighteyes just then, not even to hear the kindly memories others had of him. "So," I said when a moment of awkward silence had passed. "Did all go well this evening? The betrothal ceremony and all?"

"Oh, that was just the welcoming ceremony. The formal betrothal will not take place until the new moon. Night after tomorrow. All the dukes must arrive before we can hold that. Buckkeep Castle will be packed to the rafters with folk, and all of Buckkeep Town, as well."

"I saw her. The narcheska. She's only a child."

A strange smile lit Chade's face. "If you say she is 'only' a child, then I doubt you actually saw her. She is . . . a queen in the bud, Fitz. I wish you could meet her and speak to her. By the greatest good fortune, the Outislanders have offered us an extraordinary match for our Prince."

"And does Dutiful concur with that?" I prodded.

"He—" Chade drew himself up abruptly. "And what is this? Asking questions of your master? Report, you young upstart!" His smile took any sting from his words.

And so I did. When the water boiled, Chade brewed a tea for us, and later he poured it from the pot, stinging and strong. I don't know what was in it, but the haze of weariness and wine lifted from my mind. I told him all the events up to the time when we reached the inn at the ferry landing. As ever, his face was still as he listened. If he heard anything that shocked or dismayed him, he covered it well. He only winced once, when I spoke of slamming Dutiful flat onto his back on the beach. When I was finished, he drew in a long breath through his nose. He stood up and walked a slow turn around the room. Then he came back and sat down heavily.

"So our Prince is Witted," he said slowly.

Of all the things he could have said, this most surprised me. "Did you doubt it?"

He gave a small shake of the head. "I had hoped we were wrong. That these Old Blood folk know he carries that blood is a knife in our ribs. At any time, the Piebalds could choose to drive it home, simply by speaking what they know." His eyes turned inward. "The Bresingas will bear watching. I think, ah, yes, that Queen Kettricken will ask Lady Bresinga to take a certain young woman into her household, a girl of good blood but poor prospects. And I shall look into Laurel's family connections, as well. Yes, I know what you think of that, but we cannot be too careful where the Prince is concerned. A damn shame you let the Piebalds ride away, but I see there was nothing you could have done about it at the time. If it were but one man, or two, or even three, we could end the danger. But not only a dozen Old Bloods, but those Piebalds know as well." He considered a moment. "Can their silence be bought?"

It disheartened me to hear him plot, yet I knew it was his nature. As well fault a squirrel for hiding nuts. "Not with gold," I decided. "Actions might keep them content. Do as they asked. Show good will. Have the Queen move more strongly to protect the Witted ones from persecution."

"She already has!" Chade replied defensively. "For your sake, she has spoken out, and more than once. Six Duchies law forbids that any Witted one be killed simply for being Witted. Other crimes must be proved."

I took a breath. "And has that law been enforced?"

"It is up to each duke to enforce the laws within his own duchy."

"And in Buck?" I asked softly.

Chade was silent for a time. I watched him gnaw briefly on his lip, his eyes staring deep into nothing. Weighing. At last he asked, "Do you think that would content them? Stricter enforcement of the law within Buck Duchy?"

"It would be a start."

He took a deep breath and sighed it out. "I will discuss it with the Queen. It will not take much urging on my part. In truth, I have played the opposite role up until now, urging her to respect the traditions of the folk she has come to rule, for she—"

"Traditions!" I burst out. "Murder and torture as 'traditions'?"

"She bestraddles an uneasy alliance!" he finished more strongly than he had begun. "Since the end of the Red Ship War, it has been a juggler's trick to keep the Six Duchies in balance. It takes a light hand, Fitz, and the sense to know when to take a stand and when to let things go."

I thought of the smell that had hung near the river, and the cut rope left hanging from the tree. "I think she had best decide to take a stand on this."

"In Buck."

"In Buck, at the least."

Chade covered his mouth and then pulled at his chin. "Very well," he conceded, and for the first time I perceived that I had been negotiating with him. I had not, I reflected, done very well at it, but then I had supposed I had merely been reporting. And whom had I expected to speak out for the Old Blood? Lord Golden? Huntswoman Laurel, who would just as soon not be associated with them? I wished I had been more forceful. Then I reflected that I still could be, when I spoke with Queen Kettricken.

"So. What did our Queen think of Prince Dutiful's bride?"

Chade looked at me for a long moment. "Are you asking for a report?"

Something in his voice made me falter. A trap? Was this one of his trap questions? "I merely asked. I have no right—"

"Ah. Then Dutiful was mistaken, and you have not consented to teach him?"

I worked the two ideas against one another, trying to see how they fit. Then I gave it up. "And if I have?" I asked him cautiously.

"If you have, then you not only have a right to the information, but a need. If you are going to educate the Prince, you must know everything that affects him. But if you are not, if you intend to go back to your hermit's hut, if you are asking but for the sake of hearing family gossip . . ." He let his words trail off.

I knew that old trick of his. Leave a sentence dangling, and someone will leap to fill in the end, and possibly betray their own thoughts in doing so. Instead, I sat regarding my cup of tea and chewing on the side of my thumbnail until he leaned across the table and in exasperation slapped my hand away from my mouth. "Well?" he demanded.

"What did the Prince tell you?"

It was his turn to hold his silence for a time. I waited him out, wolf-wary.

"Nothing," he grudgingly admitted at last. "I was but hoping."

I leaned back in my chair, wincing as my aching back touched it. "Oh, old man," I warned him, shaking my head. Then I found myself smiling, despite myself. "I thought the years had rounded your corners, but they haven't. Why are you making it like this between us?"

"Because I am the Queen's Councillor now, not your mentor, my boy. And because, I fear, there are days when, as you put it, my corners are rounded, and I forget things and all my carefully gathered threads turn suddenly to a snarl in my hand. So. I try to be careful, and more than careful, in every aspect of all I do."

"What was in the tea?" I asked suddenly.

"Some new herbs I've been trying. They were mentioned in the Skill-scrolls. No elfbark, I assure you. I'd give you nothing that might damage your abilities."

"But they 'sharpen' you?"

"Yes. But at a cost, as you've already surmised. All things have a cost, Fitz. We both know that. We'll both spend this afternoon abed, don't doubt it. But for now, we have our wits about us. So. Tell me."

I took a breath, wondering how to phrase it. I glanced up at his fireplace mantel, at a knife that still stood embedded in the center of it. I weighed trust and youthful confidences and all I had once promised King Shrewd. Chade's gaze followed mine. "A long time ago," I began softly, "you tested my loyalty to the King, by asking me to steal something from him, just as a prank. You knew I loved you. So you tried that love against my loyalty to my King. Do you recall that?"

"I do," he responded gravely. "And I still regret it." He took a breath, and sighed it out. "And you passed his test. Not even for love of me would you betray your King. I know I put you through the fire, FitzChivalry. But it was my King who asked that you be tested."

I nodded slowly. "I understand that. Now. I too made my oath to the Farseer line, Chade. Just as you did. You vowed no loyalty to me, nor I to you. There is love between us, but no oaths of fealty." He was watching my face very carefully. A frown divided his white brows. I took a breath. "My loyalty is to my Prince, Chade. I think it must be up to him what he shares with you." I took a deep breath, and with great regret, severed a portion of my life. "As you have said, old friend. You are the Queen's Councillor now, no longer my mentor. And I am not your apprentice." I looked down at the table and steeled myself. The words were hard to say. "The Prince will decide what I am to him. But I will never again report to you about my private words with my Prince, Chade."

He stood, quite abruptly. To my horror, I saw tears welling in his sharp green eyes. For a moment, his mouth trembled. Then he walked around the table, seized my head in his hands, and bent down to kiss my brow. "Thanks be to Eda and El both," he whispered hoarsely. "You are his. And he will still be safe when I am gone."

I was too astonished to speak. He walked slowly around the table and resumed his seat. He poured more tea for both of us. He turned aside to wipe his eyes, and then looked back at me. He pushed my cup across the table toward me and said, "Very well. Shall I report now?"

chapter XXIX

BUCKKEEP TOWN

A good bed of fennel is an excellent addition to any cottage garden, though one must be wary of it spreading. Cut it back each fall, and gather the seedheads before the birds can scatter them all through your garden, or your spring will be spent pulling up the lacy fronds. All know the sweet flavor of this plant, but it has medicinal uses, as well. Both seed and root of this herb aid the digestion. A colicky babe will take a tisane of fennel, and much good with it. Chewed, the seed will refresh the mouth. A poultice of the same will soothe sore eyes. Given as a gift, the message of fennel is said by some to be "Strength" and by others, "Flattery."

MERIBUCK'S HERBAL

As Chade had warned me, I slept away not only the afternoon, but part of the early evening, as well. I awoke in the utter blackness of my little chamber, in the total solitude of myself, and suddenly feared I was dead. I rolled off my bed, found the door by touch, and lunged out of it. Light and moving air stunned me. Lord Golden, impeccably attired, sat at his writing desk. He glanced up casually at my abrupt entrance. "Oh. Awake at last," he observed congenially. "Wine? Biscuits?" He gestured at a table and chairs by the fireside.

I came to the table rubbing my eyes. Food was artfully arranged on it. I dropped into the closest chair. My tongue felt thick, my eyes sticky. "I have no idea what was in Chade's tea, but I don't think I want to try it again."

"And I have no idea what you're talking about, but I suspect that that is just as well." He rose and came to the table, poured wine for us, and then glanced over me disparagingly. He shook his head. "You are hopeless, Tom Badgerlock. Look at yourself. Sleeping in all the day, and then appearing with your hair half on end in a worried old robe. A worse servant a man never had." He took the other chair.

I could think of no reply to that. I sipped my wine gratefully. I considered the food but found I had no appetite. "How was your evening? Did you enjoy a dance with Huntswoman Laurel?"

He raised one eyebrow at me, as if my question puzzled and surprised him. Abruptly, he was my Fool again as a smile twisted his mouth. "Ah, Fitz, you should know by now that every moment of my life is spent dancing. And with every partner, I tread a different measure." Then, adroit as ever, he changed the subject, asking, "And are you well this evening?"

I knew what he meant. "As well as could be expected," I assured him.

"Ah. Excellent. Then you will be going down to Buckkeep Town?"

He knew my mind before I had even thought it. "I'd like to check on Hap and see how his apprenticeship goes. Unless you need me here."

He studied my face for a moment, as if waiting for me to say more. Then he said, "Go to town. I think it an excellent idea. There are, of course, more festivities tonight, but I shall endeavor to manage my preparation without you. Do, please, try to make *yourself* a bit more presentable before leaving my apartments, however. Lord Golden's reputation has been tarnished quite enough of late without it being said that he keeps moth-eaten servants."

I snorted. "I'll try." I rose from the table slowly. My body had rediscovered its aches. The Fool ensconced himself in one of the two chairs that faced the hearth. He leaned back in it with a sigh and stretched out his long legs toward the warmth. His voice reached me as I moved toward my chamber.

"Fitz. You know I love you, don't you?"

I halted where I stood.

"I'd hate to have to kill you," he continued. I recognized his adept imitation of my own voice and inflection. I stared at him, baffled. He sat up taller and glanced over the back of his chair at me with a pained smile. "Never again attempt to put my clothing away," he warned me. "Verulean silk should be draped for storage. Not wadded."

"I'll try to remember that," I promised him humbly.

He settled back in his chair and picked up his glass of wine. "Good night, Fitz," he told me quietly.

In my chamber, I found one of my old tunics and some leggings. I put them on, and then frowned at the fit. The leggings sagged on me about the waist; the privations and steady exertions of our expedition had trimmed my body. I brushed at the shirt, and then frowned at the stains. It had not changed since I came to Buckkeep, but my eye for it had. It had been fine for my farmstead, but if I were going to stay at Buck and teach the Prince, I would need to dress as a townsman again. The conclusion was inevitable and yet it felt oddly vain. I washed my face with the stale water in the ewer. In my small looking glass, I tried vainly to smooth my hair, then gave it up as a bad cause, and put on my cloak. I put out my candle.

Lord Golden's chamber, as I ghosted through it, was now lit only by flickering firelight. As I passed the chair by the hearth, I offered, "Good night, Fool." He did not speak, but lifted his graceful hand in farewell, his flicking forefinger gesturing me toward the door. I slipped out, feeling oddly as if I had forgotten something.

The keep had a festive atmosphere as all prepared for another night of feasting, music, and dancing. Garlands dressed the door arches, and far more folk than usual moved

through the halls. A minstrel's voice drifted from the lesser
hall, and three young men in Farrow colors chatted near the
door. My worn clothing and badly cropped hair drew a few
bemused glances, but I was generally unnoticed among the
newcomers and their servants, and unchallenged as I left
Buckkeep and headed down toward the town. The steep
road was still busy with folk coming and going from the
keep, and despite the steady rain, Buckkeep Town was live-
lier than usual. Any occasion up at the keep stimulated trade
in the town, and Dutiful's betrothal was a major occasion. I
wended my way through merchants and tradesmen and servants on errands. Nobles on horseback and ladies on litters
passed me, on their way up to the keep for the evening's festivities. When I reached Buckkeep Town itself, the press of
folk in the street only became thicker. Taverns were full to
overflowing, music swelled out to lure in passersby, and children raced past, enjoying the excitement of so many
strangers in town. The holiday aura was infectious, and I
caught myself smiling and wishing many a stranger good
evening as I made my way down to Jinna's shop.

But as I passed one doorway, I saw a young man chivying a maid to stay and talk with him a moment longer. Her
eyes were bright and her smile merry as she shook her dark
curls at him in sweet rebuke. Raindrops jeweled their
cloaks. He looked so earnest and so young in his entreaties
that I averted my eyes and hurried past. In the next moment, my heart ached as I realized that Prince Dutiful
would never know a moment like that, would never taste
the sweetness of a stolen kiss, or the elation and suspense of
wondering if the lady would grant him another moment of
her company. No. His wife had been chosen for him, and
the freshest years of his manhood would be spent in waiting
for her to grow to womanhood. I dared not hope they would
be happy. The best I could manage was that they would not
make one another miserable.

These were my thoughts as I found my way down the

winding little street that led to Jinna's door. I halted outside it, and sudden awkwardness flooded me. The door was closed, the windows shuttered. A little glow of candlelight leaked out through one ill-fitting shutter, but it did not look welcoming. Rather it spoke of the intimacy of home within those walls. It was later than I had thought it was; I would be intruding. I smoothed my hacked hair nervously and promised myself that I would not go within, only stand at the door and ask for Hap. I could take him out to a tavern for a beer and some talk. That would be good, I told myself, a good way to show him I considered him a man grown now. I took a breath and tapped lightly at the door.

Within, I heard the scrape of a chair, and the thud of a cat landing on the floor. Then Jinna's voice came through the shuttered window. "Who's there?"

"Fit . . . Tom Badgerlock." I cursed my awkward tongue. "Look, I'm sorry to call so late, I've been away, and thought I should check on—"

"Tom!" The door was flung wide to my hasty excuses, nearly hitting me as it opened. "Tom Badgerlock, come in, come in!" Jinna had a candle in one hand, but with the other she caught the sleeve of my shirt and drew me inside. The room was dim, lit mostly by the hearth fire. There were two chairs pulled up there with a low table between them. A steaming teapot sat brewing beside an empty cup. A heap of knitting, the needles thrust through it, occupied one chair. She pulled the door firmly shut behind me, and then gestured me toward the hearth. "I've just put on elderberry tea. Would you like a cup?"

"That would be—I didn't mean to intrude, I only meant to check on Hap and see how—"

"Here, let me take your wet cloak. Ah, it's drenched! I'll hang it here. Well, sit down, you'll have to wait, for the young scamp isn't here. Truth to tell, I've been thinking to myself that the sooner you came back and had a word with the lad, the better for him. Not that I wish to be telling tales on him, but he wants someone taking a hand with him."

"Hap?" I asked incredulously. I took a step toward the fire, but her cat chose that moment to wrap himself suddenly against my ankle. I lurched to a halt, barely avoiding stepping on him.

Make a lap. Near the fire.

The assertive little voice rang in my mind. I looked down at him and he looked up at me. For an instant, our gazes brushed, then we both looked aside in instinctive courtesy. But he had already seen the ruins of my soul.

He rubbed his cheek against my leg. *Hold the cat. You'll feel better.*

I don't think so.

He rubbed against my leg insistently. *Hold the cat.*

I don't want to hold the cat.

He reared up suddenly on his hind legs, and hooked his vicious little front claws into both flesh and leggings. *Don't talk back! Pick up the cat.*

"Fennel, stop that! Where are your manners?" Jinna exclaimed in dismay. She bent toward the ginger pest, but I stooped swiftly, to unhook his claws from my flesh. I freed myself but before I could straighten up, he leapt to my shoulder. For all his size, Fennel had amazing agility. He landed, not heavily, but as if someone had put a large, friendly hand on my shoulder. *Hold the cat. You'll feel better.*

Steadying him as I stood up was easier than plucking him loose. Jinna clucked and exclaimed, but I assured her it was all right. She drew out one of the chairs that faced the small hearth and smoothed the pillow on it. I sat down, and it tipped back under me. It was a rocker. The moment I was settled, Fennel moved down to my lap and settled himself in a warm mound. I folded my hands atop him in a show of ignoring him. He gave me a slit-eyed cat grin. *Be nice to me. She loves me best.*

It took me a moment to find my thoughts. "Hap?" I said again.

"Hap," she confirmed. "Who should be abed right now, for his master expects him earlier than the dawn tomorrow.

And where is he? Out dangling after Mistress Hartshorn's daughter, who is far too knowing for her tender years. She's a distraction to him, that Svanja, and even her own mother says that she would be better at home, tending to work and learning her own trade."

She nattered on in a voice of mixed annoyance and amusement. The level of her concern astonished me. I felt a twinge of jealousy: was not Hap my boy, for me to worry about? As she spoke, she set a cup at my elbow, poured tea for both of us, and resumed her chair and knitting. When she was settled, she glanced over at me and our eyes met for the first time since I had knocked. She started, and then leaned closer, peering at me.

"Oh, Tom!" she exclaimed in a voice of deep sympathy. She leaned toward me, studying my face. "Poor man, what's happened to you?"

Empty as a hollow log when the mice are eaten.

"My wolf died."

It shocked me that I spoke the truth so bluntly. Jinna was silent, staring at me. I knew she could not understand. I did not expect her to understand. But then, as her helpless silence lengthened, I felt very much as if she might understand, for she offered no useless words. Abruptly, she dropped her knitting in her lap and leaned across to put her hand on my forearm.

"Will you be all right?" she asked me. It was not an empty question; she genuinely listened for my reply.

"In time," I told her, and for the first time, I admitted that was true. As disloyal as the thought felt, I knew that as time passed, I would be myself again. And in that moment, I felt for the first time the sensation that Black Rolf had tried to describe to me. The wolfish part of my soul stirred, and, *Yes, you will be yourself again, and that is as it should be,* I heard near as clearly as if Nighteyes had truly shared the thought with me. Like remembering, but more so, Rolf had told me. I sat very still, savoring the sensation. Then it passed, and a shiver ran over me.

"Drink your tea, you're taking a chill," Jinna advised me, and leaned down to toss another piece of wood on the fire.

I did as she suggested. As I set the cup down, I glanced up at the charm over the mantel. The changeable light from the flames gilded and then hid the beads. Hospitality. The tea was warm and sweet and soothing, the cat purred on my lap, and a woman looked at me fondly. Was it just the wall charm's effect on me? If it was, I didn't care. Something in me eased another notch. *Petting the cat makes you feel better,* Fennel asserted smugly.

"The boy's heart will be broken when he hears. He knew the wolf would go after you, you know. When the wolf disappeared I was worried, but when he didn't come back, Hap told me, never fear, he's gone off to follow Tom. Oh, I dread your telling him." Abruptly, she reined her flow of words. Then she stoutly declared, "But in time, like you, he will recover. Oh, he should be home by now," she worried, and then, "What will you do about him?"

I thought of myself, so many years ago, and of Verity, and even of young Dutiful. I thought of all the ways that duty had shaped us and bound us and held back our hearts. Truly, the boy should be home by now, getting sleep the better to serve his master on the morrow. He was an apprentice yet, and his prospects were not yet settled. He had no business showing an interest in a girl. I could take a firm hand with him and remind him of his duty. He would listen to me. But Hap was not the son of a king, nor even a royal bastard. Hap could be free. I leaned back in my chair. It rocked and I absently stroked the cat. "Nothing," I said after a moment. "I think I'll do nothing. I think I'll let him be a boy. I think I'll let him fall in love with a girl, and stay out later than he should, and have a pounding headache tomorrow when his master chides him for being late." I turned to look at her. The firelight danced over her kindly face. "I think I'll let the boy be a boy for a time."

"Do you think that's wise?" she asked, but she smiled as she said it.

"No." I shook my head slowly. "I think it's foolish and wonderful."

"Ah. Well. Will you stay and have another cup of tea, then? Or must you hurry back to the keep and your own duties?"

"I have no duties tonight. I won't be missed."

"Well, then." She poured another cup of tea for me with an alacrity that was flattering. "You'll stay a while here. Where you have been missed." She sipped from her cup, smiling at me over the rim of it.

Fennel drew breath and began a deep, rumbling purr.

EPILOGUE

There was a time when I thought that my life's significant work would be to write a history of the Six Duchies. I made a start on it any number of times, but always seemed to slide sideways from that grand tale into a recounting of the days and details of my own small life. The more I studied the accounts of others, both written and told, the more it seemed to me that we attempt such histories not to preserve knowledge, but to fix the past in a settled way. Like a flower pressed flat and dried, we try to hold it still and say, this is exactly how it was the day I first saw it. But like the flower, the past cannot be trapped that way. It loses its fragrance and its vitality, its fragility becomes brittleness and its colors fade. And when next you look on the flower, you know that it is not at all what you sought to capture, that that moment has fled forever.

I wrote my histories and observations. I captured my thoughts and ideas and memories in words on vellum and paper. So much I stored, and thought it was mine. I believed that by fixing it down in words, I could force sense from all that had happened, that effect would follow cause, and the reason for each event come clear to me. Perhaps I sought to justify myself, not just all I had done, but who I had become. For years, I wrote faithfully nearly every evening, carefully explaining my world and my life to myself. I put my scrolls on a shelf, trusting that I had captured the meaning of my days.

But then I returned one day, to find all my careful scribing gone to fragments of vellum lying in a trampled yard with wet *snow blowing over them. I sat my horse, looking down on them, and knew that, as it always would, the past had broken free of my effort to define and understand it. History is no more fixed and dead than the future. The past is no further away than the last breath you took.*